THE SECRET MARRIAGE
A totally addictive and absolutely unputdownable psychological thriller
Mikayla Davids

For Charlotte and Rachel

Prologue

My husband has been lying to me.

I never thought this would happen. Not in a million years did I imagine that my relationship with the man I love would lead me here, but it has.

I crunch along the gravel driveway, towards the wooden entrance gate that's half hidden by overhanging trees. Gazing up at the grey sky above, I shiver. Thunder has been rumbling for the past ten minutes. I can feel the intensity building. This is the moment before the storm unleashes, and who knows what havoc it will cause.

The wind whips around me as I flatten against a tree trunk. Tucking myself as far under the foliage as possible, I make sure I'm hidden from view, my dark brown Barbour jacket helping me blend into my surroundings. The green leaves are starting to turn to orange, gold and yellow.

Just then, a vehicle rounds the corner and pulls up to the large wooden gate. I suck in a breath as I realise that was a close call – just a few seconds later and I would've been seen.

My heart beats wildly as a tall man, his jet-black hair flecked with silver, jumps out of a deep green Range Rover and strides in shiny Hunter wellies towards the white-washed building. My attention is on him, watching his every move – because he's the reason I'm here.

The farmhouse door opens and I gasp as I see my husband step into the arms of another woman. My heart feels like it's going to burst. I want to scream but I stay silent, unable to tear my eyes away from the scene unfolding in front of me. I suspected he was cheating on me but I'd hoped – I'd prayed – that it wasn't true. Now, seeing the two of them together, their bodies entwined in a tight embrace, I can't pretend any more.

An image of my husband and I on our wedding day flashes in my mind. Our smiles were wide, confetti in our hair. We were so in love. Or at least I was. But was any of it real? Or has he been deceiving me since the day we met? I'm frozen with shock, unable to turn away. I'm rooted to the spot.

Thunder claps overhead as he leans in and kisses the woman. She throws her arms around his neck, pulling him even closer to her. I can't quite see her face but even from here it's clear she's a natural beauty. She's tall and willowy, her casual but expensive clothes hugging her figure, and she wears her long, straight hair in an effortless ponytail. The early evening light is still good enough for me to see the gold wedding band that glints on her finger. My stomach drops. Why is there a ring on her finger?

The seconds feel like hours as I analyse every movement, every interaction between the two of them, my heart thudding in my ribcage. I want to believe this is just a simple affair. I've researched the statistics and affairs are more common than you think. But there's something about the look that passes between my husband and this woman, along with the circle of gold on her finger, that gives me goose pimples. Instinctively, I know there is more to this. And the fact she's here, looking so familiar with the house, makes me wonder how deep my husband's lies run.

I don't have to wait too long until my fears are confirmed. After they've finished smooching on the doorstep, he says, 'I've missed you wifey.'

His words carry clearly to where I'm standing. He's always had a deep, commanding sort of voice and there's absolutely no mistaking what he said.

My world shatters.

My husband has married someone else. When he's still married to me.

They both disappear inside. Heavy drops of rain begin to fall, running down my face, mixing with my tears and blurring my vision until I can no longer see. I place my hand on the trunk of the tree, the gnarled bark rough beneath my fingertips. I try to take regular breaths to steady myself. As the fresh country air hits my lungs, my emotions shift from shock to anger. Boiling, white hot anger. The kind that burns deep into your core. He has betrayed me in the worst possible way. Hatred twists in my heart and lights a fire in my belly.

Lightning flashes overhead and at the same time, a bolt of rage surges through my body. But, as much as I want to act on my feelings right now, I know I need to bide my time. So I stay where I am; watching and waiting.

And plotting my revenge.

Chapter One
Kirsty
Now

'Isn't this just perfect?' I smile at Nicholas.

Candles flicker, music is playing softly in the background and my wine glass is filled to the top. My handsome husband sits opposite me, reclining in his chair.

'How much of that have you drunk already?' Nicholas jokes, his blue-green eyes twinkling as he indicates towards the wine bottle.

'Just one glass,' I laugh. Although I take a few more sips of the rich red wine, enjoying the sweet taste of cherries as I drink.

Stretching my arms across the table, I hold his hands in mine. I've been married to Nicholas for six months now, and I have to pinch myself when I wake up in the mornings. Only a few years ago, my life was a constant struggle and now I feel like I've stepped into someone else's shoes. This beautiful house in the heart of the English countryside is to die for. And I never dreamt I would be the wife of a successful man like Nicholas.

'We're so lucky, aren't we? To have this amazing home and each other.'

Nicholas takes my hand to his mouth and kisses my fingers lightly. I'm still adjusting to being Mrs Johnson and sometimes the intensity of his gaze when he looks at me feels overpowering.

I feel content that the evening is going well. Nicholas works so hard and often he comes home stressed after a long day, so it's a treat to have a Friday night together that's quiet and uninterrupted. His laptop remains firmly closed on the other side of the room and he hasn't been forced to disappear into his home office to take a long work call.

'More wine?' Nicholas doesn't wait for me to answer; he just goes straight ahead and pours a generous measure into my glass until it is once again full.

'Are you trying to get me drunk?' I raise an eyebrow at him.

'Merely tipsy.' He grins back, his upper-class British accent coming through strong as he teases me.

I blush slightly. The attention of this smart, handsome older man still feels very new.

'That dinner really was delicious,' Nicholas says, his eyes roving over our empty plates. 'Where did you learn to cook so well?'

A laugh escapes me. I'm sure Nicholas wouldn't be impressed if he knew I learned to cook in busy city cafés and noisy pubs. If he'd met me back when I worked long shifts in tiny kitchens, often with a grease-stained apron tied around my waist and my hair stuffed under a very unflattering white cap, I'm sure he wouldn't have been quite so enamoured.

Nowadays, I usually have my locks pulled back in a ponytail or a bun but today I spent ages blow-drying my hair until it was glossy and shiny, allowing it to hang loose around my shoulders. I twirl a strand of my long, straight hair around my finger.

'What's for dessert?' Nicholas asks, not waiting to hear about where I picked up my culinary skills.

I'm relieved to have a more straightforward question to answer. 'I made the salted caramel cheesecake that you like.'

Nicholas pats his stomach, 'You're spoiling me. I'm going to have to do more hours at the gym at this rate.'

We sit in comfortable silence. A fire is burning in the grate, the curtains are drawn and we're in our own cosy little world. It's bliss. Our sausage dog Luna barks in the background and the sound nudges me out of my reverie.

Clearing away the dinner plates, I take them through to the kitchen and dump them in the big butler sink. I'll take care of them later: I don't want to interrupt the flow of the evening by dealing with the clearing up now.

Leaning against the worktop, I allow myself a two-minute breather to admire the vast room I'm in. I've spent my adult life working with food, in a few nice restaurants as well as the cafés and pubs, and none of them have had kitchens on this scale. I'm in my element here and the endless days I'm on my own have given me the opportunity to lose myself in recipe books and experiment with new dishes. Although I must admit I miss having people around me to chat to.

Nicholas has every appliance I could hope for and the cupboards are brimming with fancy plates and glasses for different occasions – and there's even a pantry that's the size of a small room. Every time I go into it, I'm convinced I might have just gone through the wardrobe and into my very own magical world.

At the far end of the kitchen there is a wooden table, with bench seats either side, where we sit in the morning to have our breakfast. The table is positioned in front of the bi-fold doors which open onto a patio and pretty garden beyond. It's a gorgeous view to look out on while we're eating.

As I open the double fridge and take out the cheesecake, I recall that when Nicholas asked me to marry him, he told me he wanted me to move into his home and it's easy to see why. The window is slightly ajar but all

I can hear is the rushing water of the nearby stream. There's nothing but countryside for miles and miles. It's all so tranquil. So very different to the frenetic pace of London, the city I'd lived my whole life in.

I didn't hesitate; I agreed to his suggestion of starting our married life here straight away. In the same conversation, Nicholas told me there was no need for me to work; not while his business makes so much money. To avoid any embarrassment on my part, Nicholas assured me that giving up my whole world – my friends, family, living in the city – to be with him was a big deal. He didn't want me to have the pressure of trying to commute to work from out in the sticks, especially in the wintertime when the roads can get so iced up.

I was more than willing to give up working fourteen hours a day on little pay and move away from the place that held so many painful memories, to join him in his carefully curated world where money isn't an issue. It's been a relief not to have to worry about how to keep a roof over my head, but I couldn't give up the independence of working so I've started my own freelance baking business. Although money isn't the reason why I married Nicholas. It couldn't be further from the truth.

I take the dessert and carry it through the dining room, placing it gently on the table. Portioning out some for both of us, sticky caramel oozes onto the small plates that I had already laid out on the table. I've made the salted caramel cheesecake a few times now, so it didn't take me too long to prepare earlier on today while Nicholas was at work. I bite into my own slice, and the taste of soft, sugary deliciousness tantalises my taste buds.

'Mmm,' Nicholas comments. 'This is even better than I remember. Did you change something?'

I nod. Nicholas is a man with a keen eye for detail, so I'm not surprised that he's noticed I've tweaked the recipe a little this time and increased the caramel. I'm secretly pleased that he likes it. I take another mouthful and appreciate the contrast of sweet and salt. We both polish off our food and then Nicholas leans back in his chair, running a hand through his dark hair.

'Kirsty, there's something I need to tell you.'

I look up from my plate sharply; the tone of my husband's voice tells me I'm not going to like what comes next. I put my spoon down.

'What is it?' We've only been married for a short time and Nicholas keeps his cards close to his chest, so I have no clue what he's about to say.

'I know this isn't what you're going to want to hear...'

My brain immediately jumps to the worst-case scenario. Has he realised that we're both from completely different worlds and I don't fit into his golden lifestyle? Since we got together, this is an insecurity that has niggled at me.

'I'm going to have to go on another work trip next week. I'll be going to Edinburgh. I know it's not ideal so soon after the last one, but there's a big contract I need to tie up and I have to be there in person to do it.'

Relief floods over me. 'Oh, don't worry. It's fine...' I stumble. 'I understand.'

I take a gulp of wine. Nicholas's life is always so busy; he's forever preparing for an important work meeting or jetting off to one. Suddenly, I realise what this evening has been about. This is why his phone has been noticeably absent and he hasn't been checking his laptop every half an hour. He was building up to telling me that he'd be leaving again.

'How long will you be gone for?'

'This is going to be a two-week stretch I'm afraid. Will you be okay?'

'Of course I will,' I say, trying to keep my voice as even as possible.

I stand up and stack the dessert plates and cutlery. Then I hurry into the kitchen, as I don't want him to guess how I feel about him being away again. He didn't used to be gone quite so frequently when we were first dating or when we were engaged. But I know he's got an important deal that he's trying to get over the line and his business means a lot to him. Lost in my thoughts, I start filling the dishwasher.

'Hey, I'm sorry.' Nicholas comes up behind me and kisses my neck. 'I can try to—'

'No, honestly, I'll miss you but I do understand.' I turn to face him as I want him to believe that I'm still supportive.

'Are you sure?' Nicholas asks, a look of concern crinkling across his face. 'I don't want you to regret moving here, to regret marrying me.'

'Don't be silly,' I turn around in his arms and sweep my hand along his jawline. 'I'm the luckiest woman in the world.'

He hesitates and looks like he's going to say something more but I intercept his doubt. 'Seriously, I adore living here and I adore you.'

'Good…' He sighs deeply, as though he's reassured. 'Well let's snuggle up and—'

At that moment, the familiar sound of his mobile ringtone cuts through our conversation. Typical timing.

I step back. 'Answer it,' I encourage him.

'No, no. I'll ring them back.'

He pulls his phone out of his jacket pocket but when he catches sight of the caller ID on the screen he frowns. He flicks his eyes from me then back to the screen and I can tell from the look on his face that this is a call he needs to answer.

'You get it and I'll wait for you upstairs. I'll take the wine up.'

'Sorry, this is something urgent I need to deal with.' Nicholas distractedly kisses me on my forehead and then he's disappearing through the door.

I hear him answer in a hushed, urgent tone that's nothing like his usual confident, businesslike manner when he's on the phone. It makes me question who is calling him at this time of night and what is so important. I shake the thought away. Nicholas's company keeps him busy, and I knew that when I married him.

Swinging open the fridge door, I grab another bottle of red and get to work on twisting open the cork. As the cork pops, a memory hits me like a body blow. Clearly in my mind, I can see a different moment in my life... a glimmer of happiness on a champagne-filled evening. I can almost hear the laughter and feel the warm embrace of the person who was the most precious to me. But I can't go there, I can't dwell on what might have been.

I have to look forward; not back. After all, I've been through much worse and I've always found a way to get through hard times.

Now, I have to keep Nicholas happy. I have to be the wife he expects me to be.

Because everything depends on it.

Chapter Two
Eva
Then

'This is it!'

Nick swings open the gate and grasps my hand tightly as he pulls me along after him. His face is alight with excitement as he gestures towards the tumbledown house at the end of the gravel driveway. We stand together and survey the property in front of us. The paint on the door is peeling, some of the upstairs windows are covered in ivy and there are slates missing from the roof. Run-down would be a generous description.

'Eva, come in and have a look.' He guides me eagerly into the farmhouse.

It looks as though nobody has lived here for years and yet, beneath the dust, there are still homely signs about the place. A forgotten vase on a window ledge, faded pastel curtains and a pair of old boots by the back door. Despite the plaster flaking, the stained carpets and the enormous amount of work that will need doing to make this building liveable, I can see its potential. I can see why Nick is thrumming with enthusiasm.

'What do you think?' He looks at me, like a child waiting for approval.

'It feels like home.' And I mean it. Standing here with him just feels right.

Nick and I have been through so much. Together, we've built a thriving business empire. It's taken a lot of hard work but we've done it and we're finally in a position to create our dream house.

We stand at a window and look out at the fields that come with the farmhouse. A woodland area and a river running at the edge of the land belongs to Orchard Farm. There's so much space here and it could all be ours.

This is everything I've ever wanted: the opportunity to create a beautiful home for us both. My parents divorced when I was nine-years-old and since then I've wanted to recreate the warm, safe environment I remember from my early childhood. Both my parents have passed away and I have no siblings. Nick has a similar lack of family so he is my absolute world and I can't wait to step into this next phase with him. I'm hoping for a slower pace and more time together.

'Shall we go for it then?' he asks, snaking an arm around my waist.

'Yes!'

Nick envelopes me in a hug before kissing me on the lips. 'I knew you'd like it too.'

I smile back at him. 'This is it, our forever home.'

'Our home. Forever,' he agrees.

Chapter Three
Kirsty
Now

Making my way upstairs, I remember the first time Nicholas showed me around. I had to hide my surprise at how sprawling the property was. The ivy-covered, limestone farmhouse looks impressive from the front but the inside is even more dazzling. It's like stepping into a high-end magazine where every room is perfectly coordinated. There isn't a chair or a curtain out of place; the palettes have been selected to complement each other and a theme of rustic charm runs throughout. It's so beautiful it's almost stifling.

In our bedroom, I place the two wine glasses on my bedside table before glancing around. There's only one word for this space: luxurious. On the wall behind the velvet headboard there's midnight blue panelling. This colour scheme runs across the room and the bedding, curtains, rug and lampshades are all a similar dark blue. The effect of the deep colour is cosy and welcoming; every time I come in here, I feel like I'm walking into a warm hug. I've never slept so well in my life. The orthopaedic pillow and high-thread count sheets have felt like a real luxury compared to the thin duvet and hand-me-down mattress I had growing up.

Moving into the bathroom, the midnight blue theme continues. The sink is white, set into a deep blue cabinet; there are blue and gold marble-effect tiles in the spacious double shower along with blue mats on the white flooring. The enormous white clawfoot bath tub has gold taps which match the gold-rimmed mirror as well as the gold trim and taps in the shower. Nicholas must have spent a fortune on whoever he hired to do the interior design.

Staring at my face in the circular glass, I observe my long eyelashes and dark, thick brows that come naturally to me but also happen to be in fashion. I never used to wear much make-up but Nicholas has made approving noises when I add blusher to my cheeks and paint my lips red, so I've found myself adding eyeshadow and eyeliner to my morning routine as well in recent months.

Now, the lipstick has faded and the red wine has stained my lips in its place. My straight hair falls around my shoulders, golden threads mixed with a light brown. I give it a quick brush through with a comb, wash off my make-up and then brush my teeth. That done, I come out of the bathroom and go into my walk-in wardrobe.

It's fairly sparse in here as I barely have enough outfits to fill a quarter of the space Nicholas has assigned to me. As I distractedly run my hand along the hangers of beautiful items, I still can't believe they are mine.

For our first Christmas, Nicholas spent a ridiculous amount of money on new clothes for me: warm layers for when I'm walking the dog as well as expensive scarves and bags, and a few dresses for when we go out for meals. To begin with, I felt like an imposter wearing these expensive things, but I've come to appreciate the quality material and the beautifully made designs. The clothes have helped me to fit in and feel a little less like a fish out of water in Nicholas's world, and they've also helped me to play the part of the perfect wife.

Nicholas hasn't come up to the bedroom yet; I can hear the faint rumble of his voice downstairs as he continues to talk on the phone. I stand and look out of the window; the moon is bright and the stars are shining against a canopy of ink-black sky. Everything is so quiet; there's no sounds of cars or lights from surrounding dwellings. There's something calming about looking out across the blank fields but there's also a part of me that finds this strange as well.

I'm used to looking out over the bright lights of the city, hearing cars at all hours of the day and night, surrounded by the constant thrum of people living in the overcrowded flats above and below. I thought I'd feel relieved escaping the push and pull of living in a busy area but I miss the hustle and bustle more than I thought I would. I just keep reminding myself this is an adjustment and I'll get used to it.

The nearest house to this one is down a winding country lane to the left. The couple living there, Jed and Tiggy Spencer, are early retirees in their late forties. They both had high-flying jobs in London and made plenty of money during their city careers and married each other later in life. They're often away on trips, so I've only seen them fleetingly. But Tiggy has been enthusiastic whenever I have seen her. She brought over a bottle of Bollinger champagne and a delicious Fortnum and Mason's hamper as a wedding gift.

Past the Spencer's home is the Robinson's farm. They've been farming there for centuries and currently they're a multi-generational family living in various accommodations on the land and working together. I've stopped by a few times to buy eggs and milk in their farm shop. Beyond the Robinson's, the lane opens up to a small area where there's a cluster of thatched roof cottages owned by older residents. The village of Waterbridge is to the right of our property and that's where I've been gravitating towards on my walks with Luna.

I guess if we were living somewhere a bit more populated there would be more opportunities to have a wider social circle. Right now, I just have two friends here in Waterbridge. I met Bex one day in the woods when we were both out walking our dogs. She has a German Shepherd named Trudie. Trudie and my tiny dog Luna look a bit ridiculous walking along together, like little and large, but the two animals rub along well. Then there's Jean who runs the local café; she's about twice my age and more of a grandmother figure but I've found myself perched at her cake counter for a chat at least once a week.

I take a sip of my wine before flicking through the TV channels. I skip aimlessly, hoping that Nicholas will appear before I settle on something. By the time I've finished drinking, my eyes are getting heavy and the room feels like it's getting colder. I think about going downstairs to try and persuade my husband to put his work phone away but I don't think he would like to be interrupted. His shoulders tense every time we discuss the business deal he's trying to pull off. He says it will be his biggest win yet if he's successful.

I select a rom-com movie that must be about twenty years old. I haven't seen this film since I was a teenager but it used to be one of my favourites. I watched it with my best friend so many times that I'm sure we could've recited most of the dialogue off by heart.

A pang of nostalgia washes over me as the opening credits and comforting music roll. The last time I watched this was before the events that changed me forever, the turning points in my life that in a strange way led me here to Orchard Farm and Nicholas.

I lean back against the headboard and try to focus my attention on the familiar storyline and noughties fashion. As my body relaxes, I can feel my limbs growing heavy and my head nodding. I reach for Nicholas's glass of wine and tip the liquid into my mouth, hoping it will help me to stay awake...

***

Hours later, I peel my eyes open. My throat feels like sawdust and my body aches from the uncomfortable position I've been laying in. The room is dark but I don't remember switching off the light. I turn over to find Nicholas snoring gently beside me; his back is to me and he's facing the other way. The last number I remember seeing on the clock was 12.30 am; he wasn't upstairs at that point so whoever was on the other end of the call kept him in his office for hours.

Disappointment pools in my stomach. I waited hours for him to come upstairs but his work kept him away. It's not the first time an evening has ended like this. I rub my stiff neck. Last I knew, I was sitting up in bed, having drained both my wine glass and his, and the TV mounted on the wall was still on. Nicholas must've slid me under the covers – either that or I slipped down under them in my groggy state. Stretching out, I find myself wondering why his business calls take so long. What on earth can he possibly be discussing at such length?

I tiptoe to the bathroom and slurp water greedily from the tap. Next, I find a pair of pyjama bottoms and socks and pull them on my bare legs and feet. I feel cold and I know I'll sleep better if I'm a little warmer. I'm about to get back into bed when I notice a little yellow glow coming from

Nicholas's side. It's his phone lighting up in the darkened room. This is unusual as he normally tucks it away in the drawer of his bedside table, choosing to use an old-fashioned alarm clock instead of the alarm on his phone.

I'm about to ignore it and snuggle down under the covers when the mobile device glows brightly once more. There's absolutely no way I'll get back to sleep if the light keeps flashing. So I softly move round to Nicholas's side of the bed, intending to put the phone away for the evening. Except when I pick the phone up, I can't fail to see there are six missed calls from the same number. Six missed calls from a contact named Cath.

Why is another woman calling my husband in the dead of the night?

Before I can put the mobile back down a hand shoots out in the darkness and grabs my wrist.

'Kirsty? What are you doing?'

Chapter Four
Kirsty
Now

A shiver runs down my spine.

'Kirsty, what are you doing?' Nicholas repeats his question. His eyes are wide open, staring at me, and his hand is still circling my wrist, his grasp tight.

I know how this looks; it must seem like I'm snooping on his phone. 'Um,' I stutter, tugging my arm away from him. 'The light on your phone was bothering me.'

Nicholas sits up slowly and flicks on the bedside lamp. His eyes bore into me. I look away, heat rising in my cheeks. I wish I could stop the blood flooding into my face, I've done nothing wrong so why is Nicholas looking at me like I've committed a crime?

'Really?' Nicholas snaps.

Swallowing hard, my mouth feels dry. 'Nicholas…' I give an uneasy laugh. 'I was just going to put your phone away in the drawer. That's all.'

His eyebrows shoot up as he continues to glare at me. 'Ok, fine.' He lets go of me and then says, 'You know I've got nothing to hide, don't you?'

'Of course!' I reply carefully. 'I wasn't…' I gesture at his phone. 'I mean, if you think I was trying to look at your phone then…' My voice fades out as I try to find the right words. My mind is jumbled and I'm still half-asleep.

'Good. Because I'd hate to be married to someone who doesn't trust me.' Nicholas's voice is low and hard now.

'I do trust you,' I say in a small voice, finding it hard to believe the turn this conversation has taken.

He nods, holding the mobile device out to me. 'Here, take a look if you want to.'

'What? Nicholas, I'm not interested in what's on your phone. I don't want to take a look.'

He places the phone in the drawer, slamming it shut a little harder than necessary. I flinch in response. This scenario feels all wrong to me. Nicholas is usually so patient and understanding, so full of good humour. Why is he being so tetchy about this?

'Let's just go back to sleep,' Nicholas says, a note of exasperation in his voice.

He lays back down and I do the same. As I stare up at the ceiling, unable to drift off again, his words circle round and round in my head. Nicholas's mobile is often clamped to his ear or in his hand because of his job and his heavy phone usage is something I've got used to.

My jaw clenches as I think of all the potential reasons behind why my husband behaved like that. He'd just finished a long work call so maybe he was stressed and overtired. It could be that and nothing more. I'm probably overthinking things because it's so late. So far, our relationship has been all hearts and roses but the way he's just acted feels completely out of character from the man I've been getting to know.

Unclenching my jaw, I take some deep breaths in and out through my nose and mouth. I can't let this keep me awake for the rest of the night. Nicholas is snoring gently now; our tense exchange is obviously not keeping him from sleeping. I turn onto my side, squeezing my eyes shut and willing myself to drop off.

Then I remember the caller ID. Who was the woman ringing him in the middle of the night? Cath... Is she just a work contact, or someone with a more personal connection? Our marriage is still very new and there's so much I need to find out about him.

I've been lying in a foetal position, my legs drawn towards my chest, my muscles scrunched up and tense. Uncurling, I straighten out my limbs and try to stretch out the tightness in my calves and the stiffness in my shoulders. But it's no good, my body is aching. Sitting up, I swing my legs over the side of the bed and take a deep breath in and out. Trying to keep my breathing steady, I continue to inhale and exhale until I'm finally feeling a little bit calmer. Nicholas remains asleep.

I lay down on my back and attempt to switch off my busy mind. It's very late, and thinking through things at this hour isn't going to be helpful. I flip over onto my other side in an attempt to settle. I'm facing Nicholas now, although his back is turned to me. I can just about make out the shape of him.

My husband's words come back to me then. *'I'd hate to be married to someone who doesn't trust me.'*

I don't want him to have any reason to believe that I don't trust him. If he did, he might start to question other things about me.

And that can't happen.

Chapter Five
Eva
Now

I've returned to the farmhouse again. I know I should stay away but it's like a magnet drawing me to it. I've tried so hard not to come back here but tonight I found myself following the familiar route to the place I once called my home. As I made my way down the narrow country lane, memories of the day when my husband and I first got the keys for Orchard Farm flooded my mind.

Orchard Farm: the beautifully refurbished house that I spent countless hours lovingly restoring before my life changed. I did everything from choosing the paint colours to sanding and polishing the original oak flooring. Now another woman is cooking in my gorgeous kitchen, dancing under the moonlight on my patio and sleeping in my king-sized bed with my handsome husband. This is the perfect life I created. It was meant to be mine.

Have I lost it all – forever?

Now I'm standing in the shadows, waiting to see if I can catch a glimpse of my husband. Even though I discovered his deception a long time ago, the betrayal still burns in my stomach like acid. When I think of all the years of my life I've dedicated to that man, all the energy and love I poured into our relationship. He was my everything. And this is how I've been repaid.

I glance down at the three rings on my left hand. One is a simple plain wedding band. It didn't cost more than two hundred pounds at the time – it was all Nick could afford in those days. The engagement ring is similarly inexpensive, a single red ruby set against an old-fashioned art deco band. I can't help but smile as I remember how overjoyed Nick was at finding this piece of jewellery in a small, second-hand jewellery shop by the sea. He proposed to me less than half an hour after buying it, down on one knee on Brighton Pier. It was a stormy February morning and the sea was raging. At the time, I thought it was romantic but perhaps the weather was a sign of how turbulent our marriage would become.

The third ring is gold again but much higher quality than the other two pieces. It's set with several rubies and I know it cost Nick a small fortune. But less happy memories are attached to it. I can't even bring myself to recall what happened in the months after Nick presented me with this ring. I grit my teeth and turn my thoughts to the present.

Nick is now a different person to the tousled-haired teenager I fell in love with. The more successful he got, the more strained our relationship became. I thought it was something we could work through; despite everything I still loved him – still love him – and I want to go back to those loved-up days of our youth.

But Nick always goes to extremes. He couldn't just have a simple affair like any of his business pals. No; he had to go further than that. He thought he could remove me from my house, my life and get away with it. He thought he could have a marriage with her while he was still married to me.

He was wrong.

Chapter Six
Kirsty
Now

For the first time in our marriage, Nicholas has made me feel unsettled. My head is thumping and I feel off-kilter, so I hook my hair up into a messy style bun as it's the least amount of effort. Getting ready for the day, I feel like I'm wading through mud, feeling slow and sluggish after so little sleep.

I select a loose, white top, knee-length skirt and tights as an easy outfit for the day. I replay last night, the call from the mystery number and Nicholas's reaction when he thought I was trying to look at his phone. What is he hiding?

When Nicholas enters the bedroom, a white towel tied around his waist and his hair dripping wet, I expect him to greet me with the accusatory tone of the night before. Instead, he comes over and gives me a quick kiss on the cheek. There's no mention of his sharp words. I decide that I will take his lead and wait to see if he brings it up.

When my make-up is applied, I head downstairs. My first ritual of the morning is always to make a fuss of Luna and fill her bowl with her breakfast. Once that's done, I fire up the coffee machine, adding an extra shot of caffeine into my Americano. Nicholas is going through his own regular morning routine, whistling as he reads the daily newspaper. It seems like such an old-fashioned thing to do when the news is readily available online, but Nicholas says he prefers to digest world events in print. He flicks through, the pages rustling as he turns them. He appears to be in a good mood so I say nothing but the way he's acting is unnerving.

I can't help thinking about the caller ID. Again, I wonder who Cath is and why Nicholas was rattled about me seeing her name flash up on his phone screen.

'Let's go to Waterbridge today,' Nicholas declares. 'It's beautiful outside.'

He's not wrong. Pale golden light is streaming through our bi-fold doors. Normally this would put a smile on my face but today it just hurts my tired eyes. My husband isn't the only one who is eager to get outdoors; Luna has been running between me and the front door for the last few minutes. Like Nicholas, Luna is very routine based and she's making it known that she wants her first walk of the day.

Nicholas chuckles. 'Luna thinks it's time to go too but let's just make this a trip for the two of us.'

Waterbridge is very dog friendly, both the café and the pub allow four-legged friends inside and most of the shops are welcoming as well. Usually, I take Luna everywhere with me – she's my little shadow and I can't see a reason to leave her behind but now is not the time to resist Nicholas's suggestion.

'I'll just give her a quick run around the field then, so she's had some exercise before we leave.' I'm keen to escape the house and have some time to think.

He shakes out his paper and goes back to perusing the news. I hurriedly pull on my Wellington boots, knowing that Nicholas might get restless if he's kept waiting too long. Luna follows me into the back garden, her tail wagging, and we then go through the gate to the field beyond. She is so happy to be out here, sniffing at everything and then running back to me.

We walk past the old stables. The farmhouse itself is glorious but the outbuildings on the land have been neglected for years. Just before our wedding day, I asked Nicholas if we could bring life back to the farm. I told my husband-to-be that I would love a greenhouse and a vegetable garden. I also hinted that I'd like a few animals as well: dogs, cats, chickens, maybe even a cow. I remember he laughed good-naturedly as I'd rambled on, my imagination running away with itself.

But then he'd drawn back from me, his face clouded with a serious expression. 'Animals aren't going to lead to something else though, are they?'

'What do you mean?' I'd responded.

'I mean, make you broody?' His bottom lip had jutted out as he said this.

'Of course not!' I'd replied. 'We talked about this already and we're on the same page. No children.'

I've never asked Nicholas why he doesn't want children. He fits the stereotype of the sort of man who might want a son and heir but he's also created a very high-end lifestyle for himself, so it's easy to see how children don't factor into his world.

His shoulders had untensed and he'd pulled me back into his arms and kissed me on the top of my head. 'Good. As long as we're sure of that: just you and me.'

'You, me and the animals.'

'And the animals.' He'd laughed gruffly.

I meant it. I spent my childhood raising my younger brothers and sisters. Living in a cramped three-bedroom flat on one of the highest floors of what felt like the tallest tower block, my mum had produced a newborn every other year, almost like clockwork, until the space we lived in was bursting at the seams. While my mum was nursing or birthing, I cooked and cleaned. I wiped snotty noses and sang bedtime lullabies. I loved each of my siblings equally and they loved me back. But it was a lot of responsibility at a young age.

Often, they'd run to me first if they'd scraped their knee or had a bad dream. I was their second mother. But every evening I'd sit and look out from our bedroom window, wishing for something more for me and for them. All five of them have their own lives now. Two of them are travelling together, one is married and growing a flock of her own, another is a singer trying to make it in a band and the youngest one has just started university. I'm proud of them all but I've done my mothering and, at twenty-six, I want to invest in my own future now.

I carry on walking and, in the space of fifteen minutes, my mind feels a lot clearer. I was worried that what happened last night might have escalated this morning into our first argument but Nicholas appears to have forgotten all about it. Having thought about it further, I decide the simple explanation for his snappiness is the fact that he'd just been woken up and been kept up by a late-night work call.

And yet, there could be another reason. If there is, I fully intend to find out what it is.

Chapter Seven
Eva
Then

Our chipped mugs clink together, the prosecco sloshing about inside. Our grins are wide, matching each other.

'Happy new home,' I say in a sing-song voice, before swigging my drink. Nick takes a slug of his own.

I glance at the shiny silver key on the kitchen worktop. It represents a new chapter in our lives, a new beginning and one that I am so ready for. Moving to the countryside has been a goal for both of us. We spent almost a year searching for the right property – I would be very happy never to step into an estate agent's office ever again – and then we found this, our dream house. The home we've chosen to live the rest of our lives in.

'I wonder what the neighbours are like,' I say, full of curiosity. I don't care too much; I mainly voice the thought because I know it will interest Nick. I'm the kind of person that keeps themselves to themselves, I don't often seek company outside of my marriage. Nick is the sociable one of the two of us. The only thing that matters is that Nick and I are happy here.'

'The area comes highly recommended from Ray Clarke and I remember it a little from when I was a child. I'm going to check out that golf club as soon as I can!'

Laughing, I say, 'I think we've officially entered middle age!'

He smiles back at me. 'And there's no one else I'd rather have by my side.'

He clears his throat and pulls me to my feet. 'Just stand there,' he instructs. 'And now close your eyes.'

I do as he says.

A few minutes later, Nick says, 'You can look now.'

I open my eyes and see that Nick is down on one knee in front of me. He's holding an open jewellery box, with an expensive-looking gold ring set with rubies nestled inside.

'This is an eternity ring for you Eva. You deserve it and I want this to be a new start for us.'

Happy tears roll down my cheeks. 'Oh Nick, it's gorgeous. Thank you.'

He slips the ring on my finger and it fits perfectly. Nick has always been a romantic. I can count on him to have flowers and cards organised for every birthday and anniversary. His natural charm is half the reason his business is so successful as well. Although our marriage hasn't been completely smooth sailing. We'd been navigating a tricky patch due to Nick's long hours at work. I hope things start to change for the better now.

Our belongings are all in storage so we're sitting on a set of old chairs that we found discarded in the garage. Bending down, I pick up the greasy paper and boxes that half an hour ago contained the piping hot fish and chips that we devoured far quicker than we should have. The oven isn't working and it's also far too dusty here to make a proper meal so we decided to have takeaway food as our first meal in our new home. Nick is usually quite particular about his food but he has a weakness for fish and chips. It reminds him of his childhood.

Dumping the rubbish in a black bag, I walk the length of the kitchen. I can see in my imagination exactly how we can change things to make the most of this house. I want to add an extension and create a brand-new kitchen area flooded with natural light – the space we're in now will become a utility and larder.

'Isn't this exhilarating?' Nick stands beside me and pulls me close.

We gaze out of the window onto the land that is now ours. My heart bursts with hope for everything that this will become. We've agreed that Nick will continue to steer the business full time and that I will step back from the admin and organisational role that I've played in the company so far to focus my time fully on the refurbishments.

'Thank you,' I say to Nick, kissing him full on the lips. 'Thank you for finding this place. It's going to be incredible.'

'It absolutely will be –' he chuckles, '– because you'll be behind every detail. Project management is your speciality after all.'

He's right, I will put all of my energy into ensuring this house looks like it belongs in a glossy magazine by the time I'm finished with it. In the meantime, we will be splitting our time between a hotel a few miles away while the renovations are underway and the small flat that we own in London. It's a one-bedroom flat that's tiny in proportion but in a fantastic location in the city. It gets a little cramped with both of us staying there but I'm confident we will make things work in the short term and it will all be worth it once we've finished remodelling the farmhouse.

Nick has promised that this house is going to be our happily-ever-after. And I believe him.

Chapter Eight
Kirsty
Now

Returning back indoors, I find Nicholas ready and waiting for me.

He checks his watch and announces, just like he always does whenever we go out somewhere together, 'We'll take the Range Rover.'

Nicholas guides me outside the front of our house. He isn't keen on walking places, not when we're so far away from everything.

'Sure.' I smile back at him.

The Range Rover is his pride and joy. I often see him polishing it so that it's always at its gleaming best. Today it's so clean I can see my reflection in the paintwork. I've put in my silver earrings and added a dash of blusher to my cheeks to make a little effort.

Nicholas presses a button on his key fob to open the security gates and then says, 'One sec, I just need to go back inside for my phone.'

My stomach flips again at the memory of the horrible exchange we had last night. Perhaps the retrieval of his phone will make him remember it. I lean against the vehicle, waiting for my husband and weighing up whether I should bring up what happened last night or not. It feels wrong to just leave it hanging awkwardly between us. Although maybe he feels he said his piece at the time and doesn't need to say any more. I muse on this; it would fit with his character as he's a very 'in the moment' sort of person.

'Hello!' A female figure comes up the sweeping driveway and walks through the open gates, waving enthusiastically. 'I'm so glad I caught you, hi!'

In an instant, I'm being swept up in the arms of someone wearing a very pink outfit and am engulfed in a thick cloud of perfume.

'We just keep missing each other, don't we?' The woman steps back. It's our nearest neighbour Tiggy. 'Our fault as we're always jetting off on some trip or another!' She makes a sound that's somewhere between a squeal and a high-pitch laugh and it cuts right through me.

Attempting to answer, I find myself in the middle of a coughing fit. The intensity of her perfume has tickled the back of my throat.

'Oh dear, are you okay?'

But I can't answer her. I'm properly choking now. My throat is on fire, my lungs feel as though they're burning and my eyes are watering. What on earth is in her perfume? Perhaps it's something floral that's setting off my allergies. Is that why I'm having such a reaction?

Tiggy's face blurs a little in front of my eyes. She must notice me swaying because she grabs me with one hand, her sharp nails digging into my flesh, and slaps me hard on the back with the other. I just about manage to heave in a few lungfuls of fresh air. And then a few more. After a minute or so, the coughing subsides a little and I'm breathing almost normally again.

'You need a drink of water,' Tiggy says authoritatively.

Before I can say otherwise, Tiggy is ushering me inside my house. I'm taken by surprise as Tiggy, one hand firmly on my back, steers me through the entrance. Judging by the way she finds the kitchen so quickly, I'm certain she must have been inside previously.

Tiggy opens the cupboard where the glasses are kept and hooks one down. She then fills it using the filtered water dispenser inbuilt in the front of the fridge. I now have no doubt that she's been here more than once given that she's able to navigate her way around the kitchen space so easily.

'Here you go,' Tiggy says, handing me the glass. 'Sit down.' She gestures to one of the chairs at the breakfast table.

Anyone would think that Tiggy was the host and I was the guest. I do as she says and I slowly sip the cool water. It soothes my throat.

'Sorry about that,' I splutter.

She's still standing up and, for a brief second, this makes me feel like a child who's been playing make-believe in this grown-up house and now someone who's really suited to being here has stepped in and taken over. I mentally shake my insecurities away.

'I'm fine now, thank you,' I say with a small smile. Although I'm burning with embarrassment.

'Good.'

I clear my throat. 'We were just about to head into Waterbridge. What are your plans for the day?'

Nicholas doesn't like to be derailed when he has a plan and the scent of Tiggy's perfume is starting to irritate my throat again now we're inside so I try to gently hint that this isn't the time for a social call.

'Oh, no big plans.' Tiggy looks at me pointedly then. It's clear she doesn't want to leave anytime soon. I get up and throw open a window.

'Would you like a coffee?' I ask politely.

'That would be lovely.' Tiggy plants herself down in a chair then. The satisfied look she has on her face makes me think she was eager to come inside and jumped at the first opportunity.

'Such a beautiful room, so much light,' Tiggy observes.

She tosses her hair over her shoulder. 'I've been on at Jed for years about extending the back of our place like this. It feels so airy in here and it's just such a gorgeous room in the summertime...'

Tiggy continues to talk, her words definitely designed to let me know that this isn't the first time she's been to this house. But then I guess that's not unusual. Jed and Tiggy are my husband's nearest neighbours and I'm sure he must have had them over for dinner from time to time.

'The problem is, we have a seventeenth-century cottage and the planning permission on doing anything is a total nightmare. Jed keeps saying it's a headache we could do without. I suppose I do agree as we're only there for part of the year and in winter it's so cosy. But then I step into this room and it makes me think it would be worth us taking on the project.'

I'm not too sure how to respond so I take a small sip of my coffee, which is still slightly too hot and it burns my tongue.

'I'll have to try and persuade Jed to think about it again.' Tiggy exhales dramatically and then focuses her attention on me. 'So how are you settling in?'

I wrap my hands around the warm mug to anchor myself. A number of Nicholas's acquaintances have asked me this question already. I've tried to reassure myself it's an expected question but there's something in the tone that each of them has used that sets off my paranoia. It's clear for them all to see that I'm not one of them and I'm sure that Tiggy will be watching to see whether I sink or swim in this marriage.

'I love it here. Everyone's been so welcoming.'

'We are a tight-knit community,' Tiggy replies. 'Most of us have been here for decades though!' Her laugh is harsh. 'There's not many people your age living around here; so many people move away for jobs. Although plenty return once they've made their fortunes.'

It's clear that Tiggy wanted to work in the mention of the age difference between Nicholas and I into our conversation. At forty-five, he's nineteen years my senior. It's not something that I've dwelled on too much and when we're together I don't find that the age gap is an issue. But it's true that there aren't many people in their early thirties living in the village.

'Age is just a number,' I trot out a cliché phrase. 'I'm just happy to get to know people.'

Tiggy roars with genuine laughter at this. 'Well, if that's the case and you don't mind socialising with the oldies then I'm sure you'll fit in well here. You should come along to one of the golf club events, it would be good to see you there. Everyone is dying to meet you.'

Nicholas is yet to invite me to accompany him to his golf club. I got the impression from him that it was a kind of boys' club situation but it's clear Tiggy is a regular there. I wonder why Nicholas hasn't suggested this but perhaps he's waiting for the right event or when his work has settled down.

'I'd love that,' I say.

'Good, we'll have to get on to Nicholas about arranging it then.'

She fiddles with a gold earring and looks as though she's weighing up something. She glances over her shoulder, as if to check that Nicholas isn't nearby, and then leans forward conspiratorially.

'You do know he's been married before, don't you?'

Chapter Nine
Kirsty
Now

I almost spit my coffee out.

'Oh, are you okay?' Tiggy jumps up, her hands flying to her face.

I recover myself almost immediately. 'I'm fine, I'm fine,' I protest.

'Thank goodness,' Tiggy sits back down in her seat, concern etched across her forehead. 'You did know, didn't you?'

'Of course,' I reply quickly, not wanting to give Tiggy further room to speculate. 'Of course I did.'

'Gosh, I'm glad. I thought I'd just put my foot in it!'

Annoyingly, my cheeks begin to burn bright at this. I bet this has been the topic of conversation at the golf club.

Did Tiggy come here just to find out how I was doing and whether I knew about my husband's relationship history? Even though I was already aware he had a wife before me, I don't know too much beyond this. It's not something that Nicholas has spoken much about, despite me trying to encourage him to open up about it.

I shift uncomfortably in my seat and wonder where Nicholas is. He was only supposed to nip upstairs to get his phone… I imagine he's got caught up with some work emails or even another phone call.

'Well, I just hope you don't get too bored here in this big house. I said to Jed, it can't be fun for you to be here all on your own when Nicholas is off on his business meetings.'

'I've got Luna here with me,' I say.

As if on cue, Luna appears in the kitchen. She looks sleepy – she'll have been snoozing and the commotion just now will have woken her. She walks lazily across the kitchen, stops to give Tiggy a small sniff and then comes to sit on my feet.

Tiggy doesn't make any mention of Luna or her appearance, which makes me think she can't be a dog person. 'Well, it must be lonely at times so take my number. Have you got a pen and paper?'

I hop up, disturbing Luna, and grab a pen and a Post-it note. Tiggy then scribbles her name and number down on it.

'There you go.' She looks up at me. 'If you need anything – anything at all – then don't hesitate to call me.'

'That's very kind of you.'

She gives me a practised smile and I notice how perfectly straight and dazzlingly white her teeth are.

I'm still standing, hoping this is a hint that our little chat is coming to an end. My mind is whirring – I can't work out if Tiggy really is being neighbourly or if she's just come here to stir things up.

'I mean it, if things are ever difficult—' Tiggy touches my arm.

'Tiggy!' Nicholas appears at the door before she can say any more. 'How are you?'

I watch as the serious look on Tiggy's face immediately disappears and she puts on an excellent display of being excited to see Nicholas.

'Nicholas! Darling! It's been far too long!'

They kiss each other on the cheek, both beaming at each other like old friends.

Did I just imagine the intent look on Tiggy's face when she urged me to reach out to her if ever I needed anything? And what did she mean by 'if things are difficult', was she referring to me being here by myself or was there something more to it? I watch her now and there's no trace of any hostility towards Nicholas from her – in fact quite the opposite.

'You keep spending months and months in the sunshine,' Nicholas teases her. 'What's wrong with Waterbridge?'

'I could say the same thing about you, I hear you've hardly been home since you married this poor girl.'

My cheeks flush at this. In just one sentence, Tiggy has made it sound like I've been complaining about my husband whilst also choosing to use 'poor' and 'girl' in her description of me. It could be coincidence, or maybe I'm being highly sensitive, but she's managed to both highlight the difference in my social background and the fact that I'm nearly two decades younger than the pair of them in one cleverly crafted sentence.

Nicholas looks over at me then and, despite the broad smile on his face, I see a harder look in his eyes. My stomach drops a little as I don't want him to think I've been sitting here lamenting my life, when nothing could be further from the truth.

Nicholas chuckles in response. 'Let's arrange for you and Jed to come over one evening, we'd love that.'

Tiggy looks delighted with the invite. 'Wonderful. But do bring Kirsty to the club as well, I can't believe you haven't already.' Tiggy gives Nicholas's arm a playful tap.

'I'm sure Kirsty doesn't want to spend her evening with a bunch of—'

'Choose your words carefully,' Tiggy interrupts, laughing.

I stand up then. 'I'd love to go to one of the golf club events, it'll be so nice to meet everyone.'

Nicholas looks a little surprised at this.

'There, that's settled then,' Tiggy declares. 'It'll be lovely to see more of you.'

Tiggy comes over to me and grasps my hands in her beautifully manicured ones. 'And remember what I said,' she says in a low voice before kissing me on the cheek.

'I'd best be off.' Tiggy gives Nicholas a hug and he escorts her to the door. I can hear them still talking, their voices light and teasing.

Tiggy glances back over her shoulder at me and the look on her face makes me wonder: are they talking about me?

Chapter Ten
Eva
Now

As I walk along the lane, a blanket of brown and red leaves underfoot, I remember the exact moment I set eyes on Nick Johnson. Tall, dark-haired and classically handsome, I spotted him across the room at a friend's party. I knew when I saw him that I wanted him. It was love at first sight for me.

I went up to him to say hello and we hit it off immediately. Once we started talking, it was like there was no-one else in the room. Since that day, Nick has been the only one for me.

We were a team. I did everything I could to support him when he was building his company. I believed that counted for something. Nick and I were married for fifteen, mostly happy, years before things started falling apart.

I thought we'd be there for each other no matter what.

Some days I talk to him as though he's still with me; I long for the conversations we used to share. Yes; it's true I want some kind of revenge. I want him to hurt in the same way he's made me hurt. But, more than that, I want things to return to the way they used to be.

I love him.

I miss him.

I will get him back.

Chapter Eleven
Kirsty
Now

Sitting down heavily, I try to process Tiggy's whirlwind visit. I have no idea if she was genuinely concerned about me or not. She definitely couldn't help herself when it came to making those not-so-subtle digs. Perhaps she's like that with everyone, or maybe it's her way of attempting to assert herself as the alpha female with other women.

Tiggy is so well put together, her make-up flawless and her designer clothes a clear signpost of her wealth. If I'm going to be at Nicholas's side in these circles then I need to up my game. Perhaps that's why he hasn't taken me to his golf club? Maybe he thinks I won't fit in. It's true, I'm far more comfortable in my dog-walking clothes – usually a chunky hoodie and equally chunky, mud-caked boots. But I can scrub up well if I need to.

I'm also trying to build up my freelance cake making business in the local community. So far, I've made a number of birthday and celebration cakes, including a dark chocolate ganache creation that went down particularly well at a recent baby shower. Getting to know my husband's circle of friends at the golf club could help me to make more connections. And maybe I'll discover if any of his friends there are called Cath…

Luna nudges my foot. I bend down and stroke her silky head. It gets lonely here sometimes during the day and even though I have Luna for company, it's not the same as having another adult to talk to. I like to be busy – I'd go mad if I didn't keep myself occupied. Despite Nicholas assuring me there's no need for me to work, I want to.

'Ready?' Nicholas pops his head through the kitchen door, startling me out of my musings.

I nod and then go outside to take my place in the passenger seat. Switching the radio on, I rearrange myself until I'm comfortable, leaning my head against the chair rest. I'm grateful to have the ride into the village today and the opportunity to get out of the house. It's such a pretty home to live in but I do sometimes miss being around other people. And I want to make sure things have been properly smoothed over with Nicholas in the aftermath of his cross words last night.

'Had to take a call,' Nicholas explains as he jumps into the driver's seat. 'It was nice to see Tiggy briefly.'

'It was,' I lie, wishing he hadn't been gone for so long. I don't find Tiggy an easy person to be around. And then I ask, 'Did you shut the kitchen door?' concerned he may have left it open, leaving Luna to roam the whole house while we're gone. I know she settles best in the kitchen, by the aga, if ever I'm out.

He arches an eyebrow. 'One step ahead, I knew you'd ask me that.'

There's absolutely no trace of the man who snapped at me. In the time we've been together, he's never raised his voice and we've never had an argument. It's true that he's an ambitious and laser-focused businessman but I don't see that side of him when he's with me at all. Right now, he appears to be relaxed and ready to embrace the weekend, so I decide to go with it in the hope that last night was a one-off.

He puts the car into gear and moves smoothly down the drive and through the gates he opened earlier. He presses his key fob so they close behind us. Nicholas is obsessive about security and has a high-tech system in place.

'It's a gorgeous morning, isn't it?' he says. 'Can you pass me my sunglasses from the side door?'

I do as he requests. Nicholas turns up the music on the radio a little and begins faintly singing along. He's so upbeat this morning, I'm finding it hard to wrap my head around him being so jovial. He puts his foot down as we move along the country lane. The speed he's going at feels too fast to me but I know he's very familiar with driving up and down this stretch. Hardly anyone uses these roads: only us, the neighbours and the odd person who's taken a wrong turn.

When we first moved here, Nicholas told me he'd buy me a car of my own. He insisted, promising that we'd go and look around some car garages so I could pick out something I liked. Since then, he's never mentioned it again.

Nicholas begins to whistle and the sound hurts my eardrums.

I keep wanting to bring up the subject of the car. I haven't mentioned it again because I don't want him to think I'm taking advantage – and I would love to try to get the money together myself to buy a little runaround. Yes, I'm married to a man who's worth a couple of million, but I want to retain some of the independence of my previous life.

That's why I've started to build a freelance catering business for rich clients in the surrounding areas. Cooking has always been my passion. My mum put me in charge of making meals for my siblings from a young age. We had little money, so I had to get creative to make the ingredients stretch. I'm keen to grow my own food on the farm as well. Nothing major: tomatoes and green beans would be a good start. I'd love to be able to cook with fruit and vegetables I've grown by myself but all of this is going to take time.

I swallow my pride and decide to remind my husband of his offer to buy me a vehicle. 'Nicholas, could we perhaps go and look at some cars?'

'Cars?' queries Nicholas, as though the idea is news to him.

'Yes, you know we spoke about getting a small car for me. I don't need anything fancy, just something to get me from A to B. It would help me to build my catering business. At the moment I have to ask customers to collect from here. If I had my own car I could offer delivery.'

'Ah of course. Sure, we can go and take a look.' Nicholas sounds a little non-committal about this.

Keen to pin down a plan, I make a suggestion. 'How about tomorrow?'

Without a car, most days I stick to taking Luna for long walks around the land we own – the endless fields, the woodland beyond the river – and then a few times a week, weather permitting, I walk into the village so I can pick up some shopping and see some other human beings. I want the freedom to get out a bit more as well as the increased opportunities for my new business.

'I can't tomorrow darling, you know I've got this work meeting to prep for. Things are very hectic for the business right now.'

His tone is firm but he's always busy at work and having my own vehicle will help navigate my new area in more ways than one so I try again.

'It's just winter is around the corner and you said it would be best for me to have a car in the colder months.' I feel so awkward reminding him of this conversation but I don't want the possibility of a car to slip through my fingers.

'Quite right, you'll need one by the winter. Don't worry, we'll find something.' He puts a hand on my knee as though to reassure me but still doesn't commit to a time to go browsing for one.

He then promptly changes the subject, reeling off what he wants to get in the village: bread from the bakery, meat from the butchers and he needs to collect a parcel from the post office. There's nothing unusual on his list, partly because of the limited places that we can go.

I'm frustrated but I try not to let it show. He's made it clear that he's done with the conversation, so for now it looks as though I'm still going to be limited in my options without a vehicle. Especially with the weather getting worse and Nicholas due to be away for two weeks.

'We could stop at the café; it'll be a nice treat,' Nicholas says.

'That'll be nice.' I plaster on a smile, telling myself I'll try to pick up the car conversation again soon.

He continues talking and I let his words wash over me as I take in the scenery. To distract myself, I think about the cream bun that I definitely shouldn't have but absolutely want to order at the café.

'Here we are,' Nicholas remarks, slowing to twenty miles an hour as we draw into Waterbridge village. It's a gorgeous setting, with beautiful limestone buildings arranged around the village square. There's a large field on one side – where cricket is played in the summer – which is flanked by farmers' fields and in the distance, gives way to the woodlands that stretch to the back of Orchard Farm.

I muse to myself that only just over a year ago, I thought that my life was never really going to get started. I was still at the flat where I grew up, paying my mum's rent and feeling trapped in my bedroom in the clouds. Until I took a weekend trip to the countryside, to this picturesque village with its old houses. I'd dropped a penny in the wishing well on the green and asked the universe for something.

That night, I met Nicholas in the quaint local English pub with its cosy fire and welcoming atmosphere. I was perched on a high-top chair at the bar, sipping vodka and orange, when I spotted him across the room. His eyes locked with mine. Not long after, he sat beside me and ordered another round of drinks for us both.

He took me back to his house that night and I've barely left since. I never thought we'd wind up being married. I wouldn't have believed that Nicholas would marry someone like me, so different from the wealthy, stylish women he's so used to rubbing shoulders with. Now we're about to spend a lazy Saturday afternoon enjoying home-cooked food, selecting groceries and likely ending up in that same pub for a few glasses of red wine to round the day off. My mum once told me that if something seems too good to be true, then it usually is. I don't know what makes me think of this but I try to push the thought away.

Nicholas pulls into a parking spot and pecks me on the cheek before jumping down from the jeep with his usual burst of energy. I watch as he raises his hand in greeting to one of the locals.

'Hello Harry, how are you?' he says, and the two men begin to chat.

I vaguely recognise him as someone Nicholas plays golf with. I'm starting to put more names to faces and am getting to grips with Nicholas's social circle. He's so embedded in village life.

Keen to make a good impression, I smooth down my knee-length skirt and attempt to climb out of the vehicle as gracefully as I can. It's a bit of a step down, so I hesitate. Nicholas realises I'm trying to avoid tumbling down from the Range Rover in the way I've done so many times before and he's at my side, taking one of my hands in his and placing his other firmly on my waist to guide me smoothly onto the pavement.

He beams down at me, before propelling me towards his acquaintance, one hand on the small of my back.

I know just how important these kinds of interactions are to Nicholas. So I do my best to laugh in all the right places, say the right things and flatter when appropriate. When we part ways with Harry, Nicholas seems pleased with my performance and nods approvingly.

I let out a small sigh of relief. That's the thing about luck, you have to make it yourself. And that's exactly what I intend to do.

Because my first encounter with Nicholas wasn't fate, it wasn't random chance.

I planned it.

Chapter Twelve
Eva
Then

'So what's next, Mrs Johnson?'

My hand is in his, our fingers entwining like they have a thousand times before, as we stroll together under the sun-dappled trees. The leaves above us are just starting to turn oranges, yellows and golds. It's been a blissful weekend; we woke up late and had a leisurely breakfast and now we're exploring the woodland just beyond the borders of Orchard Farm and discussing the next phase of the renovation.

'A lot of the boring but necessary jobs are out of the way now, the next step on the project is the kitchen extension,' I tell him.

'So the big one then?'

'It's going to completely transform the space downstairs.' I beam.

I've been pushing the other updates on the house forward as quickly as possible. We now have a new boiler, a complete rewire throughout and the ivy that was growing across so much of the front of the house has been tamed. Now it's time for the more exciting parts of the renovation to begin.

'I'm going for the bi-fold doors, the big kitchen window at the end and the skylight in the ceiling to maximise the light,' I update him.

'And how much is all that costing?' Nick teases me.

'It'll be worth it once it's done, you'll see,' I assure him.

'I know, I've seen the designs,' Nick says. 'It's coming together beautifully.'

'We've still got a long way to go though,' I remind him. 'I want to add a patio outside the kitchen extension and remodel the garden area. And we need to revamp a few more of the bedrooms.'

'Do you think we'll be in soon?' Nick queries.

'Definitely not.' I laugh.

His step falters then, causing us to walk out of sync.

'Is that okay?' I ask.

'It takes as long as it takes,' Nick says, but there's an edge to his voice that I know means he's disappointed.

He's being completely unrealistic to think we could be moved into the farmhouse any time in the next few months. And there's no way Nick would tolerate living here while there's still building work going on.

'We'll be settled in soon enough,' I remark.

Then I rattle off my ideas for the garden, detailing everything from where I want the seating and the BBQ to go to what kind of roses I'm going to plant. Nick is quieter than usual as we weave our way out of the woods, across the bridge over one section of the river and back to Orchard Farm.

I keep talking, filled with energy and purpose, and it's only when we get to our back door that I realise Nick hasn't said another word.

'Is everything alright?'

He nods curtly and swipes a hand over his forehead. 'I can feel a migraine coming on. I'm going to go upstairs and lie down. Don't come up for a while.'

Before I can say anything else, Nick has let himself inside and is disappearing into the house. I run back over my words. Did I say anything to annoy or upset him? Anything that might cause him to be in a grump with me?

It's been such a wonderful day together but when Nick gets into one of his dark moods it is hard to coax him out of it. I've learnt the best thing to do is to give him space rather than try to press him to explain what's wrong.

It's not ideal that we won't be moving into Orchard Farm this year. But it'll all be worth it. We'll have the perfect home and the perfect life.

Won't we?

Chapter Thirteen
Kirsty
Now

'You want to watch him...'

Jean, the older woman behind the counter in the village tea shop, gives me the hint of a smile, but there's something in her tone that sounds more serious. Like she's warning me.

At least once a week, my dog walks with Luna involve popping by the tea shop for a hot drink and sweet treat. Jean's baking is the best I've tasted yet and I've enjoyed our chats over the past few months, swapping recipes and tales of working in the food industry. It's been nice to connect with someone who has similar passions and I've appreciated her kindness.

Now, her words are completely unexpected. We've never really discussed Nicholas before. But something in her manner tells me she's been holding her tongue on the subject for a while.

'What do you mean?' I ask, glancing back at Nicholas, who is sitting at a table by the window – and staring in our direction.

She looks a little flustered and drops her voice to almost a whisper. 'Oh, nothing dear, I just mean there will always be women who are interested in men like him, just like you were. Take it from me, I've seen it all in my time.'

'Thanks for your advice, Jean,' I respond in an equally low voice, 'but Nicholas and I haven't been married for very long. We haven't even been on our honeymoon yet!' I laugh but it sounds forced, even to my ears.

She raises her barely-there eyebrows and I shiver slightly, pulling my jacket a little tighter around me.

When she doesn't say anything more, I give her a faint smile and politely say, 'I'd best get on before our drinks get cold, thank you.'

Taking the tea tray, I carefully weave my way towards my husband, making a mental note to bring up the subject with Jean again without Nicholas in earshot. There must be a reason why she decided to warn me.

My hands are trembling so I focus on balancing the tray and putting one foot in front of the other, willing myself to reach the table without dropping anything. I was always a terrible waitress and better suited to working in the kitchen. Finally setting the tray safely down, I sink into the chair, glad to sit after half an hour of running errands around the shops.

'My legs ache!' I joke. With the recent weather, I've mostly been wearing trainers or Wellingtons but today I'm in calf-length boots. They have a small heel and they aren't designed for too much walking.

'Well, they look good from where I'm sitting.' Nicholas winks.

His comment steadies my nerves. Jean's words have bothered me but I remind myself that she doesn't know anything about our marriage. Instead, I try to distract myself by admiring the tea shop. The food is served on china plates, detailed with intricate blue patterns, and the drinks are in delicate china cups. The frilly curtains, wooden Welsh dresser and cracked teapots look vintage. This week Jean has put up cute little Halloween decorations, including crocheted witches and ghosts.

I take a sip of the peppermint tea but immediately put the cup back down as the hot water scalds my tongue. Nicholas has told me I should have at least one herbal tea a day as they're good for health. But I'm not really enjoying the taste of them and I'm now longing for a cold drink.

'Is there anything else you need to get before your trip to Edinburgh? I ask Nicholas, trying to take an interest in his week ahead.

'Nope, I've got everything now.' He leans across the table and links his fingers through mine. 'Are you sure you'll be ok?'

'Of course I will be,' I answer quickly, eager to dispel any doubt. 'I'll have Luna for company.'

He kisses my hand and then takes a gulp of his cinnamon-spiced latte. Our conversation turns towards his plans for the business. I ask him a few more questions than I normally would and he opens up to me about various different goals he has for where he'll be at the end of the year. I listen intently, trying to glean as much as I can about his professional life from what he tells me.

As Nicholas and I talk, I'm aware of Jean's eyes on us. Every time I move my head in her direction, she averts her gaze away from our table, but there's no mistaking that she's watching us with interest. There are only two other tables occupied. At one of them is a woman in a smart black ensemble, tapping away on a laptop. At the other is a young mother, who is trying to persuade her little boy to eat the rest of his ham sandwich. I can see why Jean's attention is drawn to us – a successful man who is well-known in the community and his new wife – but I feel uncomfortable knowing our conversation is being observed.

I bite into the toasted teacake; I'd been keen to have one of Jean's delicious cream buns but Nicholas was ordering and he said we needed to keep the calories down a little after last night's cheesecake. A dollop of raspberry jam slides off the teacake and onto my white blouse.

'Oh no!' I cry.

Nicholas stops what he's saying and gives me an endearing look. He grabs a napkin and helps me wipe up the mess, but my cheeks are glowing hot knowing that Jean's eyes are still trained on our interactions. An unwanted thought occurs to me: is everyone comparing me to Nicholas's previous wife? How well did they know her? I imagine them whispering about how beautiful and elegant she was; how different I am in comparison.

'Thank you,' I whisper to Nicholas.

My husband demolishes his teacake but I've lost my appetite. He then proposes that we make our way along to The Rose and Crown. He always takes charge of our plans in this way, but I'm happy to agree today as a glass of wine might help me relax a little after Tiggy's visit and now Jean's advice.

'But first, let's stop at the florist's. I'm going to buy you some flowers.'

He takes my arm and leads me out of the tea shop. The bell tinkles and Jean shouts her goodbyes; I can feel her gaze on me as we leave.

Classic Blooms is the next shop along. There's a huge autumnal flower wreath on the door, bursting with oranges and golds. The second I step inside; my senses feel assaulted by the assortment of strong floral scents.

'What would you like?' Nicholas asks.

I open my mouth to speak but before I can respond, Nicholas is off, heading for the roses, and he selects a dozen of the deep red variety.

'I hope you like them.' His blue-green eyes meet mine, and once again I find myself suckered in by him.

'Hi Nicholas,' says the young shop assistant, instantly breaking the eye contact between us. She greets him like she knows him. I catch sight of her name badge. '*Francesca*' is written in neat black writing. I'm certain I've not encountered her before or heard my husband mention her.

'Ooooh,' says Francesca. 'A dozen red roses.' She eyes me up, clearly trying to assess whether I'm the wife or the mistress.

I make my left ring finger visible so she can see the white gold wedding band and the diamond ring to match.

'We don't get much call for red roses, apart from on Valentine's Day – and when someone's done something wrong.' Her words are loaded with meaning.

Francesca flicks her auburn hair off her shoulders and rings up the price on the till.

'Why wait for Valentine's Day to spoil my wife? I'll buy her red roses every week of the year if she wants me too.' Nicholas is confident, brandishing his credit card as he pays for the bouquet.

'Well make sure you get them all from Classic Blooms if you do,' she responds with a wry smile.

First Jean and now this. I'm starting to feel like the whole village knows something about the man I married – and I don't.

I watch how Francesca interacts with him as Nicholas chats easily to the young woman. She's over-the-top, almost like she's trying too hard. But then she switches her gaze to me and I swear her lip curls disdainfully. I'm sure she probably hates me. I used to envy the women who seemed to have it all when I was doing shop jobs and waitressing. And now, somehow, I'm one of them.

Francesca can see Nicholas's extravagance – the amount of money he's spending on me – and his dimpled smile. But she has no idea what our marriage is really like.

Or how much we're both hiding from one another...

Chapter Fourteen
Eva
Now

It's strange being back in Waterbridge. This was the place where I thought that Nick and I would grow old together. Things haven't quite worked out the way I'd expected.

I've hired a car and organised a short-term rental in a neighbouring village so that I can keep a close eye on Nick. I observe him now in the village. Nick gets out of the car, pocketing his keys, and marches confidently along the high street. He's always been self-assured and in control. There was a time that I walked like that as well, with my head held high. Like my privileged life was untouchable. I've well and truly learnt my lesson.

And now it's time for my husband to learn his.

I watch as Nick and his new wife walk along the cobbled street together, past the corner store, with its colourful Halloween display in the window, hand in hand. Peering over the rim of my huge sunglasses, I'm certain that Nick won't notice me at this distance as I sit behind the screen of my car. They stop in front of the florist's, admiring the impressive autumn wreath on the door. He smiles down at her before they both disappear inside the shop.

Nick has no idea I'm here and that in itself gives me a sense of power. An upper hand.

I've been watching and waiting. And now Nick's time is nearly up.

Chapter Fifteen
Kirsty
Now

Suddenly, the inside of the florist's feels too claustrophobic, too overwhelming. The strong scents tickle my nose and throat, almost making me gag. I've always been sensitive to floral smells. Nicholas is completely oblivious to how I'm feeling and continues chatting to Francesca. This is what he's like when he starts a conversation, he gives it his complete attention.

I remember the first time we spoke. He made me feel like the only person in the world and I was completely drawn in by his ability to laugh so easily. I know now this is his way with everyone. As I battle to keep my composure, I tune back into what my husband is saying. It sounds like Nicholas knows Francesca's family, which means he could be here a while catching up.

My head starts to spin. I can't take it anymore; the scents in the shop are just too overpowering.

'I'm just stepping outside.' My voice comes out in a squeak.

Missing the small step down from the shop to the pavement, I manage to catch myself on the window ledge before I do any serious damage. Gulping down the fresh country air, I start to feel a little better.

Another ten minutes pass and I can feel myself getting more agitated. What is Nicholas doing in there? The longer I wait out here, the more I turn over today's events in my head. And it's like the floodgates have opened; all of my niggling doubts and insecurities come rushing to the surface. Could I lose Nicholas's attention just as easily as I've gained it?

Jean's words have put me on edge. They circle round and round in my mind. Is it possible there's any truth in what she said earlier? Could she know something about the mystery middle-of-the-night caller - is she aware of who Cath is? I shake my head. This is ridiculous because my dashing husband has just bought me a big bunch of roses. I should be floating on air, not feeling like I've got lead in my stomach.

Glancing into the florist's, I see Nicholas is still immersed in conversation. Francesca is frowning a little now and I long to go back inside to find out what they're talking about. But I don't want to come across as an interfering wife. I lean against the window ledge and survey the view in front of me.

The shops are situated around the village square in pale, limestone buildings that must be more than two hundred years old. The doors are painted only in primary colours and each entrance has some kind of adornment around it – mostly ivy, or roses twisting in natural arches. Every time I step foot here, the essence of this place seems to weave deeper into my soul as I notice new and enchanting things about this community that is so particular and protective of the idyllic spot they live in.

The houses nearest the shops are tiny terrace cottages with wicker hearts hanging on the doors and square bronze signs that proclaim names such as 'Unicorn Lodge' and 'The Old Post Office' inset into the stone, giving each otherwise identical home an identity of its own. To distract myself from my troubled thoughts, I play a game where I guess who lives in each home. I don't know the residents well enough yet to match them to their addresses, but it's fun to imagine the bespectacled eighty-year-old woman who only drinks whisky and sits quietly in the corner of the pub living in 'Reading Room House' or the large, bear of man with the big, bushy beard who often stomps about the village living in 'The Wee Abode.'

I notice a woman sitting on the bench across the road. I have no idea who she is but her eyes are narrowed and she's staring at me. If looks could kill, I'd be dead. The heat of her gaze makes me want to walk away, to shake off her attention. But Nick is still in the florist's so, instead, I tilt my chin and look in the other direction.

A light rain is falling, a complete contrast to the bright start to the day. Checking my watch, I hope Nicholas will hurry up and leave the florist's soon. This morning's sunshine has faded and the temperature is now feeling much chillier. I contemplate going inside to encourage Nicholas towards the pub, like we planned.

The next thing I know, the woman who was sitting across the road is deliberately knocking into me, jarring my shoulder and causing me to stumble back a few paces. I gasp in shock. Up close, there's something familiar about her but I can't put my finger on what it is. She doesn't apologise, she just shoves past me and then throws me a withering look over her shoulder.

I watch as she forces open the door to the flower shop and immediately slams straight into my husband.

'Jane!' Nicholas says in surprise, as he puts out a hand to steady her.

Then I realise why the woman looks so familiar. She must be Francesca's mother – they have the same shade of auburn hair and the same big green eyes.

'Nicholas, how interesting to see you here,' Jane's voice is cold and hard.

'Jane –'

Before my husband can say any more, Jane moves past him and disappears inside. Nicholas looks bewildered but then says a polite goodbye as he exits the shop and joins me outside.

'What was that all about?' I ask.

'Did she say anything to you?' Nicholas checks.

I shake my head. 'No, she just pushed past me.'

Nicholas glances at the shop and then back at me, his brows furrowed.

'Was that Francesca's mother?' I query.

'Yes,' he responds. 'That's Jane Thomas. She can be...' He pauses and then says, 'a little emotional at times.'

'That wasn't emotional, that was aggressive,' I remark, rubbing my shoulder. 'There was no need for that.'

Nicholas murmurs his agreement and then says, 'Are you okay?'

'Yes, just a little sore.'

'Let's go to The Rose and Crown and get into the warm,' Nicholas wraps his arm around me.

As we walk away from Classic Blooms, I'm certain that I see movement behind the window which makes me think that someone was standing there watching us. Jane and Francesca both gave me the impression that they didn't like me.

'Do you know Jane and Francesca well?' I glance up at Nicholas as I ask my question.

'Not especially,' Nicholas answers. 'Francesca seems like a nice enough young woman but I'd keep clear of Jane. She's been known to stir up trouble.'

'What kind of trouble?'

'Let's just say she's got a reputation for not telling the truth.'

Nicholas words hang ominously in the air between us. Has my husband has been on the receiving end of Jane's untruths? I recall how icily Jane had spoken to Nicholas.

And I wonder if there's more to this than Nicholas is saying.

Chapter Sixteen
Kirsty
Now

'Forgive me,' Nicholas says in a mock pleading tone, 'for keeping you waiting.'

He hands me the bouquet of red roses and the heavy feeling in my stomach lifts. 'Of course,' I reply, standing on my tiptoes to kiss him. Even in heels, he's still a few inches taller than me.

As we walk, my attention is pulled beyond the village square to the heath, where a number of people are walking their dogs. It makes me feel guilty that Luna is at home on her own today. Then I spot a woman patting the head of a German Shepherd and my heart leaps. It can only be one person.

'Bex!' I yell, my words disappearing in the wind. 'Bex!'

I met Bex recently when we were out walking our dogs. As is often the way with dog walkers, we said our hellos and exchanged small talk. Bex seemed happy to chat and soon we'd found ourselves ambling along for twenty minutes, talking about anything and everything. It's fair to say that we clicked straight away. We arranged to meet again and we've been seeing each other about three times during the week to exercise our canines and set the world to rights. Bex is a lifeline in an otherwise quiet existence during Nicholas's working week.

'My friend Bex is over there. Come and meet her,' I say to Nicholas, turning my attention back to him.

'The wonderful Bex, I wouldn't miss the chance.'

Linking my arm through his, I pull my husband towards the heath. My eyes scan the green space but now I can't seem to see her at all.

'She was here, just a second ago,' I bluster. 'Over there, by the oak tree.'

'Are you sure? There are a lot of people wrapped up in black jackets and woollen hats.'

'Absolutely, I recognised the dog with her.'

We pause, both scanning the heath. Nicholas breaks the silence, 'She must've gone.'

'But where?' I turn on my heel. I can't fathom how she managed to cross the heath and disappear in the short time I looked away to greet Nicholas. 'I was excited for you to meet her,' I tell him.

'Perhaps she's gone into one of the shops or along to The Rose and Crown?' he suggests.

My spirits lift a little at this. I really would like Nicholas to meet Bex; it would show him that I'm creating a life here for myself. And for once, it'd be nice to introduce him to someone I know. I'm often so out of my depth with the exchanges Nicholas has with his friends and acquaintances – it's all politics, business or sports – and most of the people he knows are around his age or older.

'Well, let's go and get a drink in the warmth, it's starting to get cold out here.' Nicholas slings an arm around my shoulders and we make our way past the limestone buildings to the other end of the street. Then it's just a short walk along an adjoining road to The Rose and Crown. Even in the five minutes it takes us to get there, Nicholas raises his hand and greets several people. I nod and smile, trying to look friendly.

I hadn't realised how isolating it would feel to move away from my family, to an area of the country I'd never lived in before. That's why my blossoming friendship with Bex is so important to me. The last time I saw her, she mentioned introducing me to a few friends that she's made through a dog training group. I'm keen to build a social circle so I've got a support network of my own. After all, you never know when you might need a friend.

The centuries-old pub building comes into view. A signpost just outside has the emblem of a rose and a crown and above the doorway, the number '*1710*' signals the date the property was built. Despite it being so ancient, it's been well looked after. Halloween lights are strung around the windows, an inviting glow comes from inside and I can't wait to be sitting near the log-burning fire within.

The feeling of warmth immediately washes over me as soon as we enter. It's busy: several men with half-drunk pints of beer are propped up at the shiny dark wood bar and groups of people are finishing their lunchtime meals. Scanning the bar and restaurant areas, there's no sign of Bex but she could be in one of the other rooms.

'I'll order you a red wine,' Nicholas tells me. 'You go and get some seats.'

I slide past the bar, avoiding meeting the eye of Robert, the landlord. Recently, I stepped in to help cater for a wake. I'd been in here having lunch, just me with Luna at my feet, and Robert mentioned in passing that they were short-staffed. I offered to lend a hand preparing the buffet for later on in the afternoon and ended up doing the whole thing myself. Robert was delighted with my cooking. He'd even asked me if I would consider doing a regular slot making meals for their weekly 'Food from Around the World' evening. My imagination had immediately run away with itself – I was already envisioning the dishes I might make for Italian or Turkish-themed meals.

I enjoyed the few hours working here; it felt like familiar territory for me. Not only that, it was nice to share the camaraderie with the other staff. The freelance baking comes in bursts and you don't get to make proper connections with people in the same way as when you're working in a team. Robert said he'd call me to discuss it further, but I haven't heard from him since and that was over a month ago.

I stick my head into the snug, where there are a few wooden tables and leather-clad benches. Two older men play a game of chess, a teenager is absorbed in their phone, and what looks like a mother and daughter are having a heart-to-heart. But there's no sign of Bex. At the back of the pub, is a covered area with outdoor heaters and rattan garden furniture. People often smoke or vape out there, and it's well used in the summertime for lunchtime meals and evening drinks, but today it's completely empty.

Turning inside, I head to the space I love the most in this building. I have to duck slightly under the low door to pass into it but, once in the room, I instantly feel enveloped by its cosiness. There are dark wood beams across the ceiling and on the far wall, in the centre, a log fire burns bright. Freshly cut logs are piled up, ready for use, in the nooks either side of the fireplace. Rubbing my hands together, I glance around.

A group of women, who I know are part of the Women's Institute, are playing cards, and a middle-aged man is having a drink by himself. Bex definitely isn't here. I resolve not to allow the disappointment to spoil my afternoon. Nicholas and I can relax here for an hour or so, maybe even get some dinner, before we head home.

My favourite spot near the fireplace is available, so I make a beeline for the table. Sinking into the high-back chair, I let my eyes rove over my surroundings, appreciating them once more. In one corner, a battered oak cupboard is stuffed full of board games and on the other side of the room, there's a rickety shelf of brass tankards. I get the sense of walking into the past every time I come in here, like I've gone through a gateway into a simpler time.

Just then, Nicholas appears in the doorway with two drinks in hand and has to duck lower than I did to enter the room. He then meanders around the various chairs and sets our drinks down on the little table in front of me.

'Result,' he says, pointing at our chairs.

Outside, it's just started raining again and big splodges are hitting the windows in a heavy, rhythmic way, adding to the sense of cosiness inside these walls. I tip my head back and close my eyes briefly. When I open them again, Nicholas is grinning at me.

'The perfect place for an afternoon like this.'

I murmur in agreement. 'We got inside just in time to avoid the downpour.'

We drink companionably and Nicholas asks me a few questions about my upcoming week. I tell him about the birthday cake I'm making for an order and the new sweet potato lasagna recipe I'm planning to try. Then he goes to get a deck of cards from the communal stack of games. 'A game of rummy?'

'I thought you'd never ask.' I laugh, taking the cards from his hands so I can shuffle them.

The next hour passes and we chat between games. Nicholas furnishes us with more drinks, deciding that we will get a taxi home. It's a blissfully peaceful afternoon and I feel my muscles relaxing. Nicholas makes me laugh a lot with his anecdotes about work, the golf club and his business contacts. I can tell that he appreciates me listening to him. I've allowed myself to fall under his spell and he's almost made me feel like this marriage could be for keeps.

Nicholas had started to convince me that he's a good husband who couldn't possibly be capable of bad things. But in the last few days, the chinks in his armour have started to appear.

Last night jolted me out of my make-believe.

And reminded me why I really married this man.

I'm here to find out the truth about his last wife.

Chapter Seventeen
Eva
Then

'Nick? Nick, are you there?' I try. 'Nick when you get this message can you call me back please.'

I stare at my phone, willing my husband to ring me. But it doesn't happen. The clock on the wall ticks loudly, as though it's mocking me. Time continues to march on but it's over thirty hours since I last heard from Nick.

Sitting crossed-legged on the pristine white sheets of the hotel bed, I almost hit the call button again but I manage to stop myself. I know he's on an important business trip to New York and there's a time difference. There's likely a whole host of rational reasons why Nick hasn't replied to any of my texts or calls in the last day, but none of those possible reasons stop me worrying about him.

We've never gone this long without speaking in the entirety of our marriage. Even when Nick has been away on business before, he's always returned my messages or called me to say goodnight. I've even emailed his work email address, just in case there's something wrong with his phone. But there's been no response.

I spin my wedding ring around on my finger and pray that Nick is okay. I'm terrified that something awful has happened to him because surely that's the only reason he hasn't been in touch with me? I picture him lying in a hospital bed and a jolt of fear runs through me.

Pacing the room, I tell myself that I need to keep myself occupied, otherwise I will go crazy with worry. I decide that I'll wait another few hours – by that time it will be lunchtime in New York, and if I've still heard nothing then I will contact his new secretary to see if she can tell me what's going on. In the meantime, I'll head back to Orchard Farm to distract myself.

An extended hotel stay may sound glamorous but it's not a normal way of living. The hotel is comfortable and has everything I need to function but existing in one room is starting to make me feel a bit stir crazy. As I navigate the country lanes towards Orchard Farm, I feel jittery with anxiety.

My phone is on the loudest volume setting as I don't want to miss a call or a message, but it continues to remain silent. Pulling into the driveway of Orchard Farm, I see the builder's van still parked where it was first thing this morning. This means I can busy myself making the contractors hot drinks and answering their various questions until hopefully I hear something from my errant husband.

I allow myself to sit in the car, for just a little while, resting my pounding head on the steering wheel. The more time stretches on, the less excuses I have for Nick not to call me. If he had lost or damaged his phone then he could have found a way to contact me to let me know. Likewise, if he was lying in a hospital bed then I would have been phoned by now as his next of kin. He never travels without any ID on him. My concern is starting to morph into anger. Nick must have some concept of how I'm feeling; he must understand that not hearing from him for this period of time is going to send me into a spiral of anxiety...

Thinking over the last few months, I acknowledge that my husband has been more distant than usual. He's thrown himself into a new work project while I've thrown myself into the remodelling of this house. We haven't seen each other as much as we usually would because Nick has been staying at the flat in London more and more while I've been at the hotel nearby to Orchard Farm so I can be on hand to manage the progress of the project.

We started off with such grand plans but then slowly we've become ground down by late-running builders, missing orders and the exhaustion of managing a big house renovation with no previous experience. I've tried to keep things on an even keel as much as possible but I know I've become tetchy and tired. This in turn has had an impact on my relationship with Nick.

The reality of doing a house makeover has been a lot more stressful than I imagined. I have to be around to ensure that every last detail of the plan is being carried out. I'm the one who has been here to let in builders and plumbers and electricians. I'm the one who has accepted the deliveries, co-ordinated the different contractors and dealt with flaws in the designs. Not to mention putting up with all the dust and the dirt and the noise. It's been all consuming.

The whole experience has certainly been more complicated than many social media videos led me to believe. In real life, it's not possible to wave a hand or click my fingers and find a whole room effortlessly updated. I've been completely immersed in everything going on here, so have I missed something?

Thinking back over our interactions – or lack of them – recently, I can count on one hand how many times we've seen each other in the last month. A gnawing feeling grips my stomach.

Was something up with Nick even before his trip to New York?

Chapter Eighteen
Kirsty
Now

I intend to make the most of this evening so that Nicholas misses me while he's away. I've organised a cosy evening in with a film and treats in front of the fire. It's important that Nicholas keeps believing that I'm completely in love with him. I'm hoping that the more he trusts me, the more chance I have of getting him to open up about his past.

As I pad through the house in my bare feet, the oak floorboards feel cool against my skin. Along the hallway, I pass the front door: it's heavily bolted and there is also a smart security system that acts as another layer of protection. It's all controlled by an app on Nicholas's phone. I've asked him how it works but he prefers to manage it himself. He's given me a set of keys to use with strict instructions about double locking the doors when I go out.

It's not hard to see why he's so obsessed about security when you look around at the contents of this house: everything is high-quality and expensive. My feet sink into the luxurious deep-pile carpet as I enter the lounge area.

'Luna!' I call, and my little dog comes running. Stopping by my ankles, she looks up at me with her big brown eyes. Bending down to scratch behind her ears, just as she likes, I smile at my sweet little pup.

Nicholas full belly chuckles and then scoops Luna up under one arm. 'Come on little doggy,' he says to her. 'You can come and sit with us.'

He plonks himself down on the L-shaped sofa and sits Luna across his lap, stroking her fur.

'Cute,' I say, pulling out my phone and snapping a photo of them together.

'Don't go posting that anywhere,' Nicholas says, 'I've got a reputation as a ruthless businessman to uphold.'

We both laugh at this – Nicholas has told me that most of his deals are struck on the golf-course or over dinner. I can just imagine him, charming his way into new opportunities and loosening his opponents up with as much alcohol as possible. It's amusing to think about when right now he's showing his softer side with our dog cradled in his arms. But it makes me wonder, which version is the true Nicholas Johnson?

Luna has only been with us for a few months but I can't imagine life without her now. I smile, thinking back to the crumpled sign I saw tacked to the corkboard in the tiny village post office. The handwriting was barely eligible, smudged and scrawled, but I managed to decipher it enough to understand an elderly couple were moving away from the area and they couldn't take their little dog with them. There was a grainy black-and-white photograph of Luna pinned next to the barely readable message. My heart melted.

I remember tentatively broaching the subject that evening with Nicholas when he returned home from work. Sliding my phone across the dining room table, I showed him my screenshot of the advertisement.

He'd wrinkled his nose. 'What does it say?'

I explained a small dog needed rehoming due to an older couple moving into a retirement home across the country to be nearer to their grandchildren. Nicholas knew how much I loved animals and how keen I was on filling this farm with creatures. To my joy, he immediately agreed that I should go and look at the sausage dog. He said it would be good for me to have some company around the house during the day.

I'd hastily dialled the number to see if she was still available. Thankfully, she was, and Luna came dashing into my arms as soon as she saw me – so it felt like I was meant to have her. This is just one of the many things that made me doubt my preconceptions about Nicholas.

'Sit next to me.' Nicholas grins widely.

As I slide myself down beside him, Luna leaps off Nicholas's lap and disappears out of the room. It's her dinnertime and she sticks to her routine like clockwork, so I know she will be dashing to the utility room where I've already put her food out.

After I set our big bowl of sweet and salty popcorn onto the table, Nicholas covers me with the fleecy, chocolate-coloured throw and puts an arm around me. He flicks on the TV and scrolls until he lands on the latest episode of the most recent bingeable drama that we've been watching together.

Half an hour into our chilled evening, Nicholas's phone rings. It's on the arm of the sofa and he snatches it up immediately. Before he does, I'm almost certain I see the name 'Cath' on the screen once more.

'I've got to get this,' he says gruffly.

I prepare myself for another evening where my husband does a disappearing act. However, Nicholas quickly returns to the room.

'Is everything ok?'

He nods curtly.

I'm desperate to ask him who Cath is but there's no way I can say this outright after how he snapped last night. I'm going to have to think of a subtle way to find out. Once again, I tell myself that it's more than likely something work related. Swivelling my attention from the TV to my husband, I take in the deep-set scowl across his face. Whoever Cath is, she doesn't seem to be the bearer of good news.

As the evening wears on, the tension exudes from Nicholas. He fidgets, unable to relax, and answers me in monotone. Eventually, he announces that he's going to bed but there's no invitation for me to join him. He mumbles something about an early start in London tomorrow as an excuse.

He's made it clear that he wants some privacy, so I stay where I am. Then, once a decent amount of time has passed and I'm confident Nicholas isn't going to reappear, I open the internet browser on my phone. I pull up my most looked at tab: it's a news piece from almost eighteen months ago. I know the words off by heart but I scan back through it again anyway.

The article details an accident on one of the winding, narrow country roads just a few miles from here. It's only a few paragraphs long, outlining a late-night collision that saw a car spin out of control. At the end of the article, there's an appeal for members of the public to come forward with any information and the telephone number of the local police station. It strikes me as being a very short article, lacking detail, in contrast to other news reports of the same nature that I've compared it to.

The name of the woman involved in the accident is one that I'm more than familiar with. It's the woman who lived in this house before me: Nicholas's last wife. And someone very important to me. Nicholas won't speak about what happened to her; he's a closed book. All I know is that he finds it too traumatic to talk about the other Mrs Johnson.

I've heard a few whispers from the locals over the last few months, usually when I go into Waterbridge without Nicholas. Nothing concrete but I've caught sidelong glances, curious looks and snippets of conversations where the words 'wife' and 'accident' have been clear enough to hear.

Nicholas only tells people what he wants them to know, and that includes me. I've observed his conversations enough times now to understand that when he interacts with another person, he showers them with interest and praise. He will ask plenty of questions but is well-practised in holding back information about himself. You wouldn't notice if you weren't looking out for it. It's an art form, a skill.

I've discovered just how difficult it is to get past the protective layer my husband has built around himself – but I've vowed to find out everything I can about Nicholas Johnson.

And that includes what happened on the night of his last wife's accident.

Chapter Nineteen
Eva
Then

I rang Nick's hotel, holding my breath, and was eventually put through to my husband's suite. He answered groggily and told me he'd had a fever. He said he'd lost track of time as he'd slept his way through the worst of his illness. Everything he said sounded plausible but there was something about the way he spoke that made me question if he was telling me the whole story.

He stayed in New York for another two weeks and was then in London for a few days before he came back to Orchard Farm. They were the longest two and a half weeks of my life. His contact was minimal during that time. I could feel my marriage slipping away from me, without really understanding why.

When I finally saw him again, I flung my arms around his neck. He put his arms around my waist in response but it was perfunctory – I could feel him pulling away even though he was right there with me. I tried to be bright and chatty, updating him on the progress of the renovation work, but he seemed disinterested. It was like someone had replaced my husband with a clone who looked and sounded like him but had no emotion towards me.

I was due to have dinner in London with him the following week but he cancelled on me at the very last-minute when I was already on the train to meet him. He said he had an important video call to attend. I was furious with him for forcing me to get off the train at the next stop and travel all the way back to the home I'd been building for us, without seeing him.

Now, another week on, things still haven't been resolved. I keep trying to arrange a time to speak with Nick properly but, for one reason or another, it doesn't happen or our conversation is dominated by the latest mishap to happen with the builders we've employed. A few days ago, I asked him if he would be coming down to Orchard Farm at the weekend and he told me bluntly that he didn't want to be living in a construction site and he would be staying in the city.

My eyes are raw from crying and my throat feels sore. Today I feel empty. I just want things to go back to normal, to have my best friend back. The hope I'd felt months ago, when we first stepped into Orchard Farm, has shrivelled and dried. I need to take action, to go to London and find out what's going on in Nick's head. But I'm afraid of what the truth might be and what it might do to our relationship.

Tapping the unlock code on my phone, my fingers begin to type a message to my husband. I delete and rewrite sentences, trying to find the right words to express how I'm feeling and how much I need to see him. Before I can hit send, a message from Nick flashes up.

He's coming to Orchard Farm tomorrow and he wants us to talk. Finally, a chance to be with each other and clear the air. Whatever drama is going on with the refurbishment, it can wait. This conversation is more important. I roll my shoulders, releasing some of the pent-up tension. Tomorrow we can sort everything out and move on. Perhaps we can book a holiday somewhere – it's exactly what we need. Some time out of our hectic lives to reconnect and relax.

Smiling, I decide to drive to the nearest town and buy a new outfit to give me an extra boost of confidence for tomorrow. I feel strangely nervous, like I'm going on a date or something. I shake my head at the thought; I'm just making an effort for my husband. I tell myself he's just been preoccupied with work and everything is fine. We will catch up and then I will make food for us both. I imagine us talking late into the night, over a bottle of wine, like we used to do.

I'm sure my world will feel right again soon. And that I've been worrying over nothing.

Chapter Twenty
Kirsty
Now

Only half an hour ago, the sky was clear but it starts to rain as I step outside the farmhouse. I'm not going to let that stop me though. I zip up my waterproof jacket and lock the door.

'Come on Luna,' I call. She follows me obediently.

Nicholas is in London today working on the preparations for his meeting. When he goes into the city he sets off for the first train and often isn't back until the day is almost done. I expect that he won't crawl into bed tonight until well after I'm asleep so I have the whole day to myself.

Striding along the path that winds through the trees, I suck in the fresh country air and tread the familiar route to a popular woodland walking spot. The leaves on the trees are an array of oranges and reds. They've already started scattering on the ground all around me and creating an autumnal carpet. It's my favourite season of the year and I intend to make the most of my first autumn living in the countryside.

Checking my watch, I see the time is already 10 am but as I head into a clearing, where a number of wooden picnic benches are positioned, there's no sign of Bex. We'd arranged to meet here with the dogs. I wait for ten minutes and then decide there must be traffic or similar, so I occupy myself by practising some commands with Luna. I set up a small obstacle course for her with a number of large sticks and logs and I'm completely absorbed in my task until a passerby stops to praise Luna. It's only then I check my watch for a second time and realise it's now closer to half past ten.

I start to question if I'm in the wrong meeting place. Pulling out my phone, I see there aren't any missed calls or messages but I've also only got one bar of signal, and that's flickering, so my phone might be too out of range to receive any updates. The signal in Waterbridge is completely unreliable. I clip Luna's lead back on and begin walking towards the car park, where the signal is better so I can use my phone to make a call.

As I'm rushing along, I see the face I've been waiting for.

'Hi!' I wave at the woman walking towards me; she's red-cheeked and looks flustered.

'I'm so sorry I'm late. I got stuck behind a tractor on the way here.'

'No worries.'

We hug briefly and I bend down and make a fuss of Trudie, her German Shepherd, who is standing obediently by Bex's side, and then instruct my own dog to sit. Luna gets so excited whenever she sees Trudie and her tail is wagging madly now.

I'm equally delighted to see Bex. She messaged me this morning to ask if I was free for a walk with the dogs. It was perfect timing with Nicholas working in London today.

'Want to walk further into the woods?' Bex asks.

I nod and we amble together, chatting away. Bex always has a list of TV shows to recommend and amusing anecdotes about what Trudie has been up to.

'How's your week been?' Bex enquires.

'The usual, I've been baking loads and Luna keeps me busy. Although Nicholas is going on a work trip later in the week... He'll be away for two weeks so I'll have to find something to occupy me while he's gone.' I try to make this sound light-hearted but I worry there was a wobble in my voice that's made me sound a little emotional.

'You should come along to the dog training group I've just joined, it'd be good for Luna,' Bex says kindly.

'That would be great. When is it?'

'It runs twice a week, on a Tuesday and a Thursday evening in the next village over.'

'Oh...'

'You're free, aren't you?' Bex asks me quizzically.

'I don't have a car,' I confess.

'No problem, I'll come and pick you up.'

'You don't have to do that—' I start to say.

Bex talks over me, 'Of course I will. What are friends for?'

'You're a gem, thank you.' My heart lifts. It may only be a small thing to some people but the possibility of having two evenings a week to socialise with a group of fellow animal lovers fills me with joy.

The rain begins to increase, but I don't care. I'm happy chatting with Bex and the trees provide some shelter.

Soon, the splattering of water gets heavier and the pathway underfoot begins to turn into muddy puddles.

'We better get going!' Bex laughs, as we race our way back to the entrance of the wooded area. We stop in the car park by her SUV.

'Do you want a lift home?' she asks.

'No, it's fine. I'm only across the way.'

We say our goodbyes and then I make a run for it, picking up Luna and tucking her into my waterproof jacket. Her dog coat has protected her from the worst of it but I don't want her to get any wetter. Tumbling into the house, I then spend half an hour drying us both off and changing into new clothes.

Looking outside, the bad weather looks set to continue for the rest of the day. I decide to make a pumpkin pie for Nicholas, so there's something for him to eat if he wants it when he gets back.

Tying my apron around my waist, I pull my hair back into a bun then wash my hands thoroughly before I get stuck into my task. With the radio on, and nostalgic music from my teenage years playing in the background, I lose myself in making shortcrust pastry and singing along to the tunes of my youth.

Once the pie is done and in the oven, I decide to watch one of the TV programmes Bex mentioned. Before I leave the kitchen, Luna paws at the patio door, her signal for wanting to be let out to do her business. I open the door and as Luna dashes out, I immediately realise something is wrong. I locked the back door. I'm certain of it.

And yet it was open.

My stomach somersaults. Surely, I wasn't so careless as to leave it unlocked earlier? I feel nauseous at the thought. Or perhaps Nicholas has been back here? But that's not possible because he's in London and, even if he had come back for some reason, there's no way he would forget to secure the house.

I pinch the bridge of my nose and try to replay the morning. Except I can't think straight because I know that Nicholas only activates the extra layer of electronic security on the locks when we're both out together or at nighttime. He trusts me to keep the place locked up during the day when

I'm popping out for a walk with Luna or to the village. And if he finds out I haven't done that, he's not going to be pleased.

I scan the room. My eyes alight on the silver key with its one heart-shaped keyring attached. It's on the kitchen worktop by the bread bin. This isn't where I usually leave my key. The only places I normally leave it are either in the door or on the hook in the utility room.

I can almost picture myself turning the key in the lock before I picked up Luna's lead. My pup comes bolting back into the house, shaking out her fur as she does and I'm back to scrambling for a towel to dry her again. I try to reason with myself that I just made a mistake and I need to make sure that it doesn't happen again.

Knowing I won't be able to settle down to watch something now, I wander through the house checking that everything looks okay. As I'm halfway up the stairs, I notice the door to Nicholas's office is open. This strikes me as strange as he always shuts it behind him – in fact it's usually locked. He's told me specifically not to go in there. Backtracking down the hallway, I reach out and put my hand on the silver door handle.

Unable to resist, I step inside. I tell myself that I have to make sure that no one else has been in here. The room is neat and ordered. It's exactly how I imagined Nicholas's office would look. I exhale with relief when I realise that it's undisturbed and there's no one else here.

I want to have a look around to see if anything he keeps locked away in here might tell me more about my husband. About his past – and maybe even about Cath. But I remember the security cameras that Nicholas has in place on the ground floor of the house, so I reluctantly close the office door firmly shut behind me. I can't slip up. I have to play the game properly. And that means coming back and looking inside this room when the camera isn't on.

When I moved in, Nicholas showed me where the cameras are. He told me that he'd had them installed to increase security and to keep me safe. I asked him how they worked, so that I could switch them on and off if needed. But his answer was for me not to worry and that he'd take care of them. Over spring and summer, I spent most of my time outdoors or in the kitchen so I'd almost forgotten the security cameras were there. I'm pretty sure Nicholas only turns the cameras on at night but as I peer at the one in the hallway opposite the office, I can see a small green light shining on it. I definitely don't want him to catch me snooping when he's been very clear his office is off limits.

My nerves are starting to fray. Both the patio and the office door were unexpectedly open... What does this mean? Has someone been in the house? Or is someone still here? Quietly, I go upstairs, telling myself that I'm just being paranoid. There are five bedrooms up here in total; I check every single room but there's nothing out of place. And no one else here.

Flinging myself on the king-sized bed in the master bedroom, I stretch my limbs and try to relax. It's been incredible to live in a house where there's so much space but finding the doors open while I'm home alone has made me feel on edge. I dial my mum's number; it rings and rings but there's no answer. She usually picks up the phone almost immediately so I'm surprised when I don't hear her voice greeting me. There was a time when I knew her daily plans just as well as my own.

I've been too out of touch lately. I know I should call more often but moving here and becoming Nicholas's wife has been a bigger change than I'd imagined. I also wanted to give myself the chance to settle in without being too distracted by my mum's many dramas. Falling out with her neighbour… falling in love again… falling behind with the rent… I've always been there to help her, but it was exhausting. I realised I needed to give my own life more focus so I decided to lessen my involvement when I moved here.

At that moment, my phone rings, the device vibrating too near to my ear.

'Hello,' I answer.

'Kirsty, it's your mum,' the voice at the other end of the line replies. 'Remember me?'

From the way she speaks, I can tell that she's not happy. I brush past the question and say, 'Mum, I was just calling to catch up.'

'It's about time too, I haven't heard from you in over a week.'

'Sorry,' I mumble, instantly feeling like I've been reduced to a teenager being told off.

'Enjoying your new lifestyle in your fancy house, are you?' Mum retorts back.

Taking a deep breath, I say, 'It's lovely, yes.'

'When are you going to invite me to visit then?' she asks, not for the first time. 'It's been six months since you married and I've still not set foot in your house.'

Nicholas and I had a small, intimate wedding at a tiny chapel a few villages over with a couple of Nicholas's friends as witnesses. We went to a nearby boutique restaurant for dinner and drinks afterwards. I didn't want a big fuss and Nicholas was happy for the nuptials to be about us and not other people. I made the decision not to invite my mum and many siblings, as it would've changed the size and feel of the day. It wasn't an easy decision but, given that I wasn't planning to be married to Nicholas for very long, I thought it was for the best. Trying to coordinate when they were all in the country and available would've been a nightmare. And I knew my mum was likely to get drunk and make the whole day about her, which I could absolutely not allow to happen. My siblings understood but my mum still hasn't forgiven me. One day I'll be able to explain to her why I made that choice.

'Nicholas is a busy man,' I repeat the line I've said to her before.

'So you keep on saying.' Her words run into each other and it makes me think she may have started drinking during the day again. I feel guilty that I'm not there to monitor her alcohol intake but it's something that I tried to help her with for years.

He is very busy but, in truth, I'm trying to put off any kind of meeting between my mum and my husband. They're from two different worlds and I very much doubt they'll have much in common. I also can't risk anyone from my family letting anything slip about my past.

This conversation isn't going well and I start to wish that I hadn't called her.

'He's going away on business for two weeks...'

I hear my mum scoff at the other end of the line. 'Business? Again? He's only just come back, hasn't he? For two weeks this time? And you believe him?'

I roll my eyes, 'Of course I do, he owns the company.'

'You've only been married for six months. You're not so naive you don't realise that if he owns the company, then he doesn't need to schedule so much time away?'

She's touched a nerve: this is something I've thought about myself.

'Kirsty, I wish you'd let me meet him. Every time I speak to you, I end up more worried. This doesn't sound like the behaviour of a newly married man. Why don't you come home?'

'You don't understand—'

'Oh, I do. You think I don't because you're now surrounded by people who wear expensive clothes and live in big houses but I still understand, alright.'

I'm shocked by her words. My whole life I've spent putting my younger siblings first and yes, my fortunes have changed but I'd hoped that after all I'd done to help her, my mum would be happy for me – or at least supportive. But it seems there's no chance of that.

'Mum—'

'You listen to me, there's something that doesn't add up about Nicholas Johnson. How much do you really know about him?'

'Please mum, don't—'

She continues to rant. She won't pause to hear me out and by now I'm sure that she's been drinking so I end the call.

Dragging myself off the bed, I feel terrible for hanging up but I've had this kind of conversation with my mum a hundred times before when she's had too much to drink and I know that it will only end in an argument. I've spent much of the last ten years trying to help her get sober but she doesn't seem to want to help herself and I got to the point where I had to step away for my own sanity.

I go and splash my face with cold water, trying to clear my mind. I wish that her words didn't bother me so much. Because what she said was right, there's so much about Nicholas that I don't know.

But I'm not the all-trusting wife she thinks I am.

Chapter Twenty-One
Kirsty
Now

The rain is still falling hard outside, so I busy myself indoors. After folding some washing and cleaning the house I drift upstairs with a mug of hot chocolate. I need something comforting after the call with my mum. I know she's upset that I haven't welcomed her into my new home yet, and I can understand why. I feel bad, but I need to make sure that nothing ruins my plans.

I go into the small upstairs bedroom that Nicholas has gifted me to do what I like with. I have a comfortable pale pink snuggle chair in here where I sit with my feet tucked underneath me as I look out of the window to the rolling fields beyond. I've adorned the walls with prints of my favourite quotes, whimsical sentiments that resonate deeply with me. Normally this space feels so calm but right now I'm still wound up by the phone call with my mum.

Sitting down, I contemplate inviting my mum to Orchard Farm while Nicholas is away. That might satisfy her for the time being and it would give me a chance to see how she's doing. Leaning back in the comfortable seat, I close my eyes. I found it hard to adjust to this house in my first few weeks of living here. The generous space felt so alien and every room is immaculate so I felt on edge about making the house look in any way unruffled.

I'm used to living in a noisy, chaotic home where people come and go, dirty dishes are left in the sink overnight because everyone's tired and the walls all have scuff marks because it's been years since they've seen a fresh lick of paint. In this house, I always feel like I have to be on my best behaviour. So it's nice to have a space of my own, where it doesn't matter if I leave a coffee cup out or I don't straighten the cushions perfectly. I can just shut the door and know that Nicholas won't disturb me.

Luna settles down on the geometric patterned rug. Checking my watch, I see the afternoon is wearing on. Nicholas won't be home for hours yet and I still can't shake my mum's words. I decide to have another look around the house, to scrutinise it for clues of the wife who lived here before. I've done this a number of times since I moved in as I've been curious to find out more about his previous marriage. However, I've uncovered nothing so far. There are no photos to evidence his previous marriage and because of the minimalist decor there are no ornaments or trinkets with any sentimental value.

But perhaps I just haven't been looking in the right places. As there are security cameras downstairs, I'm limited to looking upstairs but there are plenty of rooms up here to search through. Moving back through to the master bedroom, I check in Nicholas's bedside drawers and in his wardrobe but there's nothing out of the ordinary. Just neatly arranged clothing. I scour every inch of the other bedrooms, mostly finding the usual contents you'd expect in the cupboards, such as spare bedding and towels.

I direct my attention to the chest of drawers in the second biggest bedroom. It contains a spare throw for the bed and a handful of knick-knacks including a number of reed diffusers still in their packaging. Nicholas likes to be organised, even down to buying the same scent of reed diffuser in bulk. I pick up one of the reed diffusers and note it's a Jo Malone Orange Blossom scent. I know that Nicholas prefers more musky and woody scents so perhaps this wasn't chosen by him and was bought by the woman who lived here before me.

I'm about to close the bottom drawer when a glint of something in the left-hand corner catches my eye. My fingers feel around in the space and I hook out something cool and delicate. It's a bracelet. A woman's gold bracelet, with a daisy chain design. It looks familiar, and I'm certain it's a Marc Jacobs' piece. I hold it in my hands, noticing that the clasp is broken. Nicholas is so meticulous about his house being in order so it surprises me that anything has got past him, even something tucked away in a dark corner.

Pulling the drawer completely free, I look down the back but there's nothing else hidden here. I pocket the item and decide to stow it away at the bottom of my own jewellery box for now. The bracelet doesn't really tell me anything but it spurs me on to keep searching. The sun is setting outside but I'll still have a good few hours before there's any chance of Nicholas returning so I decide to look in one more area of the house.

I head into the boot room. I'm sure there aren't any cameras inside – as far as I'm aware there's one positioned above the front door, covering the drive, and another in the internal hallway. We keep our outdoor wear in here and I use some of the storage for Luna's variety of dog coats, leads and training equipment. If Nicholas did ever ask me why I was rummaging around here, I could easily explain it away by saying I was trying to find one of Luna's leads or treats. Concentrating on my task, I look high and low in every crevice for any information that might tell me something more about my husband.

I pat down all of his coats and delve into each pocket. In the very last one, a warm winter coat, my fingers wrap around a discarded receipt. It's for a restaurant called Fin in the Scottish Highlands. Looking at the items listed it seems the bill was for one person, albeit with a number of whiskies ordered. The date on the receipt leaps out at me: it was exactly a week before the day Nicholas and I got married. My pulse speeds up. The weekend before we wed, Nicholas was supposed to be with friends. He'd said the evening wasn't quite a stag do – he claimed to be too old for something like that – but more of a small gathering ahead of his nuptials.

My mind goes into overdrive. Nicholas had told me he'd be in Oxford for the night and most definitely not in the Scottish Highlands. There could be so many explanations for this: perhaps it's a receipt he picked up off the floor and meant to put in a bin to reduce litter, maybe this isn't his coat but one left earlier in the year by a guest... I scramble for possibilities but, try as I might, the fact that his favourite whisky is listed on the receipt and the food choices match my husband's preferences is beyond doubt.

If he lied to me about that – just before our wedding day – what else has he lied about

Chapter Twenty-Two
Eva
Then

It's a hot, summer's evening. The kind when it's so humid that your clothes cling to you and sweat trickles unpleasantly down your back. I place a jug of ice-cold water on the garden table and arrange the chairs just so. I've already sent the builders home early, so that I could spend some time tidying things up a little and making everything look a bit more presentable inside the farmhouse. Outside, the new patio is in place and the garden landscaping is almost finalised; there are just a few more flourishes to add. Nick hasn't seen any of this yet and I'm excited to show him how the vision for our house is finally coming together. It's resembling less of a building site and feeling more like a home.

Once he sees how much things have progressed, I'm sure he will start to feel more positive. By my calculations, we're only about a month away from him being able to move in. Everything will have been painted and the dust settled by then. It'll be a relief to be living together again, under the same roof. The renovations have lasted for almost nine months. It's been a big upheaval for both of us. But I feel confident things will go back to normal once we've moved into our dream house.

Everything is in place. I collected a picnic hamper full of delicious goodies this morning. I made sure it included some of Nick's favourites – sundried tomatoes, a selection of cheeses and scotch eggs – along with a bottle of wine and two glasses. I'm looking forward to kicking off my sandals and relaxing in the nearly-finished garden.

I hear his Range Rover pull up on the drive and I feel strangely nervous. I want everything to be perfect this evening so we can get our relationship back on track. Smoothing down my hair, I make my way through the house and Nick is already stepping through the front door by the time I get there.

'Hello.' I beam, pecking him on the cheek. 'Welcome to our home.'

He opens his mouth to speak but I cut in.

'There's so much that you haven't seen – we're almost done! Come and have a look.' I beckon him to follow me, walking ahead of him and talking non-stop about the colour scheme in the hallway.

'Your office is just through here and is complete. I made sure it was the first room to be finished.' I fling open the door to reveal the room that I spent the most amount of time selecting different furnishings for. I'm proud of the end result; it's exactly to Nick's taste.

He steps inside and gapes a little. 'Eva...' he breathes. 'You have done an incredible job.'

Nick stands there in the middle of the room, absorbing it all. My heart swells. It's taken a lot of effort and tears but tailoring each room to create the home that we will live in for the next phase in our lives has all been worth it.

'The lounge is next.' I take the lead again but this time Nick hangs back.

'I should've saved the office until last.' I smile, thinking that he doesn't want to move from the room that I've shaped just for him.

'Eva, we need to talk.' Nick's face is serious and suddenly I feel a little light-headed.

'Yes, yes. Sorry, I was so eager to show you everything that I'm forgetting you've had a long journey. Come out to the garden, I've got refreshments waiting.'

'Eva...'

But I don't turn around, I plough through the freshly painted rooms. Barely glancing at the newly-installed kitchen and the impressive skylight that fills the space with light, I stumble out of the patio doors and position myself by the garden table where the picnic hamper is on full display.

'Wine or fruit juice?' I babble. 'Let me guess, wine. And there's olives in here, the scotch eggs you like and—'

'Stop.' Nick's voice is stern. 'I don't want a drink and I don't want any food. I think you know why I'm here.'

'I... I...' Speech momentarily fails me.

'It's over.'

The two words hang in the air between us.

Then I bluster, 'Yes, it's nearly over. The renovations are almost done and we can be together again. It's been so strange without you here but this will be a fresh, new start for us.'

'No, Eva. I'm sorry, I can't do this anymore. I can't pretend everything is ok when it's not. It hasn't been for a long time. I'm leaving you.'

Picking up the wine bottle, which I uncorked earlier, I start to pour the liquid into one of the glasses with shaking hands. Then I drink it down in one gulp. My worst fear is coming true. I knew, deep down, that a seismic shift was happening between us. But not for a second did I imagine that it was something that would permanently destroy our relationship. We've been together so long, we've been through so much, I assumed our foundations were solid.

Looking up and into Nick's handsome face, I take in the familiar sight of him. The man I married, the man I've grown with for so many years. How can he stand here and tell me our marriage is over? And why?

I laugh then.

'Is this a joke?' I hear myself saying.

'It's no joke Eva,' Nick tells me. 'I mean it.'

'I don't understand… Nick, what's going on?'

'It's over Eva,' Nick repeats, a little more gently now as he swipes a hand through his short hair.

The softening of his voice makes my skin prickle. I can feel anger building inside me. How dare he come here and break apart our lives like this. Does he expect me just to smile and move on?

'Tell me why,' I demand, not wanting to know the answer but needing to.

'I've met someone else.'

And that's when I realise he's not wearing his wedding ring. It's gone from his finger, like it was never there. Like I never mattered. This is real, he is really saying this.

'No!' I scream, flying towards him.

'Enough,' Nick orders, catching my outstretched hands in his.

'You're deluded if you think I'm just going to walk away from our marriage,' I heave, as he roughly shoves me away from him. 'After everything I've put into this, all the sacrifices I made when you were starting the business. And now, after I've spent months creating the home we always wanted!'

Nick just stands there, silent and unmoving. As though my emotions aren't any concern of his anymore.

'You're having a midlife crisis,' I spit at him then. 'Who is she? Someone younger, thinner, prettier?'

He reacts then – I'm obviously right.

'Oh, classic hit middle age and replace your wife with a younger model. I thought you were better than that Nick.'

'Think about why I've been having an affair,' Nick retorts back. 'You've been unbearable! You've been obsessive about me and this house. It's been too much. And even before then, we were drifting apart. We aren't the same people we were when we first met. I'm not the same person.'

My mouth hangs open as I take in his words. I've tried to be the perfect wife and this is how he repays me.

'We're getting a divorce,' he says flatly. 'My solicitor will be in touch with you this week.'

'Nick, this is insane.'

He moves away, as though he's done with the conversation.

'Nick, you can't just leave!'

He turns then and glares at me icily. 'I can Eva and I will. You just need time to adjust, to understand this is how things are going to be.'

As Nick walks away from me, my heart feels like it's on fire. And then he turns. Has he changed his mind?

'Oh, and you'll need to drop the keys to the solicitor.' He gestures towards the farmhouse. 'It's in my name.'

I've watched Nick being utterly uncompromising in business deals but I never thought that I would one day be on the receiving end. It hits me that Nick has been planning this. Of course he has. He will be strategic and make sure that financially he comes out as the winner. He won't understand that I lost everything the moment I lost him – our shared memories and the future we were creating. All destroyed in a few sentences.

And then there's his new relationship. He won't want me to get in the way of it.

A boiling rage courses through my veins. I feel like a woman possessed, with no control over my actions.

Or what happens next.

Chapter Twenty-Three
Kirsty
Now

'Good morning,' I greet Nicholas with a tray laden full of breakfast food. I was up early this morning and I made a full English fry up, complete with bacon, eggs, sausages, hash browns, beans, toast and a cup of tea. I'm surprised that the delicious smell wafting through the house didn't wake Nicholas up before now.

He stretches, sitting up and rubbing bleary eyes. A smile tugs at his mouth when he sees the feast I have presented him with.

'It's the full works,' I say, setting the tray down on the bedside table.

'Wow, what've I done to deserve this?' Nicholas pulls me towards him and kisses my hand.

'You've been working so hard, I thought I'd set you up for the day.'

He runs a hand through his tousled hair. 'You, Kirsty Johnson, might just be the best wife ever.'

I'm pleased by his reaction. As I lay in bed last night, waiting for Nicholas to return from working in London, I decided to pull out all the stops so that by the time he leaves for his trip to Edinburgh he's completely convinced that I'm his utterly devoted wife. And then when he's away, I'll have more opportunities to dig into his past.

'What a morning this is.' He rubs his hands together gleefully before transferring the tray to his lap and tucking in.

'Enjoy,' I say, kissing him on the forehead. I then turn to pull open the curtains and fling one of the windows open.

'I'm working at home today,' Nicholas reminds me.

I nod. 'I've left a salad in the fridge for you for lunch, I thought it might balance what you're having for breakfast.'

'Thank you, I think that's wise,' Nicholas agrees.

'I'm going into Waterbridge this morning, is there anything you need?'

'No, thanks.'

I leave my husband to eat his breakfast and then head out with Luna. It's drizzling outside again so I put sturdy boots on as the road leading from our house to the village is extremely muddy from all the rain we've had. Luna is in a full doggy raincoat but, even with this on, her paws are immediately caked in mud.

After I've been walking for five minutes, a car whizzes past and then comes to a halt abruptly in front of me.

'Hiiiii!' A head sticks out of the passenger window; it's Tiggy.

'Jump in!' she calls to me.

I trudge over to her. 'Hi Tiggy, thanks for the offer but I'm covered in mud – and so is the dog!' My eyes roam over the gleaming Jaguar and I squirm at the idea of Luna and I covering the upholstered leather seats with dirt.

'Don't be silly! Get in!' Tiggy insists.

'Are you sure?'

'In!' she orders.

I self-consciously slide into the seat behind her. Placing Luna on my lap, I try very hard to keep the mud contained to one area. Jed's face is peering at me from the driver's seat and it's clear from his expression that he's not quite so relaxed about his precious vehicle becoming dirty.

'Hi Jed,' I say as calmly as possible.

'Heading to the village?' he asks.

'Yes, thanks for the lift.'

'We couldn't leave you slipping and sliding down the road like that,' Tiggy exclaims. 'How long are you going to be out for? We might be able to give you a lift back as well.'

'Oh, please don't put yourself to any trouble,' I say awkwardly. I was planning to have a leisurely browse in the village and not really put a timer on my outing so I'd much rather make my own way.

'No trouble. Just message me when you're on your way home and if we're heading back around the same time you can jump in with us,' Tiggy tells me breezily.

'Thank you,' I reply.

'Awful weather isn't it,' Jed comments.

'Can you not think of anything more interesting to talk about than the weather,' Tiggy teases her husband before turning to speak to me. 'Kirsty, let me know your availability for dinner and we'll get something in the calendar. If we leave it up to the men, a year will pass and nothing will happen.'

'Nicholas is away for a few weeks with work, so it'll have to be more towards the end of the month.'

'Ah yes, of course he is,' Jed says then. 'He's got that big pitch coming up, I hope the old chap gets it as he's been working hard enough.'

'He certainly has,' I agree.

'You're a saint to put up with him,' Tiggy says. 'I couldn't bear being alone while my other half swanned off every five minutes. Why don't you go with him?'

'As Jed says, this pitch is a big one,' I reply.

'Well, if you want my advice,' Tiggy says, 'I'd go on a trip or two with him. It doesn't go well if a husband and wife are apart for too long in my opinion.'

The hedgerows and fields flash by as Jed races along the country road at a speed that is far too high for my liking. And now my heart rate feels as though it's matching the speedometer on the dashboard.

'Tiggy!' Jed admonishes his wife, and I observe him giving her a warning look.

'It's ok,' I reassure. 'I'm new to being married and very happy to hear any advice Tiggy has.'

Jed throws back his head and gives a sharp laugh. 'Oh, please don't encourage her Kirsty. You'll open the floodgates now.'

'She's a sensible girl,' Tiggy shoots back at her husband. 'Jed and I have been married for five mostly happy years —'

'And we've still got plenty more mileage left in us, haven't we my sweet?' Jed interjects, laughing some more.

'Exactly, so feel free to come to me with any problems,' Tiggy says.

I join in with their laughter but I know my own sounds forced. Tiggy might be a useful source for me to find out more about Nicholas's previous marriage but I have to be careful about what I ask her.

'Here we are, in the beating heart of Waterbridge,' Jed announces as he pulls into a vacant parking space near the village green.

We all step out of the car and I make sure to dust down the seat as best as I can. There's not much I can do about the muddy floor though.

'Thanks again,' I say to the pair of them.

'Have a good day.' Jed says, before striding off towards the post office.

Tiggy doesn't make a move to go just yet. 'I meant what I said, just think of me as your resident agony aunt.'

'I will do,' I tell her. 'Actually Tiggy, there is one thing I wanted to ask you about.'

'Go on.' Tiggy's curiosity is clearly piqued.

'Can I ask you about Nicholas's previous marriage?'

'Well,' Tiggy says conspiratorially. 'That's a long story. There's a lot I can tell you about what went on there.'

I'm a little concerned that Tiggy might go back to my husband and tell him that I've been prying. 'It's only because I want to avoid the same thing happening again,' I say in a low voice. I hope this sounds convincing enough, so that Tiggy doesn't have any cause to think there might be any other reason.

Tiggy raises her perfectly shaped eyebrows. 'And I expect now that you've landed in such a dreamy home, you want to do all you can to stay between the bedsheets?'

My mouth drops open. I can't believe Tiggy just said that.

She grins like a Cheshire cat. 'Oh, come on Kirsty. This is woman to woman; you can be honest with me. After all, that's why I married Jed at first. Love came afterwards.'

Shaking my head, I insist, 'No, I know I'm younger than Nicholas but money is not the reason I married him.'

'Well, if that's what you like to tell yourself but, honestly, I understand what it's like with men like Nicholas. They have everything: the money, the looks, the power. It's hard to resist. In fact, there was a time – and this was a very long time ago – that Nicholas and I had a fleeting moment, which could have taken us down a very different path.'

Tiggy looks wistful now. I'd suspected as much from the way they both interacted with each other. I'm guessing that she was always going to drop this nugget of information into conversation with me at some point, to let me know that she got to Nicholas first.

'Although,' Tiggy goes on, 'Nicholas had a few dalliances with people in the village. He was quite the popular bachelor back in the day.' She laughs. 'For a time, I thought he would end up with Jane Thomas...'

I recall the cold way Jane spoke to Nicholas in the doorway of the flower shop the other day and how he told me to steer clear of her. Something doesn't add up, and I immediately realise what it is.

'But Nicholas only moved into Orchard Farm about three years ago so how did he know both of you?'

Tiggy looks amused at this. 'Hasn't he told you? Nicholas grew up in Waterbridge, we all went to the village school together when we were small. Nicholas of course went off to boarding school but we used to spend the summers together as teenagers.'

I can't believe Nicholas hasn't shared this information. But I can't dwell on this right now as Tiggy hasn't told me what I actually want to know yet.

Looking over my shoulder to make sure there's no one nearby, I assure her again that things are different between Nicholas and me. 'Tiggy, there is just one specific thing I wanted to ask you about.'

I'm pretty certain now that, despite her friendship with Nicholas, she's likely to spill the beans about his past. She just can't help herself.

'I heard something about Nicholas's wife being involved in an accident, is that right?'

Tiggy goes still then. 'Who told you that?'

'I can't remember, I overheard it somewhere. At The Rose and Crown perhaps, but I wanted to know if it was true.'

Tiggy exhales, pulling a cigarette out of her purse and lighting it up. She blows out a stream of smoke before replying. 'I guess you were bound to find out some time or another,' she says. 'Yes, it's true there was an accident. Such a tragic state of affairs. Poor Nicholas was devastated.'

She blows out more smoke and I try not to recoil. I wait for her to elaborate further but, just as she opens her mouth again, Jed emerges from the post office.

He calls over, 'Tiggy, I'm sure Kirsty has better things to do than listen to you gossiping all day long. And I want to get a round of golf in before the weather turns again.'

Jed couldn't be more wrong; I've been hanging on to every word Tiggy has said.

Tiggy is turning to go so, before it's too late, I blurt out my other burning question, 'Is there anyone called Cath at the golf club?'

She turns back and gives me a quizzical look. 'No – well not any more. There used to be Cathy Locke, but she moved away years ago, before Nicholas returned to the village. I believe she's living it up in Spain now with her younger—'

'Come on Tiggy,' Jed calls, a note of exasperation clear in his voice.

'Sorry darling,' Tiggy apologises. 'We'll have to talk more another time. Let's arrange a drink one evening and then I can tell you all about it. Jed and I are going to Cyprus for a week but I'll be in touch when we're back.'

'Thanks Tiggy.' I watch as she stubs out her cigarette before tottering off after Jed. The pair of them link hands and disappear into the bakery.

It's frustrating that our conversation was cut short. But I feel as though I've started pulling at the right threads and Nicholas's history is now beginning to unravel.

But will I find what I'm looking for?

Chapter Twenty-Four
Eva
Then

Shattered glass surrounds me. I can feel tiny cuts pin pricking my body and my hands are bleeding. But the pain on the outside is nothing compared to how I'm feeling inside.

My mind feels strangely blank as I sit rocking amongst the chaos I've caused. I'm aware of the blue ambulance lights flashing on the driveway, just beyond the office window. A paramedic places a silver foil blanket around me and gently helps me up.

I can't believe what I've just done.

Never in my life have I behaved in this way. But Nick sent me over the edge. It's all his fault.

I smashed the wine glasses and water jug on the patio. After that, I tore through the house, pulling apart everything I could. Tearing mirrors and pictures off walls, kicking over plant plots and finally entering the office and sweeping Nick's whisky collection – which I'd carefully lined up on the shelf hours before – onto the floor. I feel like I've had an out-of-body experience and now I'm a shivering wreck.

Nick is a smart man. He filmed it all on his phone without me noticing. When I was in the midst of a breakdown, he was recording it to use to his advantage. The wail of the sirens finally jolted me out of my rage. Nick had called the ambulance and not the police. But that's not because he was trying to help me.

I can hear him now, standing in the hallway talking to another one of the paramedics. He's just said the word 'sectioned' and I know, without a doubt, that's what will happen to me. Nick knows enough people to pull strings to make things happen – and he always gets his way.

As the paramedic leads me out of the office, I catch a glimpse of myself in the cracked mirror. My eyes are bloodshot, my hair is wild, and mascara is streaked all down my cheeks. I don't look like myself. I don't feel like myself. Is this what life is going to be like from now on?

I'm placed in the ambulance, they lay me down, and then I feel a needle go into my arm as I'm given a shot of something. I don't have the energy to fight back or question it. I just stay where I am and close my eyes.

I loved him. And he betrayed me.

Chapter Twenty-Five
Kirsty
Now

After a long walk with Luna, I make my way to The Rose and Crown. Nicholas has hinted a few times that he prefers for me not to be in the house all day when he's working at home. I guess when he's taking calls or trying to concentrate it might be distracting knowing I'm in another room and not working. In the summertime, there's been no issue as I've gone out on long walks but, as the weather turns, I realise that I need to find some indoor alternatives for when Nicholas is working from home. In a rural place like this, and without a car, I know it won't be an easy task.

At the bar, I'm greeted by Robert. 'Hi Kirsty, how are you?'

'Good thanks, and yourself?'

He nods to indicate all is well. My eyes snag on the specials board: there's a message written in capitals to announce a Swedish food evening next Wednesday. Once again, I find myself wondering why he never got back to me about the 'Foods from Around the World' cooking opportunity. Robert follows my gaze.

'It was a pity it didn't work out with you working here one night a week for the specials evening,' Robert says slowly, running a hand over his stubbled chin. 'You would've been perfect for the role.'

My mouth gapes open. He didn't ring me back, so what's he talking about?

'I can understand though if Nicholas wasn't keen on you working here, when he has a certain image to uphold.' There's a hard edge to his words.

I try to recover myself but Robert realises something is wrong. I guess the look of confusion on my face is obvious.

'He did speak to you about it, didn't he?' Robert leans on the bar, his brows knitted together.

'I... I...'

'He came in here and told me outright that you wouldn't have the time to commit to the job.'

I swallow. 'Yes, I'm sorry. I'd forgotten all about it until I saw the sign,' I lie, not wanting to betray that I've been kept in the dark about this. 'It would've been lovely to be part of it but Nicholas and I will come along one evening to enjoy the food instead.'

Robert gives me a strange look, as though he doesn't believe what I've just said.

'It's just an orange juice for me,' I say quickly, changing the subject.

'Sure, coming right up,' Robert replies. He opens his mouth as if to say something else but then closes it again and sets about making the drink I've ordered.

Once my orange juice is in hand, I go into the cosy room at the back and sit in the same seat where I was only the other day with my husband. Unease snakes around my gut. I've always thought that Nicholas was considerate and caring to me. So why wouldn't he speak to me about this? Why would he just take the choice away from me?

As I stare out the window at the pouring rain, I feel like my eyes are being opened. The way he handled the conversation with Robert feels controlling. He made a decision for me without seeking my opinion. If he'd shared whatever reason he had with me then we could've talked it through. Instead, he's taken an opportunity right out of my hands and hasn't even had the decency to tell me.

The best thing for me to do is to go back and ask Nicholas why he told Robert I wouldn't take the job – and to ask him outright about his last marriage. Except the thought of doing so makes my heart squeeze with panic. Nicholas won't like being asked – and I might not like the answers I receive.

The fire is simmering in the log burner but I still feel chilly. I don't want to head back to Orchard Farm yet so I go to the counter and order a mozzarella, tomato and pesto panini with chips. Thankfully another member of the bar staff serves me this time so there's no further awkward conversation with Robert.

Scrolling through my phone as I wait for my meal to be delivered, I look back through images of Nicholas and I, flicking right back to when we started dating. In every picture we look happy and relaxed together. I remember that when I set up my initial encounter with Nicholas, I expected to meet a cold, aging businessman. He was so different to the person I'd built up in my head – his chiselled looks, sense of humour and zest for life knocked me off guard.

A sinking feeling sweeps over me. I've been drawn in by him; I allowed him to win me over too quickly when I should've kept up my guard and questioned things more. I was at a crossroads in my life, unsure what path to take next and emotionally wrung out. Nicholas, with his smooth conversation and offer of an easier life, was more gentlemanly and attentive than any of the men I'd dated before. I didn't mean for my head to be turned by the man I was suspicious of. It's all such a mess.

But since our low-key wedding day, things between us have been changing. Nicholas is very particular and likes to be in control of everything. To begin with, I thought his offers of shopping trips and the way he's encouraged my culinary skills were sweet and generous at first. However, if I scratch the surface, perhaps he's just been trying to shape me into being exactly who he wants me to be.

With each passing week, his expectations of me become more specific. Hinting at how he prefers me to do my make-up and telling me when he wants his dinner on the table. Yet, he says things in such a way that it's hard to say no to him. I've told myself these are small compromises, considering the lifestyle he is giving me. Our relationship is a more traditional one but is that all it is, or is there something more sinister going on?

I try to eat my lunch; it's delicious but I have trouble swallowing it. My mouth feels dry as troubling thoughts circle my brain. The way people have mentioned his previous wife and the rumours of the accident are making me wonder if my initial suspicions about Nicholas were correct.

Outside, the wind has picked up again and dark clouds are gathering overhead. I send Tiggy a message, not relishing the idea of walking back in this weather. She replies immediately to say that she's still at the golf club and will be there until the evening. I decide it's best if I gather my things and go, as judging by the last few days, the weather could get worse.

I brush the crumbs from my clothes and clip the lead back on Luna. Just as I'm about to leave, I hear someone clearing their throat.

Looking up, I see an older man with a glass of beer sitting at a table a few feet away from me. I give him a small smile but I don't say anything.

'You're Nicholas Johnson's new wife,' he says, telling me rather than asking me this. His words slur slightly and he looks as though he's had a few drinks already today.

I don't respond but I'm curious about what he has to say.

He mutters something under his breath and then says more audibly, 'She's dead.'

'Who is dead?'

'His last wife.'

'And I think your husband had something to do with it.'

'Sorry, what do you mean?' I'm stunned by how forthright he's being. My eyes dart around the room but there's no one else in the room. It's just me and him.

The man sneers then. 'I wouldn't want to be in your shoes for all the money in the world.'

Before I can respond, he says, 'You have no idea what Nicholas Johnson is really like. He ruined me. He ruined my business. My whole life.' He slams his glass on the table, making me jump. 'And that's not all he's done. It won't be long now until his lies come tumbling down around him.'

And then he abruptly stands up. 'Leave while you can.'

I watch as the man half-staggers out of the room.

I'm rooted to the spot. Should I take the advice of a stranger and run? Or do I stay and find out the truth?

Chapter Twenty-Six
Eva
Then

I'm alone and I'm afraid.

They keep coming in, a conveyor belt of nurses wearing the same outfits. Only their faces change.

Every time my memories start to creep in, they inject me with something. I feel groggy again. It's like the whole world has been covered in fog.

I don't know how long I've been here. I can barely remember my own name.

But his face stays with me. I will never forget his face.

And one day I will remember who I really am and what it is I need to do.

Chapter Twenty-Seven
Kirsty
Now

I leave the pub feeling unnerved. Who was that man? And what did Nicholas do to him to make him so bitter? If he really was an old business associate, then he could be deliberately stoking the rumours about Nicholas's previous wife's accident to tarnish my husband's reputation.

I need some time to think. I can't go back to the farmhouse just yet so I decide to run a few errands while I'm in Waterbridge.

I make a hairdresser's appointment and discuss a fiftieth birthday cake order with the occupant of Sweet Pea Cottage but all the while I'm thinking about the stranger's words. I walk along to the tea shop. Peering inside the window, I can see that every table is occupied and Jean, zigzagging between the tables, looks rushed off her feet. I was planning to stop in for a chat to find out what she knows about the wife who came before me but it looks like now isn't a very good time.

I'm about to walk on by when Jean looks up from the customer she's serving and waves me in. The scent of warm pastries and coffee fills the air and the place is buzzing with chatter. A few heads swivel in my direction as the bell tinkles above the door and the room quietens a little. I stifle a laugh. Exactly how long will it take for me to stop being the new arrival that everyone is curiously interested in? Or are they interested in me because of who I'm married to?

Jean makes her way over to me.

'Kirsty, how are you?'

'Ok. It's busy Jean, shall I come back another time?'

'Nonsense!' Jean exclaims. 'The lunchtime rush is about to quieten down. I'm just going to clear this table and then I'll say hello properly.'

Heading to the counter, I order a herbal tea and a square of shortbread from Lottie, a waitress with long black hair. By the time the sugary biscuit and steaming hot mug has been placed on the counter, Jean is standing next to me.

'Oooh, I'll have a piece of shortbread as well Lottie,' Jean chirps. 'Can you bring it through to the back room?'

I follow Jean as she guides me out of the seated area at the front of the shop to a room at the back of the building, which overlooks a pretty courtyard garden. There are more tables and chairs here but there aren't any customers around.

'I try to keep this space free for larger groups,' Jean tells me. 'There is a method to my madness!'

We sit together and exchange small talk about the weather and the upcoming autumn festival. Luna curls up under my chair as Jean tells me about her pumpkin soup recipe. I start to wonder how I'm going to steer the conversation around to my husband.

Jean puts down her cup. 'I get the feeling there's something on your mind Kirsty?'

'Is it that obvious?' I chew my lip.

'Is everything alright?' Concern crinkles her face.

Taking a deep breath, I say, 'I wanted to ask you about Nicholas... I've been hearing a few things about him and, well, I was hoping that you might be able to put me straight.'

'I thought that might be it.' She looks at me with her pale blue eyes and then says, 'I try not to interfere with my customers' lives – it's one of the reasons I've stayed in business so long!' Her laughter tinkles, reminding me of the bell over her shop door.

'I don't want to put you in an awkward position Jean—'

She holds her hand up at this. 'I was just going to say I've been wanting to say something for a while but I didn't want to overstep the mark.'

'It's okay, I'd like to hear it.'

Jean nods sagely. 'I'll tell you what I know. Nicholas's wife was involved in a nasty car crash. I heard she was carted off to hospital, not a local one but a private one up north somewhere. Her injuries were extensive.'

'Were?' I query.

'Nicholas told everyone that she died, although there wasn't a funeral. It happened a few months before you started dating him.'

My heart is in my mouth. The information I'd discovered online about his previous wife had already suggested that she had died. Hearing it from Jean as well confirms it.

'That's so sad.' I respond, trying to keep the depth of my emotions in control.

'I'm guessing that people thought not having a funeral was unusual?'

Jean hesitates. 'Nicholas is both someone who keeps his private life quiet and a man who is highly regarded in the community, he donates to many causes and he's on the right side of lots of people. The majority have moved onto gossiping about his new marriage to you.'

I shudder at the thought. From the expression on Jean's face there's more she wants to say. 'Is there something else?' I ask.

'I've lived in Waterbridge all of my life and I know most people well. There was something I found out at the time, something that the wider community isn't aware of.'

My jaw tenses.

'The car accident that his wife was in…' Jean fidgets with her napkin and then says, 'Well my brother-in-law Roy is a police officer at the local station and he told me that Nicholas was in the car when it went off the road that night. He was in the passenger seat.'

I inhale sharply. I knew it was a car accident – the internet had given me that information. But I had no idea Nicholas was involved.

'Are you sure?'

'It was hushed up. I don't know all the ins and outs of it but Nicholas is good friends with the Chief Superintendent. Roy wanted to blow the whistle on it but he's nearing retirement and knew he'd risk his reputation and police pension if he did. After weighing it up, he thought his word wasn't going to win against the higher ups.' She shrugs.

My body goes cold.

'It probably was just a very tragic accident,' Jean says softly. 'But I've come to like you Kirsty, so please take care of yourself.' She pats my hand.

Opening my mouth, I want to ask so many more questions but I can't seem to form the words. Before I can say anything, the door clatters open and Lottie bursts in. Luna jumps under my chair and gives a little whine.

'We've just had a group of ten hikers turn up,' Lottie tells Jean, her face flushed. 'We're going to need to seat them in here.'

'Righto!' Jean is up and out of her seat in a flash.

Lottie disappears back through the door. Before Jean leaves, she turns to me and says, 'I didn't mean to scare you Kirsty but you wanted the truth so I've given it to you. Let's talk again soon. And you take care of yourself.'

Jean has told me so much more than I could glean from a few paragraphs on a news website. But she's also given me more questions than answers.

Was the car crash really an accident? Or was it deliberate?

Chapter Twenty-Eight
Eva
Then

Outside are fields and fields of endless purple heather. That's all I can see for miles. I've been here for at least four months now. I only know this because whenever I remember, I make a pen mark on the wall behind my mirror when they aren't looking. But I don't know how often I remember to do this and some days I don't get a chance to make the mark, even if I want to.

It's less frightening here. The other place I was in, the hospital, was sterile and cold. I couldn't think straight, I could barely sit up and there was always someone in a medical uniform by my bedside. This is a calmer environment. I'm in a house, I have my own room. I'm starting to recognise the people who look after me. I'm their only patient.

I know I'm in Scotland because I've heard the radio playing and my watchers talking about their lives. They talk over me a lot of the time, like I'm not there. They must think I'm not taking anything in. But since I started holding the tablets they give me under my tongue and then hiding them in the hollow space I discovered in the brick fireplace in my bedroom, the fog has been lifting. I remember who I am now. And I know what Nick has done to me.

My husband has played the oldest trick in the book. Like Mr Rochester and Bertha Mason in *Jane Eyre*, he's had me locked away. He doesn't want me to interfere in his new life. He wants me out of the picture.

I need to get myself stronger, mentally and physically. Some days I have to swallow the tablets, others I succeed in getting rid of them. But, however long it takes, he won't keep me here.

I will find a way out.

Chapter Twenty-Nine
Kirsty
Now

I push open the door to Orchard Farm and wonder if I should turn around and leave. I don't like the things I've been hearing about my husband today and I considered inventing a reason not to return to the farmhouse. But there's nowhere else I can go, not without Nicholas questioning why. He's only here for another few nights and then he's away for two weeks, so I've decided it's best to stay to see if I can work out if the rumours about him being involved in his late wife's accident are true. Over the next fortnight, I will have time to weigh everything up and to consider what my next move is.

There's no sign of my husband so I guess he must still be in his office. I begin the process of cleaning up Luna and then myself afterwards. I run a warm bubble bath in the freestanding tub in the main bathroom and then sink gratefully into the water. Scrubbing my body, I listen to some calming music and try to relax. When I'm done, I wrap myself in a fluffy white bathrobe.

Stepping into the hallway, I almost jump out of my skin when I realise someone is standing at the top of the stairs.

'You frightened me,' I tell Nicholas.

'Sorry my sweet,' he says, coming towards me.

I wrap my arms around his neck and kiss him on the lips. I don't want him to guess that I'm starting to view him in a different light so I've decided it's best to try and act as normal as possible around him. Plus, there's more chance of me uncovering the truth if Nicholas isn't aware that something's wrong.

He kisses me back and then wraps an arm around my waist, tugging at the tie keeping my robe together.

'No!' I squirm. 'I need to get dinner ready.'

It's a lame excuse but as much as I want to pretend everything is ok, I feel wary and I can't bring myself to be close to him after what I've heard.

I pull away but he catches my hand in his. 'Later then,' he says.

Smiling briefly, I head into our bedroom and quickly get dressed. The day has passed faster than I'd expected. As I gaze into the bathroom mirror, sweeping my hair back into a ponytail, I have the strange sensation that I'm hurtling towards something unknown, something that will send me towards a dangerous cliff edge. Even though I can sense it coming, it feels like there's no way of slowing down time or jumping off the path that I'm speeding down. I shake my head, trying to dislodge my confusing thoughts.

Looking outside, I see that all the light that shines through the glass during the day has been replaced by the pale light of the full moon. There's something about the eerie lighting that makes me go cold. For the first time, I feel properly afraid.

The fact that it really is just me and Nicholas here at Orchard Farm is starting to bother me. Tiggy and Jed are too far away to provide immediate help, even when they're not on holiday, and our other neighbours are even further away. I think back to the crowded tower block where I grew up.

There was always someone nearby – you could never go up or down the stairs without bumping into another person. There was a community of people around me, all in the same boat, and most willing to lend a hand if needed. But here, if anything bad happened then no one would know.

Flicking on the light, I try to reassure myself that my mum and my siblings are just a click of a button away if I ever needed to call them. Although Mum seems less quick to pick up these days and my siblings are in a multitude of different time zones, so they couldn't do much if there was a real emergency. There was one person who I used to be able to rely on, one person who always had my back but calling them is no longer an option.

These negative thoughts crowd my brain and I need to shake them off before I speak to Nicholas, otherwise he's going to guess something is up. Pausing by the hallway window that looks out over the front of our property, I try to distract myself by looking outside.

And that's when I see it.

The movement in the trees.

I blink and then refocus my vision. Of course there's movement out there, it's October and it's rainy and windy.

But this is different. Because trees and branches don't move in that way. And they don't look like the thing that I'm staring at right now.

I can see the shape of a person, standing behind the gates to Orchard Farm in a cluster of small trees. I stare harder. The glow from the house floodlights and the low-hanging moon illuminates the outline in a way that makes me certain there's definitely a person there. Wearing a dark coat, with the hood pulled up and a thick, woollen scarf wrapped around the lower part of their face obscuring their features.

I swallow. Who is it? And why are they there?

'Nicholas!' I shout, my voice coming out shaky.

There's no response so I try again. 'Nicholas! Can you come here?' I yell louder this time.

Seconds later, I hear my husband's footsteps on the stairs along with the pitter patter of Luna's paws. I tear myself away from the silhouette.

'Nicholas, there's someone standing out there, by our gate. I can see them in the shadows of the trees.'

'What?' A frown creases his forehead. 'Are you sure?'

A rumble of thunder sounds outside, making me jolt. Nicholas and I both turn to look out the window and then a second later there's a crackle of lightning. It can't be far away because it lights up the entire sky. In that brief moment, it's clear there is no one standing amongst the trees by the gate. No one at all.

'Where did you say they were?' Nicholas checks.

I point my finger towards the spot that's now empty. 'There,' I confirm.

'Your eyes must've been playing tricks on you,' Nicholas says, slinging an arm around my shoulders. 'It must've been the shadows.'

'No,' I protest. 'There was definitely a person there.'

The frown on his face deepens. 'Who would walk down here on a night like this? You'd have to be crazy. Especially standing under a tree in the middle of a thunderstorm.'

Another boom of thunder sounds as if to illustrate his point. 'Come on, let's go downstairs,' he says.

Pressing my face to the window, I try to work out where the figure has gone. But there's no sign of anyone whatsoever – they've melted into the stormy night.

There's a second flash of lightning, which makes me spring back from the glass. It feels too close for comfort and I hope that the storm has scared away the person in the trees.

Because whatever my husband says, I know what I saw.

Chapter Thirty
Eva
Now

Both of them are in the house this evening. The thought of the two of them together makes my skin crawl. This wasn't how things were meant to be. He was mine. She wasn't supposed to have him.

Standing in the shadow of an old oak tree just beyond the farmhouse gate, I can see them in the lounge. The wood burner is warming the room and they're curled together on the ginormous beige sofa. I'm entranced as I observe them laughing as though neither of them have a care in the world. I shudder, cold seeping into my bones despite the thick coat and sturdy boots I'm wearing.

I've tried not to come back here. I've really tried not to do this to myself. I've had every kind of therapy going but nothing has helped. And I've attempted to distract myself – with exercise classes, binge reading books and TV shows, learning a language and brushing up on my culinary skills – but he's always in my thoughts. Nick Johnson.

How could I move on from him?

It's torture thinking of Nick in there with her. She's living the life that I'm meant to have. The familiar feeling of jealousy snakes around my body. She doesn't deserve him. She doesn't know him like I do, the things he is capable of, the secrets he hides.

I can't go on like this. I have to do something. I want to burst through the door right now but I know that I can't. I have to be clever about this. I have to follow my plan because I can't go on with things as they are. The thought has occupied my mind for weeks, circling round and round. I have tried to walk away, to forget Nick but it didn't work. So this time, I've got to do something different. I have to do something to stop this pain.

And I know there's only one way for all of this to end...

Chapter Thirty-One
Kirsty
Now

I barely slept last night. The storm continued to rage outside and I couldn't stop thinking about the man who told me to run and Jean's suspicions that Nicholas was involved in his wife's accident. Nor could I shake the image of the person I saw at the gates of Orchard Farm. I know I wasn't imagining things; I saw the silhouette with my own eyes and it was real – whatever Nicholas might think. My husband wouldn't discuss it further; he refused to believe that anything untoward was going on so I had to swallow down my fear.

At least whoever was there didn't try to come inside. I try to tell myself it was someone who got lost along the country lanes – maybe a late-night delivery person or someone who lost battery on their phone when navigating the countryside in the poor weather. I have no idea how long they were there – it could've been hours or minutes – but I try to believe it was the latter and that their intentions weren't sinister.

This morning, I considered calling the police but then, when I thought it through, I realised there's probably not a lot they could do about my concerns. If I rang them to say I'd seen someone on our land but I didn't have a proper description or any proof then it wouldn't give them much to go on. And as Nicholas wasn't convinced there was anyone out there he'd be displeased if I got the police involved over something he didn't believe was an issue.

Instead, I've soothed myself by pouring over my recipe book before deciding to make my favourite comfort food: chocolate chip cookies. As I pulled the ingredients from the various cupboards, I hoped that Nicholas was right and that my imagination was just going into overdrive last night.

'Mmmm, what's that smell?' Nicholas says as he sticks his head around the kitchen door.

'I'm baking cookies.'

His eyes light up. 'How soon until they're ready?'

'They've only just gone in the oven.' I laugh. 'About another fifteen minutes.'

He groans.

'I have a spoon you can lick though?' I point at the cake mix left in the bowl.

Nicholas shakes his head. 'I'd better not have uncooked eggs before the trip.'

'Fair enough.'

Nicholas leaves the kitchen, so I push the spoon around the bowl and nibble at the remains of the mix, having no such concerns myself. There's nothing quite like the taste of cookie dough.

By the time I've cleared up the kitchen and wiped the worktops clean, the timer on the oven pings. I peek inside. The cookies look perfect and the delicious smell makes my stomach rumble. I leave the oven door ajar and let the cookies soak up a little more heat. Then I remember I left a bag of small Tupperware boxes, which I purchased while I was at the village shops, in the boot room. They will be ideal containers to load the cookies and other treats into for my husband's journey.

Autumn sunlight is streaming through the windows at the front of the house, making me eager to get outside for a short walk with Luna. I'm about to go back inside, when I decide to check our post. Nicholas has a black, lock box attached to the fence running alongside the security gate. It's big enough for parcels as well as letters and means anyone delivering items to us don't have to be let in and out of the gates. But sometimes I can go a week or more before I remember to check it. I press the correct button on my key fob and open the gates. There's a handful of letters in the box and, at the very bottom, is a small brown paper parcel. I pull it out and take a look. The label is addressed to 'Nick Johnson'.

I raise my eyebrows. I've never heard anyone refer to my husband as Nick before. He's been Nicholas in every interaction I've seen between him and his business associates or our neighbours. I wonder who has sent him this.

Coming back into the main house, I call out, 'Hey, where are you?'

Nicholas immediately springs out of his office. 'Are the cookies ready?' he asks eagerly, like a small boy hoping for his favourite sweetshop to be open.

I nod. 'Yes, and also there's a parcel for you here... Nick.' I say this teasingly, trying out the shortened version of my husband's name.

He goes pale.

'Don't call me Nick!' my husband snaps.

I can feel my mouth forming a little 'O' shape. Why has he reacted like this?

'Why on earth would you call me Nick? My name is Nicholas!' His voice is hard and sharp.

'The parcel,' I stutter. 'It's addressed to Nick Johnson.'

His face turns red. 'What?'

He snatches the object from my hands. I watch as he stares at the words on the printed label and he seems to turn a shade redder.

'Where did you get this?' Nicholas demands, his face twisted into a grimace.

'It was in the letterbox. The postman must've left it there yesterday and I've only just seen it.'

He half turns away from me, feeling the brown packaging with his hands as though he's trying to work out what's in there.

'Is everything okay?' I ask apprehensively.

But my husband doesn't even look at me. Instead, he strides back to his office and slams the door. The noise seems to reverberate around me as I'm left standing in the hallway on my own. I'm stunned.

I try to absorb what just happened. His emotions have been all over the place in the last week. It could be down to his upcoming business meeting but usually he's so calm and controlled. These unpredictable outbursts along with the rumours about him are worrying me.

Feeling shaken, I drift through to the lounge. I switch on the latest series I've been binge watching in the hope that it might calm my nerves and distract me. But I can't concentrate on what's going on so I switch off the screen and stare into space, trying to sort out my turbulent emotions.

Luna comes and sits by my feet, curling up around my slippers, and then drops off to sleep. Her presence is reassuring and I'm glad she's here with me. Although I'm aware that the longer I sit here, the more of anxious I'll become, so I decide to go and occupy myself in the kitchen. Passing through the hallway, I pause outside Nicholas's office door. There's no sound coming from inside. I raise my hand to knock and then think better of it. He'll come out when he's ready.

I've pre-made a lasagna for today, so I pop it in the oven to heat it up for lunch. Nicholas has already told me that he wants a hot meal and some salad at lunchtime and a simple soup later for our evening meal. I busy myself by getting everything ready, chopping some cucumbers and tomatoes and then washing the lettuce leaves. As I'm doing this, I replay the conversation about the parcel over and over in my head. Why would he react like that – about a different version of his name? Puzzled, I decide I have to confront him about it and to talk to him about his behaviour over the last few days. I'm hoping the conversation might unlock some answers.

Time goes by and I wait to see if Nicholas will reappear from his office or if I'll need to go and let him know that the lasagna is ready. I'm just about to leave the kitchen when Nicholas enters. He comes towards me with a sheepish expression on his face.

'Sorry, sorry…' He grasps my hands in his. 'I'm sorry my love, I shouldn't have shouted. It's just I really don't like being called that.'

I frown. There's not liking something and then there's the reaction he displayed. What could make him so touchy about shortening his name?

He sighs. 'It's a childhood trauma thing…' He squeezes my hands reassuringly and then steps back. He's not looking at me; his gaze is directed over my shoulder, looking out in the distance to the countryside beyond. He seems lost in thought.

Nicholas has never shared any information about his childhood. I asked him about his background in the early days of us dating but he told me he had no family left and he liked the past to stay where it belonged: in the past. It's something I've wondered about a lot, especially now I know he grew up in Waterbridge, but I've never had a reason to ask him about it again, until now.

'It's okay,' I say gently. 'Do you want to talk about it?'

Nicholas rubs his forehead. 'Not really.'

'Okay...' I study his face, trying to work out what's going on with him. 'I get that it triggered something difficult and I promise I will never call you that again.'

Nicholas nods appreciatively.

'We're married now, we should talk about this. It's clearly something that's had an impact on you.'

His eyes are on me once more and I wonder what's he's thinking.

'It was a long time ago. It doesn't matter now, I'm over it. I just don't want my name to be shortened by you or anyone else.' His tone is clipped.

I swallow back my next question, wanting to probe more but he's already shutting the conversation down.

'You can't speak to me like that and not expect me to be hurt,' I say steadily, hooking a stray strand of hair behind my ear as I speak.

Nicholas pulls me towards him, wrapping his arms around me. 'I know. I was out of order. It won't happen again.'

He kisses me on the cheek. 'I've been really stressed with all this work stuff but there's no excuse, I shouldn't be taking it out on you.'

I can't help feeling that I might have seen a glimpse of the real Nicholas this week, the person underneath the man who has been so perfect since the day we met.

Right now, Nicholas seems back to his rational, loving self.

But how long will it last?

Chapter Thirty-Two
Eva
Then

'It's for your own good.'

Nick sits across the table from me, steepling his hands. He looks the same but different. He's had his teeth whitened and lost weight. I'm sure these changes have been influenced by his desire to impress a younger woman.

'I've done this all for you. I'm paying for everything; this whole house. All of the staff. I'm doing it to keep you safe.'

I don't respond. I can't trust myself to say anything. I'm avoiding the tablets more often than I'm taking them. Quite often my watchers will just hand them to me now and they no longer stand over me until I've gulped them down with water. They think that because I haven't caused them any issues so far that I'm not going to be a problem for them.

This is the first time Nick has been here. I heard him say to Cath, the tall woman with high-cheekbones who's been here with me from the start, that this was my review. So he's here to check on my behaviour for himself. I just hope this review doesn't result in any changes, not when I've been doing so well at finding tiny slices of freedom in the day.

'You know this is the way things have to be, don't you?' he asks me.

My eyelids flicker at this. I nod slowly.

'Good.'

He checks his watch and stands up. What he's doing hurts so much. But one day Nick will see the error of his ways. At some point, the shine of his new relationship will wear off and he will understand what he's thrown away.

The door shuts but I still catch snippets of the conversation beyond. Nick seems to be telling Cath that he's pleased with how she's handling me. Like I'm some kind of animal. I keep quiet.

Because to have any chance of escaping, I have to play the long game.

Chapter Thirty-Three
Kirsty
Now

I wake up with a start. Nicholas is on the sofa beside me, his head lolling back, his mouth open wide as he softly snores. We'd been watching the news and we must've both fallen asleep. The TV is still on and the fire in the grate has burnt down to embers and the room is now freezing. Standing up, I get the sense that something isn't right. I can't put my finger on it but I get the feeling that something is amiss in the house.

The clock in the hallway is showing the time as almost 1.30 am. We've been crashed out down here for way longer than I thought.

When I step back into the kitchen, that's when I notice it. That's what's wrong. The patio door is wide open. The coldness creeping through the house is coming from here. I'm certain the door was shut before we went into the lounge this evening. It was pouring with rain so there was no way I would've left it open. My stomach somersaults, this is the second time I've found this door unlocked.

And then my stomach flips again. If the door is open, is Luna still inside?

Her dog bed is in the utility room, adjoining the kitchen. It's a nice cosy space and it keeps warm. I flick the light on, but the bed is empty. It's not unusual for her to sleep elsewhere; she's probably found another nook in the house to curl up in. Rushing from room to room, I call out the name of my beloved pet. My voice becomes higher and more shrill when I can't see her anywhere.

'Nicholas!' I run back through to the lounge, shaking him firmly.

'What is it?' He's wide-eyed.

'Luna's not in the house, I can't find her.' I'm breathless and panicky. 'The bi-fold doors are open.'

'Did you leave the doors open?' His tone is low and rough. The hairs on the back of my neck stand on end.

'No... At least I don't think I did.' My voice wobbles with emotion.

'You're either certain or you're not,' Nicholas snaps at me.

I gulp, tears stinging in my eyes. Now is not the time to go to pieces.

A vein is pulsing in his neck and his eyes are narrowed. It's like I'm staring at someone else. Someone who looks like my husband but isn't him.

Nicholas looks down on me. 'In case you hadn't noticed, this house is worth a lot of money. And so are the things in it.'

My body thrums with emotions. I'm stunned that his first focus is the contents of the house and not the safety of our dog. 'We need to find Luna. Every minute we're standing here is a minute when we could be looking for her.'

I turn away from him and step out into the rain. The outside lights snap on, activated by my movement, and along the path I see Luna's favourite toy. It wasn't out here earlier on, so this convinces me that she must be outside.

'Luna!' I shout into the night, my words instantly disappearing in the wind. I try to think rationally. Hopefully she's nearby and just needs coaxing back inside.

Almost immediately I hear a sound – it's a dog barking.

'Is that...?' I trail off. Nicholas is standing just behind me. 'Can you hear that?'

Hope blooms in my chest. I don't wait for his reply; I race through the garden gate. My feet slip in the thick mud, and I almost topple over. Rain slides down my face, my neck, and inside my jacket. This is my worst nightmare.

I hear the sound again. It's unmistakably Luna's bark, coming from the direction of the woods. I speed up. As we pass the stables, Nicholas stops.

'Wait,' he calls to me.

I don't want to pause; I just want to find Luna. But it's hard to see where I'm going so I do as he says. He rummages around near the entrance to the stables and a few moments later there's a beam of light as Nicholas flicks on a torch.

A forceful gust of wind hits me and I stumble a few paces. I put my hand out and catch Nicholas's arm to steady myself. But when I look into his face, dripping with rain, there's no concern – only anger in his eyes. I quickly turn away from him.

'This is ridiculous!' Nicholas bursts. 'We're both drenched. We'll catch pneumonia if we stay outside in this weather for too long.' He starts to march past me, so I snatch the torch from his hand. He looks at me, his lip curling, and then he strides away to the farmhouse.

A strange feeling washes over my body. It's clear where my husband's priorities lie, but I'm shocked he's being like this. I always thought he loved Luna as much as I do.

Reaching the entrance to the woods, I can just about see that a few branches have already come down. It's probably unwise to be searching amongst the trees when the storm is this bad but I won't stop until I've found her.

I hear her bark again – once, twice, three times.

I follow the sound, going as fast as I can on the uneven ground. Then, finally, I see her.

The poor little thing is shaking, half hidden under a thorny bush, and wet through but otherwise unharmed. I cross the distance and pull her into my arms, holding her close and kissing her head.

'It's okay Luna, I'm here.'

I can't speak; there's a lump in my throat and I cling onto my little dog. All I can think about is the fact that Nicholas has gone inside knowing that Luna was still out here. I can't begin to imagine what might've happened if I hadn't found her when I did.

Entering the house, I'm soaked to the bone but all my focus is on Luna. Nicholas bangs the bi-fold door behind us and immediately locks it. I move past him.

'What are you doing?' Nicholas growls at me.

'Going to sit in front of the fire to help her warm up…'

'You're dripping mud and water everywhere!' The anger is back in my husband's eyes – I didn't imagine it. 'You'll ruin the carpet!'

I knew my husband was particular but I can't believe he's so bothered about the flooring given the circumstances. I hesitate, unsure how to react and trying to keep my own emotions from boiling over.

'Seriously Kirsty, be sensible. Get undressed.'

I think he's going to make me strip in front of him but instead he takes Luna, disappears into the utility room and comes out with a bathroom towel around his waist and one of the dog's towels swathed around Luna.

He glares at me in a way that makes me understand that he's not happy because I'm not following his instructions.

Realising that I'm still trembling all over, I follow Nicholas's lead and head into the utility room to get undressed and find clean towels. I pat myself down and then wrap a towel around my body. When I walk into the lounge, I find Luna curled in front of the fading fire. She looks dry, even though there are still clumps of mud entangled in her legs.

Nicholas looks up at me and there's still a hard expression on his face. 'Go and shower,' he tells me. 'I'll sort Luna out.'

'She needs some water,' I reply.

'I know,' he shoots back at me, his words clipped. 'I'll deal with this. Go upstairs.'

I'm stunned. Without saying anything more, I retreat up the stairs. My heart twinges and I long to look after Luna but something tells me not to do anything that could potentially irritate Nicholas any further this evening.

Instead, I hurriedly shower. The warm water brings up my temperature and washes away the dirt. I feel much better once I've washed my hair and soaped my body but my mind still feels all over the place. Dressing in cotton pajamas, I brush my hair and quickly blast it with the hair dryer.

I'm desperate to go downstairs to my dog but I tell myself that I will go back down to her once Nicholas has gone to sleep. My whole body is thrumming with overstimulation so I breathe deeply in and out to try and calm myself.

Everything about Nicholas's behaviour tonight is ringing alarm bells for me. It's now clear to me that beneath my husband's charismatic personality is something much darker.

I've allowed myself to settle into this life of luxury when I should've been more alert. Tonight, Nicholas's mask has slipped. Again.

And I'm terrified.

Chapter Thirty-Four
Eva
Now

That was fun. Tormenting them like that. The fear written across Kirsty's face made it all worthwhile and it was good to see Nick so wound up.

This evening was intended to spook them. I'm glad it did. The way he spoke to her was a glimpse of what Nick Johnson is really like. I should know because I've been married to him for long enough.

I feel bad about the dog though. I didn't think it would come outside when it was raining so hard. But I kept my eye on it, and of course I would've made sure no real harm was done. I might be out for revenge but I'm not a monster.

Deep down I realise Kirsty isn't really in the wrong here. She probably doesn't even know that I exist. Nick isn't the type of person who would go into great detail about his past; he's someone who is always focused on the present. And whatever opportunity he is chasing.

Nick also keeps his cards close to his chest. He may come across as charismatic and sociable but I noticed over the years a pattern in his interactions with other people. He has this knack of making other people feel good, like his full attention is on them, and he knows how to compliment others in the most natural way, without coming across forced. In doing so, he puts people at ease and then they're quite happy to answer his questions. But he'd have an agenda to every conversation – and he'd more often than not come away with the answers that he was seeking. He only ever shared things about himself that he wanted other people to know. He'd feed his outward persona in a way that somehow wasn't boastful but perfected his image.

You learn a lot about a person when you live with them. Especially when you're with someone for decades, like Nick and me. You learn all about their quirks and preferences. You discover a million little things that you love about them. You also find out their worst traits. Things that no one else would ever guess.

Then of course there are the secrets. Everybody has them. Everyone has something to hide. It might be something small and relatively harmless or it could be something darker, something more explosive.

It's just a matter of time before they come to the surface. You might discover them early on in a relationship and be able to accept them and navigate your way through them, or you'll have the luxury of stepping away before you get in too deep. But if you're unlucky, your other half's secrets might surface much, much later on. Sometimes too late.

That's what happened with Nick. I'd spent half a lifetime with him – my love for him ran through my veins like my own blood. No matter what he'd done, no matter how bad, there was no way I could switch off my feelings for him. He's like a magnet, constantly drawing me to him.

I'm in too deep. Right now, I hate him as much as I love him. I want him to hurt as much as I have. But once I've succeeded in splitting him apart from Kirsty, I know we will be together again.

Because I'm never letting him go.

Chapter Thirty-Five
Kirsty
Now

'I'm so sorry about yesterday,' Nicholas says, his voice full of remorse.

He's just walked into the kitchen, still wearing his pyjamas. On anyone else, the blue and grey plaid trousers might look dated but he wears them hung low around his waist and the white T-shirt clings to his torso. I can just see the outline of his abs but instead of being attracted to him, I feel repelled.

Luna is on my lap. When I was sure Nicholas was asleep, I crept downstairs to check on her. She seemed absolutely fine, her tail wagging as soon as she saw me. This morning, I got up early to give her lots of cuddles. She's enjoyed the attention and the extra treats and seems her normal self.

I'm still shocked that she got out of the house. As Nicholas said, it must've been my fault. I must've left the door open or unlocked. There's no other way it could've happened. There was no sign of a break in, nothing taken, and – despite my fears – there was no sign of anyone else involved. At least she wasn't hurt but I'm still wracked by guilt.

Putting Luna down, I turn away from him and press the button to start the coffee machine. Instantly it begins to whirr, the noise giving me a chance to gather myself. He terrified me yesterday and part of me wants to walk out of this house right now. But what would I do if I left now? Where would I go? Besides, I came here in search of answers so I can't leave just yet. I square my shoulders and steel myself to carry on.

'Come on,' Nicholas says, 'Don't be like that.' I can hear him crossing the kitchen.

Pretending to be absorbed in the business of making a much-needed drink, I pull a spoon out of the draw and let my silence speak for itself. I've been tip-toeing around Nicholas and his mood swings but I'm an emotional wreck after last night and I'm struggling to be in the same room as him.

'Hey.' Nicholas is behind me now, his breath on my neck. 'Are you upset with me?'

Remaining with my back to him, I hook down my favourite mug from the overhead cupboard. It's handmade ceramic with a little heart in the middle and I love its size and shape: it's just right. It's funny how you can take comfort in such little everyday things. I place the mug under the stream of coffee and inhale the scent that begins to fill the room.

'I'm sorry,' Nicholas repeats. His arms are around me and he's nuzzling my neck. 'I was a jerk,' he whispers in my ear. 'Forgive me?'

I shiver at the contact but I don't want him to suspect that anything is wrong, so I slowly turn around in his arms and look up at him. 'I need you to be on my side,' I say to him quietly.

'Of course I'm on your side,' Nicholas replies swiftly. 'I was just rattled by Luna's disappearance, that's all.'

'Promise?'

'Promise.'

He kisses the tip of my nose and then I pull away. I just want to make it through the remaining time before his trip without any more clashes between us. While he is away, I will have time to work out what I'm going to do next. It was never my plan to stay with Nicholas long-term, I was only meant to be here until I discovered what I needed to. It's more complicated now that we're married. And, for the first time ever, I'm not just scraping by. I can see a future with the charming and kind version of Nicholas. But there's no way I can stay if the man I've seen over the last few days is the real Nicholas. Or if it turns out that he's responsible for his late wife's death.

'Do you want a latte?' I ask, knowing Nicholas prefers milky coffees, just like I do. My plan is to avoid angering him at all costs today.

He nods, still standing very close to me.

I create some distance by moving around the kitchen to organise his breakfast. I made pastries and croissants a few days ago; they are long-game effort because it's important to give the dough time to chill and there are various stages involved, but it's definitely worth it because they taste so much better if they're made properly. Now, they just need warming. Concentrating on what I'm doing, I put a tray of breakfast goodies in the oven to heat up and while they're in there I set out the jam, honey and chocolate spread and lay the table.

The morning light is flooding through the big windows and there's no hint of last night's stormy weather. Nicholas sits down and browses through the morning paper. The timer on the oven pings and I transfer the pastries to ceramic serving platters.

'Here we are,' I say, as I put the two platters down, one containing the buttery croissants and the other an assortment of pain au chocolat, Danish pastries and cinnamon rolls.

'Wow,' Nicholas comments, 'this is quite the spread.'

'Well, I thought you could take a few of these on your journey. I can take any leftovers round to the Robinsons, to be neighbourly.'

'Mmmm.' Nicholas is savouring an almond croissant. 'I don't think there will be any leftovers – I'm sure I can make room.'

He swallows another bite and then winks at me. 'You're the perfect wife, you know that?'

Given how he spoke to me last night, I'm taken aback. I was preparing myself for an argument this morning, instead Nicholas has turned on his charm.

Nicholas clears his throat, 'I wasn't going to say anything yet...' He's smiling at me now.

Nicholas's mood is swinging from hot to cold and I can't predict what he'll say and do next. My jaw clenches as I wait for him to continue.

'This was going to be a surprise when I came home but I want to give you something to look forward to. And you've served just the right food so this seems like the time to tell you. I know I've been away a lot so I'm booking for us to go to Paris.'

'Paris!' I cry, unable to stop myself.

He nods. 'We're going to do the whole works: the Eiffel tower, the Louvre, everything! I can't wait to wine and dine you.'

I'm stunned; I wasn't expecting this. I should be so excited but instead a feeling of dread swirls in my stomach.

I rearrange the expression on my face and then I throw myself into his lap and put my arms around his neck. 'Thank you, I've always wanted to go to Paris.'

And it's true. When I was in my early twenties, I had the opportunity to go travelling. I was desperate to explore the world and discover a life beyond London. But my mum and younger siblings were relying on my wages. I couldn't let them down, so I stayed working fifty-hour weeks in busy pubs and cafés while my best friend went and had the time of her life. Since then, I've vowed that I would go to Europe one day. But I didn't imagine it would be like this.

'We can have some quality time together. It'll be so romantic.' Nicholas kisses me on the cheek.

'Romantic like a honeymoon?' I question. Nicholas told me he wanted to take me on a lavish trip somewhere for our honeymoon but it hasn't happened yet due to his work commitments.

Nicholas shakes his head. 'Think of it as more of a mini moon. I've got big plans to go further afield for our honeymoon. Maybe Thailand. I really want to spoil you. I just need to catch a break with work and then we can start planning it together.'

'When are we going?' I ask, the sense of dread increasing.

'Soon, we'll look at dates when I'm back.'

Removing myself from his lap, I reach for a pastry to try and distract myself, and Nicholas goes back to reading the newspaper as I'd hoped. Biting into the pastry, I think about all the times I've dreamt of going to Paris. Experiencing genuine French cuisine is at the top of my bucket list. I'd be in my element browsing menus and tasting dishes, getting inspiration for my own cooking. But I can't go with Nicholas.

As I place our plates in the sink to soak, I feel as though my time at Orchard Farm is running out.

I need to find the answers I came here for before my relationship with Nicholas gets too dangerous.

Chapter Thirty-Six
Eva
Then

There's a knock at the door. It's Nick.

He's visited me twice in recent months. One time was another scheduled review and the other seemed to be a surprise visit. Cath and the other staff certainly had to scramble when he arrived. They hadn't cleared up the remnants of lunch even though it was mid-afternoon. It was quite comical to see them dashing about while Cath kept Nick in the hallway for as long as she could.

The house is large, with high-ceilings and drafty rooms. I'm in my bedroom, sitting in the chair and staring out over the fields again when Nick enters the room. Perhaps he wasn't as satisfied by my warden's work when he dropped in unannounced not so long ago and is checking up on them again. Or maybe he's starting to miss me. A little glow of hope blooms at the thought.

'Hello Eva,' Nick says, just like he used to when he returned home from work.

'Hello,' I respond, keeping my voice neutral.

He sits in the armchair across from me and begins to talk to me. Just like old times. I let myself pretend we're just on a weekend break, like any other husband and wife.

His phone rings. I'm used to him being at the beck and call of his mobile. He checks the number and lets it ring out.

Nick leans forward suddenly. 'Do you like it here Eva?'

My eyes widen.

'You always did like our trips to Loch Glass, didn't you?'

I smile. Nick's just given away where I am. I suspected the location but I didn't know for sure. I squirrel this piece of information away.

The phone ringtone goes again. Nick looks annoyed. This time he cancels the call. I can't see the name of the person ringing.

We sit in silence for a while, looking out over the view. I recall the times we used to sit companionably together – I'd usually have a romance novel in my hand while Nick scoured the stock market.

His phone rings for a third time and Nick leaves the room. I hear his muffled voice on the other side of the door; he's speaking sharply.

I catch a few words. 'I've already told you… Don't keep ringing… Calm down.'

I'm done raging and screaming now. I've accepted Nick is going through some kind of extreme midlife crisis.

Despite what he's done to me, I will always love Nick – it's the core belief that runs through me. I meant my wedding vows, and my love for him is endless. He's all I have. So, even now, I hold onto the belief there is a future for us and the conversation going on outside reignites that hope.

I can hear him leaving. He hasn't said goodbye but that's okay. I'm certain I will see him soon.

Chapter Thirty-Seven
Kirsty
Now

I've been baking most of the day. It's what I do when I'm feeling stressed. Weighing out the measurements, mixing the ingredients soothes me. The repetitive action of whisking the mixture and the satisfaction when the food comes out of the oven, keeps my mind occupied and my hands busy. I make the final flourishes to the pink icing on the birthday cake I've made before placing it carefully in the fridge. It's the only order I've had this week but I've enjoyed making it.

Nicholas has been in his office but he will be leaving soon. I parcel up the remaining pastries along with a few pieces of fruit. Nicholas left his rucksack in the downstairs hallway, so I unzip the bag and put the food inside so it's ready for him. I would never normally go into the rucksack Nicholas uses for work but I just want to help his departure go as quickly and smoothly as possible.

As I slide the Tupperware box of food inside, I can't help but notice the plane ticket that's poking out of the inside pocket of the bag. The words printed on it shock me. I rub my eyes, feeling heavy from the lack of sleep, and try to refocus them, convinced I must've read the text wrong.

But no, instead of his outbound ticket being for Edinburgh, like he told me, the destination says Inverness. Why would Nicholas tell me he's flying direct to Edinburgh if he is in fact going further north, into the Scottish

Highlands. I search for an explanation but I can't recall him telling me there was a change of plan. Nicholas has definitely said on a number of occasions that his important meeting is being held in Edinburgh.

Before I zip the rucksack back up, I spot the silver key, attached to a green fob, that I know opens up Nicholas's office. Hurriedly, I snatch them up and shove them into the deep pocket of my cord trousers. Nicholas is lying to me so I see having the keys to his office as playing him at his own game. I can feel the shape of the keys pressing into my leg, and I hope I get the opportunity to use them.

My heart is thudding in my chest as I return to the kitchen. I need to handle this strategically – I don't want my husband to think I've been snooping but I also want to get to the bottom of why he is flying to Inverness. I'm sure there's a logical reason – the flights were changed, or he has a meeting in Inverness first – but I need to know for sure.

Nicholas enters the room. His shirt doesn't have a single crease and he's adjusting his tie so it's perfectly centred. He gives me a megawatt smile as I hold out a can of diet coke to him.

'Ah, I need this,' he says gratefully, pulling the tab and immediately taking a gulp of the fizzy drink.

'Your food is in your bag,' I inform him.

'Thanks.' He bends down to Luna and scratches behind her silky ears.

I grit my teeth, remembering how he abandoned her outside but I keep my anger to myself and don't say anything.

'Are you sure you're going to be okay here on your own?' His blue-green eyes bore into me and I know he's thinking about the house security.

'I'll be fine,' I say as breezily as I can muster. 'I'll triple check the doors are locked, don't worry.'

He swigs back the last of his drink.

'I hope you enjoy Edinburgh,' I say.

'Well, I'll mostly be in a white-washed conference room.' He chuckles. 'But if I clinch the deal, I'll definitely find somewhere to celebrate.'

He didn't correct me. I was expecting him to say I'd got the airport or the location wrong. So I try again, just to make sure he's heard me right.

'Edinburgh must feel like a home from home now, given how much you go up there? I guess there's not the same novelty of exploring the city once you know it so well.'

Nicholas looks at me sharply. 'Sorry...'

Is this it? Is he about to tell me his travel plans changed?

'I knew I shouldn't be heading off again so soon—'

'That's not what I meant—'

'Next time I go, why don't you come with me? Edinburgh's a great city, there's plenty for you to do there while I'm working. And we could take in some sights and go for some nice meals in the evenings, what do you think?'

'I'd love to,' I try to keep my voice even. 'I hear the Highlands are beautiful, perhaps we could take a trip there too?'

Nicholas doesn't react to this; he simply puts his mug in the dishwasher and then turns to me. 'Sure, that sounds great.'

I know that tone of voice, he's distracted and his mind is elsewhere now. I'm certain he's already mentally finished with our conversation and is thinking about something important for his work trip. Although I'm now questioning if he is going for work and whether the really important meeting even exists.

My thoughts roam back to the receipt I found in his jacket pocket. Is there something or someone important in the Scottish Highlands?

'Nicholas?' I want to ask him outright, to find out what's going on.

'Uh, I've got to go darling,' Nicholas says, as he moves out of the kitchen and into the hallway. Moving rapidly, he flings open the door to the boot room and begins pulling on his coat and shoes. 'Don't forget I've set the security alarm for 10 pm so I don't have to manage it while I'm away. Make sure you're upstairs when it goes on,' Nicholas instructs. 'And I'll call you when I can.'

I nod obediently. I don't have access to the security app so I will need to do as he says. Annoyance flickers inside me. Nicholas has done this to control what time I go to bed and so he knows exactly where I am in the evenings. Did he treat his last wife like this too?

I can't ask him to give me access now. Just like I can't ask why he's flying to a different airport. There's no way I can delay his journey – he'd be angry again. And maybe I'm just reading too much into this, maybe Inverness airport was a cheaper flight...

Nicholas dips back into the hallway and slings the rucksack over his shoulder. 'I'm going to miss you wifey.'

He pulls me into a quick hug but the rucksack slips forward and bashes me on the shoulder, causing me to step back. My husband doesn't even notice – he's too intent on getting out the door.

'I love you,' he calls over his shoulder.

Standing in the doorway, I wave to his retreating figure and watch as he enters the Range Rover, clips his seat belt in and gives me a small wave from behind the window. I'm about to blow him a kiss but his attention is straight ahead.

The car pulls away. I go back inside, making sure the front door and the internal door are both bolted behind me. Luna is at my feet so I scoop her up under my arm and carry her into the front room with me. Once there, she flumps down on her favourite rug and promptly falls asleep. I wish I could join her and I'm very tempted. But I'm not the sort of person who wakes up refreshed after a nap.

Glancing in the mirror, I see that my eyes are puffy from lack of rest and my body feels as though all the energy has been leached from it. I know that coffee will be my friend so set about making a double espresso. Even the smell of strong, black liquid makes me feel more awake. After just a few sips, I can feel it working its magic.

I tidy away my baking equipment from the worktop. I'm about to sweep an empty paper flour bag and the offcuts of some greaseproof paper into the bin, except I notice the brown package pushed down to the bottom of the new black bin bag.

Intrigued, I tug the parcel out of the bin but as I do so the contents fall free from one end of it. Blinking, I realise that dried purple wildflowers are scattering on the floor all around me. I pick up a few of the long, green stalks and examine the fragile, purple flower more closely. It's not lavender but dried heather. I chew my lip. Who would be sending my husband a bouquet of dried flowers in the post? And why?

Delving into the remnants of the parcel, I find more handfuls of the wildflowers but no note or indication of who has sent these. I check in the bin itself but there's nothing. Frowning, I gather the parcel and flowers and put them back into the bin bag. The questions I have about my husband are growing every day.

There are a number of people I want to talk to while Nicholas is away. I decide I'll go and see Jean tomorrow to have more of a chat with her. And while I'm in the village it could be worthwhile to strike up a conversation with Francesca to see if she knows the truth about how close Nicholas was with her mother.

There's plenty to be getting on with. I need to be proactive. After all, knowledge is power.

After his turbulent emotions in the last few days, I've felt less and less safe in my husband's house.

One thing is for sure, Nicholas Johnson is a clever man. And what's more, a man who clearly won't appreciate me trying to unearth his buried secrets.

I need to be careful. Very careful.

Chapter Thirty-Eight
Eva
Then

'My husband cheated on me,' Cath tells our new cleaner. They whisper together about how awful men are. The cleaner – I think her name is Aileen – consoles Cath, who looks pale and drawn. Not a lot of cleaning is done today.

I know this is my opportunity to get Cath on my side. I bide my time and wait until Cath takes me up to my room for my enforced bedtime. Like so many things about living in this house, this bedtime routine makes me feel like a child but change is in the air; I can feel it.

As Cath plumps my pillows, I reach for her hand. I take it in mine and say, 'I'm sorry.'

She shakes her head, pulling her hand away. 'What for?'

'That your husband cheated. Mine did too.'

Cath looks surprised and then her expression goes curious. 'Is Nick your husband?'

'Yes. He cheated on me after fifteen years of marriage. He replaced me with a younger woman – and then locked me away here.'

Cath's brows raise a fraction. 'Come on now, don't go making up stories.'

'I'm not.' I make sure to look straight at her. 'Nick has money and he obviously didn't want me ruining his new plans, so he locked me away so I was out of the picture.'

'I think you're feeling groggy after your evening medication,' Cath says gently, looking away from me and straightening the bedsheets.

'I haven't taken my medication for weeks. All of the tablets are hidden in a little nook at the bottom of the fireplace over there.' I point towards the old-fashioned brick fireplace that dominates one side of the room. It's a risk telling her this, and I pray that it works.

Cath inspects the hollow space and then gasps when she finds the stash of little pills exactly where I said they would be. Once she's recovered herself, she says, 'But you've behaved beautifully. No problems at all, and Mr Johnson said you were reliant on it...'

She stares at me. 'You're telling the truth, aren't you? I can see it in your eyes.'

I nod, and hold my breath. She's starting to believe me.

'But why? Why didn't he just divorce you?' Cath asks, sitting down heavily in the chair beside my bed.

'You have no idea what he's like, the level of control he needs to have over every aspect of his life. The idea of me being untethered – even when he didn't want me anymore – isn't something he could allow to happen.'

Cath's hand flies to her mouth now. 'Oh, my goodness, I've been part of this... He told me that you were a distant cousin that he'd been charged with keeping safe. He said it was to protect you because you were a danger to yourself as well as others when you're unwell.'

'That's not true,' I say calmly.

She looks horrified. 'I have to admit, I thought that something wasn't right...'

A single tear runs down my cheek. She believes me. If Cath believes me then there's a chance my plan will work.

'He lied,' I say firmly.

'They all lie in the end,' Cath says, a faraway look in her eyes.

And that's when I know she will help me.

Chapter Thirty-Nine
Kirsty
Now

I can finally stop pretending that I'm the perfect wife. Nicholas has messaged to say he is about to board his flight and I feel myself breathing a little more freely knowing this. All this deception is more exhausting than I thought it would be but I've got this far and I have to keep going.

I cast my eye over the other phone notifications and see I've got three missed calls. All of them are from my mum. She's probably annoyed because I put the phone down on her. It's not something I'd normally do but I didn't want to say something that I'd regret. I'm not in the right frame of mind to ring her back, so I swipe down to see my other notifications.

There are a number of friend requests from social media. I click into my app and see one of the requests is a woman I made a birthday cake for and the other is from Tiggy. I accept them both immediately, feeling a surprising little glow that I'm starting to create a network of women around me. At that moment, the home phone rings. Nicholas is the only one who ever gets calls on the house phone so the caller must be for him.

I pick it up but I don't say anything immediately, debating whether I should answer the phone in a certain way now I'm married to Nicholas. And if so, what should I say: *Hi, it's Kirsty* or *Hello, it's Mrs Kirsty Johnson speaking*. This is the sort of thing that Tiggy would know.

The voice on the other end of the line speaks before I get a chance to decide. 'It's Francesca, thanks for popping into the florist's the other day. It was good to see you.'

Why is Francesca from the florist's calling my husband?

'Nicholas? Are you there?' she asks.

Clearing my throat I respond, 'Hi Francesca, it's Kirsty Johnson speaking, Nicholas's wife, can I help you with anything?'

For some reason it felt important to reinforce my status as Nicholas's spouse. There was something about the tone in Francesca's voice when she thought she was addressing my husband that felt a little off to me.

'Oh, Kirsty, hi...' Francesca seems a little flustered. 'I was just calling Nicholas back, um, about an order he'd placed.'

'An order? What for?' I ask directly.

'Oh...' Francesca clearly didn't expect me to answer the phone. 'For some flowers, I probably shouldn't be telling you this...'

I'm on high alert now. Is there something Francesca knows that she's keeping from me?

'The bouquet is for you,' she clarifies.

'Right, I see.' I release the breath that I had been holding. 'In that case, we'll say no more about it.'

'Thanks Kirsty,' Francesca's voice sounds distant now, as though she's moved away from the phone.

'Francesca, can I ask you something about your mother. About Jane.'

'I better be going, have a nice day,' she says hurriedly.

With that, the line goes dead. Francesca's call was probably completely innocent and perhaps Nicholas really has ordered a bouquet of flowers for me. It sounds like the sort of thing he'd do, and arranging for a delivery while he's away is incredibly sweet. I just wish the informal way in which Francesca initially spoke because she believed Nicholas had picked up the call hadn't unsettled me in quite the way it has.

Francesca is of course young enough to be Nicholas's daughter. But that's what I'm worried about: not that he's having an affair with her but that he once had an affair with her mother and therefore could potentially be the florist's biological father. The thought has been niggling at me since Tiggy mentioned Nicholas's connection with Francesca's mother. And there are enough similarities between Nicholas and Francesca: they both have dark hair, almond-shaped eyes and are taller than average.

'Enough,' I say to myself aloud. This way madness lies. I've been on my own for less than twenty-four hours and I'm already imagining that Nicholas has an illegitimate child in Waterbridge. I need to keep myself occupied otherwise I'm going to go completely crazy over the next weeks.

The rain is hammering down now which means there's no chance of going into the village. I decide to tackle the housework because Nicholas expects me to keep on top of things while he's away. First, I go round with the duster. I used to do more than my fair share of housework at my mum's flat but keeping a five-bedroom house pristine, just the way Nicholas likes it, takes a lot of work. Nicholas did say he'd continue to employ his cleaner when I moved in but it didn't feel necessary when I was going to be at home.

As I'm dusting in one of the spare bedrooms, I find a camera on top of the wardrobe. I frown, I'm certain this wasn't here before. Nicholas told me that he only had a few security cameras downstairs and I know where all of those are. So what's this doing here?

As I continue cleaning upstairs, I find another new camera in the hallway positioned just outside our bedroom, tucked away on the thick frame of an abstract painting

I know Nicholas is hot on security but this feels like too much. Hooking a strand of hair behind my ear, I peer more closely at the camera and notice the brand name. Turning away, I type it into my phone. My mouth hangs open when I see the price tag attached to each of the cameras. My husband really is taking the security of the house seriously, but why?

Flicking through the product details, I try to find out how the cameras operate. I'm not very technically minded but I'm curious to know if there's a central system where the footage is saved. From the information online, I glean that the cameras are linked to the same app Nicholas uses for the security system. Whoever has the app can access the camera footage at the click of a button on their phone. This means that Nicholas can quite easily monitor what's going on in his house.

It makes me wonder how often he's checking the footage: is it something he looks at regularly? And how much attention is he paying to what I'm doing during the day? The thought makes me feel sick. Has he been watching me?

I try to reason that it's likely that all of his golf club friends have similar costly security systems in place for their own homes and that he's so busy with his work he probably wouldn't have the time to keep constant tabs on what I'm doing. I try to shake the thought away but my brain feels stuck on the question of why Nicholas has installed extra cameras upstairs.

Hoovering the carpets, I turn over the idea that the cameras at the front of the house may have captured who posted the mystery parcel addressed to 'Nick'. Has Nicholas already checked the footage and does he know who delivered the brown package? Is this something else that he's keeping from me?

The cameras aren't just unnerving, they also prevent me from properly scouring this house for clues about my husband's past. I feel like I'm up against a dead end. One night last week, I made countless searches online when Nicholas was asleep to try and uncover more information about him. I've searched for his name online on a number of occasions, but this time I tried all sorts of new combinations of Nicholas's name and surname but the only online references I could find to Nicholas Johnson were business related.

The hoover cuts out. I'm only halfway through cleaning the carpets. I tut, expecting there to be an issue with the filter but when I check it looks clear. I flick the switch on and off again but there's nothing. Heading into the kitchen, I see the clock on the oven is blank which means there's been a power cut. When this sort of thing happens, the power usually comes back on quite quickly, so I'm not too concerned. I leave the hoover where it is and get on with mopping the kitchen floor, a task that I always find strangely satisfying. Once I'm done, I go back to the hoover but the power still seems to be out.

If the power doesn't come back on soon then I will need some temporary lighting as it's starting to get dark outside. I remember that Nicholas had a torch outside when we were looking for Luna. But where did he put it? I cast my mind back and try to think. There's no point in trying to message Nicholas, as I know from previous trips that it takes him an age to reply. I take a look in the boot room but I can't locate it in there.

I'm straining my eyes now in the poor light and I'm starting to panic about the possibility of not having any light at all when the evening wears on. I check my phone and I still have sixty per cent of battery but I'm guessing as soon as I switch the torch function on it will drain the battery faster than I'd like. The house phone is a modern cordless one and won't work while the electricity is down. I have no idea who the electricity provider is so I can't even try to call them to find out what the issue is and how long it might last.

Not for the first time, I really wish Nicholas had followed through on the idea of getting a car for me. At least I could leave the house. Instead, I'm trapped inside this beautiful prison while the heavens pour outside.

After flicking several switches on and off again, it becomes clear that the electricity might be out for the rest of the evening. And with another storm raging outside it's not hard to see why. I decide to put the log burner on as this will give me a few hours of dim light in this room while I eat a cold meal and read a book. Hopefully things will have sorted themselves out by then but, if not, I'll just go to bed early tonight. I find that having a plan is always reassuring and the panicky feeling in my stomach begins to calm down.

The firelight is soothing and I try to appreciate the moment. It's not often nowadays that we experience time disconnected from modern day conveniences. Some people pay a lot of money to go on retreats specifically to untether themselves from gadgets and modern devices. I try to convince myself this as a good thing, an opportunity to unwind, and perhaps going to bed earlier in the evening will help to reset my circadian rhythm.

Just as I'm starting to appreciate being in the present with my little dog by my side, a full stomach and a cosy fireside seat, I hear something that makes my blood run cold. There's a noise outside. It sounds like something being dragged across the gravel driveway.

Leaping up from the sofa, I run to the window and peer out into the darkness. Normally, the floodlights at the front of the property would give me a clear view but all I have to aid me tonight is the light of the moon.

My heart is thumping wildly but I can't see anything unusual. The trees are blowing in the wind and the rain is still coming down, although not as heavy as it was earlier on. Has my mind just conjured up the distinct sound of scraping across gravel in the silence, or is there something or someone outside?

Feeling jittery, I breathe deeply and try to regain control over my racing thoughts. I can't stop thinking about the figure that I thought I saw. I wish that Nicholas was home and that I wasn't here all by myself. Or even that I had some neighbours that were nearby. If anything happened here while Nicholas was away, literally nobody could hear me scream.

Panicking, I check my mobile phone. My battery is still ok and I have a few bars of signal. If I needed to call someone I could. It would be ridiculous to phone the police about something that could just turn out to be a figment of my imagination. I could ring my mum or one of my siblings but they wouldn't be able to get here tonight and Tiggy is away on holiday. Bex isn't far and Trudie would be a good guard dog in a tricky situation. I call her number, but there's no answer.

I stand frozen, straining my ears and expecting to hear the unnerving sound once more. Holding my breath, I wait and wait but the sound doesn't come. Did I imagine it or did it really happen?

Everything is still and silent. As I'm staring out of the window and turning over my predicament, the realisation hits me that the cameras won't be working while the electricity is down. I've got used to having a layer of security at times when Nicholas is away so I feel even more unsafe knowing they're not on.

I consider leaving the house. I could find a hotel to stay in overnight, somewhere where I'm surrounded by other people. But I don't know of any dog-friendly hotels nearby and Nicholas would go mad if he found out I'd left the house while the security system was down. I give myself a little shake; I'm just being silly. It was probably just a fox knocking over the bin or something like that. I'm still not used to all of the nighttime noises in the countryside.

It would be easy to let my imagination run away with itself while I'm here in the darkness so I try to focus on something else, something more practical to distract myself from worrying about noises outside. It occurs to me that the security system not working gives me more freedom in the house. And then I realise that the camera outside Nicholas's office door won't be working right now. This is the ideal time for me to go and take a look in his office.

It's now or potentially never, so I switch on the torch on my phone and head to Nicholas's sacred room. Hooking out the keys that I'd hidden in my pocket earlier, my heart hammers faster.

Unlocking the door, I wonder what I'll find in here…

Chapter Forty
Eva
Now

She still has no idea. I can't wait to see the look on her face when she discovers who I am. She won't have to wait long now.

I've been waiting months and months for this. All my careful planning, my late nights tossing and turning as I go through everything in detail, is coming to fruition now.

I've hated her – *really* hated her. The woman whom my husband has married... the woman he has committed bigamy with. She probably doesn't realise any of this but I hate her all the same. The thought of her living my life, in that house has been torture.

Yes, I admit, part of this is because I want someone to feel the pain I've been through – and Kirsty serves that purpose. But really this is, of course, all about Nick. I want him to see how clever I've been. Above all, I want him to understand how much I love him and why he should never have played me like this. I've been devoted to him, his one true wife, and I deserved to be treated better.

Nick is going to get his comeuppance. He needs to be taught this lesson once and for all. Then we'll be even and we can start again with a clean slate.

And then we will be together.

For eternity.

Chapter Forty-One
Kirsty
Now

I feel a mix of euphoria that I've finally made it in here and anxiety about what I might find. The light of the phone torch roams over the well-proportioned space. I can see there is a desk at the far end of the room, under the window, and a number of filing cabinets running along one wall. On another wall there's a huge whiteboard that is currently blank. As is typical of Nicholas, everything is organised. There's no sign of anything out of place so I need to be careful about what I touch in here and make sure that I put everything back where it belongs, otherwise he'll definitely notice.

Pulling out his desk drawers, I find only office stationery and business documents. Turning my attention to the filing cabinets, I comb through the contents and again find various files relating to his business. A lot of the information seems to be many years old; some of the paper is even yellowing. I guess these are files Nicholas has kept hold of and his more recent business documentation must all be digital.

Maybe the only reason Nicholas didn't want me in here was because of sensitive business files? Perhaps he really does just prefer to keep his work and home life separate. Moving the torch around the room again, my heart jolts when I see there's a door to the side of the filing cabinets. I hadn't noticed it previously but it looks like some kind of inbuilt storage. I turn the handle only to find it's locked.

The only thing between me and my husband's secrets might be this locked door. I'm so close to finding out more about Nicholas – and yet still so far. Feeling deflated, I cast around the room to see if there's any sign of a key that might fit the lock.

I'm about to give up, when I notice the computer monitor isn't straight, but sitting at an angle on the desk. This strikes me as something that would bother Nicholas, usually he likes everything to line up so maybe the monitor has been moved. It's heavy but I wiggle the base to one side and it becomes clear there's something stuck underneath the monitor. I set my phone upright with the torch light shining on the desk and then raise the monitor up with one hand and reach under it with the other.

'Got it!' I say aloud to myself as I clasp the small silver key in my fist.

Setting the monitor back down, I make sure to position it exactly how I found it. Then I insert the key in the silver lock and open the door. As soon as the door swings open, the smell inside the cupboard hits me. It's musty and stale, like this space has been shut tight for a long time. Suddenly, I feel nauseous. It's partly the dank smell and partly because this is like opening Pandora's box. What am I going to find? Is it the truth I'm searching for?

The inside of this cupboard is large: it's almost as big as the tiny bedroom I had in my mum's flat. Two of the walls are lined with shelves that are brimming with books and the noticeable difference is there isn't any kind of order going on in this space. Everything is topsy-turvy; the books aren't lined up in alphabetical order or coordinated by cover colour as I would've expected from Nicholas. They look like they've been stuffed onto the shelves at random, some of the books stacked upright and others vertically. In amongst paperbacks and hardbacks are small trinkets and photographs, each one looking as though they hold a story.

Picking up a polaroid photograph, I'm confronted by the image of my husband looking youthful and carefree. He's grinning into the camera lens and it makes me want to know who was taking the picture, who was making him smile like that. I scan over the bookshelves. There's a glass pyramid and a heart-shaped vial full of coloured sand wedged between an assortment of cookbooks. They must be remnants of trips gone by and they must mean something to Nicholas in order for him to have kept them. But it's the pictures that interest me the most.

I'm drawn to an image of a couple holding hands, their outlines contrasted against a sunset backdrop. They're facing away but I can tell the man is Nicholas. Another photograph is lying face down, I pick it up and see it's of a girl in her late teens riding a bike. But it has been crumpled up and unfolded again many times and the damage this has caused means that it's hard to see her face properly.

The power might come on again at any moment and the longer I stay in here, the more chance there is of me disturbing things and Nicholas finding out I've been in here. But I keep looking. I'm certain there are things hidden in here that Nicholas doesn't want me to know about; why else would he be so guarded?

My eyes alight on a thin, beige folder. It looks as though it has recently been thrown in the cupboard, on top of the jumble of other items that all have a light covering of dust. Snatching up the folder, my fingers tremble as I pull out several sheets of paper.

Scanning the first, I nearly drop the folder. It's a DNA test report. Three names I recognise jump out at me. Under the mother column is the name Jane Thomas and a series of different numbers. Next to this is a column marked 'child' and the name Francesca Thomas. Again there are various numbers under the name that mean nothing to me but must contain relevant information for the DNA test. The third column is title 'alleged father' and printed very clearly is the name Nicholas Johnson.

I crumple to the floor. Nicholas has been hiding more from me than I imagined. Blinking I try to decipher the rest of the information. The date at the top shows the report was generated five years ago. Francesca is in her mid-twenties so this means Nicholas received this report after she reached adulthood.

There are rows upon rows of numbers, some of them circled and some of them not. At the very bottom of the page is the sentence: *Probability of paternity.*

One hand flies to my mouth as I take in the next piece of information. The paternity probability is 0%. The report goes on to say that the alleged father is excluded as the biological father of the tested child because the genetic markers don't match. I'm stunned. I thought I was about to find out that my husband had a child. But all this tells me is there was a query over the identity of Francesca's father.

Is this what Nicholas meant by Jane being capable of stirring up trouble?

How deep does the bad blood run between my husband and this woman?

And could Jane be the figure I've been seeing outside our house?

Chapter Forty-Two
Kirsty
Now

I'm reeling from the information I've just come across. On the one hand, Nicholas wasn't hiding a secret daughter from me but, on the other hand, he also hasn't been honest with me about his history with Jane. He made out like he barely knew her, but this suggests otherwise. Because if he agreed to take a paternity test there must have been some kind of romantic relationship between them.

I place the DNA report back in the folder and then rub my temples, I have a tension headache starting but I'm not going to give up. I feel like I'm getting closer to the answers I've been searching for.

My eyes alight on a blue velvet box on one of the lower shelves. Intrigued, I spring it open and find rows of art deco-style jewellery inside. Running my finger over them, I admire their beauty. These items are insights into Nicholas' history, I just need to work out what how significant they are.

There's a second box next to the velvet one, this one is black. Opening it up, I discover it's another jewellery box but the items in here are very different to the previous box. This one contains contemporary pieces of jewellery from Tiffany's and Gucci. I see a number of bracelets and rings. My breath catches in my throat as I see a Marc Jacobs necklace; it has a thin gold chain and a tiny lock hanging from it.

Picking it up, I turn it over in my hands. This is a tangible link to Nicholas' past – and mine. Then I pull out a silver Kate Spade necklace, with the letter A hanging on the chain. I swallow back tears. This was hers; this belonged to the woman I'm here to find out more about. I can't put it back, not when it reminds me so much of her, so I fasten the silver chain around my neck and tuck it into my top.

Hands trembling, I open a medium-sized wicker basket and find stacks and stacks of letters inside. I pick up the first one and begin reading, it's addressed to 'My dearest Nick'. I skim read and take in the outpouring of love scribbled hastily across the page. Peering into the wicker basket, it's clear to me that all the letters in the box are written in the same handwriting, from the same woman. Every single one of those letters is signed, 'With all my love, Eva.'

This was not the name I was expecting to see. Because I thought the name of Nicholas's first wife was Aimee.

So who is Eva?

Nicholas has never mentioned her name to me before.

After spending another half an hour in the office, the only thing I gain is an understanding of how intense Eva's love was for Nick. Her words are declarations of her feelings and show an attachment so strong that it's obsessive. The wicker basket does not contain the responses from Nick but there are enough letters to suggest that the relationship went on for a long time.

Whatever happened between him and Eva must have left deep scars because when I called my husband 'Nick' the other evening, he told me that being called by that name was triggering and traumatic. He put it down to something in his childhood but he clearly lied to me. That's when I recall the parcel. It was addressed to 'Nick'. A chill runs through my body. Does that mean that Eva sent it? Is she still in contact with my husband?

I have so many questions that it's hard to know which answer to look for first. Scouring the shelves, I find a poetry book with the name *'Eva Johnson'* written inside in curly script that matches the handwriting in the letters. Turning the book over and over in my hands, I wish it could speak and tell me about its owner. But no such luck.

I'm about to give up when my fingers alight on a small, silver heart-shaped box. I open the lid and see that nestled inside is a simple gold wedding band. Picking it up and shining the torch light onto it I see that the outside of the ring is fairly worn, certainly not new, and it looks like it would fit a man's finger. There's a name engraved on the underside of the ring. I know what it's going to say before the beam of light from the torch picks it up.

Eva.

Hastily, I make sure the cupboard door is locked and the tiny key is returned to its hiding place. I leave everything just as I found it. There should be no way that Nicholas will ever know that I've been into his private room or accessed the cupboard where he keeps his past locked away from the rest of the world.

Taking the stairs two at a time, I run into my bedroom and fling open my husband's half of the wardrobe. Pushing aside his freshly pressed shirt and suits, I pat down every inch of the space. My fingers fly across the rows of his neat, polished shoes in the rack at the bottom of the wardrobe. I don't know what I'm expecting to see or find. All of his belongings are perfectly organised, as they always are.

I continue to pull the room apart like a whirlwind. But there's definitely nothing out of the ordinary in this room. Everything is in its place, just the way Nicholas likes it.

Suddenly, the light from the phone torch cuts out. Damn. I try to get it back on again, but nothing works. My phone battery is now at 10% and the torch won't work when it gets this low. I check the light switch once more but the electricity remain stubbornly off.

It's only eight o'clock but there's not much I can do without any light. If I stay up, I'll likely just drive myself crazy with paranoia in the darkness so I decide to try and get some sleep. I don't bother getting changed and instead slide into bed fully clothed. Luna circles round a few times at the end of the bed and then plops down to settle on the duvet. Nicholas doesn't allow Luna to sleep in the bedroom. But seeing as he isn't here, he can't complain and I will feel more reassured if she stays up with me tonight.

Closing my eyes, I try to remember if Nicholas has ever mentioned Eva to me and it's somehow slipped my memory. But no, I'm certain that I've never heard her name before. I picture the moment Nicholas told me about his previous marriage. It was a month or so after we first met. We'd been spending more and more time with each other – our relationship was galloping along at speed and Nicholas had been encouraging me to stay at Orchard Farm for longer than a night or two.

'You're not like anyone I've dated before Kirsty,' Nicholas had said to me. 'You make me feel calm and peaceful when I'm with you.'

'That doesn't sound very exciting!' I'd joked.

'It's a good thing,' Nicholas had reassured. 'There's been too much turbulence in my past. I need someone like you in my life.'

'Your previous girlfriends can't have been that bad.' I'd smiled and looped my arm through his.

Nicholas had shrugged then, and a faraway expression washed over his face. I didn't press him while he was lost in thought.

Eventually he said, 'I should probably tell you that I've been married before.'

I didn't respond, giving him space to go on.

'Maybe it's not so much of a shock, after all I'm nineteen years older than you. At my age, there's not many men who don't have some kind of baggage.'

'Stop it, you're only forty-five.' I tried to make light of his comment.

'Does it bother you?' he'd asked me then, glancing sideways at me as we walked.

'No... should it?' I'd responded to his question with another question.

He blinked and looked away before saying, 'Marriages can be complicated. But there's nothing you need to worry about now.'

'What was her name?'

He hesitated and then said, 'Aimee.'

I wish now that I'd questioned him further that day. But he'd looked so sad and I planned to gently ask him more about his marriage as we got to know each other. I didn't want him to be suspicious about my motives for asking. And I was starting to think that Nicholas was a good guy. But every time I've tried to bring up the subject again since, he's shut me down. He's made it very clear that he doesn't want to talk about his past.

Was he married to Eva before Aimee? And if so, why hasn't he told me about her?

Chapter Forty-Three
Eva
Then

They say hell hath no fury like a woman scorned and they'd be right. And two scorned women are double the fury. From the moment I got Cath on side, things began to change. Cath made sure she was always the one administering the medication so that I didn't have to take it. She took over most of my care, allowing me more time in my room on my own and giving me access to books, magazines and TV while I was in private. Small luxuries that I hadn't had for so long. She tailored the menu to food I liked and made sure I was comfortable. As the weeks went on, I felt as though I was slowly regaining my true self, the person who'd been locked away inside me for so long.

We have to be careful because we can't allow any of Nick's other employees in the house to notice the shift in my treatment. There are four others in total, although they work on a rota basis so there are only ever two people here with me at any one time. They haven't questioned any of the subtle adjustments so far. Cath has always been in charge of making the decisions on my care so this hasn't been out of the ordinary. Cath taking on more of the time with me also means they are doing lighter duties, such as cooking and washing. Plus, they're not exactly complaining about Cath starting to relax their hours on Fridays and at the weekends.

Cath pops her head around the door. 'I've got something for you.'

I sit up straighter in my chair, eager to find out what it might be.

She crosses the room and presses a small mobile device into my hands.

'Oh Cath, thank you! This will help so much!' My eyes fill with tears at her generosity. It's an old, beat-up phone but it's my line to the outside world.

The first thing I do is go to the maps app so I can see exactly where I am in Loch Glass. I commit the information to my memory. Then I access my bank accounts. Incredibly Nick hasn't frozen them. I guess he must've thought I would never manage to escape the set-up he put in place. He has the details of my main bank account so I can't access that in case he has tabs on it but I'm certain he doesn't have the information on my savings account or my investment account so I have a way of getting to some of my money.

He underestimated me. He always did.

'Is everything ok?' Cath asks.

'More than ok. I can access some of my bank accounts. I'm going to repay you for everything you've done for me Cath.' I clasp her hands in mine, my excitement building.

She flushes red. 'You don't need to do that. We're both in this together.'

The sums of money available to me are substantial. I always had a generous salary from Nick's business which has built up over time. I know that just a fraction of this money would transform Cath's life. I vow to repay her kindness as soon as I can.

'I'll be back in half an hour.' She smiles. 'Molly is glued to a reality show downstairs and I may have accidentally made an error in the rota so that there's a gap of a few hours where the night and day shift staff don't cross over, so it'll just be you and me in the house for a while.'

Good. This means we can talk more freely and start putting some plans into place. Opening up the social media app, I go straight to Nick's account. Knowledge is power so I need as much information as I can get.

A picture of his sun-tanned face pops up on screen but I scroll down only to be disappointed. Nick's account is behind some kind of privacy wall. I can't see any new posts. The most recent posts I can view are photos of us from ten years ago. Images of us smiling at Christmas time, on sunny beach trips and in the garden of our old house fill my vision. How I long to go back to that time.

Before I exit the app, I click on his followers and happen to see the name Aimee W listed. I click onto the page to find that Aimee doesn't have her social media locked down. There are regular posts and it's clear she's the type of person who is happy to share every inch of her existence online. Her pinned posts include a close-up shot of an engagement ring with a huge oval diamond and a black-and-white photograph of her in a wedding dress. Below this are recent images of dreamy sunsets, delicious food and an artfully captured wine glass.

Then I see an image I'm all too familiar with. It's the view from one of the back bedrooms at Orchard Farm. Frowning, I keep scrolling and then I inhale sharply.

There she is, resting her head on my husband's shoulder; holding his hand on a country walk; and the pair of them grinning goofily at an ice rink. Scrolling back up, I click on the photograph of her engagement ring and then of the one of her in a breathtakingly beautiful wedding dress. The comments tell me all I need to know.

This woman isn't only in a relationship with my husband – she's married to him too.

Chapter Forty-Four
Kirsty
Now

I'm in a car. My foot is pressed down on the accelerator and I'm going faster than I should along these winding country lanes, but I'm in a hurry. I crank up the music, exhilarated by the feeling of freedom as I hurtle along the maze of roads.

But then a bright beam blinds my vision. The fog lights of the car coming towards me are on full beam. I swerve and press down hard on the brake but nothing happens.

And then my whole body jerks forwards.

I feel the impact of the other car. A pain shoots along my temple.

And I gasp.

I'm jolted awake, sweat dripping down my back. I realise that I'm sat up and my mouth is open in a silent scream.

It's a dream. A nightmare.

It's always the same one; and it always ends in the same way. It's like my brain is caught in a loop, unable to stop imagining that terrible night.

The night Aimee died.

I wasn't there, but I can picture what her final moments were like.

I grope for my bedside lamp and shakily flip the switch. There's still no electricity. Grabbing the empty glass on my bedside table, I fumble my way to the bathroom and fill the glass to the brim with cool water before greedily gulping it down. My body temperature feels too hot, like I'm running a fever, and my chest is tight. This has happened many times before.

Back in the bedroom, my eyes snag on the empty side of my marital bed. I don't usually get spooked but being here on my own but tonight I feel scared.

Luna looks up sleepily from the bottom of the bed. I pick her up and cradle her in my arms, stroking her soft fur which immediately has a calming effect. I've had a nightmare, that's all. It's normal to feel off-kilter when your sleep has been disturbed. I just need to get back into bed and go to sleep because things will feel better in the morning. Except my mind is racing at a hundred miles an hour. I can't stop thinking about everything that's happened.

The parcel. The figure in the trees. The letters from Eva. And Nicholas…

I feel like I'm playing a game of dot to dot but I can't find the connecting thread. Am I just being paranoid or am I right to feel anxious?

There's so much that I don't know about my husband and his life before we got together. When I sought out Nicholas, I had one objective: to find out what happened to his last wife, Aimee. My best friend. We were by each other's sides since the age of five, going from our first day of school all the way to our very last day. I couldn't have imagined my life without Aimee. But when she went to university and I didn't, everything started to change.

Despite what happened between us before she died, she still meant the world to me. We'd promised to be there for each other no matter what, and at the end of her life I hadn't been.

I overheard someone talking about her death in the restaurant I was working in at the time. I was stunned, I couldn't believe Aimee was gone. Her parents abruptly moved away from their family home where they'd raised their only child; they didn't even speak to me about Aimee's passing. Even though we'd grown up as close as sisters.

And there was no funeral. It all felt so unreal and like something didn't add up. I was determined to find out what really happened to her. I just didn't realise how far I'd have to go in my search for answers.

Now, I'm starting to feel like I've got myself into a situation that is way out of my depth. I resolve to call my mum in the morning and to arrange to go and stay with her for a few days. A change of scenery will do me good – and if I'm at my childhood home over the weekend, there's a chance I might cross paths with one or two of my siblings. It's about time I visited.

When I think of the crowded, noisy flat it makes me feel nostalgic for the years gone by when my family were all together. It was tough at times, particularly as I shouldered the responsibilities of stepping up to be the second parent when my father left, but I love all of my little brothers and sisters fiercely. I've been so consumed with Nicholas in these last few months that I've not seen any of them. Stepping away from the four walls of Orchard Farm for a little while might be just what I need.

Knowing I have a plan in place makes me feel better. I'm about to climb back under the bed covers but, before I do, something stops me. I feel a strange, inexplicable pull towards the bedroom window. Setting Luna back down on the bed, I walk towards the window and then fling the curtains open. The storm is still blowing but it's less violent than it was earlier on.

A movement catches my eye. It's in the same place again, over by the trees near the entrance gate. I blink rapidly. It's dark out and yet there's a flash of yellow, like a torch light. But when I focus my gaze, I can't see it. Was it really there? Or is my mind playing tricks on me again?

Fixing my eyes on the spot where I thought I saw the light, I concentrate and try not to blink or look away. I'm near to giving up when I see it again. *Flash. Flash. Flash.* The light flickers on three times.

I don't move, frozen in fear. I glimpse something in the trees – the shape of a person. I'm definitely not seeing things. The light was really there. Still rooted, I know that I can't step away from the window now. If anyone is out there, I have to stay here and keep watching until I know who it is.

Gripping the windowsill for support, I remain at my post. I expect to see the light again but it doesn't appear. And it's too dark outside to see anything without it. But whoever it is, I have a feeling that they wanted me to know they were there.

Bang. Bang. Bang.

The sound ricochets through me. I know instantly what it is: someone hammering on the door. A shadow in the trees couldn't possibly make a sound like that. The threat outside is real, and now it wants to get into the house. It wants to get to me. Luna jumps up and begins barking.

I remember that the security system is down, so the only thing standing between me and whoever is outside is the front door. A wave of fear washes over me, I curse the storm, wondering why this is all happening while Nicholas is away.

Bang. Bang. Bang.

The sound is loud and clear. And it's not going away. Luna is barking in a frenzy now. I scramble for my mobile phone, my fingers shaking so much it's difficult to enter the passcode. I'm going to call the police. It could just be someone perfectly innocent, like a passerby with a broken-down car, but I'm not going to risk it at this time of night. As my home screen flashes to life, my stomach sinks like a lead balloon. The battery is completely drained.

Bang. Bang. Bang.

It's clear the person at the door is not going to go away so there's only one thing for it. I'm going to have to go down and face whoever it is. I pull a jumper on over my flimsy pyjama top and then grab my deodorant spray. My mum always told me to keep one of these in my hand if I was walking home by myself from my late-night restaurant shifts. I've never had to use the spray as a form of self-defence before and I pray that I don't have to tonight.

As I make my way downstairs, I pause where the house phone is and pick the handset up. If this is working, then perhaps I might be able to call the police after all. But the line is dead and my hopes are dashed.

Bang. Bang. Bang.

Luna runs ahead of me and barks incessantly at the front door. I really don't want to have to go through it and find out who is outside. But the alternative is to remain inside, not knowing who is trying to get into the house. I decide to confront whoever is out there.

My fingers touch the cold, metal door handle and I take a deep breath. I press the handle down but, instead of the door swinging open, I meet resistance. I frown and press the handle down again, this time with a bit more force. But it doesn't budge. I try pushing my shoulder against the solid wood but it stays resolutely shut. The door is locked. Usually, the key to this door is left hanging in the lock – it must have fallen out.

The banging outside has now stopped. I strain my ears, listening intently to see if I can make out any unusual sounds at all. But everything is completely silent.

I wait and wait and wait. After ten minutes have gone by, I exhale and almost laugh with relief. The locked door was a blessing in disguise: whatever happened to the key, it stalled me and meant that I avoided a potential nasty encounter with the person outside.

And yet my nerves feel frayed and I'm not convinced the events of the night are fully over. What if the person is still outside, prowling round the grounds of the farm? And where is the front door key?

The thought sends shivers through my body. So I go through to the kitchen. What I really want is a large mug of black coffee to keep me awake until dawn arrives and with it, the feeling of safety but as there's no power, I'll have to seek out the next best alternative, a can of sugary drink.

Fizzy drinks aren't something I have very often but Nicholas is partial to a Jack Daniels and coke so there's always some in the house. I root through the cupboard until I find what I want. I take a big swig, feeling the bubbles dance on my tongue before they fizz in my stomach. I drink a can in one go and then crack open another. All the while listening out for any unusual sounds, but there's nothing. I check my phone. There's still no signal and the battery is getting dangerously low. This makes me feel even more agitated than I was before.

And that's when I notice it.

The key to the bi-fold patio door isn't in the lock either. It's gone.

I try to slide the door open in case I've accidentally left it unlocked again. But it doesn't budge. I'm certain that I locked the door last night – I've been so paranoid about it because of recent events, that I checked it over and over. My head spins as I grapple with what this might mean.

I locked both the back door and the front door and left the keys in the locks. Neither of them are there now. So if I haven't moved them, then someone else must have. My stomach is gripped with fear. Someone is playing a game of cat and mouse with me. But who?

I run around the house and try every single window. They are all locked. Not one of them is open. All the keys are gone.

And then the realisation hits.

I'm trapped.

Chapter Forty-Five
Eva
Then

Cath is my angel in disguise. She's successfully engineered a trip to London for the two of us. She's booked a medical appointment for me and has fabricated a reason why I need to see this particular consultant at this particular hospital. The rest of the staff have been given leave. She fudged the details with Nick – all he knows is that I need this appointment urgently.

We're on the train and about to pull into St Pancras station. I can't quite believe it. We did it.

The whole journey has been stimulating, watching the sea and the cities fly by the train window; listening to the conversations of normal people with normal lives all around me. I can almost pretend that I'm one of them. All these things that I used to take for granted and never will again – if only our plan works.

We go for lunch in Covent Garden and lose ourselves amongst the tourists. I need to attend the appointment for appearances' sake but it shouldn't take long. Then I've told Cath I need to see an old acquaintance, someone who might be able to help me with my finances and my situation. We're staying in a hotel overnight and will go back to Scotland tomorrow, all being well.

I didn't want to lie to Cath but it was a necessity. There is no acquaintance – unfortunately all my relationships were in some way or another interlinked with Nick. I can't think of a single person who I could go to who would be able to get me out of this mess and who wouldn't potentially go back to Nick with everything I've said.

The truth is, I'm not going to see anyone I know. I'm going back to Orchard Farm. I'm hoping that Aimee will be there by herself. Because I need to get rid of her to pave the way for the return to my marriage.

By the time I'm back on that train to Scotland, I want Aimee out of Nicholas' life.

Chapter Forty-Six
Kirsty
Now

The noise startles me. I sit up in bed, still half-asleep, trying to work out where it's coming from. I stretch out and find the other side of the bed empty. Where is he? Where's Nicholas? It's still dark outside so he should be beside me.

Fragments of my latest dark dream seep into my waking moments: someone outside in the trees; Nicholas absent; a woman walking towards me but I can't see her face and the overwhelming feeling that something bad is going to happen.

The shrill sound has stopped. Is it an alarm? Was it part of my dream or did it really happen? I wait, straining my ears to see if I can detect it, but there's nothing.

I lay back down, pulling the bedcovers around me like a cocoon, snuggling back into the warmth and closing my eyes.

And then I remember the events of the night before. The banging at the door. I couldn't get out of the house. I tried every door, every window but they were all locked. In the end, I retreated to my bedroom in the middle of the night, with Luna by my side. I was completely wired with adrenaline, fearful that someone had deliberately locked me in. As the hours ticked by, exhaustion took over so I dragged a chest of drawers in front of the bedroom door to give me some kind of protection. I told myself the electricity was down and this must be causing an issue with the security system. The security system has a layer that locks the doors and windows. It's the only rational explanation and, trying to ignore the fact I couldn't find my keys, I slipped into a fitful sleep.

Then the noise slices through the silence again. I'm not dreaming or imagining it. It's real.

I sit bolt upright again, trying to work out what it is. I hear Luna starting to bark downstairs. It sounds like an alarm. I've never heard the security alarm go off before so I can't be certain if that's what it is. Last night all the electrics were out but they could be working again now. If the alarm is going, does that mean that the person who was lurking outside the house is now trying to get in?

Leaping out of bed, I creep along the hallway and downstairs. The noise is getting louder here. And then I wake up properly and realise it's not the alarm; it's just our house phone. We barely ever use it and the first time I'd ever picked it up was when Francesca rang the other day, so I'm still not familiar with the ringtone. My shoulders untense. It's just the phone, it's fine, and at least it means the electricity must be working again.

I pick it up and the shrill ringing stops. Before I can say hello, a voice I don't recognise says, 'Do you know where your husband is?'

The voice at the other end of the line is barely a whisper so I'm not sure I've heard right.

'What did you just say?' I'm caught completely off guard, still feeling disorientated. I wasn't expecting a phone call and especially not at this hour. I glance at the hallway clock: it's just before 7 am.

There's no response. Just silence.

'Hello? Did you hear me?'

I'm starting to wonder if I'm imagining things. The line crackles with static and then the call goes dead. I stare at the device in my hand. It must've been a wrong number. Or perhaps I'm just so tired I really am imagining things. The call has made me feel weirdly unsettled. I wish that I wasn't here by myself.

Scraping my long hair back into a ponytail, my eyes alight on the photo frame on the centre of the mantlepiece. Picking it up, I gaze at the image of my husband. It's a recent picture of us, looking windswept on a beach walk. Nicholas had spontaneously snapped a selfie with the endless sea in the backdrop. He's smiling broadly, an arm thrown around my shoulders. I'm turned towards him, my cheeks flush pink with exertion and my golden-brown hair streaming out behind me. We look like two people utterly in love. But photographs don't always show the truth.

I draw back the curtains. It's still dark outside at this hour. The sky is a gunmetal grey, heavy with thick clouds. A thought occurs to me: what if something is wrong? Maybe he's had an accident? Or he's unwell?

Pulling my mobile hastily out of my pocket, I see I have one bar of signal so I scroll down to Nicholas's name and tap on it. The dial tone kicks in; I hold my breath, waiting for him to answer. But it keeps ringing and then goes to voicemail. He doesn't pick up. He last messaged me yesterday, saying he was fine and had arrived.

I pace up and down before finding myself back at the window. Pressing my forehead against the cool glass of the windowpane in the lounge, I tell myself to get a grip. Nicholas is probably still in a hotel bed asleep. He'll call back when he can.

Sitting down at the breakfast table, I try to make sense of what the call meant. Just as I'm beginning to calm down, telling myself it must've been a wrong number, the house phone rings again. I sit bolt upright.

My stomach swoops with dread. Rushing towards the sound, I speed along the hallway and press the handset to my face.

'Do you know where your husband is?'

There's no mistaking the question now. I definitely didn't imagine it. A million thoughts crash through my mind at once.

'Who is this?'

There's a chuckle at the other end of the line.

'Are you sure you want to know?'

I can't place who it is but it's definitely a woman, and it sounds as though the voice is being distorted in some way. Like she's talking under water.

'I'm not playing silly games, either tell me or I'm phoning the police,' I say clearly and firmly.

'Oh, you don't want to do that…'

The sentence is left hanging and I know the caller is trying to bait me. I'm about to hang up when she says something that sends shivers down my spine.

'Your husband is in danger.'

'What? Is he hurt?' I ask in a rush.

I hear the person at the other end of the line breathing. Are they telling the truth or is this some kind of hoax call?

'Who are you?' I repeat.

'I'm your husband's secret wife.'

Chapter Forty-Seven
Kirsty
Now

My pulse rate speeds up and I try to process what this means.

'Yes, that's right Kirsty. I was married to him first. And I still am actually. He has a secret marriage. I bet he never told you that, did he?'

I drop the phone. It clatters to the wooden floor, making me jump. This can't be happening. What I've just been told can't be true.

My mouth is dry and I feel overwhelmed with confusion. I need to find out more. Grabbing the phone, I say, 'You're lying! What do you really want?'

But there's no one there. The woman claiming to be married to my husband has gone.

Damn. I shouldn't have dropped the phone.

Fumbling with the buttons, I try to find out the number of the caller but again I'm met with an unknown number.

My heart thuds hard against my ribcage. I slump down on the bed, my head in my hands. *Think. Think. Think.*

Why would someone call me to tell me that my husband is a bigamist if it wasn't true?

I rub my forehead and try to work out what to do next. Seconds later, the living room door creaks open. I spring back in shock. Is there someone else in the house? Has the woman on the phone somehow got into my home?

The door creaks open a little further and I hold my breath.

And then Luna sneaks around the doorframe and bounds into the room, her little brown tail wagging enthusiastically.

'You scared me,' I whisper to her softly.

Pulling her on my lap, I stroke her silky fur. She looks up at me with big brown eyes and I swear they're filled with concern.

'What would you do Luna?' I often find myself voicing my thoughts to my canine companion.

I go over the words of the caller again. She said Nicholas was in danger. What if it was true? The woman claiming to be his other wife could be delusional, or unwell. Maybe she believes she's married to Nicholas. Maybe she's hurt him. There are so many possibilities. She could really be his other wife.

One thing is for sure, whatever Nicholas has done in the past, I have to make sure he is safe.

Because that's the only way I'll find out the truth about Aimee.

Chapter Forty-Eight
Eva
Now

Poor Kirsty.

I think we might have been friends if our paths had crossed at a different time and in a different way. It's a shame that she met Nick and got caught up in all of this.

But she has, and so this is the way that it's got to be.

It's time to put the next phase of my revenge into action. Things are about to get serious.

Don't get me wrong; I've had many wobbles about doing this. I almost backed out of everything yesterday. But today is a new day and I'm going to see it through.

You never know what obstacles life is going to throw at you or what paths you will end up travelling down. The past few years have taken me to places that I could never have imagined, even in my worst nightmares.

I've done things that I never thought I was capable of.

But I can't stand the thought of anyone else having my Nick. So this is the only way forward.

Chapter Forty-Nine
Kirsty
Now

Shaking, I open the door and exhale with relief as I see a familiar face.

'Come in, come in.' I smile broadly, but my smile is not returned.

In the shadowy light, the expression on my guest's face makes me freeze.

She laughs. 'Really? Haven't you worked it out yet? Or do you finally get it now?'

There's a whooshing sound in my ears, as understanding washes over me.

'I'm Eva,' she confesses.

'You're Eva?' My jaw nearly hits the floor. 'You? But... how? Why did you...'

My voice trails off because I don't need to finish my question or wait for the answer. It's clear the woman standing in front of me has deceived me in every single interaction that we've ever had.

'Why didn't you tell me you were married to Nicholas? And how is that even possible!'

'I thought you'd work it out eventually...' She smirks at me.

My head is spinning. Looking at her again, I take in how pleased she seems with herself. The expression transforms her face and suddenly she looks so different to the woman I thought was my friend.

'Bex? Just tell me what the hell is going on!'

She looks at me with amusement. Then her eyes fix on mine as she says, 'Not Bex... Eva. And don't worry, I intend to tell you exactly what's going on. Just have a little patience.'

Crossing my arms protectively across my chest, I observe her now through a new lens. Bex, the only person I've felt a real connection with since moving here, turns out to be someone else entirely. How much of the Bex whom I was getting to know is real? Or was everything about her fake, designed to trick me in some way?

'Why don't we go and sit down?' she says, trying to step through the door as though this was an ordinary social call.

Shaking my head, I stand firm and reply, 'No, tell me why you're here first.'

Eva raises an eyebrow. 'I'm here because Nicholas Johnson is a bigamist and it's about time that he stopped playing both of us for fools.'

Tucking a strand of hair behind my ear, I think for a minute. How do I even know that what this woman is saying is the truth? She's already lied to me about who she is so she could be lying to me again. She could just be a crazy, deluded person, with no connection to Nicholas at all, who is targeting our marriage because she wants money – or something else. Then I remember the letters. If I hadn't discovered them yesterday and seen the name Eva signed off on every single one, then I would just pick up the phone and call Nicholas or the police right away.

But something tells me that I need to hear what Eva is about to say.

'Ok,' I reluctantly agree. 'Come through.'

Eva sashays past me and heads straight for the kitchen, suggesting that she's familiar with the layout of the house. She sits herself down at the breakfast table. I take the seat opposite, curious to hear what she has to say for herself but also fearful of the truth.

'Look,' Eva says, her tone gentler now. 'I'm on your side. I was in your shoes once and that's why I had to come here to tell you everything.'

I know this might all be an act but Eva's words seem genuine. It's hard to believe that the time we've spent together talking and walking the dogs has all been a pretence. Or is she just a very good liar?

She moves closer to me, her features serious and her words urgent. 'I need to warn you about Nick. I have to make you understand what he's like. Because you're not safe here, not with him.'

'Has he hurt you?' I ask her.

She throws her head back and gives a strangled laugh. 'Nick has hurt me in more ways than you can imagine. I just don't want you to end up like me in ten years' time.'

'And you said you're still married to him?' I press, trying to put the pieces of the puzzle together.

Eva nods her head. 'I am.'

She reaches into her crossbody bag and pulls out a folded piece of paper. She smooths it out on the table and points to the details. 'See, Nicholas Johnson and Eva Tennant. We were married on a hot July morning over twenty years ago.'

Scanning the paper, the printed text confirms what she's saying. Although I'm still dubious. The only other marriage certificate I've seen is my own. This could easily be a fake, or it might well be a real certificate but there could have been a subsequent divorce that Eva isn't revealing.

'And you never divorced?' I question her, my arms folded defensively.

Her eyes glitter with an emotion I can't quite decipher. 'No,' she confirms. 'We never divorced. You can search all the records but you won't find a divorce registered for Nicholas and me – because there hasn't been one.'

'I don't understand...' I shake my head. 'How could Nicholas get remarried if he hadn't divorced?'

'If you get married in a different location and give false details about yourself, it's possible to do. I've looked up other cases of bigamists online. Nick and I married in Scotland two decades ago and he has a fairly common name,' she shrugs.

I inhale sharply, trying to take this information in.

'I don't know how he did it, but he did. Nick knows enough people in the right places that he can get away with a lot of things,' Eva says starkly. 'Anyway, there's something else you need to know about Nick.'

I'm not sure I'm ready for whatever Eva is about to tell me but there's no doubt I'm about to find out.

'It's best if you hear it from him.' Eva stands up then. And, before I can stop her, she snatches my phone from me. 'Come with me,' she instructs.

'Where are you going?' I have a bad feeling about this and, despite Eva showing me the marriage certificate, I still don't quite believe everything she's saying.

'I'm taking you to Nick.'

'My husband Nicholas is on a business trip,' I explain.

She shakes her head, a slow smile spreading across her face that stretches until it becomes a grimace. 'He's not on a business trip. He's been with me.'

My heart flips. Has Nicholas not really been on a business trip? Has he been with another woman instead – with Eva?

She goes out the patio door and begins striding across the garden towards the gate that leads to the rest of the land surrounding the farmhouse.

'Where is Nicholas?' I shout towards her retreating back.

'Oh, he's not very far at all.'

My brain is screaming at me to get away from her and to extract myself from whatever game she is playing.

I don't trust her.

But I've come this far and now I have to follow her.

Because I can feel myself getting closer to the truth.

Chapter Fifty
Kirsty
Now

I can't believe what I'm seeing.

In the darkened outbuilding, my husband Nicholas is tied to a chair. He's gagged and his head is slumped over his chest and the rope bites into his wrists and ankles. For a horrible second, I think he might be dead.

But then his head snaps up as Eva clicks on the overhead light. The scene before me becomes even more real.

'Hello Nick,' Eva says. Her voice is so icy it sends a chill through me.

An expression of pure terror shoots over Nicholas's face and then he clocks me standing next to her. A desperate look comes into his eyes and he starts to rock on the chair, as though trying to topple himself over.

'Now, now Nick. Don't get too excited.' Even though Eva's voice is steady, her eyes are wild and unfocused.

I rush over to my husband.

'What have you done to him?' I shriek at Eva.

I fumble with the material around his face, desperately trying to remove the gag so he can speak.

'Well, being silent and keeping secrets is his thing, so I didn't think this would make too much of a difference.'

Nicholas's eyes lock with mine. He seems to be trying to tell me something but, until I can loosen this knot, I have no idea what it is.

'Why are you doing this?' I round on Eva.

'Like I said, it's a long story. And I'm happy to share it with you now.'

Her features have hardened once more and all the concern she showed for me during our chat at the kitchen table has fallen away. Did she trick me into coming into this outbuilding?

Thoughts hurtle through my brain. Eva clearly has a plan but I have none. I need to make sure I can extract myself from this situation – I can't end up bound to a chair like Nicholas.

'How long has he been here?' I cry.

'Well, let's just say he didn't make it very far along the lane when he left for the airport.'

'But he messaged me to say he'd arrived –'

'You received a message from Nick's phone,' Eva corrects, as she pulls his mobile phone from her pocket and holds it up for me to see. She then tosses it onto the top of the pile of boxes next to her.

Eva has planned all of this. The realisation sinks in that she's the person who has been watching the house too. Then something else occurs to me.

'What about the open doors and the security system trapping me inside last night. Has all of that been you as well?'

'All me,' she confirms. 'I knew where the gaps in the hedge were to access the farm through the back fields. And I'd hidden a spare set of keys in one of the large plant pots in the garden when I was renovating the farmhouse, just in case I ever needed them. I wasn't sure they'd still be there but Nick hadn't discovered them. So yes it was me who kept opening the patio door.'

'But how did the cameras not pick you up?'

'I still had the login details for the security system. Cath got a phone for me so I was able to download the app and view the camera footage.

I was also able to use the security controls so that any time I was on the property I could close off any cameras that I needed to. Last night, I shut down everything – the phone line, the lights, the locks.'

Clamping my jaw tight, I grind my teeth. I can't believe that the woman I believed to be my friend has been behind all this. But I keep my shock to myself because I don't want to give her the satisfaction of knowing how much she's got to me. Instead, I study Nicholas more closely: his face is ashen and he has a nasty bruise on his cheekbone. He gulps in a lungful of air as soon as I remove the gag.

'Nicholas, are you ok?' I drop to one knee and assess him further. His lips are cracked and dry – he's obviously dehydrated and there's a purple bruise on his temple. A small part of me feels sorry for him, but the rest of me wishes I'd never set eyes on this man.

'Water,' he pleads.

I look up at Eva but she shakes her head. 'Not just yet, he can wait.'

She inspects her nails and then fixes me with a stare. 'You've asked a lot of questions and now I'm going to answer them.'

Eva pauses dramatically, her words hanging in the air between us. I wait with bated breath.

'The truth is that Nick and I have been married for a long time,' she says. 'He was my first love, my only love, and he promised that we'd be together forever.'

He opens his mouth but she doesn't give him the opportunity to speak; she just ploughs on. 'We met during our first week of university and we were inseparable from then on. We were the couple that everyone was certain would get married. And they were right. Nick proposed to me the year after we graduated. Then we had a blissful summer travelling around Europe together. It was the happiest time of my life.'

Eva talks with such emotion in her voice that I believe what she's saying. Looking down at Nicholas, I notice that a deep crease has appeared between his brows.

'After that, Nicholas wanted to pursue his dreams. He'd studied business and wanted to be an entrepreneur; he wanted to take a risk and build his own empire. I took a job as a legal secretary to keep us going. My dream was to become a barrister but I put that aside to support the man I loved...' Eva looks sad as she recounts this.

I'm fascinated by the history between Nicholas and Eva. Their connection runs deep and I can't help but wonder what went wrong between them.

'We had a good life, a strong marriage – or so I thought.' The tone of Eva's voice goes from emotional to bitter.

Eva is raking her hands through her hair and she looks completely unhinged. Her movements are jerky, erratic. Nothing like the smiling, kind woman I thought she was when she introduced herself to me as Bex.

She paces up and down, muttering under her breath. This is it. This might be the only opportunity I get. I swiftly set to work on the rope binding Nicholas's hands. I'm not sure if I'm doing the right thing by untying him. Maybe I've got too caught up in the pretence of being married to Nicholas and I should wait to hear more. Although, if I free him, then surely he'll become an ally to me because I've helped him.

My hands struggle at the knot – it's frustratingly tight and I'm not sure if I'm going to be able to unravel it without Eva noticing. But she turns her back to us and I'm able to start loosening it. I keep my eyes on Eva and as soon as it looks as though she's going to turn, I spring away from Nicholas.

'He betrayed me,' Eva says, now facing us both once more. 'It was the classic mid-life crisis, Nick cheated on me with a much younger woman.'

'Eva—' Nicholas tries, but his voice gives out before he can go on.

'I should have seen the signs: the late nights at work, the changes in his behaviour. Maybe I did recognise what was happening but I didn't want it to be true.'

Eva pulls at her hair then in anguish. 'How could you Nick? How could you do it to me?' she screeches. 'After everything we'd been through! After the life we'd built together. And all the sacrifices I made for you!'

She darts forward, levelling her face so that it's only inches from his. 'You're nothing but a liar and a cheat.' She spits at him.

And then, without warning, she slaps his face hard. A red imprint of her hand is left on his right cheek. He cries out in pain.

'It's nothing more than you deserve,' Eva says to him through gritted teeth. Then she rounds on me. 'You'd better listen if you know what's good for you. Because Nick didn't just shatter our marriage, he tried to break me as well.'

'What do you mean?' I ask.

'Nick didn't want to lose his riches to the woman who'd stood by his side while he built a successful company. Oh no, he decided to play dirty, didn't you darling?'

My ears prick and I realise this is the missing piece of the puzzle that might change my view on everything.

'Nick didn't want me to have anything – the house, the money, any of the assets that had been accumulated during our marriage. So he tried to get rid of me.'

'To get rid of you?' I question.

'He had me locked up in an old stone cottage. It reminded me so very much of Orchard Farm, I'm sure he did it deliberately. There was no one else for miles – just endless fields of heather. He made sure I was in a remote spot in the Scottish Highlands where no one would think to look for me. He had me drugged up and under constant surveillance. He told everyone I'd gone mad.'

I gape. Could Nicholas really be capable of this?

Nick croaks, his voice coming out in barely a whisper.

'Oh, fine!' Eva shouts. 'I suppose you'd better say whatever it is you want to say.'

She grabs a bottle of water from a stack of boxes that are leaning haphazardly against a wall. She roughly tips the bottle to his lips and lets him drink for a few seconds. Half of the liquid is just dribbling down his stubbled chin but Eva quickly withdraws the water in one swift movement. She makes a show of screwing on the lid and then discarding the bottle on the floor.

My eyes are trained on Nicholas now. Did he really have Eva imprisoned in a remote house to remove her from his life? Just the thought of this makes me feel sick. Could he really be that controlling?

'Eva, you know that's not exactly what happened,' Nicholas says slowly. 'I was trying to help you.'

'No, you weren't. You just wanted to get your own way, just like always.' Eva heaves in a breath and then says, 'And now you're going to pay for what you did to me.'

'Eva, think about what you're doing.'

'Oh, I have thought about it, Nick. I've had plenty of time, while I've been under lock and key, to think about this moment.'

'Kirsty: don't listen to her.' Nicholas turns his attention to me. 'That's not what happened.' He descends into a coughing fit, as though the words are too much effort for him.

Eva rolls her eyes.

'Yes, we split up...' He manages to say, 'But it's not uncommon. There were a lot of... issues... in our marriage.' His voice crackles.

'Of course you'd say that,' Eva counters.

Nicholas tries again, this time communicating in short sentences. 'It's lies. The divorce papers are in my office. Kirsty believe—' His voice gives out once more.

Eva launches into another barrage of accusations at Nicholas. As I stand between the two of them, I try to work out who is lying and who is telling the truth. I don't remember seeing divorce papers in his office.

Should I believe my husband? Or the woman claiming she's trying to save me?

Chapter Fifty-One
Eva
Then

'It was your fault!'

I look at him blankly. It's been a long time since I saw Nick – and over four months since the car accident. At first, I was going out of my mind. I thought he might be injured, or worse. I was devastated, I thought that I'd lost the love of my life. I wanted to rewind time and stop the whole incident happening. I couldn't stop thinking about that night.

Cath tried to contact Nick but there was no answer. I searched the internet for news stories but even though the accident was reported there was only the mention of a woman being badly injured. So all I could do was wait. Then a couple of weeks after the car crash, Cath finally heard from Nick. It was a perfunctory phone call followed by another a fortnight later. At least I knew he was alive.

Now he's here, I'm so relieved to see him. But he looks so angry.

He slams his hand down on the kitchen table. 'It's your fault she's dead!'

I remain mute. I'm speechless. I'd assumed that Aimee had survived because Nick did. The social media account belonging to her had been set to private the week after the accident so I had no way of knowing what happened to her.

'You—'

Before I can react, Nick's hand is in my hair. He's dragging me from my seat and out of the room. My scalp is on fire and I yelp in pain.

'What are you doing?' I manage to gasp.

'What I should have done sooner,' Nick says darkly.

He hauls me up the stairs and I stop trying to resist because it makes the pain worse. He hurls me into my room and I slam into the bed with force and crumple on the carpet.

'Nick?' I sob.

He pulls me roughly onto the bed, pinning me to the sheets with one strong arm. I struggle, trying to fight back as I see what's in his other hand.

'No! Don't do this!'

The pillow comes down over my face. He's pressing it down over my nose and my mouth with both hands. I can't speak; I can't breathe. My body begins to thrash in response. I'm aware there's only a short amount of time I can hold on for. Black spots appear in my vision, and I fling my arm wide. Something on the bedside table knocks over.

The pressure on my face is unbearable. I'm not sure I can hold on for much longer. I think this might be the end.

And then the door bursts open. Whatever fell to the floor may have just saved my life.

'Get off her!'

The pain stops and the pillow slips away from my face. I suck air into my lungs; all I can focus on is breathing in and out. Trying to get my body working again.

'She murdered Aimee, I know she did!' His voice cracks.

'What? That's impossible.' It's Cath, coming straight to my defence.

Cath's cool hand sweeps my forehead. 'What have you done to her?'

'Nothing that she doesn't deserve.' Nick curses.

'I can assure you that I've been by Eva's side constantly, just as you've instructed.' Cath sounds prim and professional. And convincing.

Opening my eyes, I see Nick looming above me. 'I don't know what I'm going to do with you Eva, but you mark my words, I'm going to do something!'

The door slams, practically bouncing off its hinges. I wince.

'Are you ok?' Cath eases me into an upright position.

'Cath – you saved me.'

'It was the lamp that saved you.'

We both look at the upturned light on the floor. If I hadn't moved my arm and the lamp hadn't fallen, then I could be stone cold dead by now.

'I can't believe...' My words fall away. Nick just tried to kill me. He almost succeeded.

'I'm calling the police,' Cath says in a fluster. 'He can't get away with this.'

Shaking my head, I signal that I don't want her to do this. 'Water,' I croak.

When Cath returns with the glass, I sip slowly. The liquid slides down and cools the burning sensation in my throat.

'We can't involve the police.' I insist.

Cath raises her eyebrows and then asks, 'Did you kill Aimee?'

'No,' I shake my head. 'It was an accident.'

'Tell me the truth Eva.' Cath's voice is firm.

'I didn't plan it. Yes, there's been times when I've wished Aimee dead but this wasn't some cold-blooded murder. It was a car crash. An accident.'

I can tell that Cath isn't sure whether to trust my word or not.

'If it was anything more, then I would tell you.' I can feel my eyes watering as I speak, my emotions are getting the better of me. 'You've been such a good friend to me, I should have told you about this before but, believe me, I'm not lying.'

She stares down at me, looking as though she's trying to work out the answer to a puzzle.

'It's been eating me up that I hurt someone but I didn't know she was dead until Nick said just now. But I'm also not sorry she died. The universe has its own ways of working, and she deserved it.'

Cath stays silent for a little while longer and then, finally, she says, 'He was going to kill you in your bed. He will try to do it again.'

My tongue feels too thick in my mouth and I can't respond.

'I can only protect you for so long. What if he tries to move you elsewhere? You need to run while you still can.'

Tears pool in my eyes. With Aimee gone, I had this fantasy that Nick would come to Scotland and take me home. I believed her death would end the spell Nick has been under, but I was wrong.

'No' I manage to say faintly. 'I want to stay here with you.'

'But—'

'I mean it.'

'I thought you might say that,' Cath sighs. 'Ok, well there might be another way to keep you safe…'

Chapter Fifty-Two
Eva
Now

Everything is going to plan.

I've got Nick right where I want him. And I've certainly got Kirsty's attention.

Although she was never meant to be part of all this. I liked spending time with her on our dog walks; even though initially it was all an act. Trudie isn't really my dog. She belongs to the man living in the house next to my short-term rental. He'd just had a hip operation and needed a temporary dog walker and having a dog was an easy way for me to get close to Kirsty. My plans came together better than I could've hoped. But my walks with Kirsty took me by surprise, she was nothing like I'd imagined her to be. And I meant what I said: we could've been friends if things had been different.

I'd been so careful not to get too friendly with other women. Just in case they decided they wanted to get close to my perfect husband. The more successful Nick got, the more paranoid I became because having a rich husband made him more of a target for the kind of woman who was looking to secure a certain type of lifestyle. In the end, it wasn't any of the polished, glamorous golf club wives who made a move on him. No, instead it was the age-old cliché of a much younger woman.

It's not my fault Kirsty's been drawn into the swirling, dangerous tides of mine and Nick's relationship. Nick had to go and get married; he had to complicate things – just like he always does. I may have forgiven him in time if it was a simple affair. Or maybe not. Maybe I would have been filled with as much rage as I am now.

What Nick did was unforgivable. He broke my trust. He broke years of love and memories. He betrayed me in the worst possible way. And then he went one step further. I refused to divorce him when he asked me. I didn't want him to have the freedom to walk away and start over. Not when I felt as though my heart had been ripped out.

He played dirty. He tried every trick in the book, wheedling and persuading. If only he'd tried that hard to save our relationship. I wouldn't bend to his demands. And that made him very, very angry. He told me I couldn't stand in his way.

He deceived me. He trapped me in that remote house in the Scottish Highlands that reminded me so much of the home we'd renovated together. Dumped me there like forgotten luggage. I can never forget the eyes of the people paid to watch me constantly. A needle always in hand, ready to keep me docile, to keep me obedient.

But I escaped.

Now, unluckily for Kirsty, she's too embroiled in the situation for me to let her go.

Nick holds my gaze. Behind his eyes I know are a thousand words he wants to express, but he's too weak to say them.

It's clear that I'm the one in control now. I'm the one pulling the strings. The puppet has become the puppet master. I'm sure that Nick doesn't appreciate our roles being reversed but I'm rather enjoying being the one with the power right now. What happens next is totally down to me.

'Eva,' Nick stutters.

'Yes, my love?'

'Let me go.'

'Oh, come on now. That's not very polite, is it?' I tease him.

'You can't keep him locked up here forever,' Kirsty says gently. She's standing with her hands hanging by her sides, watching my every move.

'Oh, can't I?' I question.

'Well, no...' Kirsty trails off.

'Because I think I'm the one making the decisions here, don't you?' I indicate to the shotgun that's leaning up against the wall to the right of us.

Kirsty's eyes widen.

'How else did you think I managed to get Nick tied up?' I chuckle.

'Eva, think about this. Nicholas is dehydrated; it's inhumane keeping him like this. You could stop all of this now, before things go too far.'

Her words are calm and measured. I'm impressed that she's still talking so boldly, despite the threat of the gun in the corner of the room.

'Thanks for your advice, Kirsty. It's a shame you weren't there to step in during all the time Nick had me locked away.'

I watch as Kirsty hesitates.

'Can you imagine what that must've been like for me?'

She shakes her head.

'And do you know how long I was there?'

She shakes her head once more.

'Three and a half years.' I let the information sink in before continuing. 'That's a long time. A long time in which Nick could've changed his ways. He could've shown me some compassion, after all we've been through together. So a few days is nothing.'

'Eva...' I hear the note of exasperation in Nick's voice. At the same time, Kirsty snatches up the bottle of water and places it gently to his lips. He slurps greedily, this time managing to drink more than is spilled.

I don't move – after all we may as well have this conversation. It's been a long time coming, and I'm curious to hear what Nick has to say now that he's had a taste of his own medicine.

Nick licks his lips, closes his eyes and takes a few deep breaths. 'Eva,' he says, his voice sounding stronger now. 'I didn't tie you up like this. You weren't locked away in a prison or a derelict house! You're making it sound worse than it was. At first you were at a rehab centre, a luxury facility, to help you. And then you were resting in a beautiful house. Cath was looking after you, it was for your own good.'

'It's not nice when someone betrays you, is it Nick?'

Nick stubbornly holds my gaze and says nothing.

I laugh out loud. 'This was your chance to redeem yourself. To at least say sorry. But you couldn't even do that, could you?'

I can't deny that I'm disappointed by Nick's response. I thought there might be a chance that he would be forced to confront his mistakes and that he would ask for my forgiveness. But even when the tables have been turned and we're at the last stop before the point of no return, he won't admit that he's been in the wrong.

This is so infuriatingly like my husband. But we're not just having a small argument about how to decorate the bedroom or where to go for a weekend break. No; this is much more serious.

This final showdown between us is a matter of life or death.

Chapter Fifty-Three
Kirsty
Now

'Kirsty, help me,' Nicholas begs, his eyes flicking towards the shotgun and then back to me.

I have to choose carefully between Nicholas and Eva, because my life might just depend on it. The thought terrifies me. But how can I decide between two liars? Eva, who has already deceived me, reeling me in with a false friendship. And my husband, who has lied to me about so many things.

'So Kirsty, who's it going to be?' Eva asks, slicing through my thoughts as though she's just read my mind.

'Me or him. Him or me?' Eva laughs again, the sound grating like chalk on a board.

The more Eva says, the more she scares me. But I don't say anything, allowing her to keep going because the more she talks, the more knowledge I'll have. And knowledge is always power.

Eva cocks her head to one side, considering me. 'You know, I think there's more to you, Kirsty, than meets the eye.'

My heart rate begins to speed up. Does she know my secret? Or is she just playing a game?

Crossing my arms defensively, I still don't say anything, waiting to hear if Eva has figured out the reason why I married Nicholas.

'It's always the quiet ones you have to watch, isn't it?' Eva is enjoying this, toying with me.

When I still don't respond, I think I see something like annoyance flicker in her eyes. She turns her attention back to Nicholas.

'I bet you wish you'd been a better husband now, don't you?' Eva spits towards him.

'Eva—' Nicholas begins.

But Eva launches into a tirade of all the hurts she's endured from Nicholas over the years. His head bows, not looking at either of us as her words fly like arrows towards him. It's clear she's been waiting a long time to say all of this.

Nicholas looks up at me again, pleading in his eyes. His handsome face suddenly appearing aged. He doesn't need to speak this time; I know he is begging me to help him. Eva's rant will come to a stop eventually, and then what will she do?

Nicholas looks up at me with real fear etched across his face. He knows I'm his only hope of escape now but should I help him? He's potentially a bigamist who locked up his first wife when she became inconvenient to him. And Eva is unhinged; her obsession with the man who betrayed her is clear. Not to mention the fact she has deliberately placed a gun in the room.

I need to make my mind up fast. Whose side am I on?

One of the two people in this room has killed before. One of them is already a murderer – a murderer who killed the one person I loved most in the world.

But which one of them is it?

Chapter Fifty-Four
Eva
Now

'I'm still waiting for my apology,' I say, moving closer to Nick and crouching down so that our faces are merely inches apart.

Nick parts his lips before clamping them shut again.

'So no apology then?' I wait, holding my breath. I reach out a hand and brush a lock of hair off his forehead but he turns his face away from me.

I stand up and pace the room. I count in my head.

One. I just have to be patient. I have to give him a chance to reply.

Two. All he has to say is sorry. Just one small word and we can figure everything out.

Three. There's still time for him to say it.

Four. Why won't he just say it? I thought he would finally give in.

Five. His time is up.

I turn, narrow my eyes and regard my husband, the love of my life – no, more than that: the centre of my world. Now I have to make a choice. Pick left or right. Live or die.

'I don't love you,' he says.

'What?' My eyes widen in shock.

'I don't love you,' Nick repeats. 'I haven't loved you for a long time. You've got nothing to gain from this.'

My world tilts on its axis.

This feels like the final crack splintering through my soul. Not long now and it will shatter completely.

'I loved you once but I don't love you now,' he says more gently. 'We have to move on from this. You've got to let go of the past Eva. And so do I.'

He continues on. Something about honouring our relationship and finding the future happiness we deserve. But I can't hear his words properly – how could I? His voice is drowned out by the pounding of blood in my ears as my heart slams against my ribcage. Nick has hurt me in so many ways but those four little words have broken me.

I don't love you.

I don't love you.

I don't love you...

Chapter Fifty-Five
Eva
Now

'Eva.'

Someone is calling my name but the sound is small, muffled, as though it's coming from a long way away.

'Eva?'

Blinking several times, my eyes swimming with tears, I manage to swivel my head in the direction of where the sound is coming from.

The voice is louder now and the face of the person speaking comes back into focus.

'Eva, I know this is hard but let's go back to the farmhouse and talk about things properly. We can't stay out here, like this.' Kirsty's expression is full of concern as she speaks slowly and calmly.

She might genuinely want to help me. Or she might just be trying her best to get Nick untied and to exit the situation she's found herself in. But she's gone totally the wrong way about doing it.

Orchard Farm was my house. It was my renovation project. I poured blood, sweat and tears into making it my home. And now Kirsty is inviting me back there for peace talks like I'm a guest, a stranger instead of the person who lovingly restored every single room.

What does she think I'm going to do, accept her offer of a cup of tea and a chat? Does she think I'll back down now that Nick has made his feelings crystal clear?

'Eva, you can put a stop to this before things go too far. I know you're hurting; I can see that. But don't make things worse for yourself. You can still find happiness.'

My blood begins to boil. Does she think she can stop me with kind words and a reassuring hug? And does she really think that Nick would let me just walk away after what I've done?

I try to fake a smile but it ends up being more of a sneer. I try again. I need to keep her on side to stop her from doing anything rash.

'Kirsty, it's so cosy out here that I think we should stay a while longer. Especially now that we're sharing our truths, there's something else I want to share with you.'

'Eva,' Nick says in a warning voice, like he knows what's coming. But he no longer has the upper hand, I do.

Kirsty's eyes dart from me to Nick and back again. She really is stuck completely in the middle of all of this. But I can't stop. I plough on, down the only path that I can see for myself.

'There's something else about Nick's past you don't know about. Or should I say someone else.'

Kirsty's attention is back on me, a curious look in her eyes.

'There's a reason why I've been looking out for you Kirsty, trying to keep you safe. Because Nick has quite the track record when it comes to his wives. He didn't quite go through with getting rid of me, though he's kept me locked away and controlled for long enough. But his second wife had things even worse.'

'His second wife?' Kirsty questions.

'The wife after me. The younger model that he dumped me for. She was beautiful, but she had no idea what she was getting herself into. By all accounts, she wasn't happy to just submit to Nick's rules and orders.'

'Don't listen to her,' Nick urges.

'And because of that she ended up dead, didn't she darling?' I snap.

'Eva, what are you doing? You know full well that you caused Aimee's death.' Nick's voice is still hoarse and rough as he speaks.

'Kirsty,' I grab her arm, my fingers circling her slim wrist tightly. 'It was his fault. It was all his fault.'

Then I snatch up a thin length of wire and, in a flash, I'm behind Nick and I have the wire pressed to his neck.

'Eva, no!' Kirsty springs forward, her arms outstretched.

'Our husband here is a dangerous man. He will break your heart, like he broke mine. He will dispose of you once he's done with you, like he did to me and to Aimee. Aimee died because of him. There's a pattern of behaviour here and you're not too precious to escape it.'

I press the wire more firmly into Nick's flesh.

'He will try to kill you. It's him or us. This is the only way to end things...'

Chapter Fifty-Six
Kirsty
Now

'Wait!' I yell.

Taking Eva by surprise, I manage to spring forward and whip the wire from her hand and away from Nick's neck. There's a nasty indentation running across his skin, but it didn't go deep enough to do any proper damage.

Aimee. My head spins. Her name is out in the open now. This is what I've been waiting for.

'It wasn't just an unfortunate car accident,' Eva snarls. 'It was his fault.' She jabs a finger at Nicholas.

'Believe me Kirsty. It wasn't me, I didn't do it,' Nicholas is clearly struggling to speak but he goes on. 'Eva was jealous…' His voice breaks with emotion, like a man genuinely saddened.

But is he for real, or is this all an act?

'I should've known she'd do something like that, I should've protected Aimee better.'

An unexpected tear runs down Nicholas's cheek. He gulps a few times before then saying, 'I honestly thought Eva was secure with Cath watching over her and that she wouldn't be able to escape.'

So that's who Cath is. She was the person looking after Eva. It all makes sense now.

Nicholas looks at me. 'I'm sorry Kirsty, I've failed you as well as Aimee.'

'Oh, come on, you're not going to fall for that, are you?' Eva spits.

I look from her face to his. There's no way for me to tell who the liar is.

'Tell me what really happened to Aimee,' I say very clearly, directing my question to Nicholas. Even though it pierces my heart, I need to hear more so I can work out who was responsible for her death.

'Why do you care?' Eva asks, her eyes narrowed.

'Because Aimee was my best friend!' I explode. 'She was more than that: we were like sisters.'

A lump forms in my throat as I clutch at memories of my best friend: our first day at school, the summer we spent together in Cornwall, the day Aimee passed her driving test and the champagne-filled party she had to celebrate her eighteenth. Aimee was so full of life. She was too young to die.

Nicholas looks shocked. 'You knew Aimee?'

'Yes, we grew up together,' I say, my voice quieter.

This new information hits Nicholas and Eva in different ways. Nicholas's face is a picture of confusion, trying to connect the dots. Eva looks outraged that she wasn't the only one dealing in secrets.

'Aimee never mentioned you. I never met you, why?' Nicholas's eyes are locked on me, trying to figure out why he didn't know about my connection to his previous wife.

'We had a falling out. Aimee wouldn't speak to me in the months before she married you. And her mother wouldn't tell me where she'd moved to, despite our years of friendship. Her mother never liked me, she always looked down on my family.'

Aimee had gone travelling and I couldn't afford to go with her. She was an only child who was lavished with attention by her wealthy parents. Even though we were worlds apart in our upbringing, we were kindred spirits. I thought she'd come back home and things would go back to normal. But she'd changed. She'd met Nicholas while she'd been away. They'd hooked up in New York. He'd been there on business and she'd been staying there for a few weeks. It was meant to be a pit stop before she went to Costa Rica but fate had other plans. They had a whirlwind romance and Aimee cut her travels short.

She had been completely loved up. I should've been more understanding but the truth is I was afraid I was losing her and a little bit jealous that her life was going onto a new phase. We'd always been inseparable. I wish I could go back and change things. If I'd still been in her life maybe I could've prevented her death. That's why I've needed to try and find out the truth and get some kind of justice for her.

'So, when we met...' Nicholas begins to ask.

'I knew you'd been married to Aimee,' I tell him.

Eva starts to laugh then. 'Are you saying the only reason you got together with old Nick is because you were trying to find out what happened to Aimee?'

I stick my chin in the air and defend myself. 'Yes, I thought Nicholas might be responsible.'

Nicholas looks even more aghast now.

'I was prepared to do whatever it took to find out what happened to her. Although when I got to know you, I thought you couldn't be behind it and, well, despite myself, I started falling for you.' I hold his gaze; for some reason, it's important he knows that I didn't fake our entire relationship.

'I could see why Aimee loved you. And being at Orchard Farm made me feel closer to her.'

My feelings have been so mixed up; I didn't mean to get so close to Nicholas. For a few months I got caught up in the idea of being Mrs Johnson. Although I kept telling myself that being at Orchard Farm was the best way to uncover what happened to Aimee. Then when Nicholas's behaviour started to change, I knew I'd been too complacent and that I had to refocus on finding out what really happened to my best friend.

'Enough,' Eva roars. 'If you think he cared for you then you're deluded. He didn't love Aimee and he certainly didn't love you. Nick has made it clear today that he only loves one person: himself.'

'Then why are you here?' I challenge her.

Colour floods into Eva's cheeks. 'All you need to know is that he killed your precious friend. And you should be grateful that I'm stepping in before you meet the same fate.'

'Did you kill Aimee?' I demand of Nicholas.

I watch him shift in the chair. I hold my breath, waiting for the answer.

He hesitates and then shakes his head slowly. 'No. I had nothing to do with it.' His words then tumble out in a rush. 'Eva was in the car that ran her off the road—'

Eva cuts in. 'Don't listen to him! Nick was in the car with Aimee.'

'Is it true? Were you in the car with her? Did you have something to do with it?' I ask Nicholas.

'Of course he did,' Eva scoffs, without missing a beat. 'Aimee's death was all on Nicholas.'

'Well then how...?' I try to ask.

Before I finish my sentence, Nicholas is lurching forward. He's freed his hands completely from the ties that bound them. He's going for Eva, hands outstretched, with a look of pure hatred on his face. Their bodies collide and Eva shrieks, the sound high and shrill. Nicholas is pushing Eva down onto the chair, working fast to try and secure her to it – to turn the tables.

Eva furiously stomps on Nicholas's right foot and then lashes out at him. She strikes him across the face. He stumbles back, stunned. Eva uses his surprise to her advantage. She manages to push Nicholas to the floor, and his ankle twists as he falls.

I'm about to spring forward and help my husband up when Eva gives him a hard kick in the ribs and he yelps. Everything I've seen from Eva suggests that she is the more violent one of the pair.

'Kirsty, run! Run while you've got the chance – and call the police,' Nicholas urges me.

I'm beginning to believe that Nicholas might be innocent in all of this. Eva is clearly deranged and she has a murderous look written all over her face. She reaches for a shovel and her intentions are clear.

I can't leave and allow Nicholas to be bludgeoned to death with a blunt instrument. I barrel into Eva, knocking her off balance before she can strike.

Nicholas shouts out at Eva, 'You're crazy!' He manages to haul himself to standing.

'If I'm crazy, it's because of you!' Eva yells back at him.

'Listen to yourself Eva. Nothing is ever you, is it? There's always someone to blame.'

Suddenly, he turns to the side, pushing a stack of boxes with all his might. They topple down, creating a barricade between him and us, blocking the way out. Eva grabs the shotgun but she reacted too late. We hear the sound of the door being thrown open.

Turning to Eva, my blood runs cold. I'm now alone with her. She's got a gun in her hand.

Nicholas has left me, after I helped free him.

Was he lying after all? And will I survive this?

Chapter Fifty-Seven
Eva
Then

I've just seen Nick with his new wife. I'm a mess. I can barely breathe. I need to get back to the station, I have to make my train because Cath is waiting for me in London. I can't be late but I also can't think straight. Coming back here was a mistake.

As I go down a narrow road, the satnav beeps at me. I've taken a wrong turn. It's the last thing I need. I swing the car round; it's been such a long time since I've driven and the hire car Cath has organised is alien and unfamiliar. The gearstick feels too stiff and it's hard to see along these unlit country lanes.

I switch my full beam lights on and press down hard on the accelerator. I need to get out of here.

Turning the corner, I see the car too late.

I brace myself for the impact but the other driver swerves at the final minute. In that split second, I realise the vehicle sliding past is a green Range Rover. The man in the passenger seat is my husband, and the woman driving is his other wife.

Slowing my speed, I look in my rearview mirror. The other car spins and then skids across the road. It hits the barrier. But the force is too much and the barrier buckles. The vehicle flips over the edge, into the deep ditch running alongside the road.

I hesitate. I want to help; I want to see if they're okay. Except if I get out, they'll know it was me. They won't believe this wasn't deliberate.

My pulse races. I wanted revenge although not like this.

Putting my foot down, I drive on. I make an anonymous phone call to the emergency services. But I can't help thinking: they deserved it.

Chapter Fifty-Eight
Kirsty
Now

Eva turns to me, brandishing the gun in her hand. 'See what you've done! You should never have trusted him.'

My stomach is churning with fear. I haven't exactly appeased Eva while we've been in here and I have no idea what she will do next.

'Sit down!' She orders, pushing me into the chair that Nicholas was previously sitting in.

I hope she's not going to tie me up now. Or worse, shoot me with the weapon she's still clutching. But she appears distracted and doesn't look at me again.

'Stay there,' she barks.

I watch as she disappears off into the depths of the outbuilding. As soon as she's out of sight, I don't waste any time.

I move quickly, lifting the boxes to clear a path to the exit. I'm furious with myself for having allowed Nicholas to draw me in again and furious at myself for helping him. Now he's escaped and I'm left in this outbuilding with Eva.

Crashing through remaining boxes, I bolt through the door and half fall outside, gulping down the fresh air. Eva could easily emerge from the outbuilding and drag me back inside, so I run a few metres before scanning my surroundings. Nicholas is making his way across the field. He's limping and his ankle appears to be hindering his progress. I can see exactly where he's headed: his Range Rover, parked in the distance by the hedgerow. Nicholas is set on his escape route – and his own survival.

I need to get as far away from the outbuilding and put as much distance as possible between me and Eva. So instinct drives me forward, in the direction of the farmhouse. My heart is thumping loudly in my chest and I'm willing every muscle in my body to work as hard as it can to keep me moving.

Glancing over my shoulder, I see Nicholas reach his car and he gets in. The ignition starts up and he pulls away, heading in the direction of the gate in the far corner of the land belonging to Orchard Farm. The back gate swings open as the vehicle approaches. I watch as Nicholas drives towards safety but then, just as he pulls out of the gate, I see something that doesn't look right.

Blinking several times and straining my eyes, I half wonder if I'm imagining things but there's definitely an outline of a figure in the back of the car. Rising up and reaching forwards.

It's Eva.

I watch in horror as the Range Rover lurches forward. Nicholas seems to have put his foot down as he tries to escape.

But all along, the greatest threat was in the car with him.

Chapter Fifty-Nine
Eva
Now

This is it. Our last journey together.

I watch as Nick's hands grip the steering wheel, his knuckles white. The engine revs loudly as he puts his foot down, his eyes fixed on the dirt track that leads to the rear exit of the farm. He presses the button on his key fob and the gates begin to swing open.

He thinks it's almost over. He thinks he's going to escape.

I never, ever thought this would happen. Not in a million years would I have imagined that my relationship with the man I love would lead me here. The same thought has been on loop in my mind for months.

He has turned me into a scorned woman.

A woman driven mad by love.

Someone who has plotted and planned their revenge.

And now, this is it.

Because I can no longer live in a world where Nick doesn't love me. In a world where I'm not his wife – his only wife.

The man I loved to the depths of my being has taken everything from me. I can't go on, knowing what I've lost.

So this is the moment where everything ends.

I'm going out with a bang and I'm taking the man I married with me.

Nick moves into third gear as the vehicle hurtles along the bumpy road.

I start to rise up, ready to pounce. Ready to make my move.

There's a scream from behind us. It's Kirsty. She's obviously seen me moving in the back of the car.

Nick twists in the direction of the sound. He's expecting to see the retreating farm out of his rearview window but instead he sees me. And the shotgun.

His face goes pale.

'What the—?'

Nick whips his head back as his beloved Range Rover shoots out of the gates. He doesn't turn in time, so the vehicle bumps across the road and down the grassy verge.

I lean forward, digging my nails into his shoulders. He cries out and immediately uses one hand to fend me off.

In any other situation he would likely overpower me. He's bigger and stronger. But he's currently pinned into a chair in a vehicle that's careering down an incline.

Clawing him again, I go for his neck. Sinking my sharp nails into his soft skin, I draw blood.

'Get off me Eva!' he demands.

But he's powerless now.

I throw my body at him, grabbing the steering wheel and yanking it further to the right. The Range Rover swerves in the direction I intend it to go.

In his panic, Nick's foot goes down on the wrong pedal and we accelerate even faster.

'Eva, stop!'

My weight is pressing down on him now; I am pulling at his hair, scratching his face, pummelling the back of his head. Years of hatred and anger come pouring out.

Nick manages to shove me backwards with one arm and I fall into the back seat. The reality of the situation, as we pick up speed, suddenly hits me hard. But it's too late to change the course I'm on now. I've made my choices.

Nick gasps as the bottom of the verge comes into view, and he remembers what we're racing towards. He slams on the breaks but this propels me forwards, crashing me into the back of his seat. I hook one arm around his neck and with the other I reach for the wheel again. No amount of braking is going to stop us now as gravity pulls us downwards.

'We'll be together forever,' I whisper in Nick's ear, tightening my grip around his neck. He struggles for breath, unable to respond to me.

The Range Rover nose-dives into the rushing river and the impact causes me to let go of Nick. He's thrown forward and his head hits the steering wheel with a sickening thud.

I smile as the water rises up around us.

And I murmur, 'Til death us do part.'

Chapter Sixty
Kirsty
Now

The vehicle disappears out of the gate. I'm expecting to see it swing left and down the hill. Instead, I hear a crunching sound. Immediately, I know what's happened. The car has gone across the dirt track. On the other side of it is a steep bank and at the bottom of it is the river.

My stomach clenches. There's nothing I can do for Nicholas now. And he didn't think twice about me.

There's no doubt in my mind that Eva will have planned all of this: leaving the Range Rover where it was, pointing towards the back exit of the farm.

I'm torn. The human part of me says I should try help Nicholas and Eva. Try to stop the madness. But I'd only be putting myself in danger. They're locked in their own battle and they won't stop until at least one of them is dead.

I can't trust either of them; they're both as bad as one another.

My survival instincts kick in, urging me to keep heading back towards the farmhouse.

I just hope I can get myself to safety before anything else happens...

Chapter Sixty-One
Kirsty
Now

'Police! Please... Come quickly!'

The operator asks me a series of questions. I manage to communicate that I'm in the grounds of Orchard Farm and I'm scared for my life and my husband's. It's as if someone else is talking, like it's not really me and this couldn't possibly be happening. I managed to race back to the house and make the call, but my words fall out, jumbled. My nerves are shot to pieces after the chilling encounter with Eva.

The soothing tones of the man at the other end of the line reassure me that help is on its way, and he promises to keep talking to me until the emergency services arrive. As the operator continues to update me on the progress of those coming to my aid, my mind races over all the possible scenarios that might happen. Have they crashed into the river? Will Nick die in that car? And Eva too?

I came here to find out the truth about what happened to Aimee and to get my revenge, but I would never have gone as far as killing someone. Taking a life to avenge Aimee would have made me as bad as her killer. I just wanted justice for her, to discover who was responsible for her death and to make sure they were locked away for a very long time.

At first, I believed Nicholas had to be to blame but the more I got to know him, the less convinced I was. But was he just a brilliant liar? Did he fool me the same way he fooled Eva and Aimee? Or is he really innocent?

And is Eva the victim she makes herself out to be? Or did her love for Nicholas push her to the very edge? Is she the reason my best friend died? I have so many questions but they can only be answered by the two people who I last saw disappearing down the hillside. Will I ever uncover the truth?

Minutes later, I hear the sirens screaming in the distance, growing louder as they approach Orchard Farm. Dropping the phone, I rush to the front of the house. I watch as a police vehicle and an ambulance swing onto the gravel driveway, their lights still flashing.

'Are you Mrs Kirsty Johnson?' A young police officer asks me as he strides towards me and reaches the door.

I nod in response. 'You have to be quick,' I tell him, my words coming out in a rush. 'I think she's going to kill him!' My voice rises an octave as I speak.

'We're here now and we will do all we can.'

Two other officers and a number of paramedics follow me into the house and I take them through to the kitchen. My heart is pounding as I tell them where I last saw Nick and Eva in the Range Rover.

There's a flurry of activity: radios crackle with static, voices fill the room and they ask me question after question. This all feels like it's taking too long. I just want them to leave and find out what's happened to Nick and Eva. Not knowing is making me feel frantic.

Everyone speaks kindly and patiently to me, as though they're dealing with a small child. The police officers and two of the paramedics leave, following my directions. One remaining paramedic drapes the throw from the sofa around my shoulder and makes me a cup of too-sweet tea. It's clear she is well-versed in her role and she remains calm and professional. But I can detect the undercurrent of tension. It's like she can tell this isn't a false call and that she's preparing herself for a body – or two.

And I feel the same. My muscles are tight as I wait for news. I have no idea what way this is going to go or what the outcome of today's events will be. Nicholas's drawn face flashes in my mind, followed by Eva's heartbroken expression. I just pray this nightmare will be over soon.

I stand up and pace the room, unable to stay still. Luna is at my heels, matching my steps as I walk up and down, up and down the length of the kitchen. The clock on the wall ticks loudly. Finally, after what feels like forever, the paramedic's radio crackles. She exits the room, going out into the hallway to talk rapidly to the person on the other end of the line. I dig my nails into the palm of my hands. This is it.

When the paramedic returns, there's a strange look on her face as her eyes land on me. She quickly rearranges her expression so that it's more neutral.

'You'd better sit down,' she says gently.

I can feel the energy draining out of me as I take a seat at the kitchen table again.

'How many people did you say were in the vehicle?'

'Two,' I reply instantly. 'Nicholas and Eva.'

She nods.

'Are they ok? Have you found them?'

She says nothing, walking back out to the hallway where she speaks into her radio in hushed and urgent tones. She's out there longer this time. I strain to hear what she is saying but I can't make out her words. When she returns to the kitchen, there's a male police officer with her.

He sits down heavily in the seat opposite me.

'Have you found Nicholas and Eva?' I repeat.

The policeman looks at me, as though he's assessing my character. 'I just need to ask you a few questions.'

Glancing between him and the paramedic, I try to work out what's going on.

'How long have you been married?'

I'm slightly thrown by the question but I answer it anyway. 'Almost seven months,' I say, 'although we dated for around six months before we got married.'

I swear the police officer's eyebrow raises a fraction as he jots the information down on his notepad.

'And can you tell me about your marriage?'

'About my marriage?'

'Yes, what has your relationship with your husband been like?'

I stutter and stumble over my words, 'Fine. I mean, more than fine – amazing actually. We're planning our honeymoon – we're still very much in the newlywed phase. Everything's been wonderful. Until Eva showed up today.'

It wouldn't be wise for me to mention that I only married Nicholas to uncover what really happened to my best friend Aimee. The truth about Nicholas and his marriages is just too complicated to explain and I don't want to be accused of being responsible for anything that's happened today.

'And can you repeat the information you told us on the phone earlier about Eva.'

'Eva was my husband's first wife. I knew Nicholas had been married before but I didn't know much about her. When she arrived on my doorstep this afternoon, it turned out she was a woman who had befriended me over the last few months and given me the false name of Bex. She told me this afternoon that she was still married to Nicholas.'

'And you're certain Eva was here today and she got in the car with the man you believed to be your husband?'

'Yes,' my reply betrays my exasperation. 'Why are you asking me all of this?'

'I just need to make a record.'

'Why?'

'Kirsty...' His voice softens and I know what is coming. 'I'm very sorry to inform you that Nicholas Johnson has died.'

I inhale sharply, and the paramedic inches closer to me. 'He's dead?' I murmur.

'Yes, his Range Rover crashed into the river running outside of your property. It seems he sustained a head injury and drowned.'

'Oh no!' My hand covers my mouth as I try to take this in.

'There was no sign of anyone else in the vehicle.'

I frown. 'Eva was in the back, I saw her.'

'We're searching the immediate area in case she has somehow got out of the submerged vehicle.' He pauses. 'Are you certain that Eva was in there?'

I nod.

'We will continue to search for Eva and keep you updated.'

A sense of panic washes over me as I understand why he's asking me this. Eva isn't at the scene of the crime and if she's not found, there might not be anything to link her to Nicholas's death other than my word. But I am here; the police know that I have interacted with my husband today so they will want to establish whether I'm lying or not.

My husband is dead. Eva is missing. And the eyes of the law are on me.

I saw for myself that Eva caused the car crash that resulted in Nicholas's death.

She could be anywhere now.

And she could be coming for me next...

Chapter Sixty-Two
Kirsty
Now

It's quiet. So very quiet.

They've all gone now – the police officers, the ambulance crew, forensics. Every single one of the emergency workers that swarmed over the grounds of the farm have left.

Three days later, I'm sitting in the kitchen where I was questioned by one police detective and then another, surrounded by coffee-stained mugs and half-drunk glasses of water that I just haven't had the energy to deal with since. The simple task of collecting all the dirty cups and plates and stacking them into the dishwasher has felt like too much.

Instead, I'm staring into space again while my brain tries to process the new reality of my life.

My husband is dead.

His body was found in the river, cold and lifeless. He was pronounced dead by the paramedics and then his body was whisked away for investigation.

It all happened so quickly, I can't believe it's real.

Eva still hasn't been found – dead or alive – and this meant the police at first didn't know whether to believe my story or not. They asked me to repeat what had happened over and over again in my home and then later on at the police station. I knew I needed to be clear and to be consistent but every question they asked seemed designed to trip me up and trick me.

For a few fearful hours, I felt as though I was being treated as a criminal. I was afraid they'd blame me for Nicholas's untimely death. After all, Nicholas had done a good job of covering up his first marriage. Not many people in the area knew about Eva, as she hadn't got to know the locals while she was renovating the farmhouse. She kept herself to herself. Nicholas hadn't introduced her to his old school friends.

Thankfully, the police found the shotgun in the car and Eva's mobile phone. And then technology came to my rescue. The police were able to trace the call Eva made to me and our security cameras showed her prowling around Orchard Farm just before she deactivated the security system. The evidence of her trespassing has resulted in the police backing off from their questioning of me.

The police liaison officer asked me if there was anyone she could call to come and be with me at this difficult time. I desperately wanted to speak to my family but I didn't want my mum or any of my younger siblings getting caught up in this. Not while Eva's whereabouts remains unsolved. There's no way I'd forgive myself if any of them came to stay here with me and then... I can't bear to think about it.

They've asked me to remain at Orchard Farm while the investigation is ongoing but they don't seem to be treating me as a suspect. They told me they would be checking regularly on the property and gave me the direct number of someone at the local station in case I needed it.

I can't relax, I can barely sleep, because the situation is far from resolved. The police have also been looking into Nicholas and Eva's marriage. So far, they've been unable to get their hands on any official divorce papers which means that my marriage to Nicholas might be void.

The police have told me they're still searching the river and it can take some time before a body is recovered. But I know they won't find her. Some primal instinct is telling me that Eva isn't dead.

The security system is back up and working now, after the security company gave me access to it on my phone, but even with this in place I still feel afraid here. Every second of every minute of the day, I'm expecting Eva to burst into the farmhouse and come for me next.

Will there ever be an end to this nightmare?

Or will I always be looking over my shoulder?

Chapter Sixty-Three
Kirsty
Now

I've been a nervous wreck over the past few days. My doctor has prescribed me sleeping pills, but I don't want to take them because I need to stay alert.

Now, it's the middle of the night.

My eyes fly open in the pitch black. Even though I can't see anything, I know that something is wrong.

'Hello Kirsty.'

I bolt upright, gathering the covers around me. I can see the shape at the foot of my bed.

It's her.

She's back.

'I'm sure you've been expecting me.'

'Eva!'

I've thought about what might happen if this woman did return and how I might handle things but now it's actually happening, I freeze and the words I want to stay stick in my throat.

Luna barks loudly. I can hear her snapping around Eva's heels. I silently thank Luna for reacting on my behalf.

'Go away!' Eva shouts at my dog and then clicks on the bright overhead light.

Momentarily, I'm blinded and then I hear Luna whimpering. My eyes adjust in time to see Eva shoving my beloved Luna into the walk-in closet.

I'm filled with rage. Eva accused Nicholas of so many things but all I've witnessed her do is lie and inflict pain. I still feel numb about the events of the last few days; confused about who was really responsible for Aimee's death. And overwhelmed with the fear that I might never discover the truth.

Except now I know. Eva is standing over my bed, glowering down at me and she doesn't need to say anything more. I can feel it in my bones.

'It was you! You killed Aimee!'

I throw myself towards her, our bodies collide and we end up in a tangled heap on the carpet. 'You killed Aimee!' I repeat, yanking her hair back as I pin her to the floor.

Eva yelps in pain and tries to push me off her, but she doesn't succeed. I yank her hair a second time. 'Tell me the truth!'

Eva laughs then, that same grating laugh that's been haunting my dreams for the last few nights. 'I was in the other car, I was the reason why she crashed. But it was a mistake!'

My mouth gapes open. The weight of her words is like a fist to my stomach. I slam her head on the floor. She yelps.

'She took everything from me: my husband, my home, my whole life.' Tears stream down Eva's face now. 'I just wanted her out of the way so that Nick and I could be together again. But I didn't mean to kill her.'

I'm left reeling from the confession. At first, I suspected that Nicholas was responsible for Aimee's death. Except, the more time I spent with him the more he charmed me. Nicholas is like that. He pulled me into his orbit and I can see why Eva was so obsessed with him. He had it all. He was handsome, rich and successful.

And now Eva has confessed. Finally, I know the truth. It won't bring my best friend back but now I can try to get justice for her.

I tighten my grip around Eva's wrists. 'Did you really think you could go back to the way things were? That you could save your marriage?'

'Yes,' Eva replies through gritted teeth. 'I would've done anything to have Nicholas, and you would know that if you'd really loved anyone.'

'I loved Aimee,' I say quietly. 'She was my best friend. She was next to me for every step of my childhood.'

I stare down at her then. This is the woman who killed both Aimee and Nicholas. My feelings about him are all jumbled now that I know he didn't cause Aimee's death.

'He may not have killed her,' Eva said. 'But he cheated and married her illegally when he was still my husband. He set the chain of events in motion.'

'No one forced you to run the car she was driving off the road.'

'We're not so different,' Eva sneers. 'The only reason you're here is to avenge your friend. So go ahead, this is it. This is your moment.'

Staring down at the woman who killed my best friend, it's tempting to hurt her. But I'm not like Eva.

'Yes, we are Eva. Because I'm not going to kill you.'

A confused expression sweeps over her face. It's then I notice the dark rings under Eva's eyes and how thin she looks. Her fingernails are caked in dirt and there's a small graze along her left cheekbone. How did she manage to escape the watery grave that Nicholas ended up in and where has she been since? She looks as though she's had a rough few days, which could be to my advantage. If she's weaker than usual then I might stand a chance of trapping her – and calling the police.

'You're going to do as I say,' I tell her calmly.

I ease off her and she remains still. So I haul her to her feet and, before she can react, I propel her towards the bathroom and slam the door shut. Pressing my back against it, I suck in a breath.

Eva is completely quiet, which feels more unnerving than if she had been noisily trying to get out. I drag the chair from the dressing table and jam it up against the door handle. I search my bedside table and amongst the bed covers for my mobile but frustratingly I don't lay my hands on it. Cursing under my breath, I check under the bed but it's not there either.

After frantically turning the room upside down, I still can't locate the device. It's my lifeline to the outside world and it's vanished. Moving back towards the bathroom door, I strain my ears to hear what Eva is doing on the other side. But there's nothing. I would've expected her to be throwing herself against the door or at least screaming to be let out but there's no noise whatsoever.

'Eva?' I call.

There's no response.

'Eva, speak to me,' I shout louder.

I wait but she doesn't answer.

I'm now regretting taking my eyes off her. I have no idea what she's doing and no way of telling other than going in there. She could be passed out or she could be biding her time, waiting to pounce or flee as soon as the door swings open.

Time ticks by and my heart pounds louder in my chest with every passing second. What is she doing in there?

I can't stand it any longer. I decide to go in. I need her somewhere where I can see her.

Casting around the room, I grab my clothes steamer and clutch it in one hand. Quickly I yank the door open and step into the bathroom. I blink in disbelief.

It's empty. There's no one here. Eva's gone.

The window is wide open. Running across the room, I look down at the roof of the kitchen extension below. Eva's escape route is easy to see. I scan the area around it but there's no sign of her. She probably clambered out within minutes – she could be halfway down the lane by now.

The thought gives me some comfort. If Eva has run away that means I don't have to deal with her in the short term but it's a problem if she's out there lurking, waiting for her next chance to come for me. And I desperately want her to be locked up, the key thrown away, after what she did to Aimee.

Placing the clothes steamer on the floor, I know that I need to report Eva as still alive – and a threat to me.

Before I can turn around; I feel a hand on my shoulder.

And I scream.

Chapter Sixty-Four
Kirsty
Now

It's Eva.

She grins at me manically. 'You're not going to win this,' she taunts, her face now inches from mine.

'What do you want?' I demand. Adrenaline is coursing through my veins.

'You.'

A shiver runs down my spine. Eva wants me dead and she isn't going to stop until she's achieved it.

'Why?' I push her. 'You said you didn't mean to kill Aimee, so why are you coming after me? And you said you wanted to be with Nicholas. You had him, you were with him in the car. So why leave him?'

I take a few steps back, to create some space between us. I also want to get closer to the window, which is my fastest escape route. The idea of trying to scramble out onto the roof below fills me with fear but it's my only hope of getting away from her.

'I haven't left him,' Eva cries. 'We're going to be together soon. I was holding him – we were in the water together. But then I realised I couldn't allow you to just take everything. I didn't really care about what happened to you before then. Live or die, it made no difference. Except you lied to me Kirsty.'

Laughter bursts out of me. I can't help it, after all this woman has done and lied about.

Her hand shoots out and grabs my arm. 'You lied. You wormed your way into this house and all because of that bitch Aimee. You did it for her and she was nothing but a selfish, man-stealing—'

I slap Eva hard with my free hand. It stuns her. So I jerk my arm from her and make a run for it. As I hurtle through the bedroom, I can hear Luna whimpering in the walk-in wardrobe. My heart twinges as I want to go to her but I make the split-second decision that she's better off away from what's going on between Eva and me. And I don't want to draw any attention to Luna in case Eva decides to hurt her.

My legs propel me along the hallway and down the stairs. Instinctively, I run towards the front door. I need to get away from this house and I might have a better chance of hiding along the lane in the hedgerow and trees that run along it. Or I might even be able to make it to Waterbridge. If I stay at Orchard Farm, Eva will find a way to trap me. She knows the farm inside out.

I hear Eva gaining on me. She's down the stairs and then only steps away as I wrench open the door. Forcing myself to move faster than I've ever moved before, I run. My lungs are burning and I'm gasping for breath but I know I have to keep going. The alternative is much, much worse.

I glance back and see that Eva has tripped. This gives me a burst of hope and energy, and I surge forwards. I focus on putting one foot in front of the other; it's all I can do.

Then, without warning, a force shoves into my shoulders. I land face first on the rough ground, pain searing through my head and my torso. Eva presses a foot into the small of my back, pinning me where I am.

'Got you,' she crows.

I try to fight back but I smacked the ground hard and my head is throbbing with pain, making me feel off-balance and dizzy. She drags me back, and I'm half walking, half falling as she pushes and prods, kicks and spits, digging her nails into my flesh and doing everything she can to force me to go where she wants.

Blood pounds in my ears. My body feel bruised and battered. Eva marches me past the house, through the garden and out onto the field. She's herding me towards the far corner of the grounds. My brain catches up and I know she's trying to get me to go towards the river. That's where she's planning to end my life.

Struggling, I try with every ounce of strength I have left to break free of Eva's clutches. But it's no good, she claws at me and whacks me around the head, zoning in on my new weak spot. The pain intensifies. The bank at the top of the river comes into view and I feel like I'm out of options. The end is near.

'There, right where I want you,' Eva says, with a satisfied smile. 'You don't deserve that house. It's mine and it will always be mine.'

'What's the plan?' My words slur together. 'You kill me and then go back to living in the house of your dreams, like nothing happened?'

'No!' Eva snorts. 'Of course not.'

'You won't get away with it,' I press.

'I'm not intending to. This is where it ends for me too. I'm going to join Nick. I just wanted to make sure you were dealt with first.'

'You're insane!' I cry.

'Are those your final words?' Eva gloats.

I can feel myself swaying on my feet. My vision blurs but there's no mistaking what Eva pulls out of her pocket. It's a knife.

'Well, it's been a pleasure knowing you,' Eva says, her voice suddenly turning serious. 'This needs to be over now. You've been an inconvenience, a blip in my plans. I should've died with Nick the other day. But I'm going to be with him very soon.'

'No, Eva. Don't do this, I—'

But I don't get to finish my sentence, because she thrusts the knife forward. Miraculously, I manage to dodge to the side. The tip of the knife stabbing the air next to me. I see a flash of movement. A snapping sound.

Suddenly she's disappeared. I blink. My vision comes back into focus and I peer over the bank that Eva has just fallen down. I hear her shriek as the knife she was trying to murder me with embeds in her stomach. And then she disappears from view as she tumbles down the steep slope, gravity pulling her down to the spot where she ended Nicholas's life a few days ago. I think I hear her body hit the water and her screams stop.

Sinking onto my knees, I'm in no fit state to move. My whole body is trembling with shock. I think I might pass out but then I feel a warm, familiar shape lean into me. It's Luna. I fit the pieces together. It was Luna who raced towards Eva, snapping around her heels. Eva must've been startled by her. That's what sent her over the edge of the bank.

Luna saved me.

She must have nudged open the closest door in order to get out here. I gather my pup into my arms, whispering my thanks. If she hadn't appeared then Eva would've killed me. I have no doubt about that. I hug her to me, relief flooding my body. I want to move away from this place but my head swims again, my eyesight flickering.

And I pass out.

Chapter Sixty-Five
Kirsty
Two weeks later

I push open the door and the tiny bell tinkles overhead. By now it's a familiar and comforting sound.

'Kirsty!' Jean beams at me with a wide smile and greets me with open arms. I step gratefully into them, appreciating Jean's warmth.

'Now let's have a look at you,' Jean says, holding me at arm's length and assessing me. 'You're still looking a little too pale for my liking. A cup of tea and some chocolate cake is in order,' she announces.

I bite back a smile. Jean's answer to every problem is tea and cake. She has kept me in good supply of both in the last few difficult weeks. And she's right, tea and cake do make things feel a little better.

'Go and sit down,' Jean instructs, 'and I'll bring it over.'

I weave my way between the tables, Luna trotting at my heels, and sit down at my favourite window seat. I lean back in the wooden chair and close my eyes, breathing in the delicious smells of coffee and baked goods that hang in the air. This place feels safe. Here, I can forget about the events of the past few weeks.

After I passed out, Luna stayed by my side. The postman arrived at Orchard Farm not long after and found the door to the house still wide open. He'd heard enough through the village grapevine to suspect something might be wrong and raised the alarm. Luna heard the police searching for me and barked and barked until the officers found me. She truly was my saviour.

The security cameras picked up enough of what happened – Eva entering the house, taking a knife from the kitchen and chasing me out the front of the house and then dragging me back to the property – to understand her murderous intentions. They found her body and the kitchen knife and they believed my version of events. Since then, I've been concentrating on healing myself. I had a nasty concussion and a broken rib but I'm lucky the damage wasn't any worse. I'm lucky to still be here.

Luna nudges my leg so I bend down to stroke her silky ears. Glancing around, I notice a few of the locals sitting in the café. Of course, as soon as I survey the room the people who have just been staring at me with undisguised curiosity quickly avert their eyes. I know my life is the subject of gossip; it's hard to avoid tongues wagging in a small place like this even when just a minor scandal occurs, so I'm certain the events that have taken place at Orchard Farm are likely to keep the neighbours talking for years to come.

'There we go,' Jean says, setting down a daisy-patterned mug and a very generous slice of chocolate cake.

'Thank you so much, you've been so kind to me,' I say in a low voice.

'Oh, nonsense,' Jean proclaims. 'Providing some liquid and sustenance is the least I can do for you.'

I know Jean has been behind the home-cooked meals that keep appearing on my doorstep and I've been touched by her thoughtfulness. She always makes me feel welcome every time I come into her quaint little tea shop, and I've been stopping in more often than usual. Jean has been one of the friendliest faces that I've seen in the aftermath of Nicholas's death. And, in truth, most days she's been one of the only people I've spoken to.

I take a bite of my cake and enjoy the rich taste of the chocolate.

The locals initially eyed me with suspicion. I'm the younger woman who married a rich man, a pillar of their community, so of course when my husband was killed the finger of blame was pointed at me. I can just imagine Tiggy and Jed discussing Nicholas's untimely demise with their close circle at the golf club. I'm sure the words 'gold digger' and 'murderess' would have been paired with my name.

Mercifully, the security footage proved my innocence but adjusting to the aftermath hasn't been easy. Every time I close my eyes, I see Eva falling backwards and I hear her scream. Ultimately, she was going to kill me and if Luna hadn't been there, it's likely I'd be dead now.

I try to tell myself that Eva was on borrowed time anyway – she should've perished in the water when Nicholas did and, given the extent of her obsession with him, it's somehow fitting that they both took their last breaths in the same way. She wanted to die, that much was clear. But being entangled in the whole messy business is going to take a long time for me to process.

I hear footsteps behind me and they make me jump. I exhale when I see it's another customer walking past my table. I still don't feel completely safe. I'm constantly looking over my shoulder, fearful that Eva has somehow bounced back from the dead a second time, despite the fact I went to view her broken body. I know she's gone for good but it's going to take a long time for that fact to sink in.

The customer pauses at my table, hovering at my elbow. I squint, the pale morning sunshine briefly blinding my eyesight as I try to work out who it is.

'How are you?' She sits down in the seat opposite me. It's Tiggy.

'Um...' I scramble for something else to say. There's no way I could put how I feel into a few short sentences.

'I've been so worried about you. I wanted to call in and check on you but I wasn't even sure if you'd still be in Waterbridge.'

I take another bite of the cake to stall for time. I can't work out if Tiggy is genuinely concerned or if she's just prying.

Silence stretches between us and eventually she says, 'We've never had anything like this happen in the village before.'

I find myself nodding in agreement with her.

'And to think, Nicholas Johnson... None of us would ever have suspected a thing!' Tiggy continues, seemingly oblivious of the impact Nicholas had on me and instead focuses on the ripple effect in the community. 'He was always so charming.'

For a second, I think her line of conversation is going to turn accusatory but then she says, 'Still, you never really know what a person is like behind closed doors.' Tiggy considers me then, before asking, 'And you had no idea about Eva?'

My blood turns to ice. What does she mean?

'Eva?' I stutter.

'Yes, you didn't know Nicholas was still married to her?'

'Oh...' My shoulders sag in relief. 'No, I didn't.'

She looks at me sympathetically then. 'He really did pull the wool over your eyes. Over all of our eyes.'

Jean and I have discussed everything that happened with Nicholas in detail. I couldn't understand why I didn't hear more mentions of Eva or Aimee when I was out and about in the village. It turns out that Jean and the locals didn't know about Eva being Nicholas's first wife. They'd never met her because Eva kept herself to herself while she was working on the renovations. Nicholas hadn't moved into the farmhouse or reconnected with his old friends at that point. Since then, he'd told his friends at the golf club that he hired a project manager to restore Orchard Farm. He'd erased her from his history.

Everyone did know about Aimee and the accident. But, as Jean said, newcomers are weighed up and considered before they're accepted in this village and I was still a newbie. And of course many of them were friends with Nicholas. It was highly unlikely that any of them would break rank and dredge up Nicholas's previous marriage to his new wife, not when he was so respected in the community – and he donated so much money to local causes.

'I had no idea about Eva,' Tiggy confirms. 'He was married to her in the years when he was living in London, and he didn't keep in touch during that time. None of us can understand why he lied. Why didn't he just divorce her?'

'I've wondered the same,' I reply.

It's a thought that's occupied me since I discovered that my marriage to Nicholas was void because he was already married. Nicholas's actions seem to have been a result of arrogance. I think he believed he would get away with it, and that his money put him above the law. But more than that, it was another form of control. He didn't want to deal with a pay-out to Eva and nor did he want her interfering in his new relationship. He thought he could just pay to have her shut away when what she really needed was help for her obsessive behaviour.

'Who did he leave it to then?' Tiggy asks, abruptly changing the subject.

'What?' I'm thrown by her new line of questioning.

'The house? Orchard Farm? Is it yours now?'

I'm so taken aback by the forthright way in which she asks, as though she's entitled to an answer, that I suck down air the wrong way and end up spluttering. Tiggy thumps me on the back and, once I've recovered, she repeats the question.

Staring at Tiggy I think to myself that I would never dream of asking something so personal to someone I didn't know very well but, as the whole village is undoubtedly buzzing with theories about Nicholas's estate, I guess this is my chance to set the record straight.

'Yes, it was left to me.'

Tiggy's eyebrows shoot up an inch.

'Despite the fact we weren't legally married,' I explain, 'Nicholas had named me as the beneficiary of his estate in his will.'

'Ah,' Tiggy says, 'at least his web of lies hasn't left you destitute then.'

Her words are sharp and matter-of-a-fact but I can't help but be touched by them. She could have expressed the opposite opinion. I was expecting her to be disgruntled and to perhaps hold the belief I wasn't entitled to anything given that my relationship with Nicholas was relatively short and our marriage was a sham, not legal in the eyes of the law.

'No. Everything he owned has come to me.'

'Good,' says Tiggy, satisfied. 'At least he didn't take you down with him.'

I smile because she's right about this in more ways than one. My life hung in the balance too and I know how fortunate I am to have survived the fallout from Nicholas's lies and Eva's vendetta.

'And will you be staying or selling up?' It's obvious from the eager way in which Tiggy asks that if I were to say I'm selling up then she would no doubt put in an offer on the house. She's been very open about how much she loves it.

'I'm staying.'

'Really?' Tiggy gasps.

She'll be dining out on this conversation for the next few weeks. But I decide it's best I share the news with her; she'd find out eventually anyway and at least I can try to control the narrative.

'Yes, there's no point in running away from things. I'm going to rebuild my life here, in Waterbridge.'

'Well, I can't deny I'm surprised. You're built of sterner stuff than I gave you credit for.' Tiggy looks impressed.

It's a decision I've only come to in the last few days. I could just sell up and start again somewhere else in the country, or even abroad, but I have no idea where I'd go. Orchard Farm is a beautiful home, so I've decided to wipe the past clean and start anew right where I am. Besides, I also figured it's unlikely that lightning will strike twice in the same place.

'Good luck to you Kirsty; call me and we'll arrange drinks soon.' With that Tiggy nods her head and sweeps out of the tea shop.

'Was she bothering you?' Jean enquires after Tiggy has left.

'No, it's ok,' I say. 'She just wanted to know if I was staying or not.'

'And are you?' Jean asks softly.

'Yes.'

'Oooh, good.' She claps her hands together delightedly. 'We'll show you that this place isn't all bad.' Her eyes twinkle as she gives my shoulders a squeeze before she moves on to collect the crockery from the table next to me.

I can feel a small glimmer of hope building up inside me. I just pray I'm making the right decision to stay. I'm picking up two kittens next week. I can't wait to have more animals in the house and I'm sure they'll be the perfect distraction.

'Kirsty, I meant to tell you,' Jean comes back to my table with the teapot, filling my mug back up to the brim again. 'Someone's rented Acorn Cottage.'

'Oh really?' I feign interest, only half-listening as I'm not sure why Jean is telling me this.

'I met the woman who is moving yesterday. Sweet lass she is.' She chuckles. 'I thought you might want to knock on her door, perhaps introduce yourself. It might be good for you to have a friend around these parts who's more your age. I think her name is Catherine or Cathleen or something like that.'

'Jean, that's very kind of you. I'll think about it.'

She bustles off then, no doubt pleased with herself that her good deed for the day is done.

As I gaze out of the window to the village green beyond, I decide not to follow up on Jean's suggestion. I still crave the idea of finding someone to share my life with – the other half of me, whether that's a platonic or romantic relationship. I guess it's human nature to want that closeness with someone. But then a montage of moments with Aimee, Nicholas and Eva dance through my mind. Every second of heartache that I've experienced has been caused by trusting and loving a little too much.

Especially in the case of Aimee. Since Nicholas's death, I have been seeing a therapist. It's something that I could never have afforded before. She has helped me to see that the lengths I went to because of our friendship and the loyalty I felt to her, even when it wasn't always reciprocated, were too extreme. I can acknowledge that, now that the madness has come to an end, and I've had a lot of time to reflect. When I love, it's deeply and wholeheartedly. I guess I had that in common with Eva.

Jean's grandmotherly attentions are appreciated and I still have my gaggle of siblings to keep tabs on and live vicariously through. I'm also talking to Robert about doing a few evenings cooking at The Rose and Crown. That's enough for me. I don't think I'm ready to open myself up to any other friendships right now.

Clipping Luna's lead onto her collar, I pull her close and nuzzle into her neck. From now on, I think I'll avoid toxic relationships and stick to spending time with my animals instead.

'Bye Jean!' I call as I exit the teashop.

I walk the familiar route back to Orchard Farm with Luna by my side. Standing at the gate, I drink in the white-washed building. I can't believe that it's all mine. I know I need to properly let go and get on with my life, so I carry on walking past the farmhouse, past the outbuildings and down to the stream where Nicholas and then Eva died.

The delicate necklace with the letter 'A' hanging from it has been permanently around my neck in the last few weeks. But now I unfasten it and then hold the chain out in front of me.

I take one last look and then throw the necklace into the stream. It immediately disappears into the water. I whisper my goodbyes to Aimee, to the best friend who meant everything to me, and I finally walk away.

Back to my home, and to my future.

Epilogue
Cath

I can't believe that Eva is dead.

After everything we went through together. My only comfort is that, according to what I've heard, she succeeded in killing Nick first. But my heart feels sore with missing her already. She came into my life and turned it completely upside down but, in a strange turn of events, we ended up supporting one another.

Walking along the cobbled street, I think back on how Nicholas Johnson fooled me when I first met him. But Eva confided in me, told me all about how controlling he'd been as a husband and what her life had been like. And then how he locked her up so that he could get on with his new life. Eva trusted me.

It was a crazy situation to be thrown into but I did everything in my power to help her because I know what it's like to be cheated on and pushed away, like all the years of loving someone meant nothing. Like I meant nothing.

Opening the small, wooden gate I step through the graveyard. There was a light frost this morning and very soon autumn will give way to winter. I stand by the small wooden cross bearing Eva's name in the crematory garden. I arranged for a small plaque to be placed here for her.

Dropping to my knees, I whisper a small prayer for Eva. She didn't deserve Nick and everything that happened to her. What he did to her was enough to send anyone mad. I told her to run far away and start a new life elsewhere. I told her to forget about her husband. If only Eva had listened to me, she might still be alive now.

Standing back up again, my knees creak a little as I walk away and back down the path towards the cobbled main street. After Aimee's death, I couldn't get Eva to leave the house in Scotland. So I did the only thing I could do, and I blackmailed Nick to try to protect Eva. I told him that I'd filmed him trying to suffocate Eva with the pillow and I used what he did as leverage for more money as well as to stop him visiting Eva. Eva was safe with me and I wanted to protect her from him.

But then Eva insisted that she wanted to have a conversation with Nick. She came up with the idea of me calling Nick to ask him to come to Scotland, with the fabrication that Eva's behaviour had taken a turn for the worse. Eva then plotted how she would get Nick on his own, to properly listen to what she had to say.

I had a bad feeling about it but Eva wasn't going to give up so I thought it was better to help than not. We agreed that I'd call Nick and harass him to come up to Scotland. He was reluctant at first but I told him that I was finding it difficult to handle Eva and that I needed his help. So he booked his ticked to Inverness airport to come and assess the situation. Except Eva hadn't been in Scotland for almost eight weeks. She'd been in Waterbridge.

The plan was for Eva to get into the back of Nick's car and for her to reveal that she was there on the way to the airport. She told me that if she could make Nick sit with her and engage in a meaningful conversation then she might be able to make him see how wrong his actions were towards her. She wanted him to see sense and give her back her freedom. Except she took it too far; way too far. And now both Eva and Nick are gone.

Before she left Scotland, Eva transferred the remaining money in her bank accounts to mine. She said it was for safe keeping but maybe she didn't tell me everything. Maybe she was planning her death. There's only one person who will know the answer and that's Kirsty. So now that I'm in Waterbridge, I've decided to stay for a while.

I've already made friends with a woman called Jane Thomas, who seems to have loved and hated Nick almost as much as Eva did. Apparently, Nick fathered Jane's child, Francesca, but he denied it. And then when Jane tried to get him to do a DNA test to prove his paternity it came back that there was zero chance of him being Francesca's father. But Jane swears that that there has been no one else and he must have faked the document.

One thing I do know is that Eva desperately wanted to reclaim Orchard Farm, the house she'd renovated. From what I understand, Kirsty wasn't even properly married to Nick and the short time she'd been with him was nothing in comparison to all the years Eva had endured. It's not right that Kirsty inherits the farm and all of Nick's money.

I've decided I'm going to make Eva's last wish my own – and I'm going to do whatever it takes to make Orchard Farm mine.

If you were gripped by *The Secret Marriage*, check out *The Christmas Party*- an absolutely addictive psychological thriller with a jaw-dropping twist by bestselling author Mikayla Davids.

Mikayla's next page-turning psychological thriller, *The New Boyfriend*, is available for preorder now!

Extract: The Christmas Party

Prologue

I spin with my sister in the middle of the dance floor, our hands clasped tight, whirling round to the music just as we did when we were children. The DJ is playing yet another classic Christmas tune and we both shout along at the tops of our voices, smiles wide, eyes bright, mirroring each other. Rainbow-coloured disco lights shine across the vast room and the crowd around us shimmers and sparkles.

The moment I've been hoping for is finally here. After ten long years, my family are together under the same roof again. My two sisters, my mother, our children and our husbands. We're reunited after a decade of not speaking. But I don't want to think about the terrible night that shattered our family because I've waited for this day for a long time.

As the song ends, I stagger, wobbling on my high heels and putting a hand to my throbbing head. I feel a steadying arm loop through mine and I'm guided along the edges of the friends and family gathered here to celebrate in this exquisite hotel. The hotel that my wealthy husband and I own. We've spent the last five years remodelling the place and I've poured everything into making this building a beautiful home as well as a successful business. I've worked hard to be where I am today. I may have had a little help with my husband's money and contacts but I came from nothing. So tonight I'm proud to show off amongst my nearest and dearest. And I know I've earned every single one of the admiring looks that have come my way this evening.

Everyone else seems to be in the moment, lapping up the festive atmosphere, but I'm on edge and I can't seem to properly let my hair down, despite the champagne that's flowing. A huge Christmas tree dominates one corner of the room, while the warm gold and red colour scheme spills out across the rest of the space and throughout the multitude of plush rooms beyond. Everything looks perfect on the surface. But, right now, I need to get away from the party.

When I exit through the double doors, the noise instantly dims and I feel like I can breathe properly again. I make my way along a winding corridor, my sister's hand in mine, and then we swing open another set of double doors into the grand foyer. This is the dazzling focal point of the building, with its curved marble staircase and sweeping gallery complete with a glittering crystal chandelier.

The first thing I notice is the strange silence. The music from the party shut out by the soundproofing.

The second thing I notice is the dead body. Lying spread-eagled on the white marble floor, a pool of dark red blood surrounding the head like a halo.

I'm stunned, surely this can't be happening? But my sister inhales sharply next to me so I know I'm not imagining this.

This is not a horrible dream. It's real.

My heart is hammering in my chest and my mouth feels dry. I lift my chin and make myself look once more at the person lying on the floor. I immediately recognise the broken figure at the foot of the steep marble staircase.

And I scream...

Check out my novel *The Christmas Party*. Available to read now!

Also by Mikayla Davids

The perfect vacation... or the perfect murder...

Alicia Silver is spending her first Christmas holiday with her handsome new husband **Jack** and his family in their remote, luxurious lodge in the snowy Irish mountains.

The Silver family are wealthy and beautiful, and Alicia is determined to live up to their high expectations for her marriage. But with the festivities in full swing, Alicia quickly discovers that behind their perfect image, her new in-laws are hiding plenty of secrets...

The gorgeous husband

The jealous sister-in-law
The glamorous step-mother
The controlling father-in-law

Before the vacation is over one of them will be dead.

Who would kill to protect their shocking secret? And will Alicia survive this Christmas holiday?

The Christmas Holiday: A totally gripping and addictive psychological thriller

A luxury island. A dangerous secret. A honeymoon to die for.

On the balcony of our gorgeous villa, I clink glasses with my handsome new husband, **Owen Turner**. As I gaze into his mysterious brown eyes, a shiver runs down my spine. I can barely believe it: true love, palm trees, turquoise sea, white sand. **Everything should be perfect...**

Except last night Owen and I had our first argument. My husband drank too much and he said something that made me wonder if there's a darker side to the man I married. I remember the warnings from my family, they're worried he's only after my money. But Owen loves me, doesn't he?

This morning, I woke up early to go for a walk along the cliff-tops and clear my head. As I climb down the sandy steps to the lagoon, my heart hammers in my chest when I see a trail of blood spots.

At the bottom of the cliff is the body of a woman... who looks just like me.

Does someone want me dead?

Can I really trust my new husband?

And will I make it off this beautiful island alive?

The Couple on Holiday: A completely addictive and gripping psychological thriller with a heart-stopping twist

On a dark and stormy December night my family are gathered at an isolated hotel in the English countryside. We're reuniting for the first time since the accident that shattered our lives ten years ago.

It's a time for love and forgiveness. But more than one guest has an ulterior motive:

The perfect daughter

The alcoholic

The single mother

The liar

The handsome husband

The adulterer

The beautiful sister

The jealous sibling

The murderer...

As the clock strikes midnight, one member of our party is found dead at the foot of the grand marble staircase.

Everyone is a suspect. But which one of us is a killer?

The Christmas Party: An absolutely addictive psychological thriller with a jaw dropping twist (The Bailey family psychological thrillers Book 1)

This family reunion should've been a fresh start for us all... but now someone is dead.

My heart is thumping with fear as I stare out at the snow-capped mountains. This ski trip to the French Alps was meant to be a chance for me and my two sisters to put the past behind us after years of not speaking.

Instead, I'm expecting the police to knock on the door of our chalet.

I'd planned for our families to get to know each other, sipping hot chocolate while laughing together around the fireplace.

I didn't think our winter getaway would end in murder…

Any one of us could be the killer. We all have a motive. And we've all been lying.

I should never have come here. If anyone discovers my secret my life will be in danger.

Can I trust my own family?

Or am I next…?

The Family Secret: A completely gripping psychological thriller full of incredible twists (The Bailey family psychological thrillers Book 2)

A family party. A terrible secret. A celebration that will end in murder...

I gasp out loud as I step through the door of the beautiful country hotel.

My hands fly to my mouth in shock as I see the room is filled with my friends and family, my grown-up daughters and grandchildren at the centre, gathered to celebrate my special birthday.

Everyone raises their glasses to toast me. I should be enjoying the moment but I'm on edge and I can't relax. Who organised this surprise party? How did they know I was going to be here?

Because I didn't come back to Burcott House to drink champagne and dance. Ten years ago, someone was murdered at this hotel. Tonight, after years of heartache, I planned to bury the past once and for all.

I look around the crowd of smiling people and my heart thuds as I see the frown on my eldest daughter's face and the way my youngest daughter is smiling widely but her eyes are puffy, like she's been crying. I think about the one person who should be here who isn't...

My family's secrets and lies swirl around my mind. Can I trust anyone in this room? Can I even trust my own daughters?

I was going to finish off what happened all those years ago but did someone else have the same idea? And will I survive my own birthday party…?

Her Daughter's Lies: An addictive and unputdownable psychological thriller with a killer twist (The Bailey family psychological thrillers book 3)

Dear reader,

Thank you for choosing to read *The Secret Marriage*. This is my sixth psychological thriller and I loved exploring the characters of Eva and Kirsty. The prologue of this story came to me one day and I was intrigued by the character of Eva and what had happened to her – and the lengths she might be pushed to.

If you enjoyed reading and would like to find out about my new releases, you can sign up to my mailing list via the following link: https://subscribepage.io/MikaylaDavidsBooks

Subscribe!

I hope you were gripped by The Secret Marriage! If you were, I'd be so grateful if you could post your review on Amazon. Reviews on Amazon make such a huge difference, and they really help other readers to discover new stories.

Leave a review!

If you would like to get in touch with me, you can do so via my Facebook page, through Twitter or Goodreads.

All my thanks,

Mikayla Davids

Follow me on Twitter: **@MikaylaDBooks**

Follow me on Instagram: **mikayladavidsbooks**

Find me on Facebook: **Mikayla Davids Books**

Visit my website: **www.mikayladavidsbooks.com**

Copyright © Mikayla Davids, 2025

Mikayla Davids has asserted her right to be identified as the author of this work.

All rights reserved. No part of this publication may be reproduced, stored in any retrieval system, or transmitted, in any form or by any means, electronic, mechanical, photocopying, recording or otherwise, without the prior written permission of the author.

ISBN: 978-1-917018-03-6

eBook ISBN: 978-1-917018-02-9

This book is a work of fiction. Names, characters, businesses, organisations, places and events other than those clearly in the public domain are either the product of the author's imagination or are used fictitiously. Any resemblance to actual persons, living or dead, events or locales is entirely coincidental and unintentional.

MIKAYLA DAVIDS

THE SECRET MARRIAGE

Made in United States
North Haven, CT
11 October 2025

The Face of an Actor

The Life and Films of
Tatsuya Nakadai

MARTIN DOWSING

For Leslie Megahey

Copyright of illustrations reproduced in these pages is the property of the production or distribution companies concerned. These illustrations are reproduced here in the spirit of publicity, and while efforts have been made to trace the copyright holders, the author apologises for any omissions and will undertake to make any appropriate changes in future editions of this book if necessary.

Copyright © 2021 Martin Dowsing

All rights reserved.

ISBN: 9798476336891

'True strength is the ability to keep going.'
Ken Ogata says that in my film *Man Walking on Snow*.

Not everyone can be Tatsuya Nakadai.
No, no matter how hard we try, we cannot become Tatsuya Nakadai.
It took a tremendous amount of effort to become him.
And, of course, talent.
And luck too. Intelligence too.

However, if you believe that 'true strength is the ability to keep going', try hard and carry on, you will surely acquire luck and intelligence. Then, even if you can't become Nakadai, you should be able to get closer to the person you want to be.

Isn't it enough to believe that?

Masahiro Kobayashi

CONTENTS

Prologue 6

1. A Boy Named Moya 11

2. The Haiyuza Gang 19

3. TB or Not TB 31

4. Black River, Golden Temple 44

5. Kaji 61

6. From Humanist to Human Beast 73

7. The Snake and the Octopus 86

8. Expanding the Range 96

9. A Servant of Two Masters 105

10. Seeing Ghosts 119

11. The Return of Kihachi Okamoto 128

12. Mr Chalk and Mr Cheese 139

13. A Little Bit of Everything 147

14. Spaghetti Samurai 159

15. Having a Slash with Mishima 168

16. *Portrait of Hell* 175

17. Samurai Socialist 180

18. Samurai, Soldier, Criminal 187

19. Back to School	202
20. Of Cats and Corruption	210
21. Another Fine Mess or Two	223
22. Divided Loyalties	232
23. The Big Five-O	240
24. From Folly to Reason	254
25. Pedigree Chums	263
26. The Small Screen Beckons	272
27. From the Sublime to the Ridiculous	279
28. Triumph and Disaster	288
29. A Comeback and Two Farewells	299
30. The Stage is Where It's At	304
31. The Other Kobayashi	314
32. Omnipresent Octogenarian	328
33. Not the End	338
Bibliography	351
Acknowledgements	353

Prologue

Toho Studios, Tokyo, 1953.

Akira Kurosawa is 33 years old and enjoying a newfound status as a result of the international success of his 1950 film *Rashomon*. The film had won the prestigious Golden Lion Award at the Venice Film Festival the following year and sparked an interest in Japanese films abroad. This unexpected triumph had vastly mitigated the failure of Kurosawa's next film, a version of Dostoyevsky's *The Idiot*, enabling him to save face and continue to make the kind of films he wanted. Kurosawa has by now already redeemed himself in the eyes of the Toho executives with another film, *Ikiru*, about a meek civil servant who discovers he has terminal cancer and becomes determined to ensure that his remaining time will not go to waste. *Ikiru* has been both a commercial and critical success and now the director is mounting his most ambitious production to date – *Seven Samurai*.

Until the 1950s, Japanese cinema had always lagged behind Hollywood and Europe. Censorship stifled creativity throughout the war, and the conflict also limited the resources available to the film industry, but these problems are by this point a thing of the past. Japan has recently regained independence and is recovering economically. Television is still in its infancy, and cinema-going has reached an alltime high, as has the number of films being produced. These circumstances mean that directors such as Kurosawa are indulged and have the freedom to create films of considerable artistry and depth.

Kurosawa is one of the most painstaking perfectionists in cinema and, while he will pay a price for his obsessive attention to detail in later years, at this stage in his career he has the power to do things his way. However, this does not mean that he has carte blanche to do whatever he wishes. Kurosawa will go massively over-schedule and over-budget on *Seven Samurai* and come close to being replaced as a result. But it is the fact that he is *not* replaced which is significant.

When Kurosawa's team begin auditioning actors for the many roles to be filled in the film, a number of male actors from the Haiyuza theatre group attend the auditions. Several are successful, including Yoshio Tsuchiya, who will play the young farmer eager to fight the bandits, and Yoshio Inaba, who is cast as the cheerful Gorubei Katayami, one of the seven samurai of the title. However, Inaba's inexperience will lead to him receiving regular tongue-lashings from Kurosawa. Another Haiyuza actor, a skinny but handsome 20-year-old named Tatsuya Nakadai, is also given a role – a non-speaking part as a hungry-looking *ronin* who walks past when the farmers have come to town in search of warriors to defend their village from the bandits stealing their rice. Nakadai is still in training at Haiyuza's drama school, so he considers himself lucky even to be given a role such as this, and is thrilled to be in a Kurosawa film as he has seen much of the director's previous work. He assumes that little will be required of him – after all, he only needs to walk along a street, and his part will be filmed in one shot…

Shooting of the scene begins at 9.00 a.m., but Kurosawa is dissatisfied with the way that Nakadai is walking, feeling that he is not carrying himself like a samurai. At Haiyuza, the emphasis is on modern plays, so Nakadai has never played this type of role before and, in fact, it is the first time he has worn a kimono and carried a sword. Frustrated, Kurosawa shouts at Nakadai and makes him walk along the street over and over again while the rest of the cast and crew of 200 people wait, many of them looking on with growing impatience. Nakadai can hear them grumbling and even saying things like, 'Who is that guy? He doesn't deserve to get any lunch!' He is also acutely aware that two of his acting idols, Toshiro Mifune and Takashi Shimura, are among those observing the scene. Kurosawa angrily asks Nakadai where he is from and, upon hearing he is from Haiyuza, retorts, 'What are they teaching you there?' By this point, Nakadai is also becoming angry and struggling to keep his temper, but manages to control himself enough to continue. Ultimately, it takes until 3 p.m. for Kurosawa to be satisfied. Nakadai feels completely humiliated by the experience and resolves never to take a role in a Kurosawa film again. He even begins to consider himself unsuited to film work, and especially to period dramas. As a newcomer, he was perhaps unaware that Kurosawa was quite such a perfectionist and many directors would probably have printed the first take. Unable to understand at the time why Kurosawa did not simply replace him, he later comes to realise that, however much Kurosawa might berate a member of the cast or crew, he would not fire them if he thought they were trying their best. In the finished film, Nakadai appears around ten minutes in for approximately four seconds. His unshaven scalp and face indicates that his character is down on his luck, but he walks proudly along the street with a noble bearing. This is no doubt exactly what Kurosawa was after.[1]

Around seven years later, Nakadai is in demand, mainly as a result of his success in Masaki Kobayashi's epic World War II trilogy *The Human Condition*. Kurosawa decides that he should play the pistol-toting villain facing off against Toshiro Mifune in *Yojimbo*. However, Nakadai, recalling his experience on *Seven Samurai*, declines. Kurosawa tries again. Nakadai again declines, but discusses the matter with Kobayashi, who advises him to take the part on the grounds that it will make a good contrast to the role of the humanist, Kaji, in *The Human Condition*.

Kurosawa then visits an inn at Shibuya where Nakadai is part of a gathering with Kobayashi and others, and asks him why he has rejected the part. Unsure whether Kurosawa remembers the incident, Nakadai says bravely, 'To be honest, after *Seven Samurai*, I decided I didn't want to work with you again!' Kurosawa replies, 'I remember that – that's

---

[1] In his book *Japanese Portraits*, Donald Richie describes a time when he visited the set of *The Hidden Fortress* and Kurosawa shot a scene with Mifune over and over again. Between takes, the director spent his time trying to fix a ballpoint pen which had stopped working instead of simply replacing it. He was eventually successful in doing so, and Mifune remarked that he felt a lot like the ballpoint pen.

why I wanted to use you!' After this response, Nakadai feels he can no longer say no, and agrees to take the role, beginning what will eventually become one of the most significant actor-director relationships in Japanese cinema. Nakadai will also play a memorable second fiddle to Mifune in both *Sanjuro* and *High and Low*. Later, when a chasm opens up between Kurosawa and Mifune, he will be awarded the leading roles in Kurosawa's late samurai epics *Kagemusha* and *Ran*, making his place in cinema history secure.

If Nakadai had only formed such a relationship with Kurosawa, it would be impressive enough, but what is especially remarkable is the number of major Japanese film directors he worked with repeatedly. He made ten films with Masaki Kobayashi (including *Harakiri* and *Kwaidan*), eleven with Kihachi Okamoto (including *Sword of Doom*), five with Mikio Naruse (including *When a Woman Ascends the Stairs*), six with Kon Ichikawa, ten with Hideo Gosha, and two with Hiroshi Teshigahara. Other notable associations were formed with directors less well-known outside Japan but highly regarded at home, such as Satsuo Yamamoto (six films), Shiro Toyoda (four films), Hiromichi Horikawa (four films), Masahiro Kobayashi (three films), Koreyoshi Kurahara (two films) and Kei Kumai (two films).[2] It is difficult to think of an actor who has had an equivalent career, even outside of Japan. Although there are many famous actor-director associations, such as those between Martin Scorsese and Robert DeNiro, and between John Ford and John Wayne, few (if any) actors have enjoyed such ongoing collaborations with so many important directors, several of whom were notoriously hard taskmasters. Taking this into account, it may seem surprising that Nakadai considers himself primarily a theatre actor, a side of his work which is almost entirely unknown in the West. Nakadai is also unusual in the range of parts he has played – throughout his remarkable career, he has alternated between heroes and villains, leads and character parts. At the time of writing, more than

---

[2] These figures exclude television and narration work.

67 years since he first stepped before a camera, Nakadai is not only still acting, but continues to play leading roles at the age of 88.

This book will attempt to show how Tatsuya Nakadai managed to achieve such a unique position in the world of Japanese theatre and film, and to shine a light on parts of his life and career which have received little attention abroad, while not neglecting the most famous works for which he has become so popular with enthusiasts of Japanese cinema in the West.

Chapter 1 – A Boy Named Moya

Tatsuya Nakadai was born Motohisa Nakadai on 13 December 1932 in Gohongi, in the Meguro district of Tokyo, but the family soon moved to Tsudanuma, a suburb of Tokyo located in Chiba prefecture, as it was more convenient for his father's job. Nakadai's father, Tadao (b. 1900), was a tall, well-built man who worked as a train driver on the Keisei line. Opened in 1912, the line originally ran only between Takasago and Edogawa, but was later extended until, in 1933, it ran all the way from Ueno to Narita (although there was no airport at Narita until the 1970s). Tsudanuma, located around 30 km east of Ueno, was one of the stops on the Keisei line, and Nakadai attended the local primary school there. His mother, Aiko (b. 1910), nicknamed him 'Moya' meaning 'mist' or 'haze', which seemed appropriate as the young Nakadai was something of a daydreamer, and those close to him continued to call him this even after he began to use 'Tatsuya' as a stage name.

Aiko was his father's second wife – Tadao had married her after becoming a widower – and the two had met while she was working at the pharmacy run by her family, where he was a regular customer. She had lost her own mother at an early age and been raised by her father alone. Living in Gotanda in the Shinagawa ward of Tokyo as a young woman, Aiko had a reputation as a local beauty. She was short-tempered and feisty, and married Tadao rather suddenly despite the disapproval of her parents, who objected to the idea of her marrying a man who already had one child, a baby daughter named Ikuko. The couple decided to bring Ikuko up believing that Aiko was her real mother. After Nakadai was born, Aiko opened a small tobacco store to help support her family. Nakadai's first memory was of her pursuing a shoplifter down the street with himself an infant strapped to her back, as she shouted, 'Thief!' at the top of her voice until she caught up with the man and took back the cigarettes he had stolen.

Nakadai's maternal grandfather had been a spy during the Russo-Japanese War. Disguised as a Chinese – a language in which he was fluent – he had travelled to Russia on a secret map-making mission, but been exposed as a foreign agent by the way he washed his face, which he had inadvertently done in the Japanese rather than Chinese manner. As a result of this unfortunate error, he was shot.

Nakadai also had a younger brother, Hideyuki, who later became a successful pop singer under the name of Keigo Nakadai, and a younger sister, Tokie.

Tadao had become ill with tuberculosis four years after Nakadai was born, spending much of his time thereafter in bed or at the hospital. There was little effective treatment for tuberculosis at the time, and many died within five years of becoming infected. Aiko had been told by a doctor that Tadao should eat a raw egg every day. As it was a time of hardship, eggs were something of a luxury item, and she sometimes had to go to considerable lengths to acquire them, but it seems that Tadao was not always appreciative, and the couple frequently quarreled. There are hints that he was a womaniser, and this was another cause of their fights. In any case, Nakadai and his younger siblings got used to accompanying their mother on trips back to her hometown after these arguments.

Tadao's condition improved for a while, and he returned to work, but the hours were long and he soon took a turn for the worse. He had to move into the hospital for a longer stay, and Aiko spent most of her time there taking care of him, so the children were looked after by their grandparents. Nakadai was displeased when his grandmother cultivated a small vegetable patch in the garden and grew spring onions with the aid of manure, which created an unpleasant smell. As a result, he developed a lifelong dislike of spring onions.

When it became clear that Tadao would not survive the disease much longer, he was sent back home, and he called each of his children in to say farewell. Despite the fact that Nakadai was a quiet child and not especially troublesome, Tadao told his son that he thought he was a bad boy and would be a failure unless he changed his ways. Was this a calculated piece of psychology on Tadao's part in the manner of the father in the later song 'A Boy Named Sue', immortalised by Johnny Cash? If so, it certainly had its intended effect and seems to have provided the driving force which was to see Nakadai through a lot of hard times until he finally achieved success.

Tadao passed away at the age of 42 in May 1941, when Nakadai was 8. He later recalled feeling a greater sense of relief than sadness, and believed that this feeling was shared by the rest of the family, who had stuggled to care for him for years. Nakadai had no memories of playing with his father as a child, although Tadao had taken him to the cinema from time to time, and so was responsible for his son's first exposure to the art form through which he would later make a living.

The family had been living in accommodation supplied by the rail company, and were now forced to move. Tadao had owned a field inherited from his family, so they sold it to raise some much-needed cash, then relocated to Yoga, a neighbourhood in Setagaya City in the south-west of Tokyo quite far from the centre. Nakadai's mother found work there in a textile factory, and his big sister, Ikuko, at a homeware company. However, these jobs paid little and the family struggled to get by. Meanwhile, Ikuko received a shock when she needed to produce a copy of her birth certificate for employment purposes and discovered that Aiko was not her real mother. Then, around the time of the attack on Pearl Harbour which brought Japan into the Second World War, they again relocated, this time to Aoyama, a wealthy neighborhood just east of Shibuya, where they lived rent-free above the offices of a law firm in return for performing simple chores such as serving tea in the office and keeping an eye on the building when the office was closed.

Nakadai attended Seinan Elementary School and suddenly found himself among the sons of politicians and army chiefs, including those of Admiral Yamamoto and General Anami, the War Minister. In normal times, a boy from a poor family would have been unable to attend such a school, but during the war pupils in Tokyo had been assigned to their schools based purely on location, presumably in order to minimize unnecessary journeys. However, the situation was not entirely positive, as some of his fellow pupils as well as members of the staff resented his presence. On one occasion, Nakadai's mother marched down to the school and confronted one of the teachers who had made it clear that he considered her son an interloper.

Nakadai attended four different elementary schools in total, and this frequent changing of schools often caused him to be bullied simply for being the new boy. When he went home in tears, Aiko would find out who was responsible, then go down to the school the next day armed with the bamboo sword used for kendo practice, ready to give the bully a good thrashing. Nakadai became so embarrassed by this that he learned to endure the bullying and hide it from his mother.

Meanwhile, the American forces were getting closer to Japan, and the danger of air raids was increasing. Nakadai and his brother were evacuated, Nakadai to a temple (possibly Jindai-ji) in what is now Chofu, on the western outskirts of Tokyo, Hideyuki to another temple a few stops away. One of the first air raids was on nearby Nakajima, where the military had a base, so Nakadai was by no means out of danger. When the bombs fell, the children had to go and hide in the local cemetery. Nakadai began wetting the bed on an almost daily basis. His feelings of shame led him to wake up early and take his bedding to the cemetery to dry out before anyone else was around. One morning, as he lifted his bedding off the tombstone upon which he had laid it to dry, the tombstone fell over onto his foot, causing considerable pain. Nakadai thought this must have been a punishment for drying his urine-soaked sheets on a grave. He began to feel increasingly alienated from the other children, looking on in envy as their parents visited with packages of food while his own mother never came to see him. Becoming more and more despondent, he began to wish he had never been born and found himself crying frequently. The only ray of light was one of the teachers, a Mr Eryo, who began to take charge of the food packages brought by the wealthier parents and divided them equally among the children, something which won the admiration of Nakadai at the time as he mostly saw people acting in their own self-interest. Mr Eryo later came to see some of Nakadai's stage performances and was the only teacher who made a significant impression on Nakadai during this period.

Despite Mr Eryo's best efforts, food became scarce, so the children ate toothpaste instead, and Nakadai later recalled that some were so close to starving they even ate their own faeces. Meanwhile, soldiers came to the school and trained the children how to attack the enemy with bamboo spears in the event of an invasion. The children were indoctrinated with the idea that the greatest honour they could ever receive would be an opportunity to die for the Emperor.

In April of 1945, Nakadai graduated from primary school and returned home, where he was displeased to discover that his mother had had another baby by one of the lawyers, a married man with whom she had been having an affair. This man agreed to provide financial help, and found a better place for Aiko and the baby boy to live, in Shibuya. However, the situation worsened the already strained relationship Nakadai had with his mother, and he avoided the man's company as much as possible. After an air raid, the family relocated to Chitose Karasuyama, an area to the west in the Setagaya district of Tokyo, and Nakadai began attending Kitatoshima Kogyo, a high school some distance away to the north. This necessitated a long train journey involving two changes, and Nakadai often found himself travelling to school while the air raid sirens were sounding. During the most intense period, the air raids occurred on an almost daily basis and he frequently saw dead bodies in the street, making him acutely aware that any day could be his last. He later estimated that around half of his fellow students were killed in these raids. The worst raid was on the night of 9 March 1945, when 16 square miles of Tokyo were destroyed, leaving an estimated 100,000 dead and over a million homeless. This remains the most destructive air raid in history; the fatalities were three times those caused by the later atomic bombing of Nagasaki, and equivalent to those in Hiroshima.

One day, on his way to visit a friend in Aoyama, Nakadai found himself caught outside in the middle of an air raid as incendiary bombs fell one after another all around him. Seeing a girl of five or six years of age trying to run for cover on her own, Nakadai grabbed her by the arm to help her and they ran towards shelter together. Before they could get there, the girl was hit by one of the incendiary bombs and killed instantly. Nakadai, shocked to find himself holding an arm with no body attached, threw it away in horror and managed to reach safety. He later expressed regret that he had not disposed of the girl's arm more respectfully, and the incident continued to haunt him in his dreams until many years later.[3]

In order to avoid the long, frequently-interrupted and dangerous train journey, Nakadai changed to a new high school in Setagaya, and the war finally ended shortly after, on 14 August 1945. Two weeks later, the American occupation began. Nakadai joined forces with his uncle (Aiko's elder brother), who had just returned from the war, and Hideyuki in a family business making rice snacks and, later, Chinese noodles. However, their success was short-lived and they had to give it up. The struggle to obtain enough food dragged on and Nakadai's education was being neglected, partly because his mother put little value on it, viewing education as a luxury they could ill afford. She would even shout at her children for reading books, considering it a complete waste of time. Needless to say, Nakadai saw things very differently. He attended evening classes for four years while working at two schools during the day to earn some much needed money. His tasks included making tea and copying documents on a mimeograph, the machine used before the photocopier was invented. Nakadai and his fellow students were all in similar situations, and it was not unusual for any of them to doze off during class. The teacher understood that they were suffering from exhaustion and lack of food and let them sleep.

---

[3] The harrowing air raid sequence in Tadashi Imai's 1991 film *War and Youth* (Sensou to seishun) provides some idea of the traumas that Nakadai must have experienced during this period.

Others he knew turned to petty crime such as burglary or pickpocketing to survive, but Nakadai was dissuaded from following their example by the memory of his father's final words. The influence of communism had begun to spread, teaching that everyone should be equal, but Nakadai had begun to regard the words of others with scepticism as a result of the lies he had been told during the war. The staff at the school asked him to get lunch for them while he was struggling to feed himself and, when he managed to provide them with some croquets, he looked on hungrily while they devoured the food without offering to share.

Nakadai also witnessed how quickly people's attitudes towards Westerners changed after the war, noticing how many who had vilified them previously now performed an abrupt volte-face and became pro-American. This inconstancy deepened Nakadai's mistrust of adults yet further and he developed a strong dislike of dealing with people. Shy by nature, during this period he seems to have become almost dangerously withdrawn. Acting was the furthest thing from his mind, and he was not even part of the acting group at the school. Meanwhile, he realised that those who graduated from the night school were finding it very hard to find decent jobs. A lack of money meant that a university education was out of the question, and the situation was little better for university graduates in any case. He later described this period as his 'dark nihilistic youth.'

Nakadai found some work as a security guard at Ohi Racecourse (aka Tokyo City Keiba) in Tokyo's Shinagawa Ward, a horse-racing track built in 1950, where his job was to help crack down on illegal tipsters. In his spare time, he enjoyed reading French poets such as Baudelaire and Rimbaud, as well as Japanese writers like Natsume Soseki and Osamu Dazai, and began to think of becoming a writer. He wrote a short book entitled 'At the Race Track' about the characters he had observed while working, but when he took it to a publisher, they turned it down flat and he abandoned the idea. He tried boxing, but gave it up after receiving a particularly bad beating and deciding he did not much enjoy being punched in the nose. Then a colleague told him that he was quite handsome and suggested that he had the face of an actor.

The young Nakadai

Chapter 2 – The Haiyuza Gang

Nakadai had never even been to the theatre as a child, and this was the first time he had considered acting as a possible career. However, he had become an avid cinemagoer after the war, seeing around 300 films a year and often skipping meals in order to pay the admission. The cinema provided such a welcome escape from the harsh reality surrounding him that a missed lunch was a small price to pay. He had been put off Japanese films by the fact that those made during the war years had mostly been full of nationalistic propaganda, while those made between 1945 and 1952 were all subject to American censorship. The number of Japanese films being produced at the time was in any case low due to the state of the economy, so most of those he saw were American or French, but he preferred the latter. Among the classics he saw during this period were *Les Enfants du Paradis*, *Casablanca* and *The Third Man*. A particular favourite was Jean Renoir's *La Grande Illusion* – not seen in Japan until after the war – which he saw around ten times. No doubt one reason for Nakadai's admiration of Renoir's film was its anti-war message. As a result of his own experiences and observations, it became important to Nakadai to denounce war at every opportunity, and in his career as an actor he would frequently appear in films and plays with such a message.

In 1950, at the age of 17, Nakadai saw a production of Molière's *The School for Wives* presented by Haiyuza ('The Actor's Theatre') and directed by Koreya Senda, the founder of the theatre, who also played the lead. Learning that Haiyuza was also an acting school, Nakadai eventually decided to apply after many of his co-workers at the racing track had chipped in to raise the 2,000 yen necessary to take the entrance exam and even arranged transportation for him. However, when he arrived, Nakadai was presented with a written task about Stanislavski, of whom he knew precisely nothing; seeing no alternative, he left the paper blank. For the performance part of the test, he had to mime the part of a young man on a date who is initially cheerful until discovering that he cannot find the cinema tickets, but then finally discovers them in one of his pockets. Nakadai had an attack of nerves and his mind went blank. In the next stage of the exam, he was given a text to read aloud, but found it hard to focus as there were two well-known actors he had seen in films scrutinising him. One of these was Chieko Higashiyama, familiar to Western audiences as the mother in *Tokyo Story*.

Nakadai was so convinced he had failed this first round that he neglected to go and check the result, but a while later he received a letter asking why he had not attended the second round despite passing the first. He returned to the school and completed the other rounds. After the final stage was complete, the names of those who had passed were posted on the wall at the school. As Nakadai nervously approached, he noticed a fellow applicant, Ken Utsui, beaming cheerfully. Both actors' names were on the wall, and Nakadai received a delighted hug from Utsui – an actor whose career would go in a very different direction to Nakadai's, as he was to become best-known for playing the part of 'Super Giant' in a series of science fiction B-movies.

Nakadai joined the school in 1952, the same year that Japan regained its independence. He was one of 36 applicants selected out of a total of approximately 600, and was genuinely surprised to have passed. He was a 'fourth generation' student – in other words, he had joined during the fourth year of the school's recruitment. Later, he heard that the school had been looking for tall actors with loud voices, and these factors may have been the reason for his acceptance as he was indeed tall for a Japanese at around 5'8" (177 cm) and had a loud voice when he chose to use it.

Koreya Senda had founded Hayuza in 1944 along with his wife, Teruko Kishi (the pickpocket who steals Toshiro Mifune's pistol in Kurosawa's *Stray Dog*) and fellow actors Eitaro Ozawa (the peasant desperate to become a samurai in *Ugetsu Monogatari*), Sugisaku Aoyama (the elderly priest in the same film), Sachiko Murase (the grandmother in Kurosawa's *Rhapsody in August*), Eijiro Tono (the tavern-keeper in *Yojimbo*) and the aforementioned Chieko Higashiyama. The first

Haiyuza production was a version of Nikolai Gogol's *The Government Inspector* in March 1946, co-directed by Senda and Aoyama. At first it was a theatre company only, but in 1949 Haiyuza began taking on students annually to train over a three year period. Its actors were trained in the performance of *shingeki* ('new theatre'), a style which had emerged in the early 20th-century and was heavily influenced by Western realism, staging translations of Western classics as well as occasional new works by Western-influenced Japanese playwrights.[4] Haiyuza was one of three leading *shingeki* companies, the others being Bungakuza (founded 1937) and the Mingei Theatre Company (founded 1950). All three had a strongly left-wing stance and a considerable number of Communist Party members within their ranks.

The majority of Nakadai's theatre work was to be in translations of Western classics which retained their original settings – in other words, Nakadai has usually played Westerners on stage. This may seem a strange concept from a Western perspective – after all, there is no equivalent Western tradition of performing Asian classics, but there was an appetite for Western culture in Japan, especially after the war, when the traditional theatre of Noh and kabuki seemed less relevant. *Shingeki* had been largely suppressed during the war due to its strong foreign influence, but the occupying Americans actively encouraged it in the post-war years, somewhat naively believing that it would promote Western values, which was not always necessarily the case – or, at least, not always the Western values the Americans wished to promote, as socialist and communist ideas were commonly found in *shingeki*.

---

[4] One of Kenji Mizoguchi's lesser films, *The Love of Sumako* (Joyu Sumako no koi, 1947) is set in the world of *shingeki* during its early years and features Kinuyo Tanaka as Sumako Matsui (1886-1919), the first big female star of the genre, as well as Koreya Senda in a small part.

Koreya Senda

Koreya Senda, born the son of an architect in Tokyo in 1904, was eventually to become the teacher with whom Nakadai developed the closest relationship, and it could well be said that Senda was Nakadai's most important mentor. Nakadai would later act alongside him in a number of films and frequently be directed by him on stage, including in a version of *Hamlet* in which Nakadai played the title role and Senda was Claudius. During Senda's scenes without Hamlet, Nakadai would watch from the wings every night. He later credited Senda with being the main influence on the way he speaks as an actor.

Koreya Senda was not his real name. In the aftermath of the Great Kanto Earthquake of 1923, there had been an outbreak of anti-Korean sentiment. Senda, then named Kumiyo Ito, had been mistaken for a Korean and badly beaten, so his adoption of the name 'Koreya' was an acknowledgment of this defining event in his life. Senda became a communist as a young man, spending time in Soviet Russia and also in Berlin, where he was once shot at by Nazis. As a result of his ideals and experiences, his work often had a strong social conscience. Returning to Japan in the early 1930s, he staged plays by Brecht and others which soon fell foul of the authorities, leading to a lengthy spell in prison in the early '40s. Senda must have received harsh treatment at the hands of the police during this time – beatings were commonplace, and one friend of Senda's was actually tortured to death. After his release, he founded Haiyuza with the aim of developing new talent and becoming a progressive leftist force in Japanese theatre.[5] In 1949, he published a book, *Modern Acting*, which became the bible of the *shingeki* movement. With his swept-back hair streaked with grey, Senda also became a familiar presence in Japanese films after the war, playing professors in Toho monster movies and kindly but distant fathers in films such as Masaki Kobayashi's *Sincere Heart* (Magokoro, 1953) and Tomotaka Tasaka's *A Slope in the Sun* (Hi no ataru sakamichi, 1958). However, for Teinosuke Kinugasa's *Gate of Hell* (Jigokumon, 1953), he shaved off his trademark hair to play a different type of character, appearing as the powerful Lord to whom Kazuo Hasegawa makes his request for the hand of Machiko Kyo as a reward for his service in battle. Further evidence of his versatility can be seen in Keisuke Kinoshita's *The Good Fairy* (Zen-ma, 1951), in which he plays a slimy, corrupt politician abandoned by his wife. For his final film role, he wore a moustache and dyed his hair black to play Japan's wartime Prime Minister, Prince Fumimaro Konoe, in *Tora! Tora! Tora!* (1970), but was featured in only a couple of scenes.

In order to afford the monthly tuition fee of 900 yen, Nakadai had to get used to attending Haiyuza during the day and working in a pachinko parlour at night. When learners missed a payment, their name would appear on a list on the noticeboard – a kind of wall of shame – and Nakadai's name was usually to be found at the top. The fee was frequently paid for by Ikuko, who was working in a restaurant. She also chose his stage name of 'Tatsuya' – a reference to him being a Sagittarian, who are supposedly single-minded in their pursuit of a goal.

---

[5] For more on Senda, see 'Senda Koreya: Theatre for Change' by Ayub Khattak at www.international.ucla.edu/institute/article/40075 and the lecture 'Berlin in Tokyo: Senda Koreya, Brecht, Shakespeare' by the American academic J. Thomas Rimer on YouTube.

He often went to sleep at 3 a.m. and rose at 7 a.m., then caught the train to Shibuya, jogging from there to the school in Roppongi three kilometres away in order to avoid paying a second train fare. He wore similar clothes in summer and winter, simply wearing them in layers when it was cold.

Another of Nakadai's acting teachers was Eitaro Ozawa, a busy actor then in his 40s who had made his film debut in 1935. Nakadai was reticent and slow of speech in his youth, and Ozawa advised him to try and become more talkative as good articulation was a necessary skill for an actor. Despite the discomfort it caused him, Nakadai forced himself to overcome his shyness by announcing to his fellow passengers on the train that he was studying to be an actor and requesting they listen to him reading from a script, which he then proceeded to do loudly, if with a red face.

When he began at the school, Nakadai was taken aback to find that he was given no lines to learn and was instead repeatedly instructed to 'be a lion' or 'be a bear'. Much of his time was spent making animal noises, but he came to realise that this was necessary training for his vocal cords. The students were also taught how to project their voice even when whispering and how to walk naturally in front of an audience – a skill he said took him two years to master. In fact, for their first two years, the students had only theatre studies, voice training and English literature, and learned ballet and fencing, but no practical lessons – these did not begin until the third year. Even then, Nakadai found that the opportunities for acting practice were limited, especially as turns were taken in alphabetical order, meaning that 'Abe' was called far more frequently than 'Nakadai'. The students with names like Abe soon tired of being called first all the time, while those lower down the alphabet wanted more practise, so they sometimes attempted to subvert the system by swapping names without the teacher realising, but this ruse helped only a little. The atmosphere was apparently friendly yet competitive, and the teachers were very strict. Eitaro Ozawa, for example, would not allow a student on the stage if they had been even a minute late for rehearsal.

Another well-known teacher was Sugisaku Aoyama, an actor and director who had directed films in the 1920s. As part of his welcome speech, Aoyama told the new students that he thought only one out of the 36 would go on to become a successful actor. However, Aoyama's assessment was in this case too pessimistic, as Nakadai's fellow students included Kei Sato, Ken Utsui and Ichiro Nakatani, while one year below him was Mikijiro Hira and three years below him were Hisashi Igawa and Kunie Tanaka. The last of these was the same age as Nakadai but had failed the entrance exam two years running before finally being accepted on the third attempt. He would go on to become one of the most peculiar and instantly recognisable faces in Japanese cinema, appearing in many films with Nakadai, and is probably best-known in the West as one of the foolish samurai Toshiro Mifune takes under his wing in *Sanjuro*. Along with Go Kato, who joined the school after Nakadai had graduated, these actors all went on to have long and successful careers. This was just as well, as Haiyuza relied on its actors to donate a large part of their salaries from film and TV work to keep the theatre going. In Nakadai's case, he apparently donated 70% to Haiyuza, keeping only the remaining 30% for himself.

The fact that so many of the school's graduates went on to success was no doubt due partly to them having been in the right place at the right time. Throughout the '50s and early '60s, cinema-going was hugely popular in Japan. There was a demand for product, and the number of films produced each year frequently far exceeded that of Hollywood. Of course, this meant there were a huge number of parts requiring actors to play them. Film directors often visited the school on the lookout for new talent, or to fill out their casts – Kurosawa used a number of Haiyuza actors in *Stray Dog*, for example. However, many theatre actors looked down on film acting, seeing it only as a handy means of earning cash as it was impossible to make a living on theatre acting alone. As a film fan, Nakadai himself felt differently, but he and his friend Kei Sato pretended they had no real desire to act in films and feigned indifference. They failed auditions nine times in a row. One of the parts they both tried for was that of the ungrateful son who spurns his mother in Keisuke Kinoshita's *A Japanese Tragedy* (Nihon no higeki), a role that went to a fellow student, Masami Taura. Nakadai came closer to being cast in Nobuo Nakagawa's *Fountain of Youth* (Shishun no izumi), but ultimately lost out to Ken Utsui. Nakadai felt that he and Sato were probably passed over due to their poverty – at the time, the two were not only skinny, but tired-looking due to their night work, and often went without a bath for a month. After this string of failures, Nakadai decided that films were not for him and he should concentrate on theatre work. Feeling dissatisfied with Haiyuza, Nakadai, Sato and Nakatani began plotting the formation of a new theatre company, a plan which went awry when Sato contracted tuberculosis and returned to his hometown. The other two graduated from the training school and were accepted as members of the theatre company, deciding to remain at Haiyuza as a result. Meanwhile, some of the other students did leave to form a new company, resulting in less competition for Nakadai.

Haiyuza had been operating across various venues when Nakadai joined, but had been building its own theatre, which finally opened with around 300 seats on 20 April 1954 in Roppongi. Nakadai's Haiyuza debut was in June of that year in *The Red Lamp* (Akai ranpu), a new play written by the Western-influenced playwright Yutaka Mafune. Directed by Koreya Senda, it dealt with the Japanese occupation of Manchuria. Nakadai's second appearance on stage was also under the direction of Senda in *Youths, Resurrect Yourselves!* (Wakodo yo yomigaere) by Yukio Mishima.[6]

During this period, credited under his real name of Motohisa Nakadai, he played a small part as 'Kazuma Yamagami' in a now-forgotten Toho production entitled *The Freedom Bell is Ringing* (Kakute jiyuu no kane wa naru), but it is doubtful whether he even had any

---

[6] Despite criticising Mishima for lacking a social conscience, Senda appreciated the quality of the young writer's work. In early 1949, Haiyuza had been the first theatre to stage a play by Mishima, *The House on Fire* (Kataku), in which Senda played the lead. A year later, Mishima had also directed a play of his own there. See *Persona: A Biography of Yukio Mishima* by Naoki Inose and Hiroaki Sato for further information.

lines. The story concerned the young Yukichi Fukuzawa (1835-1901), an important historical figure considered one of the founders of modern Japan. Directed by Hisatora Kumagai, who had been directing since the early '30s, it starred kabuki actor Koroemon Onoe II as Fukuzawa. Chieko Higashiyama from Haiyuza was also in the cast (perhaps explaining Nakadai's presence), as was another Chieko – Chieko Nakakita, who had been the female lead in Kurosawa's *One Wonderful Sunday* (Subarashiki nichiyobi). The film also marked the debut of Akira Takarada, who went on to become well-known for his roles in a number of Godzilla films.

Nakadai actually turned down a major part in a film at this time because he found the script uninteresting. *The Human Torpedo* (Ningen gyorai kaiten) told the story of the men trained to pilot the *kaiten* during the Second World War. *Kaiten* were manned torpedoes, the naval equivalent of the planes used by the air force in kamikaze attacks. Presumably, Nakadai was offered the part of the young lieutenant played by Ken Utsui in the film. He would later provide narration for a more interesting film on the same subject, Kihachi Okamoto's *The Human Bullet* (1968).

The following year, 1955, Nakadai made his TV debut in *Eventually the Blue Sky* (Yagate soko), a comedy series about two old male friends, in which he played the son of one of the main characters. Produced by NHK (the Japanese equivalent of the BBC), the programme aired for several weeks over the summer. He also appeared in supporting roles in at least seven plays at Haiyuza, including translations of works by Western playwrights such as Molière and George Bernard Shaw, as well as the occasional Japanese one, such as *Slave Hunting* (Dorei gari) by Kobo Abe. [7]

The same year, Nakadai performed his first speaking role in a film in Satsuo Yamamoto's *Floating Weeds Diary* (Ukikusa nikki). Yamamoto, born the same year as Kurosawa, was at the time making independent

---

[7] This production of *Slave Hunting* was filmed and broadcast on NHK television on May 3rd 2008.

films after having been exiled from the major studios for being a member of the Communist Party. *Floating Weeds Diary*, a comedy drama based on a play by Miho Mayama entitled *The Story of the Ichikawa Bagoro Troupe*, tells of a travelling kabuki company whose star actor runs off with all their money, leaving them stranded in a coal mining town where a strike is in progress. They are rescued by the union, who ask them to perform a play written by one of their members about a similar strike. Despite their lack of experience in contemporary works, they succeed and are well-rewarded as a result. The film was a collaboration between Yamamoto Productions and Haiyuza, and featured many Haiyuza actors, including founders Eijiro Tono and Eitaro Ozawa as the head of the troupe and the troupe's bad apple respectively. As kabuki was neither taught nor performed at Haiyuza, the actors had to receive special training and must have found it ironic to be cast as a kabuki troupe tasked with performing in modern, Western-style clothes for the first time. Nakadai, who received a screen credit, has a few lines towards the end of the film playing a cheerful young miner who is a member of the union. Yamamoto later became a major director in Japan, but has remained largely unknown in the West. Nakadai would appear in a trio of significant films for him around 20 years later.

Nakadai in *Floating Weeds Diary* (screenshots).

Another Haiyuza production Nakadai appeared in at this time was *The Living Forest* (Mori wa ikiteiru), an adaptation of a fairy tale play entitled *The Twelve Months* by Russian writer Samuil Marshak. Although his part was a small one, *The Living Forest* would prove to be personally significant for Nakadai – while performing in it, he met his future wife, actress, writer and stage director Yasuko Miyazaki.[8] She was playing the leading part of the spoilt young queen who, on a whim, offers a fortune to anyone who can find a specific type of spring flower in the middle of winter, while Nakadai had just two lines of dialogue in the play as a soldier protecting the princess.[9]

Yasuko was a pretty and petite young woman with a ready smile, optimistic by nature and of cheerful disposition. Born on 15 May 1931 in Nagasaki, she was a year and a half older than Nakadai. Having joined Haiyuza in 1950, she was in the third year there when he was in the first. The two young actors had to take the same train line home; as they lived the furthest away of all the cast members, their group would gradually dwindle as the others got off one by one until he and Yasuko were left alone. At first they both felt self-conscious and their attempts at conversation were somewhat awkward but, as the play was successful, it ran for some time and they gradually relaxed in each other's company. Nakadai soon found himself waiting for Yasuko in the dressing room after the play each night and, before he even knew it himself, the other members of the company had decided that the two were officially 'going out'. He began to be invited to her family's home for dinner regularly, and their relationship deepened, but it was nearly cut short when Nakadai suffered a health scare.

---

[8] 'Yasuko' is sometimes incorrectly translated as 'Kyoko', as the *kanji* can be read either way.

[9] The Haiyuza production of *The Living Forest* became a film the following year, with Yasuko again in the role of the queen. However, it seems that Nakadai did not appear in the film.

Chapter 3 – TB or not TB

After undergoing a routine medical examination, Nakadai was told there was a possibility of tuberculosis, the disease which had killed his father and afflicted his friend, Kei Sato. Tuberculosis seems to have been especially prevalent in Japan during the post-war years, and Japanese films of the period with contemporary settings frequently featured tubercular characters. Indeed, this was common to the extent that, if an actor coughs in such a film, the viewer can be certain their character is doomed to die from the illness a few reels later. Nevertheless, what rapidly became a cliché was based on numerous real-life cases. One famous example is Fumio Hayasaka, the composer of the score for *Seven Samurai* and other Kurosawa films, who died aged 41 as a result of the disease at around this time.

Knowing how serious tuberculosis could be, Nakadai had no wish to burden Yasuko. He invited her to spend the day with him at Hamarikyu Gardens near Tokyo Bay, intending to use the occasion to break off the relationship. However, Yasuko dismissed his concerns, saying that the disease could be cured and she would support them both if necessary – at this point, she was better established in the acting profession than he. Moved by her attitude, Nakadai allowed himself to be persuaded, and the two began to talk of marriage. Later, he underwent a further check up which revealed that the shadow on his lung was in fact an old injury which had long since healed.

Nakadai's first major part at Haiyuza was as Oswald, the son who has inherited his father's syphilis, in the company's version of Ibsen's *Ghosts*. His casting caused resentment among some of his approximately 100 seniors, many of whom had been with the company for years and never received such a good role. As Nakadia's seniors, they were entitled to criticize his performance, and many did so mercilessly, but he soon learned to distinguish those who had something constructive to say from those who were merely bitter.

Haiyuza lacked the funds to spend on wigs for their actors, so Nakadai was obliged to dye his hair blonde in order to look more Western. In the 1950s, it was extremely unusual for a Japanese person to colour their hair in this fashion, so Nakadai felt embarrassed when away from the theatre. His character's mother was played by Chieko Higashiyama and the priest by Koreya Senda. Although the play was successful enough to win an award, the wages were low, so Nakadai supplemented his income at this time by working on radio dramas. The lead actress in one of these was Yumeji Tsukioka, who had starred in numerous films and been especially memorable in the lead role of the poet suffering from breast cancer in Kinuyo Tanaka's *The Eternal Breasts* (Chibusa yo eien nare, 1955). She was due to appear in the film *Firebird* (Hi no tori), a Nikkatsu Studios production to be directed by her husband, Umetsugu Inoue, and based on a 1953 novel of the same name by Sei Ito. The project, a love story, called for Tsukioka to be cast alongside a 'new face' as a troubled youth. Tsukioka, intrigued by Nakadai's dyed blonde hair and amused by his embarrassment, became interested in him, deciding that he would be ideal; after seeing Nakadai perform in *Ghosts*, her husband agreed. Umetsugu (or Umeji) Inoue was a prolific and versatile director who worked in many genres, including musicals, crime dramas and samurai films. Few of his films have been seen outside of Japan in recent years, but his version of Edogawa Rampo's *Black Lizard* (Kurotokage, 1962) and especially his excellent *Kagemusha* predecessor, *The Third Shadow Warrior* (Daisan no Kagemusha, 1963), suggest an above-average talent, although *Firebird* was to be the only occasion on which he worked with Nakadai.

The story concerns Emi Ikushima (Yumeji Tsukioka), a star actress at the Rose Theatre, who is approached for a part in a film entitled 'Firebird'. When she goes to the studio for a screen test, she meets an ambitious young actor, Keiichi Naganuma (Nakadai), and the two hit it off. Emi wins the part but, on the day of the preview, Naganuma participates in a demonstration against the studio and is arrested. However, he is soon released, and Emi feigns illness to have a day off from the theatre so they can spend a romantic day at the beach together in Tsujido. Unfortunately, her lie is discovered, and she suffers humiliation in front of her colleagues, nearly losing her job at the theatre. When she receives an inheritance from her recently-deceased father, she quits the theatre, splits up with Naganuma and concentrates on her film career.

On the first day of filming at Chigasaki Beach in Kanagawa, Nakadai had to play a love scene opposite Tsukioka, and was shaking with nerves at the thought of acting in his first substantial film role opposite a major star. Tsukioka slapped his behind and told him to pull himself together which, fortunately, he did, getting through not only the first scene but the rest of the film successfully and becoming a lifelong friend of Tsukioka in the process. However, the film itself seems not to have been especially notable and is now almost completely forgotten.

Like *Floating Weeds Diary*, *Firebird* was produced by Masayuki Sato (b.1918), who ran the film production section at Haiyuza and had become Nakadai's manager, a professional relationship that would last for decades. Sato was a former scriptwriter who had been part of a film production unit sent to Manchuria during the war, after which he had been detained in Siberia until his repatriation in 1948, when he joined Haiyuza as a producer. Nakadai said in later years that he regarded him as a father-figure to whom he felt grateful for not pushing him to accept roles he had no desire to play, estimating that he had declined around 50% of the roles he was offered. Sato would diplomatically tell those whose offers were being rejected that Nakadai felt he was not right for the role. Nakadai also asked Sato not to let him know how much money was being offered for each role as he wanted to make his choices based solely on the scripts. However, sometimes there was a more mundane reason for saying no – Nakadai was a poor swimmer and would turn down any parts involving swimming scenes.

Back at Haiyuza, Nakadai appeared in three plays during 1956, including an adaptation of Gogol's *Dead Souls*, and works by Catholic playwright Chikao Tanaka and his wife, Sumie Tanaka, who was also a successful screenwriter, most notably for director Mikio Naruse.

During the year following *Firebird*, Nakadai had roles of various sizes in a number of now-forgotten films produced by Japan's largest film studio, Toho. The first of these was *Barefoot Youth* (Hadashi no seishun), a romance set on a small island populated by two rival fishing communities, one Japanese Catholic, the other Buddhist. A young Catholic (Akira Takarada) has fallen in love with Kikue (Kyoko Aoyama), from the Buddhist group, but her father (Eijiro Tono) wants her to marry Yuji (Nakadai), another Buddhist. The two young men fight over her, but ultimately decide the winner by means of a sardine-fishing contest. The film was shot on location on the island of Kuroshima in Nagasaki Prefecture, which boasted a large church and was home to a real Catholic community who had once had to practice their religion in secret. *Barefoot Youth* was filmed in Eastmancolor and directed by Senkichi Taniguchi, whose career had begun well in 1947 when he directed Toshiro Mifune's impressive debut film, *Snow Trail* (Ginrei no hate), from a script by his friend Akira Kurosawa. However, by the time of *Barefoot Youth*, he had failed to fulfil this early promise and was regarded as a fairly minor director. Based on a novel entitled *Thirty Pieces of Silver* (Gin sanju-mai) by Ashihei Hino, the screenplay was written by Masato Ide, who would himself become an important Kurosawa collaborator many years later, co-writing the screenplays for *Red Beard*, *Kagemusha* and *Ran*.

Next up was the musical family comedy *Sazae-san*, a live action version of the most popular Japanese comic strip of the day. Created by Machiko Hasegawa and first published in a local paper in 1946, it soon became a phenomenon and ran until 1974. In 1969, it was turned into a cartoon series for television which continues to run at the time of writing, making it easily the world's longest-running animated programme. Sazae-san, played by actress and singer Chiemi Eri in the film, is a cheerful young housewife with a strange hair-do who, despite having a salaryman husband, is the real head of her household. In the early days of the strip's appearance, she would have seemed quite a modern character, and the situation of her family (who have to scrimp and save to get by) reflected that of many in post-war Japan. However, although it continued to run for such a long time, there was little modernization of the characters (who never aged) and it was later popular mainly for reasons of nostalgia. (In fact, the character of Sazae-san seems to inspire similar feelings of comfortable familiarity to that of Tora-san, the 'loveable loser' played by Kiyoshi Atsumi in no less than 50 feature films.) Nakadai played Norisuke, Sazae-san's journalist cousin, a role he repeated in the second of nine sequels, *Sazae-san's Youth* (Sazae-san no seishun), and which was perhaps the most lightweight part he ever played. In the first film, a very boyish-looking Nakadai can be seen holding hands with the other members of Sazae-san's family as they dance around a table singing 'Jingle Bells' together.

Nakadai's next film was *Lovebirds' Gate* (Oshidori no mon), a vehicle for real-life mother and daughter Isuzu Yamada and Michiko Saga, who also played mother and daughter in the film. Yamada is perhaps best-known in the West for her chilling Lady Macbeth equivalent in Kurosawa's *Throne of Blood*, whereas Saga will be known to some for her triple role in *The Mad Fox* (Koiya koi nasuna koi, 1962). In *Lovebirds' Gate*, Saga played Ashiko, whose mother leaves her father and goes to live with another man. This causes Saga to run away from home and find a job which will also provide accommodation. While working as a maid at a hot spring inn, Ashiko receives attention from a number of men, including the middle-aged Echigo (Ken Uehara) and the younger Ando (Nakadai), who looks after her when she falls ill. Based on a novel by Seiichi Funabashi, the film was written and directed by the capable but largely forgotten Keigo Kimura, whose films *The Life of a Horse Trader* (Bakuro ichidai, 1951) and *Diary of a Mad Old Man* (Futen rojin nikki, 1962) are worth seeking out.

Oban, released the following year (1957) was the first in a series of four films based on a contemporary novel of the same name by Bunroku Shishi. The novel, serialized in the *Asahi Shimbun* from 1956-58, was apparently a roman-à-clef based on the life of self-made businessman Kasaburo Sato, President of Godo Securities, known to his familiars as 'Boo-chan.' The films featured chubby character actor Daisuke Kato in a rare starring role as Yunosuke Akabane, a young man born to a poor farming family in Uwajima in Shikoku's Ehime Prefecture. When he gives a love letter to Kanako (Setsuko Hara), the daughter of a local bigwig, it causes a scandal and he flees to Tokyo. The year is 1927. Finding work as a stockbroker's assistant in Kabutocho (Tokyo's financial district), he learns quickly and improves his position, making a considerable amount of money and earning himself the nickname 'Gyu-chan' in the process. Returning to his hometown in the hope of impressing Kanako, he arrives only to find that she too has moved to Tokyo and is already married. He returns to the capital himself and eventually becomes a financial guru. Nakadai played the main character's best friend in all four films, all of which were directed by Yasuki Chiba, a prolific veteran who had directed his first feature in 1930 and would work with Nakadai on other occasions. Although it was not a terribly interesting part, he received a good review for his performance and came to the attention of director Mikio Naruse via producer Sanezumi Fujimoto. As a result, he was offered a part in Naruse's next film. Nakadai had grown up watching the films of Mikio Naruse, so he accepted eagerly.

Untamed (Arakure) was Naruse's version of the classic 1915 novel of the same name by Shusei Tokuda, translated into English as *Rough Living*. Another Toho production, it was the most notable film in which Nakadai appeared before becoming known. The film starred Hideko Takamine as Oshima, a young woman whose feisty character and refusal to play the meek and obedient Japanese wife sees her go through a series of disastrous marriages before she finally takes control of her own destiny. Nakadai had a few minutes of screen time towards the end of the film as Shinkichi, a handsome young tailor who works in the shop she owns with the last of her husbands, the lazy and unfaithful Onoda (played by *Oban* star Daisuke Kato). Oshima decides to leave him and set up a new shop with Shinkichi, with whom it is implied she will have more than a mere business relationship.

Naruse (b. 1905) had begun his directing career in 1930 and was one of Japan's top filmmakers. By the time Nakadai worked with him, he already had around 60 features under his belt and had won a number of domestic film awards. Most of his films were serious contemporary dramas concerned with the struggles of ordinary women. Naruse must have been pleased with Nakadai's work as he went on to cast him in larger parts in a further four films.

Nakadai had also been watching the films of Hideko Takamine for most of his life. Takamine was eight years his senior, and a rare case of a child star who had made a smooth transition to adult stardom. Her first film was made in 1929, when she was just five years old, and she had already made over 150 pictures at this point. She had also appeared in several films on which a young Akira Kurosawa served as assistant director, culminating in *Horse* (Uma, 1941), credited to Kajiro Yamamoto, but said to have been largely Kurosawa's work. Legend has it that Kurosawa, 14 years her senior, fell in love with Takamine but his feelings were not reciprocated. This would certainly explain why Kurosawa never again worked with the woman who became Japan's top film actress of the '50s and early '60s.[10] In her younger days, Takamine had projected an image of cheerful optimism, but bitterness bubbled away beneath the surface, and the disillusioned characters she played for Naruse and others better reflected her true personality. Her mother had died when she was 4, and her father sent her to live with an aunt who pushed her into child stardom. Takamine's education was neglected as a result and she had to teach herself to read. In a 1983 interview for the *New York Times*, she said of her acting career, 'Every day I hated it. For 50 years, I hated it but a sense of professional pride drove me on.' Nakadai admired her greatly and was understandably nervous about working with such a high-profile star who was also a consummate professional and superb actress. Takamine was critical of theatre actors moonlighting in films and showed little patience when Nakadai made a mistake or was unsure of himself. Nevertheless, Nakadai was careful to treat her with great deference and he survived the experience to make a further five films with her. She must also

---

[10] As Takamine went freelance in 1950, the two could certainly have worked together if they had wished.

have taken a liking to him eventually as, before he travelled abroad for the first time (to France), she gave him advice from her own experience as well as a farewell gift. Nakadai would later credit Takamine with teaching him many useful things about film acting.

Untamed is well-made and acted, especially by Takamine, but is not quite Naruse at his best. At two hours, the film feels long, and the dialogue-heavy script by the director's regular collaborator Yoko Mizuki means that its literary origins are all too obvious.

Nakadai returned to Haiyuza to play Valère, the young romantic lead, in a version of Molière's *Tartuffe* with Koreya Senda in the title role, and then, for Tokyo Eiga Productions (later Toei), appeared in *Daughter of Shadow* (Hikage no musume), a drama which reteamed Kyoko Kagawa and Isuzu Yamada from the previous year's *Shozo, a Cat and Two Women* (Neko to Shozo to futari no onna). Kagawa played the abandoned daughter of a geisha who stays with her aunt (Yamada) in another geisha establishment but wants to escape the geisha life. Hoping to find a man she can trust, she begins to lose hope until she meets a sincere student (Nakadai). The film was based on a novel and directed by Shue Matsubayashi, who had previously offered Nakadai his first major film role in *The Human Torpedo*. Matsubayashi was a former Imperial Navy officer who subsequently had a long but largely undistinguished career as a film director. Screenwriter Kaneto Shindo, on the other hand, would go on to be internationally known as both a writer and director for his superb film *Onibaba*, among others.

By this time, Nakadai had been seeing Yasuko Miyazaki for around two years, and she was still living at home with her family in Hatsudai, a district of Shibuya. After the tuberculosis scare had passed, the prospects for them marrying remained uncertain due to the low status of Nakadai's family, his limited education and dubious career. Yasuko, unsure her parents would approve of the match, had been considering marrying Nakadai without their consent if necessary. However, she preferred to avoid this if possible, so she had encouraged him to visit her family often in the hope they would come to accept him. Nakadai was only too happy to do so as he had very little money in the early stages of their relationship and it usually meant a free meal courtesy of Yasuko's mother, Tomoe, an excellent cook. He also enjoyed the opportunity to experience the sort of warm family atmosphere he himself had missed out on as a child due to his father's illness and early death.

Nakadai and Yasuko

Yasuko's father, Ryuzo, was a judge-turned-lawyer and a man of few words. Nakadai had initially found him intimidating, but this was balanced somewhat by the presence of her more cheerful younger sister, Fusako (b.1944). Nakadai visited so frequently that he began to feel guilty about consuming so much of their food, but when he had been absent, Tomoe would look worried and ask why he had not joined them, so it seemed that Yasuko's plan was working. At the end of each meal, Yasuko's father would go to his upstairs study and the others would relax and begin to chat freely. Nakadai would usually leave at 10 or 11 p.m., but if he forgot the time, Mr Miyazaki would come back down to give him a hint that it was time to go home.

One day, Mr Miyazaki finally asked his daughter if she was planning to marry Nakadai. Yasuko said she was thinking about it, but her father did not respond. However, the following day, he discussed it with his wife, saying that he felt Nakadai was not foolish and spoke his mind, which he approved of. Tomoe passed this on to Yasuko, who in turn told Nakadai. Emboldened, the young couple decided it was time for Nakadai to speak to her father properly about the marriage. However, nerves got the better of him on his first two attempts, leaving him unable to get the words out, much to the amusement of the females in the family. When he finally managed to say he wanted to marry Yasuko, Mr Miyazaki again said nothing in response and just went off to his room as he usually did. Tomoe told Nakadai not to worry, and he eventually obtained permission to marry Yasuko, which he did on 22 April, 1957 with 47 guests in attendance. An evening cocktail reception followed, with the guest list expanded to 200. As the couple had little money at the time, the guests had to pay a fee to attend. Afterwards, the couple went on a modest honeymoon, taking the train to Atami in Shizuoka prefecture, where they spent one night at an inn. The following day, they travelled further south by car to the coastal city of Ise in Mie prefecture, staying a further two nights before returning to Tokyo.

The couple moved into a modest second-floor apartment a few minutes' walk away from Nakadai's in-laws' house. Yasuko's father had insisted on keeping her room unchanged in case the marriage failed and she wanted to return, but fortunately this proved unnecessary. She decided to give up acting after she was married, despite Nakadai's best efforts to persuade her otherwise. Aside from the film version of *The Living Forest*, she had only appeared in a couple of other pictures. The first of these, Heinosuke Gosho's *Dispersed Clouds* (Wakare-gumo), had been made as early as 1951. A well-reviewed film by one of Japan's most respected directors of the day, it concerned a moody and self-centred Tokyo student, Masako (played by another newcomer, Keiko

Sawamura), who joins some female student friends on an extended trip into the countryside only to fall ill at the first stop. Forced to stay behind in an unfamiliar town, she encounters some selfless people who influence her for the better and becomes a completely changed person. Yasuko played one of Masako's more cheerful friends, giving an entirely natural performance, but was only featured in the early scenes. In 1953, she had also appeared in a supporting role in the Haiyuza-produced film *Loneliness in the Square* (Hiroba no kodoku) based on a prize-winning novel by Yoshie Hotta. Distributed by Shintoho, it was directed by star Shin Saburi and concerned a journalist reporting on the Korean War.

Yasuko had fared better in television, but now that her husband was getting a decent number of film roles, she decided that the best role for her was to support him as a housewife, allowing him to devote all his energy into his budding career. Nakadai was also doing bits of live television drama himself around this time. This format, also common in Europe and the USA in the late '50s and early '60s, not only meant there was no possibility of shooting a scene again if an error was made, but provided minimal opportunities for preparation due to tight schedules and budgets, causing many a sleepless night for an actor as a result. Nakadai later recalled an incident during a scene set in a kitchen with Junzaburo Ban.[11] Unbeknownst to him, Ban had written some of his lines onto a piece of Chinese cabbage, which Nakadai inadvertently threw into a pot of boiling water, much to Ban's chagrin. Nakadai had his own strategy in case he 'dried' on live television – if he forgot the words, he would simply continue moving his mouth so that the viewer would blame the fault on a technical problem instead.

Nakadai returned to Toho for the kidnap drama *A Dangerous Hero* (Kiken na eiyu), directed by veteran Hideo Suzuki and starring Shintaro Ishihara, a writer of fiction who had a brief career as a film star during

---

[11] Ban (1908-81) was a well-known comic actor who later played Yukichi Shima, the man who becomes violent in defence of his uncouth wife in Kurosawa's *Dodes'ka-den*.

this period. Ishihara had won the coveted Akutagawa Prize for his story *Season of the Sun*, but it was a controversial choice and his books were regarded by many as substandard, rather sordid literature. He subsequently became a right-wing politician and was elected Governor of Tokyo many years later. *Season of the Sun* (Taiyo no kisetsu) and another Ishihara story, *Crazed Fruit* (Kurutta kajitsu), had been rapidly snapped up and filmed by Nikkatsu Studios in 1956, while Kon Ichikawa had filmed yet another, *Punishment Room* (Shokei no heya), the same year for Daei. Being the first Japanese films to feature teenage delinquents as their main characters, they proved highly controversial, but also tremendously successful at the box office. Inspiring a vogue for films about amoral, hedonistic young men which became known as 'sun tribe' movies, they were in many ways the equivalent of American films of the time such as *The Wild One* and *Rebel without a Cause*. Nakadai, despite being an ideal actor for the genre, did not appear in any sun tribe films.

One of Ishihara's conditions in selling the rights to *Crazed Fruit* had been that his brother, Yujiro Ishihara, must play the lead role, which he did, rapidly becoming one of Japanese cinema's biggest stars as a result. Nakadai had in fact shared a dressing room with him when they were both starting out; *Crazed Fruit* was made at Nikkatsu, where Nakadai was appearing in *Firebird* at the same time. However, Shintaro Ishihara's own career as a film actor was much less successful, and *A Dangerous Hero* was the third and final film in which he played a leading role. In *A Dangerous Hero*, when the son of a wealthy businessman is kidnapped on his way to school, the boy's older sister (Yoko Tsukasa) receives a message demanding that one million yen be delivered at Shibuya station by the following morning. She decides to go to the police and tells an inspector (Takashi Shimura) what has happened. Their conversation is overheard by a reporter, Imamura (Nakadai), who subsequently goes to the inspector for further information, but is persuaded to delay publication of the story for the child's safety. Unfortunately, their conversation is overheard by Fuyuki, a less scrupulous tabloid journalist (Ishihara), who throws a spanner in the works by publishing the story in his paper's evening edition.

Eitaro Ozawa appeared as Fuyuki's boss, while the kidnapper was played by Seiji Miyaguchi, and Toshiro Mifune popped up in a guest part as a professional baseball player who makes a televised appeal to the kidnapper to release the boy. Unfortunately, the bizarre nature of this cameo apparently provoked laughter from the audience, and Ishihara's performance was also poorly received, explaining the abrupt end to his acting career, with the exception of a few cameos in films such as Masahiro Shinoda's *Samurai Spy* (1965).

Nakadai was next featured in *Skin-Coloured Moon* (Hadairo no tsuki), an ironic thriller based on a novel by Juran Hisao. The film starred Nobuko Otowa, considered by many to be one of Japan's greatest actresses. Best-known in the West as the older of the two women in Kaneto Shindo's *Onibaba* (1964), she was in fact Shindo's long-term mistress before they finally married after the death of his wife in the late '70s. Otowa played a television actress who, after losing a major part and having her heart broken by a playboy (Nakadai), decides to commit suicide. She drives to Izu and checks into a lakeside inn under an assumed name with the intention of drowning herself. However, when a fellow guest (Koreya Senda) apparently dies, she finds herself accused of murder before she can go through with it. The film was directed by Toshio Sugie, who had been chief assistant director on Kurosawa's debut film, *Sanshiro Sugata*, in 1943 and went on to direct over 50 films himself, but remained a journeyman.

After these appearances in more than a dozen movies, it was Nakadai's next film which finally put him on the map and began the most important collaborative association of his career.

Chapter 4 – Black River, Golden Temple

Masaki Kobayashi (b. 1916) graduated from Waseda University with a degree in Oriental Art and begun working as an assistant director at Shochiku studios in 1941. This fledgling career was interrupted almost immediately when Japan entered the Second World War and he was conscripted, serving first in Manchuria before being sent to defend Okinawa. If Kobayashi had reached Okinawa, he would almost certainly have died there as the Japanese forces stationed on the island were wiped out by the Americans in the Battle of Okinawa. However, Kobayashi survived due to a quirk of fate when his ship was diverted to another island, Miyakojima, en route. Miyakojima saw no such battle, and Kobayashi spent the rest of the war there helping to build an airfield. Nevertheless, the lack of control he had felt over his own life and the things he had seen and experienced during the war left a deep impression. One result of this was a deep-seated mistrust of authority and a refusal to bow before it which was especially unusual in Japan. His lack of enthusiasm for the war meant that he never rose above the rank of private despite the fact that university graduates were encouraged to apply for officer training.

When the conflict ended, the Allies had kept Kobayashi in a prisoner-of-war camp on Okinawa for a year before finally sending him back to mainland Japan. He had then rejoined Shochiku and worked as an apprentice under director Keisuke Kinoshita before directing his first film in 1952. As early as 1953, he had courted controversy with *The Thick-Walled Room* (Kabe atsuki heya), from a screenplay by Kobo Abe which dealt with the sensitive topic of Japanese prisoners awaiting trial for war crimes. The film made the studio bosses nervous, and they initially refused to release it before finally relenting three years later. Kobayashi had played it safe for the remainder of his early films, making romantic dramas in the Kinoshita vein until 1956, when he made a film about corruption in the world of baseball entitled *I Will Buy You* (Anata kaimasu). When *The Thick-Walled Room* was released the same year, it won the Japan Cultural Council's Peace Culture Award and Kobayashi was by then in a position to make the kind of films he wanted.

A year and a half earlier, Nakadai had auditioned unsuccessfully for a supporting role in a Kobayashi film entitled *Fountainhead* (Izumi).[12] Now, much to the actor's surprise, Kobayashi called him back to test for the leading role of a poor student, Nishida, in his new film, *Black River* (Kuroi kawa). However, during the rehearsal process, Kobayashi changed his mind and decided that Nakadai would be more effective as the film's villain, a young *yakuza* known as Killer Joe. But one problem remained. Nakadai had committed to a minor role in a play called *Bright Lady* (Rikona o-yomesan) for Haiyuza, and the shooting schedule of *Black River* overlapped by ten days. Nakadai was ready to give up the film so as not to let his colleagues down, but fortunately a senior Haiyuza actor, Eijiro Tono, stepped in to help. Tono had been cast in a smaller role in *Black River* and would not be needed as much, so he suggested filling in for Nakadai in the play for ten days, a suggestion which satisfied everyone.[13] The role of the student in the film was taken by Fumio Watanabe. Kobayashi's change of heart worked out very well for Nakadai, as the part of Joe was the flashier of the two and he would end up receiving far more attention for his performance than Watanabe would for his.[14] The director later said that it was Nakadai's eyes which had first made an impression on him.

Black River is a very well-made but not entirely successful mixture of neo-realism and melodrama. Nishida is a student who moves into a slum to save money. The building is little more than a huge shack and is falling apart. Most of the other tenants are pimps and prostitutes whose main source of income is the American soldiers stationed at a

---

[12] Nakadai's potential part must have been as one of the two young war veterans engaged in a feud (played in the film by Fumio Watanabe and Ryohei Uchida).
[13] Nakadai did not appear in Masaki Kobayashi's *The Thick-Walled Room*, nor did Kobayashi discover Nakadai while the latter was working as a clerk in a department store, as some sources state.
[14] Fumio Watanabe also went on to have a successful film career and became a notable associate of director Nagisa Oshima.

nearby air base. When Nishida is transporting a cartload of books in the street, a few fall off and a passing waitress, Shizuko (Ineko Arima), picks them up for him. Apparently, this is all it takes for the two to fall in love. However, a young *yakuza* gang leader known as Killer Joe has also taken a fancy to Shizuko. For him, she embodies purity and is a contrast to the women he usually associates with. He arranges for her to be abducted by his cronies, who bundle her into a car and drive her to a quiet spot. Shizuko believes she is about to be gang-raped when Joe turns up and stages a fake rescue. The rest of the gang flee and, when she does not immediately fall into his arms in gratitude, Joe rapes her himself. The following day, Shizuko, who has rather traditional ideas, visits Joe and says she wants him to marry her. He laughs but swears that he loves her and makes her his 'girl'. When Nishida becomes aware of Shizuko's relationship with Joe, he is consumed by jealousy. Meanwhile, Joe has been paid by the landlady to strongarm her tenants – including Nishida – out of her property so she can sell the land to a speculator who wants to build a love hotel there.

Although it seems as if Nishida will be the main protagonist at the beginning, the character of Joe comes to dominate the film, just as he dominates all of those around him. When Nakadai is playing introspective characters, he often directs his gaze away from those with whom he is sharing a dialogue. However, in *Black River*, he looks directly at those he is talking to, which fits the character as Joe is mostly concerned with the effect he has on others and whether they are doing what he wants – there is nothing introspective about him.

Nakadai cut a memorable figure in the role, chewing on a matchstick and wearing shades, a Hawaiian shirt and a white suit, with the jacket draped carelessly over his shoulders. Although Joe is a nasty piece of work concerned exclusively with his own gratification, he genuinely seems to believe that he loves Shizuko. This gives him a little more depth than the average *yakuza*, but the fact that he terrorizes, rapes and beats her makes it impossible to feel any sympathy for him, and his comeuppance, when it finally arrives, feels long overdue.

It was a smart move on Kobayashi's part to cast Nakadai in such a role as his good looks somehow have the effect of magnifying the character's cruelty. As Nishida, Watanabe has the more difficult part as a not-very-heroic hero. The fact that he wears exactly the same kind of floppy hat which was a trademark of the director's suggests that he is perhaps a Kobayashi substitute in some way, although the director has no writing credit on *Black River* – the screenplay (from a story by Takeo Tomishima) was by his regular collaborator, Zenzo Matsuyama, who had married Hideko Takamine in 1955.

As Shizuko, the versatile Ineko Arima handles the many emotional changes of her character with apparent ease. Arima was actually one of the film's producers. Signed by Toho as a 'new face' in 1951, in 1954 she founded the production company Ninjin Club with fellow actresses Yoshiko Kuga and Keiko Kishi. All three were popular stars as well as genuine talents with whom the top directors were keen to work. Arima left Toho in 1955 and transferred to Shochiku, where Kishi was under contract. Shochiku agreed to help finance *Black River* and loan studio facilities in return for distribution rights. [15]

In one scene, Nakadai had to slap Arima several times in the face, and Kobayashi instructed him to do it for real. This approach was far more common in Japanese cinema at the time than in American films, in which slaps were almost always faked. Arima's face swelled up, but she endured it without complaint. However, the following day, the head of Shochiku, Shiro Kido, gave Nakadai a severe reprimand, demanding to know what he had done to one of their best actresses and what he was going to do about it.

---

[15] *Black River* was the second film produced by Ninjin Club, the first having been Miyoji Ieki's *From Heart to Heart* (Mune yori mune ni) in 1955.

With Ineko Arima in *Black River* (screenshot).

Despite the title, there is no river in the film – rather, the title stands as a metaphor for something pure that has been polluted. Kobayashi shows how the American occupation of Japan led to lawlessness and vice, although his Japanese characters are not necessarily innocent victims, and many are all too complicit. The air base in the film is Atsugi Naval Air Facility, located in Kanagawa Prefecture and built in 1938. After Japan surrendered, General Douglas MacArthur landed at Atsugi – an event captured by newsreel photographers and seen around the world. The Americans subsequently took control of the base and later stationed pilots there during the Korean War. The U.S. Navy continues to operate at Atsugi at the time of writing, together with the Japan Maritime Self-Defence Force.

The blaring jazz score, high-contrast cinematography and use of real locations evokes American films of the period, while the milieu of the tumbledown apartment building featured in the film is similar to the one in Kurosawa's version of Maxim Gorky's *The Lower Depths*, released in Japan just three weeks before *Black River*. The landlady – a grotesque money-grubber with bad teeth – is portrayed by Isuzu Yamada, who had played the equally unpleasant landlady in Kurosawa's film. Nakadai had made two previous films with her and later said that she taught him the importance of learning the lines of his co-stars even before learning his own in order to respond naturally.

Although *Black River* is surprisingly misanthropic for its time, the motivations and actions of the characters do not always convince, and the love triangle plot sometimes sits uncomfortably alongside the social criticism of the eviction story. For these reasons, the film is not quite on a par with the run of Kobayashi masterpieces which were to follow and which would also prominently feature Nakadai. However, it was well-received by critics and public alike, and Nakadai made a significant impression on both for the first time.

After making *Black River*, Nakadai at first returned to more routine assignments, co-starring with Kyoko Kagawa in *Cheers! Arranged Marriage* (Kampai! Miai kekkon), a 46-minute Tokyo Eiga B-movie. Nakadai played a groom having second thoughts on the eve of his wedding as he gets drunk on highballs and reminisces about an old flame (Setsuko Wakayama), while the bride (Kagawa) has doubts of her own after realising that her friends all married for love. One of the friends was played by Yasuko, making it the only film in which both she and Nakadai appeared.

This was followed by a supporting role for Toho in *A Boy and Three Mothers* (Haha sannin), which featured Michio Aratama as Kazuko, a young single mother. The father, Seiji (Frankie Sakai), has abandoned her and is now living with Keiko (Minoru Chigure), who runs a bar. As Kazuko has to work as a maid at an *onsen* (hot spring inn) in Izu, she is unable to care for the child herself, so 'Mami' Natsu (Isuzu Yamada) looks after the young boy at her teahouse. Meanwhile, Kazuko falls in love with Kensaku (Nakadai), a road construction engineer who has to relocate to Osaka for his work and wants to marry Kazuko and take her with him. Seiji then reappears in her life, saying that he wants to raise his son in Tokyo with the help of Keiko. Kazuko begins to think that a Tokyo education might be better for the boy; however, the protective Natsu has no intention of giving him up so easily.

A Boy and Three Mothers

Next was *The Gion Tempest* (Yoru no hamon/'Night Ripples') for Shochiku Kyoto. Set against the backdrop of the annual Miyako Odori cherry blossom dance festival in the Gion district of Kyoto, it starred Hizuru Takachiho as Kyoko, an ambitious young geisha striving to play a leading role in the dance. Nakadai appeared as a civil servant who pays Kyoko for sex with stolen money and is later arrested for embezzlement. The film was directed and co-written by Seiichiro Uchikawa, who had worked as an assistant director under Kon Ichikawa, Yasujiro Ozu and Kenji Mizoguchi, but been fired by the latter after a disagreement during the making of *The Life of Oharu*. Nevertheless, he had been promoted to director the following year and would go on to make a total of 34 feature films. A modest success with *Samurai from Nowhere* (Dojo yaburi, 1964), based on a story by Shugoro Yamamoto, seems to have brought him to the attention of Akira Kurosawa, who was producing a remake of his own debut film, *Sanshiro Sugata*, and hired Uchikawa to direct. However, the film met with hostile reviews which put the blame on Uchikawa and effectively ended his film career – it would be four years before he made another film, and he was reduced to making a vehicle for a boy band known as The Tempters (featuring a future co-star of Nakadai's, Kenichi Hagiwara). Kurosawa later scripted a remake of *Samurai from Nowhere* under the title *After the Rain* (Ame agaru). Directed by Takashi Koizumi after Kurosawa's death, it featured a brief cameo from Nakadai.

Nakadai then appeared in *All about Marriage* (Kekkon no subete), a romantic comedy notable as the first film by director Kihachi Okamoto, then aged 35, and Nakadai's senior by nine years. Okamoto and Nakadai had already known each other for nearly two years at this point as Okamoto had been assistant director on *Barefoot Youth*, during the shooting of which the two had become good friends. Although Nakadai's part in *All about Marriage* was a minor one, the two would go on to forge a fruitful collaborative partnership. Nakadai later recalled:

> Okamoto was 'the Buddha.' He was a very kind man. I met him before I was famous, when I was still a starving actor. Every night I'd visit him at his house and drink. There'd be about 20 people there. He took care of young people in the industry and of his protégés.[16]

---

[16] From the interview 'Tatsuya Nakadai on Five Japanese Masters', © 2017 The Criterion Collection

All about Marriage

All about Marriage featured Michiyo Aratama and Izumi Yukimura as sisters with different attitudes to marriage – the former has a typical arranged marriage to a rather boring associate professor (Ken Uehara), while the latter wants a marriage that is passionate and exciting and gets engaged to a young businessman (Nakadai). As a studio assignment, Okamoto's debut film was remarkable for its style rather than its content, but it was well-received and he would go on to become one of Japanese cinema's most idiosyncratic auteurs. The film also featured Reiko Dan as a 'bad girl' and an uncredited guest appearance from

Toshiro Mifune as an acting teacher, both of whom Nakadai would later co-star with on a number of occasions.

As Nakadai's film work increased, his stage appearances became less frequent and, in 1958, he appeared in just one play at Haiyuza, the Swedish playwright August Strindberg's class-themed drama from 1888, *Miss Julie*. However, Nakadai played the male lead for the first time on stage, and all of his subsequent roles for Haiyuza would be leads. He was cast as Jean, a servant who allows himself to be seduced by his mistress, compromising both their positions and turning their world upside down as a result. During this period, he also played his first leading role for television as Tadanao Matsudaira (1595-1650) in the Nippon Television (NTV) series *Lord Tadanao's Travel Diary* (Tadanao kyo gyojoki). Matsudaira became a powerful *daimyo*[17] at the age of 12, later taking part in military campaigns as an adult with mixed success. Feeling that his exploits had not been sufficiently rewarded by his seniors, he began to behave badly and was banished to an obscure domain where he became a Buddhist priest and lived out his life in peace. Matsudaira was later portrayed by Raizo Ichikawa in a 1960 film of the same title.

Nakadai also had a short-lived second career as a pop singer at this time, and released three singles on the Nara-based Teichiku label during 1958. One of these, 'Ginza Rock' (Ginza rokkun), features a photo on the label with Nakadai sporting a half-hearted quiff but, for a supposed rock 'n' roll song, it manages to sound surprisingly square. Another song, 'Goodbye Tokyo Lights' (Tokyo no akari yo sayonara), was a jazz ballad with a slower tempo. It seems doubtful that he might have had any future as a Japanese Elvis as his voice, though by no means terrible, was not quite at the standard of a professional singer.

Further routine film assignments followed, including *Go and Get It* (Buttsuke honban/'Action without Preparation'), a movie about a newsreel photographer, played by the popular comedian, actor and musician Frankie Sankai in one of his more serious roles – it ends

---

[17] *Daimyo* were feudal lords who owned large amounts of land.

tragically with his character squashed by a train he failed to see coming while preoccupied with getting a good shot. Apparently based on the life of a real person by the name of Hisaya Matsui, it also featured Keiko Awaji as the wife, while Nakadai played Sakai's assistant. The film is perhaps notable as one of the few motion pictures to feature a newsreel cameraman as the protagonist, while Japanese reviewers have praised the location work, saying it provides a valuable picture of postwar Japan. Although director Kozo Saeki made 110 films between 1937 and 1967, he has remained entirely unknown abroad.

With Frankie Sakai in *Go and Get It*.

Next was a repeat of Nakadai's recurring part in the fourth and final *Oban* film, followed by a minor role in *Diary of an Elegant Hot Spring* (Furyu onsen nikki), in which the lives of the staff at a hot spring resort are affected by a variety of guests, including newlyweds, adulterous couples, a fraudster, and Nakadai's character, who checks in with the intention of committing suicide. Also featuring Reiko Dan, Daisuke Kato and Ken Uehara, it was Nakadai's second and final film for director Shue Matsubayashi.

Diary of an Elegant Hot Spring

After these unremarkable roles, the *Black River* effect finally kicked in and Nakadai was approached by director Kon Ichikawa to play a major part in an important film, an adaptation of Yukio Mishima's novel *The Temple of the Golden Pavilion*, to be filmed under the title *Conflagration* (Enjo).

Due largely to the recent international success of his 1956 film *The Burmese Harp* (Biruma no tategoto), Ichikawa (b.1915) had by this time become one of Japan's top directors. When *Conflagration* went into production at Daiei, Ichikawa was 43 and, like Masaki Kobayashi and

Kihachi Okamoto, was another hat-wearing chain-smoker. One of Japan's most prolific filmmakers, he had already made around 35 feature films at this stage in his career, many of which had been literary adaptations co-written with his wife, Natto Wada.

Yukio Mishima had been a literary superstar in Japan for some years at this point, and had already begun to receive attention abroad. His novel had originally been published under the title *Kinkaku-ji*, the Japanese name for the Golden Temple. Mishima had based it on a real incident that occurred in 1950 in which a mentally-unbalanced young monk training to become a priest deliberately burned down a 500-year-old temple regarded as a national treasure.[18] Believing that it would not be possible to do justice to the novel, Ichikawa initially turned down Daiei producer Hiroaki Fuji's request to direct the film version, but changed his mind three months later, having decided that the project posed an interesting challenge. Nevertheless, it was far from plain sailing even once Ichikawa was on board, and the film was nearly cancelled when the priests of Kinkaku-ji objected to it being made at all. A compromise was reached when Ichikawa agreed not to use the name of the temple in the title and to refer to it under another name (Ginkaku-ji) in the film. He was also forbidden to film the real temple. Ichikawa then decided to focus on the trainee monk's troubled relationships with his mother, teacher and best friend rather than the more abstract themes related to beauty and its destruction which are the focus of the novel. Mishima, an avid cinemagoer, co-operated with Ichikawa and visited the studio during shooting but allowed the director complete freedom. Nakadai later recalled that, 'He often came to the shooting of *Enjo*, to drink or dine with Ichikawa and the crew. I remember how careful he was not to tremble while holding his cup of

---

[18] Yoken Hayashi, the monk responsible, attempted suicide with poison but failed and was sentenced to seven years in prison. He was released due to illness in 1955 (the year the temple was rebuilt) and died of tuberculosis the following year.

saké! Yet he was very simple, natural, full of gaiety, never showing himself as intellectually superior.'[19]

For the leading role of Mizoguchi, the stammering arsonist, Ichikawa originally intended to cast Hiroshi Kawaguchi, the star of his 1956 film *Punishment Room* and Yasuzo Masumura's *Kisses* (Kuchizuke, 1957), but was forced to reconsider when Daiei president Masaichi Nagata would not allow it (for unknown reasons). Ichikawa then made a surprising choice and cast former kabuki actor Raizo Ichikawa (no relation), known for his good looks and skill in choreographed swordfighting. Again, the director had to fight off objections from several quarters, but had his way on this occasion as Raizo Ichikawa was not only keen to accept his first contemporary role, but was also a star with some clout. Kon Ichikawa's instincts proved to be correct, and his star's performance went on to be widely-acclaimed, while his casting of Ganjiro Nakamura as the head priest, and Nakadai as Mizoguchi's crippled friend were also excellent choices.

Not every aspect of the film is successful, however. In attempting to stick as closely to the dramatic events in the book as the censors would allow, Ichikawa badly fudged one key scene. In the novel, an American GI visiting the temple has an argument with his drunk Japanese girlfriend, who is pregnant. He knocks her down and then bullies Mizoguchi into treading on the woman's stomach in an attempt to abort the baby, a task which the young man perversely enjoys. Such a scene would not have been acceptable in a film at this time. Ichikawa's solution was to have Mizoguchi accidentally push the woman to the ground when she tries to enter the Golden Temple without permission. Ludicrously, this in itself is enough to convince the GI that the baby has been aborted. Not only is this implausible but, by making the action accidental, the point of the scene is completely lost. Another key scene in the novel featuring a woman who squirts milk

---

[19] From an interview with Max Tessier for *Cinemaya* magazine, 1993. Translated from the original French by Aruna Vasudev.

from her breast into her soldier husband's green tea had to be omitted completely.[20]

Otherwise, the film is highly effective. Apart from the perfect casting, it also benefits from the subtly unsettling music score of Toshiro Mayuzumi and the black-and-white widescreen cinematography of Kazuo Miyagawa. (Widescreen became standard in Japanese films at this time, and virtually every film Nakadai made from this point on until the early '70s was shot in this format.) Ichikawa admired Miyagawa's work on Kenji Mizoguchi's *Ugetsu Monogatari* (1953) and resisted studio pressure to film in colour in order to capture both the gold of the temple and the flames in the fiery climax, which he felt would have looked 'cheap' shot in such a way.

Conflagration was the first film that Nakadai made in Kyoto, much of it being shot at the Kyoto branch of Daiei studios. In contrast to the smarter modern studios in Tokyo, the atmosphere at the Kyoto studio was far more old-fashioned and traditional, and Nakadai found this intimidating at first. He also came in for some criticism from Ichikawa who, like Kurosawa and Kobayashi, was known for seldom giving his actors an easy ride. On one occasion, Nakadai was reprimanded when the director caught him checking his script, which he was expected to have learnt fully in advance. Ichikawa also took issue with Nakadai's walk. Despite the fact that the actor had researched how people with his character's disability walked and copied it faithfully, Ichikawa wanted something far more pronounced, and instructed him to walk like someone who had a leg missing below the knee. Ichikawa even encouraged Nakadai to use bad language, and laughed at his efforts to do so, saying in front of everyone that he should not be taking the money if he could not perform properly. However, Nakadai soon realised that he was merely being teased and took no offence, while

---

[20] It is interesting to compare Ichikawa's film with Yoichi Takabayashi's 1976 adaptation, which lacks the stellar cast of the earlier version, but faithfully replicates both of these key scenes.

Ichikawa must have been pleased with the final result as he would go on to cast Nakadai in a further five films.

If Nakadai felt intimidated by Ichikawa at first, he had a much better experience with Raizo Ichikawa, with whom he became good friends. The two often went drinking together and enjoyed discussing their contrasting acting backgrounds. However, as Ichikawa was under contract to Daiei and Nakadai (despite being freelance) was mostly employed by Toho, *Conflagration* would be their only film together.

As the supremely cynical and misanthropic Kashiwagi, Nakadai had a plum role and made the most of it. First appearing around 40 minutes in, he immediately makes an impression with his very un-Japanese lack of social niceties, brusque manner and mirthless laugh ('Hah!'). His final scene is also his best one, in which he veers from apologetic friend to sneering bully before finally exploding in a burst of almost hysterical self-pity, all within the space of a few minutes. It is a tribute to Nakadai's acting skills that, despite his good looks, he manages to make himself quite repulsive here.

The film was praised by Mishima despite its departures from his novel, and reputedly remained Kon Ichikawa's favourite of his own works. Meanwhile, Raizo Ichikawa and Yukio Mishima had formed their own mutual admiration society. One thing both men had in common was a sense of insecurity about their frail bodies, which led them to push themselves physically in an effort to become stronger. In the case of Mishima, he became a fully-fledged body-builder but, like Ichikawa, was able to do little to improve his weak legs. The actor subsequently planned to star in a film version of another Mishima novel, *Frolic of the Beasts* (Kemono no tawamure), but dropped out when the director, Yuzo Kawashima, unexpectedly passed away in 1963, although the film was made without him by director Sokichi Tomimoto. The following year, Ichikawa starred in Kenji Misumi's *Sword* (Ken), based on a short story by Mishima, in which he played the top student at a kendo training school whose puritanical attitude isnpires the hatred of a rival. In 1969, he was planning to appear in a stage version of the author's *Spring Snow* (Haru no yuki), but it was not to be – the actor died the same year at the age of 37 from rectal cancer. He had starred in over 150 films, an astonishing number in the 15 years since his debut.

Conflagration won a number of awards, including for its two main actors, although Nakadai was not nominated, perhaps because Raizo Ichikawa received the lion's share of the attention for having succeeded so well in a part many had thought him unsuited to. However, Nakadai also gained good notices for his performance and by now it was clear that he was going places.

Chapter 5 – Kaji

Despite offers of studio contracts, first from Nikkatsu and later from Toho, Nakadai had no wish to abandon the stage and decided to remain freelance, dividing his time between theatre and film work. Signing with a studio would have provided greater financial security, but would also have given Nakadai little freedom in the roles he played and made it difficult to get time off to appear on stage. This strategy proved to be a wise one in the long run and is one of the main reasons why Nakadai was able to play such a wide range of parts and work with so many of Japan's finest directors. It also helped that he was not egotistical by nature and did whatever he was asked without complaint. Although the studios continued their attempts to entice Nakadai with offers of a house or a round-the-world trip for him and his wife (and he often witnessed how stars with a contract received preferential treatment), he held his ground and remained a freelancer for his entire career. Having said that, so much of his work ended up being at Toho that many assumed he was under contract to them.

Nakadai was not a money-motivated person and he enjoyed the contrast between the worlds of theatre and film. As his film parts became larger, he began to find himself staying in private en suite rooms, whereas when touring with Haiyuza, he earned very little and sometimes had to share a hotel room with as many as ten other actors. Most film directors respected his dedication to the theatre and some even postponed their films to accommodate his stage commitments.

During this period, Nakadai found that he was being recognized in the street with increasing frequency and it was becoming awkward for him to use public transport. Despite the expense, he decided to buy a car and, because he had no wish to give up drinking, also hired a driver – something he was at pains to keep secret from his Haiyuza colleagues, most of whom had no such luxuries. When travelling to Haiyuza, he would ensure he was dropped off some distance away so he could arrive on foot.

Nakadai's next film saw him third-billed in a supporting role for Toei in *Naked Sun* (Hadaka no taiyo), from a screenplay by Kaneto Shindo. Director Miyoji Ieki had just made an acclaimed film called *Stepbrothers* (Ibo kyodai), so Nakadai would probably have considered himself fortunate to land a part in Ieki's next picture. The fact that the story dealt with the lives of poor railway workers would certainly have made the subject matter close to Nakadai's heart given his late father's occupation. Shinjiro Ebara and Michiko Hoshi starred as a young couple scrimping and saving in order to get married. Their plans become unravelled when a friend (Nakadai) urgently needs to borrow money to help his ex-sweetheart pay her sick husband's medical bills.

Few of Ieki's films are accessible outside Japan with English subtitles, although *The Wayside Pebble* (Robo no ishi, 1964) certainly deserves to be better known. Dealing with the bitter disappointment felt by a young man who longs to study but is forced by economic circumstance to work as a salesman's apprentice, it features excellent work in every department. *Naked Sun* would be Nakadai's only film for Ieki, but it was entered in competition at the Berlin Film Festival and also received a brief release in the USA.

At the recommendation of Ineko Arima while making *Black River*, Masaki Kobayashi had read the first volumes of *The Human Condition* (Ningen no joken), a six-volume novel by Junpei Gomikawa, based on the author's experiences as a conscripted soldier during the Second World War. Kobayashi identified completely with Kaji, the protagonist, and became determined to film it as his next project. With Arima equally enthusiastic, it became a Ninjin Club production, but Kobayashi was still under contract to Shochiku and had to persuade them to help finance the film in return for the distribution rights. Whereas most film-makers would have attempted to make a single film from the 'highlights', Kobayashi envisioned filming the entire novel in multiple parts. Although the book was gradually becoming a bestseller, Shochiku were wary, partly due to the scale of the project and partly because Gomikawa's unflinching portrayal of the brutality of the Japanese military was bound to be controversial and would make for grim viewing. Kobayashi began to think he should quit and take the project to another studio when Shochiku boss Shiro Kido suddenly relented and gave him the go-ahead.

There was great interest from the public as to who would play Kaji, with every young actor in Japan hungry for the part, and it took Kobayashi a long time to choose his lead. However, he found that it was Nakadai's eyes that he saw when he imagined Kaji's death scene, and that clinched it. This was a bold move on Kobayashi's part, akin to David Lean's casting of the then-unknown Peter O'Toole as the star of *Lawrence of Arabia* a couple of years later. Nakadai was not a popular choice with the studio as his success in *Black River* had been in a very different type of role and *Conflagration* had yet to be released, so he was by no means a star at this point. Shiro Kido wanted the role to go to Keiji Sada, a good (though limited) actor and popular star under contract to Shochiku who had already played the lead in four Kobayashi films. However, Kobayashi felt that Sada was not right for the part. He remained stubborn and once more got his own way. It was not only in Nakadai's case that Kobayashi gave little thought to studio politics. For the female lead, he failed even to consider casting any of the three Ninjin Club founders let alone any other Shochiku contract players, instead insisting on Michiyo Aratama, who was signed with Toho at the time.

As the story of *The Human Condition* was told through the eyes of Kaji, Nakadai would rarely be off-screen, and Kobayashi wanted the film to be as authentic as possible. In preparation for his role, Nakadai visited Junpei Gomikawa at his home on several occasions, and observed that, not only were the author's war experiences similar to those of Kobayashi's, but that the two men were almost exactly the same age and had similar personalities. Nakadai ended up basing much of his performance on his observations of Kobayashi, and this naturally pleased the director, who saw the film as an opportunity to put his own experience on celluloid. Nakadai's preparation also involved military training for a month at Shochiku's Ofuna studios at Kamakura, southwest of Tokyo. Together with the other actors cast as soldiers, he slept at the studio in pyjamas and was woken by a bugle early every morning. The young actors had to change quickly into uniform within three minutes or be slapped in the face by their trainer.

After six months of preparation, there would be six months of shooting for Part I (*No Greater Love*) then six months off while the next part was prepared, followed by six months of shooting for Part II (*The Road to Eternity*), a further six months' preparation, and finally six months of shooting for Part III (*A Soldier's Prayer*). Each part would be around three hours long and divided into two sections with an intermission in between. The six-month breaks between shooting the three parts meant that Nakadai would be free to appear in other films during these periods, and he somehow managed to fit in five or six films in each break, many in leading roles. It may seem difficult to understand today how he could have managed such a feat, but it should be noted that Japanese films generally had a shorter shooting schedule than American ones, while the Japanese crews had a much stronger work ethic. In any case, one thing is for certain – since landing the part of Kaji, Nakadai's career was well and truly launched.

In *No Greater Love* (filmed between 15 August 1958 and late December the same year), Kaji and Michiko (Michiyo Aratama) are a young couple working in the offices of a steel company in Manchuria when war with the USA breaks out. Kaji believes that the best way to get the most out of the Chinese labourers coerced into working for the company is to treat them well. He is given the chance both to test this theory and dodge the draft when offered a position overseeing the workers at a remote mine. At the urging of his best friend, Kageyama (Keiji Sada), who has just been drafted, he accepts the position, marries Michiko and takes her with him. Although Kaji's new boss (Haiyuza's Masao Mishima) is willing to let him try anything if it increases production and gets the army off his back, Kaji quickly discovers that brutal treatment of the Chinese by pit bosses such as Okazaki (Haiyuza's Eitaro Ozawa) is the norm and his ideas are unwelcome, although he finds one colleague (So Yamamura) is sympathetic. However, Kaji's situation quickly becomes untenable when he is suddenly given responsibility for 600 near-dead Chinese 'prisoners of war' who are to supply extra labour. Despite doing everything in his power to treat the prisoners as humanely as possible, he finds them reluctant to trust him due to the harsh treatment they have repeatedly received from the majority of Japanese. When one of the Chinese 'comfort women' kept on site to motivate the workers, Chun Lan (Ineko Arima), falls in love with a prisoner named Kao (Koji Nanbara), he intends to let them marry, but is unable to prevent Kao's execution after an escape attempt. Having confronted the military police in an attempt to stop the executions, Kaji is tortured as a result. After his release, he is immediately drafted into the army but allowed a brief reunion with Michiko. This final scene threatens to become sentimental, but Kobayashi avoids the standard romantic ending by having Kaji's last day with Michiko ruined by the appearance of Chun Lan who, hating him for his failure to prevent the beheading of Kao, throws rocks at him, wishes him dead and calls him a 'Japanese devil.'

The Road to Eternity finds Kaji beginning life as an army private. Unfortunately, his reputation as a trouble-maker and a 'red' have preceded him, so he is given a hard time all round. One of the few friends he makes is Shinjo (Kei Sato), who has been in the army for three years but remained a private as he actually *is* a communist. However, Kaji's abilities as a soldier save him from receiving the harshest treatment. This is reserved for Obara (Kunie Tanaka), the squad's weakling, who is eventually driven to suicide by constant bullying. Kaji's attempts to stand up for Obara cause further trouble for himself. As a result, he is transferred to the front close to the Russian border. This move reunites him with his best friend, Kageyama, now a Second Lieutenant under whom Kaji will serve. Kageyama asks him to take charge of some new recruits in order to spare them the harsh treatment they would receive from the veterans. Kaji agrees and is promoted to Private First Class, but the veterans resent the fact that he has been given the responsibility for training the new men and Kaji once again finds himself in constant battle with the army itself. Kaji and the recruits he has trained are then sent into battle, but there is little they can do to stop the Russian tanks advancing and his squad are almost completely wiped out. One of his men, Onodera (Minoru Chiaki), goes mad with fear and Kaji, trying to keep him quiet to prevent their whereabouts being revealed to the Russians, accidentally kills him.

In *A Soldier's Prayer*, Kaji desperately tries to find a way out of the war zone and back to Michiko. Initially accompanied by a couple of survivors from the tank battle, including the naïve Terada (Keisuke Kinoshita favourite Yusuke Kawazu), he picks up various stragglers along the way, including a prostitute (Kyoko Kishida), who falls for him but is subsequently killed. The party get lost in an immense forest, nearly dying of starvation before they find their way out. Eventually, they arrive at a refugee camp full of women and one old man (Ozu favourite Chishu Ryu). The leader of the women (Hideko Takamine) makes a pass at Kaji, but he rejects her out of a wish to remain faithful to his wife. When Russian soldiers arrive at the camp, Kaji decides to surrender in order to avoid endangering the women. Now a prisoner of war, he and the rest of his group are sent to a labour camp where they are worked hard and given little to eat, while the Japanese officers kowtow to their captors and live well. One of these, Kirihara (Nobuo Kaneko), works Terada to death in Kaji's absence; when Kaji returns, he kills Kirihara in revenge and escapes from the camp despite knowing that his chances of survival are poor. After walking for many miles and begging or stealing food to survive along the way, he finally collapses from the combined effects of cold, hunger and fatigue, dying in the middle of nowhere as a snowstorm slowly covers his body.

Nakadai came of age as a film actor while making *The Human Condition*. He later said it felt as if there had been two directors – the other being cinematographer Yoshio Miyajima, who had also photographed *Naked Sun*. Although Kobayashi later said that he chose Miyajima because he considered him the best cinematographer in Japan, this may not have been the sole reason; Miyajima had also served in Manchuria during the war and, as a communist, had been ideologically opposed to the military in the same way as Kobayashi and

Gomikawa. He had also been head of the Toho Employees' Union during the infamous labour dispute of 1948, when the U.S. military were called in to break the strike and surrounded the studio with tanks. Nakadai credited Miyajima with teaching him the importance of performing in the correct relationship to the camera. As a theatre-trained actor, this was something he initially found quite difficult, especially while making *The Human Condition*, which often featured complicated set-ups, long takes and mobile cameras. Another thing he found challenging was working with so many senior actors, such as So Yamamura, Eitaro Ozawa, Seiji Miyaguchi and Nobuo Nakamura, all of whom were around 20 years older than Nakadai. Not only did he feel inexperienced in relation to these old pros but, even worse, they played mahjong every night, a game which Nakadai had never mastered. Being invited by his seniors, he felt unable to decline, with the result that he lost a great deal of money during the shooting and most of his wages went to pay off his losses.

Nakadai said that, during the making of Part I, the actor he learned the most from was So Yamamura. Born in 1910, Yamamura had begun his career as a stage actor with the Bunkaza theatre company, later branching out into films. His film debut came in 1946, and he quickly found success, appearing in the work of esteemed directors such as Kenji Mizoguchi, Yasujiro Ozu and Mikio Naruse. In 1953, he became a film director himself, going on to make a total of six films. When Nakadai wanted to change one of Kaji's lines from '*So desu na*' to '*So desu ne*' (different inflexions of 'that's right'), Yamamura drew him aside and said that screenwriters spend ages agonising over each line, so he should not try to make changes. Nakadai later said that, throughout the rest of his career, he has always followed his scripts to the letter.

In general, Nakadai enjoyed making Parts II and III more than he had the first part as they provided more opportunities to work with actors of his own age, several of whom he already knew well. He was happy to have the chance to help his old friend Kei Sato when Kobayashi asked him if he could recommend anyone to play a sympathetic fellow soldier in Part II. He telephoned Sato, who was still in his hometown, where he had gone to recover from tuberculosis. By this time, he had a clean bill of health. Sato made his film debut in *The Human Condition* thanks to Nakadai, later going on to enjoy a long and successful film career which included further memorable roles for Kobayashi as well as other major directors such as Nagisa Oshima and Kaneto Shindo. Pleased with Nakadai's recommendation, Kobayashi asked if he could suggest actors for other roles, and Nakadai also became responsible for the casting of Kunie Tanaka, among others. Presumably not wishing to become typecast as weaklings, Tanaka later built himself up physically and went on to play tougher characters. Nakadai, on the other hand, seems to have already improved his physical fitness by the time of shooting Part II and looks noticeably stronger than in Part I. With the other young actors, Nakadai indulged in some heavy drinking sessions after shooting was finished for the day and often found himself acting with a hangover the following morning, but was always careful not to let it to show.

Although the film is set in Japanese-occupied China, filming on location in China was out of the question as there were no diplomatic relations between China and Japan at the time. Kobayashi and cameraman Yoshio Miyajima spent a great deal of time finding locations in Japan which could serve as substitutes for Manchuria. Most of the exteriors were shot on the northern Japanese island of Hokkaido, where the Sarobetsu Plain was especially effective for giving the impression of vast spaces a long way from civilisation. Determined to make the film as true to their memories as possible, Kobayashi and Miyajima even went so far as to delay the shooting of one scene for a week while they waited for the kind of clouds they remembered from their days in Manchuria to appear. Kobayashi's level of perfectionism rivalled Kurosawa's, and he often not only delayed the shoot while waiting for conditions to be right, but would shoot a scene over and over again until it conformed as closely as possible to the vision he saw in his mind. Such an uncompromising attitude made life difficult for cast and crew.

Kobayashi also wanted his characters to speak in Chinese where appropriate, but was unable to hire Chinese actors. Some of the actors chosen, such as Koji Nanbara, had lived in China and spoke the language, while others, including Nakadai, had to learn their Chinese dialogue phonetically.

According to Nakadai, he and Kobayashi were the only two people working on the film not to fall ill or suffer injury at some point. In Nakadai's case, his luck was remarkable as the use of stuntmen or stand-ins was almost unheard of in Japanese cinema at the time and he was often required to perform dangerous acts such as jumping into a foxhole moments before a tank passes over it, or falling into a freezing cold river. When Kaji earns the enmity of the veteran soldiers, he is assaulted repeatedly, and Nakadai had to suffer being slapped many times by his fellow actors with the result that his face became swollen. In another scene, Kaji and his fellow soldiers have to walk through a swamp. The locals warned the crew about the danger of contracting a disease from mites, so the actors wrapped themselves in plastic under their clothes and fortunately nobody caught anything.

For the final scene of the film, when Kaji escapes from the Siberian prison camp, Kobayashi instructed him not to eat for a week so that he could lose six kilos and look suitably undernourished. Nakadai took this literally and ate nothing at all for a week, while continuing to exercise. By the end of the week, he had lost the required amount of weight. Nakadai had this to say about the shooting of this unforgettable ending:

The original novel ended with Kaji collapsing and snow building up on top of him like a small mountain. Kobayashi attempted to capture this. The location of the scene was the Sarabetsu Plain in winter, where strong blizzards were frequent. There was nothing in the field. Before shooting, we made a temporary resting shelter, collected charcoal, brought a burner and waited until the conditions were right and the snow was falling sufficiently. When this happened, I [did the long walk]… and fell down to the ground. Then they filmed until enough snow had built up on top of me. My hands and feet started to become numb and it felt like I really was freezing to death, but I could still hear the camera whirring. I felt I couldn't really cope with the cold anymore, but if I stood up too early they would have to reshoot, so I waited until I heard Kobayashi say 'Cut!' The assistant director rushed over and pulled me out from the snow, stripped my clothes off and warmed me up in front of a fire, while five or six people began to rub my body to warm me up. Someone said, 'Where are the director and cameraman?' They were nowhere to be seen. After I got dressed, I thought they must have gone back to base, but they were both waiting in the backseat of the car. However, neither of them said anything, not even, 'Great work!' or 'Well done!' even after finally finishing this last scene of the film. On the other hand, Akira Kurosawa sometimes gave such praise, even though he was known to be very strict and tough, but in Kobayashi's team, there were no such words. For them, this etiquette did not exist – it was just a job which had to be done. But for four years of my 20s I worked on this film and I felt it was a good use of these years. [21]

In case this story makes Kobayashi sound like some kind of monster, on another occasion Nakadai said, 'Kobayashi was very calm on the set, extremely patient, waiting until one was ready. He had great force of character, an authority which impressed me deeply. Contrary to what one might believe, he was not strict and willingly accepted all that I did.'[22]

---

[21] From *Tatsuya Nakadai Talks about the Golden Age of Japanese Cinema* by Taichi Kasuga, PHP Shinsho, 2013, pp.58-60. Translated by Martin and Miki Dowsing.
[22] From an interview with Max Tessier for *Cinemaya* magazine, 1993. Translated from the original French by Aruna Vasudev.

Despite its deserved status as a masterpiece, *The Human Condition* is easy to find fault with, sometimes lapsing into melodrama and romantic sentimentality. The character of Kaji is saved from becoming excessively saintly as he is insufferably self-righteous at times and changes significantly as the trilogy goes on, his idealism dwindling as he finds himself increasingly ready to do anything to survive. However, many of the other characters are too one-dimensional, conveniently painted either black or white as the story demands. Nevertheless, *The Human Condition* packs an emotional wallop few films can match – not because of Kaji's efforts to fight the system, but because for nearly ten hours we follow a man who has lost control of his destiny through all of his trials and tribulations only to find him erased without a trace at the end. Michiko will never know what happened to him, and we realise that this is the story of not one but millions of men drafted by their governments in the Second World War, sent away to fight and never seen again. *The Human Condition* is one of the few films to really give the viewer some idea of what it must have been like to be a soldier during the war and leave us grateful to have been spared such an experience ourselves. Furthermore, few films have dealt with the collective war-guilt of their country so thoroughly. Kobayashi's trilogy offers no excuses or evasions, and the fact that it was seen by millions of Japanese can only have increased their resolve never to return to the militaristic nationalism of the past.

While Nakadai's impassioned acting may lack the control of many of his later performances, it fits the role perfectly as Kaji is an idealist who reacts to situations on an emotional level. Kobayashi chose well, and it is difficult to imagine another actor in the part. The director's other choices were equally wise – Miyajima's images are stunning throughout and powerfully complemented by the brooding, dramatic, cymbal-clashing musical score of Chuji Kinoshita (Keisuke Kinoshita's younger brother). Although the music lacks the subtlety of Kobayashi's later collaborator, Toru Takemitsu, it contributes greatly to the epic quality of the three films.

No Greater Love, the first part of *The Human Condition*, went on to win multiple awards both at home and abroad. Luckily for Kobayashi, it was a box office success in Japan, and its popularity spawned a 1962 television version featuring Go Kato (another Haiyuza member) in the role of Kaji. Curiously, while Michiyo Aratama won two domestic awards for her performance, Nakadai was overlooked – perhaps because the greatness of his performance only becomes evident in the later parts. However, in many ways it could be said to be the high point of his career, and the film has lived on, with annual all-night screenings of all three films remaining popular in Japan. Overseas, the trilogy was seldom seen for many years, partly due to its sheer length, but partly due to the scenes of violence, which were certainly strong for the time; the British Board of Film Censors refused to grant *No Greater Love* a certificate originally unless 45 minutes of cuts were made. Kobayashi declined to cut it, meaning it could only be shown at film clubs. However, *The Human Condition* finally found its audience in the West decades later thanks to the emergence of DVD labels specialising in film classics.

Chapter 6 – From Humanist to Human Beast

Nakadai's first leading film role after completing part one of *The Human Condition* was as Kunihiko Daté in *The Beast Must Die* (Yaju shisubeshi), an adaptation by *All about Marriage* writer Yoshio Shirasaka of a novel by Haruhiko Oyabu, who also supplied the source material for Seijun Suzuki's otherwise unrelated *Youth of the Beast* (Yaju no seishun, 1963). The original novel, written while Oyabu was still a student, had been selected for publication by none other than Edogawa Rampo (Japan's most famous author in the mystery genre), who was at the time editing a literary magazine.

The film opens with Daté killing a police officer and stealing his gun and badge. This scene is made especially memorable by having the policeman drop a clockwork toy robot he had just bought for his son – as Daté speeds away from the scene of the crime, the toy seems to follow in pursuit. The image also sets up an important motif in the film, and Daté is later himself compared to a robot. We assume that he must be a professional criminal, but soon discover that he is in fact studying criminal psychology at university and has some Raskolnikov-like theories by which he believes crimes can be justified. However, unlike Dostoyevsky's creation, Daté is entirely lacking a conscience. Although many of his fellow students are busy protesting the renewal of the US-Japan Security Treaty, Daté shows no interest in this. Using the stolen police badge to impersonate an officer, he steals a large amount of money from a couple of *yakuza* (played by Tetsu Nakamura and Makoto Sato), then hides it in his small apartment and continues life as usual. It gradually becomes clear that Daté commits crimes purely for the fun of it – he seems bored the rest of the time, and only when doing something illegal or cruel does he appear to come alive. Unlike in the 1980 remake, no other motivation is given for Daté's behaviour than the fact that he is a sociopath with a sadistic streak who gets a thrill out of leading a double life.[23] This type of antihero was rare at the time, especially in Japanese cinema, but seems a logical progression from the 'sun tribe' films. The closest western counterpart would perhaps be Patricia Highsmith's Tom Ripley, whose screen debut came the following year in the shape of Alain Delon courtesy of René Clément's *Plein Soleil*.

When Daté humiliates an elderly flower seller in a bar one night by offering her a wad of cash to sing and dance, he catches the interest of an off-duty detective, Masugi (Hiroshi Koizumi), who is investigating the murder of the officer killed at the the beginning of the film. Later, Masugi discovers that a newspaper quote regarding the case attributed to a professor at Daté's university actually came from Daté himself and he begins investigating him. However, Daté is highly intelligent, and an expert at covering his tracks. He befriends a tubercular fellow student, but only in order to use him as an accomplice in a heist, after which Daté murders him without a second thought. Audience expectations are nicely subverted when, at the end of the film, we see him flying off to Hawaii and delightedly tucking into a juicy steak on the plane.

The Beast Must Die was only the second film of director Eizo Sugawa, who had been an assistant to Mikio Naruse and co-written Nakadai's earlier film, *A Dangerous Hero*. Sugawa produced a stylish modern noir which has stood the test of time very well indeed, and provides Nakadai with a role which is not only a complete contrast to Kaji in *The Human Condition*, but also a very different type of villain to that of Killer Joe in *Black River*. Daté himself plays a number of different roles in the story, as he is a chameleon-like character who adapts effortlessly to whatever situation he is in – when speaking to a professor at the university, he is impeccably polite and respectful, and when questioned by the police, he takes it with good humour, but he

---

[23] At one point, we learn that Daté's father committed suicide after being falsely accused of embezzlement by his boss, who was having an affair with his wife. Although this may explain his twisted personality, there is no sense of him wishing to get revenge on society.

holds himself aloof from his fellow students and treats his girlfriend roughly. Nakadai plays all these variations effortlessly, making Daté believable and even likeable at times. The girlfriend is played by Reiko Dan, who would be paired with Nakadai in a number of future films, while senior Haiyuza actor Eijiro Tono appeared as the elder of the two detectives on the case. Atmospheric cinematography by Fukuzo Koizumi and a strong jazz score by Toshiro Mayuzumi, one of Japan's top composers, also help to make the film a rare gem well worth discovering.

The Beast Must Die was remade three times: by the original director himself in 1974 (with Hiroshi Fujioka as Daté), by Toru Murakawa in 1980 and by Masato Hironishi as a two-parter in 1997 (with Kazuya Kimura). The best-remembered version is the excellent 1980 film, for which star Yusaku Matsuda famously lost 25 pounds and had four molars removed, transforming himself into a very different vision of Daté from either the author's original conception or Nakadai's interpretation. In Matsuda's hands, the character became a charmless, rail-thin social misfit driven mad by the terrible things he saw working as a war photographer.

Nakadai's second film with director Kon Ichikawa, again at Daiei, was an adaptation of *The Key* (Kagi), a short novel by Jun'ichiro Tanizaki, one of Japan's most celebrated novelists. Like *Conflagration*, the screenplay was written by Ichikawa in collaboration with his wife, Natto Wada, and Keiji Hasebe. The novel had taken the form of alternate entries from the private diaries of an unnamed, ageing man and Ikuko, his 40-ish but still attractive wife, a very literary device difficult to transfer to the screen. Although they have been married long enough to have a grown-up daughter named Toshiko, the husband remains sexually obsessed with his wife and is secretly taking injections to boost his virility. Nakadai was cast in the role of Kimura, a friend of the family, who is engaged to Toshiko although it is her mother that he really desires. Noticing their fondness for each other, the husband encourages Ikuko and Kimura to spend time alone together, finding the feelings of jealousy this inspires a stimulus to his flagging libido. When Kimura lends him a camera, he repeatedly gets his wife drunk and uses it to take nude photos of her once she has passed out from too much alcohol. His obsession spirals out of control and his blood pressure climbs dangerously high.

Ichikawa and his collaborators retained almost the entire story of the novel, but fleshed out the characters – in the film, Kimura is a medical intern (his profession is not stated in the book), while the husband gains both a profession (antique expert) and a name (Kenji Kenmochi). A major twist involving a multiple poisoning was also added, perhaps due to pressure from either the studio or the censors, who may have insisted on the characters being punished for their sins. Unfortunately, this new ending is a major weakness of the film, partly because it makes little sense, but especially as the deaths from poisoning are so unconvincingly portrayed – according to this film, poison victims simply drop dead within seconds. However, it does allow for some fine comic character work from then 47-year-old Tanie Kitabayashi as the ancient maid whose colourblindness results in tragedy. Another significant change is that, in the film, we have no insight into the minds of Ikuko and her husband, and it is only Kimura's secret thoughts that we are privy to – the unusual opening sequence features Nakadai in close-up standing before an anatomical chart and speaking directly to the audience about the inevitability of the ageing process and how the decline in human faculties begins much earlier than most of us realise. Kimura looks very pleased about this, even permitting himself a little chuckle, and this immediately sets him up as an unsettling and cold-blooded character. It also frames the story as a cautionary tale about a man (Kenmochi) who tries to defy the ageing process, although the ending of the film appears to reframe it as a warning about how those who indulge in 'immoral' behaviour will at some point receive their comeuppance. Later, we hear Kimura in voiceover wondering how he can disentangle himself from the family after the death of the husband makes it clear there is little money left, revealing him to be a simple opportunist – in the book, he is a much more ambiguous character. Nakadai was again effective as another unscrupulous seducer of women, but the film provided him with only limited opportunities, and the opening was his most memorable moment.

Cinematographer Kazuo Miyagawa, who had also shot *Conflagration*, again used widescreen compositions inventively, this time in Eastmancolor. The colour of the film is rather peculiar and not very colourful, dominated as it is by tones of beige. Everyone looks very pale and unattractive, especially the women. In the case of Nakadai, this was because Ichikawa had made him wear white make-up as, even after the actor shaved, the director felt that a blue-ish stubble remained which would not photograph well in colour. Ikuko was played by Machiko Kyo, a big star in Japan, who was also known abroad for films such as *Rashomon*, *Ugetsu Monogatari* and *Gate of Hell* and had even acted alongside Marlon Brando in *The Teahouse of the August Moon*, an American film set in Okinawa. Unfortunately, in *The Key*, neither her make-up nor her hairstyle do her any favours, making it difficult to see her as the object of obsession, and she also has to play an extremely passive character.

As Toshiko, the daughter, Junko Kano suffered a similar fate to Kyo, also appearing to have been made-up to look as unattractive as possible, which in this case seems to have involved shaving the ends of her eyebrows off. It could be that Ichikawa was trying to make Kyo appear older (as she was playing older than her age) and Kano plainer, as Toshiko is supposed to lack her mother's looks. However, this choice seems merely eccentric and adds to the overall strangeness of what is already a very strange film.[24] Nevertheless, Kano gave perhaps the strongest performance as the perverse and rebellious daughter who receives no affection from her father.

Ganjiro Nakamura, who had played the head priest in *Conflagration*, gave another quietly excellent performance as the husband, portraying

---

[24] For an idea of how different these actresses looked in other films, see *Black Lizard* (1962), in which Kyo plays the whip-cracking bisexual master criminal of the title, and Kano a kidnapped heiress.

him as a ridiculous figure who falls over while trying to copy the presenter of an exercise programme on TV. Nakamura was from the Kansai region, where he had enjoyed a long career in the kabuki theatre before switching to film acting in 1957. Nakadai thought he was quite suited to his role in *The Key* when Nakamura asked him where to find the red light district in Tokyo.

The Key has a number of strengths, including a fine score by Yasushi Akutagawa, but can ultimately be seen as a fascinating, quirky misfire. Among Ichikawa's other unusual touches are the use of freeze-frames holding characters in suspended animation, and the very unsubtle montage of coupling train carriages as a metaphor for sex. But somehow the film won the jury prize at the Cannes Film Festival of 1960, sharing it with Antonioni's *L'Avventura*.

Despite its lack of nudity, the subject matter of the film appears to have been enough to see it rejected by the prudish censorship board in Britain, while it was released in America as *Odd Obsession* with the tag line, 'The most daring motion picture ever made!' which, of course, was far from true even back then.

Nakadai next appeared in Toho's *Three Dolls in Ginza* (Ginza no onechan), a sequel to the popular comedy *Three Dolls in College* (Daigaku no onechan), which may have provided some welcome light relief after the series of intense roles he had recently taken on. He played a physicist who attracts the interest of one of the 'dolls', played by Reiko Dan. Meanwhile, on stage he starred in Haiyuza's 1959 adaptation of *A Game of Love and Death*, a play by Romain Rolland about the French Revolution. Nakadai would typically manage to act in just one stage play per year from this point on, but always in a leading role, and he would never abandon the theatre as a great many actors do once they achieve film success.

Anyakoro, Nakadai's next film, was based on the semi-autobiographical novel of the same name by Naoya Shiga, which originally appeared in magazine instalments between 1921 and 1937 and was later translated into English as *A Dark Night's Passing*. The director was Shiro Toyoda, a specialist in careful literary adaptations who had been directing since the silent days. Apart from their literary origins, any unifying theme is hard to detect in Toyoda's work, which includes not only serious dramas like *Anyakoro*, but comedies such as *Shozo, a Cat and Two Women* (1956) and *The Inn in Front of the Train Station* (Kigeki ekimae ryokan, 1958), and even Toho's first special effects fantasy in colour, *Madame White Snake* (Byaku fujin no yoren, 1956), a film which looks almost as gorgeous as the better-known *Gate of Hell*. His 1940 film *Spring on Lepers' Island* (Kojima no haru), shot entirely on location, was an early example of neo-realism which treated a difficult subject with great sensitivity and won the 1941 Kinema Jumpo Award for Best Film.

Toyoda's films were always well made, but some of his choices inevitably transferred to celluloid more successfully than others. While his 1953 version of Ogai Mori's classic novel *The Wild Geese* (Gan), starring Hideko Takamine, stands alongside the best of Mikio Naruse, his 1957 version of Yasunari Kawabata's *Snow Country* (Yukiguni) fails to move. Despite the beautifully-photographed snowscapes, Kawabata's classic became an uninvolving tale of a dull-as-ditchwater Tokyo artist (Ryo Ikebe) who meets a childish and exceedingly irritating companion-for-hire (Keiko Kishi) in a mountain resort and embarks on an interminable affair. Nevertheless, Toyoda was another respected director with whom Nakadai would later form a fruitful creative partnership. However, for their first film together, Nakadai had only a small (albeit significant) part, while the leading role went to *Snow Country*'s Ryo Ikebe as Kensaku, the writer struggling to overcome his inner demons. The film apparently focused on one theme of the book in particular – Kensaku's belief that he is the product of an incestuous relationship, and his attempt to come to terms with this. Nakadai appeared briefly as Kaname, who is both the cousin and seducer of Kensaku's wife. Unfortunately, despite being a major production based on a novel widely regarded as one of the high points of Japanese literature, *Anyakoro* appears to be both forgotten and inaccessible today, although it did receive a Japanese VHS release at some point. Yasujiro Ozu, an admirer of Shiga, once apparently remarked that Toyoda's attempt at filming the book was like 'spitting in church.'[25]

After his roles in *Black River, Conflagration, The Beast Must Die, The Key* and *Anyakoro*, Nakadai came close to being typecast as corrupters of women, and it was the role of Kaji in *The Human Condition* films which allowed him to demonstrate a greater range and so helped him to avoid such a fate. After returning to this role for the second part of the trilogy, Nakadai made his second film with Mikio Naruse, *When a Woman Ascends the Stairs* (Onna ga kaidan wo agaru toki), which would eventually become the director's most famous work (at least in the West). Being a Naruse film, the main character was, as usual, a woman – Keiko, the senior hostess of a Ginza bar, who is known as 'Mama' to her colleagues and clients. As in *Untamed*, Nakadai's previous film with the director, the lead was again played by Hideko Takamine. Mama dislikes her work but feels she has no other choice after losing her husband in a road accident. Aside from prostitution, being a bar hostess is the only realisitic way of earning enough money to live comfortably while supporting both her widowed mother and her kind-hearted but weak brother and his disabled child. Mama drinks as little as possible and makes it a rule not to sleep with the customers. For these reasons, she is widely respected but nevertheless pursued by a number of wealthy men.

Nakadai was cast as the bar manager. At first, it seems like another of his callous seducer roles as he treats one of the hostesses, Junko (Reiko Dan) with indifference, only to break his own rule of 'not touching the merchandise' by sleeping with her when he feels the need. However, we gradually come to understand that he is secretly in love with Mama, and it is this which gives his role an interesting extra dimension. Having known Mama for five years, he finally makes a pass at her after learning that she has slept with one of the regulars, but is firmly rejected. A row ensues, during the course of which he loses his

---

[25] https://beatle001.hatenablog.com/entry/20070305/1173018347 /
http://blog.livedoor.jp/michikusa05/archives/51784773.html

temper and slaps Mama's face, an action which Naruse had Nakadai do for real, albeit with the admonition to hit Takamine only on the cheek and not the side of her head so as not to damage her eardrum. Nakadai later said that he had found Naruse to be the most difficult director he ever worked with, the reason being that Naruse never actually gave him any direction other than to 'be natural.' Takamine herself later made similar comments, saying that throughout their 19 films together, Naruse never once gave her any acting instructions.

With a screenplay by regular Kurosawa collaborator Ryuzo Kikushima, a suitably jazzy score by Toshiro Mayuzumi, cinematography by Naruse favourite Masao Tamai and a strong supporting cast, *When a Woman Ascends the Stairs* has an impressive pedigree which is evident in the high quality of the work throughout. Unusually, the film features occasional voiceover narration from Takamine's character, lending a documentary feel to parts of the film.

Nakadai's next film saw him immediately reunited with Naruse. *Daughter, Wife, Mother* (Musume·tsuma·haha) was a family drama in the Ozu manner featuring Hideko Takamine and another of Japan's biggest female stars, Setsuko Hara, the latter of whom was known especially for her work with Ozu in films such as *Tokyo Story*, and also for her wholesome image. *Daughter, Wife, Mother*, a Toho production, was shot in colour, an unusual choice for this type of film at the time. Unfortunately, it was a definite step down from *When a Woman Ascends the Stairs*, being a dull, excessively talky two-hour film about a squabbling family, with a syrupy music score laid on thickly throughout. Hara played Sanae, a recently widowed woman in her thirties, and Nakadai appeared as Kuroki, a young vineyard owner who falls in love with her.

Nakadai had to kiss Hara in one scene, and assumed that he need not actually touch her lips as explicit kissing in films was still largely taboo in Japan at the time. It was common practise to have the actors bring their faces close together, then cut and fade out. However, before the scene was shot, Naruse privately instructed Nakadai not to fake the kiss. Nakadai decided he should check with Hara, who raised no objection, so Nakadai went ahead only to be reprimanded by her manager as a result. Despite the fuss, the scene as it appears in the finished film is very tame – we mostly see the back of Nakadai's head, and it is all over very quickly. Still, Japanese audiences at the time were no doubt surprised to see their icon of purity being kissed in such a way.

Nakadai found Hara to be quite open-minded. One evening after shooting a rural scene on location, he was drinking with her and another actress in the cast, Keiko Awaji, and decided to teach them a card game called *dobon*. Unfortunately for Nakadai, the two actresses had a double case of beginner's luck, and he finished the evening in debt to the tune of 2 million yen. The following day, Nakadai's wife went to the pawnshop to raise the money, which he paid to the two actresses at Toho the day after.

Kuroki is a one-dimensional character, and the script gives no indication of why he is interested in the older Sanae, making this role a pretty thankless one for Nakadai. However, the combination of Hara and Takamine seems to have been enough to make the film a big box office hit in Japan and it seems only fair to point out that some consider it a masterpiece.

Fortunately, Nakadai's next role gave him something more substantial to sink his teeth into. In *The Blue Beast* (Aoi yaju), he played Yasuhiko Kuroki, a low-level executive working for a women's magazine who becomes vice-president of the labour union. However, he soon sells out the workers during a strike and exploits his position in an attempt to line his pockets and further his career. When the situation becomes dangerous, he goes to work for an important politician (played by Koreya Senda), whose daughter (Yoko Tsukasa) he makes pregnant. In order to secure his future, he agrees to get married, but receives his comeuppance when a member of the union he betrayed comes after him for revenge.

With Yoko Tsukasa in a publicity still for *The Blue Beast*.

Nakadai shared scenes on film with his Haiyuza teacher Koreya Senda for the first time in *The Blue Beast*, but it was by no means the first time he had played an unscrupulous manipulator, and it would not be the last. On this occasion, his character seems to be motivated by the temptations of money and power rather than any sadistic impulses as in his earlier 'Beast' film, to which this was unrelated in terms of story. However, like *The Beast Must Die*, the screenplay was also written by Yasuzo Masumura's regular collaborator, Yoshio Shirasaka, although in this case it was an original work.

Director Hiromichi Horikawa (1916-2012) was known for making dramas with a left-wing perspective and had worked as an assistant to Kurosawa, by whom he had been heavily influenced. The two had first met while making *Horse* (1941), on which Horikawa was a junior assistant director under Kurosawa, the senior AD. Horikawa subsequently assisted Kurosawa on his directorial debut, *Sanshiro Sugata* (1943) and a number of other films, including *Seven Samurai*. When Horikawa directed his first film in 1955, the influence of Kurosawa had led him to waste too much film and, before he could resume his directing career he was forced by the studio to retrain as an assistant under Mikio Naruse for two films in order to learn how to shoot more economically. For *The Blue Beast*, his ninth picture, Horikawa employed another of Kurosawa's regular collaborators, cinematographer Asakazu Nakai, and the film marked the first of four collaborations with Nakadai. Unfortunately, *The Blue Beast* appears to be languishing in obscurity today, but was rated highly enough at the time to receive a release in the US, where *Variety* gave it a positive review and described it as a Japanese variation on *Room at the Top*.

Like *The Beast Must Die*, Nakadai's next film was based on a novel by Haruhiko Oyabu and directed by Eizo Sugawa, although in this case the screenplay was by Shuji Terayama, who later became a well-known avant-garde director. However, although the tone and style seem to have been very similar to the team's previous film, *Get 'Em All*[26] was

---

[26] The original title '*Minagoroshi no uta' yori kenjū-yo saraba!* is translated as "From the 'Song of Annihilation'-Farewell, Gun!" in *The Toho Studios Story* by Stuart Galbraith IV (Scarecrow Press, 2008)

an unrelated story in which Nakadai played a different character. The plot concerns Kyosuke, a young man seeking to avenge the murder of his gangster brother. He comes to the conclusion that a band of criminals led by a boxer named Tsubota (Nakadai) are responsible. After stealing a gun from one of them, he finds that the weapon gives him a newfound feeling of power as he picks off the gang members one by one. In his book *Gun and Sword: An Encyclopedia of Japanese Gangster Films 1955-1980*, author Chris D. describes the film as 'A well done, edgy noir thriller with some great touches.'

The supporting cast included Tetsuro Tanba and Kyoko Kishida, while the leading role of Kyosuke was played by Hiroshi Mizuwara, a teen idol singer who had just begun a second career as a movie star. He was initially quite successful in films, and his performance was praised by Nakadai, but his addictions to gambling and alcohol damaged his career, which never fully recovered. He died of liver failure in 1978 at the age of 42, leaving debts reputedly amounting to around 90 million yen. *Get 'Em All* received a Japanese DVD release in 2006, albeit without English subtitles.

Chapter 7 – The Snake and the Octopus

On 14 January 1961, shooting began on *Yojimbo*, continuing for three months, although Nakadai would not have been present for the whole shoot as his character is not seen until 45 minutes in.[27] Whether Nakadai had any inkling that he was appearing in a seminal future classic is doubtful, but he was certainly aware that Kurosawa was an exceptional talent. Cast as Unosuke, the one 'bad guy' who represents a serious challenge to Toshiro Mifune's tough *ronin*, he gave a somewhat cartoonish performance as a villain who clearly enjoys being bad, grinning from ear to ear while casually ending lives with the pull of a trigger. Kurosawa is said to have told his two leads that he saw Sanjuro as a wolf and Unosuke as a snake. This cartoonishness is entirely appropriate as it was in keeping with Kurosawa's casting of the other roles, for which he seems to have rounded up every odd-looking actor in Japan. He even found a giant wrestler named Rashomon to play a henchman armed with an enormous hammer, while *Oban* star Daisuke Kato sportingly allowed himself to be grotesquely made-up to play the pig-like Inokichi. Also notable were Haiyuza's Eijiro Tono as the bad-tempered but good-hearted, gargoyle-faced tavern keeper, Isuzu Yamada as the scheming wife of a *yakuza* boss, and Ikio Sawamura as Hansuke, the 'constable' who scurries around town like a hyperactive mouse.

One of the touches that made Nakadai's character memorable was the tartan scarf he wore. Although he later conjectured that Kurosawa had suggested it as a means of concealing his long neck, it may simply have been part of the portrayal of Unosuke as a fashion-conscious poser symbolic of what was to come (something also evident in his use

---

[27] In recent years, Nakadai has often said that *Yojimbo* was made during breaks between filming parts 1 and 2 of *The Human Condition*, and *Sanjuro* between filming parts 2 and 3. However, the final part of *The Human Condition* was released in Japan on 28 January 1961, just two weeks after the shooting of *Yojimbo* began, so his memory must be at fault here.

of a gun as his weapon of choice). Some film critics later complained that the scarf was anachronistic as the story was set in 1860, but Kurosawa justified it by arguing that the port of Yokohama had opened to foreign trade in June 1859, making the purchase of such an item – and a pistol – entirely possible.

In the case of *Yojimbo*, Kurosawa mainly used telephoto lenses, even for close-ups, with the cameras placed far away from the actors, sometimes with two or three shooting from different angles. Such an approach was groundbreaking at the time, and it was one which Nakadai found difficult. Kurosawa adopted it partly because he felt it would help obtain more natural performances from his actors, but Nakadai was often unaware when the camera was on him and felt uncertain exactly where to place himself, with the result that he received a number of tongue-lashings from the director. Mifune, on the other hand, was accustomed to Kurosawa's methods, and seemed to have few such problems. Nakadai was greatly impressed by Mifune, who always seemed thoroughly prepared and usually able to deliver what Kurosawa wanted in one take. However, Mifune tended to give a full performance even in rehearsals, sometimes becoming so carried away that he broke parts of the set. This, of course, did not please Kurosawa so, after a while, he simply shot without rehearsal. Nakadai and Mifune became good friends during the making of *Yojimbo,* and Nakadai later said that he learnt a great deal from the older star, especially in terms of how to perform swordfighting.

Another aspect which Nakadai found challenging was the dust. Kurosawa wanted to convey the impression of an arid, windswept town, so his crew scattered dust around the set and used powerful wind machines to stir it up, making it difficult for the actors to keep their eyes open. To add to his discomfort, Nakadai spent his final three days on set lying in a pool of fake blood to film his protracted death scene. When shooting was over, he broke out in a rash, and was never sure whether this was a reaction to the fake blood or the result of stress.

Yojimbo is notable for so many reasons, it feels impossible to name them all. The unforgettable image of the dog carrying a human hand in its mouth... the attention-grabbing music of Masaru Sato... the incredibly detailed and realistic set for which a whole street and multiple buildings were created from scratch... Toshiro Mifune giving one of the most charismatic star performances in cinema history... And Nakadai too, of course, who proved such an effective adversary for Mifune that the two actors would find themselves pitted against one another in a number of memorable films to come.

As a Wife, As a Woman (Tsuma to shite on'na to shite, aka *Poignant Story*), Nakadai's fourth film for Mikio Naruse, again saw him wasted in a minor role as Minami, a man attracted to Miho, the manageress of a bar on the Ginza, played by Hideko Takamine. If this all sounds very similar to *When a Woman Ascends the Stairs*, it should be pointed out that in this case the focus is not on Miho's job, but on her troubled relationship with Kono, the owner of the bar, played by Masayuki Mori, and his family. Like the other philanderers that Mori played for Naruse and others, Kono is self-centred and ineffectual, but inexplicably attractive to women. Miho has had a 19-year affair with him, producing two children in the process, both of whom were taken from her and raised by Kono and his wife, Ayako (Chikage Awashima). The film becomes more interesting and dramatic as it goes on, and features a good role for Takamine after the rather subdued character she played in *Daughter, Wife, Mother*. Superb as usual, she never appears to be 'acting', and everything she does feels completely realistic and natural. Naruse is also successful in providing another effectively frank critique of Japan's patriarchal society. However, as far as Nakadai is concerned, there is a little to say other than that he appears as a peripheral character about whom we know very little. Minami claims to be willing to do anything for Miho, but when she really needs his help, he is too busy preparing for a trip which will take him away to Africa for several months. The character is given so little attention that it is unclear why he is even going to Africa in the first place.

Nakadai followed this with a leading role on stage in *Yellow Wave* (Kiiroi name), a drama about the atom bomb by Yushi Koyama, directed by Koreya Senda for Haiyuza. It ran from 14 May to 30 July.

His next film role was brief enough that it was probably filmed on days off. This was a cameo in *As the Clouds Scatter* (Kumo ga chigireru toki), a Shochiku tearjerker centred around the character of Misaki (Keiji Sada), a bus driver assigned to a dangerous route on a mountain road. His chance encounter with Ichie (Ineko Arima), the childhood sweetheart he was separated from during the war, disrupts his peaceful life with tragic consequences. Both characters have been scarred by the hard times they endured as a result of the war and its aftermath, and discover that it is not so easy to put the past behind them.

Nakadai appeared in a couple of flashback scenes set in 1950 as James Kimura, an American soldier born to Japanese parents in the USA, and is first seen speaking English when he arrives at a hospital seeking help for an orphan with dysentery. He falls into conversation with Ichie, who is at this point working as a nurse, and reveals that he grew up in an internment camp in Death Valley, California, where his parents were forced to stay throughout the war. He charms Ichie with his stories about Death Valley, where it was 'so hot you could fry an egg in the sun', and the two embark on a relationship which is cut cruelly short when he is sent into battle in Korea and killed. Nakadai has the peculiar challenge of speaking Japanese like someone brought up in America, but plays Kimura as such a warm and sincere character that, despite his brief screen time, we understand Ichie's profound sense of loss. Perhaps it was Nakadai's friendship with Arima which led to him taking on such a small part.

The film has a good pedigree, with a screenplay written by Kaneto Shindo (from a novel by Torahiko Tamiya), and direction by Heinosuke Gosho, a highly respected figure in Japan who had been directing feature films since 1925, his best-remembered being *Where Chimneys are Seen* (Entotsu no mieru basho, 1953). However, Yasushi Akutagawa's Spanish guitar score eventually becomes wearing, as does the relentlessly downbeat tone of the film after the misleadingly cheerful opening. Misaki dies at the end when he swerves to avoid a motorbike and his bus tumbles down the mountainside; Keiji Sada (a popular leading man and Masaki Kobayashi favourite who had appeared alongside Nakadai in *The Human Condition*) died in a very similar accident three years after the release of *As the Clouds Scatter*.

Nakadai's next film had a number of things in common with *As the Clouds Scatter*. The director was Keisuke Kinoshita (b. 1912), whose homosexuality had not prevented him from becoming one of the most respected filmmakers in Japan at the time and one still remembered today. Although not necessarily his best work, the only Kinoshita films widely seen in the West are *Twenty-Four Eyes* (Nijushi no hitomi, 1954) and *The Ballad of Narayama* (Narayama bushiko, 1958). Averaging two films a year for his first 20 years as a director, Kinoshita was perhaps too prolific for his own good and had a weakness for novelty. After directing Japan's first colour film (*Carmen Comes Home* / Karumen kokyo ni kaeru) in 1951, he embarked on a series of whimsical experiments, such as the constantly tilting camera in *Carmen Falls in Love* (Karumen junjo su), the silent-film style iris vignette used throughout *She Was Like a Wild Chrysanthemum* (Nokigu no gotoki kimi nariki) and the seemingly random splashes of colour with which he tinted portions of the otherwise monochrome *Fuefuki River* (Fuefukigawa). Nakadai's one film with Kinoshita, again for Shochiku, had its own peculiarities, but remains an impressive piece nonetheless. The Japanese title, *Eien no hito*, translates as something like 'forever human', but the film is known in English as *Immortal Love* or, more appropriately, *Bitter Spirit*. Star Hideko Takamine had already played the leading role in eight films for Kinoshita; with Nakadai, she had by this point appeared in five films – the four Naruse pictures and *The Human Condition Part III*.

In *Bitter Spirit*, Nakadai played Heibei, who returns to his rural hometown of Aso in Kumamoto Prefecture on Kyushu, Japan's southernmost main island. The year is 1932, and Heibei has been wounded during military service in Manchuria, leaving him dependent on crutches to move around (making this the second of several films in which Nakadai plays a character with a bad leg). The son of a wealthy landowner, he has always harboured a grudge against Takashi (Keiji Sada), another young man from the village who is still in the army. He also has an eye for Takashi's sweetheart, Sadako (Takamine), who is loyally awaiting the return of Takashi. Heibei rapes her, soon after which Takashi arrives home having finished his military service. Kinoshita makes an effective contrast between the two men here by essentially repeating the same scene with Takashi that had opened the film with Heibei – when the villagers had staged a parade to welcome him home, Heibei had completely ignored them, whereas when Takashi returns from his military service and they do the same for him, he acknowledges them all with a smile and a salute. Meanwhile, now 'soiled goods' and concerned that her father will be evicted from his farm if she refuses, Sadako reluctantly agrees to marry Heibei but continues to despise him, and the consequences of his actions last for decades.

Like *As the Clouds Scatter*, the film's soundtrack features Spanish music, which was presumably in vogue in Japan at the time. In this case, Kinoshita's composer brother Chuji provides full-on flamenco, complete with rapidly-strummed Spanish guitars and clacking castanets. The film is divided into five 'chapters', the last of which takes place in 1961. Each chapter is even bridged by a flamenco song sung in Japanese which tells the story of the lovers as a tragic ballad. This has the effect of lending a sense of inevitability to the drama as the characters are doomed to act out their pre-determined fate. A similar effect can be found in Kinoshita's *Legend of a Duel to the Death* (Shito no densetsu, 1963), which makes a fascinating companion piece to *Bitter Spirit*. Both films are set in rural communities in which the consequences of a far away war reverberate, and in both cases Kinoshita (with regular cameraman Hiroshi Kusuda) makes superb use of widescreen as his characters act out their tragedies on country roads in the shadow of the mountains.

Another interesting aspect of the film is the fact that, although Heibei seems very much the villain of the piece, it is suggested towards the end that the real villain may be Sadako for holding on to her hatred for 30 years, something which resulted in the suicide of her eldest son. However, it is difficult to go along with this when we have consistently seen Sadako treating others with kindness while her husband thinks of no-one but himself. Nakadai plays Heibei as a self-pitying egotist who, though perhaps genuinely in love with Sadako, eventually comes to realise that by adopting such an unethical method to force her into marriage, he has denied himself the opportunity of ever being loved in return.

In one scene, Nakadai had to slap Takamine. Before shooting, Kinoshita took Nakadai aside and explained that Heibei felt complete hatred for Sadako at this moment in the story and, to make it convincing, he wanted Nakadai to slap Takamine for real as hard as he could. Although he must have been used to slapping his female co-stars by this point, Nakadai double-checked to make sure he had understood correctly before doing as instructed. Afterwards, Takamine told him that his acting was rubbish but he could certainly hit hard. Also notable in the cast was Nobuko Otawa playing the wife of Takashi and ageing more convincingly than any of the other principals, although all the performances are strong. Another point of interest is that the film's assistant director was none other than Yoshishige Yoshida, a key figure in Japan's 'new wave' who later went on to direct *Eros + Massacre* (Erosu purasu gyakusatsu, 1969) among other films.

Bitter Spirit was Japan's submission for Best Foreign Language Film at the 1961 Oscars but, though nominated, it lost out to Ingmar Bergman's *Through a Glass Darkly*. However, both Nakadai and Takamine picked up awards for their performances at the Mainichi Film Awards (Nakadai's was also for *The Human Condition*).

Following the huge success of *Yojimbo*, the studio begged Kurosawa for a sequel. After some initial reluctance, he agreed, seeing an opportunity to resurrect an unfilmed screenplay. His adaptation of Shugaro Yamamoto's story *Peaceful Days* (Hibi heian) had for some reason been abandoned, so Kurosawa altered it to accommodate the character of Sanjuro. Planning to pass it on to his former assistant Hiromichi Horikawa to direct, he ultimately took the reigns himself at the request of Toho. Although *Yojimbo* had also been a comedy of sorts, Kurosawa decided to emphasise the humour in his follow-up, entitled *Sanjuro* (or *Tsubaki Sanjuro* in Japan, after the fake name meaning 'thirty-year-old camellia' given by the main character in the second film).

It is a measure of how pleased he must have been with Nakadai's performance in *Yojimbo* that Kurosawa invited him back to play Mifune's opponent once more, despite the fact that it was a completely different character. Indeed, it is difficult to think of another example of a director doing this. For the sequel, Kurosawa created an entirely new image for Nakadai, which may have been partly to differentiate his role from the previous one as much as possible, but was also something Kurosawa would do every time he cast Nakadai. The director had begun his creative life as a painter and seemed to conceive his characters primarily in visual terms, often neglecting to provide them with a backstory. However, this absence was seldom a shortcoming as the appearance of his characters was so detailed and the performances so strong that audiences could easily fill in the blanks. Kurosawa often spent a month or more preparing the make-up and costumes for his actors before shooting began. For Nakadai's character of Hanbei Muroto, a bald wig with top-knot was required. The type chosen was not too flattering for Nakadai, but Kurosawa liked the fact that it made him look 'like an octopus.' Nakadai had worn very little make-up for *Yojimbo*, but more was required for *Sanjuro*, as Kurosawa wanted the character to have a darker skin tone, so the actor had to spend a considerable time every day being carefully painted brown. Perhaps the idea behind the skin colouring was to accentuate the whites in Nakadai's already large eyes for effect; if so, it worked and his eye movements seem more pronounced than usual. Indeed, there are moments in the film when the expression on his face is priceless – most notably when he learns that Sanjuro (tied to a rock in this scene) has made a fool of him and, before departing, he turns back looking as if about to burst into tears.

As in *Yojimbo*, the film would climax with a dramatic stand-off between Mifune and Nakadai, ending with the death of Nakadai's character. However, in this case, there were no guns involved and both would be armed only with swords. The script provided no detail of how this was to be staged, and Kurosawa told very few of the crew what he had in mind – even Nakadai had little idea of what was to happen before they came to shoot the scene. All he knew was the sword movement he was to use, which Kurosawa asked him to prepare without Mifune. With the help of *tateshi* (sword fight choreographer) Ryu Kuze, Nakadai practised his move every day for a month while Mifune practised a different move. At the time, blood was rarely seen in films, and swordfighting scenes were mainly a matter of careful choreography. Kurosawa had already been responsible for introducing greater realism to the cinema through his staging of violent scenes in previous works, but this time he decided to go further. A hose was wrapped around Nakadai's chest and connected to a pump operated by a member of the effects team. The purpose of this was not explained to Nakadai, although of course he realised it was probably to provide blood. When the cameras were rolling, Kurosawa had Mifune and Nakadai stare each other down while his script supervisor, Teruyo Nogami, counted out thirty seconds, at the end of which the two actors made their move, both striking in single rapid movements. Sanjuro is a fraction of a second faster. As Mifune struck, the pump was released and a huge geyser of blood spurted from Nakadai's chest. Nakadai later said the pressure was so strong that it took him by surprise and nearly knocked him off his feet. Some onlookers apparently thought that Mifune had actually slashed Nakadai and were in shock. Nogami turned and fled, and Nakadai remembered seeing the blood splash the back of her white jacket.[28] The scene was shot in one take. After Kurosawa viewed the footage, there was some talk of reshooting as Nakadai had moved his eyes when, supposedly already dead, he fell slowly to the ground. However, Kurosawa ultimately decided his chances of achieving a better take were slim and left it alone. When the

---

[28] In *The Films of Akira Kurosawa*, Donald Richie states that the 'blood' was actually 'a vat of chocolate syrup and carbonated water under thirty pounds of pressure'. This suggests that the colour would have been different enough from real blood not to have fooled anybody on the set, so the stories about shocked crew members may be exaggerated.

film was released, it was another big hit for the director, and the shocking finale made a considerable impression. The result was that, for better or worse, Kurosawa was largely responsible for the introduction of copious amounts of blood into the samurai genre, many exponents of which used blood far more liberally than he would ever do himself.

Despite the blood, *Sanjuro* would be one of Kurosawa's lightest entertainments, and a film with the simplest of messages: to judge by appearances is a mistake. Never again would he make such a commercial film, and within four years he would be struggling to get his projects off the ground. For his part, Nakadai had learned a great deal about how to handle action sequences from Toshiro Mifune during the shooting of the two Sanjuro films and this was soon to serve him well.

Chapter 8 – Expanding the Range

Nakadai then appeared in three films in a row for Shochiku, first taking on a supporting role in Masaki Kobayashi's atypical film *The Inheritance* (Karami-ai/'Entanglement'). Based on a novel by Norio Nanjo, it starred another Kobayashi favourite, Keiko Kishi, in the role of Yasuko, secretary to Kawahara, a wealthy businessman dying of cancer (So Yamamura). The film begins with a montage of a carefree Yasuko window-shopping for jewellery and looking every inch the glamorous, modern, westernised young woman promoted as an ideal in the glossy magazines of the day. In fact, she is curiously reminiscent of Audrey Hepburn in *Breakfast at Tiffany's* – a film which had just been released in Japan around the time *The Inheritance* was shooting, so it seems reasonable to surmise that Kobayashi was deliberately subverting Hepburn's already iconic image.

Yasuko's day is spoiled when she is approached by a man from her past. In voiceover, she confides to the audience that she despises him, even as we watch her smile and accept his invitation to join him for tea. The rest of the story is then revealed in flashback: we discover that Kawahara dislikes his wife, with whom he has a childless marriage, and that he has three illegitimate and estranged children by three separate women. Before dying, he orders his minions to track them down so that he can judge whether or not they may be worthy of receiving a sizeable share of his vast fortune. This leads to all manner of conniving among his family and employees as they come up with a variety of criminal schemes in the hope of getting rich off the old man's death.

Nakadai played Furukawa, a particularly cold-blooded employee who uses his good looks to manipulate women into helping him outfox the other gold-diggers. Furukawa is a one-dimensional character introduced without fanfare around 20 minutes in, and Nakadai plays him in a very low-key style before disappearing abruptly some time before the end of the film. As it was similar to the corruptor-of-women parts he had played in his early career, it seems doubtful that Nakadai would have accepted such a role at this stage were it not at the invitation of Kobayashi. However, his star power at the time meant that he received second billing over Yamamura, despite having the smaller part, and was also featured prominently on the posters. As one would expect from Kobayashi, this caustic study of unfettered greed is extremely well-made, although the European feel makes it something of an anomaly among his filmography. Some critics have characterised it as a black comedy, but *The Inheritance* is a very different type of film from *Kind Hearts and Coronets*, for example, being played entirely straight and offering few (if any) laughs. While we have some sympathy with Yasuko for being treated like a doormat by Kawahara and others, she is nevertheless shallow and materialistic, and is revealed to be just as ruthless as the rest by the end. The other characters, meanwhile, are utterly despicable, and Kobayashi's dispassionate and unflinching scrutiny of their hypocrisy makes *The Inheritance* far and away his most misanthropic work. A brilliant film, then – but probably nobody's favourite movie.

Nakadai's next, *Ogin-sama* (aka *Love under the Crucifix*), was directed by Kinuyo Tanaka, one of Japanese cinema's most respected actresses. The cousin of Masaki Kobayashi, Tanaka had begun her film career in 1924 at the age of 13, going on to become a major star, perhaps most notably through her work for Kenji Mizoguchi, for whom she made 16 films. After Kurosawa won the Golden Lion at the Venice Film Festival in 1951, Mizoguchi became so incensed at having been upstaged by a junior that he immediately upped his game, producing three of the greatest classics of Japanese cinema as a result – *The Life of Oharu* (1952), *Ugetsu Monogatari* (1953) and *Sanshu Dayu* (1954). Although Mizoguchi failed to win the top prize of the Golden Lion, *The Life of Oharu* won the International Award at Venice, and the other two both won Silver Lion Awards. Tanaka had played the lead in the first of these as well as major parts in the other two, and Mizoguchi was said to have been in love with her, although it was not reciprocated.

During the 1950s, Tanaka's career as a leading lady inevitably came to an end and she turned to character parts and directing, becoming the second female (after Tazuko Sakane) to have directed a film in Japan, and the only female director active in the country during this period. After the success of her directorial debut, *Love Letter* (Koibumi, 1953), Mizoguchi had tried to sabotage her new career. As a result, she never spoke to him again and was conspicuously absent from his final four films. Despite his interference, Tanaka went on to direct a further five pictures, all of which were well-received dramas of considerable quality. *Ogin-sama*, her final film as director as well as the only period drama of the six, would be the sole occasion on which Nakadai worked with Tanaka.

Like *Black River* and *The Human Condition*, the film was produced by Ninjin Club, the company founded by Ineko Arima, Keiko Kishi[29] and Yoshiko Kuga. Arima played the lead in *Ogin-sama*, a tragic love story set in the late 16th-century and adapted by Mizoguchi's regular screenwriter Masashige Narusawa from a novel by Toko Kon. Arima's character, Ogin, is the daughter of Sen no Rikyu, the famous tea master (here played by Ganjiro Nakamura from *Conflagration* and *The Key*) ordered to commit suicide by Hideyoshi Toyotomi. The reasons for the order were never revealed, and Toko Kon would not be the only author to use the mystery as the basis for a novel.

Ogin is in love with her childhood friend, Takayama Ukon (1552-1615), a war hero and devout Christian played by Nakadai. At the beginning of the film, Ukon is already married and Ogin is forced to keep her feelings a secret and suffer unrequited love in silence. She is pressured into accepting a marriage proposal from a wealthy trader (Hisaya Ito). Meanwhile, the Japanese authorities become increasingly hostile to Christianity and make its practise illegal. After Ukon's wife dies and he is forced into exile, Ogin finally has the opportunity to confess her love. This leads to a night of passion followed by divorce from her husband, but any chance of happiness is destroyed when

---

[29] In a brief, silent cameo, Kishi appears in *Ogin-sama* as a woman tied to a horse being led off for crucifixion.

Lord Hideyoshi (Osamu Takizawa) states his intention to make her his concubine.

The star of *Ogin-sama* is not Nakadai but Arima, who suffers convincingly and displays a stubborn defiance that would have made life very difficult for a woman in this era. As the object of her affection, Nakadai looks the part and is admirably restrained – where a lesser actor may have indulged in hand-wringing or other external gestures in order to reveal the character's inner torment, Nakadai trusts the audience to understand this from the look in his eyes and what he does *not* say and do. Unfortunately, the script never allows these characters to emerge as anything more than one-dimensional, especially in the case of Nakadai, here playing one of his least interesting roles as a man who is essentially a religious bore. Donald Richie has said that Japanese drama generally deals with the conflict between *giri* (obligation) and *ninjo* (inclination), and *Ogin-sama* is the epitome of this, but detrimentally so, as the story is exceedingly predictable. Perhaps Nakadai had been enthusiastic enough about working with Tanaka and Arima to overlook the script's deficiencies. However, the film is so beautifully shot in widescreen and Eastmancolor by *Human Condition* cameraman Yoshio Miyajima that its visual qualities alone make it worthwhile. *Ogin-sama* was remade by Kei Kumai in 1978 as *Love and Faith*, with Ryoko Nakano as Ogin, Kichiemon Nakamura as Ukon, Takashi Shimura as Rikyu and Toshiro Mifune as Hideyoshi.

Nakadai and Yasuko had been married for five years at this point, and she became pregnant for the first time. Unfortunately, while getting ready to visit the hospital, she fell down some stairs. Nakadai received a call informing him that there may be some danger, and quickly made his way to the hospital. By the time he arrived, the baby had been stillborn but Yasuko was out of danger. The doctors decided not to show the baby to her, but did show it to Nakadai. It was a boy, and Nakadai thought he detected a resemblance to himself around the nose. Before going in to visit his wife, he had expected her to be distraught, but was surprised to find that she greeted him with a smile, saying the doctors had told her she should be able to conceive again.

This made Nakadai feel better even though he was aware she may have been putting on an act for his benefit. The baby was named Harujo-doji ('Spring Child') and buried next to Yasuko's father, who had passed away not long before.

Nakadai's next collaboration with Masaki Kobayashi, *Harakiri*, was loosely based on a short story entitled 'Ibunronin ki' by Yasuhiko Takiguchi, which had been adapted into a screenplay by Shinobu Hashimoto, co-writer of many of Kurosawa's finest films. The film was Kobayashi's first period piece, and he later said that the reason he used Nakadai in so many films was because he felt him to be one of the few actors who could effectively portray both modern and historical characters.

Nakadai was cast in the lead as Hanshiro Tsugumo, a masterless middle-aged samurai struggling to survive by making umbrellas while caring for his daughter (Shima Iwashita) and grandchild. Typically for Kobayashi, the protagonist is a righteous individual battling an unjust society. Only 29 at the time, Nakadai initially had doubts that he was right for the part and thought that Toshiro Mifune might have been more suitable. However, being greatly impressed by the script, he put these misgivings aside and made himself appear older by growing a beard and using the lower tones of his voice. Some subtle make-up also helped, with the result that Nakadai was quite believable as a 50-year old. A number of fellow Haiyuza actors also appeared in the film, including Ichiro Nakatani, Yoshio Inaba and Masao Mishima.

As he had to spend much of the film kneeling in the *seiza* position on a mat narrating events in flashback, Nakadai paid particular attention to the use of his voice in this role. During these scenes in the courtyard, he also had a large amount of dialogue with Rentaro Mikuni, who was playing the chief representative of the Iyi clan and was sitting on a veranda a considerable distance away. Mikuni, Nakadai's senior by nearly 10 years, was born Masao Sato and had made his film debut in Keisuke Kinoshita's *The Good Fairy* (1951) playing a reporter named Rentaro Mikuni, a name he had taken for his own. One of Japanese cinema's most peculiar stars, he seemed to delight in making himself as unappealing as possible. For his role in Satsuo Yamamoto's *Ballad of the Cart* (Niguruma no uta, 1959), in which he had to age by 40 years during the course of the story, he went so far as to have all of his upper teeth removed to make himself convincing as a decrepit old man.[30] Unlike Nakadai, Mikuni was a pure film actor with no theatrical background and was speaking softly, confident that the microphone would pick it up, whereas Nakadai thought it necessary to project his own voice to cover the distance and was struggling to hear what Mikuni was saying. The two actors got into an argument, at which point Kobayashi halted production and told them to let him know when they had resolved it – a process which took three days! Mikuni's performances were of variable quality, but in this case he was admirably restrained as an unyielding man convinced he is doing the right thing.

Another challenge Nakadai faced was the fact that, not only would *Harakiri* involve extensive swordfighting sequences, but Kobayashi wanted to increase the sense of danger by using real swords. At the time, it was standard practice to use fakes made from silver-coated bamboo or duralumin, an aluminium alloy used in the production of airships and bicycle frames. The only previous film in which Nakadai had wielded a sword was *Sanjuro*, and most of the swordfighting in that had been done by Mifune. He sought advice from Kinnosuke Nakamura, a star of *chambara* (sword-fighting) films who lived in Kyoto (where *Harakiri* was being shot) and was married to Nakadai's frequent co-star Ineko Arima. Nakamura, born a month before Nakadai, was a former kabuki actor who had made his stage debut at the age of 4. As an adult, he switched to film work in 1954, initially appearing in low-budget programme-fillers, but becoming a fully-fledged movie star by the end of the decade. The two actors met at a bar in Gion, where Nakamura offered some useful tips, such as moving the sword in the shape of the *kanji* for rice (similar to an asterisk) when attacking. In

---

[30] For more on this, see Chia-ning Chang's translation of *My Life as a Filmmaker* by Satsuo Yamamoto (University of Michigan Press, 2017).

preparation, Nakadai practised this with some fellow actors in a *dojo*[31] he had built in his garden for the purpose. Later, during filming, he visited Nakamura at his home, and they had a lively discussion about acting theory which soon became heated, with the two stars throwing whisky at each other while a tearful Arima begged them to stop. The two men calmed down and decided to continue their debate in a bar, but the influence of alcohol soon caused their tempers to flare up again and they got into a fistfight. Nakadai's swollen face caused problems for the production crew the following day, as did the condition of Nakamura's face for the film he was making at the time. They subsequently laughed this incident off and became good friends.

In one sequence, Nakadai had to fight a duel against Tetsuro Tanba, the film's other main villain, playing a more sadistic type than Mikuni. Tanba was much more confident in the use of swords and tried to reassure a nervous Nakadai that all he had to do was duck and everything would be fine. When the long-awaited violence finally erupts in the film's climax, Kobayashi's insistence on using real weapons not only made it more dangerous for the actors, but also more exhausting due to the heavier weight of authentic swords. It also meant that the battle is not elegantly choreographed but rather clumsy and messy, which seems to have been what Kobayashi, in his pursuit of realism, was trying to achieve. This sequence alone took up a week of the film's three-month shooting schedule. Nakadai later claimed that *Harakiri* was the only Japanese film to use real swords throughout.

Harakiri saw Kobayashi working once more with cameraman Yoshio Miyajima, who made excellent use of the widescreen format. Another notable element of *Harakiri* is the score by Toru Takemitsu, who cleverly utilised the *biwa* for dramatic punctuation, a type of Japanese lute traditionally used as an accompaniment to storytelling but rarely heard on film soundtracks previously.

Despite the fact that *Harakiri* is unusually talky for a Japanese film, the two-hour running time passes quickly due to the ingenuity of

---

[31] A training room for the practice of martial arts.

Hashimoto's screenplay, which is not only inherently suspenseful as we wait to see what Nakadai will do, but also contains some highly effective surprise revelations. Perhaps because *Harakiri* allowed Nakadai to express a wide range of emotions and demonstrate both his vocal and physical skills as well as play a character older than and quite different from himself – not to mention the fact that it is so well-executed in every department – *Harakiri* has remained Nakadai's personal favourite of all his films. The film was entered into competition at the Cannes Film Festival, which was attended by Kobayashi, along with Nakadai and his wife – the first time either had travelled abroad. Although Yasuko had shown no signs of depression after the stillbirth of their son, Nakadai thought that taking her along may be a good idea in the circumstances, and they had some extra money at the time due to an inheritance from her father.

Harakiri proved controversial at the festival because of the excruciating scene in which a young samurai is forced to commit hara-kiri with a bamboo sword. However, despite reports of women fainting in the audience, the film was praised by many, including Yukio Mishima, who was not present at the festival, but enjoyed the 'cruel beauty' of the film and believed that it's success was due to this, and to the fact that, deep down, Japanese audiences admired hara-kiri as an honourable and voluntary act. In saying this, Mishima was well aware that nothing could have been further from the intentions of the left-wing Kobayashi than to glorify Bushido, and it seems unlikely that many would have agreed with him.

Harakiri won Nakadai the Blue Ribbon Award for Best Actor as well as the Kinema Jumpo Award for the same category (although the latter was also partially for *Sanjuro*). Although the film lost out on the Palm d'Or to Visconti's *The Leopard*, it was awarded a Special Jury Prize which guaranteed distribution abroad. After the festival, Nakadai and Yasuko travelled around Europe for a month, visiting cities such as Paris, Rome, Venice, Florence and Vienna. Despite being a major film star in Japan, Nakadai was hardly ever recognised abroad and so felt quite relaxed, although the economic disparity made itself felt and the couple had to be careful with money, even electing to avoid the expensive hotel breakfasts and go to cheap cafes instead.

Nakadai's three period costume parts of 1962 in *Sanjuro*, *Ogin-sama* and *Harakiri* altered the course of his career. Although *Yojimbo* had also been a period piece, his role in it was to some extent deliberately anachronistic, as he was playing a character who was essentially a symbol of what was to come. Prior to 1962, Nakadai was widely perceived as an actor suited only to contemporary drama, but from this point on, he would play a roughly equal number of contemporary and period parts, becoming best-known in the West for the latter.

Chapter 9 – A Servant of Two Masters

Nakadai's next film has become one of the most obscure in his filmography. *Chibusa o daku musume-tachi* means something like 'Udder-pulling girls', but lacks an official English title.[32] The film itself told the story of workers at a dairy farm struggling to form a co-operative. Directed by Satsuo Yamamoto, who had been responsible for Nakadai's film debut in a speaking part in *Floating Weeds Diary*, it was produced by Japan's National Agricultural Film Association, financiers of Yamamoto's earlier success, *The Ballad of the Cart*.

Chibusa o daku musume-tachi

---

[32] The film is referred to as *Farm Girls* in the English edition of Satsuo Yamamoto's autobiography.

Nakadai appeared in a guest star role as Kenichi, the leader of a modernisation association in a neighboring village, while the leads were played by newcomers Yoshiko Ieda and Haiyuza student Kei Yamamoto (the director's nephew), the latter of whom was to become a close friend of Nakadai's. The supporting cast included fellow Haiyuza actor Ichiro Nakatani (as a vet) as well as Jukichi Uno, Ko Nishimura and Yunosuke Ito. After this film, Yamamoto's success with independent productions, combined with the cooling of anti-communist sentiments, saw him invited to work for a major studio once more. He made *Band of Assassins* (Shinobi no mono) for Daiei, singlehandedly inventing the ninja genre in the process. The film became a smash hit, spawning many sequels and imitations, and Yamamoto was *persona grata* once more.

Nakadai's play at Haiyuza for 1962 was a version of Carlo Goldoni's 18th-century Italian comedy *The Servant of Two Masters*, directed by Etaro Kozawa. This provided a rare opportunity to play a comic role as Truffaldino, the greedy servant who becomes embroiled in farcical complications as he flits between two masters, each of whom is unaware they are being two-timed.[33] Of course, as an actor who has always divided his time fairly equally between film and stage work, Nakadai himself can be said to be a servant of two masters. Although he has sometimes managed only one play a year, it is worth bearing in mind that these require considerable preparation, often tour and sometimes run for several months.

Madame Aki (Yushu heiya/'The Plain of Despair'), Nakadai's second film for Shiro Toyoda, again saw him in a supporting role, albeit a larger one than in *Anyakoro*. As usual with Toyoda, the film was an adaptation of a prestigious literary work, in this case an untranslated 1961 novel by the esteemed Japanese author Yasushi Inoue. The screenplay was by Toyoda's regular collaborator, Toshio Yasumi.

The story focuses on Aki (played by Kon Ichikawa favourite Fujiko Yamamoto), the wife of Katayuki, a business executive (Hisaya

---

[33] The play was reworked in 2011 as *One Man, Two Guvnors*.

Morishige) who begins a harmless flirtation with a deceased friend's younger sister, Misako (Michiyo Aratama). After seeing the two together, Aki becomes convinced that her husband is having an affair and confronts him. He admits that he finds Misako attractive, but denies having been unfaithful, although Aki is not convinced. When she meets an attractive young sculptor, Tatsumi (Nakadai), she feels free to embark on an affair of her own.

The film could not be accessed at the time of writing but, in his programme notes for a Toyoda season at the National Film Theatre in London in 1993, critic John Gillett described it thus: 'Beautifully shot by Kozo Okazaki in colour and widescreen... An all-star cast and Toyoda's knowing, ironic handling make this one of his best modern dramas.'

Madame Aki is notable as the final film of its lead actress, Fujiko Yamamoto, who had also played the author's wife with whom Nakadai's character has an affair in *Anyakoro*. Yamamoto may be familiar to many Western fans of Japanese films as the tomboyish thief in *An Actor's Revenge* and as the best friend of Ineko Arima's character in *Equinox Flower*. A former Miss Japan, she was a major star considered by many in her country to represent the ideal of Japanese beauty. However, Yamamoto, who had been starring in around ten films a year, did not retire willingly – her contract with Daiei had come up for renewal, and she insisted that changes be made. Masaichi Nagata, the head of the studio, not only refused to negotiate, but used his power to make the other studios promise not to hire her, with the result that she never appeared in a film again, although she continued to act on television and later in theatre. It is difficult to imagine this happening to a major star in Hollywood, and the incident illustrates how the Japanese studios generally refused to tolerate disobedience on the part of their stars, sometimes even working their actors to breaking point. There is no doubt that, if Nakadai had accepted a studio contract, he would have been forced to make a considerably higher number of films and given little say in which parts he played.

Kurosawa cast Nakadai opposite Toshiro Mifune for the third time in *High and Low* (Tengoku to jigoku/'Heaven and Hell'), but on this occasion they were on the same side for a change. Mifune played Gondo, the executive of a shoe company in Yokohama, who finds himself in a difficult position when a kidnapper abducts the son of his chauffeur, believing it to be Gondo's son. After realising his mistake, he demands that Gondo pay a huge ransom anyway or he will kill the boy.

Kurosawa had used a novel entitled *King's Ransom* by the American crime writer Ed McBain as his source. It seems to have been the moral dilemma of whether or not a man should pay a ransom to save the life of someone else's child which intrigued him the most, but there had also been a recent spate of kidnappings in Japan. *High and Low* is a rare example of a film being more complex than the book on which it was based, and it represents a high point in Kurosawa's artistry which was not entirely recognised at the time – the fact that it was classed as a crime story seems to have been enough in itself to prevent it being given serious consideration by contemporary critics, especially in America.

Nakadai had enjoyed reading translations of Ed McBain as a teenager, and *King's Ransom* had been among them, so he was thrilled to find himself cast as Tokura, the detective heading the investigation. Kurosawa told Nakadai that he wanted him to play the part like Henry Fonda, and had Nakadai's hairline shaved back slightly to make him look more Fonda-esque. Before Sergio Leone subverted his image in 1969 with *Once Upon a Time in the West*, Fonda had been the embodiment of a kind of basic decency without self-righteousness, and it was exactly this quality that Nakadai chose to emphasise in his performance. To a certain extent, he was also representing Kurosawa himself in expressing the director's feelings of moral indignation towards crimes of this nature. Tokura is impressed with Gondo's stoicism and has great sympathy for him. As a result, he is completely dedicated to the task of catching the criminal and begins almost to take the crime personally.

Tokura must have been a challenging part as Kurosawa not only neglected to provide him with any backstory whatsoever, but also gave him reams of detailed dialogue to deliver, most notably in the six-minute press conference scene, a near monologue in which Tokura explains the intricate details of the case before asking the reporters for their help. Nakadai thought he might have to do the scene multiple times in order to get it right, but managed to do it perfectly on the first take. Unfortunately, one of the other actors made a mistake near the end, and the scene had to be reshot, but the second attempt passed. Despite his absence for the first twenty minutes, Nakadai has almost as much screen time as Mifune, who disappears for much of the last hour, leaving Nakadai to carry half the film playing a character about whom almost nothing is known. He pulled it off flawlessly, making it hard to imagine *High and Low* working quite so well with another actor in the role.

Nakadai originally had an additional scene with Mifune which took place after Gondo visits the kidnapper in prison and was to have provided a coda. Kurosawa described the scene, filmed over a period of two weeks, in the following terms:

> We shot some long footage showing Nakadai and Mifune walking while thinking about Yamazaki. The two were full of unhappy feelings, despite having succeeded in their mission. To take this scene, we had made a huge set. They were about to part and they felt his shadow behind them. They couldn't forget him. [34]

Disregarding the considerable time and money that had been spent on it, Kurosawa changed his mind during the editing and deleted the scene entitrely. He decided instead to end with the more uncomfortable moment when the criminal is dragged back to his cell screaming and Mifune is confronted with his reflection in the glass partition.

Kurosawa shot much of *High and Low* in long takes using multiple cameras, spending more time in preparation and editing than in actual

---

[34] *Voices from the Japanese Cinema* by Joan Mellen (Liveright, 1975), p.50

shooting. In the famous bullet train sequence, when Gondo is to hand over the ransom, no less than eight cameras were used, and a retake was practically impossible. The cast were told that one mistake could cost Toho 20 million yen. Fortunately, despite the failure of one camera, Kurosawa got what he needed.

One of the director's motivations for making the film was his belief that the perpetrators of such a heinous crime should receive longer prison sentences, as some had served as little as three months, and he felt that harsher punishments would discourage potential kidnappers. Unfortunately, his film would be credited with inspiring a number of such crimes after its release, most notably the 'Yoshinobu case', in which a 4-year-old boy was kidnapped and murdered. The criminal collected a ransom of half a million yen, but was finally caught after a two-year investigation.[35] Kurosawa himself apparently received calls from people threatening to kidnap his daughter, and one from a man who said he would explode a bomb on a train unless the director paid him off. He informed the police, who sent officers to his house in case the man called back, but he never did. However, *High and Low* may have had some positive effect after all, as the law was revised the following year to increase the minimum sentence for kidnapping to three years' imprisonment.

It would be 17 years before Nakadai worked for Kurosawa again. Despite his run of commercial successes, including *High and Low*, during this period the director had been under increasing pressure to produce less costly films, just as Gondo is under pressure from the shoe company execs to churn out cheaper footwear. Kurosawa's adamant refusal to do so would lead to a falling out with Toho Studios and a much slower rate of output over the coming years.

Nakadai's next, *Pressure of Guilt* (Shiro to kuro/'White and Black'), was scripted by *Harakiri* writer Shinobu Hashimoto and directed by Hiromichi Horikawa, with whom he had previously made *The Blue Beast*. For their second collaboration, Nakadai was cast as Hamano, a

---

[35] This case formed the basis of Hideo Sekigawa's 1966 film *13,000 Suspects*.

man seen strangling a woman with a rope at the very beginning of the film. We are given no clue as to his motive until much later, but it gradually emerges that Hamano is a lawyer, the woman was the young wife of his much older boss, Munekata (Koreya Senda), and the two had been having an affair. Hamano flees the scene of the crime, and Nakadai spends most of his scenes looking sweaty and nervous while he strives to conceal his guilt. When Wakita (played by Nakadai's friend Hisashi Igawa, from *The Human Condition II* and Haiyuza), a burglar with a criminal record, is found with some of the dead woman's jewellery, the detective in charge of the case, Ochiai (Keiju Kobayashi), not only charges him with the murder, but intends to press for the death penalty. Meanwhile, Munekata, who is passionately against capital punishment, takes on the job of defending Wakita even though he believes him to be guilty, and he is assisted by Hamano. However, Wakita has tuberculosis and does not expect to live long; worn down by Ochiai's interrogations, he decides he may as well confess. Confession in the bag, Ochiai goes out with his colleagues to celebrate, but finds himself harangued by a drunken Hamano, who, not wanting to see another man executed for his crime, manages to sow seeds of doubt in the detective's mind.

There are a number of further twists and turns in the plot, which is certainly ingenious, if not altogether plausible. There are also hints of social criticism from Horikawa and Hashimoto in regard to the system which produces criminals like Wakita and the dubious justice of the death penalty, but the complexity of the story ultimately takes precedence and these themes are not pursued fully. At the beginning of the film, it appears that Nakadai is the main protagonist, but the focus soon shifts away from him and on to Ochiai as the detective who finds himself digging into an apparently solved case despite the danger to his own reputation.

Pressure of Guilt

Nakadai does well in a part which is difficult because the plot demands that his character commit actions which do not fully convince as those of the apparently rational human being Hamano is supposed to be. His best scene is the one where he is gently but doggedly questioned by Ochiai; cleaning his glasses under the table in order to hide his shaking hands, he finally breaks down under the 'pressure of guilt' which gave the film its American title. Given that a number of Kurosawa collaborators worked on the film, it may or may not be a coincidence that Hamano's eyes are often spookily seen as twin points of light reflected in his glasses, as were the kidnapper's in *High and Low*, which came out around the same time in Japan. *Pressure of Guilt* is an atmospheric piece of work which successfully keeps the audience guessing and looks and sounds great thanks to Hiroshi Murai's black and white cinemascope photography and Toru Takemitsu's impeccable score. The long unavailability of the film in the West is difficult to understand and it deserves to be more widely seen.

At around this time, Nakadai's mother made a surprising revelation about the family history. Nakadai had always been told that his paternal grandfather had been a farmer, but he now learned that he had in fact been a travelling actor who had made his grandmother pregnant while passing through on tour. Nakadai had never met his grandfather, and his father had instructed his mother to keep this to herself. Years later, during a trip to Hokkaido, Nakadai and Yasuko went to an exhibition of photographs from old theatre performances. Yasuko pointed at a picture of an actor and told her husband that the man looked just like him, but when Nakadai looked, he thought the man more closely resembled his father. However, despite this intriguing clue, he was never able to discover anything further.

Nakadai's next film role was in *The Legacy of the 500,000* (Gojuman-nin no isan), notable as the only film directed by Toshiro Mifune, albeit with some help from chief assistant director Shigekichi Takamae, whom he acknowledged in the opening credits. It was the first film produced by Mifune's newly-formed production company, and he reportedly found himself in the director's chair more as a result of necessity than any personal ambition. Feeling insecure, he surrounded himself with Kurosawa collaborators, including cinematographer Takao Saito and composer Masaru Sato. The screenplay was by Ryuzo Kikushima, who had co-written *Yojimbo*, *Sanjuro* and *High and Low*, and also written *When a Woman Ascends the Stairs*, but in this case the script seems to have been a lot less polished.

The plot concerns Takeichi Matsuo (Mifune), a Second World War survivor who now runs a small business. He is approached in the street by Mitsura Gunji (Nakadai), an old wartime acquaintance, who has discovered that Matsuo is the only person to know the location of a fortune in gold coins buried by the Japanese army in the Philippines during the war. He wants Matsuo to retrieve the treasure, but Matsuo refuses, so Gunji forces him to co-operate by threatening his daughter. Matsuo reluctantly returns to the Philippines after nearly 20 years, accompanied by Gunji's far-from-trustworthy cohorts, but when he arrives he finds himself haunted by the memory of the 500,000 Japanese who died there during the war, and his plans change.

Nakadai played Gunji as a slick, well-groomed salesman and opportunist who has clearly made his fortune on the black market after the war. He was given some grey hair courtesy of the make-up department in order to make him look a similar age to Mifune, 12 years his senior. Although the two actors had already become famous on-screen adversaries in two previous films, anyone hoping for another memorable showdown scene was to be disappointed, as Nakadai's character does not make the journey to the Philippines, and is in fact not seen again once Matsuo leaves Japan.

Mifune seems to have had ambitions beyond making an entertaining adventure film, and some straining for significance is evident throughout. Much of this manifests itself in the relationship between Matsuo and Tsukuda, a young criminal in whom Matsuo thinks he sees a glimmer of goodness (played by none other than Tsutomu Yamazaki, *High and Low*'s kidnapper). Unfortunately, this attempt at depth does not really come off as some of the story developments are none too plausible, making it hard to take seriously. In addition, as far as films portraying men falling out over gold go, *The Legacy of the 500,000* suffers greatly in comparison to *The Treasure of the Sierra Madre*. However, it remains a well-shot and competent entertainment, albeit a little disappointing overall. Much of the editing was apparently undertaken by an uncredited Kurosawa as a favour to Mifune. The film was a commercial success in Japan, but went unreleased in Europe originally, perhaps because it was felt that the sympathy the film shows for the 500,000 fallen Japanese soldiers would have been poorly received considering the lack of acknowledgement for the dead of other nations. However, it did receive a US release, although the critical response on both sides of the Pacific was unenthusiastic. Mifune had apparently inspired a great deal of loyalty on set from his cast and crew, which was just as well as directing had not come naturally to him, and after this film he kept his promise never to direct again.

Nakadai's next film, *Miren* ('Unforgettable'), was an adaptation of Jakucho Setouchi's autobiographical novel *The End of Summer* (Natsu no owari), which would be filmed again under that title in 2013.[36] The screenplay was by Zenzo Matsuyama, who had co-written scripts for a number of previous films featuring Nakadai by Masaki Kobayashi and Mikio Naruse, while the director was Yasuki Chiba, who had directed Nakadai in *Oban* and its sequels. *Miren* seems not to have been released outside Japan, but many of those who have seen it have noted its similarity to Naruse's classic *Floating Clouds* (Ukigumo), and the story is as follows:

Tomoko (Junko Icheuki) is a textile designer who has been having an affair with a failed writer, Kosugi (Noboru Nakaya), for the past eight years. Kosugi still lives with his wife, Yuki (Kyoko Kishida from *Woman in the Dunes*), but Tomoko earns enough to be independent and does not consider herself a kept woman. Kosugi divides his time between the two women, who know of each other's existence but have never met. However, this delicate triangle is upset when Tomoko runs into Ryota Kinoshita (Nakadai), an old flame she had known before Kosugi. Ryota is down on his luck, and she takes pity on him, partly because she feels a twinge of guilt about the past. It emerges that Tomoko had been married herself, and left her husband to be with Ryota, but subsequently broken off the relationship, which now starts up again.

---

[36] The novel's title was not used in 1963 as there had been an unrelated film of that name by Yasujiro Ozu two years earlier.

Although Nakadai was top-billed in *Miren*, the focus seems to have been on the character of Tomoko, and the film to have been a fairly typical example of what was generally known in those days as a 'women's picture.' Director Yasuki Chiba had a good reputation at the time but is almost forgotten today, apparently even in Japan. However, the one Chiba film to have surfaced in the West, *Tokyo Sweetheart* (Tokyo no koibito), is a beguiling comedy worth seeking out. Starring Setsuko Hara and Toshiro Mifune, it features a variety of eccentric characters struggling to get by in post-war Tokyo.

Nakadai's fifth and final film for Mikio Naruse was arguably the best – both in terms of film *and* role – after *When a Woman Ascends the Stairs*. Released in November 1963 and entitled *A Woman's Life* (Onna no rekishi), it again starred Hideko Takamine, this time as Nobuko, a war widow looking back on a life of hardship and tragedy. The film itself threatens to become quite depressing, featuring as it does no less than three bereavement scenes, and depicting a world in which it seems to rain all the time. However, a couple of welcome rays of light break through the clouds, one of which is the character of Akimoto, played by Nakadai.

Nobuko finds herself entering into an arranged marriage with Koichi (Akira Takarada), whose friend Akimoto gives a sincere speech at the wedding party saying that he will not marry until he finds a woman as beautiful and intelligent as her. He then performs a traditional Japanese song in tribute to the couple. Nobuko, who has had her eyes modestly glued to the floor throughout this episode, cannot help briefly raising them to look at Akimoto. Takamine manages to suggest a great deal with this glance – namely, that Nobuko has just realised that she has married the wrong man. Nevertheless, Koichi seems nice enough at first and the two soon have a son but, when the war comes and Koichi is killed, she discovers that he had been having an affair. After the war, she struggles to get by, but is helped by Akimoto, who is now involved in some minor racketeering. The two fall in love, but Akimoto is forced to leave town when the police are tipped off about his activities. In the chaos of post-war

Japan, Nobuko does not see him again until many years later, when Akimoto is now a respectable middle-aged married man with three daughters.

Written by the incredibly prolific screenwriter Ryozo Kasahara, the film is not based on the famous Guy de Maupassant novel of the same name, at least not directly. However, like Maupassant's Jeanne, Nobuko marries a man who is unfaithful to her before he gets killed, and she has a son who is constantly asking her for money and involved with a woman she disapproves of. In other respects, Nobuko is quite different from Jeanne, as her background is not particularly privileged and she has to work hard just to survive.

Perhaps because we see Akimoto in greatly varying circumstances over a period of many years, he seems much more of a believable human being than do the previous two characters Nakadai had played for Naruse. He also gets a chance to sing, which he does rather well, and ages quite believably throughout the course of the story, although the make-up artist also deserves some credit here. The repressed love between Nobuko and Akimoto feels convincing and it seems a shame that *A Woman's Life* was to be Nakadai's last film with the great Hideko Takamine.

Nakadai's one play for 1963 was *Everything Ends in a Song* (Mo nomina uta de owaru), a new musical by Kiyoteru Hanada about Izumo no Okuni, believed to be the founder of the kabuki theatre. A Haiyuza production directed by Koreya Senda, it opened at the new Nissay Theatre in Chiyoda, Tokyo. Nakadai played Okuni's samurai lover, Sansaburo Nagoya (c.1572-1603), while Okuni was played by the singer and actress Yaeko Mizutani. Although not a Haiyuza member herself, this was appropriate casting as she came from a family of kabuki performers.

In *Fire Ants' Strategy* (Jigoku sakusen), Nakadai played Lieutenant Isshiki, the leader of the Fire Ant Corps, a suicide squad of soldiers with dubious histories tasked with blowing up a bridge on the Chinese Front towards the end of the Second World War. The film was the seventh in Toho's *Desperado Outpost* series, but series creator Kihachi

Okamoto only directed the first three, and this entry was directed by the less distinguished Takashi Tsuboshima. In any case, there seems to have been no narrative connection with the previous films, although it repeated the combination of action and comedy pioneered by Okamoto.

Fire Ants' Strategy.

Fire Ants' Strategy was released at the end of April 1964. Nakadai, a baseball fan and supporter of the Yomiuri Giants, also contributed a cameo around this time to the baseball film *Mr Giant's Victory Flag* (Misuta jaiantsu shori no hata), in which he was briefly seen as a guest at a celebration party.

Chapter 10 – Seeing Ghosts

In 1964, Nakadai played two leading roles on stage for Haiyuza. The first was a production of the classic Japanese ghost story *Yotsuya Kaidan*, in which he played Iemon under the direction of Eitaro Ozawa. This was a highly unusual and controversial choice as it was unheard of for a *shingeki* troupe such as Haiyuza to stage a kabuki play like *Yotsuya Kaidan*. Nakadai had to have his whole body painted white for each performance. The cast also featured Michiko Otsuka as Iemon's unfortunate wife, Oiwa, along with Kunie Tanaka, Masao Mishima, Etsuko Ichihara, Mikijiro Hira, and Eitaro Ozawa himself. Despite objections from the purists, the production was successful enough to lead to a film version directed by Shiro Toyoda the following year.

Nakadai's other Haiyuza play of 1964 was *Hamlet* under the direction of Koreya Senda, who had once played the part himself. Etsuko Ichihara played Ophelia, Mikijiro Hira was Horatio and Eijiro Tono the grave digger, while Go Kato, Kei Yamamoto and Kunie Tanaka were also in the cast. When Mikijiro Hira passed away in 2016, Nakadai paid tribute to his colleague's acting skills, recalling how he had felt Hira's tears flowing into his open mouth when Horatio holds the dying Hamlet in his arms at the end of the play.

According to the American academic Thomas Rimer, who saw the production in Kobe and gave a lecture on Senda in which he discussed it, Senda cut parts of the play, but stressed the political aspects, making it clear that Hamlet was 'a product of social forces.' Rimer quotes Nakadai as saying, 'This is the hardest thing I've ever tried to do in my life. I've seen Shakespeare, but I've never acted in it and, as a Japanese man, we're not supposed to talk, you just sort of grunt, but Hamlet has all these long soliloquies and no Japanese man talks like that! How am I supposed to do this and be real at the same time?' Nevertheless, Rimer felt that Nakadai's performance was 'athletic' and 'remarkable.'[37]

---

[37] Rimer's lecture, *Berlin in Tokyo: Senda Koreya, Brecht, Shakespeare* can be found on YouTube

Towards the end of the year, Nakadai starred in the series *Shionogi TV Theatre presents Tatsuya Nakadai Hour: The Kaga Rebellion*, which depicted the feudal system from the perspective of Denzo Otsuki (1703-48), a feudal lord played by Nakadai. The script, by *Harakiri* writer Shinobu Hashimoto, was based on a novel by Genzo Murakami. Sponsored by Shionogi, a pharmaceutical company, the series was produced by Fuji TV and cast entirely with Haiyuza actors. Nakadai subsequently appeared in a number of other dramas under this arrangement.

After playing a middle-aged man for Kobayashi in *Harakiri*, Nakadai now found himself cast as an 18-year-old in the director's latest, *Kwaidan*. Based on the stories of Lafcadio Hearn, a Westerner who went to Japan as a foreign correspondent in 1890 at the age of 40, *Kwaidan* is perhaps the main reason why Hearn is remembered today. Hearn fell in love with Japan and continued to live there for the remaining 14 years of his life, producing a large number of books about the country in the process. Some were comprised of his versions of Japanese folk tales he had collected, often involving ghosts. Hearn's immersion in his adopted culture not only led to him marrying a Japanese woman with whom he had four children, but also resulted in his conversion to Buddhism. *Kwaidan: Stories and Studies of Strange Things* was published shortly before his death from heart failure in 1904.

Kobayashi based his film on four of these stories, one of which was 'Yuki-Onna', meaning 'Snow Woman.' This seven-page story became a 40-minute section of the film in which Nakadai played Minokichi, a young woodcutter who gets caught in a snowstorm in the forest along with the much older man from whom he is learning his trade. Finding shelter in a hut, they are visited by a spirit in the shape of a beautiful woman (Keiko Kishi) with very pale skin who kills the old man with one freezing breath, but spares Minokichi because he is so young and handsome. However, there is a catch – if he ever tells anyone what happened on this night, she will kill him. Time passes, and one day Minokichi meets a beautiful woman, Yuki, in the forest. She says she is on her way to Edo to look for work. He invites her to rest at his house, the two fall in love, get married and have three children. One day, Minokichi is suddenly struck by his wife's resemblance to the Snow Woman and tells her about it, causing Yuki to reveal that she is the spirit that visited him on that night.

Kobayashi was very faithful to Hearn's story, the only notable divergence being that Minokichi and Yuki have ten children in the story but only three in the film, and one can easily imagine his reasons for making this change. He also added some extra parts but, most notably, he allowed the film to take its time in building the atmosphere in a way the rather bare-bones story does not, so it is fair to say that this is a rare case of a film improving on a literary original.

Although it was pushing it to have Nakadai playing an 18-year-old at the age of 31, it works, partly because *Kwaidan* is not a film which is concerned with realism in any form. Not only does Kobayashi not attempt to hide the fact that the snowstorm scenes are all filmed in a studio, he more or less emphasizes the artificialty of the environment by using art design and lighting impossible in nature, together with surreal touches such as the eyes in the sky which seem to look down upon the woodcutter with evil intent. This image was recycled by Francis Ford Coppola in his version of *Dracula*, and the influence of *Kwaidan*'s visual design can even be seen in the films of Kurosawa, most notably the dream sequence in *Kagemusha*. Shot by Kobayashi's favourite cameraman, Yoshio Miyajima, *Kwaidan* is one of the most visually striking films ever made, and dialogue is kept to a minimum – it is a long time before Nakadai speaks, so for the first half of the Yuki-Onna section he has to rely on his expressive eyes, which he uses most effectively. He would no doubt have made an excellent silent film actor, but he does get to deliver a memorable speech towards the end when he innocently confides his secret to his wife. On the face of it, 'Yuki-Onna' is a rather silly and predictable story, but the combined effect of excellent actors, beautiful images and Toru Takemitsu's unearthly score create a truly bewitching piece of art, which also holds true for the rest of this remarkable three-hour film.

Kwaidan was reportedly the most expensive film ever made in Japan at the time, and the sets – all meticulously painted by hand – were designed on such a scale that the usual studio spaces would not be able to accommodate them. For this reason, it was shot in a huge building on the outskirts of Kyoto owned by a car manufacturer and containing a testing track for the company's new cars.[38] The cost involved eventually bankrupted the Ninjin Club (co-founded by Keiko Kishi), which was co-producing the film with Toho. Most of the cast and other staff contributed their services free of charge. In Nakadai's case, he also not only paid for his own travel expenses and accommodation, but contributed 4 million yen to the production – money he never saw again. For his part, Kobayashi was forced to sell his house and lived in rented accommodation for the rest of his life. Although he left the money to Nakadai in his will, Nakadai felt uncomfortable accepting it from Kobayashi's family and declined it.

When the film was entered in competition at the Cannes Film Festival, Nakadai and Kobayashi travelled to France to attend, and were looked after by Keiko Kishi, who had married a French film director, Yves Ciampi, in 1956, and was residing in the country. Unfortunately, Kobayashi was informed on arrival in Cannes that the film was too long and would have to be cut before it could be screened. He ended up removing the 'Yuki-Onna' sequence in its entirety, which must have felt like a tremendous slap in the face for Nakadai and Kishi. However, Nakadai was convinced that it must have been a difficult decision made simply because it had been the least damaging option artistically and Kobayashi had always put his art above all other considerations. Nakadai remained loyal and Kishi cannot have taken it too personally as she worked with Kobayashi again a decade later, appearing in *The Fossil* (Kaseki). The 'Yuki-Onna'

---

[38] This description comes from the book *Tatsuya Nakadai Talks about the Golden Age of Japanese Cinema* (Japan, 2013) and contradicts other sources stating that it was filmed in an aircraft hangar.

sequence was shortened for the film's release abroad, but eventually reinstated at its full length.

Kwaidan went on to become one of the Japanese films most widely-seen in the West, while 'Yuki-Onna' has been adapted as a feature film on at least two occasions, and also inspired a section of Akira Kurosawa's *Dreams*, in which *Ran* actress Mieko Harada appeared as a more benevolent Snow Woman who rescues a group of mountaineers caught in a blizzard.

Unfortunately for Kobayashi, after this artistic if not financial triumph, it would be largely downhill. Television had been slower to take off in Japan than in America, but many Japanese had invested in a TV set in 1964 in order to watch the Tokyo Olympic Games. As a result, audience numbers fell significantly as many families chose to save money and stay at home for their entertainment, signalling the end of the Japanese cinema's 'Golden Age'. The film industry in Japan struggled increasingly from this point on, and perfectionist directors like Kobayashi were no longer indulged with such large budgets and long shooting schedules. Although he would live for a further 32 years, Kobayashi's output dwindled to such an extent that he would only manage to complete six more feature films, and it was a similar story for Kurosawa. On the other hand, more pragmatic directors, such as Kon Ichikawa and Kihachi Okamoto, accepted the diminished scale of their films and continued to be prolific, although there was a marked decline in the quality of their later work.

Nakadai's third film for Shiro Toyoda saw him playing the lead role of Iemon in *Illusion of Blood*, a version of the 1825 play *Yotsuya Kaidan* by Namboku Tsuruya which he had performed on stage the previous year. This classic kabuki play had already been filmed many times before and remains the most famous ghost story in Japan. Confusingly, the play was itself based on a novel of unknown authorship dating from 1727 said to be based on real events, while the English translations available are based on a *rakugo* version by Ryuo Shunkintei published in text form in 1896 (*rakugo* being a form of theatrical oral storytelling unique to Japan).[39] The details of the story differ considerably from version to version.

Notable previous versions of the play included Nobuo Nakagawa's 1959 film (the Japanese equivalent of a Hammer film), and Kenji Misumi's less lurid version from the same year. However, perhaps the most intelligent film version is Keisuke Kinoshita's two-part 1949 adaptation, which downplays the supernatural element and has Iemon as a moral weakling manipulated by the poison poured into his ear courtesy of an Iago-like Naosuke. In *Illusion of Blood*, however, it is made clear early on (though not from the start) that Iemon is a thoroughly bad egg.

Iemon is a samurai who (like Hanshiro Tsugumo in *Harakiri*) has been reduced to making umbrellas after his lord has gone mad as a result of 'bad blood.' Iemon's wife, Oiwa (Mariko Okada), is pregnant but has been called back home by her father (Yasushi Nagata), who is also living in reduced circumstances for the same reason as Iemon. He plans to hire Oiwa out as a prostitute to the local brothel, where her sister, Osode (*Miren*'s Junko Ikeuchi) is already employed. Iemon visits his father-in-law in an attempt to persuade him to let Oiwa return, but the two have a quarrel during which it emerges that Iemon had stolen some money from their lord and his father-in-law knows about it, telling him, 'You'll never be a samurai again!' Iemon replies, 'As things are, the world's not worth living in,' and kills the old man. It is at this point that we realise that Iemon, an apparently sympathetic character down on his luck and missing his wife, is actually an insincere and ruthless individual who will stop at nothing to regain his former status.

Leaving the house after the murder, Iemon has a chance encounter with his friend Naosuke (Kanzaburo Nakamura XVII), who has just committed a murder of his own. Naosuke is of low status and in love with Osode, who had rebuffed him at the brothel earlier that evening. Shortly after this rejection, Osode's estranged fiancé, Yomoshichi

---

[39] For further detail, see Takashi Saito's introduction to *Ghastly Tales from the Yotsuya Kaidan* (Chisokudo Publications, 2020).

(Mikijiro Hira), had arrived out of the blue, leaving after an emotional scene. Naosuke had followed him when he left, then killed him out of jealousy; he cheerfully shows the corpse to Iemon with the boast, 'I skinned his face to be safe!' Iemon sees an opportunity to divert suspicion away from himself, and the two carry the body to his father-in-law's house, hoping it will appear that Yomoshichi had died attempting to defend the old man from an attack by persons unknown.

An opportunity arises for Iemon to gain a position through the help of Ito (Eitaro Ozawa), but this involves marrying Ito's daughter, Oume (Mayumi Ozora), so he must find a way to rid himself of Oiwa in order to do so. Bizarrely, he gives Oiwa some 'special medicine' provided by Oume's governess, Omaki (Keiko Awaji) which disfigures her horribly – a part of the story which makes little sense in this version – and he kills her shortly afterwards, but Oiwa's spirit returns to haunt Iemon and frustrate his plans.

The ghost of Oiwa can be seen equally as a hallucination brought on by Iemon's guilty conscience or a vengeful spirit with a will of its own. In this version, Toyoda and Nakadai decline to favour one interpretation over the other, but in the later stages it becomes clear that Iemon is losing his mind and the ghost is visible only to him. Like Macbeth, he has abandoned morality for the sake of ambition and will not escape the consequences. The film now seems like a warm-up for the following year's classic *Sword of Doom*, another film in which Nakadai portrays a samurai who consciously chooses the path of evil and finds himself bound for hell as a result.

In Kenji Misumi's earlier version, Iemon takes no part in the poisoning of his wife and kills those responsible when he finds out about it. What Iemon does to his wife in *Illusion of Blood* is so cruel that it subsequently becomes impossible to have the slightest sympathy for him. For this reason, Nakadai's performance inevitably becomes more one-dimensional than usual, especially as a substantial amount of screen time is also devoted to other characters such as Naosuke, and it is perhaps famous kabuki actor Kanzaburo Nakamura XVII[40] in this rare film role who steals the show with his more casual brand of villainy. Naosuke is also more interesting because, despite being capable of skinning the face of his rival, he is genuinely in love with Osode to the extent that his feelings render him as helpless as a child in her presence. A strong supporting cast also featured Eijiro Tono as a priest, while Eitaro Ozawa, who had directed Nakadai in the stage version, repeated his role in the film, as did Masao Mishima (as Iemon's servant, Takuetsu) and Mikijiro Hira, although the other principles were different.

Michiko Otsuka, who had played Oiwa on stage, had made very few films and was probably not considered enough of a name to be cast in the film. Instead, Toyoda cast Mariko Okada, a major star who had won awards for her roles in Minoru Shibuya's *Season of Bad Women* (Akujo no kisetsu, 1958), Keisuke Kinoshita's *This Year's Love* (Kotoshi no koi, 1962) and Yoshishige Yoshida's *Akitsu Springs* (Akitsu onsen, 1962). She subsequently married Yoshida and starred in most of his films. Like Nakadai, Okada had lost her father to tuberculosis, but in her case she had no memories of him as he had died in 1934, when she was only one year old. However, after attending a screening of Kenji Mizoguchi's *The Water Magician* (Taki no shiraito, 1933) as a high school student, she had told her mother about the film and been surprised when she broke into tears and revealed that the film's star, Tokihiko Okada, had been Mariko's father. Okada returned to the cinema the following day and watched it again with new eyes. In some ways, she is not very well-served in *Illusion of Blood* as she begins the film playing Oiwa as a meek doormat, and when she finally has the chance to do some real acting in the crucial disfigurement scene, the director keeps her face hidden, although she is highly effective in spite of this.

---

[40] Kanzaburo Nakamura XVII (1909-88) is sometimes confused with his son, Kanzaburo Nakamura XVIII (1955-2012). The elder Nakamura also gives a memorable performance in Keisuke Kinoshita's *Thus Another Day* (Kyo mo mata kakute ari nan, 1959).

Some of the effects in the film look rather primitive today, but this is due to the time in which it was made rather than budgetary constraints (although the budgets for Japanese films were generally much lower than those of Hollywood productions). While it is true that some former versions of the story were of the B-movie variety, *Illusion of Blood* was mounted as a prestige production and even given an extra touch of class by Toru Takemitsu's splendidly unsettling score. Working from a screenplay by his regular collaborator Toshio Yasumi, Toyoda's direction is especially effective in the very long delay (around seven minutes) before we see Oiwa's disfigured face, even if the revelation when it comes is not especially shocking. In collaboration with *Pressure of Guilt* cameraman Hiroshi Murai, Toyoda uses screens as a visual motif throughout the film, lending a sense of the characters being hemmed in on all sides. Unfortunately, the film would surely have been more effective in black and white; it seems too colourful and brightly lit for a ghost story and consequently lacks the requisite atmosphere. *Illusion of Blood* received a limited release in the USA three years later.[41]

---

[41] Internet rumours of a three-hour running time in Japan with nudity and more graphic violence are unfounded.

Chapter 11 – The Return of Kihachi Okamoto

Nakadai's third film for Hiromichi Horikawa was *The Last Judgment* (Saigo no shinpan), based on an American novel, *Heaven Ran Last* by William P. McGivern, first published in 1949. McGivern is best remembered as the author of *The Big Heat* and *Odds against Tomorrow*, both of which were turned into notable *films noir* in the 1950s. Although one could easily imagine it as a movie starring Humphrey Bogart or John Garfield and Gloria Grahame, *Heaven Ran Last* was never filmed in Hollywood, but Horikawa somehow picked up on it, as his mentor Kurosawa had done with Ed McBain's *King's Ransom*. In this case, however, other than changing the setting to contemporary Japan, Horikawa followed the plot of the novel closely.

Jiro (Nakadai) is a professional gambler having an affair with a nurse, Masako (Chikage Awashima), who is married to his cousin, Riichiro (Fujio Suga), an engineer, while the latter is away on a two-year trip to oversee a construction project in Vietnam. When Riichiro returns, Jiro and Masako welcome him home, but secretly decide to find a way to remove him from their lives so they can continue their affair. Jiro receives further motivation when offered the chance to buy two pachinko parlours owned by Asai (Masao Mishima) and Masako reveals she has a lot of money in a joint savings account shared with her husband. When she tells him that Ueno, the director of the hospital where she works (Tatsuo Matsumura), is always pestering her for a date, Jiro believes he has found a way to commit the perfect murder. However, he decides that he must first arrange things so that the police will not connect him romantically with Masako, so he begins dating a waitress, Miyoko (*Onibaba*'s Jitsuko Yoshimura), to divert suspicion. Once this relationship is established and he learns that Riichiro will soon be going away for a week on business, he tells Masako to take her husband's wallet out of his pocket just before he leaves for the airport, and to arrange for her boss to come over half an hour later. Riichiro is a jealous man with a short fuse, who also happens to own a gun, and

Jiro arranges things so that he will drive his cousin to the airport, remind him on the way to check that he has his wallet, then drive him back home to get it just in time for him to catch Ueno and Masako together. However, Riichiro does not shoot Ueno in a jealous rage as planned, but merely beats them both up and walks out. Jiro, who had been waiting outside, sees Ueno walking off in a daze and goes to check what happened. Finding both Ueno and Masako unconscious, he finds Riichiro's gun and hastily shoots Ueno, then makes his escape. As expected, the police initially believe that Riichiro is the murderer, and he looks set to be sent away for a long stretch in prison, but a stubborn police detective (Junzaburo Ban) senses something is wrong. Jiro now has further problems – Miyoko is expecting him to marry her, and he is being threatened by Ohara (Takeshi Kato), a gangster who wants control of the pachinko parlours Jiro hopes to buy. Jiro comes up with another cunning plan to make Ohara kill Miyoko, believing her to be Jiro...

Horikawa used many of the same people who had worked on *Pressure of Guilt*, including Toru Takemitsu, who once again provided the score. Nakadai was also surrounded by actors he had worked with in previous films, such as Kunie Tanaka, who had a small part, and Chikage Awashima, who had appeared in the *Oban* films, *Anyakoro* and *The Human Condition Part 1* (as the leader of the Chinese 'comfort women') as well as *Pressure of Guilt*, but who was best known for playing rather more wholesome roles in the films of Yasujiro Ozu. Her final film, *Haru's Journey*, in 2010, was also with Nakadai.

The Last Judgment, shot in black-and-white and running a concise 95 minutes, has an excellent pedigree and appears to have been well-received in Japan, but has seldom (if ever) been shown in the West.

Nakadai's next would be the only film he made at Toei's Kyoto studios. *Wanderers: Three Yakuza* (Matatabi: sannin yakuza), was (as the title suggests) comprised of three separate stories. Although the main characters are *yakuza* rather than samurai, the fact that the film is set in the distant past and featured actors in period costume playing wanderers handy with a sword makes it very different from the typical *yakuza* film of the time and gives it more in common with samurai films centred around the exploits of *ronin*.[42] Nakadai played the lead in the first and longest story, 'Autumn', as Hatsukari-no-Sentaro, a *yakuza* on the run after killing two *hasshu-mawari* (travelling policemen who operated in the early 19th-century). We first see him disembarking from a boat and walking along a hilltop wearing a *sandogasa*, a large round hat which obscures the eyes and lends a sense of mystery to a character. The *sandogasa* is often seen in period Japanese films worn by *ronin* or wandering *yakuza*. Hatsukari asks a local *yakuza* gang (one of whom is played by Kunie Tanaka) for shelter, which they reluctantly provide. While deciding what they should do about this potentially troublesome intruder, they ask him to guard Oine, an uncooperative prostitute, to ensure that she does not run away. Hearing her story, he becomes sympathetic and realises that he has fallen in with a bad lot who are using him for their own ends.

Oine is played by Hiroko Sakuramachi in an admirably intense performance. By contrast, Nakadai is quite restrained and generously allows her to steal the show. A Toei contract player, Sakuramachi made 57 films for the studio in a 12 year period from 1957-1969, but never quite made the front rank. The second story, 'Winter', featured another Kurosawa favourite, Takashi Shimura, as an ageing *yakuza* seeking redemption while attempting to dissuade a young man from leading the *yakuza* life. The final episode, 'Spring', is more comic in tone and starred Kinnosuke Nakamura as a cowardly *yakuza* tricked by some crafty villagers into agreeing to kill a corrupt official who is bleeding them dry with spurious taxes. Nakamura received top billing as he was an even bigger star than Nakadai in Japan.

Each story in the film is quite different in tone and style, but all are well-written and have satisfying twists. The colour cinemascope cinematography by Osamu Furuya is impressive and director Tadashi

---

[42] Chris D's *Gun and Sword* devotes a whole chapter entitled 'Matatabi and Period Yakuza Films' to this sub-genre.

Sawashima handles all parts with confidence and style, although Masaru Sato's cartoonish, anachronistic score is less successful.

As a *shingeki* actor from Tokyo, Nakadai had faced some hostility during his first days at the studio, and he was warned not to get into any mahjong games with the contract players if he wanted to keep the shirt on his back. When it came to the *chambara* scenes, he learned that he was expected to tip in advance every actor he cut down to ensure they died properly. Nevertheless, he enjoyed making the film once he got used to the local customs and he got on well with Sawashima, who had been directing at Toei since 1957, making historical dramas, *yakuza* thrillers and musicals starring Hibari Misora. When his contract with Toei expired in 1967 and was not renewed, like many other Japanese directors around this time, he was forced to go freelance, but he struggled to find regular employment in the film industry and switched to stage work. While Sawashima's best-known film in the West, the 1969 Toshiro Mifune vehicle *Shinsengumi: Assassins of Honour*, is decent enough, *Wanderers: Three Yakuza* is better. A quality piece of entertainment which became a personal favourite of Nakadai's, it deserves to be more widely known.

In Kihachi Okamoto's Second World War film, *Fort Graveyard* [43] (1965), Nakadai appeared as Captain Sakuma, the superior officer to Sergeant Kosugi, played by Toshiro Mifune in a typical 'gruff exterior conceals a heart of gold' characterisation. Okamoto co-wrote the screenplay with Susumu Saji, based on a story by Keiichi Ito entitled 'Kanashiki Senki'.

When Kosugi reports to the Captain for the first time, we learn that he has been exiled to a remote outpost in China as a result of striking a superior officer. Warning Kosugi not to repeat his previous behaviour, Sakuma describes himself as 'fragile' and 'not suited to

---

[43] The Japanese title, *Chi to suna*, meaning 'Blood and Sand', was understandably not used in the West as there had already been two well-known Hollywood films of that name.

fighting.' Later, during an argument over the execution (ordered by Sakuma) of a young officer for desertion, Kosugi says contemptuously that he feels sorry for the Captain for being so 'fragile', then goes ahead and strikes him in the face. Sakuma returns the blow and orders the arrest of Kosugi, who is then imprisoned. However, Kosugi's mistress intervenes, hoping to use her feminine wiles to persuade Sakuma to release Kosugi and forget the incident. She is surprised to find Sakuma nervous in her presence and she intuitively realises that he is a virgin. Bizarrely, in order to *avoid* being seduced, Sakuma agrees to give Kosugi the chance of escaping court martial and subsequently assigns him to a highly dangerous mission involving the recapture of a fort fallen into the hands of the Chinese. To assist him in this task, Sakuma allows Kosugi to take along three misfits – an eccentric mortician, a chef with anger issues, and a conscientious objector – together with a squad of new recruits. These greenhorns are 18-year-old music students, each of whom is known by the name of his instrument – Sousaphone, Little Drum, etc. They specialise in the unlikely genre of Dixieland jazz, their favourite tune being 'When the Saints Come Marching In'.

There cannot be many Japanese comedies set in occupied China during the Second World War, but this is, indeed, what we have here, complete with erection jokes and fart gags. The female lead is played by Nakadai's frequent co-star Reiko Dan, here playing Oharu, a 'comfort woman' in love with Kosugi. At one point in the proceedings, with the encouragement of Kosugi, she provides 'comfort' one by one for the entire squad. There is no hint in the film that this might be anything other than an entirely wholesome activity – something very hard to imagine in a Western film. However, despite the emphasis on sex and humour there is, as the title suggests, also a great deal of death in the film, as well as a serious intent, which is hammered fully home in the ending – ultimately, *Fort Graveyard* is an anti-war film which wants us to remember how many young lives were needlessly wasted in the pursuit of military ambitions.

Director Kihachi Okamoto's career as an assistant director for Toho had barely begun in 1943 when he was conscripted. Although he saw no combat himself, and at the end of the war was still at the First Army Reserve Officer School in Toyohashi City, Aichi Prefecture, he witnessed the deaths of many comrades in an air raid during his time there. Okamoto made a number of films revolving around the conflict, always painting a resolutely unglamorous picture and emphasizing the high cost in human life, but he also saw the absurdity of war and frequently injected comic moments which most other filmmakers would have considered out of place.

This was Nakadai's first film for Okamoto since appearing in the director's debut, *All about Marriage*, in 1958. Okamoto had actually offered him the lead in *Desperado Outpost* (Dokuritsu gurentai) back in 1959, but Nakadai had been forced to decline due to his commitments to *The Human Condition*. The role went to another Haiyuza actor, Makoto Sato, and *Desperado Outpost* became a hit, spawning a number of sequels.[44] Sato became a star as a result, but it should not be considered a missed opportunity for Nakadai as *Desperado Outpost* did not have the impact that *The Human Condition* had. Although it proved popular with young men who appreciated the irreverent anti-establishment tone of the film, *Desperado Outpost* and its follow-ups were largely dismissed by the critics. Being the first film Okamoto made from his own script, the studio only allowed him a small budget, and this is evident in the settings featured in the film, while the contrived plot makes for a surprisingly talky experience for a reputed 'action' movie.

In any case, after *Fort Graveyard*, Nakadai and Okamoto would work together very effectively on a number of further films, and Okamoto seems to have been the director with whom Nakadai had the closest and most relaxed relationship. This was probably partly due to

---

[44] In fact, *Fort Graveyard* seems to have been promoted by the studio as a new Desperado Outpost film, although Okamoto did not himself consider it to be part of the series.

the fact that he was only nine years older than Nakadai, so the age gap between the two was not as large as it was between Nakadai and Kurosawa, Kobayashi or Ichikawa. Another factor was that Okamoto was not an established name when Nakadai first worked for him, as the others were. In Japanese society especially, etiquette dictates that those who are senior in age and/or position are treated with much greater deference. Perhaps most importantly, however, Okamoto was of a more self-effacing character than the others. In any case, the two were quite informal with one another, Okamoto addressing Nakadai by his nickname of 'Moya' and Nakadai addressing Okamoto as 'Kiha-chan', although they observed the formalities on set.

Fort Graveyard has been criticised over the years for its failure to address the atrocities committed by Japanese troops in China but, to be fair, this is not the subject of the picture and there is no racism in the portrayal of the Chinese characters. A well-made film, it remains memorable mostly for the incongruity of Japanese soldiers in China blasting out brass band jazz, but the jokey tone means that it never becomes quite as moving as Okamoto seems (judging from the way he chose to end it) to have hoped it would be.

Nakadai gave a strong performance in a small but significant role, but was perhaps not the most obvious choice to play a fragile virgin. Initially, he seems to be the villain of the piece, but Kosugi and Sakuma gradually develop a grudging respect. However, fans of Japanese cinema will appreciate the chance to enjoy yet another confrontation between Mifune and Nakadai. *Fort Graveyard* was released in the USA in May 1966 and may have been an influence on Robert Aldrich's *The Dirty Dozen*, released a year later.

Also in 1965, Nakadai played the title character in *Ronin of the Wilderness* (Koya no suronin), a four-part series made by Fuji for *Shionogi TV Theatre presents Tatsuya Nakadai Hour*.[45] This was followed the same year by a couple of two-part dramas for Fuji/Shionogi – one, a remake of Yasujio Ozu's 1941 film *Brothers and Sisters of the Toda*

---

[45] The series was remade in 1972 with Toshiro Mifune in the lead.

Family (Toda-ke no kyodai), the other a remake of Mikio Naruse's 1938 film *Tsuruhachi and Tsujiro* in which he co-starred with Fujiko Yamamoto.

Around this time, Nakadai also starred in a one-hour TV drama for director Satsuo Yamamoto, entitled *One Track Road* (Hitosuji no michi). Set in 1929, it featured Nakadai as an idealistic young scientist trying to develop a skin cream to help his mother and others who suffer from dry skin. His boss is only concerned with profits, so he quits and returns to his hometown, continuing his efforts from there and using the pure mountain spring water as an ingredient. He decides to enter a competition for best new cosmetic product, and rushes to get his work finished in time. Unfortunately, he falls ill and takes to his bed with a fever, but his wife (fellow Haiyuza member Misako Watanabe) continues the work under his instruction. Finally, an effective new product is created. The drama was produced by a cosmetic company and told a true story from the company's early history. This practice of a company making a TV drama or even a film as a means of advertising itself is not uncommon in Japan. While hardly among Nakadai's most significant roles, he nevertheless gave a thoroughly dedicated performance, making the formulaic drama surprisingly watchable.

Nakadai quickly found himself reunited with Kihachi Okamoto as producers at Toho felt that a collaboration between the two could be a winning combination and suggested they make a new version of *Daibosatsu Toge* (aka *The Great Bodhisattva Pass*), a hugely popular 41-volume novel by Kaizan Nakazato which had been serialised over many years and remained unfinished at the time of the author's death in 1944. The novel's main character, Ryunosuke Tsukue, is a master swordsman and seemingly amoral killer who travels throughout Japan in the 1850s and '60s hiring himself out as an assassin to anyone who pays. There had already been a number of film versions – Hiroshi Inagaki had made a two-part film of the book in 1935-1936,[46] Kunio

---

[46] Part One originally ran 136 minutes, but only 77 minutes survive, while only a 64-second fragment remains of the 110-minute Part Two.

Watanabe a now forgotten three-part version in 1953, Tomu Uchida an excellent trilogy known overseas as *Swords in the Moonlight* (1957-59) featuring a memorable performance by Chiezo Kataoka, and finally Kenji Misumi and Kazuo Mori had directed another trilogy starring Raizo Ichikawa, which was known abroad as *Satan's Sword* (1960-61). All had been successful, so Toho must have thought they were onto a winner. Okamoto, being more interested in making anti-war comedies at the time, was initially reluctant to accept the assignment but, once he agreed, he threw himself into the project and produced what is arguably his best, if not most typical, film. He was helped in no small part by the work of scriptwriter Shinobu Hashimoto, who had previously written the screenplays for *Harakiri* and *Pressure of Guilt*, as well as many of Kurosawa's finest films.

The Daibosatsu Toge itself is a mountain pass in central Japan whose spectacular views make it a popular destination for hikers. The opening scene of Okamoto's version – known in the West as *Sword of Doom* – takes place there, as does the opening scene of *Satan's Sword*. In fact, we can see by comparing the two films that Okamoto and Hashimoto added virtually nothing new in terms of story – *Sword of Doom* is virtually a scene-for-scene remake of *Satan's Sword* (Part One). However, *Sword of Doom* is superior in every way – Hashimoto improved the dialogue considerably and fleshed out the characters, while Okamoto cast the film with the very best actors. These included Nakadai's *Human Condition* co-star Michiyo Aratama, Yuzo Kayama (Mifune's co-star in *Red Beard*), the great character actor Ko Nishimura and, from Haiyuza, Kei Sato, Ichiro Nakatani and Kunie Tanaka. However, the trump card was the casting of Toshiro Mifune – the perfect choice to play Toranosuke Shimada, the one swordsman whom Tsukue fears. Furthermore, Raizo Ichikawa, so brilliant in *Conflagration*, had been rather wooden in *Satan's Sword* and given little depth to the character, so Nakadai was a vast improvement to say the least. The cinematography, music, art direction and editing were also much more impressive, while the peerless extended action scenes made *Satan's Sword* look lame indeed.

Another significant difference between the two versions was Okamoto's view of the main character – he saw Tsukue as a more modern, nihilistic (rather than straightforwardly evil) figure. In *Satan's Sword*, the killing of the old man at the beginning is portrayed as the result of a cruel whim – Tsukue just seems to commit the murder in order to practise his technique. In *Sword of Doom*, on the other hand, Nakadai appears at the shrine on the mountain pass just as the old man is praying that he will be allowed to die soon so as not to be a burden on his granddaughter. Tsukue could be said to be merely granting the old man his wish. In both films, Tsukue later murders his common-law wife and, again, in *Sword of Doom*, she asks to be killed, whereas in *Satan's Sword*, she does not. In fact, Tsukue does not initiate any of the killings in *Sword of Doom* – he only kills those who have asked to be killed, those who are foolish enough to attack him, and those he has been hired to assassinate. However, Nakadai makes it clear in his performance that Tsukue enjoys killing, as it appears to be the only time he feels truly alive – the rest of the time, Tsukue sits at home drinking saké while ignoring his wife and staring into space, seeming bored and listless. One of the reasons Tsukue is such a compelling character is that he is difficult, perhaps impossible, to understand. Although many of the other characters refer to him as 'evil', some of these are revealed to be hypocrites and there are times when Tsukue has the moral high ground.

Nakadai is superb in the part – at times, it is remarkable how little he seems to be doing, yet he commands the attention throughout. His performance in the fight scenes has seldom been equalled in the *chambara* genre, with the exception of the lightning-fast Toshiro Mifune. In one scene, he walks almost casually along a forest path, cutting down countless opponents as he goes. In the final scene, he loses touch with reality, slicing away at imaginary enemies before they are replaced by real ones, at which point he embarks on an extended orgy of violence. The scene recalls Iemon slashing away at ghosts at the climax of *Illusion of Blood*, but Okamoto takes things much further. Nakadai spent ten days in a row doing nothing but swordfighting for this final sequence, which had been carefully stoyboarded in advance. In a sequence lasting 10 minutes, Nakadai cuts down around 65-70 opponents.[47] Real swords were used in some sequences (mainly those in which Nakadai destroyed a large number of bamboo shades), a fact which made cameraman Kazuo Yamada especially anxious when he saw Nakadai's blade stabbing the tatami dangerously close to his own big toe.

The surprising thing about *Sword of Doom* is that, despite all the undeniable improvements it made on *Satan's Sword*, it was not very well-received in Japan, with the result that the planned sequel was cancelled. This is the reason for the film's abrupt ending, for the fact that a number of plot threads are left dangling, and also the explanation as to why the anticipated climactic confrontation between Nakadai and Mifune never occurs. Perhaps Japanese audiences were not too excited about seeing yet another version of the familiar story so soon after both the *Satan's Sword* and *Swords in the Moonlight* trilogies. It also may not have helped that all versions (including *Sword of Doom*) were known under the same title (*Daibosatsu Toge*) in Japan, and also that *Doom* was in black and white, whereas the previous two had been filmed in colour. However, the new film was quite successful abroad, where audiences were mostly unfamiliar with the story, the previous versions had been little seen, and Nakadai was better known than either Chiezo Kataoka or Raizo Ichikawa.

---

[47] An equally elaborate and impressive *chanbara* scene features in the climax of Tokuzo Tanaka's *The Betrayal* (Daisatsujin orochi, also 1966), in which Raizo Ichikawa single-handedly slaughters countless opponents is a surprisingly convincing manner.

Chapter 12 – Mr Chalk and Mr Cheese

Cash Calls Hell,[48] a Shochiku-Haiyuza co-production made in 1965, marked the first of Nakadai's collaborations with 36-year-old director Hideo Gosha, whose third film it was. Perhaps due to his background and character, Gosha's route into film directing had been a highly unusual one. His family were not considered 'respectable' as his father was a bouncer and his uncle – whom he lived with for a time – a gambler. Because of this, he had been the only boy in his class to receive corporal punishment for getting into fights at school. Later, as a young army conscript towards the end of the war, he had been hit so hard by an officer for being slow in rifle training that his jaw had been broken. In fact, his life as a young man became so miserable that he joined the kamikaze in the hope of being able to die but, ironically, health issues prevented him from taking part in any suicide missions and he survived the war relatively unscathed. However, his elder brother had been killed in action and his parents' home destroyed in an air raid. These experiences had made him into a tough, stubborn character who never allowed himself to show weakness.

After the war, he worked in a shop on an American military base, where he stole supplies and sold them on the black market to support his family, eventually earning enough to attend Meiji University. Determined to become a film director, after graduating he applied to every major studio, but was rejected by all. In desperation, he went to the home of Daiei head Masaichi Nagata and begged to be given a chance, but in vain. The closest he could get was a job in radio, but this eventually led to a job with Fuji TV, whom he managed to talk into letting him direct. In 1959, he directed his first drama, a series called *Detective* (Keiji), which was filmed live. Four years later, he scored a hit

---

[48] The original Japanese title, *Gohiki no shinshi*, translates as 'Five Gentlemen'; a distortion of this, *Five Human Beasts*, has also been used as a title for the film in the West.

with the series *Three Outlaw Samurai* (Sanbiki no samurai) and was given the opportunity to make it into a movie, which was also successful. Gosha seems to have been the first director to make the leap from TV to film in Japan – prior to this, apart from the occasional screenwriter or actor who went into directing, the only way to become a film director in the country had been to be taken on by a studio as a trainee and serve as an assistant director for at least five years, sometimes ten. For this reason, Gosha had faced great resistance from some in the film industry who wanted to protect their own interests and prevent television directors from making the crossover into film. Intimidation tactics had been used in an attempt to send him packing, but life had already made Gosha into such a hardhead he was unfazed by such behaviour.

Three Outlaw Samurai and Gosha's second film, *Sword of the Beast* (Kedamono no ken), were in the *chambara* genre, whereas *Cash Calls Hell* is a contemporary crime thriller – something of an anomaly at this stage of his career as he would subsequently return exclusively to the world of the samurai before eventually revisiting contemporary Japan in the 1970s. Shot in black and white, the striking use of shadows, high contrast and unsettling camera angles in *Cash Calls Hell* place us firmly in the world of *film noir*. The opening robbery sequence is entirely in negative, which makes for an effective attention-grabber. We are then introduced to Nakadai's character, Oida, in a prison yard, as he passively allows himself to be used as a human shield during a knife fight between two other inmates before finally making a move to defend himself. A flashback sequence reveals that Oida is from a working-class family but became an ambitious careerist and social climber, even managing to get himself engaged to the boss's daughter in order to enhance his position. However, his plans came to nothing when he lost control of his car during an argument with his mistress and accidentally killed a 7-year-old girl and her father. While Oida is no saint, he does take responsibility for his actions – becoming aware of the presence of the grieving widow in the police station, he voluntarily approaches her and apologises.

During the jail time which follows, he encounters Sengoku (Mikijiro Hira), a fellow inmate in whom he confides. We later learn that he is the mastermind of the robbery seen at the beginning of the film. Nakadai makes little eye contact with the other actors for much of the time, portraying Oida as a haunted man gazing into space as if at something unspeakably sad which only he can see, his large eyes unblinking pools of sorrow.

Soon to be released and with nothing waiting for him outside, Oida accepts a job from Sengoku before fully understanding what is involved. He knows only that he must make contact with Sengoku's woman, Utako (Atsuko Kawaguchi), at the bar where she works, and that she will give him instructions. We are introduced to Utako during a dispute with another bar hostess which ends up in typical Gosha fashion with the two women slapping the hell out of each other in the ladies'. Fight over, Utako goes outside for a fag and sees a stray dog looking for food. Taking pity on it, she kicks over a garbage bin so it can eat. At this point, Oida appears and it's not long before she's offering him 15 million yen (a very generous amount in those days!) to kill three men for Sengoku: Motoki (Hisashi Igawa), Umegaya (Kunie Tanaka) and Fuyushima (Ichiro Nakatani). These were Sengoku's colleagues in the robbery, but this information is withheld from Oida. There is a weakness in the story here as it already seems clear that the last thing Oida wants to do is kill more people but, despite the unconvincing motivation, he appears to accept the job.

Oida begins by seeking out Motoki at a shipyard, the first in a number of notably unusual and unglamorous locations featured throughout the film. He tells Motoki that he's a friend of Sengoku, and the two go drinking together, during which we learn via another flashback sequence that Motoki is an ex-cop who was compromised due to an affair with the wife of a criminal. By the time they leave the bar, Motoki is quite drunk. At one point, Oida appears about to push him into the canal before experiencing a change of heart. It then emerges that Motoki has left his lunchbox in the bar; as he can barely stand, Oida goes back to retrieve it. During his absence, two gangsters appear, one of whom carries an umbrella (Hideyo Amamoto), which he uses as a weapon, and speaks in curiously-accented Japanese – it later emerges that these two are from Hong Kong. By the time Oida returns, Motoki is dying as a result of a beating from the gangsters.

The next day, Oida goes to visit Motoki's family to return the lunchbox and is moved by the plight of his daughter, Tomoe (Yukari Uehara), now an orphan. The rest of the family have no wish to assume responsibility for her care, and Oida is the only one to show her any kindness. She follows him and calls him 'uncle.' In order to divert her attention and stop her trailing after him, he sends her to buy a balloon, intending to make his escape at the same time, but finds himself unable to abandon her – the trust she has placed in Oida has begun to restore his humanity and he realises that he needs her just as much as she needs him. However, Gosha never shied away from delivering the exploitation quotient and there follows a jarring transition from this genuinely moving moment to a scene in a strip club, in which we are introduced to the second man on Oida's list. This is Umegaya, who is controlling the lighting for the strip show, the star of which is his girlfriend, Akemi (Chiyo Aoi). When umbrella man and his cohort arrive, he blinds them with a spotlight and makes his escape via the window, leading to an exciting rooftop chase sequence in the course of which he manages to shake off his pursuers. Oida (accompanied by Tomoe) arranges to meet him at night in a deserted fairground. During their conversation, Umegaya talks passionately of his love for Akemi and their dream of leaving town to 'organise private strip-joints' together (!). However, he becomes distrustful of Oida and threatens him in anger, at which point Tomoe throws one of her shoes at his face. Impressed by the child's readiness to defend Oida, he calms down.

Later, at another nightclub, Oida encounters Natsuko (Miyuki Kuwano), the woman whose family he had killed, who is now working as a hostess (Oida's surprise at seeing her is very well-played by Nakadai using facial expression only). Natsuko initially reacts with fury and expresses a desire to kill him but, when Oida asks what he can do for her, she finds herself moved by his sincerity. Meanwhile, Umegaya, learning that the two gangsters from Hong Kong have kidnapped his girlfriend, goes to meet them at a water treatment plant, which a waiter has helpfully informed him is seven minutes' drive away. He manages to escape with Akemi and another chase ensues, this time with the added danger of many rapidly-turning watermills. However, the gangsters catch up with them, the two are brutally murdered and Oida is once again too late.

The third and final man on Oida's list is Fuyushima, an ex-boxer forced into retirement when he refused to throw a fight and had his hand broken by gangsters. The Hong Kong gangsters locate Fuyushima at almost the same time as Oida, and the two flee together, ending up this time in a car breakers' yard, where another violent confrontation ensues. At the end of the film, Oida has found redemption as well as a way to make some restitution to the woman whose family he killed, but the ending cannot exactly be called a happy one.

As usual with Gosha, every scene is imaginatively staged and the visual style throughout is striking. Nakadai would later say that Gosha was a 'passionate' director but sometimes paid more attention to the visuals than he did to the story. The plot of *Cash Calls Hell* has its absurdities, but also some clever touches along the way. Masaru Sato, a prolific and often brilliant composer who had scored *Yojimbo* among many others, delivered one of his lesser works, a rather dated jazz score. The film benefits from Nakadai's sincere performance and lack of posing in one of his haunted roles, while at the same time being fast-paced and highly entertaining. It is also refreshing to see a crime film with an emotional element which moves beyond the usual clichés, and the relationship between Oida and Tomoe, which could easily have been cloying and sentimental, is treated with admirable restraint and makes the film worthwhile.

As a Haiyuza co-production, the cast was understandably packed with the theatre company's own actors. One of the producers was Masayuki Sato, the head of Haiyuza's film department and Nakadai's manager. Haiyuza had been involved in a handful of films in the mid-'50s, but then appear to have abandoned this pursuit for almost a decade before Sato began to focus his energies on film production again in 1965, co-producing Gosha's *Sword of the Beast*. Sato would go on to produce a further 11 films featuring Nakadai.

On the surface at least, Nakadai's next collaboration could not have been more different and saw him working for the first time with a director associated with the Japanese 'New Wave'. In 1962, Kobo Abe, a writer frequently compared to Kafka, had published a strange and compelling novel, *The Woman in the Dunes* (Suna no onna), about an entomologist who travels to a remote village on a bug-collecting expedition and finds himself held captive by a woman who lives in a sand dune. The book had been a hit among critics and public alike while, in the same year, Abe had written the screenplay for *Pitfall* (Otoshiana), the feature debut of director Hiroshi Teshigahara. Teshigahara was the son of Sofu Teshigahara, a renowned master of *ikebana* (the Japanese art of flower arranging) and sculpture who had founded his own school, the Sogetsu-ryu, and helped to move these arts away from rigid traditionalism, encouraging more avant-garde forms. However, according to Donald Richie, Hiroshi himself 'hated it, knew nothing about flowers' and his true passion was for cinema.[49] Another American writer who knew Teshigahara and whose subject was also Japan, John Nathan, described him as having 'so many silver spoons in his mouth that he could scarcely talk.'[50]

Hiroshi Teshigahara had begun his film career in the 1950s making short documentaries, and also working as an assistant director under Keisuke Kinoshita. Abe and Teshigahara had subsequently collaborated on a film version of *The Woman in the Dunes*, which became an international success, winning the Special Jury Prize at Cannes in 1964. Also in 1964, Abe published *The Face of Another* (Tanin no kao), a novel about a man whose face has been destroyed in an industrial accident and subsequently wears a lifelike mask which enables him to interact

---

[49] *The Japan Journals 1947-2004* by Donald Richie (Stone Bridge Press, 2004), p. 194
[50] *Teshigahara and Abe* (documentary), Criterion Collection, 2007

with others normally but changes both his appearance and personality. Unfortunately, on this occasion Abe produced an excruciatingly dull first-person narrative which reads like the incoherent ramblings of a madman. However, despite such unpromising material, Abe and Teshigahara collaborated again, turning it into a film and, remarkably, producing a masterpiece of cinema in the process.

The Face of Another was an independent production by the wealthy Teshigahara's own company, and he may have had difficulty persuading a studio to lend him a star for such an unusual project. Fortunately, he knew Nakadai through the unlikely connection of baseball – Teshigahara had been part of a team comprised of assistant directors at Shochiku and had played against a team led by Nakadai in weekly matches. This acquaintanceship, together with Nakadai's freelancer status, must have made him the obvious choice, but Teshigahara also claimed later on that he chose Nakadai 'because he had a smooth face, like a reptile's' [51] and that was the image he had been looking for.

In the leading role of Okuyama, Nakadai is first seen as a talking x-ray, then with his head entirely swathed in bandages, with holes only for his eyes and mouth. In one scene, Okuyama walks along a crowded street in Shibuya in this fashion. Shot with a hidden camera from a hotel window, the experience always stayed with Nakadai, who recalled many years later how, instead of being stared at as expected, most people looked away in discomfort and pretended not to see him.

Teshigahara deliberately denied the audience a good look at Okuyama's disfigured face, which is seen only in brief glimpses or distorted images. Perhaps he felt that the make-up was not convincing enough to bear close scrutiny, but it seems more likely that he held back through not wanting to exploit facial disfigurement for shock value in the vein of horror films such as *The Phantom of the Opera*, *Doctor X* and *Mystery of the Wax Museum*. For the most part, we see Nakadai's

---

[51] From an interview with Teshigahara by Max Tessier, originally quoted in French in *Le cinéma japonais au present: 1959-1984*. Translated by Allison Dundy for Criterion's 2007 DVD release.

own face as the 'mask', albeit with some subtle make-up applied and the addition of dark glasses, a beard and a prominent mole.[52]

The doctor who creates Okuyama's mask in the film was played by Mikijiro Hira, who had been one year below Nakadai at Haiyuza and had played Horatio to Nakadai's Hamlet. He had also appeared alongside Nakadai in *Cheers! Arranged Marriage*, *The Inheritance*, *Illusion of Blood* and *Cash Calls Hell*. The two actors remained friends after making *The Face of Another*, and Nakadai helped care for Hira in the late '90s when he was stricken by lung cancer. Hira eventually recovered and returned to acting until his death in 2016. Another Haiyuza player in the cast was Etsuko Ichihara as a young woman with learning difficulties who is the only person not deceived by Okuyama's mask. She had played Ophelia to Nakadai's Hamlet and would later win the Japan Academy Prize for Best Supporting Actress for her part in Shohei Imamura's *Black Rain* (Kuroi ame). The nurse who assists in the creation of the mask was played by the *Woman in the Dunes* herself, Kyoko Kishida, while Okuyama's wife was played by Nakadai's co-star from *The Key*, Machiko Kyo. The film also benefitted immensely from a score by Teshigahara's other important collaborator, Toru Takemitsu, who had the unusual but somehow immensely appropriate idea of introducing the film with a waltz before switching to more avant-garde electronic music for much of the film.[53] *The Face of Another* is visually stunning and ceaselessly inventive throughout in its high-contrast cinematography and bizarre art design, by Hiroshi Segawa and Masao Yamazaki respectively.

---

[52] This had been done at least once before: in *The Face behind the Mask* (1941), star Peter Lorre's own face also served as the 'mask' with some subtle additions.

[53] It may or may not be a coincidence that a later black-and-white masterpiece dealing with disfigurement, *The Elephant Man*, also prominently featured a waltz as its main theme.

Chapter 13 – A Little Bit of Everything

With the cinema industry in crisis due to the rise in popularity of television, Nakadai began to dabble with the new medium more frequently. In the summer of 1966, he appeared in a series of three dramas for *Shionogi TV Theatre* based on Shuguro Yamamoto stories, all of which co-starred Michiyo Aratama and were directed by Hideo Ogawa. The first, *Shurushuru*, was scripted by Kihachi Okamoto and also featured Takashi Shimura. The second, *Through that Wooden Door* (Sono kido o tootte), told the tale of a samurai whose life is turned upside down when a young woman suffering from amnesia turns up on his doorstep. It was scripted by Seiichi Yashiro, a former member of Haiyuza's literature department who later wrote the the play upon which Kaneto Shindo's 1981 film *Hokusai Manga* would be based. Kon Ichikawa used the same Yamamoto story as a basis for a mediocre 1993 feature film. The third, *Fishing Rod*, was the first script written by Yasuko to be filmed for television. Yasuko had begun writing seriously soon after the stillbirth of their son and shown an example of her work to Masayuki Sato, who subsequently employed her to adapt the Yamamoto story. She thought it better to use a pen name in order to save her husband any embarrassment. In tribute to her mother, she chose the name Tomoe Ryu, which she continued to use for all of her script credits. These would include writing 11 episodes of a series of stand-alone TV dramas for *Toshiba Sunday Theatre* between 1970 and 1977.

Also in 1966, Haiyuza closed its drama school, but continued to operate as a theatre company. Nakadai played the role of Count Vronsky in a stage adaptation of *Anna Karenina* for Haiyuza directed by Koreya Senda. The title role was played by Momoko Kochi, who had joined Toho studios as a 'new face' in 1953 and played the female lead in the original *Godzilla*, but subsequently struggled to get decent roles outside the monster movie genre. As a result, she had bravely quit

Toho in 1958 and enrolled at Haiyuza as a student in order to focus on a new career on the stage.

After a series of dark roles, Nakadai was pleased to be offered the opportunity to play a rare comic part which he felt was a lot closer to his real self. This came courtesy of Kihachi Okamoto once more, who cast him as the lead in *The Age of Assassins* (Satsujin kyojidai), aka *Epoch of Murder Madness*, loosely based on a novel by Michio Tsuzuki. Nakadai played Shinji Kikyo, a nerdy professor of criminal psychology with beer-bottle glasses, permanent stubble and a bad case of athlete's foot. Kikyo drives a clapped-out Citroen 2CV and talks to a bust of his mother on a shelf at home. Okamoto had rewritten a pre-existing screenplay with Nakadai in mind, and the nerdification of the main character was apparently an Okamoto contribution.

The film opens with a scene in an insane asylum of dazzling whiteness and bizarre design, where the head doctor, Shogo Mizorogi, reveals to a visiting Nazi that, as part of his plan to rid the world of 'unproductive' people, he has trained the inmates to be assassins, boasting that he can have anybody killed at any time with no risk of being caught. The Nazi picks three names at random out of a phone book and instructs the doctor to have them killed to prove the efficacy of his method. One of the names is Shinji Kikyo, who returns home after work the following day to find a chubby assassin waiting for him. The bumbling Kikyo accidentally foils the assassination attempt, killing the man in the process. When he goes to report it to the police, he encounters a female crime reporter, Keiko, and the two join forces to try and discover why somebody wanted Kikyo dead.

Keiko is played by the vivacious Reiko Dan in her tenth and final film with Nakadai, while Mizorogi is played by Hideyo Amamoto, who had also been Nakadai's nemesis in *Cash Calls Hell*. Nakadai maintains the nerdish persona for the first half hour of the film until Keiko makes him smarten up and buys him a new outfit. Clean-shaven, without glasses, and wearing clothes that make him look like a priest, he undergoes a metamorphosis which suggests that he may not be such harmless fool after all. Like many serious actors given a rare chance to play a comic role, Nakadai clearly enjoyed playing the part and gave an entertaining performance, but Kikyo is a character of little depth and can hardly be regarded as among his best work.

The Age of Assassins can perhaps best be described as a black comedy action-thriller and is the sort of peculiar film that could only have come from the eccentric Okamoto. Visually striking and entertaining it may be but, ultimately, the film falls flat – unlike the director's earlier *Oh Bomb* (Aa bakudan, 1964), which had taken a similar cartoonish approach to its material and is not only stunningly inventive but genuinely funny. The tone of *The Age of Assassins*, on the other hand, is wildly inconsistent and at times too dark for its own good, while the convoluted plot involves several twists too many, leaving the viewer feeling somewhat duped by the end. Perhaps for these reasons, the producers at Toho hated it and held it back – completed in June 1966, it was not released until February the following year,[54] when it was quietly issued on a double bill with a Hiroshi Teshigahara documentary about motor racing. As a result, it became the lowest-grossing feature film in the history of Toho and Nakadai found himself being given the cold shoulder by the studio executives for a while. However, it seems not to have caused any lasting damage to the careers of anyone involved and, in recent years, the film has attracted a small but passionate cult following.[55]

Nakadai followed *The Age of Assassins* with another light role in *The Daphne* (Jinchoge), a comedy starring Machiko Kyo as Kikuko, the eldest of four sisters. Working as a dentist, she has remained single, so her mother arranges various schemes in order to find her a suitable husband. Predictably, these all fail, but Kikuko eventually falls in love

---

[54] Some sources state that *The Age of Assassins* was made prior to *Sword of Doom*, but released after. However, in his interview in Chris D's *Outlaw Masters of Japanese Film*, Okamoto states that it was released 8 months after completion. The release date was 4 February 1967, so it must have been completed around June 1966, whereas *Sword of Doom* was released on 25 February 1966.

[55] For more on this film, see Robin Gatto's piece at www.midnighteye.com/reviews/epoch-of-murder-madness/

with and marries one of her patients, Professor Kinpira (Nakadai). It was Nakadai's final film for director Yasuki Chiba, who had made *Miren* and the four *Oban* films. Probably thanks to the presence of Kyo and Nakadai, the film received an American release the following year.

After starring in another series of *Shionogi TV Theatre* for Fuji TV (comprised of three stand-alone episodes with the umbrella title *Overseas Stories*), Nakadai next made a minor but memorable contribution to Hiroshi Inagaki's feature *Sasaki Kojiro*. Kojiro Sasaki, born around 1575, was a swordsman famous for inventing a move known as the 'turning swallow cut' and for being killed by Musashi Miyamoto in a duel on Ganryu Island in 1612. Inagaki had made a trilogy of films about Sasaki in the early '50s and followed these a few years later with a hugely successful trilogy about Miyamoto starring Toshiro Mifune, so this was familiar ground for him.

A star was needed to portray Miyamoto in *Sasaki Kojiro* and, as Mifune was by this time a little old to reprise the role, it naturally fell to Nakadai. However, although the part was an important one, it was also fairly small and Miyamoto would not appear until an hour and fifty minutes into the two-and-a-half hour film, after which he receives only around ten minutes of screen time.

In casting Sasaki, a more unusual choice was made: Kikunosuke Onoe, a 24-year-old kabuki star. Onoe had appeared in just one previous film, and that in a minor role, but had enjoyed considerable success on television in the drama series *Minamotono Yoshitsune*. Unfortunately, Onoe was lacking in movie star charisma and, in his hands, Sasaki came across as arrogant, humourless and fickle, an utterly charmless character interested only in becoming famous through his swordsmanship. Perhaps this explains why the film was not very popular in Japan, although it apparently fared better abroad. Onoe never made another film, choosing instead to concentrate his energies on kabuki, a medium in which he went on to become a highly respected figure.

In fairness to Onoe, it should be noted that he was not in any way helped by the script, which was dull, riddled with clichés and devoid of any insight into its characters. Having said that, the film is not a total disaster thanks to being well-shot in a variety of locations, with widescreen compositions that made good use of the vividly-coloured costumes. It also benefits from an excellent score by Goichi Sakide.

Nakadai is first seen from behind and we hear that distinctive baritone voice before seeing his face. When we do, he has a fiercer appearance than usual thanks to some make-up around the eyebrows. Onoe's limitations as a film presence become even more obvious whenever he has to share the screen with Nakadai, who in one scene even chisels wood with an intensity that is entirely compelling. However, the climactic duel itself is something of an anti-climax. Short and bloodless, it appears that the intention was to be faithful to one of the historical accounts, which has Miyamoto wielding a *bokken* (wooden sword) and killing Sasaki with a blow to the ribs. Any viewers unaware of this account may understandably find the duel oddly unconvincing as the blow appears unlikely to have proven fatal.

Nakadai next played the lead in *Gomez's Name is Gomez* (Gomesu no na wa Gomesu), a five-part spy drama for Fuji TV produced in association with Haiyuza. Broadcast in April and May 1967, it was subsequently re-edited as an 86-minute movie released through Shochiku with the added subtitle *Quicksand*. The series was based on a 1962 spy novel by Shoji Yuki, and had originally been planned as a Kihachi Okamoto project to be filmed in Vietnam, but the logistics became complicated and Okamoto dropped out. Osamu Takahashi took over as director, and it was filmed in Hong Kong instead. Although Takahashi had worked as an assistant for Ozu on *Tokyo Story*, his own career as a director was brief – mercifully so on the evidence of *Gomez*, which is shot with neither flair nor imagination. Perhaps he realised he was not cut out to be a filmmaker, as he later switched careers and found fame as a writer, partly due to the success of a 1982 book about Ozu.

Nakadai played Sakamoto, an oil engineer who has just finished a two-year stint working in the Middle East. On his way back to Japan, he stops off in Hong Kong, where he has arranged to meet an old student friend, Katori (Mikiro Taira), at the airport. However, shortly after the two are reunited, Katori mysteriously disappears. Sakamoto then joins forces with Katori's girlfriend, Rika (Komaki Kurihara), in an effort to try and find the missing man. Along the way, they enlist the help of a local police detective (Ichiro Nakatani) and a Japanese journalist (Hiroshi Akutagawa). Meanwhile, Sakamoto realises he is being followed by someone, but the mystery man is shot before he can question him. Before dying, he tries to say something to Sakamoto, but gets no further than uttering the unhelpful words, 'Gomez's name is Gomez', and then expires.

With Komaki Kurihara in *Gomez's Name is Gomez*.

Both the TV and film versions have deservedly fallen into obscurity today, and there can be little doubt that Kihachi Okamoto would have made something more interesting out of the routine material. If *Gomez* is to be remembered at all, it should be for featuring the screen debut of Haiyuza actress Komaki Kurihara, who would later appear alongside Nakadai again in *Inn of Evil* and *The Wolves* as well as in a number of stage plays. Other notable actors among the cast were Kyoko Kishida and, from Haiyuza, Hisashi Igawa and Mikijiro Hira.

After *Kwaidan*, Masakai Kobayashi had gone freelance, and his next film, *Samurai Rebellion*, was (like *The Legacy of the 500,000* and *Fort Graveyard*) a co-production between Toho and Toshiro Mifune's production company. Mifune starred as Sasahara, a loyal and long-serving vassal to a selfish and insensitive lord who forces Sasahara's son, Yogoro (Go Kato), to accept as a wife a concubine, Ichi (Yoko Tsukasa), who has displeased him. To everyone's surprise, the marriage is a success, but when the lord changes his mind and demands that Ichi be sent back to the castle, Sasahara feels that enough is enough and rebels. Nakadai was cast as Tatewaki, Sasahara's best friend and the only samurai in the clan who can equal him in swordsmanship. At the beginning of the film, the two are seen practicing their skills on a straw dummy, and Tatewaki remarks how useless their abilities are in this time of peace. However, we know that both will have ample opportunity to use them before the end of the film – in fact, they find themselves as unwilling opponents and the film ends with another Mifune-Nakadai face-off. Reminiscent of the one at the end of *Sanjuro*, they again have to fight in a field with long grass blowing in the wind, but Kobayashi allows the duel to go on a little longer and in this case Nakadai's fatal wound is not even noticed at first.

In some respects, Tatewaki can be seen as the ultimate jobsworth – when first asked to kill Sasahara, he refuses not out of friendship, but because such an act is not covered by his job description! Although this could be interpreted as a way of disobeying orders he dislikes without dropping himself in it, while guarding a gate later on as part of his regular duties when Sasahara tries to exit without official permission, he is quite willing to stop him at any cost. Tatewaki makes it clear that he still considers himself a friend of Sasahara and will look after his grandchild if Sasahara is killed, but his overriding sense of duty means that he never considers turning a blind eye and allowing his friend to slip out unnoticed. This contradiction between actions and feelings is something that most of the film's characters have to deal with during the course of the story, and is one of the ways in which Kobayashi and screenwriter Shinobu Hashimoto show how the feudal system exploited notions of loyalty and obedience. As in *Harakiri*, the system always wins in the end no matter how violent the protest, and self-determination is a fantasy for those serving under a feudal lord. Nevertheless, Sasahara's rebellion redeems him, at least in his own eyes – having endured a forced marriage for 20 years to a woman whose face could stop a clock, he looks understandably miserable for most of the film, only becoming cheerful when he knows he will soon be killed in a huge fight. When a maid enquires why he is covering his wooden floors with tatami, he replies almost gleefully that it is to prevent him slipping in all the blood that will soon cover them.

Based on a 1965 novella by Yasuhiko Takiguchi – who had also written the original upon which *Harakiri* was based – *Samurai Rebellion* is in many ways a companion piece to the earlier film. However, the title of the novella (*Hairyodzuma Shimatsu*), which also served as part of the film's title in Japan,[56] can be translated as 'The Thrown-Away Wife', which reflects the main difference between the two works, as in this case the plight of women during the feudal era is also a major concern. Women had even less freedom than the male vassals, and were expected to be meekly obedient at all times, so the rebellion of Ichi is even more shocking than that of her father-in-law. It could be argued that Ichi is an unrealistic character and no female in her position during the Edo era (1603-1867) would have dared to defy her lord in the way she does, but it allows Kobayashi to make the point that women must also be treated as individuals with feelings, and Tsukasa gives a powerful performance. Having said that, *Samurai Rebellion* is really the story of Sasahara; however, it was certainly unusual to see such a strong female character in a samurai film at the time.

Nakadai's character is not in present the novella, and was quite likely created in order to provide an opportunity for another confrontation with Mifune. Unsurprisingly, then, Nakadai's screen time

---

[56] *Joiuchi - Hairyodzuma Shimatsu*. The meaning of 'joiuchi' is similar to 'rebellion.'

in the film is limited and, in playing a rather formal character, there was only so much he could do with it, although he certainly looks the part and does make an impact.

Kobayashi reportedly found Mifune difficult to work with, perhaps because the film was shot on the brand new soundstage of Mifune Productions and the star was known for being obsessive about order and cleanliness. Some of his staff even called him 'old vacuum man', so he may have seemed more concerned with the state of the toilets than his acting. However, this is in no way apparent in the finished film, which features what is perhaps the last truly great Mifune performance. Although Kobayashi expressed satisfaction with the final result, *Samurai Rebellion* would be their only collaboration.

For some reason, Kobayashi broke with his regular cinematographer Yoshio Miyajima for *Samurai Rebellion*, instead using Kazuo Yamada, Hiroshi Inagaki's regular cmaeraman. Yamada's stark black and white cinematography is unflattering for the cast, but this must have been a deliberate choice on Kobayashi's part and it effectively conveys the feeling of a cold and joyless world. However, Kobayashi continued his association with composer Toru Takemitsu in their fourth film together, and the subtle punctuation of Takemitsu's score skillfully avoids any hint of sentimentality. The film is saved from becoming unremittingly pessimistic by the fact that it at least allows Sasahara's granddaughter to survive and perhaps grow up in a world in which life is a little better. *Samurai Rebellion* won a number of awards for Best Film, Best Director and Best Screenplay and has been adapted as a stage play in Japan and twice remade for TV – firstly in 1992 with original cast member Go Kato in the Mifune role, and again in 2013.

Nakadai next provided some narration for Kihachi Okamoto's uncharacteristically serious Second World War drama *Japan's Longest Day* (Nihon no ichiban nagai hi), a film originally to have been directed by Masaki Kobayashi, who withdrew for unknown reasons. It dealt with events that took place between the Emperor's decision to surrender and the broadcast of his capitulation speech, which sections of the military tried their best to prevent by means of an attempted coup. Okamoto told a complex story well, and a great deal of attention was paid to historical accuracy, although some simplification was perhaps inevitable; it could be said that *Japan's Longest Day* rather too conveniently places responsibility for the war solely on fanatical elements within the armed forces, while both the Emperor and Prime Minister are portrayed as blameless.

Nakadai was then back in front of the camera playing the title role in Fuji TV's adaptation of Shin Hasegawa's oft-filmed 1928 play *Tokijiro Kutsukake*, made as part of the *Shionogi TV Theatre* series. Broadcast in two parts on 26 October and 2 November, 1967, it had Nakadai as a wandering *yakuza* who finds himself in an awkward situation when he accepts shelter from a *yakuza* boss, thereby placing himself under obligation – a plotline reminiscent of Nakadai's segment in *Wanderers: Three Yakuza*. The character had previously been played on film by Raizo Ichikawa in 1961 and by Kinnosuke Nakamura in 1966.

Nakadai's next leading role was in *Journey* (Tabiji), a feature film version of a popular NHK morning drama, which was still running at the time and eventually ran to over 300 episodes. Nakadai did not appear in the TV series, but in the film he played Yuichiro, a train conductor in Hokkaido in the 1930s who makes a long journey south to his hometown of Owase in Mie Prefecture to make arrangements for the remains of his recently deceased parents. His uncle has also given him an introduction to a family with an eligible daughter with whom it is hoped a marriage might be arranged. However, there is no chemistry between the two, and Yuichiro prefers a different daughter, Yuri (Yoshiko Sakuma). Despite her parents' opposition, she marries him and goes to live with him in Hokkaido. Although Yuichiro's job is not well-paid and they struggle to get by, the couple are happy. Unfortunately, trouble begins when Yuichiro's former sweetheart, Michiyo (Junko Miyazono), goes through a difficult time in the wake of a divorce and he tries to help, sparking rumours in the community which soon reach the ears of Yuri.

The film was made with the co-operation of Japan's National Railway, and apparently featured enough footage of steam locomotives passing through the picturesque scenery of Hokkaido to rouse the most jaded trainspotter. Most of the shooting took place in the Kushiro area of Hokkaido, where parts of *The Human Condition* had been filmed. As with his earlier train film, *Naked Sun*, perhaps it was the chance to pay tribute to his train-driver father that appealed to Nakadai, as the soapy nature of the material was atypical among his filmography, at least during this stage of his career. It also marked his first film with Kirin Kiki, an actress with whom Nakadai would work on a number of occasions many years later, and who would eventually become well-known abroad in her old age through the films of Hirokazu Kore-eda. Directed by Shinji Murayama, who seems to have been an experienced but not especially distinguished filmmaker, *Journey* did not receive a release overseas and there is little to suggest that the rest of the world was deprived of anything very remarkable.

Also in 1967, Nakadai played the lead in a revival of Kobo Abe's 1955 play *Slave Hunting* for Haiyuza, directed by Koreya Senda from a text revised by Abe. Nakadai had played a lesser role in the original 1955 production, also directed by Senda. At the time of writing, the play has yet to be translated into English, but apparently concerns an explorer who, having caught a subhuman creature called Way on a remote island, brings him to an animal research institute. The director of the institute sees an opportunity for a profitable business in bringing more subhumans from the island to be sold as slaves.

Nakadai's singing career had a brief revival at this time when he released a single, 'Ballata per un Pistolero' on CBS Japan. Composed by Marcello Giombini, it was the theme song from a 1967 spaghetti western of the same name, with the lyrics translated into Japanese. The B-side featured a song entitled 'Your Hands' (Anata no sonote), which Yasuko had co-written with one K. Morioka. The motivation for this release is unclear, but perhaps it was inspired by the news that Nakadai was about to appear in an Italian western – his first non-Japanese movie.

Cover of the 7-inch single 'Ballata per un Pistolero'.

Chapter 14 – Spaghetti Samurai

Akira Kurosawa had indirectly created the spaghetti western genre when his film *Yojimbo* was remade by Sergio Leone as *A Fistful of Dollars*, released in 1964. It was fitting, then, that Italian producer Tonino Cervi cast Nakadai in his western *Today We Kill, Tomorrow We Die!* after having seen him in *Sword of Doom*. Cervi had produced Antonioni's *Red Desert* but, for his own directorial debut, he chose to make a film of few artistic pretensions.

For his part, Nakadai enjoyed westerns and was pleased to have the opportunity to act in one – such offers were rarely extended to Japanese actors in those days, although Toshiro Mifune had appeared in John Frankenheimer's *Grand Prix* in 1966, and would go on to make a number of other films in the West. Another motivation for Nakadai was a hope that his participation may lead to increased opportunities for Japanese actors to play non-Japanese characters in foreign films, although in this case he was to be disappointed. However, he seems to have known virtually nothing about the part he was to play until he arrived in Rome and met Cervi.

Japanese film stars were paid a fraction of their Hollywood equivalents and Nakadai was so broke at the time that he exchanged the first-class plane tickets he had been given for second-class ones and pocketed the difference. When he arrived in Rome and realised he was to be greeted at the airport, he had to ask the flight crew for permission to disembark with the first-class passengers.

Like many other spaghetti westerns, the film was shot at Elios Studios close to Rome, as well as on various locations in the surrounding area, but Nakadai found himself working mostly outdoors in cold weather. Arriving in Rome on 2 January 1968, he was assigned an Italian driver, Aurelio, who drove him to work each day while serenading him with shaky but enthusiastic renditions of operatic arias. Surprisingly, Nakadai had never ridden a horse, and so was given lessons, in the process learning a valuable new skill which would come in useful later in his career. Although one fall from his horse resulted in a day off to recuperate, he was not seriously hurt. He also had to become accustomed to handling real guns, which he found heavy and difficult to get a grip on; hours of practice at his hotel resulted in blisters.

The story could hardly be simpler: Bill Kiowa (Brett Halsey) is released from prison after serving five years as a result of being framed by James Elfego (Nakadai), who had also raped and killed Kiowa's Native American wife while forcing him to watch. In order to get revenge, Kiowa rounds up four tough guys and they ride out in pursuit of Elfego.

The screenplay, co-written by Cervi and Dario Argento, was not exactly sophisticated, and Nakadai understandably threw his usual restraint to the wind in his portrayal of the Mexican psychotic who takes great delight in his evil deeds. Making his entrance around 38 minutes in, from that point on he has a considerable amount of screen time. As the other actors are on the wooden side, Nakadai has no trouble stealing every scene he is in, making full use of his repertoire of facial expressions as the mercurial Elfego alternately leers, sneers, giggles, screams and intimidates.

Nakadai made for a reasonably plausible Mexican; unshaven, with unkempt hair, a white shirt and a dirty black suit, he certainly looked the part. Cervi even had him wielding a machete in a couple of scenes, which was presumably the closest he could get to a samurai sword without allowing things to become too ridiculous.

The film, if not exactly high quality, is at least entertaining, and the fight scenes are well-staged. Co-star Brett Halsey, who played Kiowa, had this to say about Nakadai:

> He was magnificent. You know he'd never ridden a horse before and he kept falling off time and time again but would just keep getting back on. He got injured but it never bothered him. And in the last scene when he was running through the forest there were roots and allsorts underfoot but he wouldn't look down when he was running. So he would fall and

fall but he always kept his eyes straight ahead. He was a wonderful actor to work with.[57]

The international cast, which included American, Italian, French and Spanish actors, were apparently a noisy lot, and Nakadai later recalled that his inability to speak other languages made him the quiet one. Cervi appreciated this and as a result repeatedly admonished the others to 'Be like samurai!'[58]

Nakadai originally began performing his part in English after having learned his lines phonetically, but the dialogue was often changed at short notice. When Cervi realised this was asking too much, he told Nakadai to deliver his lines in Japanese as in Italian films the dialogue was not recorded until post-production anyway, when it would be dubbed into Italian and English, often by different actors. However, Nakadai later dubbed his own dialogue for the Japanese version, which was released by Toho in November 1968 under the title *The Beast Dies at Dawn* (Yaju akatsuki no shisu).[59]

A week after returning from Italy, Nakadai was back on stage in Sean O'Casey's 1943 play *Purple Dust* for Haiyuza under the direction of Koji Abe. A curious choice for a Japanese revival, it concerns two wealthy Englishmen, Basil Stoke and Cyril Poges, who buy a dilapidated mansion in Ireland and attempt to restore it in dubious taste, bringing them into conflict with the local community. Nakadai presumably played Stoke, the younger of the two men, a bespectacled would-be philosopher. The same year, he also appeared on stage for the second time as Tamiya Iemon in *Yotsuya Kaidan* for Haiyuza, again under the direction of Eitaro Ozawa and with largely the same cast, although Go Kato replaced Mikijiro Hira, and Komaki Kurihara also appeared.

---

[57] www.spaghetti-western.net/index.php/Brett_Halsey_Interview
[58] www.youtube.com/watch?v=kfzLeFuq2jM
[59] TV Tokyo later redubbed the dialogue entirely for television and hired Eimei Esumi to dub the voice of Elfego.

Despite the disappointing box office for *Sword of Doom* and the outright failure of *Age of Assassins*, Nakadai was reunited with Kihachi Okamoto once more for Toho's *Kill!* (Kiru), an anti-samurai comedy in which he played Genta, a hungry *ronin*-turned-*yakuza* who arrives in a bleak, windswept town hoping for a meal, meets a fellow wanderer in a similar position, Hanjiro (Etsushi Takahashi) – a farmer who wants to be a samurai – and is caught up in a dispute between rival samurai factions. The film owes a great deal to *Yojimbo*, but was in fact based on the same novel by Shugoro Yamamoto which Kurosawa had used as a basis for *Sanjuro*. However, Genta is an unusually garrulous example of the stock mystery-man-from-nowhere-in-particular character. Despite having turned his back on the samurai life in disgust, he is neither world-weary nor cynical as one might expect, and maintains his friendly demeanour and good humour throughout.

At times, *Kill!* almost seems like two films spliced together – one a traditional samurai potboiler played entirely straight, the other a post-modern parody (featuring the peripheral figures played engagingly by Nakadai and Takahashi) which slyly pokes fun at both the pomposity of the samurai characters and the genre in general. On the whole, it works – largely as a result of being shot with such panache that the uninteresting plot ceases to matter. Aside from Okamoto, cinematographer Rokuro Nishigaki deserves credit for his consistently striking high-contrast black-and-white Tohoscope cinematography. Somewhat ironically, *Yojimbo* composer Masaru Sato's score, with its twanging electric guitar, seems to have been influenced by the spaghetti westerns of the time.

Nakadai then provided narration for a couple of war movies – firstly for Seiji Maruyama's *Admiral Yamamoto* (Rengo kantai shirei chokan: Yamamoto Isoroku), which featured Toshiro Mifune in the title role, then for Kihachi Okamoto's *The Human Bullet* (Nikudan, literally 'Meat Bullet'). The latter was Okamoto's most successful attempt at capturing his unique vision of the absurdity of war on film. Unable to obtain financing from Toho for the project, he had turned to the Arts Theatre Guild (ATG), an arthouse distributor which had recently begun producing films with a small, 10 million yen budget. Notable examples included Shohei Imamura's *A Man Vanishes* (Ningen Johatsu) and Nagisa Oshima's *Death by Hanging* (Koshikei). However, ATG only provided half the amount, so Okamoto mortgaged his house to raise the other half. Various friends helped out, including Masaru Sato, who secretly recorded the score at Toho while he was supposed to be working on other films. *The Human Bullet* starred a then-unknown actor, Minori Terada, as a skinny 21-year-old soldier assigned to a suicide squad towards the end of the Second World War. Also featured was Kunie Tanaka who, having been on the receiving end of multiple slaps as a weakling soldier in *The Human Condition*, on this occasion got to dish it out as the sergeant who bullies Terada. More surprising, though, was the appearance of Chishu Ryu, who was a long way from Ozu in his role as a bookseller who has had both arms blown off in an American bombing raid. Rather than the usual stentorian war-movie narration, Nakadai's contribution was more of a dry, ironic commentary on the tragi-comic events depicted by Okamoto. Despite its tiny budget, the film features excellent work all round and was well-received by the counter-culture as well as most critics, making it a modest commercial success.

Nakadai's second film with Hideo Gosha was *Goyokin*, which marked Fuji TV's first venture into feature film production and was also the first Japanese film to be made in Panavision. As one of the producers was Masayuki Sato, a number of Haiyuza actors were featured, including Kunie Tanaka, Eijiro Tono and Hisashi Ogawa, while Nakadai played the leading role of Magobei Wakizaka, a samurai of the Sabai clan, who live in the far-flung region of the Noto Peninsula, forgotten by the shogun and struggling to maintain their usual quality of life. In order to improve the clan's situation, his closest friend, Rokugo Tatewaki (Tetsuro Tanba), arranges for a passing ship transporting gold and silver[60] to be sunk, then pressgangs the inhabitants of a nearby village into retrieving the treasure before

---

[60] The 'goyokin' of the title.

massacring them in order to keep it secret. When Wakizaka discovers what Tatewaki has done, he decides he can no longer remain a member of such a clan and goes into self-imposed exile. However, three years later, he learns that Tatewaki is planning to pull the same trick again. Wakizaka then forms an uneasy alliance with Samon Fujimaki (Kinnosuke Nakamura), a *ronin* who cheerfully admits he will do anything for money. The two return to Noto in an attempt to prevent another massacre.

Due to the flashback structure of the narrative, Nakadai makes his entrance with his character already in exile. As in *Wanderers: Three Yakuza* and *Sword of Doom*, he is again first seen wearing a *sandogasa*, which was rapidly becoming a trademark. Reduced to working at a sideshow, he demonstrates his swordsmanship skills for cash – a live carp is placed on the lap of a woman playing the shamisen; with one quick stroke, he neatly slices the fish in half as she continues playing without missing a beat. Wakizaka is a man of action and few words – not unlike a samurai version of Clint Eastwood's Man with no Name, but without the ironic humour. Indeed, *Goyokin* has the feel of an Italian western in terms of its story, visual style, and music (again by Masaru Sato), even if some of the more superficial elements are quite different. Kurosawa may have inadvertently given birth to the spaghetti western genre, but by this time things had come full circle and the influence of Sergio Leone and his counterparts could often be seen in samurai films.[61]

As Gosha wanted snow, *Goyokin* was filmed not in the Noto region, but at Shimokita Hanto, a peninsula in the northernmost part of Japan's main island, Honshu, as this was a cold area in which snow fell frequently. One of the hardest scenes for Nakadai was when he had to climb to the top of an icy cliff while waves crashed into the rocks below. He asked Gosha if he was sure this was a good idea, pointing out that, if he slipped, he could fall into the sea and be killed. Gosha

---

[61] *Goyokin* was remade in 1975 as *The Master Gunfighter*, an American western

then proceeded to make the climb himself to show it was safe, leaving Nakadai little choice but to follow suit.

Actor and director enjoyed a good relationship, which Nakadai once said was similar to that of brothers – Gosha was Nakadai's senior by just three years, and Nakadai had actually made a name for himself before Gosha had, so they were on a much more equal footing. In Japanese society, this would have made it much easier for him to disagree with Gosha in comparison to directors of the older generation.

Nakadai's acting skills are not greatly stretched as the one-note Wakizaka, but he certainly looks the part – as a tall, tanned, bearded, serious samurai with blazing eyes, he appears convincingly formidable enough to take on several enemies at a time. Some years later, Gosha was asked why he cast Nakadai so often, to which he replied that it was because he had angry eyes. Nakadai objected to this statement when he heard about it, but took no offence. However, it is not difficult to see what Gosha was getting at after a viewing of *Goyokin* – Nakadai's glistening, furious, bloodshot orbs are one of the film's memorable images, and were featured prominently in much of the promotional artwork. Wakizaka is reminiscent of the character Nakadai portrayed in *Harakiri* – like Hanshiro Tsugumo, he is highly critical of the feudal system and what it has spawned, regarding most of his fellow samurai to be self-serving hypocrites whose talk of honour and ethics is a sham. It seems likely that such parts appealed to Nakadai as a result of his experiences as a young man, when he had felt betrayed by the adults who had taught him that Japan was fighting a just war in which it was his duty to die for the Emperor if necessary.

The part of Samon Fujimaki was originally to be played by Toshiro Mifune and, in fact, Mifune had not only accepted the role, but completed several weeks of shooting before making a sudden departure. The official story was that the star was suffering from exhaustion and/or an ulcer, but the real reason seems to have been a row between Mifune and Nakadai, although the fact that Mifune disliked shooting in such a cold environment may also have had something to do with it. Nakadai later said that Mifune was generally easy-going and considerate as a person, but that he sometimes became belligerent when drunk. However, the original cause of the argument remains unclear, and Nakadai has given several slightly different versions of the incident over the years. In one version, it began while they were drinking together after a day's filming and Mifune began criticising Masakai Kobayashi, whom he felt had worked too slowly during the filming of *Samurai Rebellion*, causing Nakadai to defend the director he considered his mentor and fall out with Mifune as a result. On another occasion, he said that Mifune had complained that *Goyokin* was not his kind of film, and he had responded by asking him why he didn't quit if he really felt that way. Mifune then got on a train and left. In a third version of the story, Nakadai said that Mifune had been saying derogatory things about theatre actors throughout the shoot and criticising him constantly, with the result that Nakadai finally snapped and blew up at him. Tetsuro Tanba, on the other hand, later claimed that Mifune had had a falling out with Kurosawa around this time, causing him to make a number of disparaging remarks about him to Nakadai, and that this had been the cause of the argument.

In any case, the departure of Mifune put the film in jeopardy until Nakadai's friend Kinnosuke Nakamura agreed to play the part at Nakadai's suggestion and joined the location soon after. The incident received a considerable amount of press, especially as Mifune and Nakadai were at the time advertising rival brands of vitamin pills on TV, so the media used the opportunity to make out that they were having a 'war'. According to Nakadai, Akira Kurosawa subsequently arranged for the two actors to meet at a restaurant in Asakusa, where they had a reconciliation. However, although the *Goyokin* incident may not have been responsible for ending their professional relationship, there would be only a further four films in which they both appeared (*Safari 5000*, *Battle of the Japan Sea*, *Bakumatsu* and *Port Arthur*), and their only future scenes together were brief ones in the first and last of these.

Goyokin is a visually striking film which deservedly won awards for its cinematography and art direction, but Gosha's tendency to pay less attention to plot details is also evident. For instance, in one scene,

Wakizaka is trapped in a hole with his hands tied and, although Gosha indicates how he supposedly manages to escape, he is careful not to show the actual escape as it is obviously implausible. Nevertheless, despite some flaws, on the whole *Goyokin* can be judged a success. Another asset is an excellent performance by Ruriko Asaoka as the sole survivor of the original massacre who turns to a life of crime as a result. Asaoka, a major star in Japan at the time, is little known abroad, but was a versatile actress who gave an unforgettable performance the same year in Yasuzo Masumura's *Vixen* (Jotai) and would also appear in Nakadai's next film.

Nakadai shares a joke with Ruriko Asaoka and Hideo Gosha on the set of *Goyokin*, while Kinnosuke Nakamura looks on unamused.
(Courtesy of Robin Gatto)

Chapter 15 – Having a Slash with Mishima

As cinema audiences continued to dwindle, Ozu-style domestic dramas disappeared from the big screens and found a new home on television, while the studios attempted to lure people back into theatres by offering pleasures that the small screen could not provide – namely, sex, violence, and the occasional big budget spectacle. One example of the latter was the three-hour 1968 film *Tunnel to the Sun* (Kurobe no taiyo),[62] starring Toshiro Mifune and Yujiro Ishihara as engineers supervising the construction of a tunnel through a mountain in the Japanese Alps. Another example is *Safari 5000* (Eiko e no 5000-kiro / '5,000 Kilometres to Glory') featuring the same two actors, as well as Nakadai in a cameo. Co-produced by the Nissan Motor Company, it stars Ishihara as Godai, an international rally driver who has an ongoing friendly rivalry with a French driver (Jean-Claude Drouot), but the wafer-thin story is merely an excuse to connect the impressive motor racing scenes, many of which were shot against a backdrop of real events, including the Monte Carlo Rally and the East African Safari Rally. In an obvious attempt to entice some females into the cinemas, a subplot was cooked up concerning Godai's girlfriend (*Goyokin*'s Ruriko Asaoka), who works as a model and has an on-off liaison with a smooth-talking fashion designer from Paris (Alain Cuny). Nakadai makes his entrance around 30 minutes in, playing Takeuchi, a former driver who was in an accident partially caused by Godai. No longer able to drive because a nerve was severed as a result, he wears a support on his arm and now works as 'Japan Grand Prix Commissioner and Special Testing Director'. Mifune appears as the Nissan boss who, unaware they already know each other, introduces Godai to Takeuchi. Godai feels awkward due to their past history, but Takeuchi holds no grudge and simply laughs it off; it is almost as if

---

[62] The Japanese title means 'The Sun of Kurobe', but is often mistranslated as 'The Sands of Kurobe' as the characters for *taiyo* can mean either 'sun' or 'sand'. As there is no sand in the film, 'sun' must be the intended reading.

screenwriter Nobuo Yamada wanted to dissipate any chance of drama as soon as possible. Nakadia soon vanishes from the film, having featured in perhaps five minutes of the nearly three-hour running time. All of his (and Mifune's) scenes were shot in Japan. Despite the shortcomings in the dramatic aspects of the film, the combination of big names, exotic locations and motor racing seems to have been enough to tempt the public away from their TV sets as *Safari 5000* was the highest-grossing film at the Japanese box office in 1969 – just as well, as it had cost 400 million yen to produce (an extraordinary amount for a Japanese film at the time).

The film was directed by Koreyoshi Kurahara, who had been labeled a 'New Wave' filmmaker at the beginning of his career for films such as *I am Waiting* (Ore wa matteru ze) and *The Warped Ones* (Kyonetsu no kisetsu). His most recent previous offering (an adaptation of Yukio Mishima's *Thirst for Love*) had been considered too uncommercial by the studio. As a result, Nikkatsu had barely released it and failed to renew Kurahara's contract. However, the director had enjoyed a long association with actor Yujiro Ishihara, whose production company co-produced *Safari 5000* with Nikkatsu, so Kurahara was presumably hired as a result of Ishihara's influence. With *Safari 5000*, Kurahara planted both feet firmly in the mainstream, yet still brought considerably more style to the proceedings than a more workmanlike director would have managed. He went on to become highly successful as a freelancer and would go on to direct Nakadai one more time in *Michi* (1986).

Nakadai's next, *Battle of the Japan Sea* (Nihonkai daikaisen), was a Toho war film shot in colour whose story takes place during the Russo-Japanese War of 1904-05. The nominal star was Toshiro Mifune in the role of Admiral Togo. However, he was given little of interest to do and the film is a total failure as a piece of drama, with flat dialogue and mostly dull characterizations. Chishu Ryu was badly miscast as General Nogi, a role later played by Nakadai in the superior *Port Arthur*. Unfortunately, Ryu was entirely unconvincing as a military man and had been far more at home in the many domestic dramas he had made with Yasujiro Ozu. As far as drama was concerned, the one bright spot in the film was Nakadai, who appeared in a subplot as the fictional Major Genjiro Akashi, a spy buying Russian naval secrets from Bolsheviks in Paris. Looking dapper in an Edwardian three-piece suit and waxed moustache, Nakadai portrayed Akashi as a suave charmer; remaining unruffled even under threat of imminent assassination, he clearly enjoys the element of danger in his work. Unfortunately, Nakadai's screen time was limited and the real star of the film was Eiji Tsuburaya, the famous effects maestro responsible for *Godzilla*. Tsuburaya created a number of meticulous miniatures which made the naval battles look highly convincing for their time; consequently, the film has more fans among naval history buffs than cineastes. Director Seiji Maruyama had previously directed Mifune in two other commercially successful war films but was not especially distinguished at the time and is largely forgotten today.

In *Battle of the Japan Sea*

Nakadai's second collaboration with Hideo Gosha within a year was as Hanpeita Takechi (1829-1865) in *Hitokiri*. Although it was the less interesting role of the two, in other respects the film was a quality production. Released in the USA as *Tenchu!*, it was based on a short story from 1964 by Ryotaro Shiba entitled 'Hitokiri Izo', and had a screenplay by *Harakiri* writer Shinobu Hashimoto, making it the fifth

Nakadai film from a Hashimoto script. The story is set in Kyoto against the backdrop of the end of the Edo era, as Japan was heading towards fundamental change between the time of the American Commodore Matthew Perry's forced opening of Japan in 1854 and the Meiji Restoration of 1868.

On this occasion, the star of the film was not Nakadai, but Shintaro Katsu, best-known for playing Zatoichi in a hugely successful and long-running series of films. Nakadai had first met him while working as a barman in Ginza during his student days at Haiyuza when his friend Ken Utsui turned up one night with Katsu in tow. *Hitokiri* was a co-production between Katsu's production company and the Fuji TV network. Shooting began on 16 May 1969 at Daei's Kyoto studios.

Katsu's only film for Gosha saw him cast as Izo Okada (1838-1865), one of the most notorious *hitokiri* (assassins) of his day. The film portrays him as a somewhat naïve samurai insecure about his humble social status, but lethal with a sword more as a result of brute force than finesse. He displays an unquestioning dog-like loyalty for the head of his clan, Hanpeita Takechi, who does in fact treat Okada exactly like a dim-witted but usefully-dangerous dog. Takechi wants to keep foreigners out of Japan, overthrow the shogunate and restore the Emperor to power, and he pays Okada to assassinate those who stand in the way of these objectives and instructs him to shout '*tenchu!*' ('heaven's punishment!') before dispatching them. Okada spends all of his ill-gotten gains on saké and his favourite prostitute, Onimo (Mitsuko Baisho), while his unruly ways and overly-trusting nature land him in constant trouble. At one point, roaring drunk and unable to pay his saké bill, he is helped out by a fellow *hitokiri*, Shinbei Tanaka (1832-1863; played by Yukio Mishima), but Takechi subsequently orders Okada to frame Tanaka by using the latter's sword in an assassination.

Hitokiri is more successful as the story of an unusual samurai than as historical drama, and the film does not seem too concerned with matters of historical accuracy. For example, Okada was beheaded in real life, but is crucified in the film. Katsu was a larger-than-life personality who was more film star than serious actor. His natural charisma made him highly watchable and carries him through *Hitokiri* as it did all of his other films, but he had a tendency to go over-the-top, and Gosha was not a director known for reigning-in his actors. Indeed, Nakadai later said that Gosha tended to be very hands-off in his approach to actors and that, on *Hitokiri*, he and Katsu did not rehearse together before shooting their scenes and received no notes from Gosha. For the most part, Nakadai played it low-key in contrast to Katsu, but his maniacal laugh when Takechi finally reveals himself to be the power-crazed despot he always was, is pure cartoon villainry. The best acting in the film comes courtesy of Mitsuko Baisho, the younger sister of Chieko Baisho,[63] in what was only her second film role. As Onimo, her cynical, world-weary and resolutely unimpressed attitude makes a refreshing contrast to Okada's childlike emotional-immaturity.

Perhaps under the influence of Kurosawa, Gosha was also a lover of extreme weather in his films. In *Goyokin*, he made effective use of snow, whereas in *Hitokiri* he had the first assassination scene take place during relentless heavy rain, à la the famous battle scene in *Seven Samurai*. Nakadai later said that Kurosawa once brought up the subject of Gosha when they were together, complaining that he felt Gosha copied from his films. Nakadai defended Gosha, saying that the younger director did so because he admired Kurosawa and was still learning, an argument Kurosawa seemed to accept.

The appearance of Japan's most famous writer as a skilled samurai swordsman could be said to have been novelty casting, but nevertheless works very well, and Mishima is much better here than in his only previous major film part (as a gangster in the 1960 picture *Afraid to Die*, or 'Karakkaze yaro'). Apparently, it was Gosha's idea to cast him – a suggestion to which the other parties involved, including Mishima himself, all readily agreed. However, Mishima made some of the other

---

[63] Famous in Japan for her recurring role as the sister of 'Tora-san' in the long-running film series.

actors uneasy due to the unusual degree of enthusiasm he brought to his swordfighting scenes.

Nakadai had met Mishima before, when he appeared in a play of his at Haiyuza back in 1955, as well as while making *Conflagration*, based on Mishima's novel, and perhaps there had been other encounters. Having diametrically opposed political views, they were probably not close, but were certainly on friendly terms, and Nakadai was impressed by Mishima's dedication to his role. On one occasion during filming, he asked him why, as a writer, he put so much effort into bodybuilding. When Mishima replied that it was because he intended to commit *seppuku* (hara-kiri) and had no wish to leave an unsightly corpse, Nakadai assumed he was joking, especially as Tanaka dies by *seppuku* in the film. Around a year later, Mishima did indeed famously kill himself using this method. He had also made a 30-minute film, *Patriotism* (Yukoku), from his own short story in 1966, in which he had played a young army lieutenant who dies by the same means, so it seems that these two roles may have served as grim rehearsals. Ironically, Mishima had been influenced during the making of *Patriotism* by Nakadai's earlier film, *Harakiri*, which he had enjoyed for all the wrong reasons – where most felt horror at the forced *seppuku* of a young samurai with a bamboo sword, the perverse mind of Mishima had found a strange beauty. After his death, both *Patriotism* and *Hitokiri* were withdrawn from exhibition at the request of Mishima's widow, and as a result became almost impossible to access for many years.

Hitokiri was advertised in Japan with the taglines, 'Slash! Slash! Slash! Slash with no questions!!' and 'Katsu slashes! Nakadai slashes! Mishima slashes! Yujiro slashes! No questions asked!', but was a box office hit nevertheless.

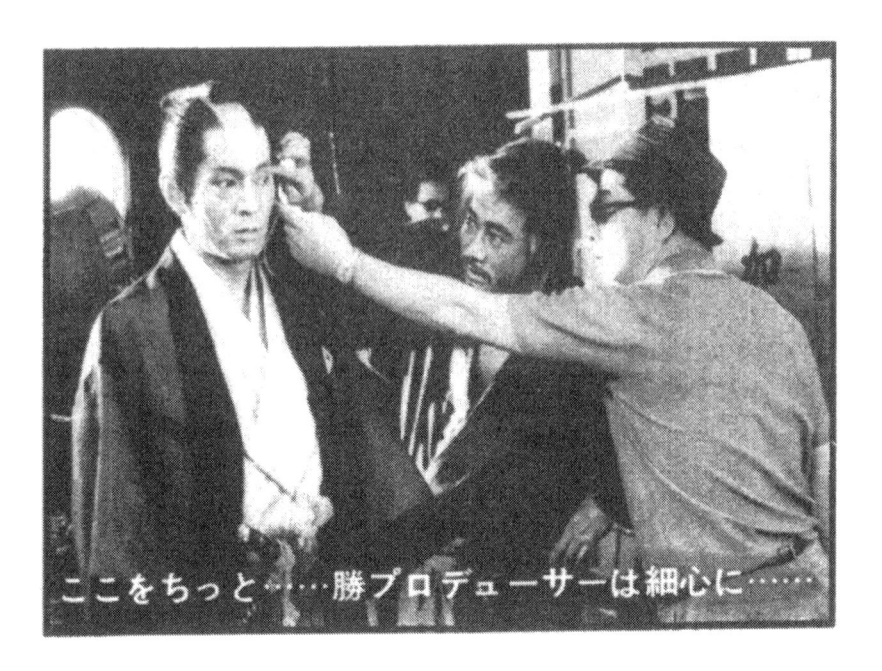

Top: Nakadai and Gosha on the set of *Hitokiri*.
Bottom: Shintaro Katsu (left) and Yukio Mishima (right).
(Courtesy of Robin Gatto)

Chapter 16 – Portrait of Hell

In his fourth and final film for director Shiro Toyoda, Nakadai played the leading part of Yoshihide, an obsessive artist. *Portrait of Hell* (Jigokuhen) was an adaptation of 'Hell Screen', a story from 1918 by Ryunosuke Akutagawa (1892-1927), one of Japan's most famous writers, upon whose work Kurosawa's *Rashomon* had also been based. Akutagawa had himself based 'Hell Screen' on a story from the *Uji Shui Monogatari*, a collection of tales thought to have been written in the early 13th-century. The original, entitled 'How Yoshihide, a Painter of Buddhist Pictures, Took Pleasure in Seeing His House on Fire', is barely a page in length, but Akutagawa expanded on this significantly, turning it into a work of around 30 pages, a substantial length for a short story. 'Hell Screen' is generally considered to be one of Akutagawa's finest stories and was adapted as a kabuki play by none other than Yukio Mishima in 1953.[64]

The narrator of the story, a servant in the household of the Lord of Horikawa, is blind to the cruelty of his master, always managing to ascribe a noble motive to an act of wickedness. The Lord frequently commissions works of art from Yoshihide, an artist known as the best in the land, and his respect for the painter's abilities makes him tolerant of his lack of manners. Yoshihide, a widower, is described as a 'thoroughly unpleasant little old man, all skin and bones,'[65] and disliked by all.

The only person for whom this misanthropic artist has anything but contempt is his teenage daughter, who works as a lady-in-waiting in the Lord's household. Yoshihide dotes upon her, but his love is a possessive one and, if any man dares to make advances, he hires somebody to beat them up. When the Lord becomes interested in her, she makes every effort to avoid his company. Yoshihide begins to worry that the Lord intends to make her his concubine. When the Lord

---

[64] A TV version of the Mishima play was produced by NHK in 1962.
[65] *Rashomon and Seventeen Other Stories* (Penguin, 2006), translated by Jay Rubin.

offers Yoshihide anything he desires in gratitude for a painting which has pleased him, the artist asks for his daughter to be released from service. The Lord is angered and refuses the request.

Yoshihide is ordered to paint a large folding screen depicting the eight Buddhist hells. Believing that he can only paint what he has seen with his own eyes, he begins chaining up his apprentices and terrifying them in order to see the expressions he needs for the sinners being tormented in his picture. He then goes even further, and purchases a large horned owl which he trains to attack his youngest apprentice, a 13-year-old boy. But Yoshihide reaches an impasse when it comes to the centerpiece of his painting, which is to be a burning carriage containing a beautiful young noblewoman being consumed by flames.

During the time that Yoshihide has been working on the painting, his daughter's situation within the household has become increasingly precarious. Again, Akutagawa skillfully reveals to us what the narrator himself is unable to see – that the Lord has attempted to rape Yoshihide's daughter. She is saved in the nick of time by her pet monkey, which manages to fetch the narrator himself to interrupt the assault.

Yoshihide visits the Lord and asks him to burn one of his best carriages to help him visualize what he needs to finish the painting. The Lord is excited to the point of madness by the idea and offers to not only burn a carriage but to put a woman inside it as well. Yoshihide is shocked but does not refuse the offer. On the night of the burning, he is horrified to discover his own daughter chained up inside the carriage. The Lord orders his men to set it alight. Yoshihide, appalled, nevertheless cannot bring himself to look away and thereby miss the opportunity to witness the burning of a beautiful young woman in order to render it accurately in his masterpiece. According to the narrator, he becomes spellbound in rapture at the sight, while the Lord looks on with what is clearly (to the reader) the sadistic glee of a madman. The narrator concludes that the Lord must have arranged the burning purely out of a noble desire to punish the painter for the sin of arrogance.

The screenplay for *Portrait of Hell* was written by Toyoda's regular collaborator, the prolific Toshio Yasumi, who had also written the scripts for *Anyakoro*, *Madame Aki* and *Illusion of Blood*. Some intriguing changes were made, especially to the character of Yoshihide, who retains the Japanese name but is stated to be Korean in the film. It is implied that he has been brought to Japan against his will so that the Lord can benefit from the services of this great artist. This change is difficult to account for – it could be that, during the course of his research, Yasumi stumbled across some stories of Korean artists being taken to Japan to work for the nobles, and decided to include it. This certainly occurred during the late 16th-century, but the film is set in the Heian period (794-1185). It could also be that he wanted to make a point about prejudice or Japan's historical relationship with Korea but, if so, it is difficult to see how these might be related to the main theme of the story, which is how pride and obsession can lead to self-destruction. Perhaps Yasumi wished to give Yoshihide an additional motive for hating the Lord. In any case, the change does no harm and certainly adds an interesting extra dimension.

As played by the good-looking Nakadai, there is no sense of the character being physically repellent as described by Akutagawa. The device of the unreliable narrator is dispensed with, and the wickedness of the Lord is evident from the very beginning. The Lord is very well-played by Nakadai's friend and *Goyokin* co-star Kinnosuke Nakamura in an atypical role.

A voiceover at the beginning of the film explains that the people live in fear while famine and disaster rule the land. The only ones who live comfortably are the aristocrats, but even they are fearful of losing their position. This set-up is reminiscent of Roger Corman's *The Masque of the Red Death*, and the Lord occupies a similar position to that of Vincent Price's Prince Prospero – another nobleman who lives for his own pleasure while the people suffer.

As the film begins, we see Lord Horikawa enjoying an excursion into the country. While he drinks saké under the cherry blossoms and watches a dance being performed, a vassal informs him in a whisper that he needs to leave as a storm is approaching. His men refuse to pay an old man (presumably a saké vendor) and, when the Lord's ox is spooked by thunder and escapes, the old man is crushed under its hooves. A circle of faces appear, looking down at the dying man, who curses the Lord. One of these faces belongs to Yoshihide. At first, he appears to be concerned for the old man, but we later realise that his eyes have been hungrily drinking in the scene so that he will be able to paint it later. In the Akutagawa story, this incident is mentioned only in passing and Yoshihide is not present, with the narrator saying that the dying man gave thanks for having been killed by 'His Lordship's own ox.' This is one of the many ways in which Yasumi's excellent screenplay cleverly expands on the Akutagawa story. Another significant difference is that, in the story, the Lord merely orders Yoshihide to paint a picture of Hell, whereas in the film, he originally requests a picture of Paradise, an assignment Yoshihide says he will not be able to carry out as there is nowhere he can see Paradise or a 'perfect virtuous face'.

At first, Yoshihide seems more sympathetic in the film. Although he is brutal towards the young apprentice in love with his daughter and sends him packing, he seems to be a champion of truth and is the only person to tell the deluded Lord what the people really think of him. He even stands up to him at the risk of his own life, and openly berates him for the corruption he encourages. However, halfway through the film, Yoshihide begins torturing his apprentice with snakes in the name of art, and naturally becomes a great deal less sympathetic as a result.[66] By the time he has finished the painting apart from the burning carriage, his hair has turned grey.

---

[66] There is no trained owl in the film. Oddly enough, there *is* an attack by a bird of prey in Corman's *The Masque of the Red Death*. This does not feature in the Poe story and may not be a coincidence as it's quite possible that the screenwriters were familiar with 'Hell Screen.'

In the story, the Lord plans to burn Yoshihide's daughter alive as soon as the idea occurs to him, but in the film it is initially a threat intended to bend the artist to his will – a threat only executed when Yoshihide refuses to compromise, perhaps not believing that the Lord will really give such an order.

Nakadai portrays both the painter's humanity and stubborn pride perfectly – we see not only Yoshihide's gruff and unyielding personality, but also how his obsession with his art has become a destructive addiction and the vulnerability he reveals concerning his daughter. Having said that, it is also implied that his interest in her may be more than a fatherly one.

Portrait of Hell is an unusual film unlikely to be forgotten by any who have seen it. In its depiction of a battle of wills between two volatile personalities which inevitably ends in catastrophe, it has a timeless resonance and, while the special effects are sometimes primitive, the visuals are consistently striking throughout. The most memorable image is perhaps that of Yoshihide's horror-struck, staring eyes as he watches his daughter burn in a blizzard of orange sparks.

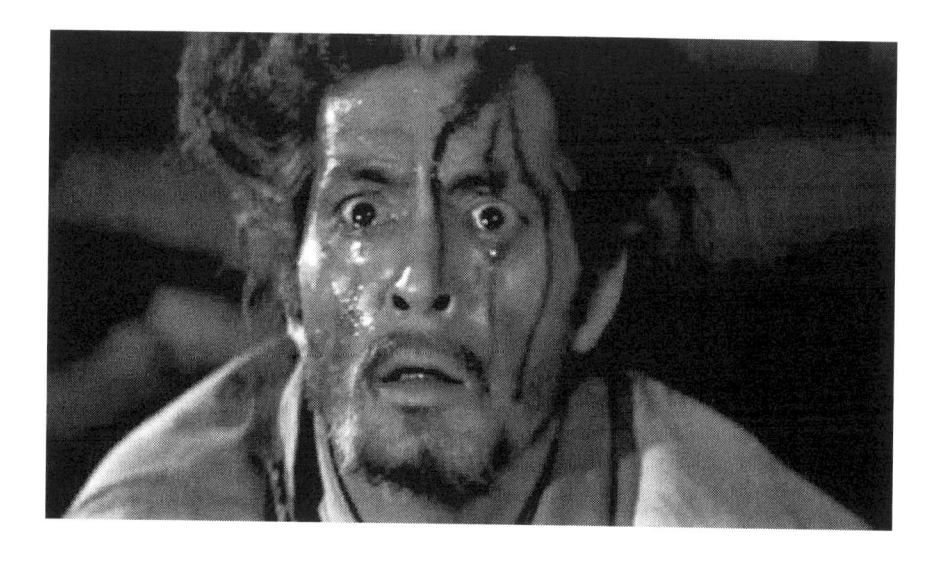

Portrait of Hell (screenshot)

Chapter 17 – Samurai Socialist

Nakadai followed this with a film for Daiei entitled *Tengu-to* ('Goblin Group', aka *Blood End*), which tells the story of the Mito Tengu group, Mito being a domain that existed in eastern Honshu during the Edo era. Active in the troubled years running up to the Meiji Restoration known as the Bakumatsu period (1853-67), the group originally consisted of samurai rebelling against the shogunate and favouring allegiance to the Emperor together with a policy of expelling foreigners from Japan. Nakadai played Sentaro, a peasant who at the beginning of the film is being brutally punished by corrupt government officials for refusing to pay the exploitative rice tax. After this pre-credits prologue, the story jumps ahead four years and we learn that Sentaro has spent the intervening period in Edo learning to be proficient with a sword in order to gain revenge. Whilst in the capital, he also fell in love with a geisha (Ayako Wakao). Returning to his native village and believing the Tengu-to to be on the side of the farmers, he falls in with them, but when infighting breaks out among the group, his naivety leads him to make a number of catastrophic errors of judgment and become hopelessly confused about where his loyalties should lie. He eventually learns the bitter truth that the samurai rebels he thought were his comrades have no genuine desire to bring about equality and still consider him their inferior after all.

Nakadai has a decent if not especially challenging part and some moments of high emotion. It was his fourth time working for director Satsuo Yamamoto, for whom he made a further three films, and it was to be these later collaborations that produced their most notable work together. Although Yamamoto's communist perspective is apparent in the film's theme of fair treatment for farmers, *Tengu-to* is barely mentioned in his autobiography, suggesting that he considered it a rather insignificant work himself. At this stage in his career, Yamamoto was dividing his time between films he really wanted to make, such as *The Great White Tower* (Shiroi Kyoto) and *Slave Factory* (Dorei kojo) and studio assignments like *The Bride from Hades* (Botan-doro/'The Peony Lantern') and *Tengu-to* (Nakadai had actually turned down a role in *The Great White Tower* due to his theatre commitments).[67] Although by no means a bad film, *Tengu-to* is far from Yamamoto's best, and the narrative becomes increasingly bogged down by an excess of talk, betraying its origins as a stage play.[68] Still, there are some good action sequences and a strong supporting cast including Go Kato and Shigeru Koyama (both seen in *Samurai Rebellion*), not to mention Ayako Wakao, perhaps the most talented of Nakadai's female contemporaries – even if, on this occasion, she is wasted in a rather small and uninteresting part despite sharing top-billing with Nakadai.

Like Nakadai, Ayako Wakao was also a favourite of multiple major directors, including Yamamoto, Kenji Mizoguchi, Kon Ichikawa, Yuzo Kawashima, Umetsugu Inoue and, most notably, Yazuso Masumura, who cast her in the lead in no less than 20 of his films. Signed by Daiei Studios in 1951 when only 18, she had won prestige when cast by Mizoguchi as the young apprentice in his 1953 film *A Geisha* (aka *Gion Bayashi*) and quickly graduated to leads. Wakao went on to play a wide range of characters in both period and modern dramas and was equally convincing whether cast as a naïve young ingénue or a scheming adulteress. Nakadai and Wakao had never worked together before *Tengu-to* as, since the beginning of her career, she had been employed almost exclusively by Daiei, where Nakadai seldom worked. By this point, the studio's output was rapidly dwindling due to financial difficulties. After Daiei went bankrupt in 1971, Wakao became a rare example of a movie star who switched almost entirely to television work.

Nakadai followed *Tengu-to* with another appearance in a left-wing samurai film set during the same period, *Bakumatsu* (aka *The Ambitious*).

---

[67] https://eiga.com/news/20180421/10/

[68] Entitled *Kirare no Senta* and written by Juro Miyoshi, it had previously been filmed by Eisuke Takizawa in 1949 under the original title with Susumu Fujita in the role of Sentaro.

Based on short stories by *Hitokiri* author Ryotaro Shiba, it starred Nakadai's friend Kinnosuke Nakamura, and would be the only film made by Nakamura's own production company. Nakamura played Ryoma Sakamoto (1836-67; previously portrayed by Yujiro Ishihara in *Hitokiri*), a samurai who abandons his clan, becomes a political radical and helps to bring about the downfall of the Tokugawa shogunate. Influenced by Western ideals of equality, he comes to believe that progress can be made only through the abolition of his own class. Nakadai was featured in a number of scenes as Shintaro Nakaoka (1838-67), Sakamoto's best friend, with whom he constantly argues. Nakaoka also believes in reform, but wants the samurai to keep their superior status.

As director, Nakamura chose 70-year-old veteran Daisuke Ito, a filmmaker he had worked with on a number of previous occasions and who was one of the pioneers of Japanese cinema. His sole surviving silent film, *Jirokichi the Rat* (Oatsurae Jirokichi koshi, 1931), remains impressive today. Ito's strengths seem to have lain mainly in aspects of visuals and movement, such as composition, orchestrating action, blocking scenes and designing elaborate crane and tracking shots. Unfortunately, he was in poor physical health at the time; speaking to Joan Mellen two years after the film's release, he commented, 'I am afraid it [*Bakumatsu*] is a failure as a work of art. My physical condition made it impossible for me to do enough retakes to be satisfied with the results.' [69] Few of Ito's films are accessible in the West (and he seems largely forgotten in Japan), but on the basis of *Bakumatsu*, *The Conspirator* (Hangyakuji, 1961) and *Osho* (1962), he allowed or perhaps encouraged his actors to go over the top (although this tendency is less in evidence in his grossly undervalued 1951 film *Five Men of Edo*/ 'Oedo go-nin otoko'). With the honourable exception of Shigeru Koyama, the main cast in *Bakumatsu* all give excessively emotional performances, and Nakadai's drawn-out death scene is far from his finest moment. The choreography in the fight sequences is also

---

[69] *Voices from the Japanese Cinema* by Joan Mellen (Liveright, 1975)

frequently unconvincing, while Ito's own script is dialogue-heavy, disjointed and confusing. Though he lived until 1981, *Bakumatsu* was to be his final work.

Nakadai was briefly reunited with *Sazae-san* star Chiemi Eri, who popped up in a cameo, as did Toshiro Mifune, although the latter had no scenes with Nakadai. Distributed through Toho and released in February 1970, the film received a limited release in the US in August of the same year, but was a commercial and critical failure.

Nakadai appeared in the first few minutes only of director Kengo Furusawa's *Duel at Fort Ezo* (Ezo yakata no ketto) a men-on-a-mission movie about a mixed group of *ronin* and criminals (led by a dishevelled Rentaro Mikuni) attempting to rescue a kidnapped Russian princess from the titular fort. Although fairly entertaining and well-made on the whole, the film features a highly unconvincing bear which trumpets like an elephant when stabbed through the heart, as well as some highly dubious sexual attitudes. The female lead is the hapless Mitsuko Baisho from *Hitokiri*, who appears here as the feisty daughter of the castle's lord. After being raped by the 'good' *ronin* among Mikuni's band of cutthroats (Yuzo Kayama), she falls in love with him and undergoes an instant personality change into a meek doormat, with the none-too-subtle implication that a good shafting was just what she needed. Presumably having nothing better to do that day, Nakadai donned a topknot wig to play the official who hires Mikuni to undertake the mission.

Nakadai's next film, *Buraikan*, was released internationally as *The Scandalous Adventures of Buraikan*, but if this title change was intended to give cinemagoers the impression it was a bawdy, *Tom Jones*-style romp, it was both inaccurate and unsuccessful.[70] However, taken on its own merits, *Buraikan* is a highly unusual and interesting film. Written by Shuji Terayama, a 'New Wave' writer-director who had penned Nakadai's earlier *Get 'Em All* and was soon to have a success with *Throw Away Your Books, Rally in the Streets* (Sho o suteyo machi e deyo), it was based on a play by the 19th-century kabuki writer Mokuami Kawatake.

The story takes place in Edo against the background of the Tenpo Reforms of the 1840s introduced by chief senior councillor Tadakuni Mizuno (1794-1851, played by Hiroshi Akutagawa). Set in a world populated by thieves and other outcasts on the fringes of society, the film presented these colourful characters with a sympathetic eye and saved its barbs for authority figures such as Mizuno, depicted here as a crank who bans everything he considers improper, from streetwalking and fireworks to the sale of actors' portraits and even female *bunraku* reciters, blind to the economic hardship that results. The other member of the ruling class depicted is Lord Matsue (Atsuo Nakamura), a sadist interested only in indulging his own pleasures no matter how much suffering it may cause others. Deprived of the opportunity to make a living, the gamblers, prostitutes and others of their class become so incensed with the situation that they plan an uprising.

Nakadai was top-billed as Naojiro Kataoka, a vain and lazy good-for-nothing who lives with his mother. He makes money by telling bogus fortunes and cheating at cards, but fancies himself an actor.

---

[70] The title has caused confusion in the West, as there is no character named 'Buraikan' in the film. Some sources state that it refers to the character played by Tetsuro Tanba, who plays an instrument called the buraikan, but there is no Japanese instrument with this name. In fact, the title may well refer to Nakadai's character, as 'buraikan' is not a name, but means something like 'untrustworthy man' or, more simply, 'villain.' But then again, this description could fit more than one of the characters in the film and could even be intended as a plural as, in Japanese, a plural noun can only be distinguished from a singular when a number or other quantifier is added. It may also be of interest to note that the 1956 western *Seven Men from Now*, in which Randolph Scott tracks down the seven men responsible for his wife's death, was released in Japan as *Shichi jin no buraikan* (i.e. 'Seven Villains').

Naojiro falls for Michitose (Shima Iwashita), a high-class prostitute who becomes equally smitten with him, but he has a rival, Moritaya (*Black River*'s Fumio Watanabe); when Naojiro makes a fool of him publicly, Moritaya swears revenge.

Other characters are also given considerable amounts of screen time, as the original play was an ensemble piece and the film remains true to this structure. Another thread involves Ushimatsu (Shoichi Uzawa), a man who returns after a year away to find that his wife and child have been stolen from him to pay off his debt to his landlord. His wife was subsequently driven to suicide by the landlord's perverted desires, while his son has been sold off to a travelling circus troupe. Ushimatsu's heartbreak leads him to kidnap a child who reminds him of his son. A further subplot concerns a father who enlists the help of palace attendant Kochiyama (Tetsuro Tanba) in rescuing his daughter from the clutches of Lord Matsue; Kochiyama disguises himself as a monk sent by a higher authority to order the girl's release.

A co-production of Toho and the briefly-resurrected Ninjin Club (the company which had previously co-produced *The Human Condition*, *Ogin-sama* and *Kwaidan*), *Buraikan* was directed by Masahiro Shinoda, known to some extent in the West for films such as *Pale Flower* (Kawaita hana), *Double Suicide* (Shinju: Ten no Amijima), and *Silence* (Chinmoku). This was to be his only collaboration with Nakadai, who rarely worked with such 'New Wave' directors, perhaps because he was considered too closely associated with the old guard of Kurosawa and his contemporaries and was seldom asked. However, he was fortunate in this case to appear in one of Shinoda's best and most accessible films.

Shinoda was in his late 30s at the time and had recently married Shima Iwashita, who had starred in most of his films and would continue to do so. According to Audie Bock in her book *Japanese Film Directors*, Shinoda felt that the plays of Mokuami 'resembled the spirit of contemporary underground theatre', which was why he chose to revive such an old play and make it in a modern 'pop art' style. *Buraikan* certainly makes memorable use of Panavision along with colourful sets and costumes to produce a stylised film full of vivid and arresting images, while Masaru Sato provided a suitably eccentric score which flits between modern jazz and traditional Japanese sounds. The result is one of the lesser-known gems in Nakadai's filmography, in which the star is perfectly cast as the amoral but charming rogue Naojiro. Despite being an entertaining comedy, the film also has a timeless relevance in its theme of the gulf between those in power and the working class, and how moralistic law-making can do more harm than good. Although submitted as Japan's entry for Best Foreign Language Film at the Academy Awards, *Buraikan* was not selected, but it did receive a limited release in the USA.

Chapter 18 – Samurai, Soldier, Criminal

Nakadai's friendship with Shintaro Katsu led to him appearing as a guest star in what would already be the 21st film in the long-running series about Zatoichi, the wandering blind masseur and expert swordsman, a role originated by Katsu in 1962. In *Zatoichi -The Festival of Fire* (Zatoichi abare hi matsuri), a blind *yakuza* boss (*Rashomon*'s Masayuki Mori in his penultimate film role) decides that Zatoichi must be eliminated as his sense of justice keeps interfering with the gang's plans to extort money from honest tradesmen. He sets a variety of traps for Zatoichi but, needless to say, Zatoichi survives every attempt on his life. At the beginning of the film, Zatoichi is massaging a rich customer at an auction where women are sold as sex slaves. The auctioneer even points out that some of the women have had their teeth removed in order to 'improve their oral skills.' When the beautiful wife of a samurai retainer fetches a high price from Zatoichi's repulsive customer, the masseur decides to rescue her. (His choice in rescuing this particular woman unfortunately implies that women from the upper classes are superior and therefore more worthy of being rescued. However, perhaps the world of Zatoichi is not to be taken too seriously.) He attacks the servants transporting her to the home of her new owner and takes her to a nearby barn to rest, but her *ronin* husband (Nakadai) arrives, assumes the two have slept together, and kills her before disappearing. The unnamed *ronin* appears sporadically thoughout the film after this with the intention of revenging himself on Zatoichi, but not too quickly as he says that his vengeance is the only thing he has left to live for (or perhaps because the filmmakers want to save their final confronation for the climax). It is never exactly explained why the *ronin*'s wife has ended up being sold as a sex slave, but presumably the *ronin* was working a con in which he profited from the auction and intended to rescue his wife himself until Zatoichi beat him to it.

This entry in the series marked Shintaro Katsu's debut as a screenwriter, and together with co-writer Takayuki Yamada, he created the role of the *ronin* specifically for Nakadai. However, he showed little imagination in this regard, with the result that Nakadai's guest part not only feels uncomfortably shoehorned into the larger plot, but also comes across as a tired retread of what was by now becoming Nakadai's angry *ronin* shtick, *sandogasa* and all. Nevertheless, *Zatoichi -The Festival of Fire* is inventive in other regards, and features a cool little alcohol-induced dream sequence for Nakadai, as well as some amusingly-staged fight scenes, perhaps most memorably the nude battle in the bath house. At one point, Zatoichi is even seduced by a gay pimp played by Peter, who would later give a memorable performance as the fool in *Ran* alongside Nakadai. Another notable actor in the film is Reiko Ohara, surprisingly moving as the woman who falls in love with Zatoichi. Ohara's career was subsequently curtailed by health problems resulting in a diagnosis of Guillan-Barre syndrome in 1975, a rare medical disorder in which the immune system attacks the nerves, but she continued acting when her health allowed. The film therefore has a very strong cast, as well as high production values, and is directed with style by Kenji Misumi, who later made the *Lone Wolf* series. Although plausibility has been thrown to the winds even for a Zatoichi film, *The Festival of Fire* is consistently entertaining throughout and a favourite among many fans of the series.

Nakadai and Katsu went drinking every night after filming, and were often out until 3 or 4 a.m. Shooting began at 9 a.m., but Nakadai had to be on set for make-up an hour beforehand and frequently found himself battling a hangover. Katsu was not an early riser and at one stage in the filming he failed to arrive on set until around noon three days running, leaving Nakadai waiting around with nothing to do. However, when Nakadai threatened to quit, Katsu apologised and changed his behaviour. Having said that, it seems that Nakadai was not always the consummate professional himself as, when not needed on set, he would often sneak off for a hair of the dog, and Katsu would then have to send an assistant to search for him among the bars of Gion.

Zatoichi -The Festival of Fire is the first film in which Nakadai appears with a scar on his left cheek. This scar was to remain for the rest of his life, although the cause is unknown – a slip of the sword by one of his on-screen opponents, perhaps?

Nakadai had a supporting role in *Will to Conquer*,[71] a biopic of Mitsubishi founder Yataro Iwasaki (1835-1885), played by Kinnosuke Nakamura. Like Nakadai's earlier *Battle of the Japan Sea,* the director was Seiji Maruyama, and the screenplay was written by the prolific Toshio Yasumi, who had scripted all of the films Nakadai had made for Shiro Toyoda. Nakadai here played Toyo Yoshida (1816-1862), a reformer who believed in opening up Japan to foreign trade and became a teacher to Iwasaki, so his role was that of an opponent of his *Hitokiri* character, Hanpeita Takechi, who appears in this film played by Isao Kimura.[72] The Mitsubishi Group provided a large part of the financing for the film, which is reportedly rather one-sided as a result. Another common complaint is that, while *Will to Conquer* begins promisingly, it becomes quite dull in the second half.

Towards the end of 1970, Nakadai played Othello for Haiyuza at the Nissay Theatre under the direction of Koreya Senda, who retired after this production. Desdemona was portrayed by Momoko Kochi, who had played Anna Karenina to Nakadai's Prince Vronsky a few years earlier, while the juicy role of Iago was enacted by another company member, Seiya Nakano. Around six years younger than Nakadai, Nakano seldom worked in film, mainly appearing on stage or television. A recording of the play was subsequently released as a vinyl LP.

---

[71] The Japanese title *Shokon ichi-dai tenka no abarenbo* translates as 'The first generation of commercial spirit.'

[72] Yoshida had also been featured in *Hitokiri*, in which he was played by Ryutaro Tatsumi.

Another supporting role followed in *Challenge at Dawn* (Akatsuki no chosen) which, like *Goyokin* and *Hitokiri*, was a product of the Fuji Television Network's forays into film production. The screenplay was co-authored by Shinobu Hashimoto, Ichiro Ikeda (*The Last Judgment*) and Takeo Kunihiro, the latter of whom had recently adapted Yasushi Inoue's novel *Furin Kazan* with Hashimoto as *Samurai Banners*, starring Toshiro Mifune. *Challenge at Dawn* was the first of several films Nakadai would appear in for director Toshio Masuda, who had just finished working on the American-Japanese co-production *Tora! Tora! Tora!* after Akira Kurosawa was famously fired.

Set in Kawasaki in 1925, *Challenge at Dawn* is based on the Tsurumi Riot Incident, which actually occurred in Yokohama that year and was sparked by corruption and *yakuza* involvement in the construction industry. When there is an industrial dispute and the workers walk out, the *yakuza* are hired to break the strike, but the workers stand up to them and the climax of the film recreates (not very faithfully) the real-life armed confrontation at dawn between the *yakuza* and the workers, in which around 2,000 people were said to have been involved. 1,500 police were dispatched to quell the unrest, which resulted in two deaths and 400 arrests. The *yakuza* were forced to back down and admit that times had changed.

Nakadai had a supporting role as Tsukagoshi, a bearded *yakuza* who commits *seppuku*, while Kinnosuke Nakamura played the main role of a worker caught up in events, Tetsuya Watari (star of the *Outlaw Gangster VIP* series) appeared as another *yakuza* and Mitsuko Baisho as a geisha. *Challenge at Dawn* received its first screening in many years in 2014, but seems unlikely to surface outside Japan.

Nakadai's next film saw him reunited with director Kihachi Okamoto for *The Battle of Okinawa* (Gekido no Showa-shi: Okinawa kessen/'Turbulent Showa History: The Battle of Okinawa'), another biggish-budget Toho war movie, albeit one cut from a rather different cloth to its predecessors – partly because it was helmed by the eccentric Okamoto and partly because of the especially horrific nature of the events involved. The real battle had lasted three months and cost the lives of not just huge numbers of soldiers on both sides, but hundreds of thousands of civilians, many of whom committed suicide rather than be captured by the Americans. In fact, *The Battle of Okinawa* probably features a higher suicide count than any other film ever made. Characteristically, Okamoto interspersed these scenes with episodes of comic relief courtesy of Kunei Tanaka's barber and Yuriko Oka's prostitute-turned-nurse which feel decidedly out of place. However, to the credit of Okamoto and screenwriters Ryozo Kasahara and Kaneto Shindo, the film is effective in showing the true cost of war, and especially the tragic waste caused by the propagation of the myth that the only way to show loyalty to one's country is by dying for it. The film finishes with a little orphan girl (seen earlier searching for a grenade to destroy herself with) finding a canteen of water from which she drinks thirstily – an inspired ending which skillfully avoids both pessimism and sentimentality.

Nakadai played Colonel Hiromichi Yahara (1902-81), a senior officer struggling to defend the island alongside Lieutenant Isamu Cho (Tetsuro Tanba), with whom he fails to see eye to eye. Both are under the command of General Mitsuru Ushijima (*Pressure of Guilt*'s Keiju Kobayashi). The role mainly required Nakadai to look serious and concerned, and so offered few opportunities to demonstrate his range, but he was no doubt pleased to be associated with another film that refused to flinch from portraying the horrors of war. In one scene, Yahara encounters a dazed woman clutching a baby's severed arm – an image which must have evoked his own traumatic experience during an air raid when he was 12 years old. Nakadai may also have appreciated the fact that Yahara is depicted as less gung-ho than his counterparts, and keen to avoid any unnecessary sacrifice of life, including his own. In fact, the real Yahara had been ordered to survive and tell the truth about events on Okinawa – an order given by Ushijima, who realised that defeat was inevitable and decided to commit suicide along with Cho. Two years after Okamoto's film was released, Yahara – who served as advisor on the film – published his account in book form, also under the title *The Battle of Okinawa*.

One of the popular aspects of Toho's war films is the use of elaborate miniatures. *Battle of Okinawa* features fewer of these than usual, but there is an impressive shot of the island under attack from the U.S. Air Force achieved by means of a 1/1100 scale model of the entire island. The film was a box-office success in Japan and received an American release two years later but, like the battle itself, it remains controversial.

The majority of Japanese films about the Second World War have performed a delicate balancing act between portraying the realities of a war impossible to justify in retrospect and fulfilling the need of the domestic audience to see upstanding examples of their countrymen on screen. *The Battle of Okinawa* was no exception, and some Western reviewers have interpreted the film as jingoistic right-wing propaganda, but this was certainly not the intent, and neither Okamoto nor Nakadai would have been involved if it had been. Part of the reason for this misinterpretation undoubtedly lies in the fact that we see only the Japanese side of the story – the Americans are simply 'the enemy' and there are no American characters. It should also be pointed out that the film frequently shows the Japanese army behaving brutally towards the Okinawan civilians, and the endless scenes of suffering and suicide surely in no way glorify military imperialism, but clearly condemn it. However, the film is guilty of some inaccuracies; for example, in one scene, American soldiers throw gas bombs into a cave in which Japanese civilians are hiding; while the Americans certainly used a variety of terrible weapons throughout the battle, gas was not one of them.

Nakadai's next film, *Inn of Evil*,[73] reunited him with director Masaki Kobayashi, but in this instance the project was instigated by Nakadai, not Kobayashi. Based on a novel by Shugoro Yamamoto entitled *Fukagawa Anrakutei*, the screenplay had been written by Nakadai's wife,

---

[73] The Japanese title *Inochi bo ni furo* is difficult to translate into English, but Kobayashi scholar Stephen Prince refers to it as *We Who Give Our Lives for Nothing*.

Yasuko, credited as usual under her pen name of Tomoe Ryu. Nakadai pitched it to the 'Four Knights', the production company formed by Akira Kurosawa, Masaki Kobayashi, Keisuke Kinoshita and Kon Ichikawa which had produced Kurosawa's *Dodes'ka-den*. Kobayashi, who had been struggling to get projects off the ground since the commercial failure of his previous film, *Hymn to a Tired Man* (Nihon no seishun, 1968), signed on as director.

Nakadai thought he saw a good role for his friend, Shintaro Katsu, who was under contract to Daiei. As the film was being co-produced by Haiyuza and Toho, Nakadai had to obtain permission to cast him from Daiei head Masaichi Nagata – the very man who had prevented his *Madame Aki* co-star, Fujiko Yamamoto, from ever working in films again. He went along with one of the producers to the studio's office in Ginza, but it took three attempts over three consecutive days before they were granted an audience. Nagata was in the middle of a dispute with the unions at the time, but when they were finally able to speak to him, he granted their request and Katsu was cast.

Inn of Evil, set in the late Edo period, tells of a group of criminals involved in smuggling who live in an inn situated on a tiny island in the middle of a river accessible only by a single footbridge. Anyone not known to the proprietor who enters the inn is beaten up and thrown out, usually after having his money stolen, and even the local police are too afraid to go near the place. The worst criminal in the group is Sadashichi (Nakadai), known as 'Sadashichi the Indifferent', who is said to have killed his own mother upon discovering she had become a prostitute. Into this group comes an innocent, Tomijiro (Kei Yamamoto), who has stolen money from his employer in a failed attempt to buy back his fiancée after her father sold her into prostitution. Tomijiro's sad story awakens the sympathies of these apparently beyond-the-pale criminals, and they decide to help him.

Nakadai's character is presented as an evil, psychotic killer in the first half of the film before it is revealed that he has been caring for a baby sparrow separated from his mother (as Sadashichi himself had been as a child). This arouses the interest of the innkeeper's daughter,

Omitsu (Komaki Kurihara), who begins to look at him with new eyes, especially when Sadashichi (after some initial reluctance) becomes the most enthusiastic about the idea of helping Tomijiro.

Inn of Evil has no pretensions to realism and comes across as quite a theatrical piece of drama, evoking the down-and-out milieu of Maxim Gorky's *The Lower Depths*, although filmed by Kobayashi with his customary visual panache, especially in the climactic sequence. Clearly inspired by a similar scene at the end of Daisuke Ito's 1931 film *Jirokichi the Rat*, this involves a night-time raid by a huge group of police, each of whom are visible only by the paper lanterns they are carrying both to identify themselves and to light their way. The screen swarms with hundreds of lanterns, which bob and weave, forming a variety of abstract patterns in a striking display of cinematic bravura.

Nakadai gave one of his most intense performances, but the transformation of his character seems rather sudden, and *Inn of Evil* is – again like *The Lower Depths* – essentially an ensemble piece. Among a strong cast, Shintaro Katsu is especially good value as a mysterious customer who comes in every night and drinks himself into apparent oblivion while the others ignore him and continue to talk amongst themselves, only to be astonished by his sudden bursts of insight before he passes out again.

Inn of Evil has not been as widely seen abroad as Kobayashi's other period films. As an uncharacteristically sentimental piece, it is perhaps one of his lesser works, but still has much to recommend it, including another fine score by Toru Takemitsu and the black and white cinematography of Kozo Okazaki. Realising the theatrical nature and potential of the property, Yasuko later adapted it as a stage play, also starring her husband.

Nakadai followed *Inn of Evil* with a fourth film for Hideo Gosha – *The Wolves*, a bloody tale of betrayal and revenge involving a conflict between rival *yakuza* gangs in the early Showa era (late 1920s). The project represented a change from Toho's usual fare, as it was Toei which had cornered the market in *yakuza* films, which typically ran 90 minutes and starred Ken Takakura. *The Wolves* was something of an attempt to beat them at their own game, with a bigger budget, an extra 40 minutes running time and a little more sophistication and depth. While the English-language title is unrelated to anything in the film, it at least sounds better in English than a literal translation of the Japanese one, *Shussho Iwai*, meaning 'Prison Release Celebration'.

Nakadai played Iwahashi, a *yakuza* serving a prison sentence for murder who finds himself released early when the new emperor decides to celebrate his ascension by commuting the sentences of several hundred convicts. Also released are Tsutomu (Toshio Kurosawa) from Iwahashi's gang and Gunjiro (Noboru Ando), one of their rivals. Having seen enough bloodshed and already spent several years behind bars as a result, Iwahashi is keen to keep the peace, and Gunjiro apparently feels the same way. However, when Tsutomu discovers that his woman is now engaged to a member of the other gang, things become complicated and violence ensues.

Nakadai's co-star, Noboru Ando, was in fact a former *yakuza* himself, having formed the Azuma Kogyo, aka the Ando Gang, in 1952. Said to be handy with a razor, Ando operated in Shibuya and reportedly had 300 members in his gang at its peak. In 1958, he sent an underling with a gun to dispatch a businessman who had not only refused to pay a debt, but had insulted him to boot. The man was shot but survived, and Ando went on the run for a month before being caught and sentenced to six years. Upon his release from prison in 1964, he put an end to his *yakuza* career and resolved to go straight. By this time, *yakuza* films were becoming popular, so a producer from Shochiku studios approached Ando and signed him as an actor, although he later switched studios and went to work for Toei (whose main producer was another former *yakuza*). Toei even produced a number of films loosely based on their star's former career and featuring the man himself, such as *The Yakuza and Feuds – True Account of the Ando Gang* (Yakuza to koso – Jitsuroku Ando gumi, 1972) and *Noboru Ando's Account of Filthy Escape into Sex* (Ando Noboru no waga toboto sekkusuno kiroku, 1976).

Nakadai later said that, when they arrived at the train station where the filming location was based, a group of local *yakuza* were lined up to greet his co-star, and that such scenes occurred wherever they went. Ando was apparently embarrassed by this kind of attention and always apologized to his co-workers when it happened. Despite being the older of the two, he was also humble in his attitude towards his co-star, and said that he would like to learn from Nakadai as he did not really consider himself an actor.

Nakadai and Gosha prepare to shoot an action on the set of *The Wolves*. Noboru Ando is next to Gosha. (Courtesy of Robin Gatto)

The female lead in *The Wolves* was played by Kyoko Enami, star of a popular film series entitled *The Woman Gambler* (Onna tobaku-shi) and future winner of the Kinema Jumpo Best Actress Award for Koichi Saito's excellent *Tsugaru Folk Song* (Tsugaru jongarabushi, 1973). Nakadai had to perform a sex scene with her (something he disliked doing as he always felt embarrassed) and asked Gosha for direction, whereupon the director proceeded to demonstrate with Enami what he wanted him to do. Nakadai said that he felt sorry for the actresses at such times.

In full-body tattoo, Nakadai looked the epitome of cool machismo in *The Wolves* and delivered a restrained performance, only letting himself off the leash during the intense fight scenes. In one of these, he cuts deep into his enemy's face, although the actor's head is replaced by a very unconvincing fake for this shot. Nakadai's finest acting moment comes when he finally realises how foolishly naïve he has been to believe in the *yakuza* code of honour, and at this point we see the tough but sensitive Iwahashi cry bitter tears of regret.

The film is slowly-paced and, at 131 minutes, considerably longer than most *yakuza* films, despite having little new to offer in terms of story other than an especially complex plot. However, what separates it from the usual formulaic genre entry is its iconoclastic presentation of notions of honour and chivalry as a mere sham – not unlike Kobayashi's critique of the samurai code in *Hara-Kiri* and *Samurai Rebellion*, although Gosha does not emphasize this theme to the extent that Kobayashi did. Unfortunately, it was perhaps this bleaker view of the *yakuza* world which made *The Wolves* a box office failure on release as the usual fans of the genre stayed away.

The Wolves looks stunning throughout due to Gosha's usual careful attention to visual design, cinematography, sets and costumes. The climactic scene of slaughter during a festival parade is particularly memorable as Gosha fills the screen in a riot of colour. Returning to the Shimokita Peninsula at the tip of northern Honshu, where *Goyokin* had been shot, Gosha once again came up with a number of striking locations. On this occasion, his great find was a windswept beach on which an abandoned ship is stranded. Other memorable additions included a terrific bar brawl featuring Kunie Tanaka, a lengthy murder scene reminiscent of the one in Hitchcock's *Torn Curtain*, and the two silent female assassins who dispatch their victims with knives concealed in the handles of their umbrellas. Aspects such as these have made *The*

Wolves a firm fan favourite over the years despite its initial lack of acceptance in Japan.

Nakadai and Gosha on the set of *The Wolves* in a rare photo featuring Nakadai's autograph in both Japanese and English.
(Courtesy of Robin Gatto)

Once the 1970s were underway, television began to seem a far more attractive prospect to actors than it had previously. While cinema attendance was declining, TV audiences were increasing, which meant that programme budgets and actors' salaries were too. Advances in technology also meant that the nerve-wracking days of live drama broadcasts were over. Although Nakadai had worked in television, up to this point he had mainly appeared in one-off dramas for a niche audience. His mother had even complained that her friends did not consider him famous as they had never seen him on TV. When Nakadai was offered the lead role in NHK's *New Tale of the Heike* (Shin Heike monogatari), this was one of the reasons he accepted even though it was a huge commitment – it was to be the channel's Taiga drama for 1972, meaning that a new episode would be broadcast weekly for a year. NHK had been producing a new Taiga drama series annually for the past decade, and Nakadai later said that he had been turning them down every year up to that point. Screened on Sunday nights at 8 p.m. in 45-minute episodes, Taiga dramas were often watched by the whole family and had become a national institution in the process – so much so, in fact, that they are still being produced at the time of writing, despite a waning audience.

The original *Tale of the Heike* dates from around the 13th-century and is an epic prose work of unknown, probably multiple, authorship concerning the battle between the Heike (or Taira clan) and their rivals for control of Japan in the late 12th-century. In 1950, Eiji Yoshikawa (the writer upon whose Musashi Miyamoto novels the famous trilogy starring Toshiro Mifune were based) began publishing a weekly serialisation of his new version, now called *New Tale of the Heike*. Using the same title, Kenji Mizoguchi filmed part of this in 1955 with Raizo Ichikawa in the lead,[74] while the length of the 1972 Taiga production made it possible for screenwriter Yumie Hiraiwa (author of Nakadai's earlier *Journey*) to cover the entire plot of the novel.

As Kiyomori Taira (1118-1181), the ambitious samurai who works his way up to become one of the most powerful men in Japan, Nakadai had to age by around 40 years during the course of the drama, and shaved his head for real – the first time he had ever done so for a part. He decided to turn the event into a ceremony with the press in attendance in order to provide some PR for the series. *New Tale of the Heike* was NHK's most lavish Taiga drama to date and benefitted from a big budget, elaborate sets and star actors – other notable cast members included Michiyo Aratama, Ken Ogata, Eitaro Ozawa, Daisuke Kato, Masayuki Mori, and Ayako Wakao. A large audience was guaranteed, and Nakadai's mother must surely have been a very happy woman.

---

[74] Mizoguchi's film had two sequels made by different directors.

Nakadai's fourth and final film for Hiromichi Horikawa was *Osho* ('King'), based on a popular 1947 play of the same name by Hideji Hojo which had been filmed twice before by the same director, Daisuke Ito, once in 1948 and again in 1962. *Osho* was a different kind of film from the three dark crime dramas Nakadai had made with Horikawa previously. The play had been based on a true story, and Horikawa's version featured Shintaro Katsu as Sankichi Sakata (1870-1946), a sandal-maker obsessed with *shogi* (a Japanese game similar to chess). Perhaps Katsu was cast in this unlikely role as Sakata suffered from an eye disease and the actor had made an unusual speciality out of playing visually-challenged characters in *The Blind Menace* (Shiranui kengyo) and countless Zatoichi films.

Set in Osaka, the story covers a period of years from 1907-1919. Sakata's obsession leads him to neglect his work, fall into debt, and drive his wife to despair. When she finally gives up trying to stop him from playing *shogi*, he becomes determined to gain the title of Grandmaster. The man he must beat is Kinjiro Sekine (1868-1946), an urbane Tokyoite he will attempt to defeat on three occasions over a number of years.

Nakadai played Sekine, while Sakata's wife was played by Katsu's own wife, Tamao Nakamura (also the daughter of actor Ganjiro Nakamura from *Conflagration* and *The Key*).

Osho is another film that was inaccessible at the time of writing. However, the 1962 version was accessible, albeit without subtitles, and proved to be a very well-made film with wonderfully fluid camerawork. Unfortunately, it is also ruined by the performance of its lead actor, Rentaro Mikuni, who goes full *daikon*,[75] affecting a bizarre manner of speech, and making of Sakata a thoroughly irritating and unlikeable character. Having said that, it should be noted that Mikuni is excellent in other films, and many must have felt differently as he played Sakata again in a sequel the following year. Still, it seems likely that Katsu made Sakata far more sympathetic.

---

[75] The Japanese word for 'radish' – the Japanese equivalent of 'ham' in relation to acting.

In the 1962 version, Sekine has very little to do, so the role of the opponent was probably beefed up a bit for Nakadai, who no doubt played him in phlegmatic fashion as the polar opposite of Katsu's unkempt and emotional Sakata, the yin to Katsu's yang.

Chapter 19 — Back to School

'I've been an actor for a long time, but I never thought I'd play a penis!' According to director Eiichi Yamamoto, this was Nakadai's reaction when he saw the character he was to voice for the animated film *Belladonna of Sadness* (Kanashimi no beradonna). This extraordinary film sprung from an unlikely source: a story from *La Sorcière*, a book on witchcraft by the French historian Jules Michelet published in 1862. Yamamoto had previously made two other full-length animated films for adults based on more familiar foreign tales, *1001 Nights* and *Cleopatra*.

Set in mediaeval France, *Belladonna of Sadness* tells the story of Jeanne, a beautiful young woman raped by the local lord on her wedding night after her husband, Jean, has been unable to pay the required wedding tax. Jeanne makes a pact with the Devil (Nakadai) in order to gain her revenge. The Devil is first seen as a small penis-like entity. Nakadai pitched his voice high during these scenes, but lowered it as the story progresses and the Devil grows and metamorphoses into a variety of different forms. Jeanne was voiced by Aiko Nagayama, who had appeared in *Kwaidan*, although not with Nakadai.

Not only was the choice of source material unusual, but no attempt was made to transpose the setting of the story to Japan. The style of the film was equally bold, and the animation differed greatly from the familiar anime type, using watercolours and a combination of still and animated images against minimal, often blank white backdrops. Some of the images were sexually explicit enough that even the film's director referred to them as porn, although it is difficult to imagine anyone getting their rocks off by watching *Belladonna of Sadness*. A psychedelic rock soundtrack was used throughout and there is one extremely trippy montage sequence, which may give the impression that the film was some kind of drug-induced '70s folly. However, this would be a mistake as the quality of the work by all involved is of an exceptional standard, which is no doubt why Nakadai chose to participate. *Belladonna of Sadness* is a mad masterpiece which has no real right to exist but has endured and become a deserved cult classic.

Nakadai's next film, *The Human Revolution* (Ningen kakumei), and its 1976 sequel were based on part of a 12-volume series of books of the same title by Daisaku Ikeda, leader of the Soka Gakkai, a religious movement inspired by the teachings of Nichiren, a Buddhist priest who lived in Japan during the 13th-century. The books had been bestsellers in Japan, where the movement had expanded dramatically after the Second World War from a handful of followers to millions. This was a result of the efforts of Josei Toda, the second president of Soka Gakkai, whose struggles are the focus of the books. Despite the difficulties involved in making feature films with a religious theme, the popularity of the books was such that a well-made film was bound to be a success in Japan at least.

Tetsuro Tanba, known for playing tough guys, was an unlikely choice for the lead role of Toda, for which he had to grow an unbecoming moustache and wear absurd-looking tortoiseshell glasses of the type favoured by Toda. However, he acquitted himself well under the circumstances. Nakadai contributed cameos as Nichiren in both films. In the first, he appears for a few minutes in a sequence visualizing a story about Nichiren which Toda relates to his followers. As the completely bald priest, Nakadai is seen calmly praying while about to be executed by decapitation. His prayer appears to summon a fierce wind which causes his would-be executioners to flee in terror. In this sequence, the words spoken by Nichiren are voiced not by Nakadai, but by Tanba during the narration of the story. The part is a very small one for Nakadai, but it is easy to see why Masuda felt he needed a charismatic star for the role.

In the second film, Nakadai is again seen for only a few minutes when Nichiren appears to Toda in a vision. Toda has been having doubts about his ability to facilitate the growth of Soka Gakkai, and Nichiren sternly berates him for his lack of faith. Nakadai is a suitably commanding presence in this sequence, this time using his deep voice to full effect. The two films were written by Shinobu Hashimoto and directed by Toshio Masuda, who had made *Challenge at Dawn*.

Next up for Nakadai was the film *Rise, Fair Sun* (Asayake no shi/'Poetry at Sunrise'), a co-production between Haiyuza and Toho. Director Kei Kumai (Nakadai's senior by two years) had been sitting on the project for some time, having originally planned to film it with actress Sayuri Yoshinaga eight years previously. However, there had been doubts about whether Yoshinaga was really suited to the part, so it was delayed until 1973, when Kumai decided to make it with the 18-year-old Keiko Takahashi and Nakadai as her father. After making her debut in 1970 in a leading role at the age of 15, Takahashi had already starred in seven films at this point and become something of an idol. For her first scene in *Rise, Fair Sun*, she had to swim nude in a lake; when this became known, around 150 people turned up at the location attempting to get photos of the naked Takahashi, resulting in a minor scandal which generated more publicity than anything else about the film.

Set in an unspoilt village in the Japanese Alps in Nagano Prefecture, the film concerns Sakuzo (Nakadai), a struggling farmer who works hard in an attempt to run the village as a self-sufficient collective through sustainable farming practices. His wife has left him because of the hardship of their lives, and his daughter Haruko (Takahashi) now looks after his two younger sons. When the representative of a tourism company arrives, a local big shot, Inashiro (Shin Saburi), colludes with him in a development deal which will make them wealthy while selling the villagers down the river. Inashiro persuades many of the poverty-stricken farmers to sell their land to him, but as they are all in his debt anyway, they receive little compensation. Others refuse to comply and the village splits into two factions. Sakuzo becomes the leader of the anti-development faction, and begins to make life difficult for the developers.

Director Kei Kumai was from Nagano originally, and *Rise, Fair Sun* appears to have been a project close to his heart. However, he apparently considered the film a failure, although the reasons for this are unclear and his opinion not necessarily shared. In any case, the film was ahead of its time in its concern with environmental issues, and it was thought of a high enough standard to be entered into competition at the Berlin Film Festival. *Rise, Fair Sun* was also notable for bringing the distinguished actor Shin Saburi back to the big screen after 12 years in television.

Kumai, who died in 2007 at the age of 77, was a highly-regarded left-wing director who began his career at Nikkatsu but went freelance in 1969. Initially known for films of social criticism, he later showed an affinity for the work of Japanese Catholic novelist Shusaku Endo, adapting three of his books for the cinema. He made some of Japan's most intensely self-critical films, including a version of Endo's *The Sea and Poison* (Umi to dokuyaku, 1986), about Japanese doctors experimenting on captured American airmen during the Second World War. He depicted an equally uncomfortable part of Japan's history in *Sandakan 8* (Sandakan hachiban shokan bokyo, 1974), which deals with the plight of girls from poor families in the early 20th-century who were deceived into going abroad to work only to find themselves forced into prostitution. Nakadai would go on to play a further leading role for Kumai some eight years later.

Nakadai was receiving few film offers that interested him during this period. He had become somewhat disillusioned with acting and spent much of his time playing golf. However, he was helped out of this rut by an offer from Kobo Abe to join his newly-formed Kobo Abe Studio and appear in two plays he had written which he would also direct. This involved not simply learning his parts, but attending unconventional rehearsal sessions in which Abe encouraged his actors to improvise and venture out of their comfort zones, so it was almost like going back to school. However, there was no escaping the fact that Nakadai was famous, and when performances began, it was clear that part of the audience were there to see him rather than the play.

Nakadai first appeared as the 'Red Doctor' in *Love's Glasses are Coloured* (Ai no megane wa iro garasu), a fast-paced comedy. Set in a mental hospital where it is never exactly clear which characters are members of staff and which are patients, it also featured fellow Haiyuza actors Kunie Tanaka and Hisashi Igawa as the 'White Doctor' and 'Man' respectively. Tanaka and Igawa had already enjoyed a lengthy association with Abe, both having appeared not only in *The Face of Another*, but in Hiroshi Teshigahara's striking debut feature, *Pitfall*, also scripted by Abe. Indeed, Igawa's rare leading part in a dual role in *Pitfall* was perhaps the high point of his career, although he also played three roles in the original 1969 stage production of Abe's *The Man Who Turned into a Stick* (Bo ni natta otoko).

The Red Doctor wears a red lab coat and glasses with red lenses, encouraging everyone to wear similar red-tinted spectacles and play table tennis if they wish to speed up their return to society. However, according to a nurse, he is a patient who was hospitalized for sexual impropriety. The White Doctor wears a more traditional white coat and is keen on tranquilizers and women, but is said by the Red Doctor to be a patient who was found guilty of indecent exposure. The unnamed 'Man' believes a rubber doll to be his wife. The play opened at the new 458-seat Seibu Theatre in Shibuya, Tokyo, on 4 June 1973 and featured music courtesy of Toru Takemitsu.

The following year, Nakadai appeared in Abe's *Friends* (Tomodachi), a black comedy again co-starring Hisashi Igawa. It was a revised version of Abe's Akutagawa Award-winning 1967 play which was itself based on the author's 1951 short story *Intruders* (Chinnyusha). Nakadai had in fact appeared in minor role in a radio version of the original story produced by Abe in association with Haiyuza back in 1955. On this occasion, Nakadai played the leading role of a man living alone in an apartment which is invaded by a strange family headed by Igawa. It opened on 17 May 1974 at the Seibu Theatre, where it ran for several weeks before transferring to Osaka's Mainichi Hall for two nights.

Nakadai was next reunited with his *Rise, Fair Sun* co-star Shin Saburi as well as director Satsuo Yamamoto for *A Splendid Family* (Karei-naru ichizoku), based on the novel of the same name by Toyoko Yamazaki, who had also written the book upon which Yamamoto's

1966 hospital drama *The Great White Tower* had been based. Like the earlier film, *A Splendid Family* was a study of corruption within an institution, in this case in the world of banking.

The large ensemble cast was headed by Saburi as Daisuke Manpyo, president of the Hanshin bank and head of the Manpyo family, a cold man who treats his wife, Neko (*Firebird*'s Yumeji Tsukioka), like a doormat and has made his children's live-in tutor, Aiko (Machiko Kyo) into his mistress. At one point, Aiko goes to Daisuke's bedroom, expecting him to be alone, but discovers him in bed with his wife; Daisuke forces his wife to remain while he makes love to Aiko in the same bed. He dislikes his cheerful eldest son, Teppei (Nakadai), as he believes that he is actually the son of his own father, Keisuke (also played, in flashback, by Nakadai), whom he closely resembles. For this reason, he does the bare minimum to help when Teppei needs a loan to build a new blast furnace in his steel company, so Teppei is forced to look elsewhere for part of the financing. Later, when he accidentally shoots his father in the head on a family hunting trip, the bullet only grazes Daisuke, but the incident sours their relationship further. Without his father's assistance, Teppei is forced to compromise on the quality of the blast furnace, which explodes, killing several of his workers. Although Teppei himself had acted in good faith, subsequent investigations also reveal irregularities in the financing of the blast furnace which will bankrupt the steel company. The once ebullient Teppei becomes increasingly depressed and eventually walks off into the mountains, where he commits suicide with his hunting rifle. After his death, Daisuke is appalled to discover that Teppei had been his biological son after all, while the rest of his family turn against him. However, the final scene shows Daisuke, having successfully completed some dodgy dealing, celebrating a bank merger that will consolidate his power. As the film ends we hear once more the rifle shot with which Teppei took his own life, reinforcing Yamamoto's message that power is built upon the misery of others. Shin Saburi is convincingly understated as the ruthless patriarch whose cruelty proves so toxic that it destroys any chance of happiness for the rest of his family, while Nakadai gives a moving performance as the kind-hearted son driven to despair and Machiko Kyo is also memorable as the scheming mistress.

Nakadai found Saburi to be rather an eccentric figure who, after a family dinner scene had been shot, ate all of the leftover food before going home. He also told Nakadai that he spent all of his money on stones, with which he filled his garden, and that these would be the only thing anyone would inherit from him.

Since Nakadai and Yamamoto had last worked together on *Tengu-to*, the director had spent the intervening years making an epic Second World War trilogy entitled *Men and War* (Senso to nigen) for Nikkatsu. Based on a novel by *Human Condition* author Jumpei Gomikawa, it was well-received but has been little seen abroad and is not held in such high esteem as Masaki Kobayashi's masterpiece. *A Splendid Family* marked Yamamoto's first film for Toho since 1947, when the studio had fired him for being a communist, and it is the only film apart from *Kagemusha* in which Nakadai plays two roles, although one of these is very brief. Yamamoto was no great visual stylist, and the film is undistinguished in this department, dominated by tones of beige and shot in the old 1:33 aspect ratio. Widescreen formats had become a lot less common in Japan after the studios began struggling in the late '60s, and the re-emergence of this older format was partly a way of saving money, but perhaps also a way of making films more TV-friendly for future sale to the new medium. Indeed, *A Splendid Family* often resembles a TV drama more than a movie and, consisting of two parts totalling 211 minutes, is perhaps better suited to home-viewing. Nevertheless, the book had been a bestseller and the cast was star-studded, and these factors combined to make the film a huge success in Japan.

Aside from Nakadai, a number of other Haiyuza actors were featured, including Eitaro Ozawa and Yoshio Inaba, while Kyoko Kagawa, Takashi Shimura, Ko Nishimura and Shigeru Koyama also appeared. *A Splendid Family* earned 420 million yen at the box office and ranked third in Kinema Jumpo's end-of-year Best Ten list (after

Kei Kumai's *Sandakan 8* and Yoshitaro Nomura's *Castle of Sand*). Toho even remade it as a TV series only a few months later in association with Mainichi Broadcasting with Yuzo Kayama in Nakadai's role of Teppei, while further television adaptations appeared in 2007 and 2021. Nakadai would soon appear in two similar films for Yamamoto which together form a loose trilogy on the theme of corruption.

The same year, 1974, Nakadai appeared on stage as Richard III in a Haiyuza production at the Toyoko Theatre directed by Toshikiyo Masumi, who had joined the company in 1951, initially serving as an assistant director to Koreya Senda. Komaki Kurihara played Lady Anne and the play ran for 119 performances.

Chapter 20 – Of Cats and Corruption

Nakadai's next film was another long one, running over three hours. *The Gate of Youth* (Seishun no mon), based on a best-selling series of novels by Hiroyuki Itsuki, was a coming-of-age story about a boy from a coal-mining family and the challenges he has to face in the tough environment of the mines. Nakadai played the boy's father, who dies while attempting to rescue some trapped miners. *The Gate of Youth* was directed by the not-very-prolific Kirio Urayama, who had made three previous features and been Shohei Imamura's assistant. Shot on location in the coal-mining region of Fukuoka, the film was a big-budget production which became a box office success and spawned a sequel. The story was also remade as another two films in 1981/82, a mini-series in 1991, and a further one in 2005.

Nakadai next contributed a cameo to Kihachi Okamoto's *Battle Cry* (Tokkan), an alleged 'action-comedy' set around the time of the Meiji Restoration. Senta (Toshitaka Ito) is a sexually-frustrated young peasant who leaves home in search of adventure and gets mixed up in the Boshin War,[76] joining forces along the way with Manjiro, a thief (Yusuke Okada). Nakadai appeared in a single five-minute scene near the beginning as Toshizo Hijikata (1835-1869), a senior member of the Shinsengumi (the band of masterless samurai formed to support the shogunate). Senta encounters him when Toshizo is resting in an inn after injuring his foot in battle. His conversation with another resting samurai (overheard by Senta) seems mainly intended to fill in some of the historical background to the story. There is not much to the part, but even after the few minutes of the film which precede this scene, it feels refreshing to see some decent acting after the relentless mugging of Ito.

---

[76] A civil war which broke out in Japan in 1868 between supporters of the shogun and supporters of the Imperial Court.

Okamoto was still making films for Toho at this time, but they declined the opportunity to finance *Battle Cry*, perhaps due to the poor script. For this reason, he was forced to make the film on a low-budget as a co-production between his own company and the Art Theatre Guild, which had helped finance many independent features by Japanese 'new wave' directors. He was also helped by Toshiro Mifune, who let him use a set created for Mifune Productions free of charge. Despite such generous assistance, the low-budget is all too obvious – the cinematography is lacklustre and Nakadai, obviously appearing as a favour to Okamoto, is the only well-known actor in the film. Sadly, the quality of this once-great director's films declined dramatically after the '60s, and *Battle Cry*, a tiresome film best forgotten, only serves to provide unwelcome evidence of this.

Although there can be few books as unsuited to film adaptation as Soseki Natsume's episodic comic novel *I Am a Cat* (Wagahai wa neko de aru; originally published 1905-06 in serial form), the enduring popularity of the work in Japan led Kajiro Yamamoto (Kurosawa's mentor) to tackle it in 1936 and Kon Ichikawa to take it on in 1975. Although Natsume's original is narrated by a cat, the main character is really the cat's owner, an English teacher named Kushami (the cat itself being more a device than a protagonist). As screenwriter, Ichikawa assigned Toshio Yasumi, a specialist in literary adaptations who had been Shiro Toyoda's regular collaborator. Yasumi abandoned the feline narration but retained both the period setting and the cat, which made frequent sporadic appearances throughout.

Nakadai played Kushami, a dilettante forever flitting from one artistic pastime to another. He frequently plays host to his friends Meitei (played by future film director Juzo Itami) and Kangetsu (Nobuto Okamoto), a student, and the three indulge in pretentious conversations in which the more sophisticated they try to appear, the more their naivety is revealed. Meanwhile, most of the women are no better – Kangetsu has begun a tentative courtship with Tomiko (Hiroko Shino), whose beauty is balanced out by her appalling table manners, but must deal with her mother (Mariko Okada, previously seen as Oiwa in *Illusion of Blood*), a snob who gossips maliciously about her neighbours. Also featured in the cast are Shigeru Koyama in a rare comic turn and Yukari Uehara, who plays Kushami's maid and previously appeared as the young girl unintentionally adopted by Nakadai's character in *Cash Calls Hell*.

In order to avoid ending up with a film consisting entirely of scenes of people talking in a room while being watched by a cat, Ichikawa bends over backwards to vary the settings in flashback and fantasy sequences. He also uses subjective camera at some points to achieve a cat's-eye point of view and, to keep things lively, even stages a battle between a rival cat and an obviously fake weasel. Despite the inherent difficulty in the material, Ichikawa's manic inventiveness is almost enough to pull it off, but not entirely – at nearly two hours, the film is overlong, and the sequence in which Kashumi is tormented by schoolboys deliberately hitting balls into his garden becomes disconcertingly violent but never funny. However, *I Am a Cat* is on the whole one of Ichikawa's better later films, and the cast are uniformly excellent, with Nakadai as the self-pitying but somehow likeable creator of his own problems giving a more subtle and successful comic performance than he had managed in *Age of Assassins*.

The second film in Satsuo Yamamoto's mid-'70s trilogy of corruption, *Kinkanshoku*, featured a top-billed Nakadai as part of a large ensemble cast that included former co-stars such as Rentaro Mikuni, Ko Nishimura, Shigeru Koyama and Machiko Kyo (although he had no scenes with Kyo on this occasion). The title resists easy translation, though the film is referred to as *Annular Eclipse* in the English edition of Yamamoto's autobiography, and a shot of a full solar eclipse is seen over the beginning and end credits. However, an alternative translation, 'Golden Ring Erosion' seems more accurate, but to better convey the meaning in English, we could adjust it to 'Golden Ring, Hollow Centre,' as the title is a metaphor describing something that looks good on the outside but is rotten in the middle. In this case, Yamamoto turns his jaundiced eye on corruption in the world of politics and the collusion between politicians and big business. Yamamoto excelled at this kind of film – his 1966 movie *The Great White Tower*, for example, shows the ruthless jockeying for position among the senior staff of a major hospital, and makes for a riveting two and a half hours.

With a screenplay by Kei Tasaka, who had co-written *Goyokin* and *The Wolves* with Hideo Gosha, *Kinkanshoku* was based on a 1966 novel by Tatsuzo Ishikawa that was itself based on a real-life scandal of 1964 in which a company was suspected of having won a government contract to construct the Kuzuryu Dam through bribery. In his autobiography, Yamamoto said that he could not help thinking of the people described in the novel as villains as 'characters in a comedy,' and the film certainly presents them as caricatures if not actual grotesques. One of the main roles was played by Jukichi Uno, a favourite of director Kaneto Shindo and the founder of the Mingei Theatre Company in Kawasaki. It would be the only occasion on which he acted opposite Nakadai. Sporting a set of fake dentures which made it look as if he had crooked, stained teeth barely hanging onto his gums, Uno played Ishihara, a shady financier who discovers the bribery and attempts to blackmail Hoshino, the Chief Cabinet Secretary, who outfoxes him. Nakadai plays the latter as an unflappable, immaculately-dressed smoothie over whom nobody gains the upper hand. Hoshino was based on Yasumi Kurogane (1910-86), and Nakadai copied Kurogane's appearance down to the last detail despite the fact that Kurogane was never actually found guilty of any wrongdoing. Nakadai later said that it was one of the roles he most enjoyed playing. Hoshino is introduced 25 minutes into the film via a shot of his shoes – snazzy two-tone Italian brogues – and is later seen with other luxury accoutrements: shiny cufflinks, a gold cigarette case, a glass of cognac. Unruffled by Ishihara's blackmail attempt, he laughs in his face and tells him to go ahead, making Ishihara briefly lose his composure. This is a marvellous scene between two greats of the Japanese acting world, and there are further pleasures to be had in seeing Nakadai trade lines with Rentaro Mikuni's blustering House of Representatives member – whose attempt to expose the corruption is rank hypocrisy as he is thoroughly corrupt himself – and Ko Nishimura's sly company head, quick to adopt whatever face he feels will best serve him at the time.

Yamamoto makes a highly entertaining film out of what could easily have seemed like two and a half hours of talk, partly by casting excellent actors, but also by dynamic camera movement and editing. In addition, he frequently adds unexpected comic touches, cutting away during a serious conversation to a shot of Ishihara's wife blubbing over a soap opera on the TV, for example, or having the newspaper editor discover his staff messing around every time he enters the office. An excellent score by Masaru Sato also helps in heightening the moments of drama and tension.

Yamamoto accentuated the venality of the characters, who are almost always eating, drinking, smoking, playing golf or cavorting with women – in other words, indulging their appetites and avoiding anything resembling actual work. Another interesting point of note is the way Yamamoto transposes the metaphor of the film's title into the set design – the construction company's boardroom has a round meeting table with a hollow centre, while Mikuni's table in a restaurant is in a sort of sunken circular booth. Like *A Splendid Family*, *Kinkanshoku* was another critical and commercial success for the director, in this case ranking third in *Kinema Junpo*'s ten best films of the year and winning a Golden Arrow Award.

With the idea of building a house for Yasuko and himself, Nakadai bought some land in early 1975 in Okamoto, located in Setagaya Ward in the west of Tokyo, close to Yoga, the neighbourhood in which he had lived for a while as a child. He soon began to invite actors over to rehearse in the field from time to time, while Yasuko offered some direction. From this spontaneous beginning, the idea of forming their own acting school began. The couple named it Mumeijuku, meaning 'Anonymous School.' Remembering how he had struggled to pay the fees at Haiyuza as a young student, Nakadai decided not to charge any tuition fees. In order to make it manageable, they would take on a maximum of five students per year.

Most of their students would join during their late teens or early twenties but, perhaps mindful of how his stint at the Kobo Abe Studio had reinvigorated his own acting, Nakadai also wanted the school to be open to established actors. One of the first students was Shinji Ogawa, then 34, who had previously studied at Haiyuza and already gained a considerable amount of experience acting for television. Nakadai would help Ogawa to get a start in films by finding him roles in two of his own, *Blue Christmas* and *The Empty Table* – something he would do for many of his students, as we shall see. However, it was in the area of voiceover work that Ogawa would eventually find his niche. He went on to dub such major Hollywood stars as Michael Douglas and Dustin Hoffman, becoming their regular voice double in the Japanese-dubbed versions of their films. He passed away in 2015 aged 74 shortly after performing alongside Nakadai one last time in the film *Before the Leaves Fall*.

Ogawa had been one of five students who joined Mumeijuku in its first year, 1975, before the school welcomed applications from the public two years later. The following year, Nakadai travelled to New York to visit The Actors' Studio, the famous non-profit school founded in 1947 by Elia Kazan and others. Nakadai spent time with the school's artistic director, Lee Strasberg, who had taught 'the Method' to future stars such as James Dean, Marilyn Monroe and Robert De Niro.

Nakadai appeared on stage in two plays for Haiyuza in 1975. The first of these was a version of the Russian writer Maxim Gorky's groundbreaking work of social realism from 1902, *The Lower Depths*, which had been filmed by Kurosawa in 1957. As the play is an ensemble piece about a group of down-and-out characters sharing a seedy boarding house, Nakadai could not be said to have had the lead role – he played Satin, the gambler, who delivers the memorable final line, 'Idiot… You ruined the song,' which brings down the curtain. The production was directed by Toshikiyo Masumi and also featured Seiya Nakano (who had been Iago to Nakadai's Othello) as Vaska Pepel, the thief.

Nakadia's second play of the year was a revival of Strindberg's *Miss Julie*, in which he once again played Jean, as he had back in 1958, while the title role was played by Komaki Kurihara. The translation was by Koreya Senda and the production was notable as the first to be directed by Yasuko (under the name Tomoe Ryu and in collaboration with Yukio Sekiya).

Nakadai then appeared in a pioneering work for television which blended documentary with fictional drama. A feature-length 'Thursday Special' for Nippon TV, the unwieldy title translates as something like *Secret Pacific War Story, 'Emergency Coded Message: Peace to the Mother Country' - with Love from Europe*. Nakadai played the leading role of a naval officer working for peace towards the end of the Second World War, while his *I Am a Cat* co-star Juzo Itami appeared as a reporter. Shot using a new, more manoeuvrable type of video camera and including scenes filmed on location abroad, nothing quite like it had been seen on Japanese TV before its broadcast on Dec 18th 1975 and it won the Japanese Galaxy Award Grand Prize for Best Programme.

Nakadai's next film, *Banka* ('Elegy'), was a romantic drama set in the city of Kushiro, Hokkaido, which he had visited on two previous occasions – parts of *The Human Condition* and most of *Journey* had been shot thereabouts. The story concerns an emotionally immature drama student with a partially paralysed left arm, Reiko, who meets a married architect, Setsuo Katsuragi (Nakadai), with whom she has an affair. Meanwhile, Katsuragi's wife, Akiko, is having an affair of her own with a medical student, but has no desire to get divorced as they have a daughter and she wants the security which her marriage provides. This delicate state of affairs comes under threat when the unconventional Reiko also finds herself attracted to Akiko and strikes up a friendship with her unbeknownst to Katsuragi, who is away on a business trip. Needless to say, upon his return, things do not end happily.

Banka was based on a novel of the same name by Yasuko Harada which had been filmed once before by Heinosuke Gosho in 1957, with Yoshiko Kuga as Reiko and Masayuki Mori as Katsuragi. The main point of interest in Gosho's film is that Reiko is a milder prototype of a character which became common in Hollywood films 30 years later – the obsessed stalker who wrecks a family. However, her behaviour is not seen in those terms by the other characters in the film, which is a rather laboured Douglas Sirk-type melodrama.

The remake was the second film to be directed by Yoshisuke Kawasaki, known to Nakadai from working as chief assistant director on *Osho*. Screened in America at some point under the none-too-subtle title *Little Serpent*, it seems to have been mainly intended as a vehicle for its young star, Kumiko Akiyoshi, who played Reiko. Although out of circulation for many years, this may be no great loss as it appears to be a relatively minor piece of work.

Nakadai followed *Banka* by reuniting with director Satsuo Yamamoto for another long corruption-themed drama based on real events. Like *A Splendid Family*, *The Barren Zone* (Fumo chitai) had a screenplay by Nobuo Yamada from a novel by Toyoko Yamasaki. Nakadai was cast in the lead as Tadashi Iki, a former lieutenant-colonel in the Japanese army and member of the Imperial Headquarters staff during the Second World War who is recruited by a powerful trading company in the late 1950s. He has spent the intervening eleven years in various prison camps in Siberia and is new to the world of business. His boss, Daimon (Isao Yamagata), wishes to expand the company by purchasing American war planes to supply to the government for Japan's 1959 Second Defense Strategy Plan. To this purpose, he exploits Iki's naivety and manipulates him into using his close friendship with a senior Defense Agency officer (Tetsuro Tanba) in order to give his company an advantage.

The story was based on the life of Ryuzo Sejima (1911-2007), whom Nakadai met a number of times in preparation for his role. The Siberian section takes up most of the first 230 pages of the 380-page English translation of the novel,[77] but is dealt with in a mere 15-minute flashback sequence in Yamamoto's three-hour film. Although the director was not an especially didactic filmmaker despite being a

---

[77] The English translation appears to be an abridged version of the original.

lifelong member of the Communist Party, his work is certainly informed by his political beliefs, and he goes far easier on the Russians than Yamasaki did in her novel – where the book depicts the Siberian prison guards as almost uniformly brutal, Yamamoto shows them offering to share their cigarettes and vodka with Iki while cheerily singing a song as they cart him off to a prison camp in the frozen wastes. Meanwhile, the corruption involved in the buying of American military jets which accounts for only a few pages in the novel becomes the main focus of the film. Unsurprisingly, Yamasaki and Yamamoto fell out as a result of the changes and never collaborated again.

It has to be said that his portrayal of Tadashi Iki is not one of Nakadai's strongest lead performances, perhaps because he had the difficult task of playing a protagonist who remains passive for the majority of the film; after following the orders of his superiors in the army, he is then pushed around by the Russians while, as a civilian, his strings are pulled by his boss, and he rarely initiates an action himself. In one scene added by Yamamoto in an effort to give voice to the anti-war sentiments of the younger generation, sympathy for Iki disappears the instant he slaps his gentle teenage daughter for criticising his involvement in the rearmament of Japan. Of course, Nakadai cannot be blamed for this scene, but it adds another factor which works against him. He also looks distinctly uncomfortable delivering his lines in English in one scene with an American actor.

Other members of the cast come off better, including the aforementioned Isao Yamagata and Tetsuro Tanba, along with Haiyuza veterans Eitaro Ozawa and Hisashi Igawa as, respectively, Tanba's nasty boss and a determined reporter. Hideji Otaki also gives a quietly impressive performance as the phlegmatic secretary of the Economic Planning Agency. The less rewarding women's roles of Iki's wife and daughter were played by Kaoru Yachigusa and Kumiko Akiyoshi (Nakadai's *Banka* co-star). Yachigusa is best known in the West for her part as the main love interest in Hiroshi Inagaki's *Samurai Trilogy* (1954-56) with Toshiro Mifune, which began filming when she was just 22. The third wife of director Senkichi Taniguchi, with whom Nakadai had worked on *Barefoot Youth* in 1956, she had also appeared alongside him in the 1965 TV version of *Brothers and Sisters of the Toda Family*, and would work frequently with him in later years, often playing the wife of his characters.

Although the film was another box office hit in Japan, *The Barren Zone* lacks the wry humour and energetic rhythm of *Kinkanshoku* and was the last of Nakadai's roles for Yamamoto. Offering little in the way of spectacle and being a long film with a complex story mainly delivered via scenes of men talking in rooms, it was not deemed suitable for release in the West. However, it won Mainichi Film Awards for Best Film, Best Director and Best Screenplay, while Hideji Otaki won several Best Supporting Actor awards for his roles in both *The Barren Zone* and Tadashi Imai's *Older Brother, Younger Sister* (Ani imoto). *The Barren Zone* has been remade twice for television – in 1979 with Mikijiro Hira as Iki, and again in 2009 with Toshiaki Karasawa in the role.

Nakadai next starred in *Castle of Sand* (Suna no utsuwa), a Fuji TV-Haiyuza co-production based on the best-selling 1961 novel of the same name by Seichi Matsumoto, a notable crime writer who introduced post-war social-consciousness to the genre. The book had previously been adapted for TV in 1962 and as a major feature film in 1974. Directed by Yoshitaro Nomura from a screenplay by Shinobu Hashimoto, the film version had been a considerable box office hit. Starring Tetsuro Tanba as the haiku-loving Inspector Imanishi struggling to solve a baffling murder, it wisely simplified the convoluted plot of the novel, but also changed the murderer's profession from avant-garde musician to composer of sentimental corn. As a result, the drawn-out climax of the film revealing his motive by portraying his childhood in flashback becomes horribly mawkish when intercut with a scene in which he performs a concert of his syrupy schmaltz.

Tanba gave a strong performance in the film, but Nakadai seems a better fit for the rather gentler character described by Matsumoto, especially as the dogged Imanishi could almost be an older version of

Detective Tokura from *High and Low*. This must have been recognized by Yasuko, who wrote the script for the TV version and also appeared in a small role as the wardrobe clerk of a theatre company. Comprising six episodes of 45 minutes each, her adaptation was likely more faithful to the book, but she did make one significant change – the killer's father suffers from Hansen's disease (leprosy) in the original, but is a victim of mental illness in her version. Supporting roles were found for Mumeijuku students Ai Kanzaki, Shinji Ogawa and Daisuke Ryu, while Haiyuza co-founder Eitaro Ozawa also appeared. The series was re-edited as a 2 hour 20 minute omnibus in 1985 and there have been several further versions since, including a 1991 TV series starring Nakadai's old friend Kunie Tanaka. In 1989, the original novel was published in English under the title *Inspector Imanishi Investigates*.

Nakadai next starred as Gonbei Yamamoto (1852-1933) in *The Sea Revives* (Umi wa yomigae eru), produced by TBS and broadcast in August 1977. Yamamoto had twice been Prime Minister of Japan, but the story (based on a novel) traced the progress of his earlier life from young Naval Academy student shortly after the Meiji Resoration to Minister of the Navy at the time of the Russo-Japanese War (1904-05). Costing 100 million yen and with a running time of three hours, both the scale of the production and its length were unprecedented for a Japanese television drama at the time. Audience figures were high, and the drama won two domestic TV awards.

Nakadai's next film saw him working under the direction of Kihachi Okamoto once more in a new version of *Sanshiro Sugata* for Toho. The original novel by Tsuneo Tomita had been the basis of Akira Kurosawa's first film as director in 1943 and was itself based on the life of Shiro Saigo (1866-1922), a disciple of judo who became a master in the 1880s. There had been at least three other versions of the story since Kurosawa's. In Okamoto's film, Nakadai played Sugata's teacher, Yano, a character based on Jigoro Kano (1860-1938), the founder of judo who had been played by Toshiro Mifune in a 1965 version. The title role in Okamoto's film was played by Tomokazu Miura, a young actor in vogue at the time, while the love interest was provided by Kumiko Akiyoshi from *Banka* and *The Barren Zone*. A strong supporting cast included Kyoko Kishida, Tetsuro Tanba, the obligatory appearances by Kunie Tanaka and Ichiro Nakatani, and cameos courtesy of Tomisaburo Wakayama and Okamoto himself. The screenplay was co-written by Okamoto and Yasuko, writing under her pen name of Tomoe Ryu. Unfortunately, while the film does seem to have been shown on Japanese television in recent years, screenings outside Japan have been rare and it is inaccessible at the time of writing.

Shortly after his appearance in *Sanshiro Sugata*, Nakadai took the lead in a TV film directed by Okamoto entitled *Mysterious Legend of Showa* (Showa kaitotsuto). Based on a novel by Koji Kata, it featured Nakadai as a Robin Hood-like serial burglar operating at the beginning of the Showa era (late 1920s). Nakadai gave an ebullient performance, adopting a series of disguises and cheerfully cocking a snook at the incompetent police trying to catch him, one of whom was played by fellow Okamoto regular Kunie Tanaka. The 71-minute comedy-drama was well-made and entertaining enough to win a domestic award for Best TV Drama.

The same year (1977), Nakadai visited Beijing as part of a delegation of filmmakers led by Keisuke Kinoshita and including Masaki Koboyashi. He also appeared on stage for Haiyuza as Marc Antony in *Julius Caesar* in a production directed by Toshikiyo Masumi and co-starring Go Kato as Brutus, while Yasuko co-wrote the screenplay for an animated fairy-tale film, *The Prince of the Swans* (Hakucho no oji).

Meanwhile, Nakadai and Yasuko had begun recruiting new students for their acting school, Mumeijuku, via open auditions and interviews. There were typically around 1,000 applicants per year, and the couple saw each one personally every February, a process which lasted around 10 days. One of the first to be accepted was a tall 20-year-old known at the time as Akio Zhang, for whom a small part was found in *Sanshiro Sugata*. While at the school, Zhang adopted the stage name Daisuke Ryu, combing elements of both Nakadai's name and

Yasuko's pen name, Tomoe Ryu. After a couple more small roles in Nakadai's films, the young actor's career got off to a remarkable start when he landed the important part of Nobunaga Oda in *Kagemusha*, a role in which he made a dramatic entrance jumping off his still-galloping horse and landing perfectly on his feet. Later in the film, he impresses when performing a song from the Noh theatre in response to the news of Shingen Takeda's death. Ryu's performance earned him a Blue Ribbon Award for Best New Actor of 1980.[78] Two years later, he won a 'new face' award for the Taiga drama *The Gunzo Pass* (Toge no Gunzo), while in 1985 he worked with Kurosawa again, playing one of the son's to Nakadai's King Lear figure in *Ran*. Unfortunately, by the 1990s, his career had become derailed due to his battles with alcohol and he was largely relegated to supporting roles. Nevertheless, he continued to work and, in 2015, he was cast in Martin Scorsese's *Silence* only to be replaced after he was arrested for assaulting an immigration official in Taiwan whilst intoxicated. The incident was widely publicized and resulted in Toei Management dropping him from their roster. It was three years before he worked on another film.

---

[78] Kurosawa held open auditions for many of the roles in *Kagemusha*, so it is unclear whether Nakadai's influence had anything to do with Ryu's casting.

Chapter 21 – Another Fine Mess or Two

The year after Nakadai's collaboration with Kon Ichikawa on *I Am a Cat*, the director had scored a box office smash in Japan with *The Inugami Family* (Inugami-ke no ichizoku), based on one of a series of best-selling novels by Seishi Yokomizo which had already formed the basis for a series of films in the 1950s. Ichikawa's film blended the comedy-horror of the Bob Hope classic *The Cat and the Canary* with an Agatha Christie-style mystery and a touch of Georges Franju (the French director best-known for *Eyes Without a Face*). The story involved a seemingly inexperienced detective arriving in a small rural community to investigate some unusual goings-on among the family of a pharmaceutical tycoon. Despite a convoluted and implausible plot, an excessively talky script consisting mainly of expositional dialogue, and an overlong running time of two and a half hours, the picture had proven inexplicably popular. Ichikawa went on to direct a further four films featuring the adventures of detective Kosuke Kindaichi (Koji Ishizaka) before finally giving it a rest after 1979's *The House of Hanging* (Byoinzaka no kubikukuri no ie).

Each of the five films is a stand-alone story, but Ichikawa repeated the recipe so precisely on each occasion that there is little to distinguish one from another. He had the same character actors doing almost exactly the same shtick from one film to the next, some of whom he allowed a little too much rope.

Nakadai appeared in *Queen Bee* (Joobachi), the fourth in the series, as one of the many murder suspects. His character does, at least, have some depth, as Ginzo Daidoji, a man with a murky past and divided loyalties, is wracked with guilt. Unfortunately, the script fails to explore this in any depth and, as in the previous entries, Ichikawa insists on peppering the movie with scenes of unfunny lowbrow slapstick. Parts of the film are also poorly edited and feature bad continuity. As for the seemingly random use of freeze frames, it remains anybody's guess what Ichikawa was trying to achieve by this.

Nakadai is first seen in a flashback sequence set in the 1930s. At this point, his character is a young student, and it has to be said that the make-up department's attempt to make him resemble a 20-year-old by means of extra hair is entirely unsuccessful. On a more positive note, he was reunited with Keiko Kishi, his co-star in *The Inheritance* and *Kwaidan*. Kishi was also guest-starring for this one film in the series, and the two even had a middle-aged love scene together. Other notable guest stars were Mieko Takamine, Yoko Tsukasa and Junzaburo Ban, making *Queen Bee* the starriest entry in the series. The presence of so many famous, in-demand actors meant that Ichikawa had to make the film on a tight schedule, so a second unit was assembled led by director Shue Matsubayashi, the former naval officer who had helmed two of Nakadai's early films.

Although Nakadai gives a good performance in *Queen Bee*, using his soulful eyes to considerable effect, the material remains stubbornly superficial and the execution is poor. However, these shortcomings failed to prevent the film from becoming another success at the box office.

In 2006, at the age of 90, Ichikawa produced a scene-for-scene remake of the first film in the series, released in the West as *Murder of the Inugami Clan*, even casting original actor Koji Ishizaka as the detective once more. Presumably for old times' sake, Nakadai appeared briefly at the beginning as the dying patriarch whose eccentric will initiates the mayhem to follow. The role itself was really a gag – in the original, it had been played by another big star, Rentaro Mikuni, and in both cases the character appears about to say something of great import, then suddenly drops dead without uttering a word. *Murder of the Inugami Clan* was Ichikawa's final film and he died two years later at the age of 92.

After a seven year gap, Nakadai next found himself working under the direction of Hideo Gosha once more. Gosha's film career had died after the financial failure of *The Wolves* and his next film, *Violent City* (Boryoku gai), forcing him to return to TV work as a result. However, he was saved from this ignominious fate by Masayuki Sato, who got him the job of directing *Kumokiri Nizaemon* (aka *Bandits vs. Samurai Squad*). Nizaemon – played by Nakadai – was a Robin Hood-like figure about whom little is really known, although he is said to have been active during the Kyoho period (1716-36). Gosha's film was based on a novel by Shotaro Ikenami serialized in the *Weekly Shincho* from 1972-74 and adapted by Kaneo Ikegami, best known for writing Eiichi Kudo's 1963 hit film *13 Assassins* (Jusan-nin no shikaku). As the project was a co-production between Shochiku and Haiyuza, a number of Haiyuza actors were featured among the large cast, together with stars including Shima Iwashita, Tetsuro Tanba and Mitsuko Baisho, while Nakadai also managed to wangle a small part for one of his Mumeijuku students, Daisuke Ryu.

The story takes place in Edo in 1722 and has Nakadai as the leader of a group of bandits, all of whom seem to revere him for reasons never fully explained. The name Kumokiri is a combination of the Japanese words for 'clouds' and 'mist', and Kumokiri does indeed disappear like mist after each crime he and his gang commits, continually eluding the special squad of samurai who pursue him. His mysterious quality is emphasized by the fact that he is first introduced when we hear Nakadai's unmistakable voice from behind a screen some 11 minutes in. By the time we actually see him around half an hour into the film, considerable interest in Kumokiri has been built up by the supporting characters talking about him. However, Gosha also grabs the audience's attention right off the bat by starting the film with an impressive action sequence which sees plenty of blood sprayed on the torn *shoji* (paper screens). Unfortunately, he fails to maintain this throughout the film's excessive 163-minute running time, which features too many subsidiary characters, leaving Nakadai absent for long stretches. Despite these longeurs, there are impressive bouts of action along the way with Nakadai on good form, including a memorable assassination by Kumokiri as, brandishing his sword, he charges a palanquin in order to assassinate Yanagi Sukejiro, 'the best swordsman in Japan' (Kyoichi Sato), successfully managing to decapitate the passenger only to find that someone else was inside.

When Sukejiro then pops up looking as hard as nails and flourishing his sword like a true expert, Kumokiri's more direct approach enables him to make short and bloody work of his enemy in a nearby paddy field. Not long after this, hamster-faced Jo Shishido appears in a guest star role as a blind masseur who threatens to unmask Kumokiri, getting a folded fan rammed down his throat for his pains.[79] Aside form these bursts of violence, Nakadai gives a restrained performance, effectively suggesting that there is more to Kumokiri than a mere bandit leader, which indeed there is. An hour and a half into the film, we learn of his former status as a samurai, and he passionately defends his life of crime as preferable to a samurai's 'staged life of falsehood'. Regrettably, the music score is heavy-handed throughout, and this big speech in particular is spoilt by some unnecessary and intrusive piano. Most of the film also looks more studio-bound than Gosha's previous features, and the impressive locations he used to great effect in his earlier work are largely absent in this case, perhaps because the production budget was lower than on films such as *Goyokin*, *Hitokiri* and *The Wolves*. His customary inventiveness also seems less in evidence, and one of the highlights recycles the famous climax from *Jirokichi the Rat* (by way of *Inn of Evil*) when Kumokiri's gang are surrounded at night by samurai holding paper lanterns.

Overall, *Kumokiri Nizaemon* fails to engage quite as it should, but the film has its defenders and certainly a number of memorable sequences along the way. More importantly, it performed well at the Japanese box office and put Gosha back on the map as a cinema director, leading to a number of fruitful further collaborations with Nakadai. It also inspired a Fuji TV series the following year starring Shigeru Amachi, along with at least four subsequent TV versions.

1978 also saw an important change in Nakadai's personal life. Yasuko's younger sister, Fusako, had become a successful TV host for

---

[79] The temple filled with grotesque statues in which Jo Shishido delivers his message was previously featured in *The Manster* (1959), when the title character goes in seeking advice and ends up murdering the priest he finds inside.

Fuji TV after abandoning acting because her diminutive stature of 4' 9" (145 cm) meant that she was considered too short for most parts. She married her fellow host, Yukio Yamakawa, and became pregnant. Yasuko stood in for her during her maternity leave, and she gave birth to a girl, Nao. However, when Fusako and her husband were divorced in 1978, the 4-year-old Nao was adopted by Nakadai and Yasuko and became known as Nao Nakadai. Nao later became a successful pop singer and also acted occasionally.

The same year, Nakadai starred in a six-part drama series written by Yasuko for Fuji TV entitled *Catch Up* (Oitsumeru), based on a prize-winning hard-boiled crime novel from 1967 by Jiro Ikushima which had been filmed in 1972 by Toshio Masuda. Nakadai was cast as a police officer who accidentally shoots a colleague, while Tomisaburo Wakayama (star of the *Lone Wolf* film series) was on the other side of the law as a *yakuza*.

Nakadai was back with Kon Ichikawa for *Firebird* (Hi no tori). Unrelated to Nakadai's 1956 film of the same title, it was based on a long-running and immensely popular manga series of the same name by Osamu Tezuka, whose own production company were involved in the film. A fantasy based on Japanese mythology and involving a quest for the legendary bird of the title (whose blood supposedly grants eternal life), it also featured Tomisaburo Wakayama as a warrior who is punished by his wicked queen by being put into 'the moat of wasps' for three days. After his release there is an odd scene in which a boy sucks the pus from his face, but despite this assistance he is left with a nose like that of a proboscis monkey until the end of the film, when he is turned into a human pin cushion by a hail of arrows à la Toshiro Mifune in *Throne of Blood*. Nakadai, sporting a bizarre haircut, played one of the film's two main villains, Jingi the Conqueror and, like the rest of the cast, clearly decided that the only thing to do with this kind of material was to chew the scenery. Perhaps in desperation, *Firebird* features a variety of ill-advised visual gimmicks including split screen and some poorly-executed animated sequences directed by Tezuka. The manga series remains popular and is apparently considered quite profound by some, but unfortunately Ichikawa's film merely feels like a badly dated children's movie which fails to engage.

Nakadai's next film was no better. *Blue Christmas* (Buru Kurisamasu) saw him working for Kihachi Okamoto once more, this time in the role of Minami, a reporter for the Japanese Broadcasting Company, who inadvertently uncovers a conspiracy. For reasons never explained, UFOs have been zapping people around the world with a laser beam and turning their blood blue. Although the only other effect of the beam is that it rids people of their neuroses, governments have begun to secretly round up the 'blue bloods' and send them to concentration camps, where many are vivisected or lobotomized. The first half of the film focuses on Minami, who appears to be the world's most incompetent investigative reporter – not only does he cause the death of an innocent person by betraying a confidence but, when sent to New York in search of Hyodo (Eiji Okada), a missing scientist, he simply wanders the streets asking random people if they know the missing man. He even makes a quick trip to Houston in an effort to uncover information about the government's secret UFO investigation committee. His method is to walk into the NASA building and ask the guy on reception about it; reception guy understandably laughs in his face, so he immediately jets back to New York, where he finally discovers something important, but only because someone from Japan has thoughtfully bothered to phone him at his hotel. As there is no indication that Nakadai's character is *supposed* to be an idiot, this can only be attributed to sloppiness on the part of Okamoto and his screenwriter, So Kuramoto. In any case, Minami's breakthrough sees him taken off the investigation and transferred to Paris, where the narrative abandons him, switching its focus to the character of Oki (Hiroshi Katsuno), a special forces member involved in the rounding up of the blue-bloods who discovers that his own girlfriend, Saeko (Keiko Takeshita), is one of them.

One has to admire Nakadai's loyalty to Okamoto in accepting such a poorly-written part. To add insult to injury, even his costumes have dated badly – first seen in a polo neck sweater and corduroy blazer, he later switches to a denim suit – and he looks uncomfortable in his role, especially when having to speak in English. Perhaps some consolation was provided by the trips to New York and Paris for location shooting, along with the opportunity to act opposite so many old friends; other familiar faces popping up among the cast included Kaoru Yachigusa and Shigeru Koyama, along with Haiyuza members Kunie Tanaka, Yoshio Inaba, Eitaro Ozawa, Kappei Matsumoto, Tomoo Nagai and Ichiro Nakatani, while a part was also found for Mumeijuku student Shinji Ogawa.

Like Okamoto's earlier *Age of Assassins*, *Blue Christmas* is a parable about the dangers of Nazi-type ideologies, a theme made explicit when we see Saeko watching a documentary about the Holocaust, and again when Minami has a secret meeting with Hyodo in a Jewish cemetery. That this allegory is manifested in changes to human blood may be a result of Japan's obsession with blood types, which many Japanese believe can influence a person's character in much the same way as Zodiac signs are thought to in the West. As some have suffered discrimination as a result of their blood type, *Blue Christmas* may in part be intended as a comment on this. Even today, the Japanese version of Wikipedia goes so far as to list the blood type of just about every domestic celebrity. For the record, Nakadai is apparently blood type B. In *The Encyclopedia of Japanese Pop Culture*, Mark Schilling writes that type Bs are 'the third largest group at twenty-two percent' and are thought to be 'impulsive, passionate, creative, and bold' while having 'a reputation for flakiness.'[80]

Although Okamoto was clearly struggling to film a complex story on a low budget – many scenes were shot on location using a hand-held camera, and the much-talked about UFOs are never even seen – this fails to explain quite why the film is such a mess. Multiple plot threads poorly woven together and an excessive running time of 132 minutes make for an unengaging experience, so it remains unsurprising that *Blue Christmas* was a flop and has been little seen abroad.

---

[80] Weatherhill, 1997. PP 28-29

In 1978, Mumeijuku staged its first play, a version of *Oedipus Rex* directed by Yasuko with Nakadai in the title role and featuring first generation Mumeijuku student Ai Kanzaki as Jocasta. Kanzaki – a trained musician whose instrument is the flute – had not originally intended to pursue acting as a career. However, after being employed by NHK as a musician on one of their programmes, she had found herself sitting next to Nakadai in the cafeteria, fallen into conversation with him and ended up joining Mumeijuku. Kanzaki won a Golden Arrow award for Best Newcomer for her performance as Jocasta.

The success of *Kumokiri Nizaemon* saw Nakadai and Gosha reunited again for the similar *Hunter in the Dark* (Yami no kariudo). Like the earlier film, it was also set in 18th-century Edo and based on a novel by Shotaro Ikenami with a script by Kaneo Ikegami – although Ikegami was on this occasion credited under the pseudonym Naoto Kitazawa as he took exception to some of Gosha's rewrites. Being another co-production between Shochiku and Haiyuza, the cast featured a number of Haiyuza veterans, including Yoshio Harada and Eijiro Tono, but non-members such as Keiko Kishi, Tetsuro Tanba and Sonny Chiba were also present, as were Mumeijuku students Ai Kanzaki and, in bit parts, Koji Yakusho and Daisuke Ryu. Yakusho, a former civil servant, had only just become a student at Mumeijuku after having been inspired to take up acting after seeing the company's production of *The Lower Depths* a couple of years earlier. Nakadai chose the name 'Yakusho' for his stage name as it can mean either 'government office', reflecting his past occupation, or 'role place', referencing his new career as an actor. He would go on to become the school's greatest success story, becoming a major star by the late '90s.

The one major difference from *Kumokiri Nizaemon* is that Masaru Sato was recruited to provide the score for *Hunter in the Dark*. A great improvement on that of the earlier film, it even won Sato a Japanese Academy Award for Best Music. Otherwise, it was business as usual – a convoluted plot with too many characters offset by Gosha's trademark sex, violence and colourful visuals. As Gomyo, Nakadai was once again top-billed as the head of a shadowy criminal gang considering retirement – despite the fact that he had even less screen time on this occasion and the real lead was Yoshio Harada, playing the one-eyed amnesiac swordsman he takes under his wing. However, the film comes alive during the inventively-staged action sequences, such as when a trio of women armed with knives attempt to assassinate Harada in the bath, a fight in a burning temple among a blizzard of sparks, or the climactic duel between Nakadai and Sonny Chiba, which takes place on a chicken farm with feathers flying everywhere. Unfortunately, the part of Gomyo does not stretch Nakadai at all – the most memorable performance in the film comes from Kayo Matsuo, who specialised in playing sexy female villains, appearing here as a knife-wielding gangsteress. *Hunter in the Dark* has been remade twice for TV – in 1994 with Takahiro Tamura as Gomyo and in 2014 with Baijaku Nakamura in the role.

Now that Mumeijuku was properly established, Nakadai had a clear conflict of interest, and so resigned from Haiyuza in 1979. Although he by no means cut his ties with the company completely, this change freed him from the obligation of donating a large portion of his salary to Haiyuza so he could use it to fund Mumeijuku instead.

Meanwhile, with director Kimio Yabuki, Yasuko had co-written the screenplay for an animated film version of *The Twelve Months* (Mori wa ikiteiru/'The Living Forest'), the play which had first brought her together with her future husband back in 1955. In the Japanese version, Koji Yakusho voiced the small part once performed by Nakadai, but the film was dubbed into many different languages in order to be shown around the world.

Chapter 22 – Divided Loyalties

Nakadai travelled to Brazil in 1979 for a three-week location shoot for *Amazon Song* (Amazon no uta), a two-hour historical drama for Fuji TV. Nakadai played Shinichi Konuma, the leader of a group of 189 Japanese immigrants who go to Brazil in 1929 to start a new life as farmers. They struggle with malaria and numerous other problems, but eventually succeed as pepper producers. Broadcast on 6 October 1979, it co-starred Kunie Tanaka as Konuma's best friend.

In order to do *Amazon Song*, Nakadai had turned down a leading role as General Nogi (1849-1912) in *Port Arthur*, a big-budget Toei war film. There had been talk of Tetsuro Tanba playing Nogi instead, but studio head Shigeru Okada hated the idea – perhaps because Tanba generally played unsympathetic parts – and Okada decided to delay the start date in order to get Nakadai, casting Tanba as General Kodama instead. However, just as Nakadai was about to return to Japan to commence shooting, he received an urgent message from Akira Kurosawa asking him to replace Shintaro Katsu as the star of *Kagemusha*, Kurosawa's three-hour samurai epic which would be his first film in five years. This was a difficult situation for Nakadai as his loyalties were split in three directions – not only was he now committed to *Port Arthur*, but he felt a strong sense of obligation to Kurosawa, while also valuing his friendship with Katsu. In fact, Katsu had asked Nakadai for advice about working with Kurosawa; Nakadai had advised him to listen carefully to everything Kurosawa said – advice which Katsu completely ignored on what was to be his first and last day on set.

Kurosawa had originally intended to cast Katsu only as the thief and to have the actor's real-life brother, Tomisaburo Wakayama, play Shingen. However, Wakayama had apparently foreseen that Katsu and Kurosawa were a marriage made in hell and decided not to be involved, so Katsu had been cast in both roles. Katsu had been excited about starring in a big-budget Kurosawa picture, especially as it was guaranteed to be widely distributed overseas and he was not well-known abroad at the time, so he had invited Kurosawa to dinner at an expensive restaurant in Kyoto before production began. Katsu had hired geisha, which was not something appreciated by Kurosawa according to his assistant, Teruyo Nogami. However, a rehearsal held the day before shooting was to commence had not gone well as Katsu had either failed to learn his lines properly or thought he could improve on the script. The following day, Katsu arrived with a video camera and a small crew, intending to have his performance filmed on videotape, supposedly so that he could play back his own performance and assess it himself. Kurosawa pointed out that *he* would provide any direction necessary for Katsu to improve his performance and that the video crew would be a nuisance. Katsu instructed them to keep out of the way, but Kurosawa still refused to allow it – perhaps the first time anyone had said no to the star in over a decade. Katsu stormed off to the dressing room, where fellow cast member Jinpachi Nezu watched him tearing off his costume and wondered if Katsu were suffering from an attack of diarrhea. A little later, Kurosawa knocked at the door with producer Tomoyuki Tanaka in tow, causing Katsu to think he had come to apologise, but instead Kurosawa dismissed him, at which point Katsu lunged at the director but Tanaka pulled him off. It seems likely that Kurosawa had already been having misgivings, and he reportedly had Nogami calling Nakadai before the dust had even settled. [81]

The success of the Zatoichi series had made Katsu one of the most powerful stars in Japan, a status he had enjoyed for more than 15 years before *Kagemusha* went into production. He was accustomed to having his own way and even directors had to pander to his whims. Despite his generous nature and undoubted (if limited) talent, he was also a show-off who went around with an entourage of sycophants trailing in

---

[81] Nogami's version of these events can be found (in Japanese) at www.dailyshincho.jp/article/2016/03080500 .

his wake like pilot fish, and it was probably this need for attention which had led him to bring a video crew onto Kurosawa's set.

It seems that Kurosawa had never entertained the idea of casting Toshiro Mifune, the obvious choice for the role, and the casting of whom would surely have made the film's producers – who included Francis Ford Coppola and George Lucas – very happy indeed. The relationship between Mifune and Kurosawa had become strained during the production of *Redbeard* (1965), which had tied Mifune up for an uncommonly long time. Although the star had voiced no complaints, it seems that Kurosawa sensed his frustration and took it amiss. There were also unsubstantiated rumours that Mifune had turned down the title role in *Dersu Uzala* (1975), quailing at the prospect of being stuck in Siberia with Kurosawa for a year or two. Nevertheless, it seems that, although Mifune was never offered *Kagemusha*, he *was* attached to *Ran* for a while in the late '70s.

Kurosawa agreed to postpone the shooting schedule of *Kagemusha* so that Nakadai could fulfil his commitment to *Port Arthur*. Nakadai wanted to gain approval from Katsu first, but Katsu avoided his calls. Kurosawa called a press conference to announce the casting of Nakadai, who was also present and took questions from reporters. Unfortunately, a number of newspapers took his remarks out of context, depictung him as a shameless opportunist with no respect for Katsu. Nakadai later said that he received a number of threatening phone calls as a result of this. A little later, he ran into Tomisaburo Wakayama, who was angry with him about his supposed lack of courtesy towards his brother. Although Nakadai's explanation was accepted by Wakayama, Katsu was less forgiving and it would be sixteen years before he spoke to Nakadai again.

It seems likely that Nakadai's part in *Port Arthur* was shot more quickly than it otherwise would have been had Nakadai not been under pressure to start work on *Kagemusha* as soon as possible. Like the earlier *Battle of the Japan Sea*, *Port Arthur* told the story of the Russo-Japanese War of 1904-05 from the Japanese perspective. In the rather biased version depicted in the film, Japan is forced into invading China to start a war with Russia because they believe it to be the only way to prevent a future Russian invasion of Japan. However, not only does the logic of this seem rather twisted to say the least, but the film omits to mention that Japan had expansionist plans of its own at the time involving Korea (a country which Russia also hoped to control). For this reason, and because it makes something of a hero of the controversial figure of General Nogi, the project was seen in some quarters as right-wing, and it is said that a number of actors had refused to participate as a result. It may seem surprising, then, to see the left-wing Nakadai heading the cast as Count Maresuke Nogi, the white-bearded, 55-year-old general burdened with the unenviable task of taking Port Arthur from the Russians. However, Nakadai appears (rightly or wrongly) to have been persuaded that the intention was to make an anti-war film, and perhaps that really *was* the intention of director Toshio Masuda – a man who had, after all, been expelled from the kamikaze during the war for his liberal views.

Despite being top-billed, Nakadai's screen time was limited and much of the narrative focused on the fictional character of Takeshi Kogyo (Teruhiko Aoi), a Tolstoy-loving schoolteacher drafted into the army as a lieutenant and forced to fight against the country he admires so much.

Port Arthur (in China) was where a large part of Russia's naval fleet was stationed, and the film focuses on the efforts of Japan to gain control of the heavily-fortified Russian base. In order to do so, they must first capture Hill 203, the strategic position which gave the film its Japanese title (*203 kochi*). It takes General Nogi four attempts to succeed in his mission, which he only manages eventually at the cost of thousands of Japanese lives. Two of his own sons are killed in the wider conflict, but Nogi represses his personal feelings and perseveres with grim determination. However, at the end of the film, after the battle is won, he finally gives reign to his emotions and breaks down in front of Emperor Meiji, portrayed by Toshiro Mifune in a cameo that was almost obligatory in a big-budget Japanese war film. Tetsuro Tanba gave his usual solid performance as Nogi's friend and fellow general

Gentaro Kodama, while Masako Natsume from the popular TV show *Monkey* provided the love interest as Kogyo's girlfriend.

Although the project was instigated by Toei president Shigeru Okada, who had commissioned Kazuo Kasahara to write the screenplay, it had a personal resonance for director Toshio Masuda. The director had turned 18 in 1945, narrowly missing military service, and majored in Russian literature as a student at Osaka University. It can be no coincidence that, in *Port Arthur*, the Russians are portrayed with considerable sympathy (by Westerners of various nationalities). After completing his studies, Masuda had decided to pursue a career in filmmaking and became Nikkatsu's top action director for much of the '60s. Aged 52 at the time of shooting *Port Arthur*, he had made over 60 films, many of which had been both commercially successful and well-received critically. He also had a reputation for reliability and so was seen in Japan — by those in the industry at least — as one of the country's best directors despite being little-known abroad. In 1969, Masuda had taken over the direction of the Japanese sequences of the Pearl Harbour epic *Tora! Tora! Tora!* after Akira Kurosawa had been fired. He had previously directed Nakadai in *Challenge at Dawn* (1970) and both parts of *The Human Revolution* (1973/76).

Port Arthur is a well-made but rather sentimental film. Running over three hours, it was screened with an interval, and the end of part one features an excessively emotional pop ballad which is repeated over the end credits. Despite this lapse, the rest of the musical score is strong, and the cinematography first-rate. The battle scenes are more convincing than usual for a film of this vintage and Masuda depicts the violence of war in sometimes gory detail. However, he also gives his actors too much rope at times and some of the characters seem to take a long time to die while making a lot of noise doing it. There is also some occasional unintended humour, such as when Kogyo's girlfriend solemnly promises to give up reading Tolstoy until he returns from the war. Nevertheless, *Port Arthur* was a hit at the Japanese box office, spawning a TV version the following year starring Takahiro Tamura as Nogi, while Masuda was nominated for Best Director at the Japanese

Academy Awards and won a Kinema Junpo Readers' Choice Award for Best Film.

Before Nakadai had agreed to do *Kagemusha*, he had asked Kurosawa to make some changes, although the precise nature of these is unclear. In any case, Kurosawa said that it was too late as shooting had begun, so Nakadai had little choice but to accept the two roles as written, playing both the *daimyo* Shingen Takeda (1521-73)[82] and the larger part of the unnamed thief pressganged into impersonating him. However, he was unable to escape the shadow of Katsu and Kurosawa even asked Nakadai to try to look more like his former friend, so he put wads of cotton in his cheeks to fill out his face. In some scenes, Nakadai appears to be mimicking Katsu, especially when the thief laughs. Another difficulty may have been the thief's lack of back story – a common trait among Kurosawa's characters, but an unusual one for the protagonist of a three-hour epic. Kurosawa also prevents us from becoming fully engaged with the thief emotionally by treating him in much the same way as the other characters. In other words, the story is not truly told from the thief's point of view – he is absent from many scenes and we mostly observe him from a dispassionate distance as there are few close-ups in *Kagemusha* and the camera assumes a consistently objective viewpoint. Nevertheless, Nakadai's performance in *Kagemusha* has been generally underrated and he communicates a great deal through his subtle use of body language. A number of commentators have suggested that the film would have worked better with Mifune or Katsu, but it is hard to see how the emotional distance would have been overcome simply by using another actor (assuming the same directorial approach were maintained). It is also difficult to imagine Katsu being able to match the look of horror on Nakadai's face as he witnesses the Takeda clan being completely wiped out in the Battle of Nagashino at the film's climax. Furthermore, while Katsu was

---

[82] Takeda had previously been played by Kinnosuke Nakamura in *Samurai Banners* (1969) and is said to have used a double to deceive his enemies.

perfect casting for the thief, it is less easy to imagine him portraying the calm dignity of Takeda.

At one point during shooting, Nakadai fell off his horse while eight other riders were following. Having been taught not to move after a fall, Nakadai remained where he was as the other horses came galloping along so close to him that some of their hooves clipped the horns on his helmet. The sword that Nakadai was wearing had pressed into his chest as he fell, resulting in three broken ribs. Kurosawa preferred not to use stuntmen but was prepared for such accidents and apparently had no less than ten ambulances on standby, one of which took Nakadai away to hospital. He was told that it would take a month for him to recover but, mindful of the pressure Kurosawa must have been under, he checked himself out after two weeks and returned to work. [83]

Along with Kurosawa and his regular team, Nakadai was also reunited with Tsutomu Yamazaki, who gives an excellent performance as Nobukado Takeda (brother of Shingen Takeda) and is unrecognizable from his role as the kidnapper in *High and Low* some 17 years previously. He won the Kinema Jumpo Award for Best Supporting actor, while Nakadai won the Mainichi Film Award for Best Actor and the Blue Ribbon Award in the same category, the latter for both *Kagemusha* and *Port Arthur* – the second time he had won the Blue Ribbon (the first having been for *Harakiri*). Filming had ended on 23 March 1980, with the film premiering in Japan at the Yurakuza cinema on 23 April 1980. Attendees included Hollywood luminaries such as James Coburn, Peter Fonda, Sam Peckinpah, Athur Penn and William Wyler. Even Toshiro Mifune turned up to show his support. When the film subsequently screened in competition at Cannes on 14 May, Nakadai accompanied Kurosawa to the festival, where it shared the Palme d'Or with Bob Fosse's *All that Jazz*. It must have seemed like Kurosawa was back with a vengeance after his years in the wilderness, especially as *Kagemusha* went on to become the highest-earning Japanese film of all time (until *Antarctica* three years later). However, 20th Century

---

[83] https://thetv.jp/news/detail/111842/

Fox, who had provided part of the budget at the behest of Lucas and Coppola in return for the American distribution rights, lost money on their investment, and Kurosawa would continue struggling to get his projects off the ground in the years to come.

Shintaro Katsu saw the film and reportedly commented that it was not interesting, but it would have been if he had been in it.

Chapter 23 – The Big Five-O

Around the time of *Port Arthur*'s release in August 1980, Nakadai had his first book published by Kodansha. Entitled *Actor Memo 1955-1980*, it featured Nakadai's musings on a variety of topics such as playing Shakespearean roles on stage, acting for Kurosawa and Kobayashi, health and diet, and even 'miscellaneous thoughts about hotels.' He also narrated a 5-hour miniseries produced by Asahi TV in association with Haiyuza. Entitled *Blue Wolf: The Life of Genghis Khan*, it was based on a 1959 novel by Yasushi Inoue. More importantly, Nakadai's house and the adjoining rehearsal hall were finally completed. This enabled Mumeijuku to stage their first entirely independent production – a version of Norwegian playwright Henrik Ibsen's 1892 classic, *The Master Builder*, in which Nakadai starred as Halvard Solness, the 'master builder' of the title. Solness, a renowned architect, receives a surprise visit from Hilda, a 23-year-old woman who claims that she had met him a decade earlier, when he had promised her 'a kingdom' while attempting to seduce her. Solness claims not to remember the incident, but is nevertheless charmed by Hilda and invites her to move in to his home as a kind of assistant. We learn during the course of the play that Solness has a strained relationship with his wife due to the fact that they had lost their children in a fire years before, and also that he believes himself to have the ability to make events happen just by thinking of them. However, he also has a fear of heights, and the play ends with him climbing to the top of a church – his latest creation – with Hilda's encouragement, only to have an attack of vertigo and fall to his death.

Directed by Yasuko, *The Master Builder* featured Ai Kanzaki as Hilda, along with Shinji Ogawa and Daisuke Ryu, and won an Arts Festival Excellence Award, but the production had not gone entirely smoothly. On opening night, thirty minutes before curtain time, a member of the supporting cast fell sick. Nakadai hastily chose another Mumeijuku student to replace him – Toru Masuoka, then in his first year at the school and working on the production as a props clerk, although he had also been studying the role as part of his lessons. He asked Nakadai to delay the start by thirty minutes and managed well enough to be kept on for the rest of the run, subsequently becoming one of Mumeijuku's success stories.

Nakadai next starred in the Fuji TV movie *Magistrate in a Nest of Vice* (Chaku nagashi bugyo) playing a samurai sent from Edo to clean up a corrupt town called Horiuchi. He uses a variety of unconventional tactics to achieve this, including martial arts when necessary. Directed by Kihachi Okamoto, it featured the director's trademark humour and a cast which combined Haiyuza veterans such as Ichiro Nakatani and Eitaro Ozawa with members of Mumeijuku's younger generation, including Koji Yakusho and Ai Kanzaki. The story it was based on, *Town Magistrate's Diary* (Machibugyo nikki) by Shugoro Yamamoto, had previously been filmed in 1959 with Shintaro Katsu and also been adapted as a screenplay by the 'Four Knights' (Kon Ichikawa, Keisuke Kinoshita, Masaki Kobayashi and Akira Kurosawa) which eventually became an underwhelming Kon Ichikawa film in 2000 under the title *Dora-heita* starring none other than Koji Yakusho. Other adaptations include a 1987 film by *13 Assassins* director Eiichi Kudo with Ken Watanabe and a second Fuji TV version in 1992.

Nakadai was reunited with *Rise, Fair Sun* director Kei Kumai in 1981 for the film *Wilful Murder*,[84] based on the 1973 novel *Murder: The Shimoyama Incident* (Bosatsu: Shimoyama jiken) by Kimio Yata, a former reporter for the *Asahi Shinbun*. Yata had been involved in the investigation of three mysterious events which had occurred close together during the hot summer of 1949, all of which had involved Japan's railways: the Shimoyama Incident, the Mitaka Incident and the Matsukawa Derailment. It was not the first time these incidents had inspired a motion picture – Yasushi Inoue's untranslated 1950 novel *Kuroi Ushio* ('The Dark Tide') had been based on the Shimoyama

---

[84] The long-winded Japanese title *Nihon no atsui hibi bosatsu: Shimoyama jiken* translates as 'Hot Days in Japan – Murder: Shimoyama Incident'.

Incident and filmed in 1954, while the aftermath of the Matsukawa Derailment had been the subject of a 1961 film by Satsuo Yamamoto.

Kei Kumai had begun his directorial career with similar material. *The Long Death* (Teigin jiken: Shikeishu/'The Teigin Incident: Prisoner Condemned to Death', 1964) dealt with the real-life mass poisoning of some bank employees in 1948, a crime known as the Teigin Incident, for which a man named Sadamichi Hirasawa was convicted and sentenced to death but never executed due to doubts over his guilt. Although Kumai's second film, *A Chain of Islands* (Nihon retto/'The Japanese Archipelago'), told a fictional story, it was filmed in a similar semi-documentary style and again concerned a mysterious murder, on this occasion of an American army sergeant in Tokyo. The writer Seicho Matsumoto and the director Yoshitaro Nomura specialized very successfully in this type of material, but Kumai's three contributions to this fascinating Japanese sub-genre – perhaps best described as socially-conscious post-war crime drama – are equally impressive. Typically beginning with the discovery of the corpse of a person killed under mysterious circumstances, films of this genre generally feature a detailed police-procedural investigation which uncovers all kinds of dark secrets and large-scale corruption. Notable examples include Nomura's *Castle of Sand* and Tomu Uchida's *Straits of Hunger*, but there are many more, and *Wilful Murder* is one which seems to have been unjustly forgotten.

Nakadai was cast in the lead as Yashiro, a reporter for the *Showa Nippo* newspaper, who investigates the death of Sadanori Shimoyama, the head of the newly-formed JNR (Japan National Railways), which replaced the JGR (Japanese Government Railways). Shimoyama's broken body was discovered on a railway track on 6 July 1949, only days after he had announced the planned redundancy of 100,000 workers. In response, the National Railway Workers' Union (aka the Kokuro) had announced their intention to call a strike. The condition of Shimoyama's body after being hit by a train made it impossible to determine whether the cause of death was suicide or murder, but the timing gave rise to the suspicion that he was killed by communists.

However, in the film, Yashiro begins to wonder if Shimoyama was murdered as part of a right-wing conspiracy intended to put the blame on the labour union and the Communist Party.

On 15 July, just nine days after Shimoyama's body was found, an unmanned runaway train caused an accident at Mitaka Station, leading to six fatalities and many injuries. In the film, Yashiro's boss, Toyama, tells him to forget about the Shimoyama case and report on this new incident, but Yashiro begins attending a forensic medicine class at the University of Tokyo to aid him in his investigation. Meanwhile, it turns out that the runaway train had been a deliberate act of sabotage as the operating handle had been tied down, suggesting that the two events may be related. The Prime Minister blames the Communist Party for both incidents, and public opinion turns against them and the union, enabling the JNR to go ahead with the planned redundancies.

Meanwhile, the US military have also been investigating and discovered a bloodstain close to the location where Shimoyama's body was found. Yashiro learns about a chemical called luminol, which can be used in forensic investigation to make traces of blood glow in the dark. He takes some to the crime scene at night and sprays the track, revealing a trail of blood which suggests that Shimoyama might have been murdered a short distance away, then carried to the railway track. Tests reveal that the blood type from the traces collected by Yashiro matches that of the victim. Yashiro takes his findings to Deputy Attorney Iba of the Tokyo District Public Prosecutor's Office, who is greatly impressed and invites him to join the investigation in an official capacity. Although this means that Yashiro will not be able to write about it in the newspaper, he readily agrees.

On 17 August, a train close to Matsukawa Station derails, killing three members of the train's crew. After it is found that sabotage was again the cause, the left-wing are blamed once more, and members of the Communist Party and the Kokuro are rounded up and thrown in jail.

In March 1950, the team responsible for the Shimoyama case is dissolved, although Yashiro and a few others continue the work on their own time. Several years pass, during which five suspects in the Matsukawa Incident are sentenced to death and another five to life imprisonment.

In September 1963, the Supreme Court reverses all of the guilty verdicts in the Matsukawa case. By this time, the statute of limitations has come into force regarding the Shimoyama case, and a man named Maruyama offers to provide Yashiro with the information he wants in exchange for 500,000 yen, which he needs in order to run away with his wife and child and ensure their safety. Maruyama says that, on the day of Shimoyama's kidnapping, he was ordered by 'the boss with a hoarse voice' to carry an unconscious man to the railway tracks and had watched, terrified, as the train drove over the body.

In 1964, Yashiro is watching the opening ceremony of the Tokyo Olympics when he receives a phone call informing him that Maruyama has been hit by a train. He rushes to the station and learns that there were no witnesses to the accident. Suspecting that Maruyama has been murdered in order to silence him, he becomes emotional and realises that the mystery on which he has spent 15 years of his life will never be fully solved.

As the story is told from the viewpoint of Yashiro, Nakadai is in almost every scene of the film and gives an energetic, committed performance. One difficulty he faced was that Yashiro continually has to react to the latest surprising development, and Nakadai does a good job of varying his reaction each time this occurs.

The supporting cast reads like a *Who's Who* of the male Japanese acting world: Ichiro Nakatani as Yashiro's boss, Eitaro Ozawa as a dodgy politician, Shigeru Koyama as a state attorney, Mikijiro Hira as a high-ranking police inspector, Kei Yamamoto as a police detective, Daisuke Ryu as an informant, and an early appearance by Koji Yakusho as a young reporter. One especially nice piece of casting is that of Hideji Otaki, who reprises the same mysterious character he had played in Kumai's earlier *A Chain of Islands*. Perhaps most memorable of all, however, is Hisashi Igawa, who seemed to specialise in playing unfortunate, downtrodden characters. In *Wilful Murder* he outdoes himself as a Korean whistleblower who, in a chilling sequence, gets pushed out of a helicopter by American military police, falling from a great height into the sea below, which swallows him up without a trace.

With Daisuke Ryu in *Wilful Murder*.

Aided by Takeo Kimura's Mainichi Award-winning art direction and the black-and-white cinematography of Shunichiro Nakao, Kumai was very successful at capturing the atmosphere of post-war Japan in *Wilful Murder*. In the early scenes especially, he fills the frame with busy background characters as if trying to outdo Kurosawa, and has them perpetually wiping the sweat off, giving an impression of Tokyo in 1949 as a hot, crowded and chaotic place. The screenplay was the work of Ryuzo Kikushima, who had co-written *Yojimbo*, *Sanjuro* and *High and Low* among others, and he manages to tell the complex story with great clarity, a feat also aided by the use of voiceover narration and archive newsreel footage at appropriate points. *Wilful Murder* was well-received in Japan and nominated for a number of Japanese Academy awards. Abroad, it was nominated for the Golden Bear at the Berlin Film Festival and received a limited US release in May the following year.

Nakadai's Mumeijuku play for 1981 was an adaptation of Machiavelli's comedy of deception published in 1524, *The Mandrake*, entitled *Posionous Flower* (Doku no hana). The play concerns a young man's convoluted plot to sleep with the beautiful wife of a foolish old man. Directed by Yasuko, it also featured Mumeijuku's own Mai Okamoto,[85] Toru Masuoka and Koji Yakusho, as well as Kei Yamamoto, one of Nakadai's juniors from Haiyuza who was also the nephew of Satsuo Yamamoto and with whom Nakadai had a particularly warm relationship. Yamamoto would go on to appear in a number of further Mumeijuku productions when there was a part calling for another experienced senior actor. *Poisonous Flower* was the first Mumeijuku play to be produced in association with the Parco organization, which hosted the 458-seat Seibu Theatre inside its department store in Shibuya. A number of Haiyuza plays had been staged there since its opening in 1973 and it would be home to all of Mumeijuku's plays for the next seven years.

Nakadai's next film found him working for Hideo Gosha once more, this time on an adaptation of Tomiko Miyao's novel *The Life of Hanako Kiryuin* (Kiryuin Hanako no shogai), which tells the story of the daughter of a *yakuza* boss and her adopted elder sister, Matsue. In Japan, the film retained the title of the book despite the fact that it focused on the character of Matsue rather than Hanako, but it was generally known abroad as *Onimasa* after the name of the *yakuza* boss memorably portrayed by Nakadai – who had more screen time and a far more interesting part than in either *Kumokiri Nizaemon* or *Hunter in the Dark*.

---

[85] Real name Wakana Maita, and therefore no relation to Kihachi Okamoto, and not to be confused with his daughter Mami, also an actress. Mai Okamoto is the daughter of composer Toru Fuyuki, known for contributing music to numerous *Ultraman* series and spin-offs. However, Nakadai helped her to choose her stage name, so a tribute to the film director was probably intended.

Masagoro Kiryuin, or Onimasa, is one of the most unpleasant characters Nakadai ever played and required an intricate full-body tattoo. His interpretation of Onimasa is of a boorish, swaggering hulk of unfettered machismo. While not exactly stupid, he is certainly uneducated and, when he does reveal a more human side, it is purely the result of a whimsical sentimentality or simplistic idea of chivalry. Assigned by his boss, Uichi Suda (Testuro Tanba), to break up a strike, he gives a vicious beating to the union leader, who continues throughout the assault to call Onimasa a 'pet dog' of Suda's. Impressed by a level of courage he has not previously witnessed, Onimasa switches sides, deciding that it is more 'chivalrous' to defend the poor. However, this new-found idealism fails to last and, a little later, he attempts to rape his adopted daughter, only desisting when she threatens to cut her own throat with a glass broken in the struggle. Nakadai's acting is surprisingly unrestrained compared to his usual style, but the choice is entirely appropriate for the character, making it one of his best performances.

Onimasa, a co-production between Toei and Haiyuza, was a project instigated not by Gosha, but by the actress Meiko Kaji (best known in the West as *Lady Snowblood*). She had read the novel and brought it to the attention of Toei producer Goro Kusakabe in the hope that she would star as Matsue alongside Tomisaburo Wakayama as Onimasa, with Yasuzo Masumura as director. Kusakabe liked the idea and bought the rights, but had to persuade Toei head Shigeru Okada before getting the go ahead. He also considered Kaji (then 34) too old for the role and wanted to cast Shinobu Otake (then 24) instead, so he arranged a reading of the two main parts with Otake and Wakayama in front of the studio heads, but the project was initially rejected by Okada as being 'too dark'.

Meanwhile, Gosha had been having a terrible time. His wife had walked out, leaving him with a huge debt, his daughter had been critically injured in a car accident, he had been arrested for possession of a firearm and, during pre-production on the film *Samurai Reincarnation* (Makai tensho), he had been replaced by Kinji Fukasaku.

Gosha had also resigned from Fuji TV and was rumoured to be depressed and contemplating suicide. Fortunately, Masayuki Sato came to the rescue once more, visiting Toei and asking Okada to give Gosha a job. When Okada suggested that he direct *The Life of Hanako Kiryuin*, Gosha jumped at the chance. However, production was delayed when Shinobu Otake refused to commit and eventually dropped out, perhaps because Gosha's reputation was low at the time and she was uncomfortable with the sex scenes. When Wakayama also dropped out, Nakadai was cast alongside Masako Natsume, a 24-year-old model-turned-actress who had appeared in *Port Arthur*.

Learning that the role of Matsue had become available, Natsume had aggressively pursued the part and visited Gosha's home, where she had apparently sat on the script and refused to leave until he agreed to cast her. Despite having previously specialized in innocent, virginal characters, her tactics worked and her persistence persuaded Gosha that she was the right choice. However, Natsume was hiding a secret which she did not reveal until shooting began – she was ill with leukemia. She also needed time off for an operation, so Gosha shot scenes with Nobuko Sendo playing Matsue as a young girl while he waited for her to recover. When she returned, Natsume explained the situation to Nakadai as she had to perform the scene in which Onimasa tries to rape Matsue and she wanted to warn him in advance about her surgical scars. Natsume also began dealing with her illness by drinking large amounts of whisky after shooting was over for the day. On one occasion, she went drinking with Nakadai and Gosha and drunk them both under the table. Nevertheless, she was always on time and ready to begin work the following morning. Nakadai was greatly impressed with her attitude in the face of her illness and later said that, if anyone asked him to name the most charming actress he had worked with, he would say it was Masako Natsume.

Nakadai again managed to wangle parts for some of his Mumeijuku students, in this case Koji Yakusho and Toru Masuoka, while the role of Onimasa's wife, Uta, was played by Shima Iwashita, who had played Nakadai's daughter in *Harakiri* and later appeared in

Buraikan and *Kumokiri Nizaemon*. Iwashita was under contract to Shochiku, who had apparently loaned her out somewhat reluctantly at the request of Gosha. She asked Nakadai for advice on how to play the wife of a *yakuza*; Nakadai, figuring that *yakuza* wives were often former prostitutes, suggested that she copy Ayako Wakao's walk in Kenji Mizoguchi's *Street of Shame* (Akasen chitai/'Red Light District', 1956), which she proceeded to do both on and off set.

In directing the sex scenes, Gosha reportedly took his clothes off and demonstrated the movements he wanted with the aid of the assistant director, who had also stripped, even going so far as to lick the toes of his junior. As a result of this example, those members of the cast who had to perform such scenes found it easier to ignore their own feelings of embarrassment – or at least more difficult to refuse.

Onimasa opened on 5 June 1982 and was a big hit at the Japanese box office, earning 1.1 billion yen. Masako Natsume won the Blue Ribbon Award for Best Actress, while the books of Tomiko Miyao received a huge boost in popularity, leading Gosha to make a further two films based on her work. In Japan, the advertising had focused on the female stars rather than Nakadai, and the success of this approach also meant that Gosha would concentrate mainly on films centred around strong female characters from this point on. The film was submitted as Japan's entry for the Academy Awards for Best Foreign Film, but not accepted, although it did receive a U.S. release in 1985.

Not long after *Onimasa*, Nakadai starred in a TV movie for Gosha, *Tange Sazen – The Pot Worth One Million Ryo* (Tange Sazen Kenfu! Hyakuman ryo no tsubo). Tange Sazen, a one-eyed, one-armed swordsman, is a fictional character created by Fubo Hayashi in the 1920s who first appeared in a serial published in one of Japan's national newspapers, the *Mainichi Shinbun*. The story of Tange Sazen and the pot containing the secret to a fortune which is pursued by multiple parties had been filmed umpteen times before, including by Gosha himself in 1966 with Kinnosuke Nakamura.

With the exception of the first scene, when the swordsman's body is still fully intact, Nakadai had to act in a gruesome make-up job and with one arm tucked into his kimono. He affected a rather unlikely swordfighting style and took a tongue-in-cheek approach to the part – appropriate as the tale is pure hokum anyway. Gosha threw everything he could at it to keep it entertaining, including a group of brightly-dressed dancing female assassins and a topless scene for co-star Kayo Matsuo (who had also appeared in *Hunter in the Dark*) as Sazen's pistol-toting sidekick. As a Fuji TV-Haiyuza co-production, *Tange Sazen* featured a number of Haiyuza actors such as Isao Natsuyagi and Ichiro Nakatani, while one of Nakadai's Mumeijuku students, Goro Ohashi, also appeared, as did *Onimasa*'s Masako Natsume.

Mumeijuku's play for 1982 was a production of *Macbeth* directed by Yasuko, with Nakadai in the title role for the first but not the last time. Lady Macbeth was played by his former Jocasta, Ai Kanzaki, while Koji Yakusho and Daisuke Ryu were also featured.

The same year, Nakadai headed the cast of a new, 90-minute version of *Inn of Evil* scripted by Yasuko for Fuji TV, this time under the title *The Law of Hell* (Jigoku no okite), directed by Akira Inoue, a former feature film director who had transferred to television. This time round, Nakadai played Ikuzo, the inn-keeper portrayed by kabuki actor Kan'emon Nakamura in the 1971 film, while Daisuke Ryu was cast as Sadashichi, the character previously played by Nakadai. Fellow Mumeijuku students Koji Yakusho and Toru Masuoka also appeared.

Nakadai's next film, *Tono Monogatari*, was based loosely on a book of the same title by Kunio Yanagita who, like Lafcadio Hearn, was a collector of folk tales – in this case from the Tono region of Iwate Prefecture in north-east Honshu. However, the script also incorporated elements from a book entitled *Waga Kakushi Nenbutsu* by Tokumi Aizen. Published in 1977, it dealt with the customs and religious practices of the inhabitants of Waga, a village also located in the Tono region. The film was made to celebrate the 30th anniversary of the Iwate Broadcasting Company, who co-produced it in association with Haiyuza and others.

Set around the time of the Russo-Japanese War, *Tono Monogatari* concerns a 16-year-old girl, Sayo, whose fiancé, Takeo, returns to their village after three years of military service. Discovering that his family has become poor in his absence, Takeo decides that he can no longer in good conscience marry Sayo. He leaves the village in the company of a mysterious wandering *biwa* player (Nakadai), but she defiantly cuts her hair and tells her parents she will wait for him however long it takes.

Director Tetsutaro Murano had embarked on a film career after seeing *La Grande Illusion* (a great favourite of Nakadai's), working as an assistant to Kenji Mizoguchi and Yasuzo Masumura before directing his first feature, *In a Snowy City* (Yuki no furu-gai ni), in 1960. He had previously collaborated with *Tono Monogatari*'s screenwriter, Yukiko Takayama, on *Gassan*, Japan's entry for the Best Foreign Film Academy Award of 1980. In the case of *Tono Monogatari*, they created a decent but rather slow-paced period romance with an element of fantasy. Playing an old man, Nakadai was given grey hair and a beard to match, but the make-up was not terribly convincing, and his character was (presumably) dubbed by somebody else during the scenes in which he sings and plays the *biwa*. At one point, Otokura explains to Takeo why he ended up as a wanderer, and there is a flashback revealing the tragedy which drove him to a life on the road. He warns the younger man that leaving the village will not erase his painful memories, as he can testify from his own experience.

The film also featured another early appearance by Koji Yakusho, while a fellow Mumeijuku student, Yoko Hara, appeared as Sayo. Parts of the film were shot at a historical building owned by the Chiba family, who were initially reluctant to allow a film crew inside. However, when one family member heard that Nakadai would be in the film, they readily granted permission.

Nakadai provided some narration for the animated feature film *Space Battleship Yamato – The Final Chapter* (Uchu senkan Yamato – kanketsu-hen), the last in a science fiction series about a space battleship named after the famous Second World War ship. The production also marked the fifth time Nakadai had worked with director Toshio Masuda, who oversaw the production and was clearly a filmmaker willing to try his hand at anything. While the quality of both the animation and the music was high, unfortunately the same could not be said for the story, especially as it took two and a half hours to tell it – an unprecedented length for an animated film at the time. During the same period, Nakadai also provided narration for *Battle Anthem* (Nihonkai daikaisen – Umi yukaba/ 'Japan Sea Battle Anthem – If I Go Away to Sea'), Masuda's follow-up to *Port Arthur*, which again dealt with the Russo-Japanese war.

In 1983, Nakadai appeared in three one-off 90-minute samurai dramas for Fuji TV, all directed by Akira Inoue. The first of these was *Shadow Hunters* (Kage gari), a remake of Toshio Masuda's 1972 film, with Nakadai in the role originally played by Yujiro Ishihara – the bearded leader of a trio of idealistic *ronin* who battle against ninjas (the 'shadows' of the title) employed by the shogunate. The second was *The Fir Trees Remain* (Momi no ki wa nokotta), scripted by Yasuko and based on a novel by Shuguro Yamamoto previously filmed as *Aoba Castle Demon* (Aoba-jo no oni) by Kenji Misumi with Kazuo Hasegawa in 1962, and also the basis of several other TV versions. Nakadai played Harada Kai (1619-71), a samurai involved in a conflict known as the Daté Uproar, during which Kai assassinated an informant and was himself beheaded as a result. The third and final drama was *Gears of Darkness* (Yami no haguruma), based on a novel by Shuhei Fujisawa, best known in the West as the author of the novels upon which Yoji Yamada's internationally-successful film *The Twilight Samurai* had been based. *Gears of Darkness* was itself made into a feature film in 2019 with the English title *The Fox Dancing in the Dusk*.

On 23 March 1983, Nakadai was one of the guests at Akira Kurosawa's 73rd birthday party. Another was Jun Norisugi, a lawyer who had once prepared a contract for a proposed '70s remake of *Woman in the Dunes* on behalf of Raquel Welch and later worked occasionally for Kurosawa. Norisugi later described the gathering as resembling the birthday party scene from the director's final film, *Madadayo*. Nakadai, meanwhile, had turned 50 at the end of 1982 and been a star for around half his life. Despite the decline in the Japanese film industry, his career remained in good shape, mainly because he had chosen his roles well. In excellent health and still able to get away with playing younger than his age, he was about to be cast as a 70-year-old by none other than Kurosawa.

Chapter 24 – From Folly to Reason

Nakadai had accepted the male lead in Hideo Gosha's next film, *The Geisha* (Yokiro), but when production was delayed he was forced to pull out as the shooting schedule overlapped with that of Kurosawa's *Ran*, so Ken Ogata took the part instead. As *Ran* was originally to begin shooting in July 1983 and would tie Nakadai up for a considerable time, the Mumeijuku production for 1983 was a version of *Hamlet* directed by Yasuko in which he did not appear. However, production on *Ran* also became delayed, in this case by nearly a year, so Nakadai could have made *The Geisha* and possibly even managed a play after all.

This unexpected extra free time allowed him to contribute a cameo as Macbeth in some dream-style sequences for a three-hour TV documentary-drama about living with cancer. Produced by TBS, *Unknown Rebellion* (Michinaru hanran) starred Kimiko Ikegami as a cancer research worker who learns that her own father (*High and Low*'s Tsutomu Yamazaki) has been diagnosed with the disease. The programme was broadcast on 24 October 1983 and won a Nippon Television Technology Award.

In 1984, Nakadai starred in his ninth role for Hideo Gosha in *Fireflies in the North* (Kita no hotaru) as Takeshi Tsukigata, the governor of Kabato Prison in Hokkaido in the 1880s. The character was based loosely on the actual governor of the prison during this period, Kiyoshi Tsukigata (1846-94). However, there seems little to suggest that his personality bore much resemblance to the demonic figure portrayed by Nakadai and, in fact, Tsukigata's grandson filed a complaint against the producers for this reason. During the period in which the story is set, Hokkaido lacked infrastructure and the government wished to exploit the island for agriculture and to build defences against Russian expansion. For these reasons, prisoners were brought over by ferry from Honshu and used as slave labour to construct roads. In the film, Tsukigata is ambitious and pushes the inmates so hard that many die as a result of overwork.

Fireflies in the North opens with a scene in which Tsukigata shows off his swordsmanship on horseback, slicing cleanly through multiple targets with little apparent effort and admonishing his men to follow his example, which none are able to do. Shortly after this display, he intervenes in the bungled execution of a prisoner, whom he beheads, causing a huge fountain of blood to gush from the man's severed neck. When a beautiful ex-geisha, Yu (Shima Iwashita), arrives at the prison in the hope of seeing her husband – an inmate – Tsukigata falls in love with her and his personality begins to soften, especially after an assassination attempt leaves him almost blind and, now vulnerable, he has to depend on her for help.

The unusual story and setting of *Fireflies in the North* works in its favour and the role of Tsukigata provides plenty for Nakadai to get his teeth into. However, the film has its flaws, including an incongruous pop ballad which blasts out on the soundtrack halfway through (complete with horribly dated '80s production), an unconvincing attack by an obviously fake bear, and some unfortunate overacting by certain members of the supporting cast. The script also lacks polish and at one point uses a clumsy device to make Tsukigata more sympathetic – with eyes bandaged, Nakadai has to deliver a monologue to no-one, revealing that Tsukigata believes himself to be doing a good deed by building new roads at any cost in order to help the farmers. This rather begs the question of why he seems so concerned with the welfare of farmers and indifferent to the fate of those he is responsible for. At one point, he states that he wishes he could at least provide enough food for the convicts, but on other occasions he treats them with brutality, and no attempt is made to account for these contradictions. Otherwise, the film has plenty to recommend it and, as usual, Gosha – along with *Onimasa* cinematographer Fujio Morita – made it a visual treat, using the wintry Hokkaido locations to full effect and contrasting the almost monochromatic landscapes with bold flashes of colour.[86]

---

[86] Some scenes were also shot in Fukui Prefecture in Honshu.

As with *Onimasa*, *Fireflies in the North* was a co-production between Toei and Haiyuza. The project was apparently initiated by Toei president Shigeru Okada, who had come up with the idea for the film after visiting a prisoners' graveyard in Sapporo. He discussed it with Yu Aku, a writer and lyricist who had also written the lyrics to the main themes for *Belladonna of Sadness* and *Blue Christmas*. Aku came up with the title, suggested a story concerning a woman who 'pursued a man to the end of the earth' and wrote the lyrics to the theme song performed by one of Japan's most popular singers, Shinichi Mori. Aku was given a rare 'supervising producer' credit, although how much input he had in the actual production is open to question. In any case, screenwriter Koji Takada was assigned to write an original script based on his ideas and spent a considerable time in Hokkaido doing research. Once Gosha was brought on board, Okada became concerned that the main theme of the story as he saw it may get lost, and reminded Gosha not to focus too much on the killing, saying, 'The point is to make a great human drama about a woman falling in love with a man like a demon.'[87] However, Gosha may not have paid too much attention, as in the finished film this aspect feels like a sub-plot and the character of Yu is not developed as fully as it might have been. Despite this failing, Shima Iwashita gave her usual committed performance in the role, and Nakadai later said that she had been so convincing in their sex scene together that Gosha asked him afterwards if they had done it for real.

Along with Haiyuza actors like Yoshio Inaba, the film also featured a number of young Mumeijuku graduates, including Daisuke Ryu and Toru Masuoka. Another member of the cast was Koichi Sato, the son of Nakadai's *Harakiri* co-star, Rentaro Mikuni. It also marked the final film credits for *Onimasa*'s Masako Natsume, who provided some opening narration, and character actor Asao Koike. Natsume's battle with leukemia ended in 1985, when she passed away aged just 27. Koike had made his film debut as a soldier in Kurosawa's *Throne of Blood* and provided the Japanese dubbing for Peter Falk's *Columbo*. In

---

[87] *Shigeru Okada's Active Life in the Film World*, Cultural News Agency, 2012, pp. 135-140, ISBN 978-4-636-88519-4, cited on Japanese Wikipedia.

order to appear in *Fireflies*, he had checked himself out of hospital against medical advice, and also passed away in 1985, in his case of lung failure at the age of 54.

Mumeijuku's play for 1984 was a stage version of *Harold and Maude*, an American film from 1971 about an unlikely relationship between a death-obsessed 19-year-old male and a free-spirited 79-year-old female which became something of a cult movie. It was a brave choice as a previous attempt at a stage version on Broadway in 1980 had closed after four performances. Once again, Nakadai did not appear, but in this case he co-directed the production with Kiyoto Hayashi, while Yasuko returned to the stage as Maude and Harold was played by 22-year-old Isao Washu. As a co-director, Nakadai had no need to attend every performance and this helped to keep him free for *Ran*.

Fireflies in the North was yet another film on which production had become delayed. Originally intended to begin shooting in January 1984, it had been postponed until 19 April, which must have put considerable pressure on Nakadai as the new shooting schedule overlapped with that of *Ran*, which was expected to begin production on 15 May, but was delayed further to 2 June and completed in March 1985. [88]

Kurosawa had written the screenplay of *Ran* with Hideo Oguni and Masato Ide in early 1976. The same period had also produced the scripts for *Kagemusha* and an adaptation of Edgar Allan Poe's *The Masque of the Red Death* which might have seen Nakadai in the role of Prospero had it ever been filmed. Of the three, the film Kurosawa most wanted to make was *Ran*, which he saw as his definitive statement on the madness of war and the folly of mankind in general. His vision

---

[88] Many sources give the start date of *Ran* as February 1st 1984, but Kurosawa's lawyer, Jun Norisugi (who also appears in the film as an extra), states on his website (norisugi.com) that shooting began on June 2nd. This seems correct, as it is otherwise difficult to see when Nakadai could have had time to star in *Fireflies in the North*. Furthermore, Mr Norisugi clearly kept records and carefully notes the dates of the events he writes about in relation to *Ran*.

was so ambitious that he used *Kagemusha* (set in the same period) as a trial run for *Ran* and was able to reduce the large budget necessary for the latter film by reusing many props and costumes from the former. Nevertheless, despite the fact that *Kagemusha* had made a tidy profit, Toho refused to finance *Ran* as they felt that the darkness of the material made it too risky a venture, so Kurosawa was once more forced to seek financing abroad. He found it courtesy of producer Serge Silberman, a Polish ex-pat based in Paris whose company Greenwich Film Productions had financed a number of films by Luis Buñuel. Silberman was an Auschwitz survivor who seems to have been sympathetic to Kurosawa's pessimistic vision. However, the relationship between the two men was an uneasy one and, when Silberman was unable to cover the entire budget, additional funding was obtained from the Japanese companies Nippon Herald and Fuji TV, together with a small contribution from Toho, who would act as the film's distributor in Japan.[89]

Kurosawa had not originally intended to make a Japanese version of King Lear, but in the process of writing *Ran*, the idea of using Lear had occurred to him and he began incorporating many elements from Shakespeare's play. Nakadai was cast as Kurosawa's Lear equivalent, the fictional Lord Hidetora Ichimonji. While writing the script, Kurosawa had intended the role for Toshiro Mifune, and Mifune had even tried to attract an American investor to provide part of the budget, but was unsuccessful. However, by the time *Ran* finally went into production, Kurosawa had long since lost interest in working with him again. The main reason for the rift appears to be that Kurosawa felt he had done much to build Mifune up as Japan's foremost film actor only to see him squander his reputation in works of poor quality. According to Donald Richie, Kurosawa told him around this time that he 'wouldn't have anything to do with actors who appeared in the likes

---

[89] For an idea of exactly how uneasy the relationship between Kurosawa and Silberman was, as well as the convoluted nature of the film's financing, see norisugi.com.

of *Shogun*,[90] the 1980 TV mini-series in which Mifune had co-starred with Richard Chamberlain. Kurosawa had actually been approached to direct *Shogun* himself and turned it down, regarding it as trash.

Kurosawa had turned once more to Nakadai, perhaps partly as a reward for having come to his rescue on *Kagemusha*. The director envisioned Hidetora's face as a sort of living Noh mask – not for the first time, as Isuzu Yamada's face had been used in a similar way in *Throne of Blood* (Nakadai, of course, had never performed in the Noh theatre). Nakadai was 51 when shooting began and had to endure three and a half to four hours in the make-up chair each morning to transform him into the 70-year-old Hidetora, complete with added wrinkles, bulging veins and a beard pasted on a whisker at a time. On at least one occasion, when he was informed after make-up had been completed that filming had been cancelled for the day, he tore it from his face in frustration – fortunately, the make-up was much quicker to remove than to apply. Another compensation for this hardship was the fact that he received the highest fee of his career for *Ran*.

At the urging of Kurosawa, Nakadai gave an intentionally theatrical performance, and he used his stage training in movement to excellent effect throughout. At the start of the film, Hidetora is a vigorous septuagenarian who has only just begun to feel the ravages of age and is still capable of killing a wild boar with an arrow while mounted on horseback; Nakadai had developed considerable prowess as an equestrian by this point as a result of buying two former racehorses and training every day for six months. Roughly midway through the film, Hidetora's stronghold is attacked, his retainers slaughtered and the castle set ablaze, triggering Hidetora's madness. Kurosawa had this to say about Nakadai's contribution:

> What I asked of him – and which he accomplished successfully – was the passage from folly to reason. It's very difficult in the same scene to go from one to the other. One of the most difficult scenes was the

[90] *Japanese Portraits* by Donald Richie (Tuttle, 2006), p.68

dungeon scene, where he begins to go mad as burning arrows fly behind him. No other actor could have done that. We shot it in the studio, and it was very intense. It was awfully hot. The crew was drenched. Makeup was streaming. The flames rose as high as the ceiling; the entire room was burning. You'd need to have great mastery of yourself to act as he acted [...][91]

Nakadai then had to emerge from the blazing castle, walking down the steps and through a parting throng of soldiers all the way out of the castle gates. The castle had been specially built in Gotemba on the slopes of Mount Fuji (where *Throne of Blood*'s Cobweb Castle had also stood) at a cost of $1.5 million only to be destroyed by fire in this pivotal scene. One mistake on Nakadai's part could have been disastrous. Concerned about emerging too quickly, he waited until the last possible moment to the point where Kurosawa became worried about his safety. Nakadai's beard was singed, leaving him with a blistered face which led to the postponement of the following day's shooting. Although the steps he had to walk down were extremely steep, he had been unable to look downwards to watch his step as Hidetora was supposed to be in a stupor, while the walk to the castle gates was also a long one. As only one take was possible, Kurosawa had no less than eight cameras covering the scene. Fortunately, Nakadai achieved it perfectly and the scene became one of the most impressive spectacles in cinema history achieved without the aid of special effects.

From this point on, Hidetora is a much more vulnerable character who flits between lucidity and madness, and his increased frailty is achieved partly by additions to the make-up, but also by Nakadai's mastery of posture and gesture. Although Donald Richie was correct when he said that Hidetora 'becomes a visible idea rather than a

---

[91] Akira Kurosawa interviewed by Kiyoshi Watanabe for the magazine *Positif*. Published in October 1985 and translated from French by Dorna Khazeni. Cited in the booklet accompanying the 2005 Criterion DVD of *Ran*.

believable person',[92] Nakadai embodies this idea perfectly. Furthermore, the overall approach of the film makes it clear that Kurosawa was not aiming for naturalism on any level, but was instead concerned with pursuing the kind of artistic vision which could only have come from a director who saw the world with the eye of a painter. This vision had, of course, been deeply thought out over a period of many years, and Kurosawa had painted many images of the scenes prior to production, just as he had done for *Kagemusha*. Even so, there remains one issue concerning Hidetora that Kurosawa failed to fully address – given that all we hear of the character's history relates to his merciless pursuit of power, why is it that Tango, Kyoami and Saburo are so devoted to him? Although he saves Kyoami's kife at one point with a well-aimed arrow and claims to have spoiled Saburo as a child, we mostly see him treating them (and others) with little consideration.

Saburo, Hidetora's youngest son and the equivalent to *King Lear*'s Coredelia, was played by Daisuke Ryu, while a number of other actors from *Kagemusha* were also given roles, including Jinpachi Nezu, who played the middle son, Jiro. In the role of the vengeful Lady Kaede, Kurosawa cast Mieko Harada as a result of seeing her extraordinary force-of-nature performance in Yasuzo Masumura's 1976 film *Lullaby of the Earth* (Daichi no komoriuta), for which the then-17-year-old had deservedly won a slew of awards. The scene in which Kaede attacks Jiro remains one of the most spectacular examples of physical acting ever captured on film. Also memorable was the portrayal of Kyoami, the fool, by the female impersonator known simply as 'Peter' – a surprising piece of casting by Kurosawa which succeeds brilliantly as Peter proves able to switch from mischievous capering to vindictiveness to self-pity with equal facility. Nakadai's former Haiyuza colleague Hisashi Igawa was also highly effective as Jiro's right-hand man, Shuri Kurogane, in a part originally intended for Ken Takakura, who had been unable to accept due to a prior commitment.

---

[92] *The Films of Akira Kurosawa* (Third Ed.) by Donald Richie (University of California Press, 1996), p.217

When *Ran* was released, it was widely seen around the world and greeted with tremendous enthusiasm by the majority of critics, although there were a few naysayers. While it won numerous awards, mainly for Best Film, Kurosawa as director, and visual elements such as cinematography and costume design, Nakadai was not even nominated. One wonders if giving such as stylized performance in heavy make-up even damaged his career somehow, as good film roles would prove to be thin on the ground for the next few years. However, *Ran* has endured as one of the great classics of cinema and rightly remains one of the films for which Nakadai is best-known.

Chapter 25 – Pedigree Chums

Nakadai followed *Ran* with a leading role for another grand master, Masaki Kobayashi – their first collaboration since *Inn of Evil* in 1971. Based on an untranslated 1979 novel of the same name by Fumiko Enchi (who co-wrote the screenplay with Kobayashi), *The Empty Table* (Shokutaku no nai ie) would become the director's final work for the cinema. In the intervening years, Kobayashi had struggled to find financing and completed only three films. The first of these, *The Fossil* (Kaseki, 1974), was a long film about an ageing businessman (Shin Saburi) who receives a cancer diagnosis. The second, *Glowing Autumn* (Moeru aki, 1978), again featured Shin Saburi, this time as an ageing artist with cancer whose mistress (Kyoko Maya) has an obsession with Persian carpets which takes her to Iran, where much of the film was shot.[93] This was followed by *Tokyo Trial* (Tokyo saiban, 1983), a four-and-a-half-hour documentary about the trials of Japanese accused of war crimes after the Second World War.

In *The Empty Table*, Nakadai starred as Nobuyuki Kidoji, an electronics expert whose son, Otohiko (Kiichi Nakai), is in prison as a result of his participation in a radical group known as the Red Star Army. The group are responsible for having taken hostages at a mountain inn, then brutally killing several members of their own organization for 'wrong thinking', after which a ten-day siege ensued, involving thousands of police and televised across the country, before the remaining members finally surrendered. This is based very closely on a real event involving the United Red Army. According to Nagisa Oshima in the documentary *100 Years of Japanese Film*, 'Coverage of the group holding off police in their mountain hide-out gained the highest rating in the history of Japanese television.' Known as the Asama-Sanso incident, it took place in 1972, and the film even appears to have

---

[93] As a result of a legal dispute, *Glowing Autumn* has fallen into obscurity, but is occasionally screened at repertory cinemas in Japan.

used some of the original TV news footage, although the characters in *The Empty Table* are fictional. In the film, Otohiko is portrayed as a naïve innocent who got mixed up with the wrong crowd and has no direct responsibility for the deaths that occurred, although his presence at the inn is in itself enough to see him imprisoned. However, there is little doubt that the five United Red Army members who surrendered in the real life incident were all guilty of torture and murder.

While the parents of the other radicals attempt to atone for the sins of their children by resigning from their jobs or even committing suicide, Nobuyuki refuses to follow suit and determines to remain strong for the sake of his wife and other children. Unfortunately, his stoicism is perceived as coldness, and his daughter, Tamae, turns against him, marries behind his back and goes off to America (Tamae is played by Kiichi Nakai's real life sister, Kie Nakai; their father was film star Keiji Sada, who had appeared with Nakadai in *The Human Condition* and *Bitter Spirit* and played the lead in *As the Clouds Scatter*; Sada had also starred in a number of other Kobayashi films before his untimely death in 1964). Meanwhile, unable to cope with the shame, ostracism, constant death threats and bricks through the windows, Nobuyuki's wife, Yumiko (Mayumi Ogawa), goes insane. In a shocking scene, he catches her eating one of her son's pet goldfish alive, then vomiting into the fish tank, after which he has no choice but to have her committed. The family dining table around which parents and children once gathered is now conspicuously empty.

While Yumiko is in hospital, Noboyuki grows closer to his wife's sister, Kiwa (Shima Iwashita), who admires his strength in adversity, although Nobuyuki himself has come to believe that he has done more harm than good by repressing his feelings. When Yumiko commits suicide, he finally allows himself to cry; later, when he realises he may never see Otohiko again, he breaks down completely. Along the way, others try to help, including Nobuyuki's lawyer friend Kawabe (Mikijiro Hira) and Kanae (Azusa Mano) a young woman studying Buddhism who becomes interested in Nobuyuki.

MARTIN DOWSING

The Empty Table

If *The Empty Table* had been produced by a regular film company, it would probably not be languishing in the obscurity it is today. Produced by the Marugen Building Group (in association with Haiyuza), the original negative is reputedly lost, while it is also unclear who owns the copyright. At the time of writing, the film can only be viewed in the West via poor quality bootleg copies made from a videotaped television broadcast, and this situation looks unlikely to change anytime soon. This is a shame because, although Kobayashi was working on a smaller scale than in his heyday and *The Empty Table* at times has the feel of a filmed play, it is nevertheless a very well-made and acted film of considerable depth. On the other hand, the themes of death, violence, madness, loss and guilt do not make for a comfortable watch; unsurprisingly, it was a box office failure, and it seems doubtful whether a re-release could have much chance of commercial success.

Nakadai gives a necessarily restrained performance as the stoical Nobuyuki, and this makes it all the more moving when the character's emotions finally begin to spill out. In her only film appearance with Nakadai, Mayumi Ogawa is equally impressive as his wife, especially in the goldfish scene, in which she appears to cram a live fish into her mouth for real. Alongside a number of Haiyuza actors in the cast, Mumeijuku's Shinji Ogawa, Daisuke Ryu and Toru Masuoka were also featured. The film is notable, too, for the music of Toru Takemitsu, who won the 1985 Japanese Academy Award for Best Score for his work on *The Empty Table*, *Ran* and Mitsuo Yanagimachi's *Himatsuri*, but it was perhaps understandably overshadowed at international competitions by the Kurosawa film.

Back on stage for the first time since 1982, Nakadai's play for 1985 was a revival of *The Lower Depths* directed by Yasuko in which he again played Satin, with Kei Yamamoto as Luka.

In *The Atami Murder Case* (Atami satsujin jiken), a film version of a comic mystery play first performed in 1973, Nakadai played the lead role of a detective investigating the case of a man who appears to have strangled his oldest friend. Unfortunately, what had been a popular item in the theatre appears to have fallen flat as a movie, perhaps because it was made by a director with no previous film experience.

The Atami Murder Case

Nakadai's next film, *Michi* ('Road'), was based on a 1949 novel by the French writer Serge Groussard about the struggles of two ordinary working class people who fall in love. Entitled *Des Gens sans Importance* ('People of No Importance'), it had been filmed once before, with Jean Gabin in 1956. Originally planned for Ken Takakura, by the time the film was ready to go into production, Takakura had become too expensive and Nakadai took over. Gabin was a favourite of Nakadai's and it is likely that he had seen the French version. However, he seems unlikely casting for the part of Seiji Tajima, a long-distance truck driver who gets involved with a much younger waitress, Kazue (Miwako Fujitani).

Kazue impulsively decides to quit her job at 'Sakura', a diner near Yonago City in Tottori Prefecture (north-west of Osaka) and catches a ride with Seiji, who is unhappily married. By the time they reach Tokyo, the two have fallen in love. Kazue finds employment at a hotel, but Seiji, who lives in Urayasu in Chiba Prefecture to the east of Tokyo and also has a daughter, soon decides he must end the relationship and reluctantly bids her farewell. Kazue returns to 'Sakura', but then discovers she is pregnant with Seiji's child. The owner of the restaurant, also called Sakura, is a friend of Seiji's, and writes to tell him of Kazue's condition, but the letter is opened by Seiji's daughter, who hides it, but later reads it aloud to her mother in order to get back at her father for a scolding she received. Seiji leaves and heads for 'Sakura' by truck, but has an accident en route. Meanwhile, Kazue is having a difficult labour and dies from severe bleeding.

Nakadai reportedly had a difficult time with co-star Miwako Fujitani, who was prone to emotional outbursts which interrupted the shooting. In fact, she had just been fired by director Yoji Yamada from his film *Final Take* (Kinema no tenchi) for that very reason. However, it should be noted that Fujitani was a talented actress who later won two major awards in 1993 for her performances in Hideo Gosha's *Oil Hell Murder* (Onna goroshi abura no jigoku) and Koji Wakamatsu's *Sosuke Loses his Lover* (Netorare Sosuke). In 2003, she caused headlines when she took a taxi to the Imperial Palace and attempted to gain admission by informing a guard that she was the sister of Princess Nori (not true) and wished to deliver a letter to her. Fujitani was refused entry and placed on the counter-terrorism list of people to be monitored, suggesting that her difficult behaviour may have been caused by an illness that was not understood. Presumably as a result of the incident, her career came to an abrupt halt at around this time.

Tajima's wife was played by Junko Icheuki, who had twice appeared opposite Nakadai over 20 years earlier, in both *Miren* and *Illusion of Blood*, while Sakura was played by Tomisaburo Wakayama. The director was Koreyoshi Kurahara, with whom Nakadai had worked on *Safari 5000*, and who enjoyed a somewhat schizophrenic career. Partly as a result of *Safari 5000*, Kurahara had developed a reputation for being good at location work, and gone on to make a couple of semi-documentary features about animals, the success of which had in turn led to him directing the big budget 1983 feature *Antarctica* (Nankyoku monogatari). For a time, *Antarctica* held the Japanese box office record for a domestic film, so it was surprising to see him overseeing such a small-scale drama as *Michi* a mere three years later. Ironically, the star of *Antarctica* was Ken Takakura and it was the success of that film which had increased his price and prevented him from being cast as Seiji Tajima. *Michi* was a modest success at the box office and received a Japanese VHS release in the late '80s, but has seldom been seen since and was not released in the West.

Nakadai's play for 1986 was *Poor Murderer* by the Czech writer Pavel Kohout, in which he starred as Anton Ignatyevich Kerzhentsev, an actor who has been playing Hamlet and come to believe that he has killed Polonius for real. Set in a St. Petersburg asylum in 1900, the original production had opened to positive reviews on Broadway in 1976 and enjoyed a successful run, but the play seems largely forgotten today. As usual, the Mumeijuku production was directed by Yasuko.

Hachiko was based on a true story about a male dog (an Akita called Hachiko) which goes to meet its master every day on his way home from work at Shibuya station in Tokyo. The dog's master is a university professor, Shujiro Ueno (Nakadai). When he dies suddenly,

Hachiko continues to wait for him at Shibuya station every day for nine years, before dying himself in 1935. The story remains famous in Japan to this day, and the statue of Hachiko outside Shibuya station has been a popular meeting point ever since it was erected. The narrative presented in the film appears to be fairly close to the reality – Ueno's sudden death in the middle of a lecture actually occurred, and the scene is shot and acted with admirable restraint. However, certain facts were changed to make the film more palatable for a family audience, and Ueno's younger girlfriend becomes his wife of a similar age in the film.

Although his character dies just over halfway through, Nakadai had the leading human part as the professor who even starts to neglect his wife and child due to his love for a dog. Nakadai had nothing too challenging to do as Ueno, but is very likeable in the part, which he plays as light comedy – the sad part of the story does not begin until after Ueno's death. In fact, the film unfolds exactly like a tragic love story except for the minor variation that one of the lovers happens to be canine. Having said that, Hachiko was not just any canine, as there were said to have been only 30 purebred Akitas in Japan at the time, hence the rather complex route by which Ueno acquires the dog, which arrives at his residence after a two-day train journey.

The film itself also boasted an impressive pedigree – the screenwriter was none other than Kaneto Shindo while the director, Seijiro Koyama, though less well-known, crafted the film with care, and Nakadai went on to make a further two films for him. The professor's wife was played by Kaoru Yachigusa, who had also appeared as the wife of Nakadai's character in *The Barren Zone*, and would do so again on several future occasions.

Nakadai was wary of dogs as he had been bitten on his right cheek by one during his first year at junior high school. At first, 'Hachiko' ignored Nakadai, so he took the advice of a dog trainer to get down on his hands and knees and play with the dog in order to make friends.

This strategy worked and Nakadai not only fell in love with his co-star for real, but overcame his fear of dogs in general.[94]

Hachiko is a very well-made film, and the Japan of the 1920s and '30s was recreated in considerable detail, suggesting not only that the production had a substantial budget, but that Shochiku had known they were on to a winner. Indeed, the film became the number one box office hit of 1987 in Japan, raking in a staggering 2 billion yen, and also doing good business in many territories abroad, so it was probably the most commercially successful film Nakadai ever appeared in. The inevitable Hollywood remake finally arrived in 2009 under the title *Hachi: A Dog's Tale* and starred Richard Gere.

The same year, Nakadai appeared in a one-scene cameo towards the end of *Trinacria Porsche 959*, a full-length TV movie designed to promote Porsche's latest model. The film featured endless driving scenes and a threadbare plot involving the hero searching for Nakadai's character, a legendary musician who has gone into hiding and is finally found in a church. This was followed by an assignment as narrator of Kihachi Okamoto's samurai mini-series *Taikoki*, while Nakadai's play for 1987 was *Lupin*, in which he played the gentleman thief and master of disguise, Arsène Lupin. Created by Maurice Leblanc in 1905, the character has been the inspiration for countless films and plays ever since, including a long-running manga series. *Lupin* was written and directed by Yasuko (as Tomoe Ryu) for Mumeijuku.

---

[94] https://2015.kiff.kyoto.jp/en/news/detail/40

Chapter 26 – The Small Screen Beckons

In 1988, Nakadai appeared in a 2-hour Fuji TV version of *Straits of Hunger* (Kiga kaikyo), a novel by Tsutomu Minakami which had previously been filmed by director Tomu Uchida in 1965 in a version also known in the West as *A Fugitive from the Past*. Nakadai played Yumizaka, the detective portrayed by Junzaburo Ban in what is arguably Uchida's finest film.[95] Yumizaka is no super-sleuth in either version, frequently managing to just miss the man he is pursuing, whom he suspects of multiple homicide. Nakadai portrayed him as slow-thinking, but possessing a dogged determination and given to occasional bursts of insight. The role was beefed up for the TV adaptation, in which Yumizaka is even seen working as a kendo teacher after leaving the police force. Yumizaka's quarry, Inugai – memorably played by Rentaro Mikuni in the original – is here portrayed by Kenichi Hagiwara, a singer and actor who had played leads in films such as Kon Ichikawa's *The Wanderers* (Matatabi, 1973), Masahiro Shinoda's *The Petrified Forest* (Kaseki no mori, 1973) and Tatsumi Kumashiro's *Bitterness of Youth* (Seishun no satetsu, 1974), as well as the son of Shingen Takeda (Nakadai) in *Kagemusha*. Hagiwara's career would come to an abrupt end in 2004 when he was fired from a film for abusive behaviour towards co-star Kumiko Akiyoshi. In response, he threatened to set his *yakuza* friends on the producers if they failed to pay his full ¥18 million fee. He was convicted of blackmail as a result. The other main role was played by newcomer and Mumeijuku student Mayumi Wakamura, appearing as the prostitute who shelters Inugai and is Yumizaka's only lead. Wakamura had joined Mumeijuku after being impressed with the company's production of *Harold and Maude*, which she had seen while still at high school. In 1987, she had won the lead role in a TV drama entitled *Hassai-sensei* after being selected from

---

[95] There had also been TV versions in 1968 and 1978 starring, respectively, Jukichi Uno and Tomisaburo Wakayama as the detective.

over 700 applicants, and she would go on to act opposite Nakadai in several films to come. Although *Straits of Hunger* was an above-average TV drama for its time and won a domestic broadcasting award, it cannot compare with the greatness of Uchida's original.

In the same year, Nakadai also contributed a supporting role to *Oracion* (Yushun), a film about a horse named Oracion ('prayer') which is born on a small farm in Hokkaido and goes on to become a racehorse, eventually competing in the Japanese Derby. Nakadai played the father of the girl who owns the horse. Based on a recent literary prize-winning novel by Teru Miyamoto, it was probably intended to capitalise on the vogue for animal films sparked by *Antarctica* and *Hachiko*, and was directed by Shigemichi Sugita, with whom Nakadai would work again. Following this, he appeared in *Another Way*, a Second World War drama based on a novel which provided Nakadai's Mumeijuku student Koji Yakusho with his first starring role in a movie. Yakusho played a naval commander who, during the last days of the war, is sent on a secret mission to Switzerland via submarine in order to purchase the uranium necessary to make a nuclear bomb. However, he ends up being persuaded to try and find a way to make peace with the United States instead. Appropriately enough, Nakadai played his boss, while the main foreign characters were portrayed by Udo Kier and Robert Vaughn. The director was Kosaku Yamashita, best known for minor *yakuza* classics such as *Red Peony Gambler* (Hibotan bakuto) and *Big Time Gambling Boss* (Bakuchi-uchi: socho tobaku), the latter a favourite of Yukio Mishima, who thought it akin to a Greek tragedy. Both *Oracion* and *Another Way* are now forgotten and have disappeared into obscurity, but *Oracion* must have been well-received at the time as it was nominated for various Japanese cinema awards, several of which it won.

Nakadai then accepted the role of Major Harada in *Return from the River Kwai*, a routine WW2 film which was not, as its title suggested, a sequel to the classic *Bridge on the River Kwai*. Towards the end of the war, Harada arrives at a PoW camp in Burma with orders to transport the prisoners to Japan. Unfortunately, the camp commandant, Lieutenant

Tanaka (*Star Trek*'s George Takei), is a brutal sadist who resents Harada's more humane approach. It emerges that Harada once lived in England and has a positive view of the British, but he is also a secret drinker – a flaw which undermines his authority but is never explained. This is perhaps unsurprising as the film hardly seems to be one in which the writers took pains over such details of character. Indeed, the role of Harada is one which could have been made much more interesting in a better film, but Nakadai's talents are wasted in *Return from the River Kwai*. It was only his second film outside Japan, and shooting took place in a variety of locations in Malaysia, the Philippines and Thailand. Other Japanese officers were played by Etsushi Takahashi (who had co-starred with Nakadai in *Kill!* and a number of other films) and Masato Nagamori, one of Nakadai's Mumeijuku students. The film is the only one in Nakadai's career for which he was called upon to speak English throughout, and the fact that he delivers his dialogue rather awkwardly would have suited the character if the writers had not decided to make him a former resident of England. However, at least Nakadai's lack of English probably prevented him from realising quite how poor the script was.

Andrew V. McLaglen, a specialist in routine war movies and westerns, directed the picture, which also starred Edward Fox, Chris Penn, Timothy Bottoms and Denholm Elliott (as surely the oldest colonel in the British army). It was released in the UK the following year to hostile reviews and went entirely unreleased in America.

Nakadai's play of the year for 1988 was not the most obvious choice – he took on the challenge of playing a woman for the first time in the title role of Bertolt Brecht's classic anti-war play *Mother Courage and Her Children*. As usual, the production was directed by Yasuko (as Tomoe Ryu) for Mumeijuku. There seems to have been no precedent for the role being played by a man – indeed, Yasuko had originally intended to cast a female. However, thinking that German women were usually on the large side, she had been seeking a suitably large Japanese actress; unable to find one ample enough, she decided to cast her husband (much to his surprise).

Nakadai then starred in a two-hour Fuji TV special, *Rest in Peace, My Friend* (Tomoyo, shizuka ni tsumure) based on a novel by Kenzo Kitakata previously filmed in 1985 by Yoichi Sai with Tatsuya Fuji. Nakadai played Shindo, a disgraced doctor who arrives in a small coastal town to help his old friend, an innkeeper who is in prison after refusing to sell out to the local bigshot.

Film work seems to have been scarce around this time, but Nakadai still had to find money to keep Mumeijuku going, which is perhaps why he allowed himself to appear looking rather foolish dancing and singing on a hilltop for a commercial advertising Citizen Watches. He made a more dignified appearance in Hideo Gosha's *Four Days of Snow and Blood* (aka *226*) as General Sugiyama (1880-1945), to whom he bore little resemblance. Gosha's film was uncharacteristically sober, with nary a catfight or bare breast to be seen, and provided a sympathetic portrayal of the army rebels who had attempted to overthrow the government on 26 February 1936. The rebels are motivated by their belief that the Prime Minister and his cronies have prevented the Emperor from realizing the extent of the hardship suffered by the majority of his subjects. One of the main roles was played by Kenichi Hagiwara from the TV version of *Straits of Hunger*, while Tetsuro Tanba, Daisuke Ryu and veteran actresses Mieko Takamine, Yoshiko Kuga and Kaoru Yachigusa also popped up in this stately-paced film. Beautifully shot as one would expect from Gosha, it was an impressive piece of work, but Nakadai's role was a tiny one obviously done as a favour to the director.

In 1990, Nakadai worked mainly in television, first starring in Fuji TV's 90-minute remake of Eiichi Kudo's 1963 samurai classic *Thirteen Assassins* (Jusan-nin no shikaku) as Shinzaemon, the character played by Chiezo Kataoka in the original film. Next up was *Letters of a Businessman to His Son*, an NHK series based on a non-fiction book of the same name by a Canadian, G. Kingsley Ward. The author (played by Nakadai) was a businessman who had written a series of long letters to his son following a heart attack in case he missed the opportunity to tell him everything he wanted before he died. The book had been popular in translation around the world, but especially so in Japan, and this appears to have been the only filmed version. It was followed by *Araki Mataemon: Battle of Kagiya no Tsuji*, a three-hour NHK special based on a novel by Shin Hasegawa which was in turn based on a true incident that occurred in 1634. Nakadai starred as Mataemon Araki (1599-1638), a skilled swordsman who helps his brother-in-law avenge his brother's death by ambushing the man who killed him, along with his party of retainers. Legend has it that 36 people died in the attack, most of them slain by Araki. In reality, only two lost their lives, one of whom was Araki's best friend, Jinzaemon Kawai, who happened to be on the opposing side. Kawai was played by Nakadai's old friend and fellow Haiyuza student, Ken Utsui. The story had also been the basis of the 1952 film *Vendetta of a Samurai* (Araki Mataemon: Ketto kagiya no tsuji), scripted by Akira Kurosawa and starring Toshiro Mifune as Araki and Takashi Shimura as Kawai. Nakadai's fourth TV drama in a row was *Battleship Yamato* (Senkan Yamato), a two-and-a-half hour special for Fuji TV directed by Kon Ichikawa. The Yamato had been Japan's biggest battleship until it was sunk by the Americans at the end of the Second World War while attempting to defend Okinawa. Almost the whole crew died as a result, and the tragedy became hugely symbolic in Japan and the basis for many books and films. Nakadai played Admiral Seiichi Ito (1890-1945), who chose to go down with the ship.

After this extended stint in television, Nakadai returned to the stage for Mumeijuku's production of *Cyrano de Bergerac*, in which he played the title role under the direction of his wife. The large fake nose he wore for the part rendered him virtually unrecognizable. This was followed by an uncredited cameo in the film *Embrace the Wind of Florence* (Firenze no kaze ni dakarete, aka *Florence My Love*), presumably done as a favour to former Mumeijuku student Mayumi Wakamura, who had the starring role.

More notable was Nakadai's final film for Hideo Gosha, *Heat Wave* (Kagero), in which he played the apparent villain of the piece, Tsunejiro 'the Immoveable', a *yakuza* with full-body tattoo who kills a gambler in front of his young daughter for refusing to pay his debts. The girl, Rin, is adopted by a well-to-do family who own a restaurant, but her father's past comes back to haunt her as a teenager and she leaves home. Rin (played as an adult by Kanako Higuchi) becomes a *yakuza* with some impressive tattoos of her own, and also an expert gambler. Unaware of the history between Rin and Tsunejiro, her boss nominates her to represent his gang in a gambling competition against his rivals, who are represented by Tsunejiro. The two should be arch-enemies but, to Rin's surprise, Tsunejiro seems keen to sabotage himself and begins to give her advice on how he might be defeated.

Nakadai used his famous eyes to unnerving effect in *Heat Wave*, but Gosha first recycled an old trick from *Kumokiri Nizaemon*, introducing him around ten minutes in, when we hear that unmistakably deep and resonant voice (in this sequence his character's face is concealed and Murai is actually played by a younger actor). Nakadai himself appears on screen 20 minutes in, after Rin has grown into a beautiful woman, and his character lives up to his nickname by barely bothering to respond when spoken to. Although Nakadai had some embarrassingly poor dialogue to deliver, his character at least has two dimensions and it helped that he played the part in a very low-key fashion. In fact, the script by prolific *yakuza* specialist Koji Takada (co-writer of *Onimasa*) is a bit of a mess, but the film looks so good and the actors play it so straight that it is easy not to notice. Kanako Higuchi gave a fine performance in a role she was perhaps not best-suited to – she seems rather too elegant and fragile to convince as a tough *yakuza* lady, although this does help to justify how easily Rin has most of the male characters eating out of her hand.

Gosha was battling cancer during the making of *Heat Wave*, and Nakadai later said that he had lacked his former energy. Nevertheless, the film is very well-made, and Gosha kept things interesting in typically shameless fashion with a gratuitous lesbian sex scene, his obligatory cat-fight, and a climax that was both bloody and fiery. Tetsuro Tanba and Ken Ogata also dropped by to contribute brief cameos. After making one further film, Gosha passed away the following year at the age of 63. *Kagero* was a commercial success and spawned a sequel some five years later, albeit one featuring neither Higuchi nor Nakadai.

Chapter 27 – From the Sublime to the Ridiculous

Nakadai's Mumeijuku play for 1990 was a revival of *Miss Julie* directed by his wife, in which he played Jean for the third time – a role he was by now becoming a little old for, as the character is usually portrayed as a man in his 20s. Mai Okamoto played Julie. He then donned a top-knot wig to play Oishi Kuranosuke (1659-1703), the leader of the 'loyal 47 *ronin*', in *Chushingura*, Fuji TV's three-and-a-half hour dramatisation of the oft-told incident in which a group of samurai banded together to avenge their late lord, whom they believed had been wrongfully sentenced to commit seppuku. The programme was broadcast on Nakadai's 59th birthday.

Nakadai was next reunited with director Hiroshi Teshigahara for the first time since *The Face of Another* (1966), although on this occasion the material was far more traditional in nature. *Go Hime* ('Princess Go'/*Basara the Princess Goh*), a historical drama based on a novel by Masaharo Fuji, is the sequel to the earlier *Rikyu* (1989), which had marked Teshigahara's return to feature films after a 17-year absence. This hiatus had been due partly to the failure of his 1972 film *Summer Soldiers*, and partly to Teshigahara's decision to take over the *ikebana* school founded by his father, Sofu, who had died in 1979, closely followed by Teshigahara's sister in 1980. Despite Teshigahara's earlier lack of interest in the art, his sense of filial responsibility had won the day and he had himself become an *ikebana* master, bringing an avant-garde approach to this traditional art. Examples of Teshigahara's *ikebana* creations can be seen in both *Rikyu* and *Go Hime*, frequently serving as transition points between scenes.

The story is set around the turn of the 16th-century. Nakadai was cast as Furuta Oribe (1544-1615), a nobleman given the position of tea master after the death of Sen no Rikyu (the leading character in Teshigahara's previous film). Oribe was said to have been uninterested in the tea ceremony when young, and in the film he becomes dedicated to the way of tea after the death of Rikyu. 'Tea' is in many ways a substitute for 'ikebana' as Teshigahara identified with Oribe, while Rikyu represented his father, Sofu. Indeed, Teshigahara wrote a book entitled *Furuta Oribe – I Saw the Avant-Garde in a Momoyama Bowl*, which was published to coincide with the release of *Go Hime* and concerns the influence of Oribe on Teshigahara's art. In 1980, the director had come across a bowl made by Oribe during the Momoyama period (1568-1600) and been struck by how similar it was to a piece of modern avant-garde art, subsequently taking up ceramics himself, which is also reflected in the film. Nakadai, then, was not so much playing the part of Oribe as he was the role of Hiroshi Teshigahara.

In *Go Hime*, Oribe's promotion comes courtesy of Hideyoshi Toyotomi (then *shogun* in all but name), who privately disagrees with the feudal system of which he is very much a part. Japan is undergoing changes during this period, and calls for reform of the feudal system are just beginning to be heard, while Christianity is also gaining an increasing foothold in the country. Oribe has sympathies for both developments. These sympathies will eventually bring about his downfall, but not before he finally allows himself to show anger and rebels. However, his final act proves to be a futile gesture as it is hushed up by those in power.

Oribe is a man of divided loyalties who is secretly in love with his tomboyish 'niece', Hideyoshi's adopted daughter, the Princess Go (1574-1634). Nakadai gives a restrained performance, expressing his character's inner conflict with the kind of subtlety which only a truly confident actor can achieve. When Oribe first hears that the princess loves his servant, Uso, he is visibly shaken; then, tending to Uso's wounds after he is attacked in the snow, she says, 'Calm your heart or it will bleed more... I know it hurts.' These words are addressed to Uso, but the camera's focus on Oribe makes it clear that he is the one whose heart is suffering. Rie Miyazawa is striking as the princess who goes from boyish teenager to dignified aristocrat in exile in a story which features a jump of around 20 years. Miyazawa was a controversial figure at this point as she had originally become known for playing wholesome young girls, but had just appeared in a book of nude photographs, creating something of a scandal. During the shooting of a scene featuring Nakadai and Miyazawa on horseback, Miyazawa fell off her horse. When Teshigahara saw that she was in tears, he suggested they stop filming for the day, but Nakadai objected, arguing that it would be better for her to conquer her fear by getting back on the horse as soon as possible. Miyazawa agreed to give it another try, and the scene went off successfully on the second attempt, leading Nakadai to feel that she had the qualities to develop into a fine actress.

Admirers of Teshigahara's '60s collaborations with Kobo Abe will find few points of comparison with his earlier work, but the film is nevertheless extremely well-made and speaks for the versatility of Teshigahara as a director. The painterly compositions of the cinematography are especially noteworthy – unsurprising, perhaps, considering his background. The cast are uniformly good, with only Paris-based international actor Katsuhiro Oida (as the tyrannical lord Hideyoshi Toyotomi) acting in a somewhat broad fashion. However, it should be noted that Oida had the difficult task of taking over the character from Tsutomu Yamazaki, who had played him in equally broad fashion in *Rikyu*, and whom Teshigahara had for some reason not hired for the sequel. Strangely, the director did re-hire Rentaro Mikuni, who had played *Rikyu*, even though the character is already dead by the time the sequel begins. In *Go Hime*, Mikuni plays Junsai, an old hermit who lives in the woods and saves the life of Oribe's servant, Usu. Another actor from *Rikyu*, Hisashi Igawa, also reappears in a new role, on this occasion playing the important part of Ieyasu Tokugawa – an unusual one for him, as Igawa was rarely cast as members of the nobility.

Go Hime is a rare example of a sequel which is superior to its predecessor. The events in the 135-minute *Rikyu* revolve around a rather reserved character and virtually all take place indoors; the result is a staid drama which largely fails to engage. *Go Hime*, on the other hand, features many exterior scenes shot on location and a variety of interesting characters, meaning that the even longer running time of 142 minutes seems to fly by in comparison. After the film's completion, Teshigahara – who was 64 when he began shooting *Go Hime* – seems to have become preoccupied with non-cinema projects once more and made no further films. He passed away in 2001 aged 74.

Nakadai's next film work was a supporting role in *Faraway Sunset* (Toki rakujitsu), a biopic of Hideyo Noguchi (1876-1928), a scientist who made important breakthroughs in research on syphilis. Based on a book of the same title by Junichi Watanabe, as well as another entitled *Noguchi's Mother-The Story of Hideyo Noguchi* by Kaneto Shindo, it had a screenplay by the latter and direction by Seijiro Koyama, the same team responsible for *Hachiko*. Noguchi was portrayed as an adult by Hiroshi Mikami, while Nakadai played his elementary school teacher. He followed this with the lead role in a samurai drama, *Kazaguruma no Hamakichi Torimono Tsudozuri*,[96] a TV series comprised of six 50-minute episodes based on a book by Keiichi Ito, who had also written the story upon which *Fort Graveyard* was based.

In 1992, Nakadai made his third non-Japanese film. On this occasion, he went to Hong Kong to appear in *Wicked City* (Yia sau dou si), a special effects laden science fiction movie based on a Japanese novel, which had previously been filmed in animated form in 1987. *Wicked City* could well be the most bizarre item in Nakadai's filmography, and one wonders if he had known what he was himself getting into. The visual style is all whacky camera angles and blue filters, and the plot is utterly incomprehensible. However, it seems to concern a kind of undercover cop whose job it is to expose 'reptoids' – intelligent, shape-shifting, reptilian creatures with the ability to take on human form and defy gravity, among other powers. Nakadai played the head reptoid, which involved appearing in four different make-up designs. As he spoke no Chinese, he was dubbed in all versions of the film. Perhaps copying the Hollywood tradition of casting British actors as villains, in the English language version, he was dubbed by an

---

[96] The author was unable to come up with a satisfactory translation of this title, although 'Hamakichi' is the name of the character portrayed by Nakadai, and 'kazaguruma' means 'windmill'.

anonymous British actor, whereas the Chinese actors are all dubbed with American accents. In one memorable scene, finding himself trapped inside a sexy female elevator, Nakadai gleefully dismantles her from the inside and turns her into a motorbike with which he makes his escape – a scene which makes about as much sense as anything else in *Wicked City*.

Also in 1992, Nakadai co-directed a revival of *Harold and Maude* with Kiyoto Hayashi for Mumeijuku, with Yasuko again playing Maude and Minoru Tanaka as Harold. He also received a French cultural award for his contributions to the arts, earning him the title Chevalier De L'Ordre des Arts et des Lettres.

Although its English title makes it sound like a sequel, *Lone Wolf and Cub: Final Conflict*[97] was in fact a one-off film based on the popular manga series by Kazuo Koike and Goseki Kojima which had provided the basis for a number of highly popular films of the '70s. These had starred Tomisaburo Wakayama as Ogami Itto, a samurai unjustly accused of a crime, who embarks on a bloody one-man battle against his accusers, the Yagyu clan, after they murder his wife. Wakayama had died shortly before the new film went into production in 1992. The original series of films had ended in 1974, although the 1980 film *Shogun Assassin* was a re-edit of the first two. There had also been a TV version starring Kinnosuke Nakamura which ran from 1973-76 and was itself re-edited into a number of movies for home video in the mid-'80s.

For the new film, director Akira Inoue took a radically different approach, downplaying the action and making both Itto and his nemesis, Yagyu Retsudo, considerably more sympathetic. In Inoue's film, both are reluctant killers forced into taking the lives of others by the vicissitudes of fate. As Retsudo, Nakadai had a sizeable role and yet another climactic duel to fight with the hero at the end. On this occasion, the duel is reminiscent of the one in *Sasaki Kojiro*, taking place

---

[97] The Japanese title *Kozure Okami sono chisaki te ni* translates as something like 'Lone Wolf with a Small Child in His Arms'.

as it does on a beach, with the waves gently lapping at the feet of the protagonists. This scene is rather more satisfying, however, as Inoue was free of any obligation to follow historical accounts and could thus have a longer battle staged with more attention to dramatic effect. Retsudo makes his way to the duel playing the *shakuhachi* (bamboo flute) and wearing a *tengai*, or *komuso-gasa*, a traditional basket-like hat which entirely obscures the face. The *komuso* were monks who believed that wearing such a hat would eliminate ego; they played the *shakuhachi* as an aid to meditation. The camera reveals that inside his *tengai*, Retsudo's eyes are brimming with tears, and this is intercut with flashback images of the family members he has lost in the feud with Itto.

Despite being produced and co-written by Kazuo Koike, one of the original creators, the change of emphasis away from violence to focus on the themes of Buddhist fatalism and the inevitability of destiny meant that the film was (also inevitably) rejected by fans of the earlier movies. The '70s films had become famous (or infamous) for their scenes of gratuitious nudity, limbs being hacked off and spurting geysers of blood. However, anyone coming to the newer version without expectations of such titillation may be pleasantly surprised to find a well-made, thoughtful samurai picture, albeit one not without its faults. The syrupy string motif repeated ad infinitum on the soundtrack is especially unfortunate.

Director Akira Inoue had worked as an assistant to Kenji Mizoguchi and been under contract to Daiei throughout the '60s, but became a casualty of the studio's financial problems and switched to television. His work in that medium had included four TV movies starring Nakadai made in the early '80s. *Lone Wolf and Cub: Final Conflict* was his first work for the cinema since 1969.

Nakadai certainly lent a strong presence to the film, but it was old territory he had traversed many times before. The star of the film was Masakazu Tamura, who had played Nakadai's son in *Bitter Spirit* over 30 years previously. A greater contrast with Tomisaburo Wakayama could hardly be imagined, but for the most part he delivers an effectively restrained performance. As an actor who specialized in playing swordsmen, he is also an excellent choice in terms of the action sequences. Other, more frequent associates of Nakadai's also appeared – Mumeijuku's Mayumi Wakamura played the part of Nanao, Lord Retsudo's daughter, while Kunie Tanaka appeared briefly as a Buddhist priest. Although Nakadai had no scenes with Shima Awashita, in the last of their eight films together she appeared in a cameo as a prostitute who has crawled into a temple to give birth and is helped by Itto.

Following *Hachiko* and *Faraway Sunset*, Nakadai's third film with director Seijiro Koyama, *Summer of the Moonlight Sonata* (Gekkou no natsu), was based on a novel which was itself based (loosely) on a true story and tells of a schoolgirl's encounter with a pair of kamikaze pilots during the Second World War. The girl, Kimiko (Mumeijuku's Mayumi Wakamura), is a talented pianist who has been given the responsibility of looking after the school's grand piano. One day, two kamikaze pilots arrive at the school and request permission to use the piano. Both are serious musicians who wish to have one more opportunity to play before being sent on a mission from which they are unlikely to return. One, named Kazama (Mumeijuku's Minoru Tanaka), plays Beethoven's 'Moonlight Sonata' with a passion and seriousness that moves the schoolchildren and teachers, especially Kimiko, who presents each with a bouquet of flowers. Nearly half a century later, upon learning that the piano, fallen into a state of disrepair, is to be thrown away, Kimiko (now played by Misako Watanabe) visits her old school and asks if she may have it. The headmaster asks why and, upon hearing her story, invites her to tell it to the pupils during assembly. Her tale comes to the attention of the local press and gradually generates national interest, inspiring Kimiko to try and discover what happened to the two pilots.

Half an hour into the film, Kazama (now played by Nakadai), who somehow survived, is contacted by the press, but claims not to remember the past and asks to be left alone. On hearing about his reaction, Kimiko writes him a letter of apology which causes him to reconsider. He tells a reporter how he came to survive and how his fellow musician and pilot was not so fortunate. According to Kazama's wife, this is the first time he has ever told the story, even to her. Doing so helps Kazama to come to terms with the past, and he agrees to return to the school to meet Kimiko and play the sonata one more time on the now-restored piano.

Nakadai's character seems cold at first, but we gradually realise that this is merely a form of defense and he has in fact been suffering from a bad case of survivor's guilt ever since he survived a mission from which none of his fellow pilots returned. In a typically restrained performance, Nakadai is very effective in portraying a man who has lived with an overwhelming feeling of sorrow for over four decades. At no point in the film does he break down, but we sense the emotion bubbling under the surface throughout. Indeed, Nakadai is one of the few actors confident enough to suggest this through a lack of animation in both voice and gesture, and this is what makes his performance ring so true.

The film was very popular in Japan, being seen by over two million people in the two years following its release, but has been little seen abroad. The story is essentially a very simple one, but its sentimentality appealed to Japanese audiences, as did the portrayal of kamikaze pilots as tragic heroes.

Nakadai followed this with another stint in television, first taking the lead role in NHK's 14-episode samurai drama *Seizaemon's Last Diary* (Seizaemon zan nichiroku), based on another novel by *Twilight Samurai* writer Shuhei Fujisawa. He then starred in *Five Pearls* (Go-tsubu no shinju), a one-off 90-minute special, as ground-breaking entrepreneur Kokichi Mikimoto (1858-1954), the first person to successfully produce cultured pearls. The script was written by Yasuko under her usual pen name of Tomoe Ryu. Nakadai next played Japanese-American sculptor Isamu Noguchi (1904-1988) in *A Silent Enthusiasm: Isamu Noguchi and the Actress* (Shizukanaru nekkyo: Isamu Noguchi to joyu'), Sapporo TV's 35th Anniversary Drama.

Nakadai's Mumeijuku play for 1993 was *Richard III*, directed by Yasuko and also featuring Nakadai's former Haiyuza colleague Kei Yamamoto, who appeared in drag as Queen Margaret. It was the first time Nakadai had played Richard since the Haiyuza production of 1974. The production toured the country, running for over 100 performances and winning the Kinokuniya Theatre Award.

Chapter 28 – Triumph and Disaster

Film work was scarce around this time, but Nakadai did contribute a cameo as a 'suspicious customer' to *Second Round Kin-chan Cinemagic* (Dainikai Kin-chan no cinemagic), a vehicle for comedian Kin'ichi Hagimoto composed of several 15-minute sketches. Towards the end of 1994, Nakadai's mentor, Koreya Senda, passed away from liver cancer at the age of 90. Senda had been long-retired by then, having made his final film (*Tora! Tora! Tora!*) some 24 years previously, and last worked with Nakadai on their production of *Othello* at around the same time. Also in 1994, the Nakadai Theatre, a new rehearsal hall also used for secret 'warm-up' performances was completed next to Nakadai's home in Setagaya.

The following year, Kihachi Okamoto made a samurai-meets-cowboy comedy western, *East Meets West*, which told a fictional story inspired by a genuine event in which a group of Japanese had sailed to San Francisco in 1860 on a goodwill mission. Nakadai appeared in a couple of scenes at the beginning of the film as Rintaro Katsu (1823-1899), the captain of the ship. Speaking slowly in a lilting sing-song voice, he gave an oddball comic performance in keeping with the tone of Okamoto's film. Although well-made, mostly on location in Sante Fe, New Mexico, *East Meets West* is scuppered by a weak script penned by Okamoto himself. With the exception of the odd moment along the way, there is a dearth of original ideas, and the lack of story and character development cause the film to fall resoundingly flat.

Nakadai next appeared in a major TV drama series, *Child of the Earth* (Daichi no ko), made to celebrate the 70th anniversary of NHK, who co-produced it in association with China Central Televsion. Comprising seven episodes of around 90 minutes apiece, it aired at 9 pm on Saturday nights during November and December 1995. Based on a book by Toyoko Yamasaki, who had written the novels upon which Nakadai's films *A Splendid Family* and *The Barren Zone* were based, it told the story of a Japanese boy separated from his family in occupied China at the end of the Second World War. His father, Koji Matsumoto (Nakadai), reluctantly returns to Japan without him, while his son is taken in by a Chinese family and given the name Lu Yixin. As he grows up, he finds himself unable to forget about his real family and is regarded with suspicion by the Chinese due to his Japanese origin. During the Culutural Revolution, he is suspected of being a spy and sent to a labour camp. Years later, learning that his son had survived the war after all, Koji returns to China in the hope of finding him.

As around two-thirds of the series was shot in China, Nakadai made three separate trips abroad during the course of a year for location work. Although he was top-billed, the main character in the drama was the son, played by Takaya Kamikawa – who had once taken the entrance exam at Mumeijuku but been rejected. Nakadai was impressed by Kamikawa's dedication in learning Chinese during his breaks and thought he gave an excellent performance, subsequently reflecting on how difficult it could be to recognize real talent in the early stages. The series also starred Nakadai's fellow Haiyuza student, Ken Utsui, as well as Yoshiko Tanaka, who had won multiple awards for her performance in the leading role in Shohei Imamura's *Black Rain* (Kuroi ame, 1989).

Yamasaki had interviewed over 300 orphans who had lost their families and had similar experiences, so the story was based on a considerable amount of historical research and helped to raise awareness of their plight. *Child of the Earth* was so well-received in Japan that an extended version with 40 minutes of cut footage reinstated was broadcast the following year.

1995 proved to be an important year for Nakadai and Yasuko when a long-cherished plan came to fruition – a new theatre resulting from a collaboration between Mumeijuku and the people of Nakajima was completed. Nakajima is located in Nanao City, Ishikawa Prefecture, on the Noto Peninsula, which projects into the Japan Sea from central Honshu. The area has been featured in such films as *Zero Focus* (Zero no shoten, 1961), *Mabarosi* (1995) and *Warm Water under a Red Bridge* (Akai hashi no shita no nurui mizu, 2001) and had been the setting for the story of *Goyokin* (filmed elsewhere). Nakadai became the first Honorary Director of the 651-capacity Noto Theatre and, from this point on, Mumeijuku's productions would be staged there every autumn.

Nakadai had visited the area some 17 years previously and casually remarked to a local that he wished he could rehearse in such a place as they were always worried about annoying the neighbours in Setagaya. He was promptly invited to bring his company to Nakajima, where Mumeijuku established a yearly training camp and gave outdoor performances. Many of the young actors stayed with the locals and a warm relationship developed, eventually leading to the plan to construct a theatre under Nakadai's supervision. One unusual feature was incorporated – the back of the stage could be opened up to reveal the woodland on the edge of which the theatre was built. Inspired by a recent trip she and her husband had made to the open-air Minack Theatre at Land's End in Cornwall for an NHK documentary, *Journey of the Heart* (Kokoro tabi), Yasuko immediately saw the possibilities, envisioning a production of *Macbeth* in which Nakadai entered on horseback through the woods and the soldiers disguised as a moving forest in the famous climax could be played by the locals.

On 12 May 1995, the Noto Theatre opened for the first time. However, the plan to launch the new theatre with *Macbeth* had to be abandoned due to budgetary concerns, so it was decided to revive *The Master Builder* instead. Ibsen's most famous drama had been the first play to be staged by the company back in 1980. Again directed by Yasuko, the revival featured Mayumi Wakamura as Hilda. Despite concern that it may not prove popular with the audience, the play was received with great enthusiasm. Nakadai and the rest of the company were in a celebratory mood when, on 13 November, he received a phone call from Yasuko's doctor informing him that she had pancreatic cancer and would need an operation soon. The doctor had disobeyed Yasuko's instructions not to tell her husband. Nakadai was shocked, especially when he found out that she had been diagnosed several months earlier and he had noticed no change in her demeanour.

Despite the fact that he later heard from her doctor that pancreatic cancer is very painful, Yasuko never complained of any pain. Although the operation went smoothly and appeared to have been a success, unfortunately the good news was not to last.

During this difficult period, Nakadai worked with Masaki Kobayashi for the last time. According to Nakadai, Kobayashi had received further offers to direct after *The Empty Table*, but found none of interest and turned them all down, making a living instead through his formidable skill at mahjong. However, he had finally begun work on a documentary entitled *The World of Aizu Yaichi: The Buddhas of Nara*. Yaichi, a former student of Lafcadio Hearn, had been a professor at Waseda University when Kobayashi was studying Oriental Art there before the war. He was also a poet whose writings celebrated the ancient city of Nara and its connection with Buddhism. Kobayashi had once accompanied Yaichi on a trip to Nara and become heavily influenced by him. When Yaichi died in 1956, Kobayashi regretted never having visited him after returning to Japan from the war, and was evidently still living with this regret some four decades later. As a tribute to his mentor, the documentary was something he was determined to complete before he himself died. However, Kobayashi was in poor health by this time and had to hand over direction of the project to Shuei Matsubayashi. Nakadai played Yaichi and was filmed reciting the latter's poems and visiting Buddhist temples in Nara.[98]

Another project which Kobayashi had fought hard to bring to fruition was a film version of Yasushi Inoue's 1959 novel *Tun-huang*, a work of historical fiction set in early 11th-century China and inspired by the real-life discovery of a huge cache of Buddhist scrolls in a cave in the early 20th-century. Inoue had created an adventure story providing a possible explanation of how the scrolls came to be hidden there 900 years earlier. With a screenplay completed by the author, Kobayashi

---

[98] For more on this documentary and Kobayashi's relationship with Yaichi, see *A Dream of Resistance – The Cinema of Masaki Kobayashi* by Stephen Prince (Rutgers University Press, 2018).

had been trying to make the film since the early '60s, hoping to shoot on location in China, where he had scouted locations with Inoue. Nakadai was to play the leading role of Hsing-te, a young scholar who becomes a warrior and is taken under the wing of his older commander, Wang-li – a part which would have been perfect for Toshiro Mifune. However, as the project was continually delayed and Nakadai grew too old for the lead, plans changed and he was himself assigned to the part of Wang-li. Kobayashi continued his efforts until well into the '80s, but was finally forced to abandon the idea. He reluctantly sold the rights to Daiei, who were interested in making a more commercial version of the novel. A new script was written without Inoue and the story was finally filmed by director Jun'ya Sato in 1988. It seems to have been Kobayashi's insistence on historical accuracy and the resulting high budget which scuppered his dream, and it has been said that he never quite recovered from the disappointment.

1996 also saw Nakadai appear in one of NHK's annual Taiga dramas for the first time since 1972. Entitled *Hideyoshi*, it was based on a trilogy of historical novels by Taichi Sakaiya. Nakadai played the famous tea master, Sen no Rikyu (1522-91), who became a trusted advisor to the powerful Lord Hideyoshi (1537-1598), but later incurred Hideyoshi's displeasure and was ordered to commit seppuku. Hideyoshi was played by Naoto Takenaka, perhaps best known for his role as mystery author Edogawa Rampo in *Rampo* (1994). In playing the role of Rikyu, Nakadai was in good company, as the tea master had previously been portrayed by Ganjiro Nakamura in *Ogin-sama* and Takashi Shimura in Kei Kumai's 1978 remake (released in the West as *Love and Faith*), as well as by Toshiro Mifune in Kumai's *Death of a Tea Master* (Sen no Rikyu: Honkakubo ibun) and Rentaro Mikuni in Hiroshi Teshigahara's *Rikyu* (both 1989). A nice touch was that Rikyu's daughter, Ogin (played by Ineko Arima in *Ogin-sama*), was on this occasion played by Nao Nakadai, although she ultimately decided to concentrate on music and has acted only occasionally. *Hideyoshi* achieved the highest audience rating of any Taiga drama, and apparently such a high rating has never since been achieved in Japanese television.

At the same time, preparations began for Mumeijuku's 1996 production, a revival of *Richard III*. Due to Yasuko's delicate state of health, Kiyoto Hayashi was assigned as co-director. Hayashi, who had known Yasuko for some 30 years and was around 10 years her junior, soon had to take over the reigns completely. Yasuko would not live to see the play open – the cancer had spread to her liver and her health was rapidly failing. She collapsed at home on 17 June and was re-hospitalised, passing away ten days later at 3.20 a.m. aged 65. Her body was cremated and her ashes placed in an urn which Nakadai subsequently kept at home.

As Nakadai and Yasuko had not only been husband and wife, but close collaborators in a demanding creative venture, there is no doubt that they were much closer than the typical Japanese couple. Furthermore, while many of his peers kept mistresses, Nakadai seems to have remained faithful throughout the marriage. Devastated by his wife's death, he fell into a depression and considered suicide. The first sign of her cancer had been a stiffness in her back about a month before she went for a check-up, and Nakadai blamed himself for not insisting she see a doctor immediately, thinking that her life might have been saved if he had done so. However, although he had been ready to give up acting and close Mumeijuku, Yasuko had left a letter asking him to carry on with the school, and this is what he eventually did. He was also spurred on by the words of someone who had seen *Richard III* and judged him to be an actor past his prime – Nakadai had always responded best to negative motivation and wanted to prove them wrong.

As if to make matters worse, it was not only Yasuko who died during this period – many of Nakadai's close friends and associates also passed away around the same time. Etsushi Takahashi, his co-star in *Kill!* and a number of other films, had died at the age of 60, also from pancreatic cancer, on 19 May 1996. Masaki Kobayashi fell victim to heart disease on 4 October at his home in Setagaya, the same district in which Nakadai lived. *The World of Aizu Yuichi* was broadcast for the first time a few days later. Nakadai's manager, Masayuki Sato, died on 16 December 1996 aged 78. In both cases, Nakadai was unable to attend the funeral due to his *Richard III* performance schedule. The fact that he was awarded the Medal with Purple Ribbon for his services to theatre the same year must have seemed poor compensation, especially as he would continue to lose those close to him as the '90s drew to a close. On 10 March 1997, Kinnosuke Nakamura, weakened by laryngeal cancer, died of pneumonia at 64, and was soon followed by Shintaro Katsu, who died of pharyngeal cancer on 21 June. Toshiro Mifune passed away on Christmas Eve the same year of multiple organ failure. In 1998, on 6 September, Akira Kurosawa died of a stroke at his home – also in Setagaya – at the age of 88, while Nakadai's mother, Aiko, died the same year, again at 88. However, the most shocking death was that of Juzo Itami, Nakadai's co-star in *I Am a Cat* and the TV drama *Secret Pacific War Story*. Itami died on 20 December 1997 after a fall off the roof of the building which housed his office. Although the official verdict was suicide, many believed he had been murdered by the *yakuza* in revenge for portraying them so negatively in his films – a not implausible theory as he had previously been physically attacked by several *yakuza* for this reason. They had beaten him badly and slashed his face, an incident which led to a public outcry and caused the government to introduce new anti-*yakuza* laws.

On the work front, Nakadai appeared in *Kenji Miyazawa, That's Love* (Miyazawa Kenji, sono ai), a biopic of poet and children's author Kenji Miyazawa (1896-1933), who had little success in his lifetime but achieved posthumous fame for works such as *Night on the Galactic Railroad* (Ginga tetsudo no yoru). It was Nakadai's fourth and final film for director Seijiro Koyama after *Hachiko*, *Faraway Sunset* and *Summer of the Moonlight Sonata* and, like the first two, had a screenplay by Kaneto Shindo. Nakadai had a supporting role as Miyazawa's father, whose wife was played by Kaoru Yachigusa – the third time she had played the wife to his character.

Nakadai had been due to begin filming the Kenji Miyazawa picture on the day of his wife's death, but the production company had delayed the schedule for a week out of respect. Even so, returning to work so soon after his loss meant that he struggled to concentrate on the project. Once the film was completed, the last few months of the year were taken up with performances of *Richard III*, after which he felt the need to get away from it all. In the New Year, he took a trip to Italy with his two sisters, visiting Yasuko's favourite cities, Rome and Siena, but found himself unable to shake his feelings of regret. In his mind, he found himself obsessively rehashing his years with Yasuko and berating himself for all the times he had taken her for granted. Nakadai avoided film work for the next couple of years while he struggled to keep Mumeijuku going and paid tribute to his wife's memory. He had helped to prepare a collection of her essays, published on 1 September 1996, while for Mumeijuku's next production, he decided to stage her final written work, a play version she had written of *Inn of Evil*. It was directed by Kiyoto Hayashi, who became Mumeijuku's principal director after Yasuko's passing. As all of Mumeijuku's previous productions had been straight adaptations of western classics, the venture marked a significant departure for the company, many of whom would be playing Japanese characters on stage for the first time. Aside from members of Mumeijuku, the cast also included Haiyuza's Kei Yamamoto, who had appeared in the original film as the innocent Tomijiro, but in the stage version played the Shintaro Katsu part of the nameless wanderer. Nakadai played Ikuzo, the inn-keeper, as he had also done in the 1982 TV version.

Opening at the Noto Theatre on 9 October 1997, where it ran for a month, the play quickly sold out after the success of the opening night performance. Attracting a total audience of around 20,000 in a town with a population of only 8,000, it caused traffic jams every evening as people drove for many miles to reach the theatre. Some customers bought tickets as part of a package which included an overnight stay and visit to a hot spring, thus boosting the coffers of other local businesses. A large number of Nakajima residents even appeared as extras, playing the lantern-wielding policemen in the climax, for which the back of the stage was opened up to reveal a specially created moat filled with water. Indeed, the townspeople embraced the theatre project to such an extent that the local high school added a theatre studies course to its curriculum. [99] In December, the company took the play to Kyushu, and then to Tokyo in the New Year. This schedule became an annual routine for Mumeijuku; each year, they would open a new play at the Noto Theatre in October or November, then take it on tour for the following five or six months, with the Tokyo performances taking place towards the end of the tour.

Nakadai next co-starred with Mayumi Wakamura once more in *Flag in the Mist* (Kiri no hata), a two-hour Fuji TV special based on a novel of the same title by *Castle of Sand* author Seicho Matsumoto.[100] Nakadai played Kinzo Otsuka, a famous lawyer who is approached by a young woman named Kiriko (Wakamura) to defend her brother on a murder charge. He declines the case as she cannot afford his usual fee, but when her brother is found guilty and dies, Kiriko blames Otsuka and decides not to let him forget it. This dark tale of revenge has been filmed on several occasions, most notably by Yoji Yamada in 1965 with Osamu Takizawa and Chieko Baisho.

For NHK, Nakadai was then reunited with actress Yoshiko Mita from *Michi* and *Faraway Sunset* in *The Mirror Never Sleeps* (Kagami ha neranai), about a woman who commits murder while apparently under the influence of a haunted mirror. Mita played the woman in question, while Nakadai was cast as her former lover, now the director of a shipping company. Comprised of five episodes of 45 minutes each, the series was based on a novel by Moriichi Ichikawa. Nakadai then played the lead in *Inspector Miyanohara*, a one-off two-hour TV special based on a novel by Kyosuke Kotani in which he was a detective investigating the fatal poisoning of a Kyoto night club proprietress.

---

[99] www.jafra.or.jp/library/letter/backnumber/1997/33/5/1.html
[100] The book was translated into English by Andrew Clare and published by Vertical under the title *Pro Bono* in 2012.

There would be no new Mumeijuku play for Nakadai in 1998 as he had taken on an unusual commitment which would tie him up for some time. He had been approached by Toshihiko Tabuchi, a producer for TV Tokyo, to make a documentary series investigating the history of the Jomon people. The Jomon were hunter-gatherers who inhabited Japan from around 14,000-300 BC, and from whom modern Japanese are partially descended. One theory about the Jomon people held that they had been ocean travellers who traversed the Pacific. Tabuchi wanted to explore this with a TV crew travelling to a number of remote islands. Although it is unclear what led him to Nakadai, given such an esoteric subject he obviously needed a famous face to attract viewers. Tabuchi's request turned out to be well-timed as Nakadai was still feeling lost after Yasuko's passing and he had been feigning a strength he by no means felt. Despite never having done anything like it before, he quickly agreed and it seems that the experience of making the series helped him regain a sense of equilibrium.

Nakadai found himself making an almost year-long 16,000 mile journey across the Pacific to South America, stopping off at various islands along the way. One journey between two islands in Micronesia took twice as long as the expected 24 hours when the weather turned nasty, and Nakadai later recalled that the sea had been so rough, it had been difficult just to keep hold of the pole inside his cabin. Thinking it might be the end, he had taken a photo of Yasuko from his travel bag and placed it in his pocket, but remained calm. When the crew of seven finally arrived at Satawal Island two days later, Nakadai was the only one who had not fallen seasick, but his hand had suffered an allergic reaction to the metal on the pole he had been clutching. Later, visiting a village on the island of Kiriwina, Papua New Guinea, Nakadai and crew were expected to provide a shark as a tribute, so they recruited some locals and went fishing. The task was accomplished, but only after battling with unusually high waves which ruined some of the filming. They later discovered the waves had been a result of an earthquake a long distance away which had killed thousands on some islands. In spite of such dangers, on the whole the journey was a calming experience for Nakadai and he was able to visit some of the most beautiful and unspoilt places on Earth. His precarious emotional state at the time suggests that it must have felt good to be along for the ride for a change and away from the pressures of running an acting school and theatre company.

Also in 1998, Nakadai found time to appear on stage for a short run as Abel Znorko in *Enigma Variations*, a 1996 play by Franco-Belgian writer Eric-Emanuel Schmitt. Znorko is a misanthropic Nobel Prize-winning writer who lives a hermit-like existence on an island in the middle of the Norwegian sea, haunted by the memory of a lost love. A journalist who comes to interview him is concealing a hidden motive, and the two engage in a battle of wits à la Anthony Shaffer's *Sleuth*. The play was a Shochiku production directed by Keiko Niyata and co-starring Morio Kazama.

Chapter 29 – A Comeback and Two Farewells

After a three-year absence from the big screen, Nakadai finally returned to films in 1999 in *Jubaku* (Kin'yu fushoku retto jubaku/ 'Financial Corruption, The Curse of the Archipelago', aka *Spellbound*), a complex financial thriller dealing with corruption in the Japanese banking system and based on a real-life scandal. Nakadai played the supporting role of Hideaki Sasaki, a senior banker who finds himself pitted against Kitano, his own son-in-law, in the latter's fight against corruption. Kitano was played by Mumeijuku's Koji Yakusho, by this time a major star thanks to the international success of films such as *Shall We Dance?* (1996), Shohei Imamura's Palme d'Or-winning *The Eel* (Unagi) and Kiyoshi Kurosawa's uniquely creepy *Cure* (both 1997).

As played by Nakadai, Sasaki is an intimidating member of the old guard who fancies himself an aesthete. We hear the actor's distinctively sonorous voice before we actually see him – not the first time a Nakadai character has been introduced in this way. He is rather inappropriately educating his young grandchildren in the art of wine appreciation. As we listen, the camera pans around his study, revealing a number of awards and framed photos (including some vintage shots of the young Nakadai) and the front cover of *The New York Economist*, bearing his portrait along with the legend 'Banker of the Year'. Admonished by his daughter for giving wine to the grandchildren, he objects that 'French kids start when they're babies!' The next time we see him, he's angrily pushing his way through the paparazzi on his way into the bank. Despite an unexplained but prominent limp, his large, tinted glasses, snazzy suits and cigars speak of wealth and power, and he's not above flourishing or slamming down his silver-tipped walking cane to emphasize his displeasure to his underlings.

Sasaki's office contains a large sculpture of a she-wolf suckling Romulus and Remus, and it soon emerges that his empire is doomed to fall just as that of ancient Rome did. Sasaki will not go down without a fight, but he is quickly moved to self-pity when it becomes clear he is in real trouble. He refuses to take a session with the lawyers seriously, nonchalantly humming classical music and humiliating a colleague in the room by recalling an anecdote involving his co-worker accidentally entering a ladies' toilet in Paris only to find himself face to face with Brigitte Bardot.

Meanwhile, Kitano claims to have evidence of collusion with the *sokaiya*, racketeers of a type unique to Japan, who extort money from banks and other big companies through blackmail. Sasaki calls his son-in-law an ingrate and a bastard. The pressure leads one of Sasaki's colleagues, Hisayama, to commit suicide. Kitano visits Sasaki at the inn of his mistress, ostensibly to provide details of Hisayama's funeral arrangements. Sasaki appears to have calmed down and even compliments Kitano on his cleverness, saying that everyone thinks that he himself is responsible for instigating the investigation by Kitano and the others. However, Kitano says that Hisayama's suicide letter said that Sasaki had been named Banker of the Year as a result of approving some dodgy loans to the *sokaiya*. Sasaki loses control of his temper and falls down some steps into the garden, looking pathetic and scared on the ground, unable to believe that this has happened to him.

The synopsis given above focuses on the parts of the story featuring Nakadai's character, but there are other equally important threads. However, Nakadai gives the most memorable performance, making every moment of screen time count, and providing a deft portrayal of an arrogant man used to having his own way, but who soon crumbles when his misdeeds come to light.

Jubaku works hard to tell a highly complex story, and is semi-successful in doing so. Director Masato Harada is known for his social criticism and there's certainly plenty of that in the film but, although it's undeniably well-made, in his efforts to keep the attention of the audience, Harada indulges in a number of eccentric stylistic touches which seem unnecessary and distracting.

The supporting cast included Mumeijuku's Mayumi Wakamura, along with Ken'ichi Endo as a prosecutor. Endo had briefly been a member of Mumeijuku some 17 years previously, but had quit after 10 days as he had found the rules too strict and the pressure too intense.

Nakadai appeared as a talking head in two Kurosawa-themed documentaries around this time – Alex Cox's 50-minute Channel 4 documentary *Kurosawa: The Last Emperor*, and Adam Low's two-hour BBC documentary, entitled simply *Kurosawa*. He also worked on a Kurosawa project for the last time. When the director had passed away the previous year, he had left a couple of recent screenplays unfilmed. One of these, *After the Rain* (Ame agaru), was an adaptation of a Shugoro Yamamoto story that had previously served as the basis for *Samurai from Nowhere* (1964) and was to be filmed by Takashi Koizumi, who had worked as an assistant director on all of Kurosawa's films from *Dersu Uzala* on. The film was very much a family affair – one of the producers was Kurosawa's son, Hisao, the costumes were designed by his daughter, Kazuko, and the cast featured Toshiro Mifune's son, Shiro, along with Kurosawa favourites such as Hisashi Igawa and Mieko Harada. Akira Terao (one of the sons in *Ran*) starred as Misawa, a *ronin* whose skill with the sword comes to the attention of the local lord (Shiro Mifune), who decides to hire him as an instructor to his men. Nakadai appeared in a black-and-white flashback sequence for a very brief cameo as Tsuji Gettan (1648-1727), the famous real-life swordsman supposedly responsible for teaching the fictional Misawa. Although there is nothing much to the part, his presence lends gravitas and was a way of paying tribute to Kurosawa. The film itself is rather sentimental and fails to reach the standards of the master's work, but is a pleasant enough entertainment.

On 1 March 1999, a short book was published featuring Yasuko's illustrations and thoughts on theatre, while Nakadai's Mumeijuku play for that year was a revival of *The Lower Depths*. Nakadai again played Satin and Kei Yamamoto was once more cast as Luka, on this occasion under the direction of Kiyoto Hayashi.

The following year, Nakadai starred in *Sodefuri au mo*, a one-hour special for NHK in which he played Iwao, a recently-widowed sword polisher who collapses in the street one day. A young woman helps him to get home and takes care of him, beginning an inter-generational friendship. This one-off drama by Hisashi Yamauchi won the Japan Media Arts Festival Excellence Award.

Nakadai's first play for both the new millennium and the 25th anniversary of Mumeijuku was *Death of a Salesman*, in which, with hair dyed brown, he played the leading role of Willy Loman after having visited playwright Arthur Miller in New York to obtain his blessing. Nakadai had had the play in mind for many years, originally hoping to play opposite Yasuko as Loman's wife, Linda. With Yasuko gone, Kumiko Komiya played the part instead, while Kiyoto Hayashi directed. The production was tremendously successful, perhaps because, after the recent collapse of the country's bubble economy, many Japanese could relate to Loman's story. Nakadai revived it only two years later with most of the same team.

In 2001, Nakadai played the title role in *Detective Commissioner Shohei Koyamada* (Shokutaku Keiji Koyamada Shohei), a two-hour TV movie in which he was a retired policeman trying to solve the mystery of his daughter's disappearance. Meanwhile, the Mumeijuku play for the year was Shakespeare's *The Merry Wives of Windsor*, for which Nakadai donned a fatsuit and fake ginger beard to play John Falstaff under the direction of Kiyoto Hayashi. He also had his second book, *Testament*, published, which focused mainly on Yasuko's battle with cancer.

The same year, Nakadai appeared in *Vengeance for Sale*, a *chambara* comedy which was to be the final film of Kihachi Okamoto, then aged 78. Okamoto had actually written the scenario many years earlier and directed it as an episode of the TV drama series *Ambush* in 1969, featuring Daisuke Kato in the role Nakadai was to play in the film. Hiroyuki Sanada, star of Okamoto's *East Meets West*, as well as the international horror hit *Ring*, played the leading role of Sukedachiya Sukeroku (the film's title in Japan), a man who returns to his native village after seven years spent wandering. He has survived during this time by helping people accomplish acts of vengeance. Sukeroku never knew his father, and discovers his mother has died in his absence, so he visits her grave, finding it marked by the most humble of tombstones. Deciding she deserves better, he goes to the local undertaker to order a more fitting monument. While there, he meets an older man, Umetaro Katakura (Nakadai) who is the object of a vendetta – a large group of men with official backing have come to the village to assassinate him in revenge for his killing of two members of their corrupt gang. Katakura knows he is outnumbered and is expecting to die. Sukeroku is impressed with his calm, gentle and dignified manner and wants to help, despite the fact that he is usually on the other side. However, Katakura realises that Sukeroku is his son and knocks him out to keep him from harm. Katakura is killed before Sukeroku is able to help, but Sukeroku realises that Katakura was his father and decides to take revenge on his murderers.

Vengeance for Sale is a throwback to the films of the '60s and '70s but, unfortunately, not a very successful one. The low budget is obvious despite some good cinematography, and the music score unwisely features some incongruous and intrusive jazz. As in Okamoto's earlier *Battle Cry* (which it resembles), most of the performers overact shamelessly, straining desperately for laughs by running about and pulling faces while shouting and screaming. Nakadai's performance is in sharp and welcome contrast to these tiresome antics but, overall, the film is further evidence of Okamoto's decline. Like Kon Ichikawa, Okamoto's later films make it difficult to consider him a truly great director. Nevertheless, when he passed away in February 2005 at the age of 82, he left behind a handful of excellent films, the best of which is probably *Sword of Doom*, although *Samurai Assassin, Oh Bomb* and *The Human Bullet* come close.

Nakadai and Okamoto had planned to make one further film together, a version of a 1976 novel, *Magic Lantern Carriage* (Gento tsuji basha), by Futaro Yamada. Set in the Meiji era, it would have had Nakadai as a former member of the powerful Aizu clan reduced to providing a taxi service in a horse-drawn carriage with his granddaughter. His wife has committed suicide after being raped by government soldiers, and his son has been killed in the Satsuma Rebellion, but both regularly appear to him as ghosts. However, when Okamoto died before production began, the project died with him.

Chapter 30 – The Stage is Where It's At

The next few years would see Nakadai's film roles become less interesting as his age meant that he was now usually cast as the father or even grandfather to one of the main characters. However, one of the great benefits of having his own theatre company was the ability to provide himself with some much more rewarding roles, as we shall see.

The film *To Dance with the White Dog* (Shiroi inu to waratsu o) was based on the 1990 novel of the same name by American writer Terry Kay. There had been an earlier film version made for American TV in 1993 starring Hume Cronyn, but the book had also been translated into Japanese and become a surprise bestseller in Japan, selling over two million copies. The story tells of an elderly farmer struggling to accept the sudden death of his wife. He finds comfort in the company of a stray white dog which disappears whenever anyone else comes near. Nakadai played the lead and related strongly to the character, called Eisuke Nakamoto in the Japanese version. Nakamoto is another character who has a bad leg. The moment of shock when he discovers his wife collapsed in the garden and rushes to her aid despite the crutch he uses is very affecting and, as usual, he gives a tastefully restrained performance. Nakadai, never a scene-stealer, has always known when to be still and do nothing – a mature approach which allows his fellow cast members plenty of opportunities to make an impression. Nakadai has no doubt been especially conscious of this when acting alongside his own students, and in this case Nakamoto's daughter was played by Mumeijuku graduate Mayumi Wakamura.

Debut director Takashi Tsukinoki shot mainly in longshots and unbroken takes, with minimal use of close-ups. The film was well-made but the story perhaps too simple to comfortably fill the 100-minute running time, and a couple of sub-plots feel like padding which add little to the film as a whole. The original book was more ambiguous about whether the dog is actually real or not, but Tsukinoki's film soon makes it clear that it is.

In *Spring Has Come* (Haru ga kita), a light-hearted Edo-era drama for NHK in six parts, Nakadai co-starred as 'Tarobei', a magistrate who loses his job and strikes up an unlikely friendship with 'Jirobei', a thoughtful ninja played by Toshiyuki Nishida (best known to viewers in the West as 'Pigsy' in the 1978 TV series *Monkey*). Jirobei is also recently unemployed, so the two decide to help each other out and begin living in an abandoned temple together, after which they have a series of minor adventures. *Spring Has Come* was based on a popular manga series of the same name by *Lone Wolf and Cub* creators Koike Kazuo and Goseki Kojima.

Perhaps as a result of acting alongside Nishida in *Spring Has Come*, around the same time, Nakadai contributed a cameo to the film *Dawn of a New Day: The Man Behind VHS* (Hi wa mata noboru), in which Nishida starred as Shizuo Kagaya. The character was based on Shizuo Takano (1923-92), an engineer who oversaw the development of the home video system which was to become the standard around the world. Nakadai appeared in a couple of scenes as Konosuke Matsushita (1894-1989), the founder of Panasonic. In the film, Matsushita is the genial big shot Kagaya has to convince in order to successfully launch his product on the market. Although there was little resemblance between Nakadai and Matsushita, Nakadai obviously went to some lengths to copy his manner and style of dress and clearly enjoyed playing the part of a good-natured man with almost god-like power. At least to Western eyes, the subject matter seems rather weird for a feature film, but there are a number of Japanese movies concerning workers engaged in a joint effort in order to achieve a technical goal – a theme reflecting the tendency in Japanese society to put the needs of the group before those of the individual. *Tunnel to the Sun* is another example, and in essence such films are similar to the American musicals in which the performers overcome various difficulties to put on a show. *Dawn of a New Day* is a very sentimental film, but well-made by debut writer-director Kiyoshi Sasabe. The strong supporting cast also featured Ken Watanabe, Hisashi Igawa and Mitsuko Baisho.

After reviving *Death of a Salesman* in 2002, Nakadai's Mumeijuku play for the following year was a musical version of *The Living Forest* (aka *The Twelve Months*) by Samuil Marshak – the same play in which he had been playing a small role way back in 1955 when he first met Yasuko, who had been appearing as the queen. Unusually, he directed the Mumeijuku production himself while also playing two roles and increasing the personal connection by casting his adopted daughter, Nao. She played the young girl who, to please the queen, is forced to search the forest in the middle of winter for a flower that only grows in the spring. Nakadai played both the old soldier who helps her and the comic role of the queen's private tutor.

Also in 2003, Nakadai appeared in a supporting role in the film *Like Asura* (Asura no gotoku), which tells the story of four sisters who are shocked to discover that their 70-year-old father is having an affair with a woman 30 years his junior. Nakadai played the father, but had little to do as the focus was very much on the four sisters. At the beginning of the film, he cuts an enigmatic figure, betraying no reaction even when confronted about his infidelity separately by his daughters. As it seems out of character, we expect that at some point we will learn how his illicit relationship began. However, such a revelation never comes and, by the end of the film, the father seems merely dignified but dull even in Nakadai's hands. The lack of background to the father's affair is typical in a script that feels unfinished and is littered with unexplained events and a general lack of character motivation but, despite these shortcomings, the film proved popular in Japan and won a number of awards.

The same year, Nakadai achieved further recognition for his services to Japanese theatre when he was awarded the Order of the Rising Sun, 4th Class. His friend and former colleague Keiko Kishi was also awarded the same honour that year.

The 2004 TBS series *Crying Out Love, In the Centre of the World* (Sekai no chushin de, ai o sakebu) was based on a best-selling novel of the same title by Kyoichi Katayama. This maudlin but popular story revolves around the character of Saku, a 17-year-old male high school student who falls in love with Aki, a female student of the same age. When Aki develops leukemia and dies, Saku dedicates his life to medical research. Looking tanned and healthy, a bearded Nakadai mostly provided comic relief as Saku's sprightly grandfather, Kentaro. However, it turns out that he has a tragic love story of his own – returning from the war to find that his girlfriend had contracted tuberculosis, Kentaro worked hard to raise money for her treatment, even committing a crime for this reason, for which he was caught. While he served time in prison, she was cured, but her family had forbidden her to marry a former convict and married her off to another man. Kentaro himself dies at the end of the second of 11 episodes. The series was very popular and a film version with an entirely different cast was produced the same year.

Also in 2004, Mumeijuku revived the stage version of *Inn of Evil*, with Nakadai reprising the role of the inn-keeper. Again directed by Kiyoto Hayashi, the tour even included Hokkaido, where several performances were held in the city of Kushiro, on the east coast. Nakadai knew the area due to previous visits for location work on *The Human Condition*, *Journey* and *Banka*.

In NHK's two-episode historical drama *The Taika Reform* (Taika no kaishin), Nakadai played a supporting role as Minabuchi no Shoan (?-?), a monk who spent 32 years in China and returned to Japan to teach Confucianism. The protagonists are Nakatomi no Kamatari (614-669) and Soga no Iruka (?-645), who become his students and start out as friends but end up as enemies when they find themselves on opposing political sides. In fact, the former is involved in the assassination of the latter, and goes on to become one of the key figures in the Taika Reform (when Japan first became a united country).

Mumeijuku's production for 2005 was Alfred Uhry's 1987 play *Driving Miss Daisy*, which had been made into a hugely successful film starring Morgan Freeman and Jessica Tandy in 1989. With darkened skin and white beard, Nakadai played Hoke, the black American chauffeur. Although this may appear to be in questionable taste and acting 'in blackface' is no longer considered acceptable in the West, the chances of finding an experienced black actor fluent in Japanese and available to tour the country were probably nil. Translated and directed by Ikumi Tan'no, the play was a co-production with another theatre troupe known as Folk Art. Miss Daisy was played by Tomoko Naraoka, a distinguished actress and founding member of the Mingei Theatre Company, established in Kawasaki in 1950. Naraoka was four years older than Nakadai, and the two stars had never previously acted together. Staged in various parts of Japan over the following four years, the play was very well-received, winning a number of awards, including the Arts Festival Grand Prize.

In the 2005 Fuji TV movie *Wish upon a Star* (Hoshi ni negaio), Nakadai played the manager of a planetarium frequented by the main character, a boy who wants to become an astronaut. This was followed by a role in *Yamato*, a big-budget war film about the world's largest battleship, which was sunk towards the end of the Second World War when dispatched on a hopeless mission to save Okinawa. The film had an unusual genesis – Haruki Kadokawa (a publisher and producer whose film career had begun in 1976 with Kon Ichikawa's *The Inugami Family*) had just been released from prison after serving several years for cocaine smuggling. Yusuke Okada, then president of Toei, had helped Kadokawa to get released and given him the job of producing *Yamato*, a project based on a book by Kadokawa's sister, Jun Henmi.

Nakadai played the fictional character of Katsumi Kamio, a 75-year-old fisherman who served on the *Yamato* and has been suffering from survivor's guilt for nearly 60 years. He finds closure when approached by a younger woman to take her on his boat to the location of the sinking so she can fulfil the last wishes of her father (another *Yamato* survivor) and scatter his ashes there. On the journey, Kamio's mind returns to his days as a teenaged sailor assigned to serve on the Yamato, and most of the film is comprised of flashback sequences featuring Ken'ichi Matsuyama as the young Kamio. Nakadai's role was similar to the one he played in *Summer of the Moonlight Sonata* – again, his war veteran character is initially reluctant to remember the past, but can only be saved by doing so, and eventually breaks down emotionally.

Yamato is the only film Nakadai made with Jun'ya Sato, a veteran director of the same age. Although overly sentimental, the film is very well-made and the battle scenes are especially impressive. Like most Japanese war films, it tries hard to strike a delicate balance between delivering an anti-militarist message and treating members of the armed forces who had lost their lives with respect. Despite featuring scenes of young sailors being brutally beaten by their superiors, *Yamato* was criticized in some quarters for glorifying the former Japanese Navy, but it certainly makes the cost of war to human lives very clear. The film also won a number of awards, including the Japanese Academy Award for Best Film, and was a huge success at the box office in Japan, taking a reported 5.9 billion yen – a good return on a production cost of 2.5 billion.

NHK's three-part 2006 drama *New Human Crossing* (Shin ningen kosaten) was based on the manga *Ningen Kosaten* by Masao Yajima and Kenshi Hirokane, which had already been adapted for TV on more than occasion. For this new version, Masao Yajima wrote the script himself but also included elements of a novel entitled *Ship with Wings* (Tsubasa aru fune wa) by Ryuichiro Utsumi. Nakadai starred as Yuji Terashima, a former newspaper reporter who, since quitting his job 20 years earlier, has been leading a reclusive existence as a farmer in Shimane Prefecture, a quiet, mountainous region in western Honshu. Terashima's grand-niece, Marie (Eriko Sato), is now a reporter in Osaka. When she comes across an old article written by Terashima, she is inspired to visit him and find out more.

Nakadai was absent from Mumeijuku's play for 2006, *Choshu ibun Shirai Iiyama shoden*, the big draw of which was the return to the company of Daisuke Ryu after a gap of 19 years. After filming his cameo in Kon Ichikawa's *Murder of the Inugami Clan*, Nakadai then appeared as a recurring character in several episodes of his third Taiga drama, *Furin Kazan* (aka *The Trusted Confidant*). The series was based loosely on Yasushi Inoue's novel published in English as *The Samurai Banners of Furin Kazan*, previously filmed by Hiroshi Inagaki in 1969 with Toshiro Mifune and released in the West as *Samurai Banners*. However, Nakadai played not the Mifune part of Kansuke Yamamoto, but the smaller role of Nobutora Takeda (1494-1574), a warlord and father of the *daimyo* Shingen Takeda (whom he had played in *Kagemusha*).

In the two-hour TBS special *Man from a Distant Country* (Toi kuni kara kita otoko), Nakadai was reunted with fellow Haiyuza graduate Komaki Kurihara, who had played the innkeeper's daughter in *Inn of Evil* and also appeared in *The Wolves*. Sporting glasses and a moustache, he played the part of Yusaku Tsuyama, who returns to Japan for the first time in 46 years to visit his mother's grave and meet an old flame,

Noriko Okano (Kurihara), to whom he had once been engaged. After leaving Japan to work for a trading company in Central America, Tsuyama had become involved in some political protests and been imprisoned as a result, causing all contact with Noriko to be lost. She had eventually given up waiting and married their mutual friend Takumi (Naoki Sugiura) instead. Tsuyama manages to arrange a meeting with Noriko through an intermediary but, when he arrives, he is surprised to find Takumi waiting for him. After some awkward conversation, Takumi agrees to let Tsuyama see his wife, and long-repressed feelings are brought to the surface once more. *Man from a Distant Country* was a well-reviewed drama written by Taichi Yamada, who had started out in films working with Keisuke Kinoshita, but later focused his efforts on television, becoming one of Japanese TV's most acclaimed writers.

Nakadai's Mumeijuku play for 2007 was a version of *Don Quixote*, in which he played the title role opposite Hatsuo Yamaya as Sancho Panza under the direction of Ikumi Tanno. Yamaya, who was one year younger than Nakadai, had enjoyed an unusual career, dividing his time between starring in Roman Porno films for Nikkatsu and performing on stage in a number of Shakespeare plays. Although not a member of Mumeijuku, he had previously appeared with Nakadai in *Buraikan*, *Inn of Evil* and *Fireflies of the North*. He passed away in 2019 at the age of 85.

Nakadai's year ended well as he was designated a Person of Cultural Merit in the 2007 end-of-year honours list, providing him with a special pension. Among his peers who had received the award previously were Isuzu Yamada and Ken Takakura.

In 2008, a season of 25 Nakadai films was presented in New York over a seven-week period. Nakadai was surprised to find every film fully-booked, and even more surprised to discover that the most popular films were *I Am a Cat* and *Sword of Doom*, as he had thought those two in particular might be difficult for Western audiences to understand. Nakadai was visiting New York regularly during these years and enjoyed going to Broadway shows, often seeing as many as ten on each trip. He also watched foreign films regularly, once naming *Dances with Wolves* as his favourite movie.

Nakadai was again absent from Mumeijuku's play for 2008, a revival of *Choshu ibun Shirai Iiyama shoden* from 2006, again with Daisuke Ryu. However, the following year, aged 76, he finally performed *Macbeth* as Yasuko had envisioned it, making his entrance through the woods and onto the stage at the Noto Theatre on horseback. The production was also notable for marking the return to the company of Mayumi Wakamura as Lady Macbeth.

In an interview around this time,[101] Nakadai spoke of how he had often felt crippled with nerves as a young actor but found that old age had released him from this, saying that he now viewed every performance as if it might be the last and gave no thought to tomorrow. He added that he had ceased to worry about the competition and begun to feel more warmly towards everyone around him.

In the episodic tearjerker *Listen to My Heart* (Hikidashi no naka no rabu reta/'Love Letter in the Drawer'), a bespectacled and bearded Nakadai played a gruff granddad. The only feature film directed by Shinichi Michi, who usually worked in television, it revolved around a female radio presenter who launches a new show allowing listeners to phone in and read out their love letters. Also featured were Kaoru Yachigusa and former Mumeijuku student Nana Nagao. Meanwhile, Nakadai's third book was published; entitled *Ageing is Evolving*, it dealt with the challenges of acting as a 70-something in the aftermath of his wife's passing.

Nakadai then played the head bad guy in *Zatoichi: The Last*, another attempt at reviving the popular character of the blind masseur-gambler-swordsman following Takeshi Kitano's successful film of 2003. The result was much the same as it had been for Nakadai's earlier film *Lone Wolf and Cub: The Final Conflict* in that fans of the original series hated it and nobody else seemed to like it much either. Directed by the 55-year-

---

[101] www.hi-carat.co.jp/column/interview/200907/entry22784.html

old Junji Sakamoto, who had made his first feature in 1989, it adopted a more serious tone than either the Shintaro Katsu series or the Beat Takeshi film, but only proved in the process that a tongue-in-cheek approauch was better when making a film about a swordsman who can survive a mass attack by a couple of dozen enemies he cannot even see.

An Edo-era style street set was built in the Shonai area of Yamagata Prefecture, where shooting began in March 2009. Zatoichi was played by 33-year-old boy band/TV star Shingo Katori, who had begun preparing for the role a year in advance by attending swordfighting lessons and playing table tennis with the blind and visually-impaired. Unfortunately, he was unable to bring the strength of personality of the previous Zatoichi actors to the role. Nakadai fared better as Tendo, a pony-tailed gourmet villain who talks in food metaphors and slices off a dining companion's hand during a meal as casually as if he were slicing a joint of meat. The film seems strangely determined to confuse the viewer, and it is often unclear who is doing what to whom and why – in the climactic duel between Zatoichi and Tendo, the two characters even vanish into thin air at one point only to rematerialize in the room next door. The reasons for this remain a mystery. Still, it was a juicy supporting role for Nakadai, who continued to cut an imposing figure at the age of 77, and he also managed to get Mumeijuku's Nana Nagao into the cast. The film did healthy box office when it first opened in Japan, but was little-seen abroad and quickly forgotten.

Chapter 31 – The Other Kobayashi

In 2009, Nakadai received his best film role in many years courtesy of Masahiro Kobayashi (no relation to Masaki), a 55-year-old independent filmmaker who had previously had a career as a folk singer under the name Hiroshi Hayashi. He began his film career in the '80s by writing screenplays for the *pinku* (softcore porn) genre, subsequently writing for television and enjoying enough success to establish his own company, Monkey Town Productions. The company's first feature film, *Closing Time*, appeared in 1996 and marked Kobayashi's directorial debut. His films are characterised by their use of real locations, long takes and an often static camera. *Bashing* (2005) concerned the plight of a young aid worker kidnapped in Iraq who returns safely to Japan only to find herself victimised by her own people, who believe it was selfish of her to put herself at risk by ignoring the government's prohibition on visiting the country. While this film resembles the work of Ken Loach, the same year's *Flic*, which portrayed the mental disintegration of a bereaved policeman, had enough strange and unsettling elements to recall the work of David Lynch. *Man Walking on Snow* (2001), meanwhile, was lighter in tone and dealt with the strained relationships between a retired widower (Ken Ogata) in a small Hokkaido town and his two sons.

Kobayashi's growing interest in the theme of ageing made him an ideal collaborator for Nakadai, then in his late-70s, although Kobayashi's overriding theme is perhaps the broader one of loneliness and isolation. Although Kobayashi had previously made a couple of successful films with another veteran star, Ken Ogata, the relationship between the two had been strained and Ogata had passed away in 2008. In any case, it seems that he had always intended the role of the elderly protagonist of *Haru's Journey* (Haru tono tabi) for Nakadai. Kobayashi had written the script shortly before 9/11, but ended up waiting eight years for Nakadai to become available. As a filmmaker, Kobayashi was heavily influenced by French New Wave directors, especially Truffaut, but with this film he decided to do something more Japanese and pay tribute to the domestic dramas of Ozu – though Kobayashi allowed his actors a lot more freedom.

In *Haru's Journey*, Nakadai plays Tadao Nakai, an elderly herring fisherman with bad legs who lives with his 19-year-old granddaughter Haru (Eri Tokunaga) in what is little more than a large shack on the coast in northern Japan. Haru has been living under his care since the death of her mother five years earlier, but really it is she who has been looking after him. As the film begins, the first thing we see is a furious Tadao burst out of the door with a worried-looking Haru trailing behind. It gradually emerges that Haru has lost her job at the local primary school and suggested to her grandfather that he go to live with one of his siblings so that she can move to Tokyo to look for work. Tadao's feelings are hurt, but the two set out on a journey to visit his three brothers and one sister in the hope that one of them will take him in. The relationship between these two disparate characters is a complex one, but we soon realise that there is a deep mutual affection between them. Tadao is a stubborn hothead who has always done as he wanted, seldom taking the feelings of others into account, while Haru feels totally abandoned by her father and perhaps appreciates her grandfather more for this reason.

For the most part, the film skillfully avoids sentimentality, presenting us with a realistic and rather bleak portrait of the problems of old age, albeit one not entirely devoid of hope. Nakadai gets the opportunity to run the gamut of emotions and gives a thoroughly believable performance – surely one of the most impressive in his career – pulling off the difficult feat of making Tadao sympathetic even while he behaves quite selfishly. Although once more playing a character with walking difficulties, Nakadai distinguishes it from his past roles by coming up with a unique walk, a kind of swaying hobble, which looks like it must have been difficult to sustain. Not to be outdone, Eri Tokunaga also developed a memorable walk for Haru, sheepishly staggering along behind her grandfather, and looking not remotely like the former model that Tokunaga actually was. Both actors were deservedly acclaimed for their performances, with the 21-year-old Tokunaga earning two 'best newcomer' awards despite the fact that she had played her first leading role in a film back in 2006.

Masahiro Kobayashi directing Nakadai and Eri Tokunaga
(Courtesy of Naoko Kobayashi).

On location for *Haru's Journey* with Masahiro Kobayashi
(Courtesy of Naoko Kobayashi).

A small role was once again found for Mumeijuku graduate Nana Nagao, while the film is also notable for featuring the final appearances of Kin Sugai as Tadao's sister-in-law and Chikage Awashima as Tadao's older sister, the only person from whom he humbly accepts criticism. Sugai was a Haiyuza graduate who had been married to Nakadai's manager Masayuki Sato until his death in 1996 and had worked with Nakadai in at least a dozen films going as far back as *Black River*, while Awashima had worked with Ozu and also been Nakadai's co-star on no less than eight occasions in the late '50s / early '60s.

Shooting began in Mashike-cho, Hokkaido, in April 2009 and continued in Miyagi prefecture in northern Honshu, with all scenes shot in sequence, so we see the beard that Nakadai shaves off near the beginning gradually grow back as the film progresses. However, it was not a continuous shoot, and filming was not finally completed until December. During the Q&A at the film's premier in April 2010, Nakadai said the character of Tadao resembled that of his headstrong mother, who could be similarly irresponsible and would indulge in gambling with her neighbours despite struggling to feed her family, while Kobayashi said that Tadao was similar to his own father. The film is partly a comment on the problem of Japan's ageing population, but it never becomes a simple 'message movie', and the two protagonists feel like real people we come to care about. Kobayashi's previous films had been poorly received in Japan but popular at overseas film festivals; *Haru's Journey* reversed this trend and became his first domestic success. Kobayashi had also found Nakadai much easier to work with than Ogata, while Nakadai had been grateful to receive such a good role and enjoyed the collaboration. The two were to work together on a number of future occasions in what would be the last of Nakadai's many notable multi-film partnerships with a director.

In 2010, Nakadai appeared in a non-Mumeijuku play – a version of Henrik Ibsen's 1896 drama *John Gabriel Borkman*, produced by Asahi TV and directed by Tamiya Kuriyama. It opened on 2 February in Ogawara, Miyagi Prefecture (near Sendai), then toured, stopping at Akita, Niigata, Koriyama, Tokyo (at the Setagaya Public Theatre),

Asahikawa, Sapporo, Nagoya, Sagami Ono, Mito, Nishinomiya, Matsuyama, Chiryu and Yamanashi before returning to Tokyo for a final two nights. It played for one or two nights in each town, with the exception of the first Tokyo stint, which lasted for nine days – a punishing schedule for a 77-year-old actor.

Nakadai played the title role of Borkman, a bank manager who, for the past eight years, has been living in exile in his own home, haunting the upstairs gallery like a ghost after bringing shame on the family name as a result of embezzling funds. Planning to use the money in a speculation and replace it before it was missed, Borkman had made the mistake of confiding his intentions to a friend, who reported him, leading to a five-year prison sentence. He claims that his actions were a result of his uncontrollable love of power, which he always intended to use in a positive way. The play, not one of Ibsen's most popular, is seldom revived in the West, and seems a curious choice for a Japanese adaptation. However, banking scandals are not uncommon in Japan, where they receive considerable media coverage, so there may have been some topical relevance, although much of the plot is concerned with three women battling for the affections of Borkman's son. Borkman's wife, Gunhild, was played by Mayumi Ozora, who had previously appeared alongside Nakadai in a number of films including *Illusion of Blood*, while his old flame, Ella Rentheim, was portrayed by Yukiyo Toake, who had featured in the 1969 film *Tengu-to*. On 21 February, Nakadai and the two actresses made an appearance on the talk show *Bokura no jidai* to promote the tour. The original play has not aged well, mainly due to its old-fashioned, melodramatic style of dialogue, but it seems likely that the adaptation by Hiroshi Sasabe was not simply a straightforward translation.

Nakadai's occasional co-star Keiju Kobayashi passed away on 16 September at the age of 86. Although little-known abroad, he was very famous in Japan and had appeared alongside Nakadai in a number of films, most notably *Pressure of Guilt*. However, despite playing a considerable number of such dramatic parts, he was at his best in comic roles, such as the enemy samurai kept prisoner in the cupboard in *Sanjuro*. A farewell party was held in his honour on 24 October with Nakadai, Kaoru Yachigusa, Chikage Awashima, Yoko Tsukasa and others in attendance.

Nakadai's Mumeijuku production for 2010 was a Japanese play about Van Gogh entitled *A Man of Fire* (Hono no hito), in which Nakadai appeared with dyed orange hair and beard as the famous artist who died at 37 (40 years younger than Nakadai was at the time). Directed by Hitoshi Uyama, a graduate of the Bungakuza theatre company who had been Artistic Director of the New National Theatre in Tokyo, it had first been performed in 1951. The author, Juro Miyoshi, had also written the play on which *Tengu-to* had been based. Nakadai had, in fact, played the painter once before 20 years earlier. Made in 1990, *The Life of Van Gogh* was a feature-length TV Asahi documentary which Nakadai also presented and for which he was filmed visiting various places in the Netherlands associated with the artist. During the play's run, a six-part series about Nakadai's career, *The Film Heritage of Tatsuya Nakadai*, was broadcast on the Nihon Eiga satellite TV channel.

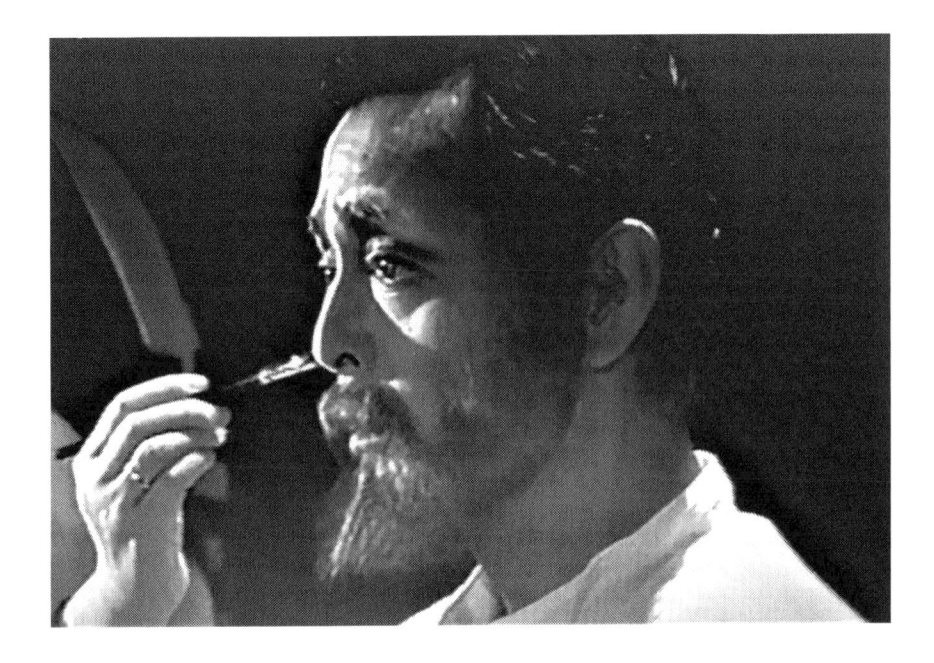

Nakadai as Van Gogh in the *The Life of Van Gogh* (screenshots).

On 14 January 2011, Nakadai was a guest on Japan's longest-running talk show, *Tetsuko's Room* along with his with brother, Keigo. First broadcast in 1975, it was hosted by former actress Tetsuko Kuroyanagi, who had also written the bestselling Japanese book of all time, a childhood memoir entitled *Totto-chan*. Nakadai would make several further appearances on the show.

His next project was *Gaku*, a movie produced by Japanese satellite TV station Wowow, for whom Nakadai had appeared in a commercial around the time of their launch in the early '90s. First broadcast on New Year's Day 2012, the title refers to Gaku (Mahiro Takasugi), a 14-year-old boy living alone in Tokyo whose parents are living and working in New York. When he catches a 4-year-old girl who lives in the neighbourhood playing carelessly with his computer, he pushes her away, accidentally killing her. Terrified, Gaku tries to hide her body, but is caught and arrested. The media soon get wind of the story and public opinion blames the absentee parents, who commit suicide as a result. Gaku becomes withdrawn and loses the will to live, but his concerned grandfather, Shinichi (Nakadai), intervenes. Shinichi is a former Antarctic explorer who believes that the boy must learn to forgive himself and may find solace in nature. Although Shinichi is terminally ill, he takes Gaku on a trip to the Rocky Mountains of Canada in an attempt to give him a reason to carry on.

Written by So Kuramoto – the author of *Blue Christmas*, no less – it also featured Nakadai's frequent co-star Kaoru Yachigusa. As the bulk of the story was filmed on location in and around Southern Alberta, it presented a rare opportunity for Nakadai to film outside his home country. Curiously, despite the fact that many of the characters are Canadians played by natives speaking English, *Gaku* appears not to have been screened outside Japan.

At the end of April 2011, Nakadai received some shocking news – 44-year-old Mumeijuku graduate Minoru Tanaka had hanged himself, leaving no suicide note. After debuting in the 1985 Mumeijuku production of *The Lower Depths*, Tanaka had gone on to play the younger self of Nakadai's character in *Summer of the Moonlight Sonata*. Although such film roles had been few, he had enjoyed a successful acting career on television and had in fact been in the middle of shooting a series when he took his own life for reasons which have remained a mystery. The news must have been especially disturbing given that his favourite own role had reportedly been that of Harold in the 1992 revival of *Harold and Maude*, a play which opens with Harold staging a fake suicide by hanging.

On a more positive note, Masahiro Kobayashi created another excellent leading role for Nakadai with *Japan's Tragedy* (Nihon no higeki), a film unrelated to the 1953 Keisuke Kinoshita picture of the same name he had once auditioned for. Like *Haru's Journey*, the film deals with the problem of Japan's ageing population and the difficulty of caring for the elderly. Such sombre material naturally gave the film little chance of being greatly profitable, perhaps explaining why

Kobayashi wrote a screenplay that could be filmed with a very low budget – *Japan's Tragedy* is essentially a two-hander set mostly in a single location, the small and unremarkable house of the widower Fujio, played by Nakadai. Using highly experienced actors and shooting long takes with a static camera, Kobayashi was able to complete the film quickly and cheaply without compromising on quality or content. This approach caused some consternation on the part of Nakadai, who later said, 'There was a lot of dialogue that I had to remember. For *Japan's Tragedy*, he kept the camera on my back for 20 minutes without cutting. That was one single cut. I was shocked by that.'[102] Some of the action even takes place off camera – the actors walk out of view and leave us looking at an empty room while the dialogue continues, lending a curiously voyeuristic quality to the film.

Japan's Tragedy begins with Fujio, a retired carpenter, being brought home from hospital by his son, Yoshio (Kazuki Kitamura), who makes the bed, offers to do the washing and makes tea, but receives no thanks from his father – by all appearances a stern and humourless curmudgeon who takes his son for granted. It is one year since the death of Fujio's wife, and we learn that Fujio himself has lung cancer, for which he has already had one operation, and is now refusing further surgery. It emerges that his wife had been ill for several years before she died and that Yoshio has been so occupied with caring for his parents over the past five years that he has been unable to work or have any kind of life of his own. He resents his father for this and has begun to pity himself.

---

[102] Karen Severns, The Foreign Correspondents' Club of Japan, 2 June 2017

A scene from *Japan's Tragedy* (courtesy of Naoko Kobayshi).

Hoping to hasten his own death, Fujio barricades himself in his room and decides to stay there without eating or drinking until he dies, but asks his son to speak to him once a day to check if he is still alive. Much of the narrative from this point on is told in a series of flashbacks featuring Fujio's wife and daughter-in-law. During one such sequence, we learn that Yoshio had abandoned his wife and young daughter some years previously, and that they had moved away before going missing in the devastating tsunami of 2011. Our opinion of Fujio undergoes a change during the course of the film, as we see him treating his son with sympathy and realise that he is trying to help by exiling himself to his room so that Yoshio can focus on finding employment while continuing to claim his father's pension for some time after his death by not reporting the event. However, Yoshio finds himself unable to simply dismiss all thoughts of his father, who for the most part remains stubbornly silent on the other side of the door despite his son's entreaties to respond. One flashback shows the family in happier times as Yoshio and his wife bring their newborn daughter to meet the grandparents for the first time. This is the only part shot in colour, and it provides an effectively jarring contrast with the cheerless black and white of the rest of the film. Nothing is resolved at the end, but Kobayashi offers us a glimmer of hope that Yoshio may be successful in finding a job and Fujio may yet come out of his room, while there is a suggestion that the ringing telephone with which the film finishes may possibly be Yoshio's wife trying to get in touch.

Kobayashi treats this uncomfortable subject matter in an admirably clear-eyed and unsentimental manner. Inspired by a true story in which a man in desperate straits continued to live off his father's pension money after his death, *Japan's Tragedy* is not an easy film to watch and is unflinching in its portrayal of problems we will all have to face but prefer to ignore. Nakadai must have felt strongly about it as he accepted immediately upon reading the screenplay in April 2011. After shooting the film in October of the same year, he even made a journey to South Korea a year later to attend the premiere at the Busan Film Festival on 12 October, 2012.

In the role of the son, Nakadai was well-balanced by Kazuki Kitamura, a well-known actor in Japan who had starred in films such as Takashi Miike's *Ley Lines* (Nihon kuroshakai, 1999) and whose emotional collapse in *Japan's Tragedy* is highly convincing. The fact that Kitamura had once followed in the footsteps of Rentaro Mikuni and Yusaku Matsuda by having a number of teeth removed for a role (nine for the 1998 film *Joker*) certainly proves his dedication to his art.

With Kazuki Kitamura in *Japan's Tragedy*
(Courtesy of Naoko Kobayashi)

Nakadai himself showed his dedication by going on a diet and shedding 10 kilos in preparation for his role. In *Japan's Tragedy*, he gives perhaps the most serious performance of his career as an ordinary man with nothing left to look forward to but misery, pain and death. It is honest, restrained acting which refuses to pull on the heartstrings or make the character of Fujio out to be anything more than the unremarkable person that he is. However, as we discover how much Fujio misses his wife and wants the best for his son, he eventually elicits our full sympathy. Nakadai was nominated for Best Performance at the Asia Pacific Screen Awards 2013, but ironically lost out to South Korean actor Lee Byung-hun for his *Kagemusha*-like dual performance in a film called *Masquerade*, in which Byung-hun played both a king and the lookalike trained to impersonate him.

The cast and crew of *Japan's Tragedy*, with Masahiro Kobayashi in the front row flanked by Nakadai and Kitamura
(Courtesy of Naoko Kobayashi)

Chapter 32 – Omnipresent Octogenarian

In the spring of 2012, Nakadai played a supporting role in *Tsunagu*, a film based on a 2010 novel by Mizuki Tsujimura. Produced by the Nippon Television Network, it was screened abroad under the title *Until the Break of Dawn*. A *tsunagu*, or 'connector', is a person who supposedly helps others to contact their deceased loved ones (i.e. what is known in English-speaking countries as a 'medium'). The film concerns a male high school student named Ayumi learning this skill from his grandmother, Aiko (played by Hirokazu Koreeda favourite Kirin Kiki), although it branches off into a number of separate stories as Ayumi meets a variety of clients, learns their reasons for seeking contact, explains the rules, and eventually realises their wishes. The clients are allowed one night only with their dear departed and, naturally, all of the stories are sad ones. Nakadai played Aiko's elder brother, who watches over Ayumi, while Kaoru Yachigusa also popped up playing one of the deceased. The film was written and directed by Yuichiro Hirakawa, who had experience in directing for both film and television. Although it appears to have been well-received in Japan, *Until the Break of Dawn* made little impact abroad.

Nakadai's Mumeijuku production for 2012 was a British comedy, Harold Brighouse's *Hobson's Choice*, directed by Ikumi Tanno. First performed in 1916, it is mainly remembered today as a result of David Lean's classic film version of 1954, which featured a memorable performance by Charles Laughton in the leading role. Set in 1880, the story revolves around Hobson, a pompous widower who owns a shoe shop in Salford, near Manchester, and has three grown daughters of marriageable age. When he realises the expense involved in marrying them off, he decides to keep them in the shop, but is shaken when the daughter he considered most reliable announces her intention to marry one of his bootmakers. He forbids the marriage, but she defies him and sets up a rival business with her fiancé. The plot shares many similarities with *King Lear*, which may have been one reason why

Nakadai was drawn to the role of Hobson. King Lear's fits of madness are replaced by Hobson's bouts of excessive drinking, and the highlight of the David Lean version is a comic drunk scene masterfully played by Laughton. Another Mumeijuku play staged in 2012, *Mumyo Choya – Another Yotsuya Kaidan*, did not feature Nakadai.

Nakadai's next project, *The Promise – The Nabari Poisoned Wine Case: The Life of a Death Row Inmate* (Yakusoku – Nabari dokubudoshu jiken shikeishu no shogai), involved him in something of a cause célèbre. Television journalist and documentary director Junichi Saito had been driven to make his first feature-length drama through the impossibility of interviewing the living person who was its subject, a death-row inmate to whom Saito was denied access. The inmate in question was Masaru Okunishi, the prime suspect in a bizarre murder that occurred in Nabari, Mie Prefecture, in 1961 when seventeen women were poisoned at a village gathering after drinking wine contaminated with pesticide. Five died as a result, including Okunishi's wife. Another of the dead women was said to have been his lover and, as Okunishi had delivered the wine and there were no other obvious suspects, he was arrested – his motive unconvincingly ascribed to a desire to end the love triangle. Okunishi apparently confessed, but later recanted, saying that he had been forced to sign the confession under duress. He was acquitted in 1964 due to lack of evidence, but the prosecutors appealed the verdict and in 1969 he was sentenced to death. Okunishi maintained his innocence and himself made a series of appeals, a process which dragged on for decades. [103]

Junichi Saito became interested in the Okunishi case and came to be convinced of Okunishi's innocence; this led him to make a number of television documentaries on the subject, for which he enlisted the services of Nakadai as narrator.[104] However, frustrated by the prison

---

[103] The story echoes another case of mass poisoning which had been the basis of Kei Kumai's debut film as a director back in 1964, *The Long Death* (Teigin jiken: shikeishu/ 'Teigin Case: Death Row Inmate').

[104] Before making *The Promise*, Nakadai had narrated *Poison and Sunflower: Half a Century of the Nabari Poison Wine Case* (2012); he narrated a further documentary on the topic for Saito in 2018 (*Sleeping Village*).

services' refusal to allow him to film an interview with Okunishi, Saito decided that to truly do justice to the story, he would have to make a feature film with an actor playing Okunishi. Nakadai was the obvious choice.

Saito created a powerful docudrama combining scenes of Nakadai as the elderly Okunishi (which make up the bulk of the film) with recreations featuring another actor as the younger Okunishi, historical newsreel footage of the case, and contemporary interviews with lawyers and other interested parties. Nakadai gave an especially committed and moving performance as the prisoner who, having seen others dragged off for execution and never knowing when his own turn might come, is unable to stop his hand shaking violently every time he hears guards approaching his cell. We see his pathetic delight when he receives a special meal on New Year's Day, and how he stands on tiptoe to benefit from a brief ray of sunlight that manages to penetrate his cell window.

At the time of filming, Okunishi was 86, in poor health as a result of gastric cancer, and had been on death row for over 43 years. Saito must have been hoping that his film would help to obtain freedom for Okunishi, but it was not to be, and Okunishi died a couple of years later at the age of 89. Although made for television, the film won the Local Drama Award at the 2012 Tokyo Drama Awards and subsequently received a domestic cinema release.

At the beginning of 2013, the book *Tatsuya Nakadai Talks about the Golden Age of Japanese Cinema* was published, featuring interviews with Nakadai conducted by film writer Taichi Kasuga. On 1 March, Nakadai appeared on TV chat show *Hello from Studio Park* (Sutajio paku kara konnichi wa) alongside Koji Yakusho. Around this time, Nakadai also narrated two documentaries for director Hidetaka Inazuka, who had previously made the documentary *Twice Bombed: The Legacy of Tsutomu Yamaguchi* (Niju hibaku – Kataribe Yamaguchi Tsutomu no yuigon) about a man who survived both Hiroshima and Nagasaki. The first was *Fukushima 2011: Records of People Exposed to Radiation* (Fukushima 2011: Hibaku ni sarasa reta hitobito no kiroku); the second, *The Weight of*

Writing (Kaku koto no omo-sa), concerned the novelist Yasushi Sato, who had commited suicide in 1990 at the age of 41 but become posthumously popular when his work was adapted for the movie *Sketches of Kaitan City* (Kaitanshi jokei) in 2010. Mumeijuku's Shingo Murakami starred as Sato, and several other members of Nakadai's company were also featured.

Nakadai next contributed a cameo to a feature film entitled *The Human Trust* (Jinrui shikin), a big budget, globe-trotting thriller in which he played the CEO of an investment company. Directed by Junji Sakamoto, who had also been responsible for *Zatoichi: The Last*, it starred Koichi Sato as a conman recruited to locate a fortune originating from a stash of looted gold hidden by the Japanese army at the end of the Second World War (shades of *The Legacy of the 500,000*). *The Human Trust* was poorly-received, but at least Nakadai had managed to swing roles in the picture for a couple of his Mumeijuku students, Aki Sugawara and Taro Kamakura.

During this period, Nakadai also provided voices for characters in two animated feature films. The first of these was *The Tale of the Princess Kaguya*, a Studio Ghibli production based on the oldest fictional story in Japanese literature, dating back to the 10th-century. The story, about a childless bamboo cutter and his wife who find a tiny baby girl inside a bamboo stalk and adopt her, had also been the basis for Kon Ichikawa's 1987 film *Princess from the Moon* (Taketori monogatari) starring Toshiro Mifune and Ayako Wakao. The Ghibli version remains the most expensive Japanese film to date at the time of writing, and it is an indication of the no-expense-spared approach that Nakadai was called in to voice the minor character of an old charcoal burner with whom the princess has a brief encounter in the forest when she returns to her village. With its tasteful watercolour animation, this charming film was extremely well-received all over the world.

The second animated film, *Giovanni's Island* (Jobanni no shima), told the story of two young Japanese brothers living on a small island occupied by the Russians at the end of the Second World War. Nakadai provided the voice of one of the brothers as an old man in the final section of the film, which brings the story up to date. *Giovanni's Island* was a more modest production, lacking the inflated budget of *Princess Kaguya*. Nevertheless, it was also well-received internationally, although Nakadai's characters were of course dubbed by other actors in the overseas versions of both films.

In 2013, Nakadai performed in no less than three separate stage productions, including his only appearance in an opera – *Bluebeard's Castle* by Béla Balázs at the Tokyo Metropolitan Theatre, in which he played The Bard, who speaks the prologue. In May, Mumeijuku staged a play about William Shakespeare for a short run without Nakadai, and followed it later in the year with an adaptation of *Romeo and Juliet* in which he played Friar Laurence, the wise priest who advises Romeo but is unable to prevent the tragedy despite his best efforts. Most notably, however, he fulfilled a long-held ambition to play the leading role in Eugène Ionesco's 1951 Theatre of the Absurd play *The Lesson*, which he had seen in Paris in the 1960s at the tiny Théâtre de la Huchette (where it continues a world-record run to this day as part of a double bill with Ionesco's *The Bald Soprano*). For the first time, Mumeijuku held public performances at their own training hall, limiting the audience capacity to just 50 seats. Directed by Kiyoto Hayashi, the production was like nothing Nakadai had done before. He played an elderly professor who welcomes an 18-year-old pupil to his home for her first private lesson. While she is initially cheerful and confident, he seems timid and apologetic but, as the play goes on, she becomes deflated and he increasingly aggressive. Ultimately, he kills her with a knife, and we learn from his maid that it is the fortieth pupil he has killed in this way; the play ends as it began with another pupil arriving for her first lesson.

2013 was also a productive year for Nakadai in terms of awards, although his age may have become a factor in his selection as he had turned 80 at the end of the previous year. First, he won the Kawakita Award, established to honour the memory of Nagamasa Kawakita, an entrepreneur who had done much to promote Japanese cinema both at home and overseas. Nakadai also became one of the few actors to win the prestigious Asahi Prize for the Arts, presented by the Japanese newspaper the *Asahi Shimbun* for his 'long years of activities as an actor and contribution to the theatre and movie worlds through nurturing of junior fellows.' This put him in very high-class company, as previous recipients had included such renowned writers and directors as Jun'ichiro Tanizaki, Akira Kurosawa, Yasushi Inoue, Kenzaburo Oe, Hayao Miyazaki and Haruki Murakami. The award included not only a bronze statue, but a monetary gift of five million yen (around £36,000 at the time of writing).

Wowow TV's five-part 2014 drama *A Sinner's Lie* (Zainin no uso) was about a battle between two lawyers. One, Takuya Kasahara (Hideaki Ito), will do anything to win a case, and manages to have a serial rapist and murderer acquitted on a technicality. The other, Masashi Kusunose (played by Mumeijuku graduate Ken'ichi Takito) is a humanitarian who had turned down the chance to defend Ito's client. Kasahara's success comes to the attention of Kenzo Haneda (Tatsuya Nakadai), the head of Nikkyo Holdings, who hires him to defend one of his subsidiary companies in a lawsuit involving a death resulting from an allergic reaction. Meanwhile, Kusunose accepts a request to represent a client bringing a lawsuit against another Nikkyo subsidiary related to a cargo plane accident.

In March of 2014, a second book of interviews related to the 'Golden Age of Japanese Cinema' was published. In this case, the interviews were conducted by Akihiko Naga and the book was given the title *Unfinished*.

Nakadai's Mumeijuku play for 2014-15 was *Barrymore*, which opened at the Noto Theatre on 18 October, 2014. Sporting a pin-stripe suit and made up with blue eye shadow, a moustachioed Nakadai played the American star of stage and screen, John Barrymore (1882-1942). It was directed by Ikumi Tanno, who also translated the original William Luce play of 1996, which had featured Christopher Plummer in the title role. Essentially a one-man play – the only other character being a stage manager heard over the loudspeaker but never seen – it depicts the alcoholic actor rehearsing for a new production of *Richard*

III shortly before his death. The play presents its leading actor with the opportunity to portray not only Barrymore but also, in effect, Richard III and sundry other characters as Barrymore reminisces about the past and indulges in mimicry of people he once knew. As his first one-man play, it represented another new challenge for Nakadai, then approaching the age of 82. Most actors find it increasingly difficult to remember lines as they get older, and Nakadai has claimed that he had found it challenging even as a young actor; in order to overcome this weakness, he developed the habit of writing his dialogue by hand on sheets of paper in careful Japanese script and posting them around his house. In the case of *Barrymore*, it took him three months to prepare for opening night.[105]

On 15 December 2014, the 90-minute documentary film *Tatsuya Nakadai – The Life of an Actor* (Nakadai Tatsuya: 'Yakusha' o ikiru) received its premiere. Directed by Hidetaka Inazuka, for whom Nakadai had narrated a couple of documentaries, it offered a rare behind-the-scenes glimpse of rehearsals for *The Lesson* and *Romeo and Juliet*, along with the Mumeijuku recruitment process and other aspects involved in the running of a theatre school – the first time Nakadai had allowed a film crew such access. Other than those close to him, few had been aware that Nakadai suffered from chronic asthma, but the documentary even showed him learning his lines with a tube up his nose to provide oxygen.

Performances of *Barrymore* continued in 2015, and Nakadai also made another stage appearance, playing the lead in Swedish playwright August Strindberg's two-part play *The Dance of Death*, first published in 1900. However, rather than a full-blown stage production, it was a performed reading – another first for Nakadai, who read the part of Edgar, an ageing artillery captain stationed on an island fortress. Edgar lives with his wife, Alice, to whom he has been married for 25 years, but their relationship is toxic and they spend most of their time

---

[105] Luce's work is extremely similar to the 1994 play *Jack – A Night on the Town with John Barrymore* by Nicol Williamson and Leslie Megahey, in which Barrymore was portrayed by Williamson.

dreaming up new ways of tormenting each other. When Alice's long-lost cousin Kurt arrives on the island, his well-intentioned efforts to help them both only seem to make matters worse. Becoming overexcited and drinking too much whisky, Edgar has a fit and blacks out, while Alice encourages Kurt to make advances towards her. Despite his failing health, Edgar then attempts to increase his wife's misery with a series of lies, but appears to be sowing the seeds of his own destruction when she believes him and decides to get revenge.

As a shameless bully with nothing but contempt for everyone except himself, Edgar hardly a likeable character. However, he has moments of pathetic vulnerability, and there are hints that his behaviour may be the result of mental illness. Laurence Olivier had given an acclaimed performance in the role at the National Theatre in 1968, an effective film of which was made the following year.

Unusually, the Nakadai reading was staged not by Mumeijuku, but by a small independent company called Major League, and it was the first theatrical work to be directed by Masahiro Kobayashi, who was working from an adaptation by Hiroshi Sasabe. Nakadai had wanted to do the play for years, originally hoping for Kyoko Kishida as his co-star, but she had passed away in 2006. In the event, Alice was played by Kayoko Shiraishi, who had previously appeared with Nakadai in the films *Queen Bee* and *Yamato*, but was best known for her stage work, while Kurt was played by Mumeijuku graduate Toru Masuoka – the first time he had appeared on stage with his former teacher in thirty years. *The Dance of Death* ran from 17-22 February 2015 at the Hakuhinkan Theater in Ginza, Tokyo, followed by two nights at Ryutopia in Niigata.

Nakadai next played the title role in the independently-produced feature film *Norin Ten: The Story of Gonjiro Inazuka*. Norin Ten is a variety of wheat created by Inazuka (1897-1988), an agronomist whose creation helped to dramatically increase wheat yields and avert famine in many countries. Nakadai played Inazuka as an old man, with Mumeijuku graduate Kenji Matsuzaki portraying the younger Inazuka in the flashback sequences. At least 15 other Mumeijuku members appeared among the cast. The film was written and directed by Hidetaka Inazuka, who was related to Gonjiro Inazuka and had also made *Tatsuya Nakadai – The Life of an Actor*. Nakadai went on record to say that 'real happiness comes to those who spend their entire life working toward a goal' and that *Norin Ten* told an important story he hoped might inspire some of the younger generation to follow in Inazuka's footsteps.

Another independent film starring Nakadai which came out around the same time was *Before the Leaves Fall* (Yuzuriha no koro), a gentle, sentimental drama which marked the directorial debut of the 77-year-old Mineko Okamoto, the widow of Kihachi Okamoto. A former producer who had worked on a number of her husband's films, she also wrote the screenplay herself and functioned as executive producer. In a role that had been written specifically for her, Kaoru Yachigusa starred as Ichiko, a retiring kimono maker who learns from a newspaper article that the works of a painter she once knew are to be the subject of an exhibition. In the hope of seeing a specific painting which holds a precious memory, she makes the long journey to Karuizawa, where the exhibition is being held. As such a trip is out of character, her son is worried and follows her. When she visits the gallery, she finds herself unexpectedly reunited with the artist, Miya (Nakadai). In an effort to promote the film, Nakadai and Yachigusa appeared together in an episode of *Tetsuko's Room*, but it was little seen abroad, with the exception of a screening at the Moscow International Film Festival. Both *Norin Ten* and *Before the Leaves Fall* were released in May 2015. The same month, Nakadai guested at a concert by his brother, Keigo, and Keigo's wife, Mito Yukishiro, and the two brothers sang Jerry Jeff Walker's much-covered 'Mr Bojangles' as a duet.

Nakadai's next job was providing the narration for *Two Death Row Prisoners* (Futari no shikeishu), a TV documentary which examined both the Nabari poison wine case and the case of Iwao Hakamada, a boxer who was wrongly convicted of murder in 1968 and sentenced to death, but finally released in 2014. By then, he had become the world's longest death row inmate. Despite no longer being in prison, he is actually yet to be acquitted at the time of writing (September 2021).

NHK's seven-part medical drama series of 2015, *Haretsu* ('Burst'/'Rupture'), was based on a best-selling 2004 novel by doctor-turned-author Yo Kusakabe. In one of the three main roles, Nakadai played Kuraki, a famous actor forced into retirement by a heart condition who offers himself as a guinea pig for a radical new medical treatment he hopes will enable him to resurrect his career. At first, it seems like the surgery is a great success, and Kuraki devotes himself to fulfilling a long-cherished dream – to make an autobiographical film about his experiences as a child in Tokyo during the war, when he lost his parents in an air raid and had to live in an underground tunnel with his brother. However, when the animals on whom the treatment was tested beforehand begin dying suddenly from a ruptured heart, it becomes clear that Kuraki could fall victim to the same fate at any time. Meanwhile, a Machiavellian health official concerned with the problem of Japan's ageing population begins to think he sees a solution in the new heart procedure.

Haretsu was a major series on which seven months of painstaking preparation were spent before shooting began in July 2015. Former Mumeijuku student Kenji Matsuzaki was also featured, while Nakadai's role had obvious echoes of his own personal history, suggesting that it had been written with him in mind. The series was well-received when broadcast beginning in October of the same year.

Chapter 33 – Not the End

Masahiro Kobayashi created another good role for Nakadai with his script for the TV movie *A Duel Tale* (Hatashiai), based on a story by *Twilight Samurai* author Shuhei Fujisawa. On this occasion, however, directing duties were undertaken by Shigemichi Sugita, who worked mainly in television but had directed Nakadai's earlier film, *Oracion*, and written and produced *Giovanni's Island*. Nakadai was cast in the lead as Shoji Sanosuke, an elderly samurai who has been living for decades as a *heya zumi*, or incapacitated person, as a result of a leg injury sustained during a duel in his youth. As a result of this and other misfortunes revealed in flashbacks (featuring a younger actor as Sanosuke), he has no position, cannot work, and must live off the charity of his brother's family. This charity is given grudgingly by his nephew's wife (played with thin-lipped malice by *Ran*'s Mieko Harada), who never misses a chance to remind him of his uselessness. However, Sanosuke finds solace in the company of his grand-niece, Miya (Nanami Sakuraba), the only member of the family who really cares about him. When threatened with a forced marriage she does not want, Sanosuke intervenes so she can elope with her true love instead.

Shooting took place in Kyoto, mostly at Shochiku's Uzumasa Studios, beginning on 3 June 2015 and finishing 15 days later. It had been many years since Nakadai had made a period drama there, and his belated return lent a sense of anticipation to proceedings. *A Duel Tale* was the sixth film in which Nakadai played a character with a walking difficulty, something which he seems to have been at pains to vary each time – here, he walks with a curious swivelling motion instead of the obvious limp. In saving Miya from a loveless marriage, Sanosuke is exorcising demons from his own past; he ended his relationship with the love of his own life after becoming crippled, fearing that he would not be able to provide for her. However, this sacrifice was to lead to further tragedy, so he has been living with regret for half a century. As the film progresses, a number of scenes subtly emphasize how the inflexibility of samurai etiquette so often led to misery. The most shocking of these is when a baby is suffocated immediately after birth because the mother's status as mistress of a *heya zumi* prohibits her from raising children. This emphasis probably comes from Kobayashi, a filmmaker often concerned with illustrating the consequences of destructive social forces.

Nakadai plays Sanosuke in an appropriately avuncular manner for most of the film, before becoming deadly serious and commanding when real danger arises towards the end. He makes this dramatic transformation entirely convincing, and it is somehow satisfying to see him finally take up the sword once more. *A Duel Tale* has a strong storyline and is well-made and acted all round, but the approach tends to underline the sentimental aspects rather more heavily than necessary, especially in the case of the musical score, which features far too many repetitions of 'Greensleeves.'

2015 had begun badly for Nakadai as Yasuko's sister (and the mother of his adopted daughter, Nao) passed away on 24 February at the age of 71 after a long illness. On a more positive note, Nakadai was the recipient of two awards the same year. The first of these, the Toshiro Mifune Award, had been launched the previous year by the Kyoto International Film and Art Festival and was intended to be awarded to the actor 'most likely to make an international impact on the film industry.' The selection committee included Kurosawa's former assistant, Teruyo Nogami, and the first recipient had been none other than Nakadai's former student, Koji Yakusho, in 2014. During his acceptance speech, Nakadai said that he had been thinking of retiring, but after receiving the award with his 'most respected actor's name on it', he felt obliged to continue.[106]

Towards the end of October 2015, it was announced that Nakadai (along with six others) was to receive the Japanese Order of Culture for his services to the arts. The award, which included an annuity for life, was in effect a promotion from his previous status as a mere

---

[106] https://2015.kiff.kyoto.jp/en/news/detail/40

Person of Cultural Merit, which he had been awarded in 2007. Previous recipients who shared his profession and had been likewise promoted included Isuzu Yamada and Ken Takakura. Nakadai gave a press conference at the Mumeijuku studio during which he sat next to an empty chair, which he said represented Yasuko. When asked about his future plans, he revealed his intention not only to continue acting on both stage and screen, but to use his work in order to express what he felt were worthwhile messages, such as educating people about war to ensure they understood the importance of maintaining peace. The award ceremony took place on 3 November at the Imperial Palace, where the medals were bestowed by Emperor Akihito, although Nakadai was not in attendance as he was booked to appear that evening in Mumeijuku's latest production.

The production in question was *We're No Angels*, a translation (by director Ikumi Tanno) of the play *My Three Angels* by Sam and Bella Spewack, which had been a Broadway hit in 1953 and was itself an adaptation of a French play of the previous year, *La Cuisine des Anges* by Albert Husson. Filmed in 1955 as *We're No Angels* with Humphrey Bogart,[107] the play is an old-fashioned comedy which seems a curious choice for a Japanese revival six decades on. Nakadai played the leader of the three convicts who escape from prison on Devil's Island and hide out in the store of a kindly shopkeeper for whom they find themselves doing a number of good deeds.

On 4 March 2016, Nakadai received yet another honour – on this occasion for Lifetime Achievement – at the 39th Japan Academy Awards. Meanwhile, in TV Tokyo's movie *Kyoaku wa nemurasenai: Tokuso Kenji no gyakushu*,[108] he played Yohei Tachibana, a fictional former Deputy Prime Minister suspected of fraud on a grand scale. Based on a recent novel by Jin Mayama entitled *Baikoku* ('Country for

---

[107] The 1989 film of the same title starring Robert De Niro was inspired by the play but retained only the basic idea.

[108] The unwieldy title translates as something like *Giant Evil Won't Let you Sleep: Special Investigator Counterattack*

Sale'), it was adapted by Arisa Kaneko, who had also written the teleplay for *A Sinner's Lie*. Acting opposite the much younger Hiroshi Tamaki (playing the prosecutor investigating Tachibana), Nakadai said in an interview that he still felt nervous when working with new people and worried that he would not be able to match the freshness of younger actors. He next appeared as a guest star in Season 1, Episode 6 of *Cold Case: The Door of Truth* (Korudo kesu: shinjitsu no tobira), Wowow's Japanese version of the popular American drama in which a female homicide detective is assigned the difficult task of closing long-unsolved murder cases. The show was scripted by Takahisa Zeze, the director of *A Sinner's Lie*, and featured Mumeijuku graduate Ken'ichi Takito as one of its regulars.

Nakadai's next film, *Lear on the Shore* (Umibe no Ria), marked his fourth collaboration with Masahiro Kobayashi, who on this occasion had not only written the role specifically for Nakadai, but had incorporated details from the actor's own life into the biography of his protagonist, Chokitsu Kuwabatake.[109] Like Nakadai, Kuwabatake is an 84-year-old actor and widower whose father died young, who joined a theatre company after high school, and who has starred in movies as well as performed Shakespeare on stage. Unlike Nakadai, he is suffering from dementia and has been put into a nursing home by his cold and calculating older daughter, Banjo, and her weak-willed husband, Yukio, who have manipulated him into naming Banjo as the sole heir in his will. The beginning of the film recalls the opening of *Haru's Journey*, in which a furious Nakadai comes out of his house heading for an unknown destination, and angrily throws his walking stick aside. *Lear on the Shore* begins with Kuwabatake emerging from a tunnel dressed in pyjamas, slippers and a dressing gown, and dragging a small suitcase behind him. He too is angry, and he kicks his slippers off his feet in frustration. He has fled the nursing home and is headed for

---

[109] The character's name is a nod to Akira Kurosawa – in *Yojimbo*, Toshiro Mifune identifies himself as 'Sanjro Kuwabatake', the latter clearly a false name meaning 'mulberry field.'

the beach, where he encounters a young woman who turns out to be his second daughter, Nobuko, born as the result of an affair. Kuwabatake's dementia means that he fails to recognize Nobuko and cannot remember their past history. When she says that she is the only one who cares about him, her words echo those of Shakespeare's Cordelia, and her father appears to think they are rehearsing *King Lear* and plays along. Meanwhile, Banjo and Yukio have been alerted to their father's disappearance and are driving around in an attempt to find him, though Banjo wishes him dead.

With Masahiro Kobayashi preparing for a scene in *Lear on the Shore*
(Courtesy of Naoko Kobayashi)

Banjo is played by Mieko Harada, who had given one of Japanese cinema's most memorable performances alongside Nakadai over 30 years earlier in *Ran*, Kurosawa's take on King Lear, and was presumably cast by Kobayashi for this reason. The part of Yukio went to Hiroshi Abe, known in the West for his roles in several films by Hirokazu Koreeda, while the 26-year-old Haru Kuroki appeared as Nobuko, who appears to be an amalgam of Cordelia and the Fool. Kuroki had won a Best Actress award at the Berlin Film Festival three years previously, so Kobayashi had assembled a very impressive cast for a low-budget film. Most of the film takes place on the beach (in Ishikawa Prefecture), and virtually the only props are the suitcase, the car and a couple of mobile phones.

In one scene, Kuwabatake falls into the sea and is pulled out by Nobuko. There was some concern about this as Nakadai was 84 at the time of filming and had never learned to swim, so Kobayashi took him to an *onsen* (hot spring) the night before this scene was to be shot in order to rehearse. After the scene was filmed, Nakadai was under the impression that Kuroki had, out of concern for his safety, pulled him out earlier than the planned ten seconds for which he was to be submerged. However, he later discovered that Kobayashi had decided to leave him under the water a little longer and had restrained Kuroki from pulling him out at the planned time.

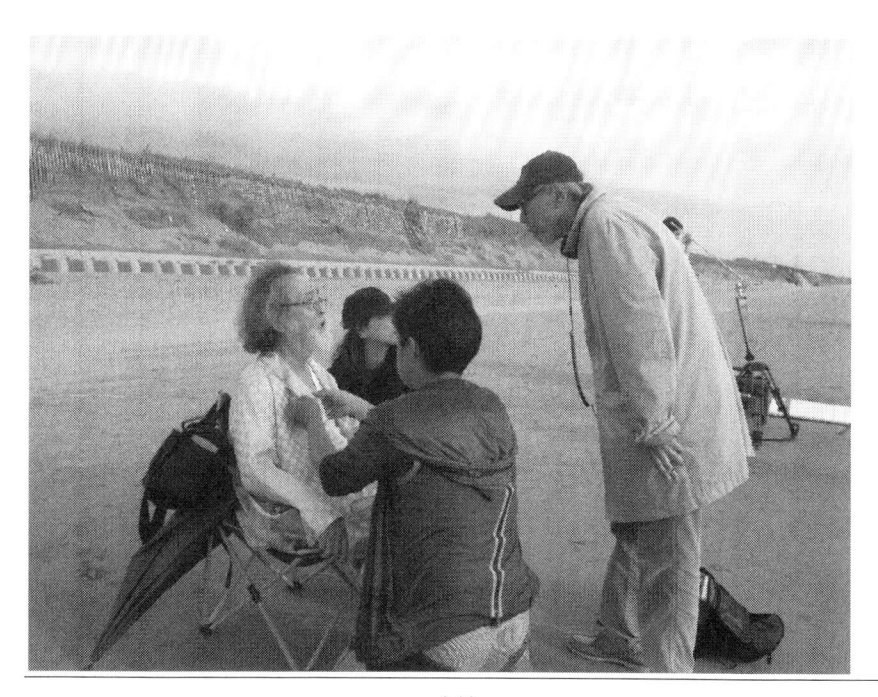

With Masahiro Kobayashi on location for *Lear on the Shore*
(Courtesy of Naoko Kobayashi)

Unfortunately, the Nakadai-Kobayashi partnership proved less fruitful here than on previous occasions. This time around, the characters are perhaps a little too unlikeable, while the film feels overlong and, like Kuwabatake himself, the story goes nowhere. On this occasion, Kobayashi has Nakadai playing not the ordinary people of their previous two feature films (both of whom had clear objectives), but a retired movie star (with no objective), and the result is self-conscious and artificial in comparison to the earlier works. Nakadai affects a curious sing-song delivery and portrays Kuwabatake as a bewildered child trapped in an old man's body. Except for the fact that it takes place on a beach rather than a stage, *Lear on the Shore* has the feel of a filmed play, and it features one of Nakadai's more theatrical performances in film. Having said that, the presence of Kobayashi's characteristic long takes and his recurring theme of problems related to old age certainly qualifies it as the work of a genuine auteur. The performances provide some compensation – the transitions in mental state from awareness to obliviousness are handled well by Nakadai, and Haru Kuroki gives a convincing portrait of a young woman in despair. Nevertheless, the film was not as well-received as the pair's previous collaborations, and screenings outside of Japan have so far been much more limited.

Nakadai showed his sense of humour by turning up at a promotional event dragging the carry-on suitcase which accompanies his character in the film. If *Lear on the Shore* had contained a little more humour, perhaps it might have found a wider audience. During a Q&A session after a screening of the film at the Foreign Correspondents' Club of Japan, Nakadai spoke of his hopes to appear in a stage version of *King Lear* and to make another film with Kobayashi, expressing a desire to play 'an incredibly nasty villain' for the director.[110]

Nakadai's other activities in 2017 included the publication of a third book of interviews, entitled *Don't Become an Actor*, with the interviews conducted by Naoko Sakanashi. Nakadai spoke about various parts of his life from his youth during the war years to running Mumeijuku. On 8 June, he made another appearance on *Tetsuko's Room*, this time alongside fellow Kurosawa veteran Teruyo Nogami. The same month, Nakadai – a lifelong baseball fan and supporter of the Yomiuri Giants team – pitched a ball at the opening ceremony of a Giants game at Tokyo Dome. On the subject of baseball, he also provided narration for *Glory Shines on You* (A eiko wa kimi ni kagayaku), a documentary about the composer of a famous baseball anthem. Another narration job he undertook around this time was for the NHK TV movie *Return Negotiator* (Henkan koshojin), which told the true story of Kazuo Chiba, a post-war diplomat who fought to reduce the American presence in Okinawa as well as to prevent its use as a base for missions during the Vietnam War and remove nuclear weapons from the island. Originally broadcast in August 2017, it received a limited cinema release the following year. Nakadai was quoted in the

---

[110] Karen Severns, *Asia Times*, 3 June 2017.

film's publicity as saying that, having visited Okinawa for his 1971 film *Battle of Okinawa* and made return visits on a number of occasions, he felt sympathetic towards the film's message and believed that Okinawa should be fully returned to the Japanese.

Nakadai's Mumeijuku play for 2017-18 was a revival of Brecht's *Mother Courage and Her Children* in which Nakadai again played Anna ('Mother Courage'), the role he had last played nearly thirty years previously. Unusually, the credited director was 'Tomoe Ryu' as it was performed according to Yasuko's production notes from the 1988 staging.

In April 2018, Nakadai had another book published, *One Body*. As usual, it was not a comprehensive authobiography, rather a collection of 35 short essays on a range of topics both personal and professional. Seven months later, another volume was published entitled *To Act is to Live*.

In the late spring of 2018, Nakadai acted in the feature film *A Town and a Tall Chimney* (Aru machi no takai entotsu). Based on a 1968 novel written by Jiro Nitta inspired by a true story, the film was directed by Katsuya Matsumura and concerned events of 1910, when villagers near the Hitachi Mine in Ibaraki Prefecture (northeast of Tokyo) discovered that smoke from the mine's chimneys was damaging their crops. Nakadai appeared as Heiba Sekine, the village leader and grandfather of the main character, Saburo, the leader of a youth group who take on the mining company. Heiba regrets having given the mining company permission to operate in the area some years previously. Saburo was played by Mumeijuku's Asato Ide in his first major film role. The 130-minute film premiered in June 2019, but the planned national release in 2020 was abandoned due to the coronavirus pandemic and it was issued on DVD instead. During this period, Nakadai also narrated *Sleeping Village* (Nemuru mura), another documentary by Jun'ichi Saito about the poisoned wine case.

Nakadai next appeared in another feature film, *The Pass – Last Days of the Samurai* (Toge – Saigo no samurai), based on a 1968 novel *Toge* by Ryotaro Shiba, who had also written the short stories upon which

Nakadai's earlier films *Hitokiri* and *Bakumatsu* (set in the same period) had been based. Directed by Takashi Koizumi, the former Kurosawa assistant who had made *After the Rain*, it also featured cameos from other veteran Kurosawa favourites Kyoko Kagawa and Hisashi Igawa. However, the star was Koji Yakusho in the role of Tsugunosuke Kawai (1827-68), a military commander who served under daimyo Tadayuki Makino (Nakadai) and tried to maintain peace in the years preceding the Meiji Restoration. The casting of Nakadai was stretching historical accuracy somewhat as Makino died in 1878 at 53 and Nakadai was 86 at the time of filming. Once again, the planned release date was repeatedly delayed due to the pandemic.

In the summer of 2019, the 86-year-old Nakadai played the lead in *The Return* (Kikyo), a two-hour TV movie made for The Samurai Drama Channel, a pay-TV service provided by Nihon Eiga Broadcasting. Directed by NEB president Shigemichi Sugita (who also co-wrote the script with Masahiro Kobayashi from a story by *Twilight Samurai* author Shuhei Fujisawa), it brought together the same combination of talents responsible for *A Duel Tale* five years earlier. Making *The Return* involved location shooting in the Kiso district of Nagano Prefecture, where ancient buildings and picturesque scenery filled with mountains and forests can be found.

'Funeral' Uno (Nakadai) is an ageing *yakuza* with a prominent sword scar down one side of his face who wanders the country living on his wits. When he begins coughing up blood, he realises his days are numbered and decides to return to his hometown for the first time in 30 years. Once he arrives, he discovers that he has a grown-up daughter (Takako Tokiwa) who is being pressured to become the mistress of the local bigwig, Kyuzo (Atsuo Nakamura), an old enemy with whom he fought many years before. Uno is still handy with a sword despite his age, and resolves to free his daughter even at the cost of his life.

The Return, which received a cinema premiere on 15 October 2019, is an engaging and well-made story although, like *A Duel Tale*, it suffers from a rather too syrupy musical score. Credibility is stretched in some of the fight scenes when a frail-looking Nakadai sees off multiple younger opponents with supposed ease, but the climactic fight between Uno and Kyuzo is much more realistic as we see two old geezers huffing and puffing, having become instantly winded by a few seconds of physical exertion. There is one bizarre scene in which Uno, finding himelf justifiably berated by his daughter for turning up three decades too late, gives her a couple of hard slaps round the head, instantly transforming her into a devoted daughter. Disappointing though it is to see such nonsense in a film made in 2019, on the whole *The Return* provides an excellent role for Nakadai, which he plays with characteristic restraint. The film was a prestige piece for NEB, whose publicity made much of the fact that it was the first Japanese period drama to be shot in the new super-high-resolution process known as 8K. In November, Nakadai received a Lifetime Achievement Award at the Tokyo International Film Festival after a screening of *The Return*.

Shortly after *The Return* had its premiere, Nakadai's friend and frequent co-star Kaoru Yachigusa passed away in a Tokyo hospital on 24 October at the age of 88. Yachigusa had often been cast as Nakadai's on-screen wife and, like Yasuko, her death was also the result of pancreatic cancer. Nakadai himself turned 88 at the end of 2020; at such an advanced age, watching his old movies has become a sad experience which leads him to realise how many of his fellow cast members he has outlived. Inevitably, there were more to come. Kunei Tanaka, also 88, died on 24 March 2021 after having retired a decade earlier due to ill health. More shocking, however, was the passing of Daisuke Ryu on 11 April 2021 at the age of 64. Ryu seems to have been almost like a son to Nakadai, at least for a while, and his death from a sudden brain haemorrhage was entirely unexpected. Dying at home, his body went undiscovered for two days.

Although it may seem that Nakadai has outlasted all of his contemporaries, at the time of writing (September 2021), the three Ninjin Club founders, Ineko Arima, Keiko Kishi and Yoshiko Kuga are all living, as are Nakadai's former co-stars Mariko Okada, Yoko Tsukasa and Ayako Wakao, along with Kurosawa's long-serving assistant, Teruyo Nogami. Most are retired now, but Nakadai himself shows no sign of stopping, although the Covid-19 pandemic has understandably restricted his activities. As an elderly asthmatic, Nakadai is especially vulnerable, but he takes good care of himself and has five doctors keeping an eye on him – one who carries out regular health checks, together with separate specialists for his eyes, ears and throat, and a dentist. He gave up smoking for the Millennium and used to go to a swimming pool regularly to walk underwater until he was 80. Although he loves beer, saké and *shochu*, these days he is careful not to drink too much. He eats a banana every morning, walks for 30 minutes every day, does abdominal breathing 100 times before bed and believes in the importance of maintaining good posture, so always keeps his back straight. Nevertheless, he suffers from pain in his lower back and knees. Nakadai also continues to present himself with new challenges – his brother gave him a guitar for his 84th birthday, so he has recently been learning to play.

The pandemic must have been difficult for him as he lives alone and was forced to curtail the activities of Mumeijuku. In the spring of 2020, most performances of the company's production of Moliere's *Tartuffe*, with Nakadai in the title role, had to be cancelled, while a group reading of Osamu Dazai's novel *No Longer Human* planned for November of that year was called off entirely. Nevertheless, Mumeijuku have continued plans for a further production, *Left Arm* (Hidari no ude) by crime writer Seicho Matsumoto. Billed as Nakadai's 70th anniversary work (marking the seven decades since he joined Haiyuza in 1952), the show is planned to tour between November 2021 and April 2022.

Nakadai has said there remain around another 30 plays he would love to perform, among them *King Lear*, and it does seem surprising that he has not yet tackled the original. Perhaps the prospect is too daunting and expectations would be too high – he is only human after all, and the part of Lear is said by some to be the most difficult in Shakespeare. Nakadai claims never to have been very good at learning lines and, as for most actors, this is something which becomes increasingly difficult with every passing year of old age. He has even said that he often forgets his lines on stage. However, he appears to feel that, were he to cease acting, he would go downhill fast and, despite suggesting a number of times that he may retire, he now seems set on continuing as an actor for as long as he is able. Could he still be treading the boards at 100? You wouldn't want to bet against it.

Nakadai's success and the longevity of his career can be ascribed to a variety of factors. His physical characteristics certainly helped: his above-average height, powerful voice, and face dominated by the large, expressive, light-catching eyes which fascinated both Kobayashi and Kurosawa and seemed to suit either heroic or villainous characters. There was also an element of being in the right place at the right time – starting out when he did with the Golden Age of Japanese Cinema in full swing meant that the number of opportunites for Japanese actors was considerable. He has also showed good taste in his choice of scripts, and being a freelancer allowed him to pick and choose. Perhaps more important than any of these, however, is his temperament. Nakadai has said that he has never had a conflict with a director, and the record suggests that when he begins a film, he puts his own ego aside and follows instructions rather than insisting on portraying his own conception of the character. Of course, some of the finest actors have been much more temperamental, but it stands to reason that directors prefer to work with those who can produce great performances without being difficult. Not every Nakadai performance is great, as he would be the first to admit, but his best work in many classics of Japanese cinema is more than sufficient to ensure that he will continue to gain new fans and not be forgotten anytime soon.

Bibliography

In English:

Japan: An Illustrated Encyclopedia Kodansha, 1993.

Akutagawa, Ryunosuke, *Rashomon and Seventeen Other Stories* (translated by Jay Rubin), Penguin, 2006.

Ashton, Dore, *The Delicate Thread: Teshigahara's Life in Art*, Kodansha, 1997.

Bock, Audie, *Japanese Film Directors*, Kodansha, 1985.

D, Chris, *Gun and Sword: An Encyclopedia of Japanese Gangster Films 1955-1980*, Poison Fang Books, 2012.
———, *Outlaw Masters of Japanese Film*, I.B. Tauris, 2005.

Galbraith IV, Stuart, *The Emperor and the Wolf: The Lives and Films of Akira Kurosawa and Toshiro Mifune*, Faber and Faber, 2001.
———, *The Toho Studios Story*, Scarecrow Press, 2008.

Inose, Naoki and Sato, Hiroaki, *Persona: A Biography of Yukio Mishima*, Stone Bridge Press, 2012.

Jacoby, Alexander, *A Critical Handbook of Japanese Film Directors*, Stone Bridge Press, 2008.

Mellen, Joan, *Voices from the Japanese Cinema*, Liveright, 1975.

Prince, Stephen, *A Dream of Resistance: The Cinema of Masaki Kobayashi*, Rutgers University Press, 2018.

Richie, Donald, *A Hundred Years of Japanese Film*, Kodansha, 2012.
———————, *The Japanese Movie*, Kodansha, 1982.
———————, *Japan Journals 1947-2004* (edited by Leza Lowitz), Stone Bridge Press, 2004.
———————, *Japanese Portraits: Pictures of Different People*, Tuttle, 2018.

Saito, Takashi, *Ghastly Tales from the Yotsuya Kaidan*, Chisokudo Publications, 2020.

Schilling, Mark, *The Encyclopedia of Japanese Pop Culture*, Weatherhill, 1997.
———————, *Shiro Kido: Cinema Shogun*, Kindle, 2012.

Yamamoto, Satsuo, *My Life as a Filmmaker* (translated, annotated and with an introduction by Chia-ning Chang), University of Michigan Press, 2017.

In Japanese:

Kasuga, Taichi, *Tatsuya Nakadai Talks about the Golden Age of Japanese Cinema* (Nakadai tatsuya ga kataru Nihon eiga kogane jidai), PHP Shinsho, 2013

Nakadai, Tatsuya, *Actor MEMO 1955-1980* (Yakusha MEMO 1955-1980), Kodansha, 1980
———————, *Ageing is Evolving* (Roka wa shinka), Kodansha, 2009
———————, *Testament* (Nokoshigaki), Chuokoron-Shinsha, 2010

Acknowledgements

I would like to express my gratitude to the following fine people:

Chris D (author of *Outlaw Masters of Japanese Film* and *Gun and Sword: An Encyclopedia of Japanese Gangster Films 1955-1980*) for some helpful advice.

Robin Gatto for providing a variety of useful material, including photos. Robin has written a two-volume French-language biography of Hideo Gosha soon to be available in English.

Luke Gietzen for the wonderful cover design.

Masahiro and Naoko Kobayashi for providing photos and allowing me to use my translation of a quote from Mr Kobayashi's blog at the front of this book.

Leslie Megahey for his help and encouragement. Leslie has written an insightful and entertaining book on the cinema of Kurosawa (yet to be published).

Masa Mitobe for handling some phone calls on my behalf; also for watching *Pressure of Guilt* with me in Japanese and patiently explaining the finer points of the plot in English.

Alan Yentob for generously writing a letter of introduction for me.

Special thanks to Miki Dowsing, who spent many hours translating Japanese sources and checking information, and without whom this book would not have been possible.

ABOUT THE AUTHOR

Martin Dowsing lives in London and is the author of ***Beware of the Actor! The Rise and Fall of Nicol Williamson*** and (as M.R. Dowsing) ***The Assassination of Adolf Hitler*** (a novel). He makes music under the name Hungry Dog Brand and has previously written for the music magazines *R2 (Rock'n'Reel)* and *Bucketfull of Brains*.

Thank you for reading.
If you have enjoyed this book, a review on Amazon or similar would be greatly appreciated.

Anyone wishing to contact the author may do so at bewareoftheauthor@yandex.com

Printed in Great Britain
by Amazon